LOVE COMES
SOFTLY 5–8

LOVE COMES SOFTLY 5-8

Four Bestselling Novels
in One Volume

JANETTE OKE

BETHANYHOUSE
a division of Baker Publishing Group
Minneapolis, Minnesota

© 1984, 1987, 1988, 1989, 2004 by Janette Oke

Edited and revised in 2004.

Previously published in four separate volumes:
Love's Unending Legacy © 1984, 2004
Love's Unfolding Dream © 1987, 2004 by Lavon C. Oke, Representative
Love Takes Wing © 1988, 2004
Love Finds a Home © 1989, 2004

Published by Bethany House Publishers
11400 Hampshire Avenue South
Bloomington, Minnesota 55438
www.bethanyhouse.com

Bethany House Publishers is a division of
Baker Publishing Group, Grand Rapids, Michigan

Printed in the United States of America

Library of Congress Control Number: 2016930587

ISBN 978-0-7642-1824-8

Cover design by Eric Walljasper

16 17 18 19 20 21 22   7 6 5 4 3 2 1

LOVE'S
UNENDING
LEGACY

Dedicated with love
to my third sister, Amy June Wilson,
who, because of her gentle
disposition, made it possible for
me to have one sister with whom I didn't fight as a kid.
We have shared many good times—
often with the help of the old pump organ.

And to my talented brother-in-law,
John F. Wilson

ONE

Homecoming

Marty's trembling hand pushed back a wisp of wayward hair from her warm, moist face as she peered once more out the window. Why was she shaking so? Was it because they had been bouncing hour after long hour in the seemingly slow-moving stagecoach, or was it her intense excitement at the prospect of once again being home? Marty made an effort to still her hand—and the tumult within her. Her slight movement must have caught Clark's eye. Though busy talking with a fellow passenger about the need for rain, he reached for Marty's hand, and she felt the pressure of his fingers, his unspoken message that he understood—not only her weariness, but her impatient longing to be home again, as well. She returned the squeeze, assuring him that she was all right in spite of her overwhelming desire for the trip to end. Clark gave her a quiet smile, then turned again to the man who was speaking. Marty leaned forward for the umpteenth time to get a better look out the small stagecoach window.

They were in familiar territory now. Marty recognized the landmarks, but they only served to make her more distressed with their slow progress. Oh, how she pined to be home again—to see the dear children whom she had not seen for so many months! Though her body was physically exhausted, her eagerness to come to the end of this journey had her sitting on the edge of her seat—every nerve and muscle vibrating with her concentrated energy. *Home! I want to get home!* She clutched at the door handle as the coach lurched through another pothole.

Clark turned from his conversation with the black-suited gentleman and gave her another understanding smile. "Won't be long now," he assured her, looking over her shoulder at the landscape. "Thet's Anderson's Corner just up ahead."

Marty knew he was right. Still, she told herself, it would seem forever before the stagecoach finally pulled to a dusty stop outside their local livery. She wondered if she would be able to keep herself in check for these last endless miles. In an effort to do so, she set her thoughts to imagining what lay ahead. Who would be there to meet them? Would firstborn Clare be the one driving the family team? Would he have his Kate with him? Or would it be Arnie who would be waiting for them? Would their youngest, Luke, be along?

Marty's thoughts switched to her home. Would it seem strange to her when she walked through the door? Would she feel she was entering the abode of someone else, or would she still have the delightful sense of fully belonging there? Would Ellie have supper waiting, impatient with the fact that the stagecoach was almost an hour overdue and things would be overcooked as the dishes waited on the back of the large, homey kitchen stove?

Marty thought of the farmyard, the garden, her chickens clucking about the pen, the spring, and the woods. She could hardly wait to see them all again. *Here I am, a grown woman, actin' like Lukey when he was a little shaver waitin' for an egg to hatch.* She smiled to herself.

She stretched her legs in an effort to relieve some of the stiffness from the long ride. Her glance fell on Clark's one booted foot placed firmly on the floor, and she knew his long leg must be even more cramped than her short ones. She did not look at the other side, the pinned-up leg of his trousers. *At least that one isn't complainin' about more room!* Clark had showed her how to treat his handicap lightly. *But it must ache, too, after this long period of forced inactivity,* she reasoned and wondered if Clark was suffering any pain with the shortened limb.

Clark must have seen her glance and read her question. He shifted his position and spoke to her. "Really takin' this jostlin' fairly well," he said, patting his thigh. "It will be as glad as the rest of me to be out of this rockin' stage, though. Seems we been shut in here 'most a lifetime."

Marty nodded and tried another smile in spite of the fact that she was hot and dusty and longed to be out in some clean, fresh air. Even the switch to the old farm wagon for those last few miles would be a welcome one.

Marty leaned for another look out the window and discovered they had covered some good distance since her last check. Right up ahead lay the last bend in the road before the small community they called *their town* would come into view. A quiver of excitement passed all through her—oh, to be home again! During the long trip home by train and stage, she realized just how much she had missed it—had missed all of them.

Her thoughts returned to Missie and Willie, Nathan and Josiah. How wonderful it had been to spend the time with them. She had learned to love and appreciate the West along with Willie's ranch and the men who lived and worked on it. She wondered how Cookie was doing. Was he progressing in his newly discovered faith? She remembered Wong and his last-minute gift of baking for their train trip home. And there was Scottie, the kind and patient man who needed to allow God to work in his life. She thought of the bitter Smith and hoped that it wasn't just wishful thinking on her part that the man's attitude was beginning to soften. Perhaps one day he would even venture to attend the Sunday services in the new church. Marty's thought of the new church brought all sorts of memories of the many people with whom they had worshiped and grown to love as neighbors and friends. How was Henry doing as he led the little flock in Bible study? Were the Crofts still coming faithfully, and had they found the peace that Mrs. Croft especially had so longingly searched for? Did Juan and Maria . . . ? And then the stagecoach driver was yelling "whoa" to his horses, and the stage was sliding to a halt in a whirl of dust.

Marty's whole insides leaped with such eagerness she felt dizzy with the intensity. Clark's hand was supporting her as she struggled to her feet. *Which of the family will be here? How long will it be until we see the others? What if they didn't get the message of our coming and no one is here to meet the stage? How can I ever bear the extra hours until we can find some way home?* Her thoughts clamored for answers. Dared she look beyond the stagecoach door?

Momentarily she shut her eyes and steadied her jangled nerves with a little prayer. Clark's firm grip on her arm calmed her. She took a deep breath and sat back down to allow the other passengers to leave the coach ahead of her, then waited for Clark to step down so he might help her as she left the coach, now finally stationary. She felt as if she were still moving—swaying slightly with the roll of the stage. Marty steadied herself, reaching for Clark's outstretched hand, and stepped down as gracefully and calmly as she could. And then the air around her seemed to explode in cries and blurred movement as family members swept toward her. Marty was passed from one pair of arms to another, crying and laughing as she held each one close. They were all there. Clare and his Kate; Arnie, Ellie, and Luke; Josh and Nandry and the children. Only Joe and Clae were missing—missing because they were still in the East, with little Esther Sue, where Joe was finishing up his seminary training.

Marty finished the round of hugs and turned to hug them all again. Wiping away tears of joy, she stood back to marvel at how much the grandchildren had grown, how pretty and grown-up Ellie looked, how Luke didn't look like a boy anymore, and how tall and manly her two oldest sons appeared. They had changed, her family. In just one short—and long—year, they had changed so much. Josh was shaking Clark's hand now and telling him how much he had been missed. Marty saw anxious glances at Clark's pinned-up pants leg, and she knew that this was a difficult and emotional time for her family. Clark put them all at ease as he expertly maneuvered his crutch and picked up some of their belongings.

"'Member how we left this place? Stuff piled up high till I wondered iffen the poor horses would be able to pull the load. Well, we came back with far less than we left with." He grinned and slapped his short leg. "Even lightened *me* up a bit fer the return trip," he quipped.

The boys laughed some, and the tension eased. The menfolk started in on the luggage and soon had it moved to the waiting wagon.

Marty turned again to the girls. "Oh, it's so *good* to be home! It's such a long trip, an' I have so much to talk 'bout I'm fair burstin'." Then she spoke to Ellie. "Thought you'd be home stewin' 'bout the stagecoach bein' so slow an' ruinin' yer supper."

"We got together an' decided to just this once be real extravagant," said Ellie, her lovely face and smile warming Marty's heart once more. "We knew you'd be tired after yer long ride, and we thought ya might need a little break before climbin' in the wagon an' headin' on home. 'Sides, we're all anxious fer some talkin' time, so we decided to meet in town an' eat together at the hotel."

Marty was surprised but, after mulling it over quickly in her mind, agreed with their decision. It would be good to just stretch a little and then enjoy a meal with the family. She would simply put off the reunion with her home and its familiar surroundings.

Marty turned to talk with Nandry, but the young woman was standing as though transfixed, watching the men move off toward the waiting wagon. The grown boys appeared to jostle for position beside their father, all talking and laughing at once. It was obvious they shared the joy of having him back. Nandry's Josh, too, walked with them, carrying their youngest, Jane, along with them. Andrew bustled along with the men, hoisting high Marty's prized hatbox. But it was on Clark that Nandry's eyes were fastened, and Marty saw deep pain in her face. Marty wanted to assure Nandry that it was all right, that the stump of leg no longer gave Clark dreadful discomfort, that he was still able to do all the things he used to do . . . well, almost all the things. He had made the adjustment well, and they had even been able to thank God for the life-changing event in their lives, since so many things had happened for God's glory from the results of the tragedy. But before Marty could even move toward her oldest daughter—this one whom she loved as truly as though hers by birth—Nandry had moved away, the pain in her eyes showing clearly on her troubled face.

It's a shock, thought Marty, *a terrible shock. She needs time to face it an' time to adjust. I didn't bear it very well at first, either.*

Ellie was speaking. "Mama, how is Pa? I know thet he seems . . . well, he seems his old self. Is he really? Does . . . does it bother 'im?"

13

"Yer pa is fine . . . just fine." Marty hoped her voice would carry to Nandry, who stood silently with her back to the group. "'Course it was hard on all of us. It's hard on you, too . . . I know thet. 'Specially at first. But ain't nothin' much yer pa puts his mind to thet he can't do. He's a big man, yer pa. A little thing like a missin' leg won't slow 'im down much. You'll—"

But Ellie was weeping. Quiet sobs shook her slight frame as large tears streamed unheeded down her cheeks.

Marty crossed quickly to her and held her close, patting her back and rocking her back and forth until Ellie had cried herself dry.

"It's okay," Marty whispered. "I had me a lot of cryin' time, too. It's all right."

Ellie dabbed at her eyes with her handkerchief. "Oh, Mama," she apologized, "I thought I was all through with such like. I promised my-self . . . but when I saw 'im . . . when I realized it was really true, I . . ."

Marty held her close. "It's just fine," she assured her again. "Why, I couldn't begin to tell ya the number of times Missie an' me cried together."

Ellie blew her nose and Kate did, as well. Marty hadn't realized Clare's young wife had also been weeping. She moved to Kate and held her new daughter-in-law for many minutes. Kate clung to her, no doubt sensing the love and strength that were being offered her by this newfound mother-in-law.

Marty turned next to Nandry. Taking the young woman in her arms, Marty could feel a stiffness in her body. No tears flowed. Nandry embraced her in return, but Marty could sense a withholding there. *Go ahead. Weep,* Marty wished to say. *You'll feel better if you do, and we'll all understand.* But Nandry was drawing away, dry eyed and silent.

The men were returning. Ellie and Kate made another effort to dab at the tears and turned to face the family.

The walk to the hotel dining room was full of loving commotion. Marty's mind went back to the morning so long ago when they had gathered together to say their good-byes. They had been noisy then, too. In fact, Clark had needed to silence his family in order to get the gathering under control. Just as these thoughts flew through Marty's mind, Clark turned to the chattering throng and held up his free hand. "Hold it," he spoke loudly. "How 'bout we git some order outta this chaos."

Tina, who appeared to have grown many inches, responded as she had a year before. "Oh, Grandpa—"

And Clark finished it for her. "I know . . . I know. How can you organize chatter?" He pulled her pigtail and they both laughed. Tina reached up for the hug she knew would be forthcoming.

Marty laughed, too, a tight little laugh that caught in her throat and brought her pain as well as gladness. *See,* she wanted to say to her gathered family, *nothing has changed—not really—at least nothing that really matters.* But perhaps they all got the message without her saying anything, for Marty noticed the changing expressions on the faces before her—the sorrow, then the acceptance, and finally the relief.

Pa was still Pa. This big man whom they knew and loved was still the same man. His accident had not altered his character. He was still in command. Oh, not of incidents, maybe, but he was in command of himself. He had not allowed something like a missing leg to shape who he was, the person he had become. He was, thankfully, still in control. No, that was not right. Clark had never claimed to be in control. That was the secret. The man who stood before them, the man whom they were blessed enough to call "Pa," the one whom they had loved and respected and learned early to obey, had always assured them that the real secret to life and its true meaning was not to try to take over the controls. The answer to a life of meaning and deep peace was to leave the controls in the hand of the almighty Father. And the fact that *He* was still totally and wisely in control was a fact not a one of them in the close little circle doubted.

Only Nandry, who stood slightly apart with eyes averted from the empty pants leg, seemed to have any doubts at all. Marty watched the expression on her face and knew Nandry was not allowing herself even to recognize any part of the situation. Marty prayed silently for this daughter who had always kept herself rather closed and alone. Nandry would need to deal with this new reality, but she probably couldn't manage it just now.

TWO

Catching Up

When the group reached the hotel dining room, Marty and Clark were pressed on every side by grandchildren who wished to sit as close to them as they could. Only Jane, who had been just a few months old when Clark and Marty left for the West, did not remember them, and she chose to cling to her father, her big blue eyes watching every move of the two strangers. Marty yearned to hold her but held herself in check, wanting to give the child enough time to get acquainted. There would be many days ahead to hold and cuddle her.

Tina, their oldest granddaughter, excitedly told them about her school and gave them a progress report on her schoolwork. Andrew boasted that he, too, was a schoolkid now and insisted on counting to ten to prove it. Mary moved closer against Marty and shyly whispered that she still had to stay home to help her mommy with Janey. Marty put an arm around her and hugged her tight.

"Well," broke in Arnie during a slight lull in the conversation, "let's hear all 'bout the West. Is it really what they claim it to be?"

Marty smiled, and Clark answered Arnie's question. "I have to admit to still preferrin' my spot right here, but the West draws one, fer sure. I can understand why Willie is so fired up 'bout his ranch. People out there are right neighborly, an' the land is wide an' open. Gives ya a feelin' of bein' free like."

"Still miles an' miles of country nobody has claimed?" asked Clare.

"Not much. Once the train tracks arrived, the available land was taken up real quick. Those ranches are so much bigger than the farms here thet one man needs far more land. There doesn't seem to be much acreage left to claim in Willie's area. 'Course, thet still don't mean a great abundance of neighbors, but they do have people all round them now. Ya just ride a ways to reach 'em, thet's all. The town has grown quickly, too. An' now they have their own little church, an' they are startin' school this fall—part-time, anyway, with Melinda teachin'—an', 'course, they have a doctor now, so things are lookin' really good."

Ellie shut her eyes. "Dr. de la Rosa," she said, trying out the unfamiliar-sounding name to herself. "Guess we owe him a lot, huh?"

Clark nodded solemnly. "Yeah," he said. "Guess we do. An' I'm countin' on 'im again, too. Countin' on 'im to safely bring into the world another of my grandchildren."

"Oh yes!" exclaimed Kate. "How is Missie?"

"She's fine. Just wished we could have been there to hold the wee one a bit 'fore headin' on home."

"Well," said Clare, reaching for his wife's hand, "maybe we can help out with thet . . . with a wee one, I mean. We thought maybe we'd just . . ."

"Ya mean . . . ?"

Kate blushed. "Oh, Clare, stop—"

But Clare, not to be deterred, went on. "Not yet," he said to the now-excited group. "We just think it sounds like a real good idea, thet's all. I can't wait to have a son of my own."

Marty sat back in her chair again, feeling a fleeting moment of disappointment. It would be so wonderful to have a grandchild right in her own yard. She wished Clare had actually meant . . .

She checked herself. There was no need to be in a hurry. She smiled at the still-blushing Kate. She was anxious to get to know her daughter-in-law better. "Never mind his teasin' none," Marty assured her. "Clare always has been an awful tease. We know him well enough to pay 'im no mind."

She could see Kate relax, and Marty decided to turn the attention of the group elsewhere.

"An' what of you, Arnie?" she asked, smiling knowingly at her son who sat across from her, acting as if he had no interest in the previous conversation.

"What of me?" Arnie repeated, as though not understanding Marty's question. But Marty could see the slight color creep into Arnie's face, and she knew he understood her well enough.

Ellie giggled. "Go ahead, Arnie. Tell 'em," she encouraged.

Arnie pretended to ignore the whole group and intently studied the pattern of the tablecloth.

In Arnie's defense, Luke spoke up slowly. "She's nice," he stated. "I don't blame Arnie none at all."

"Nor do I," Ellie added, giggling again.

Marty watched her son squirm and decided now was not the time to discuss the issue at hand.

"I will want to hear all 'bout her," she said, "just as soon as we have us a chance to talk. Right now I guess we should be decidin' what we want fer supper."

With the attention taken from Arnie, Marty turned instead to Luke. "I'm anxious to hear what plans you have, son, an' how things have been goin' with Dr. Watkins."

"Great!" was all Luke said, but he put a lot of meaning in the word. Marty assumed that Luke's plans for doctoring had not changed.

Clark turned to Nandry. "When did you last hear from Clae?" he asked.

Nandry busied herself with brushing Mary's already clean front. "About a week ago," she said without returning Clark's gaze.

"Everythin' fine?"

"Seems to be. Joe's almost finished now."

"The last we heard was 'bout a week before we left Missie's," Marty commented. "I was so glad to hear they have the boy they've been wantin'. Nice thet he arrived 'fore they have to make their move, too. Clae wrote about Joe takin' a church in the East, though. I hate the thought. Wish they were comin' back here, but I understand how Joe feels 'bout it. It would be a good experience for 'im, and he could git those extra classes at the same time, iffen it all works out fer 'im," she concluded.

Nandry only nodded.

The white-aproned waitress came for their orders then, and by the time the family group had sorted out what they wanted and the poor, confused-looking girl had left their table, the discussion had turned to other things.

Marty glanced out the window and noticed the sun no longer shone down heartily on the world. It had moved far to the west and before too long would be sinking into bed for the night. She longed to be home before dark so she might see their beloved farm, but she realized now they would not make it in time. Part of the last leg of the trip would be made by moonlight, and the men would do the remaining chores by lantern light. The boys no doubt had done all they could before leaving for town. Marty hoped silently that the meal would not take too long. She forcibly turned her attention back to the conversation, listening to the men talk of the crops, the needed rain, and the outlook for the next harvest. Marty pulled Mary up close against her and smiled across at Tina and Andrew, who sat quietly, one on each side of their grandpa. She let her eyes linger over the faces of all the family who shared the large table and inwardly thanked the Lord for bringing them home safely and for keeping the family in their absence.

Looking at Clark sitting across from her with one hand resting on Andrew's shoulder, she saw the same man with whom she had left the long year before. Marty saw the same strength, the same leadership, the same twinkle of humor, the same depth of character, and the same love for his family. These were the things that really mattered, not the stub of a missing leg beneath the table. Marty hoped these were the qualities her family saw in the man, too.

Just as Marty had suspected, daylight had been long gone by the time they arrived home. She quietly mourned the fact that she could not look around her beloved farm immediately. Though the night was moonlit and cloudless and the stars twinkled brightly overhead, she knew that to stumble around in the semidarkness would be ridiculous. So from her perch in the farm wagon, she contented herself with simply peering through the gathered night at the shapes of the buildings in the yard. She picked out the barn, the henhouse, the first little log home she and Clark and their growing family had shared, now the home of Clare and Kate. With a sigh, she allowed Clark to help her down and followed him to the house, straining as she looked out toward the garden. She wondered just what Ellie and Kate had planted and in what quantity, but the darkness of the night kept its secrets.

Ellie had already lit a bright lamp, and she watched carefully as her mother looked around at her familiar kitchen. There was Marty's beloved stove, her neatly organized cupboards, the large family table that had graced their home for years. The curtains and the pictures on the walls were just as she remembered them. Even the towel bar with its assortment of dishtowels looked the same, and familiar potholders hung from the pegs near the stove. Only the lone calendar on the wall had been changed, it now being a year later than when Marty had left her home. She sighed and turned to smile her pleasure at Ellie.

There was great relief to find everything just as she had left it. Contentment settled over her like a warm comforter. She put down the things she had been carrying and began her homecoming tour, hurrying from room to room. Yes, Ellie had kept it just as it had been. It looked like home—it felt like home. As Marty's eyes flitted over the furnishings, her mind was noting things that needed to be done in the near future. The living room could do with some new wallpaper, and the kitchen woodwork should have some fresh paint. Marty sighed contentedly again; her home still needed her. She must get busy right away and care for it—but not tonight. Suddenly she ached for her own bed. How tired she was! Because of the excitement of getting home, she had not realized her extreme weariness. Well, she knew it now. She secretly wondered if she would find the strength to climb the stairs to her own room.

Clark noticed. His eyes sought hers with an unasked question.

"I'm fine," assured Marty quietly. "Just didn't realize till right this minute how tired I am, I guess. Think I'll just go off to bed and leave the rest of the visitin' fer the morra. Plenty of time to catch up then."

Clark nodded, tucked her cases under one arm, and, with his crutch under the other, expertly maneuvered the stairway.

Marty slowly climbed after him, all her excited energy depleted. She stood at the door of her own bedroom—hers and Clark's. It had been so long since they had slept here. Her eyes lovingly caressed every inch of it. The delicate pattern of the rose wallpaper, the deep, rich look of the polished wood floor, with its thick handmade rugs, the full whiteness of the curtains at the windows, the inviting bed with its quilted coverlet. She loved this room. She wouldn't trade it for any amount of money, even for the rich hotel room where they had stayed on their trip west.

She remembered now that she had forgotten to tell the girls about the hotel room. She hadn't yet told them about her thinking Clark's watch was lost to thieves, or about the night spent with the bedbugs, or the sight of the real western Indians with their furs for sale. There was still so much to talk about, but talk would just have to wait.

Clark had placed her cases in the corner and returned to the family below.

Marty turned at a movement behind her and saw Luke approaching with the portable bathtub.

"Thought ya might be wantin' to wash off some trail dust before retirin'," he said simply and placed the tub on one of the large rugs in the middle of the floor. "I'll be right back with a couple of pails of warm water."

Marty gazed at their youngest son with deep love. It was just like Luke to realize she would want to soak in the tub before retiring.

True to his word, he was soon back, and Marty thanked him as he emptied the buckets of water into the tub.

"When yer done just leave it sit," Luke said, "an' I'll take care of it in the mornin'."

Marty nodded and Luke started to go. At the door he stopped and turned to her. "Good to have ya home, Ma," he said softly. "Been awfully lonely around here without ya. I missed ya."

"An' I missed *you*," Marty said with emphasis. "I was so afraid you'd be off fer yer trainin' an' me not here to send ya. I was so thankful when ya decided to wait fer a year. I do hope it ain't caused problems fer ya."

Luke smiled. "Did me lots of good, I'm thinkin'. Doc has been a great teacher. Can't believe what he's taught me over the last year. It did somethin' else fer me, too, Ma. There's not a doubt in my mind but thet I want to be a doctor. Some fellas have a hard time at first knowin' fer sure, Doc said, an' then it's a lot of time an' money wasted."

"An' you have no doubt?"

"Nope, none whatever."

"Then yer Pa and me will give ya our blessin'—even though I hate to think of ya goin' so far away."

Luke smiled. "Thanks, Ma," he said. "I'm ready to go now. I wouldn'ta been last year."

He was gone then, and Marty turned to her bath.

Oh, how good it feels! she thought as she climbed in and sank into its warmth. She let it wash away all of the travel grime and the extreme weariness from her aching muscles. A clean, warm nightgown, a few brushstrokes of her hair, and she was ready for her bed.

She had no more crawled in than there was a light tap on her door. After Marty's "Come in," Ellie entered.

"Just had to say good night an' welcome home," she whispered and leaned over to kiss Marty on the cheek. "It's so good to have ya home, Ma. I missed ya."

"An' I missed you. Ellie, I'm proud of the job ya did when I was gone. Everythin' looks so good, so well cared for. Makes me very proud . . . an' a little scared, too."

"Scared?"

"Yeah, scared. I have to admit, an' I hate to, thet yer truly able to make some lucky man a good wife. I don't even want to think of thet, Ellie. I hate to lose ya."

Ellie laughed softly.

"Ma, the worrier," she said as she stroked back a lock of stray hair from Marty's forehead. "Don't ya go frettin' none 'bout thet. I'm in no hurry at all to set up housekeepin' on my own."

"Yer not interested in a home of yer own an'—?"

"Now, I didn't say thet. Sure, I want a home of my own . . . an' a family of my own. I just haven't found the one I wish to share it with yet, thet's all." Then she leaned and kissed Marty's forehead. "Now, you go to sleep an' sleep as long as ya want in the mornin'. I'll care fer the family's breakfast."

Marty was just closing her eyes when again her bedroom door squeaked and Arnie tiptoed over to her bed. Marty forced her eyes to open.

"'Fraid ya might already be sleepin'," Arnie said softly. "Didn't want to waken ya iffen ya were. Clare an' Kate said to tell ya good night for them. They came over to say it in person an' found thet you'd already come up to bed."

"I shoulda thought to wait—"

But Arnie interrupted, "You've had a long, tiring day. Pa says thet yer 'bout beat. He'd chase me outta here right now iffen he knew I was botherin' ya."

Marty smiled.

"I better git," Arnie continued and bent to kiss Marty on the top of her hair. Then he whispered softly, "She's really special, Ma. Yer gonna love her. I'll tell ya all 'bout her tomorra." And Arnie, too, was gone, stepping from her room as quietly as he had come in.

Marty's weary eyes would no longer stay open. Her last thought was of Clark. Where was he? He should be in bed, too. He was just as tired as she was. And then her mind would no longer function, and Marty slipped into a deep and peaceful sleep.

THREE

Taking Stock

Clark's side of the bed was empty but still warm when Marty's eyes first opened next morning. She had not slept late. After the rest received in her own bed, she was ready to get reacquainted with her farm home. As soon as she had enjoyed Ellie's breakfast and helped with the dishes, she went out to the garden. Ellie and Kate had indeed planted it well, with more than they would be able to use. Marty smiled as she looked at the quantity and variety of growing things. She had no argument with the types of vegetables the girls had planted, and there no doubt would be neighbors who would be happy to use some of the extras. The garden was already flourishing and productive looking. Though it was still early in the season, Marty could see the potential for a good yield. Here and there she poked a plant upright or patted some extra earth around it or complimented one on its exceptional size for the time of year.

She turned from the vegetable garden to the flowers. The early blooms were already nodding in the morning breeze, dew-sparkled in the sunlight. Marty breathed deeply of their sweet scent as she moved from plant to plant. Honeybees buzzed about the flowers, sipping sweetness from the open petals.

Marty then went out toward the fruit trees. It had been a good spring for the blossoming, and Marty saw that the trees promised a wonderful harvest if the needed rains arrived in time. She prayed they would as she moved on toward the spring.

The woods were cool and green, and Marty's heart quickened with joy as she inhaled the fresh scent of the trees and the wild flowers beneath them. She hadn't known how deeply she had missed the coolness and the scent of her woods. In Missie's West they had not seen a truly wooded area. Marty stopped and watched a robin as it flew to a nearby limb with a worm in its beak. Soon tiny heads and open beaks appeared and began to chirp in unison to be fed. Marty smiled, but she sympathized with the busy mother.

Down the path she walked until she could hear the soft gurgle of the spring. The stream was down some because of the lack of rain, but the water still ran clear and sparkling. Marty bent to touch its shimmering coolness as it whispered its way across the smooth stones that formed the bottom. How inviting it looked!

Marty reached the spring, lowered herself to the ground, and reached out to trail a hand in the water. It was cold to her touch—so cool, in fact, that it made her fingers cramp. Marty wondered as before at this small miracle. How could waters gurgling forth from this tiny hillside in the woods be so cold? Where did the water come from, and how was it kept so cool in its underground travels? In her mind she could taste the sweetness of the cream and butter as they were lifted from the icy waters, even in midsummer.

She cradled her hand in her apron to restore its warmth and sat still, watching the swiftly flowing water. A woodpecker drilled on a nearby tree. There was a scampering in the grass as a wood mouse scurried past. Marty watched a dragonfly dip and swirl over the creek waters. The woods were teeming with life, much of it out of sight and sound, she knew. She continued her silent vigil, listening and watching for any movement that took place about her.

Marty loved the woods. It was such a refreshing place. Marty needed refreshing. Physically she was still bone weary from the long trip home. Emotionally she was drained from all the excitement of rejoining her family and exploring her beloved home and farm. She'd had many adjustments to make over the last year. She knew that life was full of adjustments; to live meant to change. But Marty, from the depths of her heart, thanked the Lord for the things that stayed constant in a changing world—even things as simple as a quiet stream and a gurgling spring.

And Clark. She smiled and waved as his familiar figure appeared over the hill. She could tell he was concerned about her as he drew near and searched her face for the signs of extreme fatigue that had been there last night.

"Mornin'," he greeted her as he lowered himself to a spot at her side, using his crutch for support. "Ya didn't sleep very long. How ya feelin' today?"

"I'm feelin' some rested an' *so* glad to be home, Clark!" Marty slipped her arm through his. "I'll be good as new in just a few days, 'specially iffen I can sit here by the spring a spell."

"So yer aimin' fer a life a' leisure," he teased, his loving squeeze on her hand belying his words. "Ya just go on sittin' here long as ya like," he assured her. "Ellie's got everythin' well in hand, an' she likes bein' busy."

"Thanks, Clark," Marty said and kissed him good-bye as he rose.

"I'll be gittin' back to the barn," he said, brushing her cheek with his hand. "Ya can sit here till dinnertime iffen ya want."

Yes, Clark is an unchanging part of my life, Marty thought as she watched his tall figure disappear from sight. "Thank ya, Lord," she whispered.

Eventually Marty lifted herself from the grassy bank and headed back toward the bright sunlight and the house. She looked about her as she walked, understanding better the comments she had been hearing from one person or another ever since they had arrived home. The land needed rain. The fields needed rain. The streams needed rain. Marty's eyes looked out across the neighboring pasture. The grass was short and beginning to turn brown. After coming from the arid West, even these parched meadows looked green. But Marty's memory served to remind her that things should be much greener than this in the middle of June. She looked up, but the sun shone with a dazzling light out of a cloudless sky. Then Marty looked toward the horizon. No clouds appeared anywhere over the distant hills. There was no sign of rain in the immediate future.

Marty crossed to the barn and reached a hand over the corral fence to stroke the neck of the big bay. Its teammate sauntered over for her share of the attention, and Marty patted her on the neck, too. She snorted at Marty's outstretched hand, annoyed that it held no piece of apple or lump of sugar, and walked off—heading for the shade to escape the fierceness of the sun.

Marty, too, walked on, past the chicken coop. The hens squawked and squabbled and fought over the watering trough. A big rooster strutted across the enclosure and crowed his challenge to the smaller male members of the flock. Marty noticed a number of hens with good-sized chicks scurrying about them. Ellie had cared well for the flock. There would be a fine supply of chicken for the fall and winter.

Marty slowed as she came to the little log house she had called home for so many years. She still felt nostalgic as she looked at the fluffy curtains blowing in the open kitchen window. Kate was out back hanging some wash on the line. Marty called a good morning, and Kate waved in return.

"I'm almost done. Can ya stop fer coffee?" her daughter-in-law invited.

Marty could and did. She was anxious to see the home that Kate and Clare had made for themselves in the little log house. She followed Kate through the entry and into the tidy kitchen. There had been some changes at Kate's hand—changes for the better, Marty reflected—but much of the cozy room was just as Marty remembered it.

Kate poured the water into the kettle for coffee and measured the grounds. "I was hopin' you'd have time to drop by today. I was achin' to show ya our home. Isn't it just perfect?"

Marty agreed with a smile. That's how she had always felt about this little home.

After Kate had placed the water on to boil, she offered Marty a tour, and Marty was quick to accept. They entered the family living area, and Marty looked from the fireplace to the bookshelf—familiar things—to the couch and two armchairs, the small table and the grandfather clock—all unfamiliar things. The rugs on the floor and the curtains at the window were new, as well.

They moved through the door to the room that had been Marty's bedroom, the one she had first shared with the young Missie and later with baby Clare and then with her husband Clark. Marty stopped for a moment to remember that first year with Clark and his wonderful patience with her, his gentle caring, which had broken through the walls she had built around her broken heart.

Marty looked about her at Kate's bed covered in a deep, down-filled quilt. The chest against the wall held more drawers than the chest Marty had used. There was a comfortable chair beneath the window, with a cozy cushion embroidered in butterflies. A cedar-lined chest stood in the corner. Marty openly admired the room and Kate looked pleased.

They moved on then to a simply furnished spare bedroom. It contained only a bed, a chair, and a small table with a lamp on it. It was clean and airy, and Marty was sure a guest could feel quite comfortable and at home there.

With a bit of a flush to her cheeks, Kate led her to the next room. A small workbench and a few tools lay scattered about, and Marty looked at several pieces of turned wood stacked neatly in a corner.

"Clare makin' somethin'?" she asked, and Kate flushed a bit deeper.

"A crib," she said. "We still aren't quite sure yet if we'll be needin' it, but we're hopin'. I scolded Clare last night fer speakin' up when we aren't really sure yet ourselves, but he's just so excited, an' iffen it's true an' we really are, then—well, we want our two mas to be the first to know. Clare promised I could drive on over to see my ma this afternoon."

Marty put her arms around Kate and gave her a quick hug. "I'm so happy fer ya—fer ya both. I hope with all my heart thet yer right."

"Me too," sighed Kate. "Clare would be so happy. He's been waitin' an' waitin'."

"But ya haven't even been married a year yet," Marty reminded her.

"A year is a long time when yer waitin' fer somethin' ya want so badly," Kate said in frustration and then laughed at herself.

Marty laughed with her.

"Well, I guess it really hasn't been so long," Kate went on, "but it has sure seemed long to Clare an' me."

They returned to the kitchen to enjoy their coffee, and Marty listened as Kate talked about their plans for the coming baby—if one was really on the way. As Marty left Kate's kitchen to return to her own, she prayed that Kate was right and that their dream would soon be fulfilled.

Ellie looked up from kneading some bread dough as Marty entered. Marty felt a bit chagrined when she realized what her daughter was doing.

"Oh, Ellie," she said, "I should be doin' thet instead of wanderin' about like a thoughtless schoolgirl."

"Look, Ma, I've been doin' this fer a long time now."

"I know—an' it's time ya had a break. Here I am back again, an' ya still have to do all the work."

Ellie smiled. "The work's not hurtin' me none. Do ya feel a little better now thet you've seen everythin' is as it should be?"

"Guess I do. Not thet I doubted it would be. . . . It's just thet I wanted to see iffen my memory served me accurately or if I'd built it all up to some fairy-tale dream."

"An'?"

"It's just as I remembered it. My memory played no tricks on me."

"Good," said Ellie as she continued to knead the bread dough.

"Had coffee with Kate," Marty went on.

"I saw ya go in."

"She has made Clare a nice little home. They do seem happy."

"She's been a perfect wife for Clare. Iffen she isn't in agreement with everythin' he does, I never hear about it. Kate's a dear."

Marty smiled. "It means everythin' to a mother to hear thet her children are happily married to mates who love 'em just the way they are."

Ellie nodded and kept up her rhythm with the bread. "You'll like Arnie's girl, too," she said. "Arnie's a lucky guy."

"Arnie came in to see me last night and said he'd tell me all 'bout her as soon as we find some talkin' time."

"Then I won't spill any of his secrets," assured Ellie as she efficiently placed the kneaded dough in the greased pan together with the rest of the batch. She covered it all with a white cloth and set it near the stove on a tall table built for the purpose.

"I think I'll go on up and unpack an' care fer the things from the trip," Marty said. "I was just too tired to do anythin' with 'em last night."

"Ya still look a mite tired," observed Ellie. "I think this has all been a heap harder on ya than ya will ever admit."

"I'm fine," argued Marty. "In a day or two, after I catch up on a bit of sleep, I'll be right as rain."

Ellie looked out at the brightness of the day. "Speakin' of rain," she said, frowning, "we sure are in need of some. I've already been totin' water fer the garden, an' it needs it again. We planted far too big a garden to be waterin' it by the pailful."

"It sure is lookin' fine right now," Marty encouraged. "But yer right, it does need rain."

Ellie must have read Marty's mind as she glanced at the clock. "Ya go on with yer unpackin'," she urged. "I'll look after gittin' dinner on."

Marty thanked her and went on up to her room. As she climbed the stairs, she had to admit to herself that she *was* tired. Why, after dinner she might do an unheard of thing and lie down for a little nap. She wondered at Clark's vigor. *He must be just as tired as I am, but he seems to keep goin' with no problem,* she chided herself lightly. Marty then excused herself with the promise that after a day or two of adjusting, she would be her old self again.

FOUR

Happenings

Marty and Arnie eventually found their talking time. Since Marty still had not felt too perky the next day, Ellie convinced her to sit on the porch with some hand sewing while Ellie herself continued with the duties of the kitchen. Arnie found his mother busy with some mending and sat down to talk to her about his Anne.

Anne came from a family of four and was the daughter of Pastor Norville, who was in charge of the small church congregation in the nearby town. Anne had lost her mother when she was only eleven years old, and, being the only girl in the family, much of the running of the household had fallen upon her at that very young age. Arnie spoke of her with love in his voice, and Marty was more anxious than ever to meet the girl.

"Do ya s'pose ya could bring her to dinner on Sunday?" Marty asked.

"Sure thing. I'll be seein' her tomorra night. I'll ask her then."

"Has she met most of the family?"

"All but you an' Pa."

There was a brief pause.

"Do ya have any plans?" asked Marty quietly.

Arnie colored slightly. "Sure, I got plans—but I haven't spoken of 'em yet. I wanted you an' Pa to meet her first."

"I see," smiled Marty. "Sunday, then."

Arnie, whistling, left for the barn, and Marty watched him go with both pride and a little sorrow. Soon they would all be married, her children. How would she ever endure an empty and quiet house?

Zeke LaHaye stopped by that evening. He wanted to hear all about his son Willie, about Missie and his two grandsons, and about the West they loved so much. Marty and Clark welcomed Zeke warmly, and as Marty put on the coffeepot, Zeke and Clark pulled chairs up to the kitchen table and settled in for a long visit.

Clark's enthusiasm was clear in his voice as he spoke of Willie's ranch and described the spread in detail. He told about the herd, the buildings, the cowboys, the neighbors, the small but growing town, and the prosperity that Willie had worked so hard to achieve. When Marty joined them at the table, the talk turned to the family members. They laughed as they told Zeke about the antics of their shared grandchildren. Zeke joined in the laughter, but as he listened, the hungry look in his eyes deepened.

"I think I'm just gonna take me a little trip out there," he announced at length.

"Thet's a mighty fine idea," encouraged Clark. "They'd like nothin' better. One of the last things Willie said was fer us to send ya on out."

Zeke swallowed with difficulty. "Think I'll head on into town tomorrow an' book me a ticket," he said, his head nodding slowly. "I've waited too long already."

It was hard for Marty to wait for Sunday. First of all, it would mean seeing all her friends in the Sunday morning worship service. Marty thought of Ma and Ben, and Wanda and Cameron. Though Ellie had filled her in on news of the community, it wasn't like seeing her neighbors in person.

After the service, the family would be together for Sunday dinner. They had not seen Nandry and Josh and their family since the night they had arrived home, and Marty was most anxious for another visit and a chance to get reacquainted with her grandchildren.

She was eager to meet Arnie's Anne, as well. What would she really be like? Marty trusted Arnie's judgment, but was he seeing the girl through star-filled eyes? Ellie and Luke, too, had spoken well of Anne. Marty dared to hope that Anne was all her family had claimed her to be and that God, in His love and goodness, had brought them together. Marty could hardly wait to give her blessing to the two of them.

Sunday was another bright, warm day. Ellie had worked long and hard to prepare the family dinner. Marty tried to help, but she found she still tired far too easily. Surely she wasn't *that* tired from her trip from the West! Maybe it was just that she needed to adjust to the climate again, though the weather hadn't seemed to affect Clark one little bit. He was busy every day and managed, with no apparent difficulty even with a crutch, to keep up with his energetic sons.

Marty often felt Clark's eyes upon her, but he seldom made comment except to encourage her now and then to sit for a spell or even to take an occasional nap. Marty fussed inwardly, though she dared not protest too vigorously. In fact, she forced herself to admit that she really had no energy even for argument. She was anxious to be back caring for her family again. But now it was Ellie who had to bear most of the load, though she never mentioned the fact and often asked Marty, "Now, what shall we have?" or "What shall we do?" or even "What would ya like?" so Marty might feel she was in charge.

And now, because of Ellie's capable hands in the kitchen, they were ready for Sunday and the family dinner that would follow the service. Marty wondered, a little guiltily, if she was more excited about being back in her own church and seeing her friends again than about the worship service itself. She decided that the Lord understood her feelings and didn't mind that today most of her attention was on her friends. As Marty and Clark entered the churchyard, their friends welcomed them back to the little congregation with happy smiles and warm embraces.

Wanda ran to meet Marty and clung to her; tears dampened the eyes of both women.

"Oh, I've missed you so much . . . so much," she whispered to Marty over and over. "Can you come for a nice, long visit soon, so's you can tell me all about Missie and her family?"

Marty promised she would.

Ma Graham, too, held Marty for a long time. A sob caught in her throat as she spoke of their deep sorrow when they had learned of Clark's accident. She told how, on three occasions during the ordeal, the church members had met for special prayer on his behalf. Marty thanked her sincerely and assured her that God truly had honored their prayers. Ma looked at Clark, busily shaking hands with the neighborhood men, and nodded her head slowly. "Yeah," she affirmed, "I can see thet He did. I don't see one ounce a' bitterness in the face of thet man."

The church bell called them to worship, and Marty and Clark took their familiar places with their family. It was strange not to see Pastor Joe leading the service, but the new young man whom the church had appointed did a fine job. Marty looked across at Josh and his family and realized that Nandry was not with them. She felt a moment of concern. Perhaps Nandry was busy elsewhere, she told herself, but after the service when she inquired, Josh informed her that Nandry just wasn't feeling herself and had decided to stay home. Marty felt a bit anxious, but Josh assured her that Nandry was all right, just not feeling her best. Marty promised herself that she would check on Nandry in a couple of days just to be sure. In the meantime, the family would miss them at the dinner table. Marty had counted so on all of her nearby family being there.

Anne was all that Arnie had described and more. Marty and Clark both loved her immediately. She was a rather quiet and serious girl, but her spirit was kind and gentle, and when she smiled, her whole face lit up and one could not help but smile in return. She loved Arnie—Marty could see it in her eyes and hear it in her voice. Just before Arnie left to take Anne back to town, Marty answered the unasked question in Arnie's eyes with a quick smile and an almost undetectable nod of her head. Arnie caught it and grinned. Marty had a feeling that when Arnie returned, he would have some news for the family. As a matter of fact, he did. He shared it with great gusto, and there was lots of back slapping and congratulatory hugs. He couldn't announce a wedding date yet, but he grinned and said it would be soon.

Marty did call on Wanda. They had a long visit and caught up on all of the happenings since they had last been together. Marty could see no change in her son, Rett. Though he lived in the body of a man, he had not really advanced beyond the small-boy stage. He still evidenced his uncanny ability with animals, and his menagerie had grown steadily over the years. Marty wondered how Wanda, who still clung to some of her eastern city-girl ways, managed to put up with the strange assortment of creatures with which she was asked to share her home. *Only a mother's love,* she decided with a smile as she watched the two of them.

Ma Graham came to call. She came alone now. All her children were married and had homes of their own, though Lou and his wife did live in a small house in the Graham yard and shared the farming duties with Ben. Marty caught up on all of the news of the family members and shared with Ma the latest happenings concerning Missie and her household.

Marty began rather slowly, but eventually she told in detail about the trying days following Clark's accident. Ma was the only person to whom Marty felt she could really bare her soul. As they talked and the shared tears fell, Marty felt that maybe Ellie was right. Maybe the whole ordeal had been harder on her than she had dared to admit. Maybe now that she had voiced it all, she would get back some of her old energy.

July came. Still no rain—except for a few scattered showers that didn't really count for much on the thirsty land. Daily, as a family, they prayed that the rain might come. Ellie kept busy with her watering pail trying to keep the plants from wilting. Even her brothers were not above carrying water for the very dry garden. The fields, as well, began to show the effects of the long dry spell. There was no way to bring water to the fields without the help of the Master of wind and rain.

A telegram from Missie set the whole household buzzing. It stated: *PA LAHAYE ARRIVED—STOP—SO DID MELISSA JOY, 7 POUNDS 10 OUNCES—STOP—THANK GOD FOR BOTH—STOP—ALL FINE—STOP*

The whole family rejoiced at the news, but Clare's eyes shone the brightest of all.

"Have ya told 'em?" he asked, giving Kate a nudge and a squeeze.

She answered with a shake of her head and a cheery, though embarrassed, smile. "Dr. Watkins said yesterday thet we're gonna be parents, all right."

And so there was more reason for rejoicing. Everyone in the family heartily congratulated Clare, who grinned at each comment, and hugged Kate as she flushed prettily. Marty looked at the girl's shining violet eyes and thought she had never looked prettier.

FIVE

Confessions

The storm moved in from the west with low-hanging clouds and a strong wind. Marty worried that the wind might drive the clouds right on by before the land had a chance to rejuvenate with the much-needed water. Her fears lessened as she stood at the window and watched the wind abate and the clouds hang low and heavy over the countryside. And then for three days, a continual steady rain emptied itself on the thirsty soil. When the sun returned, the growing things lifted high their drooping heads, all strength renewed. Marty felt like shouting praises. In fact, the whole family gathered together for a special thanksgiving prayer.

Kate was experiencing morning sickness. Marty felt sorry for her, but the girl only smiled. "It won't be for long," she insisted, "an' it will be worth it." Clare fussed over her and insisted that she take it easy and care for his "boy."

Already the two of them were busy with preparations for the coming baby—even though that "comin'" was more than seven months into the future. Marty, sharing their joy and enthusiasm, would welcome the wee baby, too. She suggested several home remedies to Kate that might help her over those often difficult early months of a pregnancy.

Marty continued to feel dragged out—not herself at all. She tried not to let it show, but the harder she tried to keep up with Ellie, the more it was obvious she couldn't. Clark suggested a trip in to see Dr. Watkins, but Marty shook her head. She had a suspicion that her age was showing and it bothered her some. She was an awfully young woman to be going through *that,* she kept telling herself. She did not express her concerns, but she felt her family's eyes upon her, watching with loving care.

"I'll be fine—just fine," she kept assuring them all, and she tried to be—tried with all her might to walk a little brisker, lift her feet a little higher, hold her head a little straighter. But most of the time it just didn't work. She felt tired before the day had hardly begun.

One morning she felt sick to her stomach. She passed it off as a touch of the flu. Then after an hour or two, she felt fine. But the next morning it recurred. She shrugged it off that time, too, but when it happened again on the third morning, even she was a bit worried, though she would not admit it.

"I'm as bad as Kate," she remarked to Ellie with an attempt at a light laugh.

"Well, I don't like it," Ellie said seriously. "Kate has a very good reason."

A wild thought suddenly went racing through Marty's mind, though she did not voice it to Ellie. *Ya don't s'pose . . . ? No, thet's impossible. Thet's unthinkable.* But it nagged away at her all day.

Each time it unwillingly returned, Marty tried to drive it away. *I'm past my forty-third birthday,* she kept telling herself. But inwardly she knew that really did not preclude this extraordinary possibility.

It's so silly . . . so foolish, she reminded herself. *Here I am—a grandmother many times over. I would be so embarrassed. . . .* And Marty's cheeks burned at the very thought of what might be.

The feeling of sickness continued to occur. Marty tried to hide the fact from her family. She made even more of an effort to look perky and carry her end of the household tasks. But even as she fought against it, she knew she was really being foolish.

It must be so, she finally admitted to herself and went to her room to have a rest and a good cry.

Whatever will Clark think? Here I am, a woman my age . . . and this!

Her thoughts moved on to the rest of her family. *What will Ellie think? And Missie? And Kate? Here Kate is expecting a baby of her own, and her mother-in-law, who should be long past such things, is joining her—stealing her thunder!*

And Arnie? Here he is planning his wedding, and his own mother will show up at it quite obviously with child. It'll embarrass him nigh to death!

Marty refused to share her worries with any of her family. It was the first time in her years of marriage to Clark that she kept something from him. *Maybe I'm mistaken,* she kept saying to herself. *Maybe I'm all wrong. Or, if I'm right, maybe I'll lose it. Women my age often do.*

But deep within, Marty knew she was probably correct and that the day would soon come when she would have to tell Clark. She dreaded it. Dreaded his reaction. Would he laugh? Or would he actually pity her? Marty could not stand that thought. *If he should look at me with eyes that say, "You poor thing," I'll be so mad. . . . But he just might,* Marty decided. *He just might. Especially the way I've been feeling.*

Marty decided she couldn't tell Clark—not yet. She'd wait awhile until she was absolutely sure.

Kate was now feeling a little better daily. Every time Marty saw Kate or Clare, it seemed they were talking about the coming baby. Never had Marty seen a couple anticipate a new arrival with such longing and joy. She envied them in a way. *It must be nice to be looking forward so—*

But Marty stopped herself. Hadn't she also looked forward to the arrival of each of her babies? *Each of them, but . . .* She didn't allow herself to finish it. She felt guilty about the way she was feeling toward this child. After all, this baby had not asked to be brought into the world.

She wondered what Kate and Clare would think if she suddenly were to announce, *Isn't it wonderful? I'm expecting a baby, too, and I think both babies will likely arrive about the same time.*

My, would eyes ever pop then!

But there was no way Marty would announce it like that.

Josh and Nandry were joining the family for Sunday dinners again. Marty was so glad to have them back, but she was concerned about Nandry. Something was troubling her. Quiet and withdrawn, she never looked directly at Clark unless he was seated at the table, and then her eyes seemed to slide over him. Was Nandry feeling all right? Was Marty imagining things? Was Clark's new appearance really troubling her in some way? Marty tried not to borrow trouble. At least Nandry and the family were with them, and for that she was thankful! Perhaps with a little time things would be as before.

"I've made an appointment with Dr. Watkins."

Clark made the statement matter-of-factly one night as he and Marty prepared for bed. Marty's head whipped around, concern filling her mind.

"Have ya been feelin' okay? Is yer leg—?"

But Clark interrupted. "Ain't fer me. It's fer you."

"Fer me?" asked Marty. "Whatever fer?"

"I've been worryin' 'bout ya, thet's what fer. Thought it might just take a while fer ya to get back on yer feet like, but ya haven't, Marty. Ya still have to push yerself an'—"

Anger colored her voice and face as she cut in. "Wish ya wouldn't have done thet. Nothin' wrong with me, an' there's no use troublin' Doc over somethin' thet—I'm fine, an' ya really had no call makin' an appointment without even talkin'—"

Clark reached for her and pulled her to him. Marty seldom responded in such an angry way, and when she did now, she knew he felt even more convinced that something was wrong.

He tried to hold her close, but she stubbornly stiffened her body. He did not speak, only stroked her hair.

She could not resist him for long. She began to relax against him. He went on holding her, gently kissing the top of her head. Suddenly, to his surprise, she crumpled up against him and began to cry.

Clark's grip on her tightened, and Marty knew he now was genuinely worried that something was seriously wrong.

"Please, God, please," she heard him whisper.

Marty did not weep for long. As soon as she had quieted, Clark spoke softly into her hair. "Somethin' is wrong, isn't it?"

Marty nodded her head against him, indicating that, yes, she thought there was.

"Have ya already been to the doc?"

Marty shook her head no.

"Then yer guessin'."

"I . . . I . . . don't think so," she sniffed.

There were a few minutes of silence.

"An' what are ya expectin' . . . ?" Clark didn't finish.

Marty waited for only a moment before she spoke through renewed sobs. "A . . . a . . . baby."

Clark pushed her back to arm's length, perplexity showing in his face. "A what?"

"A baby," she cried, her face crumpled with weeping.

"A *baby*?"

She nodded, wishing she could bury her head against his shoulder again so she wouldn't need to look into his eyes.

"A baby?" Clark repeated with only a shade less shock in his voice.

Marty just let the tears run down her cheeks. She closed her eyes. She wished to see neither reproach nor pity in his eyes. She stood silent and mute.

"Oh, Marty," Clark said, giving her a little shake.

Marty opened her eyes and looked directly and deeply into the eyes of her husband. There was no worry there. There was no pity. But there was love. Lots of love. Marty answered his look, and then she flung her arms tightly about his neck and wept again, tears of relief.

41

Clark held her for a long time, then pushed her gently from him. There was the trace of a smile on his lips.

"Thet's a bit of a wonder, ain't it?"

"A wonder?" repeated Marty, puzzled.

"Yeah, a wonder. Here I was a worryin'. Arnie's gittin' married soon an' movin'. Luke is goin' off to become a doctor, an' we both know there's no way we can hang on to Ellie fer long. An' here now, as I was hatin' to lose the last one, God is sendin' us another!"

Marty hadn't been giving God much credit for the whole event. She wasn't sure she liked the idea, even yet. She was a little old to be a mother again, and what in the world would her family and all of the neighbors think?

"I'd still like ya to keep the appointment," Clark was saying. "We wanta be sure thet everythin' is all right."

"Iffen ya want me to," Marty agreed, but she dreaded to face even the kindly doctor. She wished there was some way to keep her news to herself indefinitely.

"All of the family will be relieved," Clark went on. "We've all been worried thet somethin' might be wrong. It'll be a real relief—"

"A real embarrassment, ya mean," Marty interjected.

"What d'ya mean—an embarrassment? Yer simply bein' a woman the way the good Lord made ya. Nothin' wrong or embarrassin' 'bout thet."

Marty argued no further. She knew it would do no good. She also knew she was extremely tired. It was not difficult for her to agree to go to bed at Clark's gentle prompting.

SIX

Announcement

Clark pulled the team up before the house and helped Marty into the wagon. He drove to town more slowly than usual. Marty knew it was out of concern for her—and their unborn baby. She could feel her cheeks warm slightly as she wondered what Clark would think if he knew of the many times she had secretly hoped she would lose the child. Clark certainly wouldn't be having any such thoughts, she was sure.

It was a beautiful summer day. A rain shower had freshened their whole world just before dawn, and everything smelled green and growing. Marty pushed back her bonnet so she might get a better look at the familiar countryside. It had been a while since she had made this trip to town.

They passed the Grahams', and Marty waved to Ma, who was out in the garden, hoe in hand. Marty thought again of how very little of the hoeing in this year's garden she had done. Poor Ellie! She certainly had been carrying the load.

When they arrived at the doctor's, Clark helped Marty down over the wheel and gently steadied her on her feet. "I'll be in as soon as I tie the team," he promised.

Marty nodded and moved on to enter the small office. Three others were waiting, and Marty was glad to postpone her visit with the doctor for even a little while.

Clark soon joined her. The time went by too quickly, and before she was emotionally ready, it was her turn to step into the inner office. The doc began with a few preliminary questions. Marty prepared herself for the shocked look on his face when she told him what she had concluded, but it did not come. He seemed to feel it was quite the most ordinary thing in the world for a woman of forty-three, with a number of grandchildren, to be sitting in his office chair quietly informing him that she believed another child was on the way.

After the examination, Doc calmly assured Marty that she was right and that everything seemed fine. He made a few suggestions about what she might do to assure proper progress for the baby and renewed energy for herself. Marty solemnly promised to eat right and get plenty of rest.

Doc Watkins then called Clark into the room and offered his congratulations to the father-to-be. Both of the men seemed rather pleased with the fact of the coming baby, and for a moment Marty felt a trace of exasperation with them. She pushed it aside. They were right and she was wrong. There should be joy over the coming of a new life into the world. She must get her thinking into proper perspective.

When the Davises left the office, they did their needed shopping— not really all that much. In fact, it was Ellie who had prepared the list for Clark.

As they left the general store, Clark wouldn't allow Marty to carry even a small bundle. Instead, he insisted on making two trips himself, his crutch beating a rhythm on the wooden sidewalk. Marty waited rather impatiently in the shade until the groceries were carefully stored away.

"Why don't we git ya some tea?" Clark offered, and Marty agreed that it would pick her up a bit.

They headed slowly for the hotel dining room.

"Been wonderin'," Clark said as they walked, "iffen you'd like to git some things fer the new young'un while we're here. Seems to me there couldn't be much left from our previous babies."

Marty looked up at him in shock. She hadn't even thought about starting all over with the sewing of baby clothes and the making of diapers! Here Kate was as busy as could be, and their babies were due about the same time—and Marty didn't have one thing. But she took a breath and put a check on her thoughts. She just wasn't ready for that yet.

"There'll be plenty of time" was all she said.

Clark nodded and held the door for her.

All the way home, Marty's head spun. Her family knew she had been to the doctor today and were worried there might be something seriously wrong. They would need to know. She couldn't possibly continue to let them worry when nothing at all was "wrong" with her. It just wouldn't be fair. They would need to know the truth. Marty thought of asking to go to her room to lie down and letting Clark share the preposterous news. That really wasn't fair, she knew, and was the cowardly way out. Oh, how she dreaded it! How did one say it? What did you tell fully grown children? It used to be so easy. One gathered the little ones around and informed them joyfully, "We're gonna git ya a new baby. Only God knows whether it will be a new brother or a sister." And there was great rejoicing, and they would take sides as to who wanted it to be what. It was sort of like casting votes. On the day of the actual arrival, there were always winners and losers—but that was soon forgotten in the excitement of the new baby. After the initial announcement and a viewing of the new little one, everyone realized God had sent just what each one had really wanted.

Only this time, thought Marty, *we don't all want this baby. Maybe nobody really does. Oh, I know Clark will accept the new arrival all right, but is this what he really wants? Will the family really want a new baby? I know I don't. Not really.*

Marty was ashamed at the direction of her thoughts. But it was true. She hadn't planned on this baby. As much as she had enjoyed raising their family, she didn't want to start all over again with night feedings and diapers and round-the-clock care of a little one. It would not be happening had the choice been hers.

She pushed those thoughts aside and concentrated on the lazily drifting clouds overhead. It looked as though they might get a bit more rain. Well, she supposed they could use it. It seemed they never really got too much.

They passed the Grahams' again, and Marty was glad Ma was no longer in her yard. Somehow she felt that even in driving by and waving, her secret would be revealed. *Oh, what will Ma think?* And then Marty remembered that Ma had been her age when her last child was born.

But that was different, she argued with herself. *There wasn't a big gap between children, and she didn't have a whole passel of grandchildren by then, either.*

Marty's inner self quickly countered, No, *and you don't have a grand-child yet from any of the family you have actually given birth to. Nandry and Clae are both Tina's girls, and Missie is Ellen's girl. True enough now, though, you seem to be running a race with your firstborn son.*

In spite of herself, Marty smiled at the humor of it. It *was* rather funny. Why, she and Clare's Kate could well be confined at the same time. Imagine a child sharing a birthday with an aunt or uncle! She was sure there would be plenty of teasing ahead for both the little ones.

All too soon Clark was pulling the team up before the house and hopping down to help Marty. She dreaded it. Would they all storm her with questions the minute she entered the kitchen? She turned to go up the walk alone, but Clark was at her side.

Ellie met them at the door. Her eyes held her questions. She looked right past Marty and sought the eyes of her father.

Clark responded. "Ma's fine," he said with satisfaction, and the look of fear left Ellie's face, though Marty could sense that questions still remained.

Marty was surprised that Clark let it go at that, and she went on up to her room and changed into her housedress. Supper was almost ready.

It wasn't until the next morning at family worship that Clark brought up the subject. He had read a portion on the rich promises of God and the thankful response that His children should feel toward His loving-kindness. Each member of the family was invited to share something for which they were especially thankful. Clark stated that he was thankful for each family member that God, in His wisdom and love, had sent into the home, and then he led the family in prayer. After the prayer, he motioned for the little group to remain seated.

"When ya were all little an' we had a special announcement to make, we used to gather ya round us like this and share it together. Now, Luke here has never gotten in on any of those special announcements. Well, we are 'bout to correct thet. Lukey," he said, using the pet name of years gone by, "yer ma an' me got somethin' to tell ya. All of ya." Clark stopped to look around the circle. "We're missin' some of the family to be sure, but fer those of us here together, we want ya to know thet yer ma an' me are gonna git ya a new baby. Boy or girl, we not be knowin', but . . ."

Three pairs of eyes turned in unison to look questioningly at Marty. She felt herself squirm under the intensity of it. Arnie was the first to catch his breath. He gave a whoop and leaped from his chair. Luke was next. "Finally!" was what he shouted. "Finally I git my turn."

Marty couldn't believe her ears. She turned from her grown sons to Ellie, but she was crying. Oh no, did it really bother Ellie that much?

Marty moved toward her in concern, but Ellie met her halfway. "Oh, Mama," she wept, "I was so scared. So scared." And then she began to laugh through her sobs. "An' it's just a *baby*! 'Magine thet. A baby." Then she turned to her brothers. "I hope it's a girl," she stated emphatically.

"A boy!" they shouted in unison.

"A girl," insisted Ellie. "We already got more boys than girls."

"Thet don't matter," said Luke. "I still don't have a baby brother."

Clark held up his hand as a signal for silence. "Hold it," he said into the commotion. "Hold it. What it will be is already determined, an' no 'mount of yellin' on yer part is gonna change it none. I suggest we just wait an' see."

Marty looked around at her incredible family. They didn't seem to mind. They didn't seem to mind one bit. Of course, Arnie had always loved babies, and Ellie had always shown a tendency toward mothering. Luke maintained that he didn't get the fair end of things in not being a big brother to *someone*.

Marty shook her head. She might as well have purchased the materials for the making of the little garments. With a family like she had, there would be no peace until everything was prepared for the little one who was to bless their home.

SEVEN

Planning

Marty and Ellie had been invited over to Kate's for morning coffee. Marty was glad Kate was now feeling well enough to again think of serving them at a midmorning break. As yet, Marty still had no desire to eat until later in the day. She didn't say that to Kate, though. But when Kate began pouring the coffee and cutting the coffee cake, Marty asked for only a part of a cup and then generously poured cream in the cup to soften the bitter taste. Even then she was only able to sip at it. She passed up the dessert, as well. She was glad the girls did not press her.

Kate enthused about her coming baby. She seemed to expect Marty to be every bit as excited about her pregnancy as she was herself. Marty tried to show some enthusiasm. She hoped it came through as sincere. She was able to share in the joy that Kate's face held as she showed them garment after garment she had stitched.

"Clare insists it will be a boy," she laughed. "But I told him it could just as well be a girl."

"Men!" said Ellie. "They scare ya half to death with their knowledge of things to come! I'm glad when it finally does arrive, they are just as pleased with one as the other."

Marty wondered momentarily where Ellie got all her understanding of the subject. Well, she certainly had lived in a community—and a family—where there were lots of babies.

Kate showed them the nursery room, wallpapered in light green. The fluffy curtains at the windows were white, as was the painted trim. The yet-unfinished crib was quickly taking shape at the hands of Clare, who spent every available minute working on it. Kate herself was now sewing a crib quilt. To match the wallpaper, it was in a pale green calico print.

"Clare tried to talk me into blue," she laughed, "but I said I was gonna play it safe."

A small chest stood against the wall. As Kate opened the drawers, Marty saw many more already-completed baby items.

My, thought Marty, *it is still many months away. Whatever is she gonna do with all the extra time?*

Kate seemed to read her thoughts.

"I know we're gittin' ready awfully early, but iffen I get the necessary things outta the way, I can spend the rest of the waitin' time sewin' some 'specially fancy things. I wanna knit up some sweaters, too, an' I'm awfully slow at thet."

"Mama," said Ellie as they walked the short distance back to the big house, "are ya feelin' up to a trip to town?"

"I guess so. Why?"

"I'm a thinkin' it's 'bout time we got busy on this baby of ours. We don't want her comin' 'fore we're all ready."

"Baby of *ours?*" Marty repeated the words under her breath. Yes, she supposed that was the way Ellie thought of it. It would belong to all of the family.

"There's still plenty of time—" began Marty, but Ellie cut her short.

"Sure, there's lots of time, but we want lots of things fer her. I want her to be the best-dressed baby thet ever—"

"Now, hold on," laughed Marty. "She'll be properly cared fer, fer sure, but we ain't gonna go overboard. 'Sides, how any baby could ever have more'n thet little one of Kate an' Clare's is beyond my knowin'.'"

"Aren't they excited? Never seen a couple so eager fer a baby! Kate was an only child, ya know. She wanted a baby of her own from her weddin' day on. She'll make a good mother, too—I know she will."

Marty agreed. Kate seemed to be cut out for motherhood. She rejoiced with everyone who had the joy of a baby. Even the announcement of Marty's coming child had made her almost silly with happiness. Marty was glad. She didn't want the fact that she was also expecting a baby to rob Kate of any of her own anticipation. It hadn't. Kate seemed to bloom enough for them both.

"Well," insisted Ellie, "can we go shoppin'?"

Marty still hedged. She hated going into town and looking for material for baby things. Everyone would know and whisper and . . . No, she just didn't want to do that until there was simply no way of hiding it anymore.

"I'll buy it iffen ya want me to," Ellie offered.

"You?" Marty said, shocked. "Now why would I be wantin' folks to think thet *you* had need of such things?"

"Pshaw," responded Ellie. "It might be fer Kate, fer all they need to know. Or we might be sewin' fer Missie or Clae—they've each had a baby recently. An' anyway, Nandry might even—"

"Ya know somethin' 'bout Nandry thet I don't know?" asked Marty, half hoping she did. She wished with all of her heart that Nandry's somber withdrawal could be traced to something as simple as a baby on the way—although having a baby had never seemed to bother Nandry any before.

"Nope," said Ellie, "but somethin's strange, don't ya think?"

"Yeah," replied Marty with a deep sigh. "I've noticed it, too. I was hopin', though, thet I was imaginin' it."

"Yer not imaginin' it," Ellie responded. "It's there, all right. I haven't yet been able to figure out why, though. Iffen it were a baby . . ." Ellie let her thoughts hang in the air between them.

They reached the house, and Ellie continued around to the backyard to see if the wash on the line was dry. Marty went into the kitchen for a dry bread crust, in the hope that it might settle her queasy stomach. It didn't seem to help, so she went on up to her room to lie down for a spell. She would be so thankful when this dreadful morning sickness had run its course. Why was she having problems with this child, when none of her others had ever bothered her in this way? Well, Kate seemed to be fine now. If she could just hang on, perhaps the day would come when she, too, would feel well again.

Fall had brought with it both blessings and sorrows. Marty did finally feel better. It was so good to actually be hungry again. With the satisfied hunger came added strength. Marty could help more around the house without feeling completely exhausted. It was Ellie now insisting along with Clark that she slow down and not try to tackle everything in a day.

Fall was also the time for Luke to leave. Marty dreaded it. She tried to push the thought of the approaching day to the back of her mind, but it persisted to nag at her.

Again and again she reminded herself that Luke was no longer her baby. He was a young man and well able to care for himself. She had a hard time convincing herself, and as she sewed new shirts or knit new socks for him to take with him, tears often fell upon her work.

Luke was excited about his coming adventure, and it seemed to Marty that he spent far more time with Doc Watkins poring over medical books than he spent at home with his family. The doc was quite convinced that Luke would be the star pupil among the doctors in training and made no bones about telling his eastern colleagues so. Luke was to get special attention as the older doctor's protégé. Marty was glad there would be those who would be watching out for him, but it was still difficult to let him go.

She reminded herself often that Luke would be home with them again at Christmastime. Not only would it be Christmas and the family would be together, but it had been chosen as the time for Arnie's wedding, as well, so Luke could be the best man. Clark had agreed to pay for his train ticket home. Marty was glad. She would be able to judge for herself if Luke was standing the pressure of the medical training, and if he wasn't, then there surely would be some way to keep him at home.

She comforted herself with these thoughts as she worked the heel of the newly forming sock. She also faced again that it was only a matter of days until Luke and his belongings would board the stage to go meet the eastbound train.

One consolation for Marty was the fact that at the other end of the train trip, Joe and Clae and their family would be waiting. Although there was not room for Luke to be able to board with his eastern family, at least he would be able to visit them from time to time should he get lonely, Marty comforted herself. Luke had no such fears, and if Clark had, he did not voice them. He seemed to understand Marty's feelings, though, and he was gentle and reassuring as he spoke often of the short time until Christmas would be upon them.

All of Arnie's thoughts seemed to be taken with his Anne and the farm to which they would be moving following their wedding. The house that was located on the property needed repairing, and Arnie spent many hours with hammer in hand getting it ready. When other duties freed him, Clark, too, helped his son. On occasion, even Clare had some extra time that he used to help his brother with the task. The house soon began to shape up, and with it, Arnie's impatience seemed to increase.

The hammers and saws had to be laid aside for the harvest. There was a good crop to be taken in, and Luke would be around for very little of the time. Clark did a fair share. He had rigged enough contraptions together to be able to operate almost any of the farm equipment with just his one leg. The boys marveled as they watched him. He could keep up with almost anyone they knew.

All too soon the day of Luke's departure arrived. The whole family drove him into town to meet the stagecoach. Doc and his wife were there, too. Luke, near bursting with excitement, endured all kinds of good-natured teasing from his older brothers. The kind doctor had lots of last-minute advice. Marty wondered briefly if she even would get a turn at telling her son good-bye. Just before he was due to leave, he stepped over to her and hugged her close. Marty had to look up now, for her youngest was taller than she by a considerable amount.

"Ya take care, now," Luke whispered for just the two of them. "I don't want anythin' to happen to thet baby brother."

A sob caught in Marty's throat. *I'd gladly give up this baby if I could just keep you,* she wanted to say. But she didn't. Luke wouldn't want to hear that kind of talk.

Instead she held him close and said motherly things about caring for his health and getting lots of rest. She also assured him that she would be counting the days until Christmas, and he promised in return that he would be doing the same. His luggage was tossed up onto the waiting stagecoach as the restless horses stamped and pulled on the bits. The driver called, and Marty knew she must let him go. She stepped back and attempted a smile, a rather lopsided one. Luke's was broad in return. He let his hand touch her cheek, and then he wheeled and swung himself into the waiting stage. With a shout from the driver and a scattering of dust from the wheels, the coach jerked away. The horses were in a gallop before the driver had firmly settled himself. The lump stayed in Marty's throat, but she refused to allow herself to cry. There would be plenty of time for that later.

Why was life so full of good-byes? She looked over at Arnie. He would be the next one. And he was even more excited about the prospect than Luke had been. Why were they always in such a hurry to leave home?

Before Marty's thoughts could continue in this direction, Ellie was taking her arm and moving her down the street.

"Now you an' me are gonna do some shoppin'," she was saying, "an' I'm not gonna be put off any longer."

Marty nodded numbly. It was time. With Luke gone, she would need some kind of sewing to keep her hands busy. Besides, she was beginning to show—just a bit. She supposed that if people were going to talk, they would already be at it. She might as well settle their minds once and for all.

She allowed Ellie to lead her into the general store and over to the yard goods.

Little one, she apologized to the child she carried, *if you're really there—and I still have a hard time accepting the fact—you'll have to forgive me some. I just can't get excited about you—I didn't plan for you, and—*But Marty got no further, for a strange thing happened. With a suddenness that startled even her, the baby within answered with a fluttery movement. It was unmistakable, and with the movement came the clear knowledge that Marty did indeed carry within her another life. At that same instant, a love for the unborn child filled her being. Whoever this baby turned out to be, he or she was special, individual, and hers—hers and Clark's. And even though she hadn't planned it, the fact that this baby was growing, warm and safe, inside her body and would one day snuggle in her arms, impressed itself upon her.

"I hope thet yer a girl," she whispered under her breath as a tear slowly formed in her eyes.

"What'd ya say?" asked Ellie, busy laying out soft flannels and cottons for selection.

"Oh, nothin'," answered Marty, quickly disposing of the telltale tears. "Nothin' much. I'm just on yer side, thet's all. I hope it's a girl, too."

EIGHT

A Visit With Ma

Marty decided she would make a call on Ma Graham. Before word started to circulate throughout the community that the Davises were to be parents again, Marty wanted to tell Ma herself. She asked Clark for the team and bundled up snugly against the brisk fall breeze.

Even before she had the team tied at the Grahams' hitching rail, Ma was on her way across the yard, arms outstretched in welcome.

"How did ya know I've been achin' fer a good visit?" Ma called. "We haven't had us one since just after ya got home."

"I know," responded Marty. "I couldn't wait any longer."

"How ya been?" Ma asked, arm around Marty's waist on the way to the house.

"Fine—just fine."

Ma apparently let the answer go and ushered Marty into her kitchen, hanging up her coat on a peg by the door.

"Sit ya down," she said, "an' I'll put on the pot. Ya carin' fer coffee or tea?"

"Tea, I'm thinkin'."

Ma put another stick of wood in the firebox of the big kitchen stove and shoved forward the kettle. Then she joined Marty at the table.

"Yer lookin' better. Ya had me worried there fer a while. Every time I saw ya at church, I'd say to Ben, 'Somethin' ain't quite right 'bout Marty.'"

"Ya said thet?"

Ma nodded.

"My," said Marty. "I didn't have me any idea how many folks I had a worryin'. My family was frettin', too."

"But yer lookin' better."

"Feelin' much better, too." Marty smiled.

"Seen the doc?"

"I did, as a matter of fact."

"He able to tell ya what was wrong?"

Marty nodded in agreement.

"An' he was able to give ya somethin' to get ya over—?"

"Not exactly," Marty put in.

Ma's face again showed concern. "But ya said yer feelin' better."

"Oh, I am," Marty quickly affirmed.

Ma looked puzzled.

"Ya see," said Marty, "all thet is . . . I mean, the only reason I wasn't feelin' my best is thet . . . I'm . . . I'm in the family way."

Ma's eyes grew large and then her face grew into a broad smile. "Well, I'll be" was what she said. "Now, why in the world didn't I guess thet?" She chuckled and reached across the table for Marty's hand.

"Guess, like me, ya wasn't really expectin' it. I couldn't even believe it myself fer a long time."

"Well, I never," said Ma again, shaking her head with another chuckle.

"I'm showin'," said Marty and stood to her feet so that Ma could see for herself.

"Well, I declare," said Ma. "Ya are, yes, ya are."

Now Marty began to laugh and Ma joined her.

"Isn't thet somethin'?" asked Marty. "A woman of my age—an' a grandma?"

"Ya ain't so old. I had me another young'un after I was older'n you."

Marty quickly nodded.

The teakettle began to steam and Ma pulled herself up to go and prepare the tea.

"An' what does yer family think 'bout it?" she asked over her shoulder as she cut some gingerbread.

Marty shook her head. "Would ya believe thet every one of 'em thinks it's just fine?"

"Clark?" Ma asked as she rejoined her guest at the table.

"I'm afraid he has a hard time keepin' himself from bein' downright proud. He only holds hisself in check fer my sake."

Ma smiled, poured the tea, and passed Marty her cup.

"Well, thet sure beats fussin' 'bout it."

Marty knew that Ma was right.

"An' you?" asked Ma, passing Marty the gingerbread.

Marty was slow to answer. "Well, me," she said, "thet's a different story. I wasn't all thet happy 'bout the idea."

"Embarrassed?"

"Embarrassed! Scared! Worried!"

"Bein' sick like had ya scared?"

"Not really. I hadn't even figured out what was wrong with me fer a long time. When I did reckon it might be this, I was scared and worried 'bout what folks would think, not 'bout iffen I could make it okay."

"I know the feelin'," said Ma. "I felt thet way with my last one. Then I just got busy an' told myself thet it weren't nobody else's business anyway."

Marty laughed. "People make it their business," she said. But, to her amazement, she found she really didn't care anymore.

"Ya feelin' better 'bout it now?"

Marty looked into the teacup before her and watched the wispy steam rise upward. "Yeah," she said at length, raising her eyes to Ma's. "I feel better 'bout it now. After Luke left, there was a big emptiness, and then . . . well, Ellie insisted on shoppin' in town since we was already there. She's been pesterin' me 'bout gittin' some garments ready fer this here new one—an' a strange thing happened. It was the first time I felt movement. An' suddenly . . . well, I just felt a real love, all through me, fer this little stranger. I wanted the baby, Ma. I can't really explain it—I just knew I loved an' wanted this baby."

Ma nodded her understanding. "I know what yer meanin'," she said. "It's powerful hard to keep fightin' it once ya feel 'im really there."

The two women sat silently for a few moments, each deep in her own thoughts.

Finally Ma broke the silence. "Must have been awfully hard to let Luke go."

"It was. It really was. An' he was so excited 'bout it thet he could hardly contain hisself. . . . Might have been easier iffen he'd clung to me just a bit," Marty finished, her voice low.

Ma smiled. "Might have made ya feel better fer a minute, but it woulda made ya feel worse in the long run."

"I s'pose. I mighta cried all night iffen I'd felt he was hurtin', too."

"Seems they grow up too fast. Ya just git yer heart set on 'em, an' they're gone."

"It's Ellie thet frightens me."

"Meanin'?"

"Just don't know how I'm gonna stand it when it's Ellie's turn to go. She has been so good, Ma. Takin' over the runnin' of the house an' coaxin' me on. I just don't know how I'll ever manage without her."

"Ellie got a beau?"

"Not yet—but it'll come."

"I know what yer meanin'. Girl like Ellie can't hold off the young fellers fer long."

"She's never really paid thet much attention to the young men who've hung around, but one of these days . . ."

"I must confess," said Ma, "I been lookin' round me at church tryin' to sort out just which of the neighborhood fellers is good enough fer Ellie."

Marty nodded and admitted that she had been doing the same thing. Then she prompted Ma, "An' . . . ?"

"Ain't spotted 'im yet," answered Ma frankly. "Somehow it seems Ellie should have someone special like."

"Guess she'll think he's special when the time comes."

Ma reached for Marty's cup to refill it. "I know I fought it some when my young'uns were gittin' theirselves all matched up with their mates. Kinda glad it's all over now an' settled. They all chose ones I can be proud of, too. Kinda a good feelin' to know it's cared fer. They did a good job of it, too. I can sorta just sit back an' relax—an' enjoy the grandchildren."

"But yer grandkids are all nearby. Me, I've already got 'em scattered from the East to the West. I just don't think I could bear it iffen any more of 'em move so far away from home."

"Must be hard. I'd sure miss mine if they weren't here."

"Nathan an' Josiah are such sweethearts. An' there's the new little Melissa now. Who knows when I'll see her? An' Clae with her two little ones—we haven't seen her baby yet, either. Oh, I wish she could come home—even fer a short visit. It's hard, Ma. Hard to have them scatter. I miss them all so much."

Ma looked searchingly into Marty's face, then brightly and promptly changed the subject.

"An' how are Arnie's weddin' plans comin' along?"

The remainder of the time together was spent in discussing the family members who were close at hand, and Marty's spirits rose as she thought of the coming events and the happiness that was in store for each of them. And for her and Clark.

Winter settled in, and Marty was glad she had no good reason to be out as she watched the swirling snow and biting wind. Ellie was daily encouraging her on the sewing for the new baby, and it wasn't long until Marty's enthusiasm matched Ellie's.

Kate dropped in often. She obviously found great pleasure in the planning and preparations for the two babies. Clare shared Kate's eagerness, and he, too, was involved on the long winter evenings finishing the bed for the new little one who would make them truly a family.

Clark was finding it difficult to be as active as he had been in the summer and fall. The icy patches were often causing his crutch to slip, and after one or two near falls, he was content to let his grown sons handle most of the chores. He had always been easy to have around, and Marty enjoyed being with him more often.

Daily, Marty's love for her unborn child grew. She wondered how she could have ever *not* wanted it. The whole family was waiting for this baby with far more interest than they had shown for any of the others.

Most of Arnie's time and attention were given to his upcoming wedding. His little farmhouse was ready now. Anne had even hung the curtains in the windows and scattered a few rugs on the floor. Because Anne had no mother to help her with her preparations, Marty had been pleased to piece quilts and hem dishtowels and assist in any way she could. Already she felt very close to her new daughter-in-law-to-be. She was sure that Arnie and Anne would be very happy.

And so the wintry days and evenings passed, one by one. The house was brightened by friendly chatter, much coming and going, and busy activity shared by the family. Marty felt it was one of the most pleasant times she could remember, in spite of those members who were not with them.

A welcome letter arrived from Luke, and Marty opened it eagerly and read it aloud. He assured them he was fine and enjoying his studies. He stated that Doc Watkins had certainly given him an advantage over his other classmates; he understood so much that they had never been exposed to. He was boarding with a kindly old couple who fussed over him and pampered him. They had never had children of their own, and the woman was trying to catch up on all the years of missed mothering in just a few short months, Luke wrote.

He missed the family, he said, though he really had very little time even to think about it. He was going to a nearby church and had never seen so many young people gathered together before. Most of them were very kind and friendly. He hadn't seen Clae and her family very often. There just wasn't time for much visiting, but he was to join them for Thanksgiving, Clae insisted. They were all fine. The new baby was really sweet, and "Esther Sue had grown like you wouldn't believe." She had been shy with Luke at first, but she had gotten over that quickly. Joe was enjoying his seminary classes. He wondered how the little church back home had ever put up with his lack of knowledge. He couldn't believe how much there was to learn.

Luke ended his letter with a message for each of them. Marty was admonished to take care of herself and that coming baby. He would be home soon for Arnie's wedding and Christmas, and he wanted everything to be just as he remembered it.

There was a postscript on the bottom addressed to Ma. "I really won't mind if it's a girl," the sentence read, and Marty brushed at unbidden tears as she folded the letter and replaced it in its envelope.

Dear, dear Luke, she thought. *Alone and so busy—and lovin' every minute of it.*

But Luke was right. Before they knew it, Christmas would be upon them.

NINE

Ben

Marty felt like she had just snuggled down and closed her eyes when there was a pounding on the front door. Clark bounded from the bed and was pulling on his clothes while Marty struggled to a sitting position.

"What is it?" she wondered.

"Don't know—but someone seems to want us powerful bad."

Clark left the room, his crutch beating a fast rhythm as he hurried toward the stairs.

"Light the lamp," Marty called after him. "You'll be fallin' in the dark." But Clark was already on his way, no doubt feeling his way through the hallway and down the steps.

Marty left her bed and reached for her wrap. She could see Arnie beyond her door, and he had taken the time to light a lamp.

Ellie called to him from her room. "What is it?" Marty heard her ask.

"Not knowin' yet," answered Arnie. "Pa has gone to see."

He moved on down the stairway, and Marty slipped into her house socks and quickly followed after him.

Arnie turned when he heard her coming. "Ma, ya shoulda stayed in bed," he said.

"I'm all right," she insisted.

"Watch yer step," said Arnie, reaching out a hand to assist her.

Lou Graham was in the kitchen talking with Clark when the two entered. Clark looked up, and when he saw them he moved to Marty and put an arm around her shoulders. "It's Ben," he said softly.

Marty had many questions, but she could not find voice to ask any of them. Her heart was pounding as she looked from one face to the other. Surely it was serious to bring Lou out in the middle of the night. Ellie joined them, a puzzled frown on her face.

Clark moved a chair toward Marty, and she sat down.

"What happened?" It was Arnie who finally was able to speak.

"His heart," answered Clark.

A moment's silence, and then, softly, "How is he?"

"He's . . . he's gone."

"Gone?" It was Marty now. *There must be some mistake!* Her thoughts whirled. Why, she had seen Ben herself just a short time ago, and he looked perfectly well. He had taken care of the team when she was over to visit Ma and had even given out some good-natured teasing. There must be some mistake. It couldn't be Ben. Not Ben Graham.

Clark was speaking. "It happened just as he was gittin' ready fer bed. I'm goin' over, Marty."

Marty's stunned mind and emotions were scrambling to sort out what was being said—what was going on. *Ben was gone—Ben Graham— their good neighbor of so many years. Ma was a widow again. Clark was going to her.*

Marty shook her head and tried to stand. "I'm goin', too," she said quietly yet with insistence. "I'm goin', too."

She could feel their eyes upon her. Each one in the circle seemed to be saying no, even though no one had actually said it. Marty wrapped her robe more closely about her and took a deep breath. She squared her shoulders and looked at them.

"I'm goin', too," she said evenly. "Ma needs me—an' I'll be just fine."

Still no one voiced an argument, and Marty went back to her room to get dressed. Ellie followed her.

"Mama," she said, "be sure ya dress warm. It's cold out there."

Marty nodded and mechanically went on laying out her clothes.

When she went downstairs again, Clark was waiting. Lou had already gone on to take the sad news to others in the family. Arnie was heating a brick in the fireplace, and Marty knew that it was to keep her feet warm as they traveled. The team was ready, and they stomped and blew impatiently. They did not cotton to the idea of leaving their warm stall on such a night.

Without comment Clark helped Marty in, and Arnie placed the wrapped brick at her feet and tucked a heavy robe securely about her. His feelings showed without words in his extra care for her comfort and safety. Clark picked up the reins, clucked to the team, and they were off.

Marty had never experienced such a silent trip to the Grahams'. All the way there, she attempted to accept the truth that Ben Graham was dead—but it did not seem real. She wondered if Clark was wrestling with it, as well, but she did not ask.

A pale moon was shining, reflecting off the whiteness of the snow-covered fields. A million stars seemed to be blinking off and on overhead. Vaguely she wondered if anyone knew for sure just how many were up there—no, she supposed not. There were too many. Only God himself knew the actual count.

And God himself knows about each one of His children. Marty closed her eyes. He knew what had happened this night. He knew of Ben. Why, He had already welcomed Ben into the courts of heaven. Was He glad . . . pleased to have one more child at home? Marty would be. If one of her far-off children were suddenly to walk through her door, she would be celebrating. Maybe God was celebrating—celebrating because Ben was home.

But what about Ma? her thoughts went on. She was alone again now. Did God know that, too? Did He know how empty and lonely Ma would be feeling? What was it that Ma had said to her long ago about losing her first husband, Thornton? Ma had said she had wanted to die, too, that a part of her seemed to be missing or numb or something. Well, Ma would be feeling that way again. She had loved Ben so much, had shared with him for so long. Ma would be empty and hurting, and there wouldn't be any way that anyone—anyone in the world, no matter how much they loved her—would be able to help that hurt.

Suddenly Marty was crying—tearing sobs from deep inside. *Oh, Ma. Oh, Ma! How ya ever gonna bear it?* she mourned inwardly. It was true. It really was true. Ben was gone.

Clark let her cry, though he placed an arm around her and drew her closer to him. He didn't try to hush her. He knew as well as she did that she needed the release of the tears.

By the time they reached the Graham farmyard, Marty had herself under control. Lights shone from each window. Teams and saddle horses milled and stomped in the yard, doors opening and closing quietly as family arrived.

Clark helped Marty down and then moved the team on farther into the yard to tie them at a corral post. Marty waited for him, dreading that first meeting with poor Ma. She didn't want to go in by herself.

When Clark returned to take her arm and lead her to the house, they spoke for the first time.

"Looks like the whole family's here," said Marty softly.

"Yeah, Lou said he was lettin' 'em know."

"Good thet they're all close by."

"Lem was away—don't know iffen they got in touch with 'im yet."

They reached the house, and without knocking, Clark ushered them in. The big farm kitchen was full of people. Coffee cups sat on the table, but no one seemed to be drinking from them. Tearstained faces were turned toward Ma, who sat before an open Bible and, with a quavering yet confident voice, was reading to her family.

"' . . . for his name's sake. Yea, though I walk through the valley of the shadow of death, I will fear no evil: for thou art with me; thy rod and thy staff they comfort me. Thou preparest a table before me in the presence of mine enemies: thou anointest my head with oil; my cup runneth over. Surely . . .'" Ma's voice broke. She waited a moment and then went on, her voice ringing out stronger than before: "'Surely goodness and mercy shall follow me all the days of my life: and I will dwell in the house of the Lord for ever.'"

She placed both hands on the Book and closed her eyes, and everyone in the room knew she was believing its promises and silently making them her own in prayer.

When she opened her eyes again, she saw that Clark and Marty were there. Without a word she held her hands out to them as a fresh collection of tears spilled down her worn cheeks. Marty moved quickly to her and took her in her arms. They clung and cried together. Marty was vaguely aware of voices and movement about her. She knew that Clark was offering his sympathy to other family members. She must speak to them, too, but Ma came first.

After the initial expressions of sorrow, they sat around the kitchen sharing memories of Ben and discussing plans for his funeral service. There wasn't a great deal of preparation to do. The new undertaker in town would prepare the coffin. The young minister had not been called in the dead of the night—Ma insisted that he be allowed to sleep. She had her family and her neighbors, and there was plenty of time to make the arrangements. Besides, she declared, the poor young man had already lost three nights' sleep sitting up with ailing Maude Watley. Her condition seemed to have improved somewhat, and the minister finally had been able to get a night's rest.

The neighborhood men would dig another grave in the little yard beside the church. Clark offered to make sure that was done. Tom thanked him for his kindness. "But," he said, "the boys an' me been talkin', an' we'd kinda like to do it ourselves."

Clark's understanding of their desire was clear as he nodded his agreement.

Sally Anne was weeping the hardest. Marty found her in Ma's bedroom, Ben's old farm work hat crumpled up against her, the sobs shaking her entire body.

Marty tried to comfort her, but Sally Anne just cried all the harder.

"I'll be all right," she finally gasped out between sobs. "Just please leave me be." So Marty left. Sally Anne was going to need time to sort out her grief.

The day of the burial was cold. But the wind had gone down, for which all were thankful. Still, the sky was gray and the air frigid. Marty clasped her coat about her and prayed for the group of family members who were clinging tightly to one another. It would be a hard day for each of them. And when they scattered again to their various homes, what would become of Ma then?

Marty was glad that Lou and his wife and two children lived near her. At least Ma would have someone close. Still, it would be hard for her—hard to face an empty house, hard to lie alone in a bed that had been shared for so many years, hard to sit at a table where no one used the adjoining chair. Yes, she had many difficult days ahead of her. Marty was glad Ma had a deep faith in God that would help her through the days of intense sorrow. She must remember to pray for her daily. And visit her as she could. Maybe Ma would like to be included in some upcoming family dinners.

But Marty also knew that Ma wasn't likely to sit around and feel sorry for herself. What an example of faith in trying times she was to the whole community.

TEN

Good News

Life required that everybody carry on, so even though their hearts were heavy, family and friends of Ben put their minds on living and the everyday tasks that called for their attention.

It was only a few weeks now until Christmas and Arnie's wedding. Marty tried her hardest to keep an atmosphere of anticipation for the sake of her family, even though she could not get out from under the heaviness she felt for Ma and her family. Ma was often in her thoughts and prayers.

Clark returned home from town one day and hurried into the kitchen, his expression telling Marty he had news.

"Yer not gonna believe this. Guess what I just heard."

Marty looked up from the small baby gown in which she was making dainty tucks. "Couldn't guess," she said. "What's goin' on now?"

"Willie's pa has been so impressed with the West thet he's talked the whole family into goin' out fer a look."

"Yer joshin' me," said Marty, laying down her handwork in disbelief.

"Not joshin'."

"Ya mean they're *all* movin' out?"

"Not movin'. Not yet anyway. They're just goin' on out fer a look-see."

"Callie an' the kids, too?"

"Yep."

"Who's to care fer the farm?"

"Now this yer *really* not gonna believe."

Marty felt her eyes widen, wondering what in the world could be more difficult to believe than what she had already heard.

"Lane," said Clark.

"Lane?"

"Lane."

"Our Lane? I mean Willie's Lane?" Marty was stunned.

Clark laughed. "Told ya you'd never believe it."

"I can't imagine—Lane comin' back here! Are ya sure?"

"I'm sure. Zeke LaHaye showed me the letter hisself. Fact is, Lane's s'posed to arrive tomorra so's he can learn all he needs to know 'fore the LaHayes leave next Tuesday."

"Yer right—I can't believe it!" exclaimed Marty, excitement taking hold of her. "Lane comin' here. Isn't thet somethin'?"

"Ellie," she said, hurrying to the kitchen, "Ellie, Lane's comin'."

Ellie lifted her head from the potatoes she was peeling.

"Who's Lane?" she asked.

"Lane. Willie's Lane. We told ya 'bout 'im."

"Lane," repeated Ellie and frowned as she tried to remember. Clark joined them in the kitchen.

"Want some coffee, Pa?" Ellie asked, and Marty was just a trifle irritated that Ellie hadn't responded more enthusiastically to the wonderful news of their friend's arrival.

Without waiting for her father's answer, Ellie moved to reach for two coffee cups, which she placed on the table and filled.

Clark thanked her and sat down, pulling one cup toward him, and Marty took the chair opposite him and accepted the other cup. Ellie had already gone back to peeling potatoes.

"I just can't believe it," Marty said again, not willing to let the matter drop. "Lane comin'."

"How so?" asked Ellie.

"The LaHayes are goin' out to see Willie an' Missie. Gonna be there in time fer Christmas and then stay on a spell," Clark explained again.

Finally Ellie's hands stopped their busy paring, and her head bobbed up. "Really? Missie will be so excited she'll near go crazy. 'Magine thet. Havin' all thet family fer Christmas!"

Marty smiled as she pictured Missie's excitement and busy preparations. "And we can send some Christmas presents with them—"

Clark's laugh interrupted her. "Yeah, well, ya better go easy on how much you send—the LaHayes are gonna have enough luggage of their own."

"Who's gonna look after their place?" asked Ellie, and Marty noted silently that the girl hadn't been listening.

"Lane," she answered patiently.

"Oh, *thet's* why Willie's sendin'—what's his name?"

"Lane."

"Lane who?"

Clark began to laugh. "His name's Lane Howard. He's one of Willie's hands. Guess he must know somethin' 'bout farmin', or Willie wouldn't be sendin' 'im."

"I see," said Ellie, and her hands began to work on the potatoes again.

"He's such a fine boy," Marty said. "He's the young cowboy who was the first one to come to Willie's services, an' he was the first one to believe."

Ellie nodded her interest in that piece of news.

"He's a mighty fine young man," Clark agreed. He looked off into space as though seeing some events in his memory.

"It was Lane who knelt down beside Jedd Larson and joined me in prayer when Jedd was in such a bad way."

"It was Lane who rode through the cold night to get Doc de la Rosa fer Jedd, too," added Marty.

"Yeah, an' Lane hitched the team and drove back through the night to take Jedd over to Doc's house," Clark continued.

"He rode with ya, too, when ya went on over on Christmas Day," Marty reminded Clark.

"Yeah, he did, didn't he?" Clark smiled. "I can still see him climbin' down off his horse an', without sayin' a word, takin' his blanket to cover up my stub of a leg. Boy, was it cold! I think thet I'd a froze it fer sure iffen Lane hadn't done thet. An' me—I was too dumb to even think 'bout it needin' coverin'."

Ellie looked back and forth between her parents as they remembered their experiences with Lane out west.

Marty said, her voice low and husky, "Don't know iffen ya even knowed it, but Lane was the one who helped the doc when he took off yer leg. Willie wanted to, but he was afraid he couldn't stand it, so he went fer help—an' it was Lane who volunteered."

"Didn't know thet." Clark shook his head, looking thoughtful. Then he sighed. "Shoulda known it, though, thet Lane would be the one—"

"It'll be so good to see 'im again. When did ya say he's comin'?" Marty asked.

"S'posed to be tomorra."

"We'll have 'im over right away!"

"Now, hold it," laughed Clark. "Willie is sendin' 'im out here to look to his family's farm, not to spend his time—"

"I know thet," retorted Marty, "but surely we can have 'im visit now an' then without any harm bein' done. He has to eat, now, don't he?"

Clark stood up and ruffled her hair.

"Reckon we can," he said. "I was thinkin' myself thet it'd be awful nice to give 'im an invite fer Christmas."

"I hope we don't need to wait thet long to see him. I'd nigh bust by then."

Clark laughed again. "Got me a feelin'," he said confidently, "thet he'll be lookin' us up."

Marty hoped Clark was right. Lane was almost like family, like he'd be bringing a little piece of their beloved Missie's family with him.

"Look at thet sunshine," Ellie commented to Marty. "Think I'm gonna go out an' git me a little of it."

Marty followed the girl's eyes to the window. It was a truly glorious winter day.

"I was just thinkin' the same," she said. "Think I just might go on over an' have me a cup a' tea with Kate."

"Good idea. I might even join ya iffen I git my chores done in time, but don't wait on me. I might git to enjoyin' the sun so much I'll decide not to come in."

Marty smiled. Ellie had always loved the out-of-doors.

"Go ahead," she said. "It'll do ya good."

"Ya git ready," said Ellie, "an' I'll walk ya on over to Kate's so ya won't slip on the ice."

"Ya fret too much," Marty countered. "Just like yer pa. I've been walkin' on ice fer a good number of years now, an' I don't recall takin' a tumble yet."

Ellie shook her head without saying anything further, put on a light coat, and stood waiting, so Marty pulled a warm shawl about her and they started off together. The sun reflected brightly off the snow and made them squint against the glare. It felt warm on their heads in spite of the cool air.

"Hard to believe we're 'bout due fer Christmas. Feels more like spring," observed Marty.

"Doesn't it, though?" answered Ellie. "But I'm so glad it's nice. Makes it better fer Lady and her puppies."

"How are they doin'?"

"Oh, Mama, they're so cute now. 'Specially thet little black-an'-white one. He has the biggest eyes an' the floppiest ears. I hope Pa will let me keep 'im."

"We hardly need another dog around here, I'm thinkin'."

"But he's so cute."

"Puppies are all cute," reminded Marty. "When they grow up they're just another dog."

"Now, ya can't be tellin' me thet ya aren't partial to dogs," Ellie remonstrated, and Marty laughed, knowing Ellie was right. She had always loved dogs, and each time there had been a new batch, she was the one who suffered the most as she watched the puppies going off to new homes.

They reached Kate's house, and Marty was warmly welcomed in, while Ellie went on to care for her chickens.

The young man swung off his horse, tied it to the rail fence, and walked up to the door. Several knocks received no response, so he turned toward the barn, where he saw the door standing open.

After Ellie had finished feeding the chickens, she had gone on to the barn to see the puppies. The day had become so delightfully warm she hadn't gone far before removing her coat.

She had thrown the barn door wide open and let the sun stream into the building. Lady ran to meet her, four pudgy puppies tumbling and stumbling along behind her. Ellie tossed aside her coat and fell down on her knees in the warm, sweet-scented straw.

"Oh," she crooned, picking up her favorite and pressing it against her cheek. "Yer just the sweetest thing."

A small tongue licked haphazardly at her nose, and Ellie kissed the soft fuzzy head and reached for another puppy. A third one began to tug at her skirt, growling and pulling as though tackling something unknown and dangerous. Ellie laughed and playfully pushed at the puppy with her foot. The puppy swung around and attacked her shoe instead. She pulled him into her lap and reached for the last one, a shy little female, the smallest of the litter. "Come here, you," Ellie said, coaxing the little one closer. She settled herself into a sitting position and cuddled the puppies in her lap. Lady pressed herself close, taking a lick at Ellie's face, her arm, her hand—wherever she could get one in. Ellie lifted her feisty little favorite again and pressed him close against her cheek. "I must ask Pa iffen I can keep ya," she told him.

Ellie was so busy with the puppies she hadn't seen the shadow that crossed the door; nor did she notice the figure who stood there, looking at the shining golden head bowed over the squirming puppy. He watched silently. She lifted her face to the sun, and it fell across her cheeks, highlighting their glow and the deep blue of her eyes. Still she had not seen him, so enraptured was she with her little friends. She stroked the curly fur gently with slender fingers and caressed the fluffy, drooping ear.

"Yer just the sweetest thing," she went on, lifting him so she could look the puppy in the face. "How could anyone give ya up?"

Lane had not moved. He knew he shouldn't be standing there watching her with her unaware that he was present, but he couldn't bring himself to break the spell of the scene before him. Who was she, this delightful young woman? She was as pretty and wholesome as . . . as . . . Lane had nothing to compare her to. He had never seen someone like her.

It was the dog who gave away his presence. Lady turned toward him and whined, her tail beginning to wave ever so slightly. Ellie lifted her eyes from the puppy to the door. At the sight of the young stranger, she gave a little gasp and hastened to her feet, scattering the three puppies playing on her skirt into the soft straw.

Lane quickly found his tongue.

"I'm sorry, miss—to startle ya like thet. I wasn't meanin' to. I'm . . . I'm lookin' fer the Davises."

"In a barn?" she asked, but her tone held more banter than blame.

"I knocked at the house an' didn't get an answer."

When she didn't say anything, he explained, "I . . . I saw the barn door open an' I thought someone might . . ." He trailed off. "I'm sorry if I've imposed, miss."

"No harm done," she said finally and put the puppy back down with its mother.

"Am I at the right farm or—?"

"We're the Davises," said the young woman before him, reaching down to brush straw from her skirt. "Who was it ya wished to see?"

"Missie's folks," he responded. "Clark an' Marty."

Ellie felt her eyes grow wide with shock and some embarrassment, and she took a good look at the young man who stood before her, hat in hand. *This must be the Lane Ma and Pa were talking about,* she thought as she looked him over.

He was tall and rather thin, though his shoulders were broad. He had a clean-shaven face and deep brown eyes. His jaw was firm set, as though once he had made up his mind it might be hard to change it. He wasn't what Ellie would call handsome—his somewhat crooked nose prevented him from being that—but he had a certain bearing that made you wonder if he wouldn't be a nice person to get to know.

Ellie let her gaze drop, further embarrassed by her bold scrutiny of the stranger.

"Mama is at Kate's right now, an' Pa is about the farm somewhere," she explained quickly.

She moved to lead the way to Kate's house, and he fell into step beside her.

They walked to Kate's without speaking further, and Ellie rapped lightly on the door but didn't wait for Kate's answer before she entered.

"Mama," she said, "there's someone here to see ya," and she stepped aside to let the young man enter.

Marty gave a little cry and sprang up from the table.

"Lane!" she said as she greeted the young man with a motherly embrace.

Marty turned from hugging the young man to Kate.

"An' this is Kate, Clare's wife," she introduced him warmly. "An' ya already met our Ellie."

Ellie stood rooted to the spot, feeling rather self-conscious and silly under Lane's gaze. He stepped forward.

"Not really," he said. "I sorta found her—but we weren't introduced proper like."

"Ellie," said Marty, "this is Lane, the one we've told ya so much 'bout."

Lane moved closer to acknowledge the introduction.

Ellie held out her hand. "I'm pleased to meet ya," she said softly. "I'm sorry I didn't realize who ya were."

Lane took the hand and looked into Ellie's blue eyes. Neither of them spoke. Ellie was rather surprised and not a little dismayed by her tumbling thoughts. She'd had no shortage of young men who would have stood in line to come calling if she'd given the slightest hint of interest, but none of them had made her feel like this. *You only just now met this Lane,* she told herself sternly. *Now get yourself back in hand,* she finished her silent lecture.

Marty insisted that Lane stay for supper. It hadn't been too difficult to persuade him. He said he was anxious for a good, long visit with Clark and Marty. He had news concerning Willie and Missie and their family. He had up-to-date reports on the new little church and its growth since they had left. There were messages from the ranch hands. And then, he said, there was his number-one reason for being in their home that evening—the package from Missie that he was to hand deliver. He reached into his shirt pocket. "Missie sent this, an' she told me not to dare fergit."

Lane withdrew a piece of carefully folded paper.

"Missie sent ya a lock of Baby Melissa's hair." He handed the small packet to Marty. Marty unwrapped it carefully, and a tiny scrap of soft, fluffy baby hair lay snuggled against the paper.

Ellie watched her mother struggle to hold back the tears.

"Far away in the West I've got a little granddaughter," Marty whispered as she held up the tiny baby curl. She lifted it up and it wrapped around her finger. There was just a tint of red to the golden lock. Marty held it to her lips and the tears began to fall.

Marty wiped her eyes as she turned to Lane. "Thank ya," she murmured. "She must be beautiful."

"We think so," Lane said. "We all think so."

"What a place fer a little girl to grow up," Clark spoke up. "There on a ranch with a dozen men to spoil her!"

They all laughed.

ELEVEN

Ma Graham

Marty wanted to see Ma one more time before Christmas, so she asked Clark to hitch up the team for her while there was still a pleasant break in the winter weather. He reluctantly agreed because he knew how important it was to her, but his eyes showed his concern.

"Sure yer not wantin' me to drive ya on over?"

"I'll be fine," Marty assured him. "Really, Clark, I'm feelin' just fine now. Best I been feelin' fer months."

Clark eyed her rounded body. "Well, be extra careful," he cautioned.

But Marty stopped him with a playful toss of her wet dishrag. "I won't be doin' any racin'," she promised with a smile.

Though the wintry sun was shining, the air still held a sharp chill. Marty had not gone far when she was glad for the extra blanket tucked about her at the insistence of her family.

She wondered who might be meeting her in the Graham yard to take the team now that Ben was gone. He had always been so quick to greet her and hurry her off to see Ma while he tended the horses. The thought of Ben not being there made Marty's heart ache once more for the empty place left in their lives.

She thought of Ma and wondered just how she was handling the long days and nights alone. It must be awfully hard on her and even more so with Christmas approaching. Christmas was a beautiful time of year but also a very lonely time if a person had recently lost a special loved one.

When Marty turned the team into the Graham yard and alighted from the sleigh, she was soon greeted by Lou, who came from the barn. He welcomed her warmly and sent her on in to see Ma, just as his father had done on so many previous occasions.

Marty did not have time to knock, for Ma had seen her through the window and came to meet her.

"Been so hopin' ya would come!" Ma said. "Been needin' ya somethin' awful."

Marty removed her heavy coat, hugged Ma, and crossed to warm her hands at the kitchen stove.

"I was thinkin' ya might," she said, her own tears close to spilling. "My thoughts are of ya so much, an' I'm prayin' so often . . . but thet . . . even thet doesn't help much, I'm afraid."

"Oh, it helps. To be sure, it helps," Ma assured her. "I've just been feelin' the prayers of those who are upholdin' me. I have no idea how I'd ever make it without 'em."

They both were silent for a moment.

"It sure does git lonely, though," Ma went on as she motioned Marty toward a chair at the table. "Even with my family nearby—an' they've been so good, always invitin' me fer supper or coffee or just to talk. But I've got to make the adjustment on my own, Marty. At first I was over there 'most every day. Thet was fine fer a while, but I can't keep on like thet. I've just gotta make the adjustment to livin' alone."

Marty sat down, and Ma pulled out a chair across from her.

"Ya know, in some ways," Ma went on, "this time is harder than when I lost Thornton."

Marty was surprised.

"What I'm meanin' is this: when I lost Thornton, even though it was terrible hard—'cause I loved him so much an' he was so young, and I was so unprepared—still I had my young'uns, an' I knew thet I couldn't give up—not fer a minute. They sorta kept me goin', if ya know what I mean. I scarce had time to think of my own sorrow. Well, this time I'm

78

here all alone. My young'uns are grown now. It seems there just isn't a good reason to keep on a goin' a'tall."

"Oh, but there is," Marty quickly put in.

"I know. I know. I preach myself all those sermons many times a day, but I have a hard time believin' 'em."

"Ya said thet it takes time," Marty reminded Ma. "Remember? Ya haven't had much time yet, Ma." Marty reached across to grasp the work-worn hands folded one on top of the other.

Ma sat with head bowed, and Marty feared Ma would suddenly begin sobbing. Instead she squared her shoulders and looked up with a shaky yet brave smile. "Time?" she said. "It do take time, all right. Time an' God."

Marty toyed with an edge of the table, running a finger back and forth on the wood grain. "Wouldn't hurt none, either, iffen ya tried to look ahead," she said. "Christmas is comin'. Ya got a whole passel of grandchildren. Got their gifts all ready?"

Ma shook her head.

"Best ya git out yer knittin' needles and yer crochet hook, then, 'cause they're all gonna be expectin' Grandma to come up with the usual passel of scarves an' mittens."

"Oh, Marty, I just have no heart fer Christmas!" Ma mourned.

Marty rose and moved around the table to lay her hand on the shoulder of the older woman. "The hardest Christmas I ever faced was the one just after I lost Clem," she stated. "But ya know what? In lookin' back now, I see it as my most meanin'ful Christmas. Never have I felt the true meanin' of Christmas more'n I did thet year.

"I've often wondered why," she went on, sinking into the chair next to Ma, "but I think maybe it was because thet year I decided to use Christmas as a growin' time. I didn't even understand what it was all 'bout at the time, but I knew God had a far deeper meanin' fer Christmas than we usually give it. I wanted it. I wanted to find an' understand thet meanin'. At the time, all I knew was thet I wanted to give Missie a special Christmas. She had already lost so much, an' I wanted to help heal some of those painful memories. In givin' to Missie, I got far more myself. I kinda think thet's the true meanin' of Christmas. . . ." Marty paused and looked into Ma's face.

"Now, ya got a family," she continued after a moment. "A family thet ya love very much." Marty's voice was low but clear. "They are all hurtin' in their own way, but mostly they are feelin' deep sorrow fer you. Christmas isn't gonna mean much to any of 'em—unless *you* can give it meanin'. They need ya, Ma. They need ya ever' bit as much as they did when they lost their other pa."

Ma was crying softly as Marty spoke. When Marty finished, the older woman blew her nose and wiped her eyes.

"Yer right," she said. "In my sorrow I just haven't seen it. They do need me. All of 'em."

She left the table and went for the boiling coffee.

"My lands!" she exclaimed as she poured two cups and lowered herself wearily back into her chair. "I'm way behind. By this time most years I already had four or five pairs of mittens finished. I'm really gonna have to hustle, ain't I, Marty?"

TWELVE

Lane Helps Out

The LaHaye family got away on their visit west as planned, and Lane settled in to oversee their farm. There really wasn't all that much to do over the winter months. The stock needed tending, and there were two cows to milk night and morning, but he still wondered if he'd have empty hours hanging over him.

Glad that he had an excuse, he went to see the Davises and explained his predicament to Clare and Arnie. He began with, "What ya usually doin' with the long days of winter when there be no field work?"

"Well, we more'n have our days full with cuttin' the year's wood supply," answered Clare.

"The LaHayes got wood stacked a mile high," Lane informed them. "Told me not to be botherin' 'bout gittin' out any more. They gotta use thet up before it goes rotten."

"Then we've got all of the stock to care fer."

"They don't keep much stock. One sow, a few chickens, some milk cows, and a few beef cattle. They don't even have 'em a dog."

Arnie laughed. "Hope ya like readin'," he joked.

"Don't mind readin'," answered Lane, "but I sure don't wanna be doin' it all the time. Mind iffen I give ya a hand with yer cuttin'?"

"Yeah, we're gonna be gittin' out a little extra wood this year. Gonna have three fires of our own to keep burnin', what with the folks', mine, an' Arnie's here," said Clare. "'Sides, we kinda thought we'd like to add a bit to Ma Graham's woodpile, as well. Sure could use some extry help. Wanta swing an axe fer a few days?"

It was more than Lane had dared to hope for. His days would easily be filled with activity, and, in working with the Davis boys, he might even catch a glimpse of Ellie now and then. He promised Clare and Arnie he would be over the next morning as soon as he had finished the farm chores.

The chores took Lane a little longer than he had hoped, and he was concerned about the time as he hurried to the Davis farm, not even stopping for breakfast. He wondered if Clare and Arnie would be waiting or had already left for the woods without him.

He need not have worried, for the hour was still early and the Davis men were busy with the livestock when he arrived.

"Go on in an' say mornin' to Ma," Arnie called to him. "I'll be in shortly fer another cup of coffee an' my lunch. Ya might even be able ta talk the womenfolk into a cup for yerself."

Lunch, thought Lane, disgusted with himself. *I never even thought 'bout fixin' myself some lunch.*

Ellie opened the door to his knock. Trim and attractive in a dress of blue gingham with white cuffs and collar, a stiffly starched apron tied around her, Ellie smiled when she saw him, and Lane could feel his heart thumping.

"Won't ya come in?" she welcomed him. "The boys said thet ya had kindly offered to help git out the wood."

Lane entered and flipped his hat onto a peg near the door.

"Ma'll be right down," said Ellie. "She just went up to git her knittin'. Care fer some coffee?"

"Thet'd be powerful nice, ma'am," answered Lane, suddenly realizing just how hungry he was.

Ellie wrinkled a pert nose at him. "An' don't call me *ma'am,*" she teased. "Ya make me feel like an old-maid schoolmarm."

Lane grinned. "Well, ya sure don't look like one," he dared to say and quickly added "miss."

"Ya needn't say *miss,* either," retorted Ellie.

At Lane's raised eyebrows, Ellie said, "Just 'Ellie' will do."

Lane nodded and Ellie indicated a chair at the table. Lane sat down and wondered what on earth to do with his hands. They seemed too big for his lap and too awkward for anything else. Ellie was no doubt too busy pouring a cup of coffee and selecting some morning muffins to notice.

"Those sure do look good, miss . . . Ellie," he said as she set the fresh-baked pastries before him.

"Bet ya didn't even stop fer a decent breakfast," she chided. "I know how my brothers batch. They'd starve to death iffen someone didn't look out fer 'em." And so saying, Ellie went for her frying pan and some eggs and bacon.

Lane was hungry, but he sure didn't want her to go to all the trouble. Still, he wasn't quite sure how to stop her, so he just sat and watched her as she fixed the plate of food.

"There, now," she said as she placed the plate before him. "Iffen yer kind enough to work for the Davises, the least thet we can do is to feed ya." She reached for his cup to refill it but discovered he had not yet touched it.

"Ya don't care fer coffee?" she asked him.

"Oh no. I do. I love coffee. Don't know how I'd ever git by without it. Why, on the ranch—" Lane stumbled to a stop. "I was just too busy to start drinkin'," he finished lamely.

"Busy?"

"Watchin' ya," he said softly. He could feel his face turn red at the boldness of it.

Ellie flushed, too, and turned back to the cupboards. "Best ya eat 'fore it gits cold," she said, sounding a little flustered. "I've got some lunches to make."

Lane busied himself with his plate and soon had cleaned up the bacon and eggs and finished the muffins. He crossed to the stove to refill his own cup. Ellie raised her eyes from her sandwiches. Lane took a sip and then lifted his cup to her.

"Thet's good coffee," he stated.

"Coffee's always better when it's *hot*," she countered, and Lane knew she was teasing him.

Arnie came in then. He tossed his mittens in a corner and moved to the cupboard for a cup.

"Boy, but she's cold out today! Gonna hafta really work to keep the blood circulatin'."

Clare was just behind him. "Thought ya had yer love to keep ya warm," he kidded.

Arnie colored.

"Ellie, got an extra cup of coffee there?" asked Clare.

"Help yerself," Ellie responded. "Ya know where the cups are."

He reached out and messed her hair. "Boy," he said, "yer as sassy as ever. Got no one to keep ya in line since I moved outta the house. What ya need is a good boss—"

But Ellie did not let him finish.

"There," she said, putting the last bundle into a small box. "There's yer lunch. I put in enough fer the three of ya."

Clare hurriedly downed a few swallows of coffee and then set aside the cup.

"I'm gonna run over and say good-bye to Kate. Meet ya at the barn," he said to the men and was gone.

Marty entered the kitchen, her knitting basket on her arm.

"Oh, mornin', Lane," she said. "I didn't know ya had arrived. Heard about yer kind offer to help the boys cut wood. Made Clark feel better. We need a lot of wood this year, and swingin' an axe with just one good leg is a mighty hard job. 'Specially when things are all wet and slippery underfoot. With you helpin' I'm hopin' to be able to keep him at home." She hesitated for a moment. "Did Ellie invite ya to stay fer supper?"

Lane flushed again.

"'Fraid I didn't," said Ellie. "I wasn't thinkin' thet far ahead."

"Thank ya, ma'am," Lane said to Marty. "But I don't—"

"No problem," Marty assured him. "Iffen yer gonna be helpin' us out, the least we can do is to see thet yer proper fed."

Lane reddened even more. "Miss Ellie already fixed me my breakfast," he confessed, "an' sent along lunch fer my noon meal. I think thet'd be quite enough."

Marty laughed good-naturedly. "I'm glad she took care of ya. Now, ya just pop on in here an' have ya some supper 'fore ya be headin' fer home. We'll have it ready when ya get in from the hills."

Lane thought he should argue further, but he looked over at Ellie. It would be nice to see her just a bit more.

"Much obliged," he said to Marty and moved to follow Arnie out the door.

Ellie had a bad day. Something about Lane upset her. She had never met a young man who affected her that way before. Every time she thought about the way he looked at her, her cheeks felt aglow. He seemed as though he was trying to read her very thoughts—to send her strange messages with no words. It troubled Ellie and excited her, too. Why did he have to come from so far away and upset her neat and orderly world? In a few months' time, he would be heading back to the West, and what then? Would things fall back into the snug and familiar routine as though he had never been? Ellie was afraid not.

"He's nice, isn't he, dear?" Marty interrupted her swirling thoughts, and Ellie jumped.

"What?"

"Lane's a nice boy. Willie is so lucky to have him. He's been such a help on the ranch and in the church, too.

"An' then he comes on out here an' offers to go help cut wood—one of the hardest jobs there is. Sure takes a load off a' me where yer father's concerned."

Ellie agreed with her mother without committing herself in any way.

"Wonder how long he'll stay," Marty mused. "S'pose he's anxious to git on back, but they did say thet the LaHayes are gonna stay beyond Christmas, didn't they?"

"Guess so," murmured Ellie.

"Well, we should be real nice to him while he's here. Don't think he has a family of his own."

Marty went on with her knitting, and Ellie continued her kitchen tasks.

"Would be nice iffen he could go to the social at church next week," Marty speculated out loud. "Nice iffen he could meet some of our young people. Don't s'pose he's been in with fellas his own age fer ever so long. Some of those western cowboys can be a little rough. Would be nice fer him. Why don't ya ask him, Ellie?"

"Me?" Ellie's voice squeaked in astonishment at the very idea.

Marty's head came up, surprise on her face.

"Oh, now look, Ma," said Ellie defensively, "I don't go round askin' fellas to take me—"

"Oh," said Marty thoughtfully. "I wasn't thinkin' of it thet way. No, I guess ya don't. Would sorta sound thet way, I s'pose. I was just thinkin' of Lane as a friend of the family, thet's all. I'll have Arnie—"

"Arnie will be goin' with Anne."

"'Course."

"Well," said Marty, obviously not willing to give up on her idea, "I'll think of somethin'. Wish Luke was gonna be home in time. He could take 'im."

Marty busied herself counting stitches, and Ellie slipped a cake into the oven.

"Who ya goin' with?" Marty asked suddenly, and Ellie shook her head, wondering why her mother hadn't dropped the subject.

"Wasn't sure thet I would be goin'," answered Ellie honestly, thinking of the two boys who had asked her and not really wishing to go with either of them. She shrugged. "Not sure thet I want to," she continued.

"But ya should," encouraged Marty. "Ya need to git out more."

Ellie was highly relieved when her mother let it go at that.

Supper was ready when the men came in from the woods. Lane knew he really should go directly home and care for the LaHaye chores before it got too dark, but he couldn't resist spending a little more time in the same kitchen as Ellie. All day long he had thought of her. Her efficiency in the kitchen, her thoughtfulness in fixing his breakfast and sending along his lunch, her sparkling eyes and teasing smile. He couldn't get her off his mind, and he wasn't sure he really wanted to.

She served the meal, and once, when she had to replenish the plate of biscuits, she had bent near him to reach the empty dish. Lane thought surely everyone at the table must have seen how it affected him. He looked around quickly, but in truth, no one seemed to have noticed. No one but Ellie perhaps, and she was not letting on.

Lane left long after he should have and much before he wished to. It was dark riding home and a cold night for being out. He still had chores to do and cows to milk. He hoped that nothing on the LaHaye farm had suffered because of his tardiness. He wouldn't do it again, he told himself. He'd tell the Davises that he must go straight home from the wood cutting.

The next morning he was up even earlier than usual. He did the chores thoroughly and promised the milk cows that he would not keep them waiting that night.

He pushed the horse a little faster than normal on the way to the Davis', though still careful not to ask too much of it. If anyone knew how to care for his horse, it was Lane.

Again Ellie met him at the door, and Lane was surprised when he entered the kitchen to see that there was a place set at the table. Ellie pointed to it and asked him to be seated. She then busied herself at the already hot grill on the big kitchen stove, frying up a plate of pancakes. The very fragrance of them made Lane's mouth water.

She didn't pour his coffee until she had placed the stack of pancakes before him.

"Ya weren't gonna chance it gittin' cold, huh?" Lane asked softly, teasing in his voice.

If his words surprised Ellie, she chose not to show it. "Eat yer breakfast," she said in mock firmness, her words carrying with them an acknowledgment that she was aware of the strange undercurrent that existed between them.

Ellie went to make the lunches, and Marty soon joined them in the kitchen. They talked of the weather and the soon-approaching Christmas, and Marty extended an invitation to Lane to join them for Christmas Day, which he gratefully accepted.

Clark came in from the barn carrying a pail of fresh milk.

"How ya enjoyin' bein' a farmhand?" he joked with Lane. "Is it kinda nice to milk 'em rather'n brand 'em?"

Lane grinned. "Guess I'm 'bout the only cowboy who would ever admit he don't mind milkin' a cow."

Clark laughed. "Well, I don't mind admittin' it none. I kinda enjoy it myself. Had me an idea, too," Clark went on. "Since yer out there doin' my work, how 'bout I do a little of yers?"

Lane looked puzzled.

"Well, iffen ya wouldn't have to hurry on home fer the chores, you fellas could chop a few more trees. I thought I'd just ride on over and do up yer evenin' work so's you could stay on to supper here an' not be worryin' none 'bout the time thet ya git home."

"Oh, I couldn't—I was gonna tell ya thet I wouldn't be stayin' on fer supper. I'll just go on home after we finish in the woods. It won't be too late iffen I—"

"Nonsense," said Clark. "Me, I've got all day here with very little to do. I can do up the chores here and still have plenty of time to do yers, too, 'fore it gets dark."

"Oh, but I hate—"

"Won't have it any other way. Not gonna let ya work in the woods all day an' then go home to git yer own supper and do chores in the dark."

Lane could tell there was no use in arguing. He wondered if Ellie was listening to the conversation and if she was, what she thought about it.

"'Preciate it," Lane said and determined that he'd work doubly hard felling trees.

THIRTEEN

Marty Makes a Date

Supper that night was chicken and dumplings, and Lane thought he'd never tasted anything better. Ellie wore her hair pinned up, but tendrils floated loose about her face, and her cheeks were flushed from working over the stove. Arnie was anxious to eat and be off to see his Anne, and Clare had gone directly home to Kate.

After the meal, Ellie tried to shoo everyone into the family sitting room before the big fireplace. Clark and Marty were quick to respond. Lane went, too—rather reluctantly. He chatted with Clark for a few moments, more aware of the activity in the kitchen where Ellie was clearing away the table than in the responses he was attempting to make in the conversation.

When Marty started a new subject with Clark, Lane saw it as his opportunity and slipped back to the kitchen.

"Mind iffen I dry?" he asked quietly, and Ellie looked up in surprise.

"I'd think yer muscles would be tired enough after yer long day," she stated.

"I'm thinkin' thet it might take a different set of muscles to dry a few dishes."

"Then I accept the offer," Ellie said and smiled. Lane's heart did a flip.

She handed him a towel and showed him where he could stack the dried dishes. She led in the conversation, keeping it light and sticking to general subjects.

They were finished all too soon. Lane hung up the towel.

"An' how's yer young pup?" he asked.

Ellie looked surprised and then must have remembered the first time Lane had visited the farm.

"He's growin' like a weed," she said. "Pa has already given away two of the others."

"But not yer favorite?"

"Not yet. But he will. We already have enough dogs. I know thet. Pa's right. We can't keep 'em all. We'd soon be overrun."

She moved to stack dishes in the cupboard.

"It bother ya?" asked Lane.

"Guess it does." Ellie's smile looked a little forced. "But I'll git used to it."

"Anybody asked fer 'im yet?"

"I hide 'im," Ellie admitted sheepishly. "Every time someone comes to look at 'em, I hide 'im."

It was like the game of a little girl.

"An' don't ya tell," she quickly admonished, and then they were laughing together.

"How long d'ya think ya can keep doin' thet?" Lane asked when they were serious again.

"Till he's the last one," she said soberly. "Soon as the next one goes, I'm a goner."

"They don't have a dog at the LaHayes'," Lane said quietly.

"So ya said. I can't 'magine livin' on a farm without a dog."

"I've never had a dog of my own."

"Never?" Ellie's tone said she could scarcely believe that one could live without a dog.

"Never!"

"Don't ya like dogs?"

"Love 'em." Lane handed Ellie another stack of dishes, and she placed them in the proper spot in the cupboard.

"'Specially took to thet little one of yourn out there. I been thinkin', iffen ya have to give it up anyway, would ya mind if I took it?"

Ellie's eyes widened. "Not . . . not iffen you'd like 'im."

"I'd love 'im—I really would."

"He's an awfully good dog," Ellie enthused. "He's gonna be real smart—you can tell by the brightness of his eyes. An' he's from real good stock an—"

"Hey," cut in Lane, "you don't have to sell me on the pup. I'm already askin' fer 'im."

Ellie smiled. "When d'ya want 'im?" she asked.

"Well, I was wonderin'. With me gone all day, would it be too much to ask ya to keep 'im fer a while? I mean—till I'm done cuttin' logs so's I'll be home with 'im. Seems a shame to take 'im from his ma an' then not have any company fer 'im."

Ellie's grin widened. "I'll tell Pa," she said.

Lane turned to go back into the living room because all the dishes were done and there really didn't seem like any good reason for him to stay around longer. Ellie stopped him midstride by calling his name. "Lane."

He turned quickly, and she spoke softly. "Thank you," she said.

Lane wondered just how late he dared stay without being an unwanted guest. Clark challenged him to a game of checkers, and Lane was surprised that he was able to play as well as he did with Ellie sitting across the room from him, hand stitching a baby blanket. Marty was working on a tiny sweater, but Lane was scarcely aware she was there until she suddenly spoke.

"The young people of the area are havin' a little gatherin' in the church next week," she said. "Would ya be interested in goin' an' gettin' acquainted, seein' yer goin' to be in our area fer a time?"

"It'd be nice," Lane answered absently and moved a checker out of range of Clark's.

"Arnie an' Anne will be there," went on Marty, "but I don't s'pose you'll be knowin' many of the others."

"Don't s'pose," said Lane.

"Thought maybe ya wouldn't mind takin' Ellie on over. She could show ya the way an' introduce ya to the rest of the young people."

Lane moved a king directly into the path of one of Clark's men and said calmly, "Be obliged."

The game went on. Lane lost soundly. From that move on, his mind was not on the game. He didn't dare look at Ellie. He had heard a little gasp and her shocked whisper, "Mama." He was surprised she hadn't outright refused her mother's suggestion. Would she back out gracefully later? Did she already have a date for the night? Lane feared it might be so. Clark moved to put away the checkerboard, and Marty kept her knitting needles *click-clicking* in a steady rhythm. Lane rose to excuse himself, and after a mild protest on Marty's part, which Lane countered with thanks for the evening but he had to go, Marty suggested that Ellie show him to the door.

Ellie rose obediently and laid her sewing aside.

They walked silently through the room and into the kitchen, and Lane took his heavy jacket from the hook and slipped his arms into it. He pulled his mitts out of his pocket and reached for his hat. Still Ellie had not spoken.

"That wasn't yer idea, was it?" Lane asked softly.

"No," answered Ellie, not meeting his eyes.

"Iffen it's a problem, I understand."

Ellie looked at him then. "Is it a problem fer you?" she asked sincerely.

Lane looked at her steadily. "It's an honor fer me," he stated.

"Then it's no problem fer me," said Ellie simply. Lane left with his hat in his hand and his heart singing.

On the night of the social, Lane was in early from the woods, for Arnie, too, wished to be home in plenty of time to properly get ready before going to pick up Anne. Clare gave them both some good-natured teasing, but Arnie quickly reminded Clare of how he had acted when he was courting Kate.

Lane did not stop for supper, having already informed Marty not to expect him. He hurried on home, thinking of a warm bath and a quick shave. He wasn't too sure that what he had to wear was appropriate, but he would do the best he could with what he had. He couldn't believe his good fortune—that he would actually be escorting Ellie! He still wasn't sure just how it had all come about or why Ellie hadn't turned him down.

Ellie rushed through the supper dishes and hastened to her room.

Marty went up to see what was taking her so long and returned to Clark, shaking her head. "Never seen Ellie fuss so," she said. "She's had herself a bath, and she's put on and taken off more'n one gown."

"Every girl fusses when she's goin' out with a young man," Clark responded.

"Lane?" Marty's head swung around to stare at Clark. "Why, he's just like one of the family."

"And so he is," agreed Clark.

Lane was plenty early, and when he looked at the radiant Ellie, his pulse beat more rapidly. She wasn't just pretty—she was lovely.

They walked out to the sleigh, and he helped her to be seated and tucked her in carefully against the cold of the winter night.

They talked of this and that on the way to the church. When they passed a neighbor's farm, Ellie would tell Lane something of the family who lived there.

When they arrived at their destination, Lane helped Ellie down and went to tie his horses among the milling, stomping teams of the neighborhood youth. He spotted the team of bays that Arnie drove and gave one a pat on his broad rump as he walked by.

Ellie was standing just inside the door when he entered the church. She showed him where to put his hat and coat and then began the introductions.

The young people were friendly and the games lively. The evening went quickly, and Lane, who was not used to such gatherings, was surprised at the fun they had. After a snack served by the girls, it was time to go home.

Lane felt several pairs of eyes on him as he helped Ellie into her coat. He knew there were a number of neighborhood boys who greatly envied him. He could feel it in their looks and their curt manners. It made him even more conscious of the fact that he was escorting the prettiest girl in the room.

Lane did not push the horses on the way home. If Ellie realized it, she did not say so. Instead, she talked about the party, the people he had met, and his thoughts concerning the evening. He reached to tuck the blanket securely around her, wishing with all his heart that he could leave his arm around her, too. Reluctantly, he withdrew it.

"What do ya think of our country?" asked Ellie, making a real turn in the conversation.

"It's different," he answered her, "but I like it fine."

"Ya miss the West?"

"Not as much as I thought I would," he said honestly.

"But you'll be glad to git back?"

Lane thought of the wide-open spaces, the mountains in the distance, the night-crying of the coyotes, and the wind in his face and answered her, "Reckon I will."

"Guess Missie has learned to love it, too," Ellie said, gazing up at the wide, star-studded sky as she spoke.

"I think thet she does," answered Lane.

"Seems so long since I've seen Missie."

"She speaks of ya often," Lane said and went on to think about the young sister Missie had referred to and wondered what Missie would think if she could see Ellie now.

"I still miss her. She was a wonderful big sister."

"Why don't ya come on out an' see her?" *With me,* he wanted to add but thought better of it.

Ellie laughed softly. "Sometimes I get the feelin' Mama isn't too anxious fer me to go visitin' out west. I think she's afraid I might not come back."

"Do you think ya could like the West?"

Ellie sighed. "I think I could like anywhere iffen . . ." But she did not finish.

"Iffen—?" Lane prompted.

"Well," she said matter-of-factly, "no use thinkin' on it now anyway. Mama needs me at home with the new baby comin' an' all. Maybe Missie will be able to come on home fer a visit 'fore too long. I'd love to see her—an' her babies."

Lane's heart sank a little. Was there a hidden message here? Was she warning him that he had no part in her future? Mama needed her. Lane loved her for her consideration, and she was right. Marty did need her now, but surely she wasn't planning to spend the rest of her life caring for her mama's kitchen and never giving consideration to having one of her own. He wanted to ask her—to tell her—but she pointed out a falling star and began to talk of other things. He clucked to the team. The night suddenly seemed much colder.

FOURTEEN

Christmas

Marty, filled with excitement about the nearness of the Christmas season, was also anticipating Arnie's upcoming wedding. But she was absolutely overjoyed by the fact that Luke would soon be home.

Oh, how she had missed him! His letters, which seemed all too infrequent, reminded her of how lonesome she was for their youngest son.

She baked his favorite cakes, fussed over cleaning his room, insisted that his favorite foods be on hand. And even when all this had been accomplished, she still bustled about trying to think of something more to do to make sure of his welcome.

"Why don't ya just sit ya down and relax?" Clark asked her. "Yer gonna be wearin' yerself out. It's *you* the boy is comin' to see, not the house or the pantry."

Marty knew Clark was right, and she tried to hold herself in check. But it was awfully hard.

On the day of Luke's arrival, Marty suffered a disappointment. She had planned all along to travel into town to meet his stage, but the day was bitterly cold with a strong wind blowing. And Clark firmly announced she would best stay home by the fire and let them bring her son to her.

She knew there was no use arguing, but how she chafed and stewed! She finally consented, insisting that Clark and Arnie—the two making the trip to town—promise to hurry home just as fast as the team would bring them. Clark agreed and left in time to do any shopping beforehand so they could leave for home as soon as they could load Luke and his luggage.

The day went awfully slowly for Marty. Ellie shook her head at her mother's pacing back and forth to the window. "Yer gonna wear out the floor," she teased, but her tone said she understood.

At last the team was welcomed by the dogs, and Marty ran to open the door for Luke.

At first appearance, Marty felt Luke had not changed much in the few months he had been away. He had really not grown taller, and he was about the same weight. His grin was as broad and his hug still as hearty. It wasn't until they had been together for some time that Marty began to recognize little changes. Luke was no longer her "little boy." He was well on his way to being a responsible man. The knowledge both saddened her and made her proud. She felt that he was seeing her in a different way, too. Luke had always been her compassionate and caring son. Now he looked at her, as well, with the concern and practiced eye of a doctor. Oh, true, Luke had a long way to go before he would be qualified, but he was already seeing the world through a physician's eyes.

The trips to the woods were put off during the busy time of Christmas celebration and Arnie's wedding. Lane hated to think of not having an excuse to visit the Davises for a whole week, but Marty seemed to feel he was a part of the family and always found some reason for him to come over.

Lane helped Ellie set up and decorate the tree in the big family living room. The boys were busy with other things, Marty said, and it was a big job for the girl to do all alone. Lane was happy to assist and enjoyed the evening immensely. Ellie was in a carefree mood, and her light chatter and silvery laugh rather went to Lane's head. *What would it be like to share this task with this girl for the many years ahead?* he asked himself and readily admitted that he liked the idea.

Christmas Day found the house crowded with family. Children ran in and out, laughing and shrieking and exclaiming over Christmas surprises. The menfolk gathered in front of the open fire and roasted fall nuts and told jokes on one another, with much hearty laughing and good-natured backslapping. Women bustled about the kitchen, stirring and tasting and seasoning the huge pots that spilled savory odors throughout the whole house. Lane, who could not remember ever having been a part of such a Christmas before, joyfully absorbed every minute of it. Gifts from the tree were lovingly distributed, and Lane had been thoughtfully included. Marty's warm knit stocking cap would keep his head protected on cold winter days in the woods.

Eventually they were all gathered around the extended table. Chattering children were silenced for a season, joking men became serious, and the busy women laid aside their aprons and sat with hands folded reverently in their laps. Clark lifted down the family Bible and read aloud the Christmas story, as he had done on each of the preceding family Christmases, and then led his household in prayer. He remembered each of the absent ones by name—Willie and Missie and their children, and Clae and Joe and their little ones. He thanked the Lord for bringing Luke back to them for a visit. He prayed for the new family members who were yet unknown and asked that God would bless the mothers who carried them and make the new babies a blessing to many in the years to come. He asked God's blessing on Arnie and Anne as they shared the family table and would soon be establishing a home of their own. He prayed for Josh and Nandry and each one of their children. He thanked the Lord for Lane and his presence in their home and his friendship that meant so much to the family. He remembered the Graham family and this first difficult Christmas without the husband and father of the home. Last, he remembered Marty, his helpmate over the years. He thanked the Lord for her return to good health and asked God to give them both wisdom and direction as they guided the new little life with which He had seen fit to bless them.

It was a lengthy prayer, spoken sincerely. Even the children sat quietly, for Grandpa was talking to God.

In direct contrast, the meal itself was a noisy affair. Over the steady hum of chatter and loud laughter, one could scarcely hear oneself think. Lane stole a glance at Ellie. Cheeks flushed, golden hair wisping around her face, eyes sparkling with happiness, she answered some teasing coming from Clare. Lane was unable to hear her words, but from the look on Clare's face, he could guess Ellie was able to give as good as she received. After Clare's initial look of surprise at her quick response, he began to laugh and exclaimed loudly, "Well, ya got me there, little sister."

The children were excused to go back to their toys, and the adults settled down with another cup of coffee. The talk was not as boisterous now.

Clark leaned back and looked at his youngest son. "Yer lookin' good, boy. They must be takin' good care of ya."

"The Whistlers? They do all right, that's for sure. Aunt Mindy fusses even more than Ma." Luke looked at his mother with a grin.

"An' yer likin' the studies?" Clark went on.

"I love it. Learning something new every day."

"Like?"

"Ya wouldn't believe what they are able to do now—in surgery, for treatment. I'm just getting a glimpse into it, but it's a whole new world out there. In a few years' time, with what they are learning, they'll almost be able to make a man over again if something goes wrong with him."

"Guess I was born a few years too soon," Clark moaned in mock despair and brought laughter around the table.

"No fooling, Pa," said Luke. "You ought to see the artificial limbs they've got on the drawing boards now."

"Ain't no help on a drawin' board," replied Clark, and his sons laughed again.

But it looked like the doctor in Luke was not to be put off with joking. He began to explain the advancements in artificial limb design. Before he was finished, he was kneeling before Clark with the pinned-up pant leg containing its stub of a leg unselfconsciously held in his hand. He explained to the gathered family what could soon be done. "You'll forget you even have a leg missing!" he exclaimed. "I told Dr. Bush you were a natural to be one of the first to try it out. I want you to have one, Pa."

Nandry left the table. Marty thought she was going to check on the children. But when the meal was finished and the dishes were being cleared away, Nandry still had not returned.

The afternoon was spent in playing games, toasting nuts, and visiting.

"Remember the Christmas at Missie's when we all joined together in carol singing?" Marty asked Lane.

He nodded his head, remembering it well.

"Henry played his guitar," Marty went on and then interrupted herself. "Ya played your guitar, too."

"You play the guitar?" asked Arnie, immediately interested.

"Some," answered Lane.

"I always wanted to play a guitar," continued Arnie.

"Henry taught me. 'Fraid I wasn't too great a pupil, but I learned enough to sorta git a kick outta it."

"Do you have yer guitar with ya?" asked Ellie rather shyly.

"At the LaHayes'," he answered.

"I'd like to hear ya play sometime."

Only Lane and Ellie seemed to be conscious of the undercurrent flowing between them. None of the other members of the family seemed to notice that Lane's eyes followed her about the room or that her cheeks flushed when she found him looking at her. Her simple words now were more to him than a statement. They came as a request, and without a spoken word his eyes made a promise.

Nandry returned—from where, Marty did not know. Perhaps she was not feeling well. Marty hoped she wasn't coming down with something that would keep her from Arnie's wedding. Nandry stayed on the fringe of things, keeping a close eye on the children and even bustling about in the kitchen some.

The day itself was clear and bright, though the air was cold. The children begged to go out to play, but Nandry stated it was far colder than they thought it to be and the outside could just wait.

Lane, too, longed to get out. He ached for an opportunity to be alone with Ellie. He had done some shopping in the nearby town and had purchased a locket, which he had withheld from the Christmas gift exchange. He wanted to give it to her privately. But where and when would he ever find privacy on a day when the family had gathered together? He wished he were daring enough to ask Ellie to go for a walk, but he couldn't gather the courage. The day was swiftly passing, and still he had found no opportunity to speak with her. Ellie herself, perhaps unknowingly, gave him the opportunity he had been longing for.

"I'm gonna take a few goodies to the barn fer Lady and yer pup," she said. "Ya wanna see 'im?"

Lane bounded to his feet. The whole group must have thought he was uncommonly fond of his young dog.

"Better wear yer coat. It's cold out there," Ellie cautioned at the door, for Lane would have left the house in his shirt sleeves, so unthinking was he at the time.

He flushed slightly and pulled on his coat. Ellie was already bundled and ready to go.

"Yer gonna be surprised at how he's grown," Ellie told him as they walked to the barn.

Ellie threw wide the door, and the two little pups pounced upon her, licking and yapping excitedly. Ellie giggled as she tried to get them under control. Lady watched from the sidelines with a mother's pride.

"My, ya do fuss over a body!" she exclaimed and worked to settle them down so she could give them the pan of turkey meat, gravy, and dressing scraps.

"They love it," she said, watching them wolf it down. "Pa says I spoil 'em."

The pup really had grown. He was still curly haired, and he still had his long, droopy ears, and he still looked awfully good to Lane. In his mind was the picture of a beautiful girl cuddling a small puppy. He reached down and picked it up, holding the wriggling body to his chest as he stroked the soft fur. Ellie stepped closer and touched the puppy, too.

"He doesn't have a name yet," she told him. "Thought of one?"

"How 'bout iffen you name 'im?" asked Lane.

"Me? He's yer dog."

"I'd still like yer name fer 'im," Lane said, looking steadily at her. Ellie stopped stroking the puppy and stepped back.

"I dunno," she said. "I haven't really been thinkin' on it."

"What would you have called 'im iffen ya coulda kept 'im? I bet ya had a name all picked out."

Ellie's smile admitted that she had.

"C'mon," said Lane. "Out with it."

"Don't s'pose you'd want my silly name none. It's not a very sensible name fer a man's dog."

"Why? What's a sensible name fer a man's dog?"

"Oh, Butch. Or Pooch. Or Ol' Bob. We used to name our dogs Ol' Bob. We had one Ol' Bob, and when we got a new puppy, Arnie named it Ol' Bob, too. Mama told me 'bout it."

"Don't think I care fer Ol' Bob," said Lane. "Or Butch or Pooch, either. This here's a special dog. He should have a special name."

He looked at her, coaxing her to share the name that she had picked for his dog. She still hesitated.

"C'mon," he said again.

"You'd laugh."

"Never!"

Ellie began to laugh softly. "Well, ya might not laugh, ya bein' so polite, but ya sure would *want* to."

"A good laugh is good fer a body," replied Lane, and Ellie's laughter sounded like she agreed.

"Okay," she said. "An' have a laugh iffen ya want to. I woulda called 'im Romeo."

"Romeo?" and Lane did laugh.

Ellie joined in. When they had finished chuckling over the name, Ellie said more seriously, "Why don't we just call 'im Rex?"

"Rex. I kinda like thet. Though it sure be a comedown from Romeo." They laughed again.

"Promise ya won't tease?" asked Ellie.

"Tease?"

"'Bout Romeo."

"Promise," said Lane. "I might even call 'im thet myself—once or twice—in private." And he put the puppy back down beside his mother.

Ellie picked up the pan and turned to go, but Lane stopped her.

In response to the question in her eyes, he reached into his pocket and pulled out a small package.

"I wondered when I would git to give ya this," he said softly. "I didn't want to put it under the tree with the others. It's my Christmas gift to you."

Still Ellie said nothing. He passed it to her and she took it, looking down at it with confusion in her face.

"Open it," prompted Lane, and Ellie's trembling fingers began to do his bidding.

As she lifted up the delicate locket, her eyes filled with tears.

"Oh, Lane, it's beautiful," she whispered, and then the tears did spill. "But I can't take it."

It was Lane's turn to be bewildered. "Ya mean . . . what I was hopin' . . . was dreamin' . . . I didn't see a'tall?"

Ellie just stood mute, the tears continuing to fall and the fingers gently caressing the locket.

"Ya don't care fer me?" asked Lane.

"I never said . . ." sobbed Ellie.

"Then there's someone else."

"No," said Ellie emphatically.

"Then I don't understand—"

"It's Mama. She needs me."

"I know," said Lane gently, reaching out to take her hands. "I'll wait. I'm not meanin' to take ya away *now*. It won't be long—"

"But ya don't understand!" cried Ellie. "It would near kill Mama. She misses Clae and Missie so. It would break her heart iffen another of her girls were to move so far away. Can't ya see . . . ?"

"But surely—"

"No," said Ellie, shaking her head again. "I just couldn't do it to Mama. I wouldn't." And she pushed the locket back into Lane's hand and ran from the barn, leaving her pan behind her.

Lane felt a sickness sweep all through him. He loved her. Until that moment of losing her, he had not realized how deeply. He looked at the locket lying in his open hand and longed for the comfort of tears. He did not allow them. Instead he sank down upon the straw and reached for the small dog. He pressed his face against the soft fur and remembered how Ellie had looked with her face against the puppy.

"Oh, Romeo," he groaned. "I just don't know how I'll live without her. Yer a mighty poor substitute, I'm a thinkin'."

It was a long time before Lane felt composed enough to return to the house.

Arnie's wedding day turned out not to be a fair day weatherwise. The wind was blowing and light snow was swirling as Clark tucked the blanket securely around Marty in the sleigh and headed for the church. All of the others had gone on before, and Marty fretted over last-minute concerns.

"Ellie has everythin' under control," Clark reminded her. "Ya needn't worry yerself none. The weddin' dinner will happen all proper like."

Marty knew that was true. She had worked on the dinner preparations in the kitchen with Ellie as much as her family would allow her, and then her physician-to-be son had gently but firmly shooed her to bed.

"You've been on your feet long enough," Luke insisted. "I'll help Ellie with whatever she needs."

And now the rest of the family were all at the church making the final wedding arrangements and waiting for the preacher to give the signal that the long-awaited hour had come.

Clark let the horses pick their own pace. Because they hated the cold and were in a hurry to get the journey over, they trotted briskly, Marty noted with some relief as she held the blanket up to her cheeks to prevent frostbite.

Other teams belonging to family and friends stood waiting in the churchyard when Clark swung his team in close to the steps and helped Marty alight. Luke was there to assist her in and hang up her coat. She was then seated in a spot reserved for the mother of the groom and had only moments to wait until Clark joined her.

The wedding party began to take their places in the front. Marty had never seen Arnie looking happier nor Anne more radiant. Ellie seemed a bit pale and strained, and Marty chided herself. The girl had been working much too hard. She must see that Ellie got a good rest when all of this excitement was over.

It was a beautiful ceremony. The young pastor was able to give it the proper dignity and warmth of feeling that a wedding service should have. Before a caring congregation, the young couple exchanged their vows, looking at each other with expressions that said they meant deeply everything they promised.

Marty swallowed hard and blinked back her tears. Another of their children was establishing a home of his own. Soon there would be none of them left to share the big house that Clark had built for his family. And then a little jab under her ribs reminded Marty that it would be a while yet before the house would be empty, and she smiled through her tears and reached down a hand to touch the spot where her unborn child was making its presence known.

FIFTEEN

Back to Routine

Luke now had to board the stage once again and return to school. Marty sighed deeply at the thought of seeing him go, but somehow it seemed easier this time than before.

The household settled back into its routine. Arnie and his new bride took up residence in the little home that he had been so industriously preparing for them. The day Arnie had walked out the door carrying the last of his belongings from his lifelong homestead was very hard for Marty, but the broad smile on his face made her realize the truth: that all was as it should be when Arnie was looking forward to starting out on a life of his own. The thought gave her a measure of peace.

How glad she was to have Ellie as she watched Luke and Arnie leave the home. What a comfort to have at least one of her children still with her. Then Marty looked carefully at Ellie, and her eyes told her that something was not quite right. Ellie still looked pale and overtired. She had been working far too hard, with all the family at home for Christmas and then the added burden of preparing for Arnie's wedding, as well. Marty decided that what Ellie needed was to get away from the kitchen for a while. She had heard some of the neighborhood young people talking about a skating party on Miller's pond. That was what

Ellie needed. A chance to be out having fun with young people of her own age.

Marty tucked the information away in her mind, with the intention of doing something about it at her first opportunity. Marty was not concerned about who would take Ellie to the skating party. True, the girl no longer had big brothers in the house to escort her to such activities, but that would be no problem. Lane would be happy to take over that role. He was such a nice young man, and he and Ellie seemed to get along just fine. Though she would miss her brothers, Lane would be good company and sort of an "adopted" big brother.

Marty smiled as she concluded these thoughts. She tucked the small sweater that was taking form under her quick needles back into her knitting basket and went to the kitchen. She had heard the dog bark, and that must mean the men were back from the woods. This was their first day back on the job since Arnie's wedding. She hoped Arnie would stop for a brief chat before he went to his new home and waiting bride.

Ellie was busy at the big stove, stirring a pot of wonderfully fragrant stew. Fresh biscuits sat in a pan at the back of the stove, smelling as good as they looked. Marty noticed the table. It was set for four. For a moment, Marty thought Ellie had forgotten that Arnie would no longer be eating with them, and then she remembered Lane. Of course—Lane always ate with them after he spent a day in the woods. It had been a while since the men had all gone out together, and she had forgotten. She smiled again, thinking this would be a good chance for her to tell Lane about the skating party.

Marty was disappointed when Clark came in saying Arnie had been in such a hurry to get home to his Anne that he had sent his mother greetings and excused himself from coming in. He'd see her sometime soon, he promised, and told Clark to give her his love.

Lane did come in, but he seemed edgy somehow. This was the first they had seen him since Arnie's wedding, and Marty had been all prepared for a good chat. Lane, though he politely answered all the questions that were put to him, just didn't seem much in the mood for chatting. Ellie didn't seem to be too talkative, either. Perhaps they were both weary after the rush and busyness of Christmas, Marty concluded. Well, things should slow down now.

Lane had been nervous about appearing as usual at the Davis table. He had not really seen Ellie since Christmas Day, except for a few brief glimpses of her on the day of Arnie's wedding. She had been so busy then that there was no opportunity at all for him to speak with her. Lane felt it was important for them to get a chance to have a real talk. He couldn't leave things as they were when he had presented his Christmas gift to her.

Some way he had to make her understand he would never take her from her mother while Marty needed her but would wait as long as was necessary if Ellie would just give the word. But what had Ellie said in her rush of tears? *It would kill Mama iffen another of her family was to move so far away.* Did Ellie really mean that? Would it really be that hard on Marty? Lane had to know. He needed a chance to talk things out. That is, if Ellie cared—if she cared at all about him. Could he have been so wrong? Maybe Ellie didn't even—

Lane's thoughts were interrupted by Marty's words. She was asking how the logging was going. Lane answered her. He hoped that what he said in response sounded sensible. He stole a glance at Ellie. She seemed perfectly unaware that he sat across the table from her. She was completely absorbed in cutting a piece of meat into a smaller portion before serving herself.

"Ellie tells me you've laid claim on thet last pup," Clark stated.

Lane looked back to Clark and fumbled some with his fork. "Right," he finally was able to answer. "I always wanted a dog of my own an' never had me a chance."

"Think ya picked a good one," Clark continued. "Those be awful good stock dogs, an' I think thet pup be the pick of the litter. A little trainin' an' he should be 'bout able to read yer mind where stock are concerned."

Lane could feel his face get warm. What was a cowman to do with a trained stock dog? Sure wouldn't use one to be rounding up the herd.

No one seemed to notice, and Lane shuffled his feet some and cleared his throat.

"Yes, sir," he said. "He does look smart, all right."

It was time for Ellie to serve the apple pie. Though Lane's favorite dessert, somehow he had no appetite for it tonight. He did manage to swallow it, washing it down with his second cup of coffee. He stole another glance at Ellie. She still looked cool and aloof.

Clark was pushing back his chair.

"Care fer a game of checkers?"

Lane gathered his scattered wits. "No . . . no . . . I think not. Not tonight. I need to git me on home—"

"The chores are all done," Clark reminded him. "I been over and took care of everythin'. No need fer ya to—"

But Lane was standing to his feet and excusing himself. "Thanks," he said, "but I think I'd better git on home just the same. Christmas has a way of wearin' one out, an' it's a little hard to git back to work again afterward. Think I'll just go on home an' catch up a bit."

Lane was glad Clark did not argue further as he thanked them all again for the supper and the evening and turned toward his coat hanging on the peg.

"Speakin' of Christmas wearin' one out," Marty said, moving closer to address herself to Lane as he shrugged into his coat, "I been noticin' thet Ellie needs a bit of a change from all her hard work, too, an' I overheard some of the young folks talkin', an' they said this Saturday they're gonna have 'em a skatin' party on Miller's pond. Ellie knows where thet be, iffen you'd be so kind as to drive her on over."

Ellie was pouring hot water into the sink, her back to them.

"I'd be most happy to," Lane answered evenly.

Marty began to smile.

"No," Ellie said sharply without turning. "No."

Marty swung around toward her, a look of concern replacing the smile.

"No," said Ellie again. "I'm not goin'."

"What d'ya mean?" asked Marty, confusion in her tone. "Ya need to git out with the young people more. Why, ya hardly had a chance—"

But Ellie cut in with, "Mama, do you know just how *young* those young people are? Why, I wouldn't even fit in! All the young girls my age are married an' busy keepin' house. Those young people . . . they . . . they're just *kids*. I don't belong with 'em now, an' besides . . . I don't want to go . . . really I . . ." Ellie turned away. "Let's just ferget it, can we?"

Marty looked dumbfounded. She turned back to Lane with a helpless look and a shrug of her shoulders.

"Guess it won't be necessary," she said in a low voice, putting her hand on Lane's arm. "Thanks anyway, though."

Marty turned to the cupboard. "Here," she said. "Take ya home one of these fresh loaves of Ellie's bread." She hastened to wrap a loaf and hand it to Lane.

Lane took one last lingering look at Ellie. Her head was bent over the dishpan. He couldn't tell for sure, but he wondered if it was a tear that lay upon her cheek. He muttered a good-night to all of them and went out the door.

Clark followed Lane to the barn to get his horse. The young man had declared it unnecessary, but Clark insisted. He wanted to check the barn doors anyway, he declared.

As Lane went to mount his horse, he turned to Clark. "Been thinkin'," he said. "S'pose it's time fer me to do my own chorin'. Willie sent me on out here to be takin' care of things, an' I feel a bit guilty not doin' it myself. Tell the boys I'll just meet 'em in the mornin'. A bit closer fer me iffen I go straight on over from the LaHaye farm. And then iffen I go right on home at night, I'll have plenty of time to do my own chores."

Clark knew this time that Lane had made up his mind to care for the LaHaye chores himself. He didn't know what it was that had made the younger man decide as he had, but Clark put it aside as none of his business. He was sure Lane had a good reason, whatever it was. No mention was made of the meal that was always waiting at the Davis household.

"Sure," Clark said, "iffen thet's what ya want. Come anytime ya can. We're always most happy to have ya."

Lane said his good-night and urged his horse forward.

Clark returned to the warmth of the kitchen. Ellie was busy scrubbing at an awkward pan, and Marty was placing dried, clean dishes on the cupboard shelf.

Clark leaned his crutch against the wall and steadied himself on his one foot while he pulled out of his heavy coat.

"Lane won't be here fer breakfast tomorra," he said to the two women.

Two heads came up and two pairs of eyes held his. Only Marty voiced a question.

"Why?" she said simply. "What might keep Lane from breakfasting with us?"

"He thinks he should care fer the LaHaye chores hisself."

"Maybe," said Marty in a puzzled tone, "though I really don't think it matters much to Willie as long as they're taken care of." Marty paused long enough to place some cups on hangers. "Maybe he's not feelin' well," she wondered. "I noticed he didn't eat well tonight. Perhaps a few days off from cuttin' will do 'im good."

"Oh, he's still cuttin'," Clark explained. "He's just goin' straight from the LaHaye farm, thet's all."

Marty looked at him, her eyes holding more questions. Then she turned back to the cupboard. "Well, we'll see 'im tomorrow night. Maybe he'll—"

"'Fraid not," Clark said. "He told me he would be goin' straight home from the cuttin' from now on, so he won't be takin' supper with us anymore."

Marty put down the plates she was holding and placed her hand on her hip, her frown deepening. "I wonder—" she began, but Clark stopped her.

"He was sent to care fer the LaHaye farm, not to cut the Davis' logs. Guess he feels a bit bad 'bout how things been goin', thet's all. I like a fella who looks after his own responsibility."

Marty still frowned but turned back to the plates. "I'm not arguin' thet," she said. Then she continued, "But it was so nice havin' 'im round, 'specially with Arnie an' Luke both leavin'. It was like havin' another son—an' it was gonna be 'specially nice fer Ellie to still have a big brother."

Ellie swung around, her eyes large and tear filled. "Mama, please," she begged, and then she was crying in earnest.

"What—?" began Marty, her utter bewilderment evident in tone and expression as she started toward her daughter.

"I'm . . . I'm sorry," stammered Ellie, backing away. "I didn't mean . . . I never meant . . ." She brushed roughly at her tears with a corner of her apron. "I don't need . . . I don't need another big brother." And saying the words, Ellie almost ran from the kitchen.

Marty's eyes were filled with concern. "I'm worried 'bout her, Clark," she said, slowly lowering her round body to a kitchen chair. "I've never seen Ellie with all the sparkle gone from her so. I just never dreamed it would be so hard fer her to say good-bye to both Arnie and Luke."

Clark had no explanation.

SIXTEEN

Secrets

In the days that followed, Marty kept a close eye on Ellie. She still looked pale and seemed listless, but she attacked each of her many household duties with the same determination and energy she'd had before. There just didn't seem to be the joy that had previously marked her character. Marty was hoping it would return when Ellie got accustomed to being the only child left at home.

Ellie seemed to yearn to be outside. It appeared to Marty that she used every excuse possible to leave the confines of the kitchen. She was always taking food and water to the chickens. She even insisted on hauling water from the outside well—a chore Clark had never expected of his womenfolk. Mostly, though, she spent time with the young pup. The dog was of training age now, and Ellie seemed to get what little pleasure was left to her in teaching him the basics in obedience.

Whenever Marty inquired about how things were going with the dog training, Ellie's answers contained a measure of enthusiasm. Marty felt these were the only times that the heaviness lifted for Ellie—her times with that small dog. Maybe even an animal could make one forget just how much one missed an individual, Marty concluded. *It must be*

Arnie thet Ellie misses so much, she continued, *because I didn't notice this 'bout her 'fore Christmas, and Luke was gone then, too.* Marty hoped for a chance to talk to Arnie. Perhaps he could just pop in a bit oftener and say a few words to his sister. That might help her in her adjustment period.

They saw very little of Lane. He seemed to make out fine as a bachelor. Marty heard via the country grapevine that many of the neighbors—especially those with marriageable daughters—were inviting him in for meals. The only time the Davises saw Lane was at the Sunday services, and then it seemed he always had somewhere else to go. Marty did notice, though, that he was looking a bit thinner than when he had first come to their area.

"I wonder iffen Lane is missin' his West?" she said to Clark one night as they sat before the fire, Clark with a book and Marty with some sewing.

Clark lifted his head.

"Why do ya think thet?" he asked.

"Well, he don't seem as jolly—an' he looks to be losin' some weight. An' . . . an' we never see him anymore," she finished lamely.

"The fact thet we don't see 'im anymore could prove he feels more at home here—not less," Clark responded. "From what I'm hearin', he's gittin' round real good."

"Well, he still don't look happy to me," insisted Marty.

"I would love to argue with ya," said Clark slowly, "but I been thinkin' the same thoughts. Iffen it's just thet he's anxious to git on home, thet will soon care fer itself. I hear the LaHayes will be back in a couple weeks or so. Thet won't be long fer 'im to wait."

There was a soft stirring as Ellie quietly left the room. Marty could hear her in the kitchen. By the sounds that came to her, Marty knew Ellie was lighting a lantern and putting on outside wraps.

"Where ya goin', dear?" Marty called. "It's cold out tonight."

"Just gonna go check on Lady an' Ro—Rex."

"I made sure they was all shut up warm an' dry in the barn," Clark called to Ellie. "Even gave 'em some extra milk tonight."

If they expected Ellie to sigh with relief and return her coat to its peg, they were disappointed. "Still gonna go out an' see 'em," she answered, and the door opened and closed.

"She sure is powerful concerned 'bout those dogs of hers," Marty said to Clark. "'Magine goin' out this time of night just to check on 'em."

Clark picked up the book he had laid in his lap, but his eyes didn't return immediately to the open page. Instead, he sat thinking, the frown lightly creasing his forehead. Something was amiss here, but as yet Clark wasn't sure just what it was.

Ellie walked quickly to the barn, her swinging lantern making streaks of light and shadows on the snow-covered farmyard. Her heart was heavy, and she felt the tears stinging her eyelids. The truth was, she had learned to love Lane. Maybe it had been unwise, but it had been impossible for her to stop herself. She was sure he had cared for her, too. She could feel it in the way he looked at her, the unspoken and the spoken messages he had passed to her. And the locket? A man like Lane would mean a gift like that as a promise of his love—and Lane would not hold love lightly. They could have been so happy together—if only . . .

But what was the use of *if onlys*? Her mother needed her. Not just for now before the baby came but in the future, too. Marty had suffered as each of her children moved away from the family home. First, it had been Missie, and she had gone so very far away. When she had left, Marty had not even been sure she would ever see her again, would ever hold the children that would bless her home, or sit in her kitchen sharing thoughts and feelings along with cups of tea. Then Clae had gone and taken with her one grandchild and a well-loved son-in-law. Now Clae had another baby, one Marty had yet to see. Ellie knew Marty ached to see Clae and Joe and the little ones. Then Clare had married and moved out on his own. True, he was close by, and Marty could share in his life in lots of ways. Why, Marty was as anxious for that new baby of Clare and Kate's as they were themselves. Ellie checked her thoughts. *Well, not quite,* she corrected herself and even managed a wobbly smile. Nobody could be quite as excited at the prospect of a new baby as Clare and Kate were.

Ellie's thoughts continued with her brother Luke's leaving. Her mama's baby. At least for so many, many years, Luke was the baby, though his time with that position was quickly coming to an end. Ellie had seen just how hard it was for Marty to let Luke go. And close behind Luke's leaving was the marriage of Arnie. And Arnie was always so anxious to get home to his Anne that he scarcely had time for even a hello anymore. Ellie loved Arnie and was touched by his love for his Anne. When—or if—Ellie ever had the joy of being someone's wife, she hoped someone would feel the same way about her.

Again Ellie's thoughts turned to Lane, and the tears continued to stream down her cheeks. She loved him. Oh, how she loved him! How proud she would be to be the wife of such a man. But she couldn't; she just couldn't. It would be more than she could ever bring upon her mother. To ask her to lose another daughter to the West would be too much. Ellie would never do such a thing.

She fumbled with the latch to the barn door and heard excited yelps. Already the dogs were ready to greet her. She let herself in and carefully hung the lantern on the hook by the door before allowing herself to respond to their wild greeting.

"Oh, Rex," she sobbed, taking the nearly grown Rex into her arms and pulling him close. The dog seemed to sense that something was troubling her, and instead of his usual frenzied play, he crowded up against her, softly licking her tear-wet cheek. A low whine escaped him.

"Oh, Rex," she said again, the tears running more freely. "He's soon goin' back. He's goin' back west, an' I may never see 'im again. Never." Ellie buried her head against the fur of the only friend with whom she felt she could share her burden and cried out all her sorrow.

Lane, too, was in a state of torment. He had reached home from the wood cutting, done the chores, and spent a miserable evening pacing the floor. Finally he went to bed, but his troubled mind would not let him sleep. Quickly the days were passing by. It would not be long until it was time for him to return to Willie's ranch. Once back west, he would be many miles and many days away from Ellie. How could he stand never to see her again? Oh, if only he had never met her, then he would be unaware of how much he had missed—how much he loved her. She was the kind of woman he had always dreamed of sharing his life with. Her gentle spirit, the sparkle in her eye, her understanding . . .

He had felt that they were so right for each other, and he had been foolish enough to hope and dream that she felt that way, too. *She does, I'm sure she does,* Lane argued with himself. *I'm sure she could love me if only . . .* There it was again. The situation did not change in spite of Lane's yearning. It would be unfair to even ask Ellie to go west, knowing that she felt it would bring such pain to Marty. No, it would be wrong. For Ellie, being as sensitive as she was, could not know true happiness herself if she knew her mother was suffering. It was unthinkable. Even Lane, with his aching heart, knew that.

But wait, Lane checked himself. *Who says I have to go back west?* He could stay right where he was. He could farm or get a job in town. Ellie would not need to leave her mother. That was it! They would stay, and he would be free to express to Ellie his great love and his desire to share the rest of his life with her.

For a moment Lane felt wild with excitement. He could hardly wait to talk with Ellie. If it hadn't been so late at night, he would have gone to her immediately. What would the Davises think if he came riding madly into the farmyard at midnight, crying out that he had solved the problem? No, he must wait. But could he wait? Yes—wait, he must. He would go see Ellie at the first opportunity. Saturday night. In fact, he would beg off log cutting early so he could hurry through the chores. A feeling of deep relief passed through him, so thankful was he to have found a way through the muddle. "Thank ya, God," he whispered. "Thank ya fer makin' a way." And Lane turned over and slept well for the first time since Christmas.

SEVENTEEN

Letters

The long days of a snowbound January dragged slowly by. Marty had finished her preparations for the baby and now was impatient for it to arrive. On January the twelfth, she stood and stared at the calendar on the wall. *Surely the month must be further along than this,* she told herself. But no. It was right there in black and white. It was truly just January the twelfth. Marty moved about restlessly, wondering what to do with herself. She knew there were little jobs about the house she could busy herself doing, but nothing caught her interest or seemed to be worth the effort. She paced back to the window and stood looking out at the softly falling snow. Would it never quit snowing? It seemed to Marty that she had been looking at mounds of snow for months and months. She turned from the window with a sigh and stared at the calendar again. How many more weeks must they—?

Ellie must have been watching Marty's restlessness for a while. She said, "Why don't ya go an' have coffee with Kate? She's prob'ly as restless as you are."

Marty turned to Ellie in surprise. "I'm sorry," she apologized. "I'm a case, ain't I? I never remember bein' so impatient with any of the rest of ya."

"Ya were too busy lookin' after the others an' the house an' all the laundry an' the feedin' of—"

Marty's cheery laugh broke into Ellie's comments, and Marty thought Ellie looked up at her with relief.

"It's good to hear you laugh, Mama," she said. "We haven't had enough of it round here lately."

"Yer right," Marty said. "I was too busy. Havin' you here has made a lazy complainer outta me."

Ellie protested, but Marty went on. "Boy, ya must find me hard to live with. Feelin' sorry fer myself, when I've got so much to be thankful fer. But yer right. I will go see Kate. Maybe she is impatient, too, though she's had more sense 'bout all of this, I'm a thinkin'. She 'least has enough sense to stay busy."

Marty began to draw her shawl about her for the short walk across the yard. "Been worryin' 'bout Ma, too. Wonder how she's doin'. Haven't seen her fer a while, an' I just know she is missin' Ben somethin' fierce. Wish I could go on over an' see her, but yer pa will never let me—not in this weather."

Ellie looked up from the recipes she was paging through. "S'pose we could go on over an' git Ma an' bring her here," she suggested.

Marty was thrilled with the idea. "We could, couldn't we? Oh, would ya? I mean tomorra, could ya? Ya could leave right after breakfast an' Ma could stay on fer lunch. I'd do up the dishes and the mornin' cleanin' an' ya could—"

"All right," said Ellie with a smile. "Iffen it means thet much to ya, I'll go in the mornin'."

"Thank ya," said Marty.

"I'll talk to Pa as soon as he gets home from town," Ellie promised.

"Thank ya," said Marty again. And she turned with a smile to go see her Kate.

Kate was as glad to see Marty as Marty was to get out.

"Oh, I was hopin' fer some distraction!" Kate cried. "I was thinkin' of comin' up to see you, but Clare made me promise not to go out alone with it so slippery underfoot."

Marty smiled, remembering the many times when Clark had warned her of the same thing.

"I was very careful," she said, then confided, "but I've never had a lick of trouble—not with any of the babies thet I carried."

Even before Kate stirred the fire or put on the kettle, she urged Marty to "come see the baby's room."

"It's all done now," she explained as they moved to the door of the bedroom. "Oh, I just love it. Our baby just has no way of knowin' how very special he is. Iffen he knew how much his ma and pa had fussed over 'im . . ." Kate left her sentence dangling and laughed at their foolishness.

They entered the room, and Marty gasped. "Oh, it's lovely."

She crossed to the new crib that Clare had put so many hours on and ran a hand lovingly over the smoothly polished wood.

"He did a fine job on this, Kate," she said and felt that her words were inadequate. Kate must have thought so, too.

"Isn't it beautiful?" she enthused. "I had no idea Clare was so clever with his hands. I've never seen me a nicer baby's bed. An' look—he made a little chest to match it!"

Marty looked about the room—at the frilly curtains, the green walls, the handmade quilts, the pillows, the chest, the carefully chosen pictures, and especially the hand-turned bed—and her eyes shone almost as brightly as did Kate's.

"An' look," said Kate as she pulled open drawer after drawer to reveal tiny baby garments. "We are all ready now. Everythin's here . . . now we just wait."

"Wait," echoed Marty. "Sometimes it seems so long. I hope we can make it . . . both of us."

Kate reached to give her a squeeze, and the two women chuckled as they hugged over the two unborn babies.

"We'll make it," Kate promised. "We'll make it, 'cause it is so much worth waitin' fer. Oh, Mama, it's gonna be so much fun to have a baby of our own. We have been so happy, but this . . . this is gonna be . . . be . . . near to heaven."

Marty smiled. She remembered so well the excitement of waiting for the arrival of her first child. She had anticipated every one of them—that was true—but there was just no excitement like the arrival of the first one. She nodded to Kate, warm memories making her eyes mist over.

"Best we go out there an' have thet tea," she said, "'fore I git all emotional an' weepy."

Kate led the way back to the kitchen. They lingered over their cups. Marty told Kate about Ellie's proposal to pick up Ma Graham for a day's visit. "It's been so long," she said, her voice full of feeling, "an' I've been so worried 'bout her."

Kate agreed that it would be good for both of them to have a long chat. "But I've been thinkin' thet Ellie needs a break, too," Kate continued. "She has been lookin' rather peaked lately, an' she just seems . . . well . . . different."

"You've noticed it, too, huh?"

Kate nodded in agreement.

"Clark an' me's been talkin' 'bout it," Marty said. "She needs to git out more, thet's what I'm thinkin', but she doesn't really seem to want to, even when she has a chance."

"What chance?" asked Kate.

"Well, I remembered thet the young people were talkin' 'bout a ska-tin' party, an' I suggested thet Ellie go, but she wanted no part of it."

"But I can understand Ellie not wantin' to go alone."

"Oh, she wouldn't have gone alone. I asked Lane to take her."

"*You asked Lane?*" Kate's shock was evident.

"An' he said he'd be glad to," Marty assured her. "But Ellie said she didn't want to go."

"What else did Ellie say?" Kate asked thoughtfully.

"She said they were all 'kids.'"

"Maybe she just didn't want to go with Lane."

"I don't think so," Marty said slowly. "Ellie seemed to like Lane just fine. They was always laughin' an' talkin' together. Why, he helped her with the dishes, an' she gave him thet favorite dog she fusses over so. It would have been so nice fer Ellie iffen Lane had been round more, with Arnie an' Luke both gone, but he's not been back lately, an' Ellie didn't want to go to the party, an'—"

"Mama," Kate stopped her. "Do you think Ellie an' Lane . . . well, thet they had a sweethearts' quarrel?"

"A sweethearts' quarrel," said Marty in bewilderment. "Land sakes, they ain't sweethearts. They're more like brother an' sister."

Kate looked unconvinced. "Did you ever say that to Ellie?"

"Say what?"

"Thet they were . . . sorta . . . brother an' sister?"

Marty thought back. "Well, somethin' like thet, I suppose," she admitted at length.

"An' what did Ellie say?"

"She said thet . . . she said she didn't want Lane fer a brother," Marty said as she recalled the incident. She hesitated, then began to frown. "Now, why would she say a thing like thet?" she asked Kate.

"It fits, doesn't it?" Kate asked at last. "It sounds to me like Lane an' Ellie had 'em a disagreement."

"I wonder . . . ? I never had me any idea they might have thet kind of interest in each other."

Marty stirred her cup of tea around and around as she thought back over a number of things that had puzzled her. Kate might just be right. Things were beginning to *fit*.

"When I think on it," Marty admitted slowly, "they would be well suited to each other. I couldn't wish anyone finer than Lane fer my Ellie. He's the most sensitive, carin' young man I have ever met."

Marty absentmindedly continued stirring. "I wonder what happened," she mused out loud. "They seemed to be gettin' along so well together. I'm afraid I'm guilty of already seein' Lane as one of my own."

"I don't see thet as makin' a problem," countered Kate.

"Well, somethin' must have happened. I do admit it's had me worryin'. Couldn't figure out fer the life of me what got into the two of 'em. . . . Funny Clark didn't see it. He's usually so perceptive."

"Sometimes it's the most difficult to understand those closest to you," Kate said, and Marty knew she was right.

"Well, now thet we know," Marty determined, straightening up in her chair, "there should be somethin' a body can do 'bout it. Sure wouldn't want to lose Lane as a possible son-in-law." She smiled across at Kate.

"Better go slow, Mama," Kate warned her. "Maybe we are on the wrong track. An' maybe the two of them won't welcome any interference."

"I'll not jump into it," promised Marty. "First, I'll talk it over with Clark an' see iffen he agrees with us. He'll know what should be done—iffen anythin'."

They changed the subject and finished their tea.

"Thank ya, dear," Marty said at the door, giving her daughter-in-law a kiss on the cheek. "I needed that—all of it. Iffen we are right, I feel thet a load's been lifted off me concernin' Ellie. I will admit I was some worried. But I promise," she continued laughingly as she held up her hand, "not to go bargin' in."

Kate laughed with her, and Marty wrapped her shawl once more about her and headed for her own house. The air was crisp and the snow still fell, but Marty felt as though she had been given new courage and purpose to face the many tomorrows ahead.

When Marty reached the warmth of her own kitchen, she had further reason to rejoice. Clark had returned from town, and the mail he brought with him contained three letters. Letters from her children! Marty could scarcely believe her good fortune.

Missie wrote that their winter had been mild, and Willie felt it had been the easiest winter yet on the cattle. They had enjoyed the visit of Willie's brother and family. Missie didn't know how her Josiah and Nathan would ever be able to entertain themselves once their cousins had gone. They had all enjoyed one another so much.

The church was continuing to reach out. Two of the regular families had moved away, but Henry had been calling on other ranches in the area and had already recruited one new family to join them. Another family had shown some interest, and they were all praying that they, too, might soon be desiring to share in Sunday worship.

Baby Melissa was growing daily. She was such a contented child, and she already thoroughly believed that her older brothers were the most important people in her world. Everyone loved her, and Missie feared lest the ranch hands would spoil her.

The boys were growing. Nathan had started school as planned and seemed to be a promising student. He was busy trying to teach his young brother, Josiah, to read. Josiah was eager to learn and had managed, under Nathan's tutelage, to recognize half a dozen words. The family laughed about it and tried to dissuade Nathan from further teaching duties.

Missie said that they missed Lane and would be so glad to have him back again. Marty stopped her reading. For the first time since her talk with Kate, Marty realized if Lane and Ellie were truly interested in each other and they were to resolve their differences—whatever they were—Marty would be losing another daughter. It would not be easy, but this time Marty felt she would be prepared. God had helped her to give up Missie and Clae and Luke. Surely He could help her if Ellie should decide to leave them, too. Marty finished Missie's letter and picked up the letter from Clae.

Clae was all excited about the little church where Joe was serving as a part-time pastor. She had never seen her Joe happier than he was now, even though the demands on his time were so great. The people were very kind to all of them, and they felt at home among them. It was the first she had really felt at home since leaving her family behind and traveling east. Clae, at last, felt free to voice her true feelings over the move. At first, she said, she had been so homesick that she had felt she just couldn't bear it, and she had prayed daily for the time to pass quickly so they might go home again. God had now answered her prayer in an unexpected way. He had given them love and friendship and a contentment in His will that she wouldn't have thought possible. She no longer chafed for home—though she still missed them all very much—but she was quite at home where she was, as long as Joe was happy and she had her little family and their new friends.

Esther Sue was getting so grown-up. She loved to help with her baby brother. The baby was a source of joy to each one of them. He looked much like his father, although his coloring was more like his mama.

They were still thinking of accepting a church in the East for a while, although eventually they did plan to come back to the rural area. Joe felt he would be more suitably placed in a farming community than in a city, but he believed he had so much he needed to learn before leaving the area where the seminary was. He could take a pastorate and fit in some night classes for a while and better equip himself for the ministry.

They were all keeping well. It was so good to have a visit with Luke upon his return after Christmas and catch up on all of the news from home. Clae sent her thanks over and over for the parcels Luke had carried back with him from the family. She admitted to shedding a few tears as she unwrapped each one, but they were happy tears, she maintained, and came from a grateful heart that had responded to the love which came with the gifts.

Marty laid aside the letter with mixed emotions. She was so glad Clae and Joe felt at home—and at peace. How good it was to entrust them to the care of the all-knowing and caring Father.

Marty reached for Luke's letter and eagerly tore the envelope open. Luke, too, was full of good reports. He was busily engaged in his studies again. It had been so good to be home. He trusted that all the family was well. He had seen Clae and Joe, and they seemed to be happy in their new work. Joe was fairly bursting with the new knowledge he was absorbing. Especially was he excited about his in-depth study on the deity of Christ—that Christ, as Holy God, could care so much for sinful man was a truth he found staggering.

Luke was back into classes again and was even more sure than before, if possible, that his was a doctor's calling. Such strides were being made in the field of medicine, and he wanted to be right there, a contributing part of it.

The letter was short, as Luke was in a hurry. He had much work to do in preparation for his next day's classes, he stated, but he had wanted to send his greetings home and thank them for their love and support.

Marty drank in the contents of each letter, promising herself that she would read them again before retiring. As she read each page, she passed it on to Ellie, who also pored over each one.

"They all sound fine, don't they, Mama?" Ellie said as she read the last page.

"An' I'm so thankful," Marty responded, with the hint of tears in her eyes. "Nothin' makes a mother happier than to know thet her family is fine."

Ellie rose to go check on her supper, and Marty sighed contentedly as she carefully tucked each letter back into its envelope so Clark might read them as soon as he came in from the barn.

She had spoken the truth. Nothing made a mother happier than to know her children were all happy. Kate and Clare were eagerly waiting for their new baby. Missie was enjoying the visit of family and thrilled with each new accomplishment of her own little ones. Clae and Joe were happy in the work they felt called to do. Luke was thrilled with each new discovery as a physician-in-training. Arnie could hardly wait each night to get home to his Anne. Nandry's family continued to grow and flourish. That left only her Ellie. Ellie's eyes still bore a shadow. She would talk to Ellie tonight, but first she must have a chat with Clark to get his reaction to Kate's theory. Marty did so want her sweet little Ellie to be happy, as well.

EIGHTEEN

A Talk With Ellie

"Clark," Marty said softly and waited until Clark lifted his head from the page he was reading.

He didn't answer but silently looked at her, waiting for her to continue.

"Had me a talk with Kate today," Marty told him.

"Ya said ya did."

"She is so excited 'bout the comin' of thet baby. They have everythin' in readiness now. Don't know how the two of 'em are ever gonna be able to stand the next six weeks or so." Marty chuckled before she went on. "But thet weren't all we talked 'bout. She's been worried 'bout Ellie, too. She has noticed thet Ellie just isn't her usual happy self."

Clark nodded slowly, concern showing in his face.

"Kate prodded some an' got me to thinkin'. Do you think there's any chance thet Ellie is sweet on Lane? I mean thet they might sorta like each other an' have had a fuss 'bout somethin'?"

The corners of Clark's mouth turned down in surprise at the idea. "Never thought of it, but why not?" he finally said. "I mean, Lane is an attractive young man with a real love fer people, an' Ellie is a pretty an' pleasant girl. Why not? Why didn't we think of thet? It's not only possible, but it's most likely." Clark pondered a moment. "Do ya s'pose thet's what she meant by not wantin' Lane fer a *brother*?"

"I wonder iffen it might be," Marty answered him, shaking her head back and forth. "Don't know why I didn't see it afore."

"Guess we were just thinkin' *family* too much where Lane was concerned."

"Guess so. Then d'ya think it might be somethin' like thet troublin' Ellie?"

"Well, they sure could care fer each other, I see thet now. But why there should be any trouble with the carin' I still don't see. Neither of them are selfish or prideful. Don't see why they can't work out their little differences, if differences there be."

"I was wonderin' iffen we should have a chat with Ellie an' see if there's some way we could help 'em sort it out."

"Where is Ellie?"

"She left fer the barn an' thet dog of her'n again."

"Ya mean dog of *his'n*."

"Yeah, his'n."

"I don't know," Clark wondered aloud, rubbing his chin. "I've never felt it too wise to interfere where heart matters are concerned. Usually it's better to let 'em work it out on their own."

"Thet's 'bout what Kate said." Marty dropped a stitch and continued on with her knitting.

"Hurts me, though," she confided softly. "Ellie's been sufferin', I can tell. Lane don't rightly look so good, either."

"Maybe a body can beat round the bush some an' come up with somethin'."

"Ellie's pretty shrewd. Don't know iffen you'll fool her none."

"Might be easier to talk to Lane."

Marty's knitting needles stopped. "Now, what would ya say? 'Ya carin' fer my daughter an' havin' some kinda fuss? She's eatin' her heart out, an' I wanna know why'?"

"Yer right," said Clark. "Thet wouldn't be so easy, either."

Marty's needles began to slowly click again. She was usually a fast knitter, and the sound gave away the fact that her mind was not on her work. "What do ya think we should do?" she asked at last.

"Wish I knew fer sure. One thing sure is we should pray about it."

At Marty's nod, Clark bowed his head and led them in a fervent prayer for their daughter. And for Lane.

"I'm thinkin' the only way might just be to up and come right straight out with it," Clark observed after he raised his head.

"I think yer right," agreed Marty, and Clark laid his book aside and stood up.

"Guess I'll take me a little walk," he said, "an' see iffen I can discover what is so special 'bout a certain dog."

Marty's eyes looked deeply into Clark's to assure him that she trusted him to do and say the right things where their daughter was concerned, and then her knitting needles began to pick up speed.

Clark walked into the kitchen and pulled on his coat against the cold. He didn't bother to light another lantern. The winter moon shone brightly in the sky, and millions of stars sparkled above him. His way would be well lit to the barn, and once there, Ellie's lantern would light the interior for both of them.

He did not hurry. He needed time to think. He needed time to pray once more. He had no idea how to approach the delicate subject with his daughter. It helped that they had always been able to talk easily to each other. At times like this, Clark was so glad there had been years of establishing a strong connection with each of his children. It was well worth it for a father to take the time, he knew with great certainty.

The snow crunched beneath his foot and crutch, and his breath preceded him in smoky little puffs. He opened the barn door and entered, turning to close it tightly behind him. He wanted to give Ellie the advantage of adjusting to his presence before he turned to look at her. He found her sitting on a pile of straw, gently stroking the dog she called Rex.

Clark cleared his throat and crossed over to lean on a half partition. For a moment neither of them spoke.

"He's really growin', ain't he?" Clark said at last.

"Sure is," responded Ellie.

"Seems like a nice dog. He learnin' well?"

"He's really quick," said Ellie.

"You've always thought 'im kinda special, ain't ya?"

Ellie agreed that she had. Clark knelt down and stroked the dog with his large work-roughened hand. The dog squirmed with the pleasure of it but did not leave Ellie.

"Seems to me thet's more'n a dog yer holdin'," Clark observed.

Ellie's head came up quickly, but she did not ask her father what he meant.

Clark continued to stroke the dog.

"Seems like it's a dream thet yer holdin', as well," went on Clark, and Ellie's head bowed over the dog again. "A dream . . . an' maybe a love."

Tears came to Ellie's eyes and started to slide down her cheeks. Clark reached out and gently brushed one of them away.

"What is it, little girl?" he asked softly. "Do ya love a man who doesn't return yer love?"

"Oh no. He does," Ellie said quickly. "He . . . he wanted me to have a locket fer Christmas. He would have come courtin'. I know thet, Pa, iffen I would have given 'im any hope at all."

"An' why didn't ya?" asked Clark simply.

"Why?"

"Yeah, why? Didn't ya feel like he's the kinda man ya could love?"

"Oh, I do love 'im, I do," sobbed Ellie.

Clark reached out and drew his daughter into his arms. He let her cry against him, saying nothing, only holding her close and stroking her long golden curls.

When Ellie's sobs appeared to be lessening, he spoke again.

"I'm afraid ya lost me," he said against her hair. "Ya say thet he would have come courtin'—an' ya say thet ya love 'im. Then why are the two of ya so miserable an' there's no courtin' bein' done?"

Ellie pulled back and looked at her father, eyes wide in astonishment.

"I can't," she sobbed again. "Ya know thet. I can't." When Clark did not respond, she said, "Mama needs me."

The words soaked slowly into Clark's consciousness, and he pushed the girl away from him and looked into her eyes. "Whoa, now," he said. "What is this yer tellin' me?"

"Mama needs me," Ellie repeated.

"Sure, Mama needs ya, but she sure ain't expectin' ya to go on bein' her housemaid fer all the years to come."

"But the baby—"

"Mama has had babies afore—an' she's made out just fine, too. Oh, I will admit I was some worried, too—at first—but she's doin' just fine now. Why, yer mama is no softie. She can handle most anythin' thet needs handlin', an' one little baby, more or less, sure ain't gonna bother her none."

"But it's not just thet," said Ellie.

"It's not?"

"No."

"What else, then?" said Clark, fearing that a fresh torrent of tears was on the way.

"Lane is going back west as soon as the LaHayes get back to care fer the farm."

"So?"

"Every time one of us goes far away, it pains Mama. You know how it hurt her when Missie went, and then Clae, and now Luke. It would nigh kill her iffen I went, too."

"I see," said Clark. "Yer thinkin' thet yer mama just wouldn't be able to let ya go, huh?"

Ellie nodded with her head up against him.

"Well, I'm admittin' thet yer mama sure does prefer her young'uns close by. I also happen to know the thing thet Mama wants more'n anythin' in the world is fer her children to be happy. Now, iffen ya think thet yer happiness lies with a certain young man by the name of Lane, then thet's what Mama wants fer ya, even iffen it takes ya many miles away."

Ellie's eyes still showed doubt. "Oh, Pa," she said, "do ya really think so?"

"I know so," answered Clark. "Fact is, I just came from talkin' with yer mama. She is worried 'bout ya. Has been fer days. We didn't either one of us guess what was wrong, or we woulda straightened ya out long ago. It was Kate thet got suspectin'. Guess we had just thought of Lane as family fer so long thet we never even thought he might not seem like family to you."

Ellie's eyes began to glow again. "Oh, Pa," she said, "I love both you an' Mama so. I'd never want to hurt Mama. Never!"

"And yer mama would never want to stand in the way of yer happiness, either. Now wipe away those tears, and let's go see yer mama."

Ellie did so, the best she could, then bent to stroke the patient Rex once more before hurrying to the barn door. Clark lifted the lantern from its hook and followed her.

Suddenly Ellie stopped. "But, Pa," she said in deep concern, "I already told Lane no."

"I don't think Lane will be givin' up thet easy like," he assured her. "Iffen he does, he's not the man I thought 'im to be."

Some of the fear left Ellie's eyes, and she quickened her steps. Clark had all he could do to keep up with her. As he hung up his coat on the peg in the kitchen, he heard her say, "Oh, Mama," and then what sounded like both laughing and crying.

NINETEEN

Dark Shadows

Someone was knocking on the door, making far more noise than should be necessary. Marty fought for consciousness, at the same time wishing she could remain asleep. Something told her it was not time to get up yet, even though she could not see the clock in the darkness.

Clark had roused and was hurriedly dressing. Marty's mind flashed her a message of "Ben." *This is what happened when Ben . . .* But no, it couldn't be that again. Then why would someone come pounding on their door now? Fear gripped Marty's heart. It must be more bad news.

Clark left the room hurriedly without a word, and Marty heard his footstep on the wooden stairsteps. He had not stopped for boot or crutch and hopped down on one bare foot.

With an effort, Marty threw back the covers and stepped out onto the cold floor. She was glad for the rug nearby that offered some protection from the winter chill. She felt around with one foot for her bed socks and crossed to the closet hook to grab her robe. Voices drifted up to her. Excited voices. It sounded like Clare. Who had awakened Clare, and what might the trouble be?

Marty tried not to hurry down the steps. A fall in the dark certainly would be no aid to whatever the problem was. She held firmly to the rail and felt her way down carefully. Yes, it was Clare's voice. Clare's voice mingled with Clark's, Clare's muffled by horrible sobs. Marty hastened her steps.

When Marty entered the kitchen, she was more bewildered than ever. Clark had lit the kitchen lamp, and in its soft glow, she could see the outline of two men. Her men. Clark was supporting Clare, and Clare was weeping against him uncontrollably. Marty tried to voice a question, but it wouldn't form on her lips.

"It's Kate," said Clark over Clare's head. "She's in terrible pain."

"What's happened?" Marty was able to gasp out the question.

"He doesn't know. It just came on sudden like in the night. I'm gonna go git Doc. Ya think thet ya can—?"

But Clark didn't finish his question before Marty moved to her grown son and turned him toward her.

Clare seemed to get hold of himself. "Oh, Ma," he groaned, "I'm so scared. I've never seen anyone in such pain. We gotta git back there, Ma. We gotta—"

"We will," said Marty. "I'll just pull on some boots an' grab a shawl."

Clare took Marty's hand, and they hurried toward the little log house. He had taken command again now. The rough sobbing had ceased, and he was thinking rationally.

"Maybe the baby is on the way," Marty said as a means of assurance.

"It's too early yet."

"Some of 'em come early."

"Not this early."

"Maybe Kate figured wrong."

Clare made no response, and Marty thought he strongly doubted it.

"Some women do have a great deal of pain when—"

But Clare didn't want to listen. "We don't want the baby comin' now," he said. "It's still too early. It would be dang'rous fer 'im to come now."

Marty turned at the sound of someone hurrying to the barn. Clark was on his way for the doctor. She prayed him Godspeed and continued along the icy path.

"Pa's on his way," she said to Clare. "Won't be long an' the doc'll be here."

They had not yet reached the house when Marty could hear Kate. She felt Clare stiffen beside her. Poor Kate—she had never been a crybaby about discomfort. Truly Clare was right. Something was terribly wrong with her. They hastened into the little house, and Marty kicked her boots into a corner by the door and shed her shawl as she passed by a chair. Already Clare had half run through to the bedroom. A lamp had not even been lit, and Marty fumbled around in the semidarkness to find it and the matches. Kate continued to toss and moan on the bed, and Clare dropped on his knees beside her and tried to soothe her with his words and hands.

"Pa's gone for Doc, sweetheart. It won't be long now. Just hang on. Hang on."

Clare turned back to Marty and his eyes were pleading. *Do somethin', Ma*, they seemed to say. *Do somethin' fer my Kate.*

Marty moved to the bed and gently reached out to the girl, smoothing her matted hair back from her face. "Kate," she said, raising her voice to be heard above Kate's groans, "Kate, can ya hear me, dear?"

Kate responded with a nod of her head and another moan.

"When did this start?"

Kate managed to indicate that it had started about bedtime—a little—and then increased in intensity during the night.

"An' where is the pain?" continued Marty.

Kate laid her hand on her lower abdomen.

Marty placed her hand there, too. She could feel the tightening of Kate's muscles as another groan passed Kate's lips.

As the contraction passed, Marty spoke to Kate, trying to keep her voice light to ease some of the tension in the room.

"Kate," she said, "I do believe thet yer gonna be a mama."

"No!" Kate gasped out. "No! It's too early—too soon. I don't want 'im to come now. He's too little."

"Listen," Marty said sharply. "Listen, Kate. Don't fight it, Kate. Don't struggle against it. Try to relax. Maybe—maybe it will pass—but ya gotta calm yerself. Fer yer sake an' the baby's."

Marty could see Kate's big violet eyes in the dim light given off by the lamp on the dresser. Marty knew she was thinking of her baby. She wanted her baby. She would do anything that she could for his safety.

135

"I'll try," she whispered. "I'll try."

"Good girl," Marty said, then knelt down beside Clare and began to stroke the girl's cold hand. "Now, Clare, I know thet you've been prayin', but let's pray together."

Clare led them in prayer. "Our God," he said, a catch in his voice, "ya know our concern here. We don't want to see Kate in such pain, an' we don't think it's time fer the little one yet. Help us all to be calm with yer help, Lord. Help Kate at this time to feel yer love—an' our love. God, ya know our desire. We want our son safely delivered. I want my Kate—" Clare's voice truly broke here, and Marty wondered if he would be able to continue, but he quickly recovered. "But, God, in spite of our wants, we gotta say as we been told to say, 'Thy will be done.' An' we mean it, Lord, 'cause we know thet ya love us and ya want our good. Amen."

Kate had lain quietly the entire time Clare was praying. Clare leaned over and kissed her cheek as soon as he had said his "Amen." Kate stirred again, and Marty knew she was fighting to try to relax in spite of her intense pain.

"Clare," Marty said, "make us a good fire in the cook stove, will ya? And put on a couple kettles of water to heat."

Clare went to comply, and Marty moved closer to minister to the girl on the bed. She smoothed back her hair, straightened the crumpled blankets, stroked her flushed cheeks. And all the time she fussed and comforted, she talked quietly to Kate, trying to distract her mind from the pain.

Kate heroically tried—with all her being she tried. Marty could see her brace herself against the pain and then fight with all of her might to relax in spite of it. Clare started a brisk fire and filled the kettles as Marty had told him. He even brought a pan of water so Marty might sponge Kate's face. The hours dragged by. Marty felt the doctor was long overdue and feared lest he had already been called out on some other emergency. Just as she was about to give up, she heard hoofbeats in the yard. She turned to the window and breathed a prayer of thanks as she saw two riders dismount.

Clark was leading both horses toward the barn, and Doc was hurrying toward the little house with his black bag grasped firmly in his hand. Never had any man looked more welcome to Marty than did Doc.

Clare was already at the door, taking Doc's coat and giving him a report. Marty remained in Kate's room until the doctor appeared, and then she left him with the girl and went to the kitchen to wait for Clark.

She busied herself with the coffeepot. She didn't know if there would be anyone who would be wanting coffee, but it gave her something to do. With Kate now in the doctor's hands, Marty had time to think.

What if Kate's baby *was* on the way? Would it be developed enough to be able to survive? What would happen to Clare and Kate if they lost their baby? What would happen to their faith?

Marty reached down and laid a hand on her own stomach. Her baby responded with a strong kick. Marty's eyes filled with tears. "Please, God," she prayed, "don't let anythin' happen to the baby. They could never stand it, Lord. They've been workin' an' dreamin' an' prayin' fer thet little'un fer so long. It would break their hearts to lose it now. Iffen . . . iffen . . ." and Marty placed her hand over her unborn. "Iffen it has to be one of 'em, Lord, then . . . then take mine. I think I could bear it better'n Kate." Even as Marty spoke the words silently, her mind was filled with the knowledge of the great pain that losing her baby—the little unseen someone she had learned to love—would bring her. If only there was some way she could protect Clare and Kate from the awful pain of losing the baby they loved.

Another thought quickly followed, almost taking Marty's breath away. What if something happened to Kate? How would Clare ever be able to stand that? Again Marty prayed. "Not Kate. Please, God, protect Kate . . . fer Clare's sake."

Clark came into the kitchen, rubbing his cold hands together.

"Any word yet?" he asked, his face serious.

"No. Doc is with her now."

"What do you think?" Clark dropped his heavy mittens onto a nearby chair.

"I think thet . . . thet the baby is on the way."

"Can it make it?"

Marty shrugged wearily. "I don't know. It's early . . . too early. But some have. I don't know. I'm afraid, Clark, really afraid."

Clark crossed to her and drew her to him. Their baby protested, and a smile flickered across Clark's face in spite of his anxiety.

"Feisty little rascal, ain't he?" he commented and Marty eased away.

"She," she said in a whisper with a smile and moved to the stove. "Ya want some coffee?"

"Would help to warm me up some, I reckon."

Marty poured two cups. She wasn't sure if she would be able to drink from hers. She had no desire for coffee. She suddenly noticed as she crossed to the table that things were very quiet in the bedroom. It was a relief not to hear Kate tossing and moaning, and Marty hoped that the quiet was a good sign.

Clare entered the room. His eyes looked heavy and his face drawn.

"It's the baby, all right," he said in a tired, resigned voice.

"How is Kate?"

"Doc has given her somethin'. Just to help with the pain. Doc can't find a heartbeat on the little one. 'Fraid thet . . . thet somethin' is wrong."

He lowered himself onto a chair and put his head on his arms on the table. Marty was at a loss. What did one say to an aching son? This was not a childhood disappointment that they were dealing with. This was a life. Two lives. How did one give support at such a time?

Clark reached out and gripped Clare's shoulder with a firm hand. Clare did not move or respond, but Marty knew that he felt the love and support of his father.

When Clare was able to speak, he continued slowly. "Doc says Kate is strong. Her pulse is good an' she is fightin' hard. She should be fine when this is all over."

Marty breathed a thankful prayer.

"How long does Doc think it might be?" asked Clark quietly.

"Can't say."

Marty brought Clare some coffee. To her surprise he drank it, though she wasn't sure he was aware of doing so.

The long night hours slid slowly by. From time to time, members of the family went to the bedroom to check with Doc. About the only assurance he could give them was that Kate seemed to be holding up well.

Dawn came, the air brisk and wind-chilled. Ellie arrived at the little house. Unbelievably, she had slept through the commotion of the night before, her bedroom being at the back of the house. Now she came fearfully, looking for her family and wondering what were the circumstances of an empty house. Her face paled as Clark explained the situation to her, and then she went to work preparing some breakfast in Kate's little kitchen. Marty had not even thought of the need for food.

Clark left to do the chores. Clare moved as if to go with him, but Clark waved him back to his chair. Instead, Clare went to see how his Kate was. He came back to the kitchen with his face even more somber than before.

"Doc doesn't think thet it'll be long now," and he lowered himself to the chair again. Marty wondered if he might be better off choring than sitting there with Kate heavy on his mind.

Ellie served breakfast. No one ate much, but a few of them went through the motions. Marty took a plate of pancakes and some bacon and coffee to the doctor. He eased himself onto a chair by Kate's bed and ate. He knew from long experience that one must eat to maintain strength.

It was nearing eleven o'clock in the morning when the baby girl arrived, tiny and stillborn. There was nothing that anyone could do . . . or say. Clare held his infant daughter in his arms and shook with his sobs. Then he passed her to Marty, who, through her own tears, lovingly bathed the little bit of humanity who was to have brought such happiness into a home. Clare went to the baby's room and found the tiny garments that Kate had requested for their little one to wear. They had been sewn with such love and pride and were to have been worn with such happiness. Now they would represent the love wrapped snugly around the tiny baby as it was committed to the small coffin which Clare and Clark sorrowfully fashioned together.

Kate continued to hold her own. Clare was so thankful that nothing had happened to his wife. With the help of the doctor's medication, she slept through most of the first day and on through the night. The next morning, Clare spoke gently to Kate of their loss. She had been vaguely aware of the fact before she slipped off to sleep. After they had embraced each other and cried together, Clare carried the small casket that held their little daughter into Kate's room, so she might see their child. Clark and Marty went on back to their house and left the two of them alone.

The burial was a quiet family affair. The preacher spoke the familiar words of strength and encouragement to the family members who gathered around the tiny grave.

In the days that followed, Kate regained her strength quickly after her ordeal, though a shadow lingered in her eyes. She clung to Clare in their sorrow. Clark and Marty prayed daily—sometimes hourly—for their children in their pain. Marty wished over and over that she could somehow bear it for them, but she could only be there, suffering with them. Somehow they got through the first difficult days. With time it would get easier, but, oh, it was going to take so much time, and the love-built nursery room was a constant reminder of just how much they had lost. It was hard for Marty to stand the strain of the sorrow, and without meaning to—or even realizing that she was doing so—she began to draw away from the intensity of the pain.

Nandry

Lane came as soon as he heard the news, spending time with Clare and allowing him to talk out his feelings concerning the death of his infant daughter.

Ellie hardly knew how to respond to Lane, now that she'd had her talk with her ma and pa. If she was free to make her own future, as they assured her she was, then she hoped that her pa was right and Lane wouldn't give up easily. But in her heart, Ellie feared—feared that Lane might have taken her previous word as the final answer. What if he did not wish to pursue it further? Ellie would be the loser indeed. Yet could she be bold enough to approach Lane herself? It wasn't at all in keeping with how she had been brought up, and Ellie doubted very much if she could bring herself to do it.

So for now, at least, she kept her conversations with Lane courteous but brief.

Marty now had some very difficult days to live through. Each time her child moved, she remembered that she had fought against this baby. She had not wanted it. Indeed, had she gotten her way, it would not have been . . . at first. Now Marty loved this baby. Whoever it was within her had completely captured her mother love. Still . . . she felt guilty. It was true she hadn't wanted it . . . and yet it was still safe, while the small body of the baby Kate and Clare had wanted so very much right from the beginning lay in the churchyard under a heap of winter snow. It didn't seem just or fair.

So in the sorrow that Marty shared with her son and daughter-in-law, there was also mixed in a good deal of guilt. Could they see it? Did they, too, feel the circumstances were unjust, that she was unworthy to be bearing another child? True, when Kate had been in pain and her baby in danger, Marty had been willing to exchange her baby's life for the life of Kate's baby if the Lord would have accepted such a bargain. Marty was beginning to understand how very difficult it would have been for her actually to go through with such an agreement. She loved the small life within her more than she had thought possible. Yet poor, poor Kate! She had loved her baby, too. Marty wondered if Kate and Clare would be bitter toward her and the coming baby. She did not want to face them. And in the days following the death of their infant and the gathering for the burial at the church, Marty found little excuses to keep from close contact with the young couple. What could she say? How did they feel about her? About Clare's new little brother or sister soon to make an appearance?

Ellie, fortunately, had been to see Kate daily. She helped her with her housework until Kate was able once again to take over for herself. Even then Ellie went, dropping in for a chat or a cup of tea. Marty knew she must go, as well, but she begged "foul weather" and stayed close to her fire.

It was Nandry who unexpectedly brought Marty to her senses. Nandry came to call in spite of the bad weather. She had left all the children at home with Josh. Marty knew, as soon as she saw her daughter drive into the yard, that something deeper than the need for companionship had driven Nandry out alone and on such a day.

Marty was still concerned about Nandry. Something was bothering the girl—had been ever since they'd come home. Nandry never had said anything about it, but Marty knew it was there. Marty had the feeling it was somehow connected with Clark—Clark and his lost leg. But surely enough time had passed by now for Nandry to get used to the sight and the idea of Clark's need for a crutch.

Marty held the door for Nandry now and lovingly welcomed her in. Her first explanation for the visit sounded like Nandry simply had taken a notion to get out of the house for a few hours. Her small brood was driving her beside herself, she maintained. Marty nodded, remembering well the feeling.

Nandry inquired about Kate, and Marty assured her that from all reports she seemed to be doing fine, that Ellie was presently with her.

Marty busied herself putting on the coffeepot and cutting some slices of Ellie's loaf cake. Nandry talked easily of everyday things. She wanted one of Ellie's recipes for pumpkin bread. Andy had fallen and bitten his tongue. It hadn't been a bad cut, but it had bled profusely, and Mary had screamed in fright, thinking Andrew would surely bleed to death. Baby Jane had fallen down a few steps; she wasn't hurt badly, but it did frighten them all. Tina had come home from school with a gold ribbon as the best speller in the class; Josh was so proud of her. He had never been good at spelling.

Nandry, unusually talkative, continued to chat until Marty poured the coffee and settled down at the table with her. Then, with a quickness Marty found hard to follow, she changed from her current casual subject.

"How's Kate takin' it?"

Marty was taken aback. The fact was she didn't really know how Kate was taking it. Oh, outwardly Kate seemed to be handling it fine, according to Ellie. But Marty had no way of knowing how Kate was feeling deep inside. She couldn't admit that to Nandry, so she replied defensively, "She feels bad, of course."

"I didn't mean thet," responded Nandry. "I mean, is she able to accept it?"

"Accept it?"

Nandry looked at Marty searchingly, her eyes repeating the question.

"Accept it?" said Marty again. "Well, it happened, didn't it? One has to accept it—iffen ya want to or not."

"Ma," said Nandry, "don't beat round the bush. Ya know what I'm meanin'."

"No," said Marty slowly, "I'm 'fraid I don't."

"Does Kate feel God has a right—thet He was fair to do what He done?"

"God?" said Marty in disbelief. Was Nandry actually asking what it seemed like she was asking?

"Ma, we know thet God could have saved thet there baby fer Clare an' Kate iffen He had wanted to—just like He could have saved Pa's leg iffen He had put himself out some."

There. It was out. Pain showed in Nandry's eyes—pain and anger. Marty looked at the girl, shock and fear sweeping through her and making her feel heartsick.

"It's true," continued Nandry, her tone reckless. "It's true, and one might as well say it. No use just pretendin' thet it ain't."

Marty reached out a hand and laid it on Nandry's arm. She'd had no idea there was so much anger and bitterness there.

Nandry shrugged off the hand.

"But . . . but . . . it ain't like thet," began Marty, silently imploring the Lord to give her wisdom.

"It ain't? Well, how is it, then? I s'pose Pa hoppin' round on one leg is just a figment of my 'magination, huh?"

"I didn't mean thet. I mean—well, I mean God didn't just take Pa's leg to be spiteful. He—"

"How d'ya know what He did an' why?"

"At the time," said Marty quietly, "I didn't, an' I fought it, too. I had to come to the place where I could honestly say, 'Thy will be done,' an' God did His will, an' good came of the sorrow."

"Enough good to make up fer a good man losin' his leg?"

Marty hesitated at the words spat out on the table between them. Nandry had always been particularly devoted to Clark in an unusual way. Marty had hoped Nandry had long since properly sorted out the relationship with Clark as her father.

"I think so—" began Marty hesitantly. Then, with more conviction, "I know so. Why, so many things happened to show it so. The little church was started. Dr. de la Rosa went home and made peace with his family. An' the . . . the most important was what happened in the life of Jedd, yer first pa. He—"

But Nandry interrupted, rising from her chair with her eyes sparking angrily. "An' what did *he* ever do to deserve the mercy of God? Him thet run out on us, thet left Ma to die alone while he ran off to chin-wag an' chew tobacca with some old cronies. Are ya tellin' me thet God would favor a man like thet over one who was upright an' carin' an' lived . . . ?" But Nandry could not go on. She was weeping uncontrollably now, her shoulders shaking with every sob.

Marty rose to her feet slowly because of her cumbersome body. She was dumbstruck. What could she ever say to this angry and agonizing girl? How could she make her see that God *is* love? That He gives it freely whether a person "deserves" it or not? How could she ever get her to understand that bitterness and hate against her father were not in keeping with God's plan for her life—could not bring happiness or peace or anything good to anybody? Oh, poor Nandry, to have carried such a terrible burden for such a long, long time!

Marty moved to her and took her into her arms. As Marty raised her eyes, she beheld a stricken Ellie standing in silence at the kitchen door. Marty had not heard her return, and she was sure Nandry was not aware of her presence, either. Ellie stood with a white face and parted lips as though unable to comprehend. Marty wondered how long she had been standing there and how she would respond to what she had heard from the lips of her adopted older sister.

Then Ellie took a deep breath and moved into the room. She took Nandry's hand and gently led her back to her chair. Nandry sat down again, physically and emotionally spent from her outburst. Ellie passed her a hankie and Nandry blew loudly.

Ellie waited for a moment and then spoke quietly. "Nandry," she said, "I think I know how yer feelin'. At first, when I heard 'bout Pa, I wanted to fight it, too. I blamed God . . . a little bit. I blamed God fer spoilin' a good man. You know what I thought? I thought thet I might not be proud to walk down the street in town with Pa anymore. Can you 'magine that? Feelin' ashamed to be seen with a man like Pa simply because he had only one leg?" Ellie shook her head sadly, as if she felt guilty over ever having such a thought. "I always thought my pa 'bout perfect, an' I was 'fraid I wouldn't see 'im as perfect anymore. It would be embarrassin'. People would stare. I looked at the other men around. 'He's not as good as my pa,' I'd think, 'an' he's still got two legs.' I knew it was wrong—I knew it all the time—an' then God started talkin' to me 'bout it. He pointed at my own life. I had pride, I had vanity; I even discovered some deceit. 'See,' said God, 'yer not perfect. Is yer pa ashamed to walk down the street with you? He should be, iffen it's perfection yer wantin'.' I knew God was right. My cripplin' was greater and more deadly than Pa's. Mine was to the spirit; his was only the body. I prayed an' asked God to fergive me an' to help me grow from the experience of Pa losin' his leg, so the price of it might be worth somethin' in my life—both fer my gain an' so thet Pa could remain proud of me.

"Now yer pa, Nandry, had 'im many faults." Ellie's voice was gentle. "What ya have said 'bout 'im is prob'ly right. I don't know, I didn't know 'im. But God must have seen someone worth savin'. An' even iffen there wasn't anything worthy at all, God still loved 'im. An' Pa loved 'im. Loved 'im enough to want to make sure he had thet chance 'fore he died. Pa didn't knowingly give his leg fer yer pa. But I think he would have—iffen he had had some way of knowin', I think he would have. Because our pa knows thet a leg is less important than a soul.

"I think thet Pa would be hurt iffen he knew the loss of his leg somehow brought bitterness to yer soul, Nandry. He wants to strengthen ya an' help ya to grow with every experience of his life, and iffen he doesn't do thet, then it brings him pain and disappointment—far more pain than the loss of thet leg did."

Nandry had been listening silently to Ellie. Marty sat praying—praying that God would give Ellie the right words to minister to the need of the young woman, praying that Nandry would be able to understand and accept the words.

146

Suddenly Nandry began to weep again, quiet weeping now. Ellie put her arms about her and let her cry. At last Nandry lifted her head.

"Yer right," she said. "An' I've been wrong. All these years I've been wrong. My pa wasn't right in what he did, but that gave me no call to do wrong, too. I'm more guilty than 'im 'cause I know better. I shoulda been prayin' fer 'im all those years. I know Clae was. Used to make me mad at her. 'Let 'im git what he deserves,' I'd think. Thet was wrong—so wrong." And Nandry dropped her face in her hands and cried harder.

"Oh, Ellie," wept Nandry, "can God ever fergive me?"

"Iffen He couldn't," said Ellie, "we'd all be in trouble."

"Ma," wept Nandry, seeming to suddenly realize that Marty still sat nearby, "would ya pray fer me?"

Marty did. Ellie followed with another prayer, and then Nandry cried out her own pleading for forgiveness. After the prayer time, they poured fresh coffee and shared further the truths they had learned.

Finally Nandry looked at the clock and declared that Josh would wonder what had happened to her, and besides, she was anxious to talk with him about what had happened this afternoon and the lifting of her burden.

Ellie put on her coat and went with her to get her team, and Marty stayed at the table rejoicing and doing some serious thinking.

Nandry had been wrong to bundle up all of her years of bitterness. She should have been able to trust God. She had been taught ever since she had been in the Davis home that God is *God* in all circumstances of our lives, and He loves His children. Nothing happens to those He loves that catches Him by surprise. He is always there to see one through the difficulty and to bear each person up on wings of love. Good can follow on the path of sorrow. All things can work for good to those who love Him.

Marty knew it all. She even believed it all. So why was she sitting at her kitchen table when just across the yard was her daughter-in-law who needed her? *I don't know what to say,* pleaded Marty. *I just don't know what to say. I still have my baby. And, God, you know I want my baby. Is that selfish? Can I go to Kate, with me so obviously expecting my child, when she has just lost hers?* Marty wept silent tears before the Lord.

Trust Me came a quiet voice, and Marty wiped her eyes on her apron and rose from her chair. She would take Kate the new shawl she had been knitting. Perhaps something new and bright would be welcomed by her on this dreary winter day.

Marty met Ellie at the door. "I'm goin' to see Kate fer a few minutes," she said.

"Oh, good," responded Ellie. "Kate's been so lonesome fer ya. But ya know Kate. She wouldn't think of askin' ya to come out in the cold."

"She's been wantin' me?"

"Every day she mentions ya."

"Why didn't ya say so?"

"Kate asked me not to. She didn't want ya to take any chances on harmin' yer baby. She's countin' on yer little one more'n ever now, Mama."

Marty turned to hurry on out, but she did slow down and carefully place her footsteps on the path. Her eyes stung with her unshed tears. How insensitive she had been.

Kate was at her door to welcome Marty. She must have seen her coming. She ushered her into the small kitchen and steadied her while Marty slipped out of her boots. Marty noticed that Kate was still quite pale.

"How are ya, Mama?" Kate asked anxiously.

Marty felt it was she who should be asking such a question. "I'm fine, dear. An' you?"

Kate smiled. It was a courageous smile for one who had just experienced such sorrow.

"I'm fine, too . . . now. Would ya like a cup of tea?"

"I think not."

"Coffee, then?"

"No. Truth is, we just finished havin' coffee with Nandry."

"*Nandry* was over . . . on such a cold day?"

"Guess she felt she needed it bad enough to come."

"I didn't notice her come in . . . but then, Ellie an' me was talkin' 'bout that time."

Marty took a chair and produced the bright blue shawl. "Brought ya somethin'," she said. "Thought ya might be needin' somethin' new to look at."

Kate smiled. "It's lovely, Mama. I love the color . . . but ya know thet blue is my favorite color, don't ya?"

Yes, Marty had known.

Kate held the shawl, wrapping the long tassels around and around her slim fingers.

"I shoulda been here afore," Marty began slowly, "but . . ."

"It's okay, Mama. Clare an' I both know how much yer hurtin' with us. I was just so 'fraid thet the grievin' might cause harm to thet new brother or sister. Are ya sure yer okay?"

"I'm fine."

"Ya can still feel movement?"

"Oh yes. She's a busy one."

Kate smiled at the "she" and sighed with relief. "I didn't think much 'bout it at the time, but thinkin' back, I realize I hadn't felt any movement fer a few days. I thought maybe my baby was just restin' or thet I was just so used to it I didn't notice or somethin'."

"Ya think thet . . . ?" Marty couldn't voice the question.

Kate answered it anyway. "Doc said our little one died two or three days 'fore . . ."

Her voice trailed off, and Marty hurried to fill the space with words. "I'm so sorry, Kate."

Kate blinked back tears. "I'm sorry, too, Mama. But Doc also said God sometimes uses thet way to care fer a baby thet has some . . . some kind of problem. I thought of Wanda, Mama. I know Wanda loves her Rett and thet she wouldn't give him up fer the world, but I'm . . . I'm not sure I . . . I'm not sure I could take thet, Mama. Iffen our little girl was goin' to be . . . not well . . . not whole . . . then I thank God He took her. Am I a coward to feel thet way?"

"A coward? No, Kate. Certainly not. I . . . I think there are harder things to face in life than . . . than death."

"Clare an' I talked 'bout it. At first it was so hard. We wanted our baby so much, an' then Clare said, 'Let's just count the blessin's outta all this.' At first I couldn't see 'em. Clare had to remind me. 'We still have each other,' he said. 'An' we are both still well an' strong. The doctor says this isn't likely to happen again, so we'll be able to have more babies. We don't have a child who is sickly, either in mind or in body. She will never suffer. She is safe in heaven, without even sufferin' any of the pains of this earth.' So, ya see, we do have lots to be thankful fer."

Marty blinked back tears.

"We've grown through this, Mama. We've grown closer together. I've always loved Clare, but through this . . . I have learned what a wonderful, carin', unselfish, and godly man I am married to. I not only love 'im, but I respect 'im as the spiritual leader of our home."

Marty reached out and took the younger woman's hand.

"An' we've learned more, too, Mama. We've experienced firsthand that all those things we've been taught concernin' God through the years are true. He is there when ya need 'im, helpin' ya through the difficult places, easin' yer hurt. We've felt the prayers of family and friends, too. Never have I felt so . . . so . . . loved and sorta protected as I have in these last difficult days."

Marty fumbled for her handkerchief. Here she had come to minister to Kate; and instead Kate was ministering to her.

"Clare said we might go up fer supper—soon as we are invited," Kate said with an abrupt change of subject. "So how 'bout an invitation? I'm dyin' to step outside even fer a few minutes." She smiled and added, "I could bring somethin' to add to—"

Marty began to laugh through her tears. "Yer invited," she said firmly, "tonight. We'd love to have ya. We've been missin' ya so. It seems like such a long, long time."

"It does to me, too," Kate admitted. "But I'm feelin' a little stronger each day now. I'm even plannin' on going to church again next Sunday—iffen the weather isn't too bad. Doc said I should guard against a chill fer a while. I'm prayin' the weather will be nice."

"I'll join ya in that prayer," promised Marty.

"Oh, Mama," said Kate, "I'm just countin' the days now until yer little one is here. It's gonna be so much fun to have 'im to hold and play with."

"Her," corrected Marty.

"Oh yeah—her. It was *ours* who was to have been the boy. I'm glad thet it wasn't. She was a beautiful little girl, wasn't she? Clare said he learned one thing. With God makin' little girls so cute, it won't matter next time whether God decides to send a boy or a girl."

"Guess it won't matter none to me, either," agreed Marty. "It's just a little game we have always played at our house. Sorta boys against girls. Right now, the girls think they are outnumbered. They're not really—when ya count Nandry an' Clae. They count 'em or don't count 'em as suits their cause." Marty laughed.

"Maybe God would send us one of each iffen we'd ask."

"Whoa, now!" exclaimed Marty, holding up a hand. "I'm thinkin' one will be 'bout all I can handle!"

They laughed together, and Marty rose to go.

"I'm so glad ya came, Mama," said Kate with great feeling. "I've been missin' ya so. Pa has dropped in now an' then, an' thet has been a real help. It helps Clare, too, to have Pa."

Marty gave Kate a warm embrace, and both of them felt between them the struggle of the little one against the confinement.

Kate backed away laughing. "She's alive an' kickin', all right. Little rascal! I can hardly wait to meet her."

Marty could hardly wait, as well. "See ya fer supper. I'll hurry on home an' share the good news with Ellie."

"I'm lookin' forward to it. It'll be so good to be with you all again," Kate stated, then added, "You be careful on those slippery paths, now."

Marty promised and walked carefully toward her home, breathing deeply of the cold, fresh air. She really should make herself go out more often. The air was good for her. She could do with more exercise, too.

Kate needed to get out, as well. Marty prayed the weather would soon warm up so Kate might be able to get out and put some color back into her cheeks. Dear Kate. She was so brave about it all. Marty wondered about the little room. Had they left it the same? She hadn't had the heart to ask. With God's help, they would soon be needing it again.

TWENTY-ONE

Lane Comes for Supper

"Look who I talked into joinin' us fer supper," Clark announced, and Marty looked up expecting to see Clare entering her door. Instead it was Lane who stood silently in the doorway, nervously pulling off his mittens.

"Lane! How nice to see ya!"

Marty felt, more than saw, Ellie's head lift.

"We've been missin' ya," Marty went on. "How're things goin' at the LaHayes'?"

"Fine," answered Lane. "Just fine. Had a letter from the boss yesterday. He says the folks will be home next week. Mr. LaHaye, Willie's pa, has decided to stay on out west. Willie's brother might even go out there an' join 'em iffen he can find a buyer fer his place."

"He wants to sell?" Marty's voice held surprise.

"Guess he kinda likes the West," explained Lane.

"Well, come on in and warm yer hands by the fire," Marty invited. "We're havin' a nice roasted chicken fer supper, an' I think Ellie has got fresh corn bread bakin' to go with it."

As Lane moved into the room, Marty added, "Me, now, I just sit around all day an' watch folks work."

The group laughed comfortably and moved toward the table.

Lane had not dared to look directly at Ellie. He wondered if she would be able to read his thoughts.

He had pondered much how he could support Ellie, as his wife, if he stayed in the area. True, he could farm. He knew a bit about taking care of farm animals now, but he still knew nothing about planting and raising crops. He could learn, he told himself. He could ask. He would beg for the information—down on his knees if need be—if it meant having Ellie. But then, there was the matter of money. In the West, the prices were still right for the man who was brave enough to want to strike out on his own. In this farming area, all the land had already been taken and farmed. Those who might wish to sell were demanding a high price for their farms. Lane knew; he had already been inquiring. Take Willie's brother, for instance. The price he was looking for was so far from what Lane would ever be able to afford that the banker would likely laugh in his face.

No, there just appeared to be no way. No way at all that Lane could see he could ever make a decent living for Ellie in the area. And Ellie could not hurt her mama by going west. It seemed like a dead end to Lane.

He avoided Ellie's eyes so she could not read the pain in his own. Perhaps it didn't matter that much to Ellie, he reasoned. Perhaps she did not care for him in the way that he cared for her. There were many farm boys around about who would be more than happy to provide Ellie with a home of her own. Lane had seen that fact the night of the social. Ellie would be much better off—happier maybe—with one of them. And, more than anything else in the world, Lane wanted Ellie's happiness.

"I thought when ya said ya'd found someone to share our table," Marty was saying to Clark, "thet ya walked over with Clare an' Kate. They are joinin' us tonight, too."

Clark's eyes lit up. "Wonderful," he said. "Thet must mean Kate is beginnin' to feel better. It'll be great to have some of the family back again."

Ellie moved gracefully about the kitchen, putting the finishing touches to the table and dishing up the inviting food. Lane watched Ellie when he was sure she wouldn't notice. From the kitchen window she took a small violet with soft blossoms of deep purple to place in the center of the table. "Almost matches Kate's beautiful eyes," she said to Marty.

"So the LaHayes might be leavin' us?" Clark was saying, pushing a chair over to Lane. "Never thought they would be thet taken by Willie's West. Does grow on one, though."

Lane thought of the West. He loved it. Grow on one? He couldn't imagine one could live any place in the world that could be any more appealing.

"S'pose yer rather anxious to git back yerself?" Clark was saying.

Lane wished to be truthful, and he hardly knew how to respond to Clark's question. "Guess there are things 'bout here thet grow on one, too" was all he said, glad when Clark did not question him further.

Tramping on the porch announced the coming of Kate and Clare, and Clark moved to the door to welcome them and take their coats. He kissed Kate on the forehead and told her how good it was to have her able to join them.

Clare and Lane shook hands vigorously. Though it had been only a matter of an hour or two since they had been together in the woods, they had fallen into an easy camaraderie that Lane deeply appreciated.

Clark assigned seats around the table, and all of them took their places. Clark took his usual seat at the end of the table, and Marty sat opposite him at the other end. Kate and Clare sat to Clark's left, and Lane and Ellie were left with the places on Clark's right. Lane was very conscious of Ellie's closeness, but he was thankful he would not need to look into her eyes over the table.

The talk was cheery and light. Even Kate joined in with a sparkle in her eyes. Ellie was the only quiet one in the group. She stayed very occupied with making sure the bowls were kept full of food and the bread plate refilled. She fussed pouring coffee and took longer than necessary preparing the dessert. Marty wondered if she had taken time to eat anything.

After the meal was over, Clark threw more logs on the open fire in the living room fireplace and invited the others to sit and enjoy its warmth. Marty began to help with the dishes, but Ellie sent her from the kitchen, saying that Kate needed her in the living room far more than she needed her in the kitchen. Marty was finally convinced and joined the family there.

Lane puttered around, feeling rather self-conscious. He poked at the fire occasionally, adding a comment to the conversation now and then to fulfill his social obligations, and found himself shifting pillows around and around in his chair. With all of his being he ached to be in the kitchen with Ellie, yet he dared not go. He was sure he could not be trusted—he was bound to blunder and make some comment or plea that would let her know how much he cared for her. He mustn't. He knew that he mustn't. To do so would only hurt her more, and Lane could not bring her pain.

If only he could leave, he kept thinking. It was pure agony just sitting there listening to the family talk.

All the while his ears strained toward the kitchen. He heard every sound Ellie was making. He knew just how far she had progressed in the washing and drying of the dishes. There . . . she was placing the clean ones back on the cupboard shelves. Now the cutlery. Then the cups on the hooks. She wiped the table and the cupboard. Her cloth went *swish, swish* as she circled the inside of the dishpan before pouring out the dishwater. Now she was replacing the pan on the hook and hanging up the dish towels—evenly—to dry beside the big black cook stove. There . . . she was done. She would be removing her apron and wiping her hands on the kitchen towel. Would she join them, or would she excuse herself and go to her room?

Ellie entered quietly and took a chair by the fire. She sat looking into the flames, as though looking for a message there.

The evening had not gone well for Ellie. It was the first time she had really seen Lane since . . . since Christmas, except for gatherings such as the church services and the funeral for Kate and Clare's baby. She had wondered just what to say when she did see him. What would *he* say? Would he ask her if she had reconsidered? Pa had said Lane wouldn't give up that easily. Well, it appeared he had. Perhaps he hadn't really cared that much after all. *But he did,* Ellie argued within herself. She was sure of it. Then why did he say nothing . . . do nothing? Was he afraid he would be refused again? Ellie was troubled. It was hardly the place of a girl to . . . No, she wouldn't even think about it.

Ellie tried to join in with the conversation, but she soon knew it was no use. She excused herself and went back to the kitchen. Tears rolled down her cheeks as she fixed a plate of scraps for Rex and quietly let herself out of the house.

Lane stuck it out for a few more minutes. He had been right. Ellie didn't really care that much. He finally thanked his host and hostess for the good meal and told them he really should be heading for home if he was to be of use to the men in the woods the next day. The logging for the winter was almost completed. The sawing and chopping would come next.

Clark and Clare both rose to their feet with the intention of going with Lane for his horse, but he waved them both back to their chairs.

"Be no need," he assured them. "Stay here by the fire and enjoy the good company. Me, I know where ol' Jack is."

He let himself out and walked silently to the barn, his heart heavy. *Next week,* his heart kept saying, *next week and I'll be gone.*

He opened the barn door and was surprised to see the soft glow of the lantern. He wasn't aware that the Davises left a light in the barn at night. That was risky, and no farmer ever—

And then Lane saw Ellie, her head bowed over the nearly grown Rex. She was stroking him gently, and tears glistened on her cheeks.

Lane did not know whether to make his presence known or to walk home, leaving his horse. At that moment Ellie raised her head. She gasped slightly and rose to her feet.

"I . . . I . . . just came to bring 'im his supper," she explained quickly.

Lane cleared his throat. He didn't know what to say. "He's really growin', ain't he?" he finally stammered.

Ellie brushed self-consciously at her tears. "Sure is." She tried a chuckle, pushing back the tail-wagging Rex.

There was silence.

"Ya goin' home?" Ellie finally asked.

"Yeah. I was. I . . . I . . . thanks fer thet good supper. Sure beats my batchin' meals."

"Yer welcome. Anytime. Guess ya won't need to batch much longer, huh?"

"Guess not." A pause. "Sure beats Cookie's meals, too, though."

They both laughed halfheartedly.

Ellie reached and scooped up the dish in which she had brought Rex's supper. "When will ya be wantin' Rex?" she asked, "or will ya be able to take 'im?"

"Oh, I'll take 'im," Lane hurried to answer. He didn't add that he wasn't sure how he was going to get a dog out west on the train. *There must be some way,* he thought.

"I wasn't sure what a rancher would do with a cattle dog," Ellie said. "Rex is gonna be real good with cattle. He already can bring them in from the pasture. Watches their heels real good, too. He'd be great as a farm dog."

"Wish I could be a farmer," Lane said slowly.

Ellie showed surprise. "Thought ya loved the West an' ranchin' an'—"

"Oh, I do. I do, but I'd . . ." Lane stopped. "Look, Ellie," he said, "we gotta talk an' we can't talk here. Can we go back to the kitchen or . . . or somethin'?"

"We can walk."

"Ya won't be too cold?"

"This is a warm coat."

Ellie put down the dish again and reached for the lantern. Lane thought she was going to take it with her, but instead she carried it to the open door, blew it out, and set it up against the barn.

"Don't want to chance a fire," she explained. "Pa lost a barn once."

They turned toward the lane. Overhead the winter sky was clear. Stars—multitudes of stars—twinkled above them. A pale yellowy moon showed its last quarter. The wind lightly rustled the frosted branches of the trees. They walked in silence.

But the silence didn't last too long.

"I still have thet locket," Lane said.

"Oh?"

"I'd still like ya to have it . . . even though . . . even though . . ." He decided to change his approach. "I said back there thet I'd like to be a farmer. Well, what I meant was thet . . . thet iffen there was any way so's I could stay in the area so thet . . . well, so thet . . . but try as I might, I can't think of any way to come up with the money it would take fer a farm."

"Ya found thet ya like farmin' better than ranchin'?"

Lane wanted to be truthful. "No," he said. "No, I reckon I still like ranchin' the best."

"Then why would ya want to farm?"

"I . . . I thought you would know thet."

Ellie stopped and leaned her arms on the corral fence. Lane stopped beside her.

"Ellie," he said, taking a deep breath. "Ellie, I love ya. I know I have little to offer. Not near what a man should be offerin' a woman. I know ya said thet ya can't go out west 'cause it would break yer mama's heart. I'd stay here an' farm or work in town iffen only there was some way . . . some way to . . . to make a decent livin' fer ya. I've laid awake nights tryin' to sort it all out, but—"

Ellie laid a hand on his arm and Lane stopped in midsentence.

"Lane," she said softly, "ya said ya still have thet locket."

He was puzzled at her interruption but nodded his agreement.

"Do ya have it here?"

Lane lifted a hand to his inside breast pocket.

"Right here," he said.

"I think I'd like it now," whispered Ellie.

Lane pulled forth the locket with trembling hands.

"Would ya fasten it, please?" asked Ellie.

Ellie pulled aside her hair and turned around so Lane could fasten the locket around her neck. His fingers felt clumsy, and he wondered if he'd ever get the tiny clasp fastened. By some miracle he did. Ellie turned back around and, standing on tiptoe, placed a kiss on Lane's cheek. "Thank ya," she whispered.

Lane felt like he was going to come apart—hope and fear colliding in his chest.

"Ellie, please. Don't tease," he pleaded.

"I'm not teasin'."

"But—"

"A moment ago, ya said thet ya loved me."

"I . . . I . . . do—"

"An' I accepted yer gift, given with yer love."

"But the kiss—"

"Lane," interrupted Ellie, "I would never kiss a man I didn't love."

"But what about yer mama? Ya said—"

"I had a talk with my mama . . . after my pa had a talk with me. Both of 'em say I have to make my own life . . . thet they want my happiness wherever it leads me. Iffen it's the West, then—"

But Lane stopped her. "Oh, Ellie," he said, his voice sounding choked. He drew her close to him.

They walked and talked a long time in the crisp moonlight. At last they heard the door slam and voices over the frosty night air, and they knew Clare and Kate were on their way home.

"It must be gittin' late," sighed Ellie.

"Too late fer a chat with yer pa?"

Ellie smiled at him. "Don't s'pose it's *thet* late," she assured him, and they walked hand in hand toward the house.

TWENTY-TWO

Ma Comes Calling

The time for Marty's confinement was drawing near. Thinking about Ma Graham, she was concerned she had not seen her for such a long time. She knew that Ma had her family, but Marty felt maybe Ma needed her, too.

Their previous plans for Ellie to go and pick up Ma for a nice, long visit had not materialized. The unexpected birth and then the loss of Kate's baby had wiped away all thoughts of the visit from their minds. Now Marty was ready to try again. She wasn't sure if it was because she thought Ma needed her or because she knew she needed Ma.

Marty was happy to see Ellie bloom again, now that she and Lane had worked things through. She felt that, if anyone deserved to be happy, it was her Ellie. She even felt a bit of satisfaction that, in the near future, the two sisters might again have each other. But Marty was also aware of just how difficult it was going to be for her to actually give up Ellie as she had done with Missie. She needed to talk to Ma. Ma would understand exactly how she felt.

So Marty laid out her plan before Clark.

"Been thinkin' a lot 'bout Ma Graham," she began. "Wonderin' how she's doin'."

"I been thinkin' on her, too," Clark responded.

"Sure would be good to sorta check on her," continued Marty.

"I'm goin' to town day after tomorra. I can do thet. Thought I should stop by an' see iffen there's any way I could help."

For a moment Marty was silenced.

"Wasn't really thinkin' 'bout what she might be needin' from town or such," she eventually continued. "Thinkin' more along the . . . the *fellowship* lines."

"I see," nodded Clark. "Lou's wife is right there. An' I expect thet the rest of her girls git over to see her, too."

"Sometimes one needs neighbors as well as family," Marty persisted.

"I just don't think it would be wise right now."

"What wouldn't be wise?" asked Marty innocently.

"You makin' a trip out in the cold to go see Ma."

"Did I suggest thet?"

"Not in words, ya didn't, but it's what ya were aimin' at, ain't it?"

"Well, sorta . . . but not exactly. What I was really wonderin' was iffen ya would mind goin' on over an' pickin' up Ma fer a mornin' an' then takin' her on home again."

Clark laughed. "Well, why didn't ya just come out an' say so?"

"I wasn't sure what you'd think of the idea," said Marty truthfully.

"What I think 'bout it an' what I agree to do 'bout it are often two different things," said Clark wryly, "an' well ya know it."

Marty reached a hand to Clark's cheek. "I know," she said, "an' I love ya fer it."

Clark laughed and turned his head so he might kiss her fingers.

"I'll see," he said, and Marty knew that was his promise.

"Tomorra?"

"Tomorra."

Marty went to bed happy with the knowledge that on the morrow she would have a visit with her dear friend again.

When Clark was hitching the team to the sleigh the next morning to make his promised trip to pick up Ma, Lady began to bark, running down the lane toward an approaching team. It was Lou Graham.

Clark threw a rein around a fence post and walked toward the upcoming sleigh, his crutch thumping on the frozen ground.

Lou was not alone. Carefully tucked in with warm blankets, Ma Graham sat beside him.

After a neighborly "howdy," Lou explained. "Ma's been frettin' 'bout not seein' Marty fer a spell. I was goin' on by to pick up some feed barley at the Spencers', so I brought her along fer a chat while I'm gone."

"Well, I'll be," said Clark. "I was just hitchin' my team to come on over an' git ya, Ma. Marty's been right anxious to see ya."

Clark helped Ma down, and Lou prepared to be on his way again.

"I'll bring Ma on home whenever she an' Marty think they've had 'em enough woman talk," Clark joked.

"Ya mind? Thet sure would help me out some. Then I can go on back by way of town an' git some things I'm needin'."

The team left the yard, and Clark walked to the house with Ma. He would put the horses back in the barn and give them some hay until they were needed to return Ma home.

Marty couldn't believe her eyes when Clark ushered Ma into the kitchen. She knew Clark couldn't possibly have been to the Grahams' and back already.

She laughed when she heard the story and settled Ma down in one of the comfortable kitchen chairs. Ellie put on the coffee and placed the cups on the table. Then she set a plate of sugar cookies beside the cups and excused herself.

"Think I'll just run off down to Kate's fer a bit," she said.

"Not so fast, young lady," Ma said with a knowing smile. "What's this I'm hearin' 'bout you and thet there young, good-lookin' cowboy?"

Ellie blushed.

"It bein' true?" continued Ma.

"It's true—thet is, iffen you've been hearin' what I think ya might have been hearin'."

Ma pulled Ellie close and gave her a big hug. "I'm happy fer ya," she said hoarsely. "I've always saw you young'uns as sorta my own. I wish ya all the happiness, Ellie, an' God bless ya . . . real good."

Ellie thanked her with misty eyes. She and Ma Graham had always had a special relationship, as if Ma was the grandmother she did not have.

Ma turned to Marty. "So how ya been doin'?" she asked simply. "You've had ya quite a winter. I've been thinkin' so much on ya. First, ya had to git over the rather surprisin' news of bein' a mother again. Then ya had the awful hurt to bear with Clare an' Kate. Now this. Must be a little hard to take, on top of everythin' else."

Marty had known Ma would understand. Ma did not believe in talking in circles. She went straight to the heart of the matter.

"Yeah," she answered, carefully choosing her words. "Guess it has been a rather rough winter. My, it was hard to see Clare an' Kate go through thet pain. But I'm so proud of both of 'em, Ma. They have both been so strong through it all. They've showed me a lesson or two."

"I could see when I saw 'em in church thet they hadn't let it bitter 'em. I'm so glad, Marty—so glad. Bitterness is a hard burden to bear. I should know. I've had me my bouts with it."

"You?"

"Sure did. I woulda just gone on an' on a carryin' it, too, iffen ya hadn't come along when ya did an' straightened me out."

"Me?"

"You'll never know just how set I was to sit an' feel sorry fer myself before Christmas there. Oh, I know. I didn't really tell ya all I was feelin', but I was all set fer a good, long bitter spell. I felt it just wasn't fair thet I should lose two good men in a lifetime. *Some women don't even like the one they got,* I reasoned, an' here I was with two I had loved deeply an' I lost 'em both. Didn't seem fair somehow. Didn't even seem worth fightin' to keep up a good front fer the kids. Then ya came by an' made me realize it did still matter to my kids. I started thinkin' on it an' I saw somethin' else, too. True, some women don't like the man they got. Thet's to their sorrow. But I had me two good companions. Now, how many women could be so blessed? An' here I was a fussin' 'bout it."

Marty smiled at Ma's way of thinking it all through.

"So I decided," continued Ma, "thet I just should be thankin' the Lord fer all the good years 'stead of fussin' 'bout the years to come."

"An' it helped?"

"Ya bet it helped. Every day I think of somethin' more to be thankful fer. I have a good family—mine an' Ben's. We raised us good young'uns. That's truly somethin' to be thankful fer."

Marty agreed wholeheartedly. What a burden it must be to have children who fought against their parents, against the Lord.

"I have lots of good mem'ries, too, an' a mind still alert enough to enjoy 'em."

Marty hadn't thought about the "mind" bit, but Ma was right.

"So it's easin' some? The pain, I mean?" Marty asked softly.

"It still hurts. Many times the mem'ries bring a sharp pain with 'em, but each day I tell myself, *This is a new day. It can be just a little bit easier than yesterday was.*"

Marty rose to get the perking coffee.

"An' how is it fer you?" asked Ma.

Marty suddenly realized that things were just fine for her. Yes, she had wanted to bring Ma to her house so that she could cleanse herself of all of the pain of seeing her Clare hurt so deeply. She had wanted to pour out to Ma that she was going to lose her Ellie, and she didn't know how she would ever do without her. She had wanted to feel Ma's sympathetic eyes upon her, to feel Ma squeeze her hand in encouragement, to see the flicker of pain on Ma's face, mirroring her own. She didn't want that now. Not any of it. She didn't deserve it. Every mother had to watch her children suffer at times. Every mother had to someday loosen the strings and let her children go—not just one of them, but all of them, one by one. It was all part of motherhood. One nourished them, raised them, taught them for many years so that they could be free—free to live and love and hurt and grow. That was what motherhood was all about. Marty swallowed away the tears in her throat and smiled at Ma.

"Things are fine," she assured her, "really fine. We've had us a *good* winter. Kate an' Clare came through their sorrow even closer to God an' each other than before. There will be more babies. Nandry turned all her bitterness 'bout her pa an' Clark's accident over to the Lord. Ellie has found the young man she wants to share her life with, an' he will make her a good an' God-fearin' companion. An' me—well, I still have me this here little one to look forward to. Ellie an' me's been hopin' fer a girl, but I wouldn't mind none iffen it was another boy—just like his pa—or one of his older brothers."

Marty had not looked forward to coming back from the West to a church without Pastor Joe. Not only did she miss her son-in-law as family, but she knew she would miss him in the pulpit, as well. The adjustment had not been as difficult as she had feared. The young minister who now was shepherding the local flock was easy to learn to love and respect.

Pastor Brown was his name, though many of the people in the congregation called him Pastor John. He had taken a good deal of ribbing in his growing-up years. "Hey, John Brown," the kids would call, "Is yer body molderin' yet?" Then would follow a chant of "John Brown's Body." John hated the teasing. He had tried unsuccessfully to get his family to call him Jack. Perhaps then the kids would miss the pun in his name. It didn't work. His family never seemed to remember that he preferred Jack, and on the few occasions where they did remember, the kids didn't stop their teasing anyway. John decided to develop the ability to laugh with them. It was difficult at first, but it did help him to develop a delightful sense of humor. One thing John Brown was never guilty of, and that was making fun of another individual. Humor was never intended for this, he maintained. It was to make people laugh *with*, not *at* another.

Pastor Brown seemed to have a true gift of sensitivity in dealing with people. The older members of the congregation marveled at how well he could often right a difficult situation. Even the children in the church respected him. Never could he be accused of intending hurt to another.

Clark looked up in surprise from his harness-mending to see Pastor John approaching him.

"Hello there," he called. "Be right with ya. I'll just hang me this harness back up on the pegs, an' we'll go on in an' see what the womenfolk got to eat fer a bachelor preacher."

Pastor John smiled. "I've already been in the house an' greeted the womenfolk. They've already given me an invite to dinner, so I'm way ahead of you. Smells awfully good in there, too."

"Well, let's go on in an' sit a spell, then," said Clark.

"No, no. You go right on fixing your harness. I'll just sit here on this stool and watch you while I'm talking. Anything I got to say can be said right here."

Clark understood that there was something the young man wished to talk about in private, so he resumed his work on the harness, letting the preacher pick his own time and pace.

"Been a long, mean winter," spoke the parson. "Sure will be glad to see it coming to an end."

"Me too," agreed Clark. "Me too. An' I expect all the animals thet been winterin' through it, both wild an' tame, share our feelin'."

"Reckon they will at that."

"Speakin' of animals, ya got one with ya?"

"I'm riding, all right. Too hard walking in this snow."

"Best bring it on into the barn."

"Not too cold out there in the sun, and I won't be long."

"Still, it can be feedin', though," Clark responded. "Might take us a long time to eat up all those vittles the ladies are a fixin'."

John Brown laughed.

"Go ahead," said Clark. "Bring 'im on in an' put 'im in thet stall right there. I'll throw in a bit more hay." And Clark grabbed his crutch and went to do just that.

The parson brought in his horse and pulled off the saddle.

"Never could stand to see a horse eat with a saddle on his back," he said. "Makes me wonder how I'd enjoy eating if I had to stand there holding my day's work in my arms."

Clark laughed at the comparison. "Never thought on it," he responded.

The horse was tended, and Clark went back to his harness. The pastor pulled the stool closer so they could chat as Clark worked.

They talked of many things. Besides the winter, they discussed the new developments in town, the growth of the church, and the new members in the community. Clark was sure none of these subjects was the one the young preacher had come to talk about.

"Hear tell you're good at solving a man's problems," the pastor said at length.

Clark did not raise his head. "Don't know 'bout thet. I've had me a little practice. Seems I have my share of problems to solve."

The preacher reached down and picked up a long straw, which he proceeded to break into small pieces.

"You got a problem needs carin' fer?" Clark prompted.

"Sure do. And I never had one quite like it before—and I'm not sure just what to be doing with it. I've been praying about it for three days now, and something seemed to tell me to come and see you."

Clark continued to work on the strip of leather before him. "I'm not promisin' to be able to help ya, but iffen ya want to share it and work at it together, I'm willin' to listen."

The preacher cleared his throat. "It's kind of a touchy thing," he said. "I won't be able to give you too many details because I don't want to break confidence."

Clark nodded to say that he understood.

"It's one of my parishioners," the preacher began. Clark could feel how very hard this was for the young man.

"Rumor has it that he's been seen in town . . . doing . . . ah . . . doing something he shouldn't be doing."

"Rumor?" said Clark, raising an eyebrow.

"Well, a pretty reliable source, really. I say 'rumor' because I haven't talked to the individual involved yet, and a man is innocent until proven guilty, right?"

"Right," said Clark.

"Well, this ah . . . source . . . says he has seen this occur more than once. He's concerned that others have been seeing it, too, and that it will reflect on the whole church."

"I see," said Clark.

"If it is happening, and if he is doing . . . what he shouldn't be doing . . . the man's right, Clark. It could reflect on the whole church.

It's wrong . . . and it's against God's commandments . . . and I'm really not sure what to do about it."

"Did yer . . . ah . . . source say what should be done?"

"He wants him thrown out of the church."

"What do you want?"

"What I want is of no importance here, as I see it. What I want to know, Clark, is what does the Lord want?"

Clark laid aside the harness then and looked into Parson John Brown's honest blue eyes. He had just gained new respect for the young man.

"Guess we better take it a step at a time," he said and sank down onto a pile of straw, sticking his one leg out before him.

"First of all, someone . . . meanin' you, I think . . . needs to talk to the man and find out, if ya can, iffen he's really guilty as charged. Iffen he refuses to give ya the truth, then one needs to inquire further from the source an' from others. Iffen one person has seen these . . . these . . ."

"Indiscretions," put in the parson.

"This here indiscretion, then it's very likely thet others have seen it also . . . unless yer source has nothin' to do but sit him around an' spy."

"It's not like that, Clark. He's a good and reliable man, concerned only for the good of the church. He's not a busybody or a tale carrier."

"In that case, one has to pay considerable attention to his testimony."

"That's the way I feel about it. But the man accused should still have an opportunity to speak for himself."

"Agreed," said Clark.

"So I go to see him and hear his story. Now I need to know what to do about it."

"Well, let's say, first off, that he says he's innocent."

"That would be rather hard to believe, but I'd have to take his word unless we had further proof."

"Okay," said Clark, "we are thet far. He is innocent until proven guilty."

"And what if he admits to his guilt?"

"What does the Bible say?"

"You mean about taking the two or three witnesses to show him the error of his way?"

"Iffen he admits to his guilt, I don't reckon he can seriously deny the error of his way, though it's true thet some have tried."

"All right, let's say that he does admit his guilt but he has no intention to stop . . . to stop doing what he has been doing. What then? Does our little church discipline its members?"

"First, I think we need to understand what discipline is all about and why it is sometimes necessary."

"It's not easy to discipline a fellow believer, Clark. Who says that I'm so strong that I'll never fall? I'm not good at setting myself up as judge and jury."

"An' yer not the judge. God's Word is what we judge a man upon. Iffen He says thet it's wrong . . . then we can't make it right."

The young minister nodded his head.

"But should we bring judgment upon him . . . or leave it to God to judge?"

"Iffen ya committed a sin, do ya think you'd need to be making things right?"

"Certainly. I'd be guilty, and as such, I'd need to straighten the thing out with God and make restitution if necessary."

"The Bible teaches thet all the members of the church are of the same body. Iffen any part of my body sins, my whole being is held responsible. Iffen any part of the church body sins, we are all responsible to git thet thing made right. Iffen we, as the rest of the church, accept it as okay an' pass it off, then we, too, are guilty of thet sin."

The young preacher sat deep in thought. "His sin is my sin if I make no attempt to correct it when I know about it," he concluded.

"Somethin' like thet," said Clark. "I never was a theologian, so's I'm not sure how they would explain it."

"Then it's my responsibility to see that it's cared for. Boy, I hate that, Clark. It's not an easy thing to point a finger at another man."

"It's not easy. But it's not as hard as it seems when one realizes the purpose of the finger pointin', as you call it."

Clark shifted his position on the straw and continued. "Church discipline is done fer two reasons . . . to keep the body pure before God and to bring the erring one back to a fergiven and restored relationship with God. Never should it be done fer any other purpose. It's not to punish, or to make someone pay, or to whip someone into reluctant shape, or show the community thet we really are holy and pure. God already knows whether we are or not."

"'To restore them to a right relationship with God,'" mused the young preacher. "Then what about the need to send him from the church?"

"Iffen he makes the thing right before God, there's no need to throw him out. He's still part of the body . . . fergiven just like you an' me's been fergiven."

The preacher smiled. "Boy," he said, "I much prefer that way."

"We all do," said Clark, "only on occasion, it doesn't work like thet. Iffen he won't listen an' won't make it right, then comes the tough part. Then ya have to . . . to excommunicate 'im. Thet's tough, Brother Brown. Thet's really tough."

The parson sat deep in thought.

"Clark, I'm going to ask one more thing of you," he said at last. "I'm going to see this church member tomorrow. Now, I haven't told you his name or anything about him. If he sees his sin tomorrow and asks for God's forgiveness, then you need never know the particulars. If he doesn't, then I'd like you and a couple of the other deacons to go with me next time. If he still doesn't agree to do something about it . . . only then will we bring the matter to the congregation. Now, I'm hoping and praying that all of that won't be necessary, and I'd like to ask you to pray with me that God will work in the heart of the man so that we won't lose a Christian brother. I know it's hard to pray not knowing, but . . ."

"No problem," said Clark. "I've prayed fer many a need not really knowin' just what the need was, an' I certainly know thet ya need God's special wisdom an' guidance as ya speak to the fella."

The preacher nodded his agreement.

"I think thet it might be in order to take time fer some prayer right now," went on Clark.

They knelt together in the straw, earnestly beseeching God for His help and wisdom.

"Thank you," said the young parson, taking Clark's offered hand.

"Thank you for the support. I feel like part of the burden has lifted already."

"Yer doin' a fine job, son," Clark said sincerely. "I want ya to know thet we all appreciate ya an' we're prayin' fer ya daily."

The young man smiled and stood up from his cramped position. He put out a hand and helped Clark stand, passing him his crutch. Then they heard Ellie calling them to the dinner table.

"Boy," said the young preacher, "am I hungry! It just comes to my mind that I forgot all about having some breakfast this morning."

"Then I'll expect ya to eat hearty at the dinner table," laughed Clark. "Can't imagine a son of mine ever gittin' himself so busy thet he'd ferget to eat."

TWENTY-THREE

Ellie Makes Plans

The LaHayes arrived home from their trip west more than anxious to share their experiences with the Davises, so they soon came over to visit.

They were full of news of Willie and Missie and their three small children. The baby was a dear, they insisted, and she was already crawling, and Missie was extremely busy trying to keep her out of mischief.

They praised Willie's spread; they praised the little neighborhood church; they praised the school operated by Melinda; they praised the mountains, the hills, and the grazing land.

Iffen they say somethin' good 'bout the wind, thought Marty, *I'm gonna really doubt their sanity.* But the wind was not mentioned.

They had now made up their minds. They were going back. They would put the farm up for sale and leave as soon as possible.

They brought gifts from Missie for each of her family. She even sent a hand-crocheted blanket for her new little brother or sister. Marty ran her fingers over the soft wool and pictured their daughter working over it. Marty could imagine Nathan or Josiah questioning, "What ya makin', Mama" . . . and Missie's answer, "I'm makin' a blanket fer yer new aunt or uncle." How ironic it all was.

"An' ya fell in love with the West, too?" Marty asked Callie.

"I loved it," she responded with no doubt. "It took me a little longer than it took my menfolk, but when I made up my mind, I was really sure."

"Do ya have a place in mind?"

"We looked at a few. The one we liked best already has a small house, a big barn, and a well."

"How far is that from Missie an' Willie?"

"'Bout a four-hour ride."

Marty had no idea how far that would be in actual miles, but it did seem wiser to measure it in time rather than in distance.

"Plenty close enough to git together often," Callie assured her.

"What 'bout yer pa? Who does he plan to live with?"

"Willie got 'im first, an' Pa loves it there. He already has his own saddle horse—three of 'em, in fact—and he loves to help with the cattle. He'd take a daily shift iffen Willie would let 'im. Willie does humor him and lets him go out some but not on a daily basis. Willie has declared him the best fencer on the place, though. Pa loves the men in the bunkhouse, too, an' would have moved right in with 'em, but Willie an' Missie insisted that he have the small back bedroom in the ranch house. It's quieter back there, Missie says, but Pa ain't askin' fer no quiet. He loves to be right in the thick of things."

"I'm so glad he's happy out there."

"Oh, he's happy, all right. Never seen him so happy since Ma died."

"So he'll stay on with Willie an' Missie?"

"He's promised to come an' be with us some, too. He's rather anxious to help us fix up the new spread."

It all sounded good to Marty. She hoped with all her heart that it would work out well for them.

"Do ya have a buyer fer yer home place yet?" she asked.

"Not yet, but we are sure we will sell with no problem. Spring is the best time to sell—spring or late fall. Ain't too many folk out looking fer farmland with the snow piled up to one's ears."

Marty agreed.

"Will ya stay till it's sold?"

"Don't know fer sure. We're sure in a big hurry to git on back. Like to git things in order an' a small herd out on the range as soon as the spring grasses start to grow. We've talked to Lane. With a bit of persuasion, I think he would stay fer a while. Maybe care fer things till a buyer comes along. Iffen he agrees, we hope to git on back there as soon as we can."

Marty felt a small stirring in her breast, a stirring of hope. Maybe Ellie wouldn't need to leave her so quickly after all. Marty knew that Ellie and Lane were making plans, but she hadn't asked what the plans were. Ellie would tell her in her own good time.

Marty served coffee and cake to their visitors and listened to the talk circulating around and around her. It was good to share in such enthusiasm—in such dreams—even if they did belong to another.

Ellie had sat enraptured, drinking in every piece of news about Lane's West. She wanted to feel a part of it so she might feel at home when she finally arrived. She wanted to know and love it just as Lane did. She felt that something about the bigness of the West would correspond to the bigness of the man.

"Have ya heard," Ellie asked her mother, "they want Lane to stay on an' care fer the farm till it sells in the spring?"

"Is he goin' to?"

"It's sort of an answer to prayer," replied Ellie enthusiastically.

Marty looked up from her mending.

"Lane and me thought he would have to leave soon. Which meant I would need to travel alone later."

"Why later?" asked Marty.

"Oh, Mama, you know very well I wouldn't up an' leave ya before thet new baby comes. An' I don't plan to leave ya right away afterward, either. Not till yer well on yer feet an' I'm sure things are goin' fine."

"That would have been a problem," agreed Marty.

"The biggest problem would have been our weddin'. We talked of two possibilities . . . an' I didn't care fer either of 'em. We could have been married now an' Lane gone on alone an' me come later. I wouldn't like losin' a husband so soon after I'd gotten one," she said, smiling shyly.

"Or," she continued, "we could've waited an' been married when I got out there. I didn't like thet, either, 'cause it would have meant you an' Pa wouldn't have been at my weddin'."

"I wouldn't have liked thet, either," admitted Marty.

"So ya see, this is sorta an answer to prayer," Ellie repeated. "We can git married soon after yer baby is born an' I can stay on here and help ya in the daytime, an' we can live over in the LaHaye house. Callie has already promised us thet we can."

It sounded good to Marty. Ellie would not need to leave for a few months yet. Marty would welcome each additional day.

"Sounds like ya got it all sorted out."

"We been workin' on it."

"So when do ya plan the weddin'?"

"Well, thet there little one is due the end of February, right?"

"According to my calculations."

"So we thought we could be married 'bout the end of March. Thet way ya won't wear yerself all out gittin' right into a weddin' after the baby comes, an' after the weddin' I can still come over days to help ya out."

"Land sakes, girl. You've really spoiled me. Ya think I won't be able to care fer yer pa an' the little one after a month of time?"

"Well, we don't want to rush ya, Mama."

Marty blinked away tears. Ellie was more than considerate as a daughter.

"Look here, dear," she said. "I'm in no hurry to lose ya . . . ya know thet . . . but ya go ahead an' make yer plans just as ya would have 'em to be. Don't stop to fit all of yer life round me. I'm just fine now, an' I'll be just fine after this here little one gits here."

Ellie crossed to put her arms around Marty. "I'll tell Lane thet the end of March is fine, then," she said.

TWENTY-FOUR

Church and Home

Clark was out milking the roan when Pastor John rode up. His smile was broad and his handshake firm as he joined Clark in the barn. "It worked," he beamed. "We don't have to take the next step. And more importantly, we don't need to take away his membership."

Clark responded to his smile with an enthusiasm of his own.

"Just wait till I git done with Roanie here, an' I want to hear all 'bout it," he said. "I'm near done."

The pastor walked about the barn, stopped to pet a cat, and strolled around some more. Clark could tell he was anxious to share his experience. He hurried to finish up with Roanie.

Clark hung his pail, brimming with foaming milk, well out of the reach of the barn cats and pulled a stool over for himself and one for the preacher.

"Sit ya down," he offered, and the parson sat.

"Went to see him as I said I would," Pastor John began. "It was kind of tough, I don't mind telling you that. Didn't know just where or how to start, but we did get to the point. I told it to him just like it had been told to me. Then I said I wanted to hear it from him. Was it true or not true? At first, he was very ambiguous. I thought sure I would get nowhere. I was even expecting him to outright deny it. He was getting a little angry, too, and I thought maybe I had really missed it." The man looked around the barn for a moment.

"Well, I decided that we'd better stop right there," he continued, "before things got out of hand. So I said, 'Mind if we have prayer before we go on with this? I consider you my friend and brother, and I don't want to lose you as either.' He looked surprised but he bowed his head. We prayed together, and pretty soon I could hear his sobs. Clark, he cried like a baby. Don't know of anything that ever was harder for me than that man's sobs."

The young preacher stopped, his face full of emotion. "Finally, we were able to kneel down there together, and he confessed it all to the Lord and promised to make the thing right . . . as right as one can. Some sins one can't erase, Clark, but you know that. I expect that his past might haunt him more than once in the future. He knows it, too. We've got to really pray for him. It's not all over yet. Maybe never will be. That's the trouble with sin. It leaves ugly scars."

Clark nodded in agreement.

"I did leave him feeling forgiven and clean again, though. He said that he was so glad to be rid of the thing that he just couldn't rightly express it. I'm glad I went . . . though it was the hardest thing I've ever had to do."

"I'm glad ya went, too," Clark assured him.

"Well, the next thing for me to do was to go call on . . ." Parson Brown stopped and grinned, "my source."

Clark grinned, too, and nodded again.

"First time I went I didn't find him at home. Next day I got busy again and couldn't. Mrs. Watley had another bad spell, so I spent the day with the family."

"How is she?"

"She's perked up again. Can't believe the stamina of the woman. We've thought so many times that she was going, and she seems to fight it off every time. Well, I finally got back to my 'source' yesterday. I told him just what I've told you. I wasn't sure how he would respond. Thought maybe, in light of things, and fearing a public knowledge about it and all, he might still want to put the fellow out of the church. Well, Clark, when I told him, great big tears started running down his cheeks and he just kept saying, 'Praise the Lord' over and over. 'We've still got our brother,' he said, 'Praise the Lord!'"

Clark was deeply touched, and he could tell Parson John was, too. They sat in silence for a minute, each with his own thoughts. Clark broke the spell.

"So we will be worshipin' with 'im on Sunday." It was a statement, not a question.

"He's part of the body. A worthy part, I'm thinking."

"Like your 'source' says," smiled Clark, "'Praise the Lord.'"

"I'm so glad I came to you, Clark. You steered me in the right direction."

"Now, back up some," interjected Clark. "I don't recall steering you nohow."

"But you—"

"*We* talked 'bout it. We talked together 'bout what the Word says. You knew what it says. You made yer decision. You really knew what to do all along. Iffen ya think back a bit, you'll remember."

The preacher thought back a bit. He grinned. "I still needed you, though," he insisted. "Needed an older, wiser man to think it through with me. But thanks. I see now. You didn't push or steer me. You let me work it through myself—step by step, with the Word to guide me. You could have just out and told me what to do, but you didn't. Thanks, Clark. I think I've learned a bigger lesson this way. Maybe next time I'll be smart enough to go through the Word step by step on my own."

Clark put a hand on the young man's shoulder. "Ain't no harm in sharin' a burden with a brother. I'm here anytime I can be of help. Remember thet."

"I will," said the preacher. "And thank you."

"Now," said Clark, lifting the pail of milk from the hook and reaching for his crutch, "let's go see iffen the coffeepot has any fresh coffee."

Another letter came from Luke. As usual, the note was brief since he didn't have much time to write. He told them he was writing at a time he really should be studying. He was thinking a lot about his mother. Was she taking good care of herself and the coming baby? He gave doctorly advice as to what she should be eating, how much exercise she should be getting, and the danger of overdoing. Marty smiled as she read. How strange it was to have her "baby" mothering her. No, not mothering—doctoring. Luke would make a good doctor, as long as he could keep from becoming too personally involved with each of his patients. Marty didn't want to even think of the day when Luke would lose one of those he treated. The day would come. All doctors had to face it. It would be hard for Luke. He was so tender to the pain of others. Marty prayed that he might be able to handle it without too much anguish.

Clae wrote again, too. They had seen Luke briefly. He had come home with them for Sunday dinner following the church service. The kids loved him. Baby Joey had a tooth. He had been miserable cutting it but was his happy self again once the tooth was finally through. Clae hoped they didn't have to go through the same thing with each tooth that he cut.

Arnie and Anne came for Sunday dinner. It was the biggest gathering the Davises had had for many Sundays. Kate and Clare came from next door, and Nandry and Josh and the children came, too. It was so good to see Nandry able to laugh and joke with the rest of them. She looked younger and happier than she had in years. Lane came, too, as he did each Sunday. He and Ellie took much teasing, but they didn't seem to mind it. The whole house looked as if it was vibrating with the chatter and laughter. Marty looked about her and quietly thanked God for each one of them. Tina was getting so grown up. She was almost a little lady, and Marty had to realize that it would not be long until her grandchildren, too, would be leaving their nests. *My, there's no other way to say it . . . how time does fly,* she reminded herself with a wry smile.

In spite of the enjoyment of her family, Marty felt especially weary when the day came to an end and the last of the visitors had put on coats and headed for home—the last of the visitors except for Lane.

He and Ellie were still talking in the kitchen, their voices low and full of love and hope. Marty turned to Clark and said she thought she would just go on up to bed.

Clark's eyes went to the clock. "A mite early yet, ain't it?" he remarked, slight concern in his voice.

Marty, too, looked at the clock. She couldn't believe the evening was still so young. Had the clock stopped? But no, it was still ticking, and it said only ten minutes to eight. She gave him a tired smile. "Well," she said, "it was a big day. Not used to so many of 'em all at once, I guess. It's been quite a spell since they all been here together."

Clark nodded and rose from his chair. "Yer right," he said. "Yer wise to git off yer feet," and he came over to walk with her up the stairs, giving her aid without seeming to.

Marty readied herself for bed and crawled beneath the warm covers. How good it felt to just stretch out and commit one's weary body to the softness of the bed. *Yer gittin' old,* Marty told herself. *Ya gotta admit it. Yer showin' yer age.* She sincerely hoped she wasn't yet as old as she felt on this night. She was so weary, yet she didn't really feel she was ready to sleep.

When Clark came up to bed much later, Marty was still awake. She had shifted her position often, trying to find a comfortable way to rest. It didn't help much.

Clark stroked her forehead. "Are ya feelin' okay?" he asked. "Ya seem mighty restless."

"Guess I just overtired myself a bit," she responded. "Either thet or I just came to bed too early. Not used to goin' to sleep at eight o'clock."

"It's now ten-thirty," Clark told her.

"Oh," said Marty. There was a moment of silence. "Then I s'pect I'll be able to drop off anytime now."

Marty did eventually manage to fall into a light and fidgety sleep.

It was about two o'clock in the morning when Clark was awakened. He wasn't sure at first what it was that brought him to consciousness, and then he felt Marty stir and heard a slight moan escape her. He could tell she still wasn't fully awake, but he knew she wasn't sleeping soundly, either. He waited for a moment and the sound came again.

"Marty," he said, laying a hand lightly on her arm. "Marty, are ya all right?"

Marty stirred and opened her eyes. Clark could just faintly see her face in the moonlight that streamed in their window.

"Are ya all right?"

"I fergot to pull the blind," Marty mumbled.

"Ferget the blind. Are ya okay?"

Marty shook her head. "I don't know. I . . . I think so. It's just . . . just . . ."

"Just what?" insisted Clark.

"I don't know. Havin' a hard time sleepin'."

"Is it the baby?"

"The baby? The baby's all right."

"Is it time?" persisted Clark, feeling like shaking Marty to bring her to full consciousness.

"Time? Time fer the baby?" Marty's eyes flew wide open. "Clark," she said, excitement in her voice, "maybe thet's it. Maybe it's time fer the baby!"

Clark chuckled in spite of himself. "Did ya—a mother many times over—fergit thet little one is gonna ask to be born eventually?"

Marty responded with a chuckle. "Guess I got kinda used to it . . . just bein' there."

Clark rolled out of bed and lit the lamp. Then he hopped to the window and pulled down the blind. The light being on might concern Kate and Clare if they were to spot it, he reasoned, and this could well be just a false alarm.

Clark crossed back to the bed.

"Now, tell me," he said, "how're ya feelin'?"

"I don't know. I just can't sleep right, an' somethin' seems different . . . I don't know . . ."

"Think back," insisted Clark. "Can't ya remember what it was like with the other ones?"

"Clark," said Marty, sounding a bit annoyed, "any mother will tell ya thet they can all seem different. Just 'cause one bears one baby don't mean thet ya can read all the signs."

"But there must be somethin'—" But Clark's words were cut short by a gasp from Marty.

"What is it?" he asked, his hand reaching out to her.

Marty took the offered hand and squeezed it tightly, but she was unable to answer his question.

Clark was sure he knew the answer. "I'll go git Ellie," he said and hurried to dress.

Ellie was soon there, sleepy eyed and anxious in her warm blue robe.

"Mama," she asked with concern, "Mama, are ya all right?"

Marty settled back against her pillow, preparing herself for the next contraction, and assured her that she was.

Clark leaned over Marty. He was buttoning on a warm wool shirt, the one he always liked to wear when he was going out into the cold. Marty looked puzzled for a moment.

"Where ya goin'?" she asked through some kind of haze that seemed to hang about her.

"Fer the doc," he answered. "An' the sooner the better, I'm thinkin'."

Marty still didn't appear to understand.

"The baby's on the way," explained Ellie patiently as Clark left hurriedly, his crutch thumping on the wooden stairs. "Pa will be back with the doc 'fore we know it. Now, Mama, you've got to think . . . think . . ." Ellie commanded. "Is there anything I should do? I know nothin' 'bout this."

But it looked as though Marty was still thinking about something else.

"The doc," she said slowly and then seemed to fully understand. "Oh, Ellie," she said, "tell Pa not to bother. I don't think there'll be any time fer the doc."

Ellie was terrified. "There's gotta be! Ya just started yer labor an' the doc ain't thet far away. You hang on, now."

Another contraction seized Marty, and she groped for Ellie's hand. Ellie prayed, wondering if Marty was ever going to relax again.

She did, falling exhausted back against her pillows.

"Listen, Mama," Ellie pleaded. "Can ya talk to me?"

Marty nodded her head.

"Can ya think straight?"

"I . . . I think so," panted Marty.

"You've been at birthin's. Now, the doc will be here soon . . . I'm countin' on thet. But, just in case . . . just in case . . . ya gotta tell me what to do."

Marty nodded.

"Okay," she said, her face showing her deep concentration. "Here's what ya do."

Clark had never pushed his horse like he pushed Stomper that night. The moon aided him on occasion, but often he had to travel on his own instinct and that of his horse. The moon seemed to be playing games. It would bob out from a cloud just long enough for Clark to be relieved because of its light, and then it would slip behind a cloud again, leaving Clark totally on his own, traveling a rutted and snow-covered wintry road. Clark, pushing his steed as fast as he dared, learned to pace himself, riding hard by the moonlight and slowing down when he had to feel his way.

It seemed forever before he was pulling up to the doc's hitching rail. Clark prayed that he would be home and not out on some other call. Why was it that youngsters always insisted on arriving in the middle of the night?

Doc was home and quickly answered Clark's persistent knock on the door. He was not long in pulling on his clothes and grabbing his black bag.

"One thing we can be thankful for," he said, throwing the saddle on his mount, "yer wife has never had a speck of trouble with any of her deliveries."

Clark did take some assurance from the doctor's statement, but still he was feverishly anxious to get back home to Marty.

The moon again was uncooperative. Clark's horse was headed home while the doc's horse was leaving a warm stall, so Clark found himself often out in front of the doctor.

That was fine, Clark told himself. His horse knew the road better and it was good that it should lead the way.

Before they had reached the Davis farmyard, the moon had decided to disappear altogether. They were used to it by now and urged their horses on at a fast pace in spite of the darkness.

When they arrived, Doc dismounted and threw Clark the reins to his horse. Without a word, they parted company—Clark going toward the barn, riding his horse and leading the doctor's, and Doc hastening toward the house.

There was a light in the kitchen. Through the window, Doc could see Ellie moving about.

"Good," he said to himself, "she has a fire going and the kettle on."

He entered the house without knocking and threw off his heavy mittens and coat, tossing them on a nearby chair. He was halfway across the kitchen floor before he remembered his hat. He turned to throw it on the top of the pile of outdoor clothing.

"How's yer ma?" asked the doctor before starting upstairs.

"She seems to be fine," answered Ellie. "She's asked me fer some tea."

The doctor slowed midstep. If Marty was asking for tea, there was no need for him to be in such a hurry.

He stepped to the fire to warm his chilled hands.

Ellie went on with her task of pouring hot water into the teapot and setting out a cup.

It wasn't long until Clark flung open the door and burst in upon them. His eyes quickly swept across the room. Ellie and the doc were both standing in the kitchen as though nothing of importance was going on in the rest of the house. Clark was perplexed . . . and a little annoyed.

"How is she?" he asked. *Why are they both down here?* he wondered.

Doc turned to him. "She's fine. She just asked Ellie to fix her some tea."

"Tea?" echoed Clark. "At a time like this?"

He started for the stairway, the doc close behind him, and Ellie bringing up the rear with the tea tray in her hands. They entered the room together. Clark was very relieved to see that Marty was no longer tossing. She seemed quite relaxed as she lay against the pillow. *A false alarm!* Clark thought. *The false labor passed already*.

Marty looked up at the three of them. "Yer a little late," she said lightly.

"Late?" Clark responded. "Well, it weren't easy travelin'. The road was rutted, and the moon wouldn't—"

Marty interrupted him. "We won," she said complacently.

"What ya meanin'?" Clark demanded.

"Me an' Ellie. Didn't she tell ya?" and Marty pushed back the covers to reveal a little wrapped bundle on the bed beside her. "It's a girl."

Two pairs of eyes turned to Ellie. Ellie set the tea tray carefully on the bedside table. Her eyes were wide, and she shook her head dumbly. "I . . . I guess I fergot," she stammered, and then she flung herself into Clark's arms and began to weep, trembling until he had to hold her close to keep her from shaking. "Oh, Pa," she sobbed, "I was so scared . . . so scared."

The doctor took over then. Clark was patting Ellie's back and murmuring encouragement to her. After she had cried for a moment, she got herself under control again. Clark talked her into sitting on a chair and having a cup of tea along with her mother. The doctor examined both baby and mother, telling Ellie over and over what a fine job she had done. At last Clark was able to hold his new daughter. She was a little beauty, in his estimation. He smiled as he rocked her in his arms and paid her a multitude of compliments.

"Okay, you two," Clark said, turning to Marty and Ellie. "Iffen yer so smart, I s'pose ya got her named already, too?"

"No," said Marty. "We waited on you fer thet."

"Any of the names thet you've been talkin' of suits me."

"Well, it's sure not gonna be one thet you picked," countered Marty. "Henry or Isaac or Jeremiah."

Clark laughed. "Well, I won't insist."

"I was thinkin'," said Marty thoughtfully, "thet Ellie might wish to name her."

"Me?" said Ellie, both surprise and delight in her voice.

"Kinda thought since ya did so much to git her safely into this world thet ya had more right than anyone."

"I think thet's a great idea," agreed Clark.

"Well, then," said Ellie, "I like Belinda."

"Belinda," Clark and Marty both said at once.

"Belinda May," continued Ellie.

"Belinda May. I like it," said Clark. "Suits her just fine."

"I like it, too," Marty said. "An' now iffen her proud pa would just bring her on over here, I'd kinda like to git another look at our daughter."

Clark reluctantly laid the tiny baby down beside Marty again, then leaned over to kiss them both.

Doc cleared his throat.

"Well, seein' as I won't be needed here anymore tonight, I guess I'll just be headin' on home to my bed. I suspect that everyone in this house has had enough excitement for one night. Bed's a good place for all of you. 'Sides, this here new mama could do with a good rest."

They all agreed. "See ya a little later," Clark promised Marty and turned to usher all of them from her room.

"Yer not gonna head off fer home without a little coffee to warm ya up," he informed the doc.

"I'll make some," volunteered Ellie. "I need to busy myself with somethin' ordinary to unwind before going back to bed anyway."

"Coffee won't be necessary. Ya already got out the teapot an' more hot water a singin' on the stove. I'll just have me a cup of tea."

Ellie took charge in the kitchen. She was glad to be back to doing something so familiar. Looking back over the night hours she had just experienced, she decided that even though she had been frightened almost beyond herself, it had been exciting, too. To assist in the arrival of a new little life was an experience not given to many. Now that she was sure her mother and sister were just fine, she could relax and maybe even treasure the memory. One thing she was sure of: It was a night she would never forget.

TWENTY-FIVE

Sharing

The next day the household awakened early, in spite of the lack of sleep the night before. There was too much excitement in the air for anyone to be able to sleep very long. Besides, the wee Belinda awoke to insist on an early breakfast, and not being used to the cries of a new baby in the house, the whole family got up with her.

Ellie hurried across the yard over to Kate and Clare's with the good news. The commotion of the night before had failed to waken them. They immediately headed for the big house with Ellie.

Kate was the first to reach Marty's bed. Little Belinda had just finished her nursing, had her diaper changed by her pa, and was snuggled down beside her mother again for a much-deserved nap. It was hard work being born, and she had some resting to do.

Kate stood gazing at the baby, her eyes filled with love and tears. "She's beautiful, Ma," she whispered. "Just beautiful."

"Ya want to hold her?" asked Marty, seeing the longing in Kate's eyes.

"May I?"

"'Course."

"But she's sleepin'."

"She's got all day to sleep. 'Sides, she likely won't even waken anyway."

Kate picked the wee baby up carefully. "Oh," she squealed, "she's so tiny." She turned to show the little bundle to Clare. "Look here, Belinda May, this is yer big brother. Yer wonderful big brother. Yer gonna be so proud of 'im."

Clare reached out a big hand to the tiny one. Marty could see tears form in his eyes, but he blinked them away. "Hi there, ya little pun'kin," Clare greeted the baby. "Yer a pretty little thing . . . fer a newborn."

"She's beautiful," argued Kate.

Clare laughed. "Give her a few days . . . but then, my ma always had pretty babies."

At length, the baby had been inspected and fussed over enough for the present. Their attention turned back to Marty.

"An' how are you, Ma?"

"Fine. I feel just fine. But then, I had me such good doctorin'."

All eyes turned back to Ellie.

"I'm proud of ya, little sister," Clare said, tousling her hair. "But why didn't ya come fer some help?"

"There wasn't time. Not even time to think, let alone . . . but Mama was great. I woulda never been able to do it without her careful instructions. I had me no idea—"

"You were wonderful," said Marty, "never flustered or nothin'."

"Till afterward," Ellie said, laughing. "Then I just seemed to fall apart."

They all laughed together.

"Well, at least," added Clark, "ya waited till after it was all over. Ya didn't go collapsin' when yer ma needed ya."

They left the room together. It was agreed that Clare would ride on over and take the news of the safe arrival of Belinda to Arnie and Nandry and Ma Graham. Ellie was going to saddle the other horse and go see Lane. Clark would take the team and go to town to get telegrams off to Missie, Clae, and Luke. Kate volunteered to stay close beside Marty. They all scattered in various directions, anxious to share the good news.

Marty gained her strength back rapidly, in spite of her many visitors. The new baby was a good baby, demanding only a minimum of attention, much to the chagrin of the household. There were many pairs of willing arms that would have been more than happy to hold and fuss over her more, but she was content to be fed and changed and then tucked in once more to her bed for another nap. As the days passed by, she began to spend more time awake. Even then, she did not cry except when she was hungry. She didn't need to. There was usually someone there to hold her anyway. Clark was spending more and more time in the house on the wintry days.

"Little girl," Marty overheard him say to the baby, "I sure am glad ya chose to arrive in the winter when a body can be in, 'stead of at plowin' time." Marty smiled to herself. Never had Clark had more time to enjoy one of his babies.

Daily Marty felt her previous vigor return to her body. She was feeling much more like her old self and gradually took on the household duties. She felt Ellie's questioning eyes on her at times, but as Ellie could see for herself, Marty was happiest when busy. And when Marty assured her she truly had the strength and was not merely pushing herself, Ellie did not protest. Marty told her to spend some time planning for her upcoming wedding. Ellie had been collecting and preparing the things she would need for her own house.

Marty helped with the preparations, too. In the quiet of the long evenings, she pieced quilts and hemmed tea towels. Pillowcases were embroidered and rugs hooked. Marty quite enjoyed being involved and, before long, was nearly as excited as Ellie about the coming event. It didn't make her as sad as it had when she first knew the inevitable was coming and Ellie would be leaving home. Especially with Belinda sleeping contentedly in her bed or rocking in her pa's arms.

A package came from Luke. *To my new little sister,* the note read. *Bet you are really something special. I've been waiting for you for a long, long time. I finally am a big brother. We're going to love one another. I can hardly wait to see you. I'll be home just as soon as I can. In the meantime, take good care of Mother. She's someone pretty special, too. Love, Luke.*

Marty wiped her eyes as she handed the letter to Clark. Then she kissed the tiny Belinda and showed her the packaged gift. "From yer big brother," she said. "Big brother Luke. Ya wanta see what he sent?" The baby did not respond with as much as the flick of a tiny eyelash, so taken was she with sucking her fist, but Marty opened the package anyway. It was a pair of baby shoes. Marty had never seen them so small or so dainty. "Well, look at thet," she said, holding the shoes out to Clark and Ellie. "Did ya ever see anythin' like it?"

Ellie squealed with delight. "Oh, aren't they darlin'?"

Clark grinned and reached out to take one of the bits of leather in his hand.

"Most senseless thing I ever saw," he said. "But yer right—they are 'bout the cutest thing, too."

Clae also sent a letter and a package. Hers was more practical than Luke's had been—and almost as pretty. It was a little hand-sewn gown. Marty knew that Clae had not had time for all of the fancy stitching since receiving the word of the baby's birth. Her note explained it. *I took a chance that it would be a girl*, she said. *It was our turn. If it had been a boy, I'd have sent him something else—though I still hadn't figured out what—because he never would have been comfortable in all this ribbon and lace.*

In a later mail, a parcel came from Missie. Marty lifted out a carefully wrapped pale pink sweater. *I know that I sent something before for the new little sister, but I just couldn't resist doing something special just for her now that we know who she is. I've stayed up nights hurrying to get this done. I hope she gets it before she is already too big for it. It comes with love to Auntie Belinda from her nephews Nathan and Josiah, and her niece Melissa Joy.*

Marty was sure she had never seen a girl more excited about her wedding day than Ellie. Eyes glowing and cheeks flushed, she slipped into her wedding gown, her hands fairly trembling. "Oh, Mama," she said, "I can scarce believe thet it is finally happenin'! It seems I've waited so long."

"But it hasn't been long," Marty reminded her. "Not long at all. It's only been a couple of months since ya made yer plans."

"Well, it seems half of forever," insisted Ellie.

"Half of forever," repeated Marty. "Yes, I s'pose so." She gazed at her lovely daughter, wanting to hold this moment in her memory for all time. Ellie's gown, white with tiny blue flowers and ruffles at the neck and sleeves, had been carefully and lovingly sewn by mother and daughter together. *How blue her eyes are,* thought Marty. *Almost exactly the same cornflower blue as those flowers. . . .*

The wedding would be in the little community church, with a dinner following at the Davis farm. Because of the time of year and the fact that none of the entertaining could be located in the yard, only the family and special friends were invited to the dinner. Even so, Marty would be hard put to accommodate them all.

Willie's brother's family, the LaHayes, had already taken the stage to catch the train going west. They seemed almost as excited about the plans for their new home as Ellie was about her wedding day. Enough simple furniture had been left behind for Lane to be comfortable as a bachelor. Lane and Ellie had done some shopping on their own and bought a few more pieces. Ellie had hung curtains and scattered rugs and put her dishes in the cupboards. She was finally convinced that Marty was fully capable of caring for herself and the baby, so Ellie would not need to venture over every day to do the tasks for her. She looked forward to being a housewife rather than a housekeeper.

"Wear a warm coat," Marty reminded her daughter. "Thet sun ain't near as warm as it looks."

Who could worry about a coat on such a day? Ellie's expression said. But later she admitted she was glad she had listened to Marty, for indeed the sun was not as warm as it looked, and a cold wind was blowing. Ellie wondered if her carefully groomed hair would be all windblown on the ride to the church.

Clark guided the team of blacks. They were feeling frisky after the long winter of little use, and it took a good horseman to hold them back. Marty was not worried. She had complete confidence in Clark's ability to manage the horses. She held her wee daughter closely against her, making sure Belinda wasn't wrapped so tightly that she would be short of good air to breathe.

It was good to be out in the open and in the brisk air again. Marty wanted to pretend that she could smell spring coming, but in fact she could not. The air was still heavy with winter. *But it won't be long,* Marty promised herself. *Any day now and we will be feeling it.*

Marty could hear another team close behind them and turned to wave to Clare and Kate. Their horses seemed just as eager as Clark's, and Marty couldn't help but imagine what would result if the two menfolk were just to let them go.

When they pulled in to the churchyard, a crowd had already gathered. Impatient teams were tied up to the hitching rails, stomping and champing at the bits. A few were feeding, but most of them ignored the hay that had been dropped before them. They had been eating all winter. Now they simply wished to put an end to their confinement. Marty was sure she knew just how they felt.

Clark helped her carefully down from the high seat and steadied her on her feet before leaving to tie the horses.

Ellie was already on the ground, smoothing her hair and, for the first time, looking a little nervous.

"Ya look just fine," Marty assured her. "Let's go in so ya can get out of thet coat."

They walked the few steps to the church door and stepped inside. The congregation was already seated. Heads turned. Marty could feel many eyes upon them and sensed many smiles. They all seemed to blur before her. She handed Belinda to Kate, who had also entered, and reached to help Ellie with her coat. The gown was not badly wrinkled from the weight of the coat, but Marty spent some time carefully smoothing out the skirt.

"Is my hair all right?" whispered Ellie.

"Just fine. Just fine," answered Marty and brushed at it a bit just to assure the girl.

"I'm so nervous, Mama. I didn't think I would be, but I am."

"Everyone is," Marty whispered back. "It's just part of the ceremony."

Ellie tried to smile at Marty's little joke, but the smile was wobbly and a little crooked.

"Wish Pa would come," she whispered again.

"He'll be here," Marty assured her.

For the moment, Marty had forgotten all about her small daughter, so absorbed was she in the one who stood before her, fearful yet anxious to become a bride. But when she did remember the baby, she turned to look at Kate holding her. Kate stood silently back a pace, holding the tiny Belinda and unwrapping her many blankets. She was rewarded with a fleeting smile, and she hugged the wee baby close.

"Oh, Ma, it's the first time she has smiled for me," she exulted in a whisper to Marty. For just a moment the two women looked at each other, and a lump caught in Marty's throat. She knew Clare and Kate's baby would have been smiling now. Smiling and recognizing her ma and pa. But Kate's gaze with obvious love and care for the little one held no shadow, though her heart must have still been tender over their loss.

Clark and Clare entered, stamping the slush from their boots and brushing off their coats. They shrugged out of their coats and hung them on pegs by the door. Then Clark turned to Ellie. "Ready, little girl?" he asked softly. Ellie only nodded.

"We'll let Kate an' Clare find 'em a seat first; then I'll sit yer mother."

Kate and Clare moved forward to a pew near the front that had been saved for family. It was then that Marty noticed Kate still holding Belinda.

Clark drew Marty and Ellie close and, with an arm around each of them, led them in a quiet prayer. They lifted their heads, and Ellie dabbed at her eyes with the handkerchief she carried. Marty wiped her eyes, as well, then leaned to give their next-to-last born, their Elvira Davis, one last kiss. In just a few minutes, she would become Elvira Howard, Mrs. Lane Howard. *But,* thought Marty thankfully, *she will always be my daughter, no matter what her name.*

Clark offered Marty his arm and led her to a seat beside Kate. Marty intended to take Belinda back, but when she saw the way Kate looked at the baby, she let Belinda stay where she was. She looked to the front instead and saw a nervous Lane, his eyes fixed on the back of the church as he waited for his bride. Arnie stood beside him, and the young preacher stood before them with an open book.

Maude Colby, Ellie's friend from town, preceded the bride down the aisle. Ellie followed, walking sedately and purposefully on her father's arm. Marty felt such a pride well up within her. Her girl would make a good wife. And Marty couldn't think of anyone she would rather share Ellie with than Lane. Her eyes filled with tears momentarily, but she quickly wiped them away and flashed Kate a little smile.

After the ceremony and the hearty congratulations of family and friends, the wagons and buggies were loaded once again and the eager horses were allowed to run. Ellie, not in the Davis buggy now, had her proper place, tucked in closely beside Lane.

The dinner was a festive affair. In spite of the lack of room, family and neighbors laughed and chatted and ate until they could eat no more. Gifts were presented to the happy bride and groom, and Ellie exclaimed over everything with a great deal of enthusiasm. Lane gave a little speech.

"I will ever bless the day when my boss had the good sense to order me back east to care fer a farm," Lane said amid laughter. "Tell the truth, I wasn't lookin' forward much to bein' a farmer—never havin' been one. Iffen it hadn't been thet I had met Mr. an' Mrs. Davis . . ." Lane stopped and corrected himself, "Ma an' Pa here . . ." More laughter. "Well, iffen I hadn't met 'em an' looked forward to seein' 'em again, I don't s'pose even the boss coulda made a farmer outta me. Boy, what I woulda missed!" exclaimed Lane, his eyes fastened on a blushing Ellie.

Lane became more serious then. "I've got lots to learn yet in life. Lots to learn in the Christian walk, but I've already learned this. Iffen I let God control things, He sure can do a heap better job of it than I ever could. I just have no way of sayin' how thankful I am fer a girl like Ellie . . . how lucky I am to have her fer a wife. I can't express it nohow . . . but I hope to spend my lifetime a tryin' to show her how I feel."

Marty hoped no one saw her slip from the room. She needed a little time to herself. She was happy for Ellie. She wouldn't change things for the world. She just needed a little time to get used to it, that was all.

TWENTY-SIX

Family Dinner

Marty was having a hard time of it trying to convince daughter Ellie that her mother could truly manage without her.

"I might need ya, dear, I might," Marty assured her. "But it ain't to wash the dishes or to git the meals. I can care fer my own house. I haven't felt better fer months. The baby is no problem, an' yer pa fusses over me more'n ever. So it's not yer hands I'm missin', helpful as they are. It's you. Just you. Yer being here and yer company an' all."

"I miss you, too, Mama," Ellie responded, "though I must admit I'm awfully happy where I am."

Marty touched the girl's hair in silent acknowledgment that she understood and accepted the truth of her daughter's words.

"We'll come whenever ya want us to," Ellie promised.

"Then come join the family fer Sunday dinner."

"I'd like thet. I'll come early and help ya git ready."

Marty laughed. "Haven't ya been listenin' to a thing I've been sayin'?" she said, giving Ellie a playful pat on the bottom. "I'm fine. I can fix a dinner fer my family. Honest!"

"All right," said Ellie. "You fix it, an' we girls will do the cleanin' up. Fair?"

Marty laughed again. "Fair," she said and let it go.

"An' while yer a fixin'," said Ellie as she was about to leave, "how 'bout some lemon pie? Seems I haven't had a good one fer ages. I never did git the hang of makin' lemon pie."

"Okay," Marty cheerfully agreed, "lemon pie it is. An', Ellie . . ."

Ellie hesitated, her hand on the door.

"Thanks fer stoppin' by," Marty went on. "I needed a little chat. I've been missin' ya."

"I've missed ya, too," said Ellie, "an' Kate an' Pa an' even Belinda. She's growin' already, Ma. Just look at her."

Marty turned to look at the baby lying contentedly in the crib in the corner of the kitchen. She was playing with her hands and crooning to herself.

"She is, isn't she? She's already got her pa all twisted round those little fingers, I'm a thinkin'."

"Thet weren't a big job," answered Ellie. "He was a pushover the day she arrived."

Marty smiled.

"See ya both on Sunday, then."

Ellie nodded and left the kitchen.

Marty crossed to the window and watched Ellie walk out to the barn, where Clark would hitch up the team to her wagon. Marty went back to the baby, who was dropping off to sleep. "Little girl," she whispered, stroking the soft cheek with one finger, "ya have no idea what a big achin' void yer helpin' to fill."

Sunday came and with it the family. They all followed Clark and Marty's team home from church, making quite a procession. Marty smiled to herself as she thought of the sight they must be making.

The women and children were let off at the house, and the men went on down to the barn to unhitch the animals.

Soon everyone was inside, joshing and joking good-naturedly as they flocked through the kitchen. Marty shooed anyone who wasn't fixing the meal out to other places in the house. The menfolk settled themselves around the fire in the family living room. The children gathered in the upstairs hall with toys Marty and Clark had fashioned and acquired over the years. All except Tina. She insisted she was now one of the ladies and asked to help set the table. And of course Baby Belinda was too little for the children's play and lay contentedly in her pa's lap in the big, much-used rocker, obviously enjoying the motion of the chair and the solid arms around her.

Arnie cocked an eyebrow at his pa. "Been noticin' yer not as good 'bout sharin' as ya used to be," he remarked.

"Meanin'?" said Clark, frowning slightly.

"Ever'time I see ya, yer a hoggin' thet girl. She belongs to all of us, ya know."

There was laughter around the circle, and Clark reluctantly passed the small baby to Arnie.

He didn't get to keep her for long. From there she went to Josh and then to Clare, and finally Lane even got a chance to hold her. She turned on the charm for each one of them.

"I can see it all now," said Arnie. "Pa's gonna be awful busy guardin' the gate when this one grows up. Boy, ain't she somethin'?"

They all agreed, and Clark looked as if he would pop some buttons.

"Look at thet smile," said Clare. "Ever see so much sweetness in such a little mite?"

The group of men had turned their full attention on the baby, admiring and commenting on every little thing she did. Belinda cooed and squirmed and smiled at all her admirers.

It was not long until they were called to the table. They all took their places rather noisily, but complete silence reigned as Clark led them in a fervent prayer of gratitude to God. In the midst of the prayer, Marty heard a contented gurgle, and when she raised her head she saw that Clark was still holding the baby.

"My goodness," she said to him after the chorus of *amen*s, "how ya plannin' on eatin' with the young'un in yer arms?"

"It's a leg I'm missin'—I got me two hands," Clark noted with a grin.

"Well, ya need 'em both fer eatin'." Marty laughed. "My lands, she's gonna be so spoilt she won't be fittin' to live with." Marty got up from her place and took the baby girl.

"I'll hold her," volunteered Arnie quickly.

"She don't need to be held. She'll be perfectly content here in her bed." And Marty bent to lay the baby down.

"Don't seem fair somehow," put in Clare. "All the rest of the family is round the table."

"An' she will be, too—give her time."

"Aw, Grandma," coaxed Tina. "She'll miss what's goin' on."

"I don't think she's gonna miss it thet much," said Marty. "None of the rest of ya ever got so much holdin'."

"That's different," Arnie continued. "There was more babies than big folk then. Now it's been turned round. Lots of people here to hold a young'un now."

Marty looked around the table. "Yeah, lots of big folks, and lookin' round this table, I s'pect thet it could very soon be turned the other way again."

They must have caught her meaning, and Marty noticed a couple at the table exchanging glances and looking a bit sheepish.

"Anybody got anythin' to tell us?" she asked, a twinkle in her eye.

Arnie swallowed hard and looked at Anne. "Well," he said, "we hadn't planned on an announcement just yet, but yeah . . . I reckon we do."

There was laughter and congratulations for the blushing newlyweds. Marty could feel their joy, but then she thought of poor Kate and a pain went through her. Kate was slowly pushing back her chair and rising to her feet. Marty felt her throat constrict. Poor Kate. It was just too much for her. Too soon. First Belinda and now this. But Kate was not rushing from the room. Instead, she was standing with a hand on Clare's shoulder and a smile on her face. "I'm glad 'bout Arnie and Anne's announcement," she said in a clear, soft voice, "glad fer them and glad because . . . well, I just think it's important fer every child to have a little cousin 'bout his own age."

"Are ya sayin'—?" began Ellie, but Kate stopped her with, "Sure am! Just 'bout the same time as Anne. Doctor just told me fer sure yesterday."

Marty couldn't help the happy tears. She was going to be a grandma again—twice over.

TWENTY-SEVEN

Surprise

Ellie knew Lane really didn't have a whole lot that needed to be done around the farm. The animals had all been either sold or shipped off to the new ranch in the West. There were no fences to fix, no wood to cut, no harness to mend. At first he had enjoyed it since it meant he had lots of time to spend with her, but after a few days of drinking coffee and watching her work around the kitchen, she could tell he was beginning to grow restless. She didn't blame him at all. She was used to being busier herself, and now and then she, too, felt time hanging a bit heavy on her hands. At least she had baking to do, clothes to wash, a house to keep clean, and many little tasks about the home. She tried to think of some ideas for Lane to fill his hours, but nothing presented itself. It was hard for him to just sit around waiting for the farm to sell, she could tell.

"Lane," she ventured one day, "I been thinkin'. We're only a couple of miles outta town. Ya think it would matter any to the LaHayes iffen ya were to take a town job?"

Lane's expression indicated he wondered why he hadn't thought of it. "Don't rightly know what I'm fittin' to do in a town," he said reflectively, "but it sure is worth a try. Would ya mind?"

Ellie smiled to assure him. "I know thet it's hard fer ya not to be busy. An' I don't blame ya one bit. Fact is, I don't think I'd care much to be married to a lazy man. Why don't ya go on in an' make a few inquiries? Ain't a thing more in the world fer ya to do round here."

Lane saddled his horse, kissed his wife good-bye, and rode from the yard.

At first it appeared there would be no work for Lane in the small town. The bank needed another man and the town's one tailor said he could sure use some help, but Lane did not have the required experience for either job. He was about to give up and head for home again when the man from the general store waved him down.

"Hear tell yer lookin' fer work."

"Sure am. Willin' to try most anythin'. Ya need a man?"

"Not me, no. I got all the help I need, but I hear thet Matt over to the livery is down sick an' poor ol' Tom is 'bout wearin' hisself out tryin' to keep up with things. Ya might wander on over there an' see iffen he's found somebody yet."

Lane thanked him and turned his horse to the livery stable. Funny that he hadn't thought to try it first off, since he sure knew about horses.

The man was right. Old Tom did want another man, and Lane started in right away on his *town* job.

The chance to work not only helped put Lane in a much better frame of mind concerning himself, but it enabled him and Ellie to begin to tuck away a little money week by week, as well. They both felt good about it, and when Lane would ride in at night, tired from lifting feed sacks and grooming horses, Ellie was there waiting for him with a warm fire and fresh-baked bread. Their marriage prospered under such an arrangement.

One day as Ellie matched socks from the day's washing and waited for Lane to return for supper, she heard Rex barking. The sound of his bark told Ellie that someone had arrived. It wasn't Lane, she knew, and it wasn't one of her family. Rex barked as though the visitor was a stranger.

She hurried to the window and saw a tall man in a long, dark coat tying his horse to the hitching rail. Ellie had never seen the man before. "Maybe it's a buyer fer the farm," she mused and hoped with all her heart that it might be so.

She answered the knock and greeted the man cordially.

"I understand Lane Howard lives here."

"Thet's right," said Ellie. "I'm Mrs. Howard."

"Is Mr. Howard in?"

"Not at the moment. He works in town, but I'm expectin' 'im home 'fore long."

"Mind if I wait for him?" the man asked, and Ellie wasn't sure for a moment if she minded or not.

"I'll just wait out here if it's all right."

"Ya needn't do thet!" exclaimed Ellie, chiding herself for hesitating. "Ya can come on in an' have a cup of coffee while ya wait."

The man did not refuse and followed Ellie into the small kitchen. Ellie pushed the coffeepot she had in readiness for Lane's supper onto the heat and nodded at a chair.

"Just sit ya down," she offered. "He should be home most any minute."

She looked at the man. His clothes were different from what the farmers round about wore, she noticed. And he didn't really dress like the men from town, either. He must be from the city, she concluded. If he came about the farm, he must be coming on behalf of someone else. He didn't look like a farmer.

She decided to ask, but before she could speak, the man spoke to her.

"Nice farm here," he commented. "Well kept."

"First-rate," agreed Ellie, ready to give an honest sales pitch. "There's been lots of time an' money put in on it. It's in real good shape."

"Didn't see much stock about."

"Stock's all been sold right now. But it has good pastureland an' plenty of barn room. Barns fer cows, with good milk stalls, lots of pigpens, a real fine horse barn thet holds eight head, big chicken coop, five granaries . . . or is it six? . . . no, five, I think. Even got a root cellar an' a real good well."

The man looked just a shade puzzled, but Ellie hurried on. "Lots of good crop land, too. Had a first-rate stand of barley last year, and the lower field had a hay crop like I've never seen afore . . . an' thet field out back, the one ya can't see too well from the road—" Ellie caught herself. "'Course ya can't see any of the fields too well just by ridin' on by 'cause of the snow, but it'll soon be ready fer workin'. Folks hereabouts say they expect an early spring this year. Some of the farmers are already gittin' their seed ready to plant."

"Interesting," the man said, but he really didn't look much interested.

"There's a good garden plot, too," Ellie continued, since it was at least something to talk about. She reached for a cup to fill with coffee for the stranger. "Even got a few fruit trees. Pa says thet apples would do real good here, but no one's gotten round to plantin' 'em yet."

"You just buy the farm recently?" asked the man as Ellie returned to the stove.

Ellie stopped in midstride. "Us?" she said. "Oh no, it's still fer sale," she hurried to explain. "We're just livin' here till it sells. The LaHayes already moved on out west an' left us to care fer the place till someone buys it. We're goin' west, too, as soon—" Ellie stopped herself. Now, that didn't sound good. The man might think something was wrong with the farm with everyone moving away.

"Not thet we wouldn't like to buy the farm ourselves, but my husband really prefers ranchin'. An' 'sides, we don't have the money thet it takes to buy a farm. Takes a heap of money to git started farmin' nowadays." That didn't sound good, either. Might scare a body off.

"One soon is able to make it back, though, on a good farm—an' this is a good farm," she hurried on, but then she decided she'd said enough. Whatever the man was here for, she didn't want something she said to give the wrong impression.

The man said nothing, and Ellie placed a steaming cup of coffee in front of him.

She checked the biscuits in the oven and stirred the vegetables. They were ready. She hoped that Lane wouldn't be too late.

The silence now hung heavy between them. The man didn't seem too inclined toward conversation. In fact, he seemed rather impatient and kept drumming his fingers on the table, an irritating thing to Ellie. At last Ellie heard Rex bark again, and this time she could tell it was Lane who was approaching. She heaved a big sigh of relief and glanced across at the close-lipped stranger.

"Thet's my husband now," she said. "He'll be in as soon as he cares fer the horse."

The man grunted his approval. Ellie was about to start dishing up the supper but changed her mind. She'd better hold off for a few minutes while the man had his talk with Lane about the farm. Somehow, Ellie didn't expect the stranger to accept an invitation to join them at the table.

Lane came in with a puzzled look on his face.

"Lane, this is . . . is . . . I'm sorry, sir. I didn't even ask yer name."

"Peters," said the man, extending his hand to Lane and rising to his feet.

"My husband," finished Ellie lamely.

"Mr. Peters," said Lane, shaking the hand. "I believe I had the pleasure of rentin' ya a horse a little earlier."

Mr. Peters seemed taken aback. "To be sure," he said, looking more closely at Lane. "If I'd known whom I was talking to, I could have saved myself this trip. I was told that you lived on the farm."

"We do," said Lane good-naturedly, "but there's nothin' to do hereabouts right now. All the stock's been sold. We have one horse an' one dog. Don't keep a man very busy. We are just here till—"

Mr. Peters stopped him with an impatient gesture. "Your wife explained," he said hurriedly.

"Please," said Lane, "sit yerself back down an' tell me how I can help ya."

He's here 'bout the farm, Ellie started to say, but she decided she wasn't sure about that anymore.

"The matter is a private one," said Mr. Peters, pulling forth a small case that Ellie had not noticed when he had arrived.

Lane looked surprised.

"Well, I guess we are 'bout as private as we can git," he responded.

Mr. Peters cast a glance toward Ellie.

"Nothin' is so private as to exclude my wife, sir," Lane said firmly.

Mr. Peters said nothing but opened up his case and spread some papers out before him.

He pulled a small pair of spectacles from his pocket and balanced them on the end of his nose. Then he cleared his throat and said, "I understand that you are Lane Howard."

"Thet's correct."

"Who is your father, Mr. Howard?"

"Well, I . . . I don't have a father. Thet is, he died when I was five years old."

"And his name?"

"His name? His name was . . . ah . . . Will. They called him Will. His real name was William. William Clayton Howard."

"And your mother? Where is she?"

"She died only one week after. She'd been hurt in the same storm."

"And her name?"

"Rebecca. Rebecca Marie."

"Who raised you?" asked the man.

"An aunt. A maiden aunt. Her name was Aunt Maggie. Ah . . . Margery. Margery Thom."

"Is she living?"

"No, sir. I heard 'bout four or five years ago thet she had passed on."

"So you weren't with her when she died?"

"No. I left when I was fourteen."

"Why?"

"Why? 'Cause I wanted to. I didn't feel thet I should stay."

"Were you told to leave?"

Lane looked a bit annoyed. "'Course not."

"What were the circumstances?"

"The what?"

"The circumstances. Why did you go if you weren't told to leave?"

"My aunt married. She was older. Had never married before. People round town said it was gonna be hard fer her to adjust to bein' married. They also said it would be even harder with me there to . . . to . . ."

"Folks said that?"

"Well, they didn't say it right to me. They didn't know when I over-heard 'em. But I did."

Ellie felt rather unsettled. Why in the world all the strange questions? Why should this man come in from nowhere and begin to ask her husband things concerning his past? Things he had shared only with her.

"What about the man? Your aunt's new husband?" the questioner went on.

"What 'bout 'im? He was a businessman in the town. Well established. He was an undertaker."

"Were you afraid of him?"

"Afraid? No. He had never been anythin' but kind to me."

"Did he have a family?"

"No. He had never married before, either."

"But you didn't think you wanted to live with him—or with your aunt—after she married him?"

"It wasn't like thet. I hated to leave. I cried all the way to the train station, iffen ya must know. It was just thet I loved Aunt Maggie. She had been so kind to me, an' I wanted her to be happy in her new marriage."

Ellie thought she heard the stranger mutter something about busy-body tongues, but she wasn't sure.

"Did you keep in touch?" he went on.

"Till she died, I did. My last letter was returned to me marked 'De-ceased.'"

"I see," said the man, adjusting his odd glasses.

"I'm sorry, sir, but I really don't understand what this is all 'bout," said Lane. "Now, I got nothin' in my past I want to hide, but it does seem a bit unusual thet a total stranger would walk into my house and put so many private questions to me."

"I understand how you must feel," said the man, removing his glasses just a moment before they surely would have fallen. "But one cannot be too careful, and I do need to be entirely sure that you are the Lane Howard I am looking for."

"Lookin' fer?" puzzled Lane, and Ellie moved a step closer and put her hand on the back of his neck.

"You didn't mention the name of the man your aunt married," said the persistent man at the table, placing his glasses back on his nose once more.

"It was Myers. Conwyn Myers."

"Did you keep in touch with Mr. Myers at all?"

"Not really. My aunt often wrote of him, and I sent my greetings through my letters to her."

"I see," said the man. Then, "One more thing, Mr. Howard. What is your full name?"

"It's William. William Lane Howard. William from my pa. They called me by Lane so thet it wouldn't be confusin'."

"Well," said the man, shuffling through his papers, "everything seems to match."

"Match to what?" asked Lane. "I do wish, sir, thet you'd be so kind as to explain yer presence an' questions."

"Yes," said the man, "I do believe that I am free to do so."

Ellie and Lane exchanged glances.

"I am Stavely Peters," said the man, emphasizing each of his words carefully. "Stavely Peters, attorney-at-law. I am here representing the estate of the late Conwyn Myers. Mr. Myers was a well-respected and good businessman. He left everything in very good order . . . and . . . he left everything to you."

Lane slowly rose to his feet, shaking his head in bewilderment.

"He left it all to you, Mr. Howard. You were the closest of kin that he had, and he also knew just how special you were to his wife, Margery."

"But I . . . I . . ." Lane stood there with Ellie clinging to his arm. "I'm much obliged . . . to be sure," Lane stumbled over the words, "but . . . but beggin' yer pardon, what would I do with a funeral parlor?"

"He sold the funeral parlor. Sold the house, too. Said that by the sound of your letters, you loved the West and would never want to leave it."

"Oh, he's right. I don't," Lane assured the man.

"Everything that he leaves you is in cash. I have the note right here. All that needs to be done is for you to sign a few papers and then for us to visit your bank together."

"My bank," laughed Lane. "I've never had me the need fer a bank in all my life."

"Well, I'd advise you to become established with one now," said the lawyer. "It's a bit too much money to tuck in the toe of your boot." This was the closest to humor that the man had come.

"Yes, sir," promised Lane. "I certainly will, sir. Right away in the mornin'."

"I stopped by the bank on my way here and made arrangements to have it taken care of tonight. They are most anxious to have your account, I might add, Mr. Howard, and will be more than accommodating, I am sure. I am anxious to have the matter settled and to be on my way back to the city. I will confess that it has taken me much longer than I had hoped to locate you and get the estate finalized."

"I'll git my horse right away," Lane said, looking like he didn't know what had hit him.

He turned to Ellie. "Will ya be okay till I git back?" he asked her.

She clung to him for a moment. "I will iffen I don't burst," she whispered. "Oh, Lane, can ya believe it?"

Lane put her from him gently and gave her a big grin. He reached for his coat.

"I'll hurry," he promised. "I'll hurry as fast as I can. Then we'll talk all 'bout it when I git home."

He kissed her and hurried after the city lawyer.

Ellie turned back to the stove to cover the pots. Who could tell when— or if—they ever would get around to eating their meal?

TWENTY-EIGHT

Plans

"What are we ever goin' to *do* with it all?" Ellie asked when Lane returned and showed her the figure on the bank paper in his hand.

To Ellie it had seemed to take forever for Lane to return to the farm, but, in truth, the transaction had taken place very quickly. The lawyer had been right. The town banker was most anxious to be of every assistance in order to be assured of handling Lane's account. Both banker and lawyer were in a hurry to get the matter finalized.

Lane could not believe his eyes when he was shown the amount of the bank note. There it was. The large sum of money was placed securely in the bank under his name.

"I been thinkin' an' thinkin' all the way home," Lane answered Ellie's question. "There's just no end to what we can do."

"I'll git my own sewin' machine," Ellie began enthusiastically.

"Ya can have two of 'em iffen ya want to," promised Lane, and Ellie laughed.

"An' I'm gonna git those new shoes I saw in Harder's window."

"New shoes? Thet's nothin'. Won't even make a dent in the money."

"Oh, Lane. I can't believe it. I just can't believe it!"

"Nor can I. It all seems like some strange dream."

Lane pulled Ellie down on his lap and pressed his face against her fragrant hair. "The best part of the dream," he said, "is thet now I can give ya the things I wanted to . . . the things ya deserve. I was so scared thet I'd never—"

"Did I ask fer things?" Ellie scolded gently, running her fingers through his hair. "All I really wanted was you, an' ya know it."

Lane pulled her close and kissed her firmly. "I know it," he whispered. "I know it, an' thet's what makes our love so special."

"Oh, Lane, there's so much we could plan, so much to talk about—but we'd better eat this food, don't ya think?" Ellie reminded him, pulling herself free. "Even iffen we don't feel like it, we'd better eat. Thet is, if it's still fit to eat."

They began to eat their overcooked meal, but neither of them really tasted it. There was too much to think about . . . to dream of. It seemed the possibilities were endless. They talked and laughed as they ate and as Ellie cleared the table. They talked as they washed and dried the dishes together and on into the evening until bedtime. There was just so much to discuss with this unexpected turn of events.

"Ya know one thing thet I'd like to do?" asked Ellie as they lay snuggled together under the warm quilts of their bed.

"What?"

"I'd like to git an organ fer the church. Just a little organ—but a nice organ. Do ya think we could?"

"Why not? I think it's a great idea. I've been thinkin' 'bout what we could do special like fer the church—both this church an' our little church out west. Hadn't thought me of an organ, but thet sounds like a first-rate idea."

"Let's, then!" exclaimed Ellie.

Lane kissed her on the ear.

"Ya know what I was thinkin'?" he asked her.

"What?"

"We have the money to buy the farm."

"What farm?"

"*This* farm."

"Us? Why?"

"Why? Then ya won't need to leave. You'll be here, near yer ma, just like ya wanted an'—"

"But, Lane," Ellie protested, "ya don't want to farm. Ya want to ranch."

"I know, but I wouldn't mind. I'll—"

"No, ya won't. I'd never let ya. Never, Lane."

"But—"

"Listen! Mama is all prepared to let me go. It'll be hard fer her, sure, but she'll make it. She wouldn't want us to change our plans just fer her. She would be unhappy iffen she thought I was unhappy, an' I could never be happy iffen I wasn't sure thet *you* were happy—don't ya see?"

"But I could be happy, as long as I was makin' you happy."

"I wouldn't let ya do it. You've always wanted to ranch. Now ya can have a ranch of yer own. Not just a little spread to git by on, but a real ranch—one ya can be proud of. An' someday . . . someday maybe you'll even be as blessed as Willie an' have some sons to take it over after ya."

Ellie felt Lane pull her closer and kiss her hair. Then she could feel the tears on his cheeks in the darkness.

Everyone rejoiced with Lane and Ellie over their good fortune. Ellie began in earnest to prepare for their move. She was more anxious than ever now. She couldn't wait to see Lane's West, to share in purchasing a ranch and establishing a home—their home. She couldn't wait to see Missie and to once again be near to her older sister. Though they were born to different mothers, their Ma Marty had been truly a mother to them both, and they felt very close in heart, though the miles now separated them. Daily Ellie prayed that the farm might hurry and sell so they could be on their way. April passed and May came. With the warmer winds, the snow had disappeared, even in the shadowed places. Ellie fancied that soon she would be smelling spring flowers, and then the farm would sell, she was sure.

Lane continued to work in town. He still needed the activity, he said. And he and Ellie secretly slipped the extra money into the Sunday collection plate for the use of the young preacher. He needed it worse than they did, they were sure. The organ had been ordered, and there was great anticipation over its arrival. Lane and Ellie had also laid aside, in the preacher's care and keeping, a sizable amount to be spent in the years ahead as the church saw the need.

Ellie was restless each day as she waited for Lane to come home. Signs had been posted in the town that if anyone was interested in the LaHaye farm, they were to go to the local livery and talk to Lane Howard. There had been a few inquiries but none of a serious nature.

Then one day Lane came home long before his usual time.

"Yer early," said Ellie, a question in her statement as he poked his head in the door.

"Aren't ya glad to see me?" he teased.

"'Course, but supper isn't ready."

He pulled her to him and kissed her. "Fergit supper," he said. "I have some news."

"Good news?" she inquired.

"I think so."

"Then share it."

"I quit my job."

Ellie looked puzzled. "Ya quit yer job! Thet's fine. I'm not complainin' none . . . but . . . why is it such good news?"

"'Cause . . . I quit my job so I'd have time to git ready to go on home."

"Home?"

"We're free to go now. A man bought the LaHaye farm today."

Ellie threw herself into his arms. "Oh, Lane!" she squealed. "Lane, thet's wonderful!"

He picked her up and swung her around the room. "Thet's what I think!" he shouted back at her. "Finally—we are really on our way."

Marty and Clark both knew how eager Lane and Ellie were to be off to start their own home. So they rejoiced with the couple and welcomed the news of the farm's sale. It was a happy time and a sad time, and the Davis tribe gathered together to celebrate the occasion and to prepare for another good-bye. There was much excited talk around the table. Lane had already made arrangements for their train tickets. There wasn't much packing left to be done. Ellie had already carefully boxed everything she could spare, and Lane had crated it for shipment. In just a few short days they would be on their way.

Ellie was disappointed that she wouldn't be able to see Clae and Luke before she left.

"Who knows how long it will be 'fore I see 'em again?" she mourned, and tears filled her eyes that just moments before had been full of anticipation.

"Maybe Luke can pay us a visit when he finishes his trainin'," Lane said in a comforting tone.

Ellie agreed wholeheartedly, but Marty inwardly stated, *Not on your life. Don't want* Luke *staying out there, too.*

Marty remembered back to another girl, just as eager to set out for the West. She'd had to let that daughter—her Missie—go, too.

Belinda cried. Ten people stood to go to her, but Marty waved them all back to their chairs.

"I'll go," she said. "She might be wantin' to eat."

Belinda was not hungry. Only bored. Bored and in need of a dry diaper. She hated to be wet and would not bear it for long.

Marty changed her, glad for the excuse to leave the family gathering for a few minutes. She held the wee baby close and laid her cheek against the soft little head. "I'm so glad thet God was wise enough to send ya to me," she whispered. "Only *He* knew how much I would be needin' ya."

The baby grasped a tendril of her mother's hair and tried to pull it to her mouth.

"Quit it, ya hear?" reproached Marty softly. "You'll have yer fingers all tangled with it. There are better things to be eatin', I'm thinkin'."

The baby gurgled and changed her grip to the collar of Marty's dress. Marty kissed her. It seemed like only yesterday she had held the tiny Ellie in her arms, and here Ellie was on the verge of leaving.

Again Marty studied Belinda. "Well, I still have you," she whispered. "An' no matter how quickly time seems to fly, it will be some time 'fore *you* will be goin'. An' 'fore we know it, Luke will be home, too. Oh, not home to stay. Don't s'pose he'll ever be home to stay again. Not really.

But at least he'll be close enough to drop in now an' then, I'm prayin'. Close enough thet I can see fer myself just how he's doin'."

She kissed the baby again and settled her on a hip for the walk downstairs. She was ready to rejoin the others now.

On the day of Ellie and Lane's departure, they gathered at the stage station as they had done in the past.

Marty managed her emotions that day very well, she thought. In fact, she managed to hide her tears and even celebrate the occasion with Ellie.

"It's a long, long ride," she warned Ellie. "I thought me at times it would never end. Ya do eventually git there, but by then you'll have had yer fill of train travel fer a while." Ellie only smiled.

"Have ya got the package fer Missie?" Marty asked for the fifth time.

"Right here, Mama. Right here with the other things. I will see thet she gits it just as soon as we arrive."

"Ya sure ya got everythin' ya need?" This was Clark.

"Oh, Pa," laughed Ellie, "they have shops out there, too."

It was not long until their baggage was being loaded. The crated Rex complained some at his close quarters, but Lane rubbed his ear and assured him that he would be taken for a walk at every chance they got.

Ellie, who was holding Belinda until the last possible moment, bent her head to kiss the wee girl. "Know what I'm gonna miss the most?" she whispered. "Watchin' ya grow up." Then the tears were falling freely, and Marty reached out to draw Ellie and Belinda close.

The driver was soon climbing aboard and lifting the reins of the teams. The livery man held the horses' heads and tried to quiet them, but they had been trained to run and were eager to be off.

There were hurried last-minute hugs and kisses, and then Ellie and Lane were climbing into the stage. It wheeled off in a swirl of dust. Marty pulled out her handkerchief to wave the dust from her face and dry her eyes.

They all turned back to their teams; no need to linger longer. Ellie was gone now. She was on her way to her dreams, and the rest of them were left behind to carry on dreams of their own.

213

On the way home from town, Marty raised her head and took a careful look at the world about her.

"I like it here, don't you?" she asked Clark.

"Sure do," he answered comfortably and seemed to feel that his simple words said it all.

"I don't really think I'm hankerin' fer the West, do you?"

"Nope."

They rode on in silence for a while.

"We still have Nandry an' Clare an' Arnie here. An' Luke will be back, too. An' maybe someday even Clae an' Joe will be back."

"Yeah," said Clark, "maybe so."

"Thet's more'n half of 'em," continued Marty. "Thet's pretty good, huh?"

"Thet's real good—an' ya even fergot one."

Marty looked puzzled for a moment and then remembered the bundle of joy in her arms.

"Well, I did at thet. No offense, Belinda," she said, lifting the small baby and kissing her cheek.

"I guess Belinda will fergive ya—this once," teased Clark.

Marty fell silent again. She breathed deeply of the warming air. She loved the spring. There was always something so promising about it.

"Just think, Clark. 'Fore we know it, we'll have two new grandchildren, too."

Clark grinned.

"Best part of it is," went on Marty, "they'll be right here where we can enjoy 'em."

Clark agreed.

Marty looked about her. There was a nice green haze on the pastures. Leaves were beginning to open on the trees near the road. The blue sky looked as though it was willing strength to the green things to hurry and break free and come forth.

"Almost gardenin' time," mused Marty.

"Yup," said Clark, taking a deep breath.

"Ya gonna help me this year?" It was said with teasing, and they both knew she was referring back many years when he had helped a very young Marty with her first attempt at a garden.

"Will ya let me?" he teased back.

"Iffen yer good."

They both laughed.

"My, Clark," she said after a few moments had passed, "but don't thet first garden of mine seem like a long time ago?"

He looked at her, his eyes searching deep into hers. Then he reached over and took her free hand in his.

"Does it?" he asked. "Seems to me thet it weren't all thet far from yesterday."

TWENTY-NINE

The Legacy

Baby Belinda had been fed for the night. Marty and Clark lay with her between them, spending some time admiring the perfection of the tiny baby before they would tuck her into her own bed for the night. She hadn't fallen asleep yet and lay studying the faces she had learned to love. One of her hands firmly clasped a finger on her father's hand. The other tiny baby fist was knotted in the front of Marty's gown. And so she held them both. Not just with childish fingers, Marty thought, but with cords of love.

As Marty gazed at the baby lying between them, she thought again of Ellie. So much had happened to Ellie in such a short time.

"It's really somethin', ain't it?" she murmured. "I still find it hard to believe. It sounds like somethin' you'd read in a fairy tale or somethin'. Who would have thought any of ours would be left a legacy?"

"An' one of such size, too," agreed Clark. "Oh, true, Lane ain't startin' off a millionaire, but he sure has 'im a better start than a lot of young men."

"I trust 'im with it, though," said Marty. "It won't go to his head none. He'll be responsible and givin', and he'll put the money to good use."

"I been thinkin' a lot on legacies lately," Clark said, brushing one of Belinda's curls between his fingers.

"Like what?"

"Well, the kinds of legacies one can leave behind."

"Kinds?"

"Well, there's the money kind. Everyone is familiar with thet. Not thet we all git one, mind ya—but at least ya hear of one now an' then, like happened with Lane."

Marty nodded in agreement.

"But there's other kinds, too."

Marty waited for him to go on. Belinda let go of her grasp on the gown and waved a hand that hit Marty lightly on the chin. Marty caught the small fist and put it to her lips.

"Take this here little one now—we gotta plan what we're gonna be leavin' her with. An' I'm not talkin' money in the bank. I'm talkin' character—faith . . . love fer others . . . an unselfish spirit . . . independence . . . maturity."

Marty knew where Clark's thoughts were leading them. She nodded silently.

"We've got a big job ahead of us, Marty. It'll be fun—but there will be work and care there, too."

"I was thinkin' the other day," admitted Marty, "here I go again! The diapers, the fevers, the teeth, the potty trainin'. Oh, Clark. There's so much ahead of us."

"Then it will be school, an' teachin' chores, an' friendships, an' 'fore we know it—beaus!" said Clark.

"It's kinda scary," Marty whispered.

"Scary?" laughed Clark. "Maybe. It'd be even more scary iffen we didn't have some pretty good examples before us."

"Examples?"

"Our other kids. Not a rotten apple in the bunch."

Marty smiled, thinking of each one of their family.

"Sometimes I feel so proud of 'em," she admitted.

"Me too," he agreed with her. "Me too."

"Like Kate an' Clare. I was so afraid. So afraid they wouldn't be able to handle losin' thet baby. They wanted it so much, Clark. So very much. Yet not a trace of bitterness. They truly took it like real . . . real mature Christians. They even seemed to grow sweeter an' . . . an' wiser. I was so proud of 'em.

"An' Ellie," Marty went on. "The way she just stepped in an' took over when Nandry was havin' her hard time an' showed her where she was wrong without pointin' fingers or causin' hurt. Ya shoulda heard her, Clark. You'd have been so pleased.

"An' Nandry, too. I had me no idea she was carryin' all thet load of bitterness from the time she was a little girl. An' yet, when she saw her wrong, she . . . she just asked the Lord fer His fergiveness."

Clark swung his daughter up into the air and then laid her on his chest. "Yep, little one, yer gonna have to learn 'bout fergiveness, too." Belinda just stuck her thumb in her mouth and laid her head down against her pa.

"Then there's Arnie," Marty continued. "At his age, an' already a deacon in the church, an' a good one, too. An' Clae an' Joe servin' in a church, an' Missie an' Willie startin' a church out there in their own home, an' our Luke studyin' to be a doctor.

"Ya know," she said thoughtfully and with a smile, "yer right, Clark. There ain't a rotten apple in the whole bunch."

"*Luke*. I'm thinkin' we chose his name well."

"Meanin'?"

"Luke. Luke the physician."

"Never thought on thet before. Guess we did name 'im well, didn't we?"

Belinda lifted her head and reached for Clark's nose with her wet little hand. He chuckled and adjusted her to better see her in the light.

"I'm afraid yer goin' to spoil her with all yer fussin'," scolded Marty.

"Spoil her?"

"She gits held an' rocked an' cuddled so much she'll git to think thet it's all thet her pa's got to do."

"I did it with all the others, too, an' you yerself just agreed there ain't a bad one in the whole bunch," Clark reminded her.

Marty smiled. It was true. He had given a lot of love and attention to each one of the babies.

Clark turned serious. "What did we do right, Marty?"

"Is it important?"

"I think so. We've got Belinda here. We can't afford to go wrong on this one, Marty." Clark kissed his baby on her forehead.

Marty thought in silence for a moment. "Fact is," she finally said, "I don't rightly know what we did right. We made mistakes—I know I did. Lots of 'em. God knows we tried to do what was right. Maybe thet's what He honored—our tryin'."

"Lots of parents try . . . an' fail," Clark reminded her.

It was a sobering thought and one that Marty knew was true.

"We need faith, Clark," she said softly. "We need to really hang on in faith. God didn't fail us before—we need to trust 'im with Belinda, too."

"Trust 'im," echoed Clark. "Trust God—an' work an' spank an' train an' pray like we had it all to do on our own."

"Guess it all has somethin' to do with thet legacy ya were talkin' 'bout. So much depends upon what we leave our children—not *to* 'em, but *within* 'em."

"Wish it was as simple as passin' on the family heirlooms."

"Meanin'?"

"Ya don't just pass on faith. Ya have to pass on a desire fer 'em to find a faith of their own. Ya have to show 'em daily in the way ya live thet what ya have is worth livin' an' fightin' an' workin' fer. A secondhand faith is no good to anyone. It has to be a faith of their own."

"Thet's the secret," Marty agreed with feeling. "A faith of their own. I am so thankful to God thet each one of our children made their own decision to let God be in charge in their life."

"An' it doesn't stop there—it goes on an' on. They teach an' train our grandchildren, an' with God's help, they can teach our great-grand-children. It can go on an' on, an' never end till Jesus comes back," added Clark.

Marty smiled. "It's a mighty big thought," she said. She reached out a hand to touch the head of the baby Clark was holding. Their baby. "An' to think it all starts with a little bundle thet God himself dares to trust us with."

"No," said Clark, and his words were carefully weighed. "It starts long 'fore thet. It starts with a Father who loved us enough to send His Son. It starts with a man an' a woman determined to follow His ways. It starts when two people are willin' to give a child back to the Lord. It starts with all thet—but there never needs to be an end to it. It's the kind of legacy thet truly lasts."

LOVE'S UNFOLDING DREAM

*Dedicated with love and deep respect
to the memory of
three wonderful fathers—
Frederick George Steeves,
the daddy I have loved from infancy on;
John Gifford Steeves,
the uncle who was like a father to me;
Harold Edward Oke,
my kind and loving father through marriage.*

The Davis Family

The Davis family has grown in size and maturity over the years. You may need a bit of help to keep them all straight:

Clark and Marty each lost the first partner in marriage and joined together to form a new family unit.

Nandry, their foster daughter, married Josh Coffins. Their children are Tina, Andrew, Mary, and Jane.

Clae, the Davis' second foster daughter and sister to Nandry, married a pastor, Joe Berwick. Their children are Esther Sue, Joey, and Paul.

Missie, Clark's daughter from his first marriage, married Willie La-Haye, and they moved out west. Their children are Nathan, Josiah, Melissa Joy, and Julia.

Clare, Marty's son from her first marriage, married Kate, and their children are Amy Jo, Dan, David, and Dack.

Arnie, Clark and Marty's first son from their marriage, married Anne. Their children are Silas, John, and Abe.

Ellie, Clark and Marty's second child, married Lane Howard. Their children are Brenda and twins, William and Willis.

Luke, Arnie and Ellie's brother, married Abbie. Their children are Thomas and Aaron.

Belinda is Clark and Marty's youngest child.

ONE

Belinda

"Mama! Look!"

At the cry from her youngest, Marty turned quickly from the biscuits she was shaping toward the kitchen doorway. She knew by the tone of her daughter's voice that there was some kind of trouble—Belinda's cry trembled in the air between them as she stood before her mother. A chill gripped Marty's heart. *What is wrong? Is Belinda hurt?*

Her eyes quickly traveled over the slight body of young Belinda, expecting to see blood someplace. Belinda's dress, which had been clean and neatly pressed when she had gone out just a short time before, was rumpled and dirty. One of her long, carefully plaited braids had come loose from its ribbon and hung in disarray about her shoulders. Her face was smudged and tear-streaked. But to her mother's practiced eye, she seemed whole and unharmed. Marty, unconscious of the small sigh of relief that escaped her, gazed into the blue, troubled, and tear-filled eyes.

"Look!" Belinda cried again in a choked voice.

Marty's eyes went to Belinda's outstretched hand. In it lay a small sparrow, its feathers ruffled and wet, its head dipping awkwardly to the side. Even as Marty watched, she saw the small body quiver, and Marty shivered in sympathy.

Why Belinda? mourned the mother-heart. *Why did she of all people have to find the bird?* Marty knew the tender heart of her daughter. She would sorrow over the bird all day long.

Marty wiped floury hands on her apron and reached out to draw Belinda close. She made no comment on the dirty dress or the messy hair.

"Where did ya find 'im?" she asked instead, her voice full of sympathy.

"The mother cat had it!" Belinda wailed. "I had to chase her all over the barn and then . . . then . . ."

She could not go on. Tears fell uncontrollably, and the small girl buried her head against Marty and let the sobs shake her.

Marty just held her until the crying subsided. Then Belinda turned those large blue eyes to her mother's face.

"It's gonna die, isn't it?" she quavered. She looked back at the tiny bird still held carefully in her hand.

"Well, I . . . I don't know," stammered Marty and took another look at the injured bird. Yes . . . it would die. Barring a miracle, it would die. But it was difficult for her to say those words to Belinda. Besides, she had seen miracles before. *Oh, God,* she inwardly prayed, *I know it's jest a sparrow, but ya said that ya see each sparrow thet falls. If yer heart is as heavy as Belinda's over this one, then could ya please make it well again?*

"We need to make it warm," Belinda was saying hopefully.

"There's an empty basket on my closet shelf. I'll get a flannel rag from the ragbag," Marty responded.

Belinda hurried off to get the little basket, and Marty went to her pantry, where she kept the supply of old garments and sheets for cleaning purposes. She found a soft piece of flannel and returned to the kitchen just as Belinda ran back into the room.

Together they made a warm bed, and Belinda carefully deposited the tiny bird. It was in even worse shape than Marty had feared. Its little head flopped uncontrollably as it was moved, and except for a slight tremble, there was little sign of life. Belinda's tears began to flow again.

"Can we take it to Luke?" she pleaded.

Oh my, thought Marty. *A trip to town for a dying sparrow.* How many of Belinda's casualties had Luke doctored over the years? Yet he was always so patient, doing all in his power to save each tiny animal. *But this one . . . this one is beyond his help,* Marty was sure. But she didn't say so to Belinda. Instead, she said, "We'll ask yer pa. He'll be in soon."

Marty's attention returned to her biscuits. Clark *would* be in soon, and he'd be hungry and looking for his supper. She went to wash her hands so she could get the biscuits into the oven.

Belinda took the basket with its injured sparrow and settled into her favorite corner by the kitchen stove. Marty noticed the little girl's tears had stopped, but her eyes were still red and shadowed with the horror of it all. *Why do cats have to kill birds?* Marty wondered silently as she slid the biscuits into the oven. She knew it was a foolish question, but her heart ached over her daughter's sorrow. Actually, Marty knew Belinda loved the farmyard cats, too. She would have fought just as hard to save the life of one of them—and had at times, along with big brother Luke's help. But they did insist on hunting the little birds.

"It just isn't fair, Ma!" Belinda's voice burst out as her finger gently traced the curve of the feathers on the small body. It no longer even trembled.

The outer door opened and banged shut, and Marty knew before she heard the voice that Clare and Kate's oldest child was on her way in.

"Gramma?" Amy Jo called before she even entered the kitchen. "Gramma, do you know where Lindy is?"

Amy Jo was the only one who called Belinda "Lindy." In fact, Marty was quite sure Amy Jo was the only one who could have gotten away with it. Belinda was always very careful to pronounce her own name in full, but the laughing, teasing Amy Jo disregarded such personal preferences and called Belinda after her own whim.

"She's right there by the stove," answered Marty without turning from the pot she was stirring.

Marty could hear little gasps for breath as Amy Jo entered the room. She had been running again, but Amy Jo always ran.

"Do you want . . . ?" began Amy Jo as she approached Belinda's favorite corner. Then she hesitated. "What'cha got now?" she asked without too much interest. "Another mouse?"

"It's a bird," replied Belinda, her voice taut with sorrow.

"What happened?"

"The mother cat."

"Is it hurt bad?"

"Real bad."

"How come ya didn't take it to Uncle Luke?" Amy Jo was well aware of the usual procedure when Belinda found an injured creature.

"We're waitin' for Pa."

Belinda moved her hand slightly so Amy Jo could get a look at her newest casualty. For a moment Amy Jo's violet eyes widened with dismay. It was so tiny, so helpless, so . . . so crumpled.

"I . . . I think it's already dead," she whispered, now in genuine sympathy.

Belinda was about to burst into tears again when the small bird shuddered once more.

"Is not," she argued fervently. "See!"

Marty checked on the biscuits in the oven, disturbed Belinda and her precious burden for a moment to add more wood to the fire, then turned back to set the table just as the farm dog announced that Clark was on his way in. Marty's eyes swung to the clock on the shelf. She was behind schedule, but Clark was a bit earlier than she had expected.

"Grandpa," Amy Jo called to Clark from the door, but before he could even greet her, she burst out, "Lindy's got a hurt thing again."

Concern was evident in Clark's expression as he entered the room. His gaze traveled quickly over the kitchen to the young girl crouched in her corner by the stove, holding the basket tightly in her hands. His eyes went on to meet Marty's. *What now?* he silently asked. *Is it serious?* And Marty answered with just a slight movement of her head back and forth. *It won't make it. It's hurt bad.*

At the sight of her father, Belinda's eyes had filled with tears again. "It's a sparrow, Pa," she answered his unasked question. "The mother cat had 'im."

Belinda's disheveled appearance made clear she'd had quite a chase to retrieve the small bird, which no doubt told Clark as well as anything

230

what shape the bird must be in. He hung his jacket on the hook and crossed to the two girls crouching over the basket.

Clark began to reach for the bird, but he stopped and said instead in a soft voice, "It's hurt real bad, ain't it?"

Clark's hand changed directions and went instead to their youngest daughter. He smoothed her tangled hair, then gently brushed a smudge of dust from her cheek.

"I dunno," he said hesitantly. "I think anything thet we try to do fer this little bird will only bring it more pain."

Fresh tears began to course down Belinda's cheeks. "But Luke—"

"Yer brother would do all he could—you know thet an' I know thet."

The door banged open again. This time Dan, another of Clare's children, burst into the house. He was breathing hard from running and called before he was even into the kitchen, "Amy! Ma wants ya home. It's suppertime."

Amy Jo stood slowly to her feet, obviously loathe to leave the little drama and probably hoping that if a quick trip were to be made to Dr. Luke's office, she would be asked to go along.

"Are ya goin' to town, Grandpa?" she asked quickly.

Clark shook his head. "I don't rightly know. We'll need to talk 'bout it. I'm afraid . . ."

"What's wrong?" asked Dan, who had by now crossed to squat beside his grandfather and peer into the small basket.

"Oh! A dead bird," he said, not waiting for an answer.

"It's not dead," cried Belinda. "It's just hurt."

Dan's eyes moved from Belinda's face to Clark's. Had he said something wrong? Was the bird . . . ?

Clark reached out a hand and laid it on the boy's shoulder.

"It's hurt pretty bad," he said, "but it's still hangin' on."

Marty checked her biscuits, which were browning nicely. Supper would soon be ready, yet she could hardly get near her stove. Four people huddled there—all in sympathy over the injured sparrow. Marty felt sympathy herself. She did not like to see a small creature hurt and suffering. But it was, after all, the way of nature. Animals killed and were killed. It was a fact of life. Nature's food chain required it. *The mother cat has babies to feed,* Marty reminded herself. *She needs—*

But any further thoughts on the matter were interrupted.

"Are ya gonna take it to Uncle Luke?" asked Dan, his eyes round and questioning.

Clark slowly shook his head, but before he could speak, Dan commented, "Bet he could fix it."

"Yer uncle Luke is a good doctor, I'm not denyin' thet none," said Clark in a low voice, "but even good doctors have their limits. This here little bird is hurt bad. I don't think—"

"Luke says thet ya never, never give up," broke in Belinda passionately. "He says as long as there's still life, then ya fight to save it."

"To be sure," agreed Clark. "To be sure."

"Then we can go?" pleaded Belinda.

Across the heads of the youngsters, Clark's eyes met Marty's.

Surely yer not gonna . . . ? Marty's expression asked, but Clark's shoulders shrugged slightly. *What else can I do?*

Marty looked at her husband—weary, she knew, after spending a full day in the fields. True, it was easier for him now, easier with the artificial limb Luke had insisted on getting for him. But even so, planting was hard work for any man. He still had chores ahead of him, and here he was about to make a trip into town for a dying sparrow. It made no sense—no sense at all.

Marty looked back at Belinda. Surely the youngster should be able to understand reason. A girl of eleven should know by now that nature provided for its own by allowing death. But no—Belinda didn't understand. She fought death with every ounce in her tiny body, and her main ally was her older brother Luke—Luke the doctor, Luke the compassionate. Luke fought death, too. If anyone would understand a trip to town to save a sparrow, it would be Luke.

"I'll git the team," Clark was saying.

"But . . . but yer supper," put in Marty. "Yer—"

"It'll wait," answered Clark, and his eyes asked Marty to understand.

She did understand. It was not for the small bird that Clark would take the trip to town. It was for the child whose heart was breaking.

"I'm sorry . . . sorry to make ya the extry work," Clark murmured. "Don't fuss none. I'll help myself when I git back."

It wasn't the work that concerned Marty. It was Clark. He needed supper. He needed the rest. And yet—

Once again the door banged opened and four-year-old Dack bustled into the kitchen, his red hair bright and standing in disarray as usual. He was the youngest member of Clare's household and a favorite with everyone. His chubby, freckled face crinkled into a big grin as he spied his grandfather shrugging into the jacket he had removed just a short time before.

Dack's round little arms wrapped around the legs of the tall man, and he grinned impishly up at him. One small fist began pounding on Clark's leg.

"Knock, knock!" he cried playfully. "Knock, knock on wood."

Clark could not resist the small boy. He reached down and lifted him up into his arms.

"Who's knockin' on my wood?" With mock seriousness he asked the question expected of him in their little game.

"It's me. It's Dack," he announced gleefully.

"Dack *who*?" his grandfather responded next, on cue.

The little boy paused a moment to get the words right. "Dack be nimble, Dack be quick, Dack . . . Dack jumped over the candlestick!" he finished in a triumphant shout.

They both laughed together as Dack's pudgy arms squeezed Clark's neck.

"And what is Dack doin' at my house?" inquired Clark.

Dack's eyes immediately turned serious. He squirmed to get down. "Mama sent me," he said. "I'm 'posta git Amy an' Dan fer supper."

Clark looked at the two, who were still peering into Belinda's basket.

"You'd better all git," he said. "Iffen yer pa has to come fetch the three of ya, he might not be too happy."

The three "got"—Amy Jo, taking the hand of her little brother after one last glance at her grandpa in case she might be invited to go along.

Clark turned back to Belinda. "I'll be ready in a minute," he informed her. "Better grab a coat." Then he was gone.

With a sigh, Marty turned to remove the biscuits from the oven. They were crispy brown and piping hot, just the way Clark loved them. But Clark wouldn't be eating them the way he liked them. By the time he returned, the biscuits would be cold.

Just as Marty finished taking the biscuits from the pan, Belinda gave a little cry. Marty whirled to see what new calamity had befallen.

"I think it's already dead," she said in a sobbing whisper. "Look! It's gittin' stiff."

Marty looked. Belinda was right. The sparrow was already past the help of even Dr. Luke.

Belinda burst into fresh tears, and Marty put her arms around her to comfort her.

"I need to catch yer pa before he hooks up the team," she murmured, more to herself than to the weeping girl, but grief-stricken Belinda nodded her head.

Marty took the nod as consent and hurried to the barn for Clark, sighing deeply as she walked. She was glad Clark was spared the trip to town. She was glad the injured little bird was no longer in pain. But she was sorry that Belinda had to suffer so deeply every time some little creature suffered. It was good and noble for her daughter to be compassionate—but Belinda really took it too far. In many ways she was so much like her big brother Luke. So much! Yet she was even more tenderhearted than Luke. *Life is going to be so painful for Belinda,* Marty lamented. How many hurts—deep hurts—lay down the road for their youngest child? She trembled at the thought.

Clark was just leading the first horse from the stall.

"It's too late," said Marty. "The bird's already dead. Ya can have yer supper now."

Concern rather than the relief one could have expected was in Clark's face.

"She'll git over it," Marty assured him. "She'll cry for a while. Then she'll have her little buryin' and put the sparrow to rest in the garden with her other little creatures. By tomorra she'll be herself again."

They both knew the truth of it. Belinda would feel the pain of the loss for a time, but she would soon bounce back. They had seen it happen before. While Marty returned to the house, Clark took King back to his stall, the horse no doubt relieved that his supper would not be delayed either.

As Clark removed the harness, hung it on the peg and started for the house, he realized just how hungry and tired he was. But his walk was even and steady with hardly the trace of a limp. Again, Clark had a moment of thankfulness for the wooden limb that functioned almost as well as his own leg had. It was good to have his hands free. It was good to be able to throw aside his crutch. But he did get weary and sore. Right now the whole side of his body protested against the pressure of the artificial limb against the stub of leg remaining. He was anxious to take it off and stand it in a corner for the night.

But he wouldn't—not for a while. He still had chores to do. He wouldn't remove it even when the chores were all done. He knew Marty watched him carefully for signs of pain or weariness. To remove the leg before bedtime would tell Marty he was in pain. Marty worried enough about his well-being without adding this to her concern. He'd rest the leg a bit while he had his supper. By the time he went to chore, perhaps it would be feeling better.

Clark sure was glad he would not have to make the long trip into town—with a sparrow. He smiled slightly as he thought of the many times he had wished he could rid the whole world of sparrows. Such pesky little nuisances they were, even when Belinda wasn't fussing over one! And yet . . . they were God's creatures, too, and Clark would have cheerfully aided Belinda in the fight to save one little life.

TWO

Dr. Luke

Just as Clark and Marty predicted, Belinda grieved over the dead sparrow, carefully made and lined a small box for it to be buried in, called on Amy Jo and the three boys to join her in the little ceremony after supper, and wept as the small bird joined a number of other small graves at the far end of the garden. Then it was over and the girl's thoughts returned to childhood play. The Saturday evening hours ended with a boisterous game of tag, in which all five children joined.

Marty drew a sigh of relief as she threw the dishwater on her rosebush by the door. Belinda was usually a happy, well-adjusted child. *If only she did not grieve so when she found little creatures dead or dying,* Marty lamented for the umpteenth time. She did hope Belinda eventually would learn to face the realities of life with a bit less emotional turmoil. No one approved of suffering. But some pain was inevitable.

Clark came toward the house, the pail he carried brimming with white foaming milk.

"She looks fine now," he stated, nodding his head slightly in Belinda's direction with a look of relief.

"Oh, she usually comes out of it fairly soon—but, my, what a storm of tears in the meantime," responded Marty as they entered the house together.

"Guess I'd rather have her on the tender side than calloused an' uncarin'," Clark commented, but Marty shook her head and sighed. More than once she had found Belinda's tender heart a very difficult characteristic with which to deal.

"She'll grow out of it as she gets older," Clark comforted. "Jest hope she doesn't go off to the other extreme."

Marty could not imagine Belinda changing that much. "Don't think there be much danger of thet," she assured her husband.

"Jest pray all thet compassion gits put to proper use like," said Clark. "God must have Him a special place fer someone like our Belinda."

Marty thought about Clark's comment as she poured the milk through the strainer and set out the container for the cream. Clark began to turn the handle of the separator, and Marty stood and listened to the gentle hum. Soon Clark had reached the proper speed and turned the spigot to let the white milk pour into the whirling bowl of the machine. From the left-hand spout, the milk began to stream, and soon a smaller, richer cascade of cream descended from the right spout to splatter into the cream crock.

"She's so much like Luke," ventured Marty, picking up the conversation where they had left it minutes before.

Clark nodded. "Or Arnie," he said. "Arnie's 'bout as tender as a man could be."

It was Marty's turn to nod. Arnie *was* tender. He could not bear to see anyone or anything in pain. But Arnie would not openly weep as Belinda did. He would just withdraw, his eyes mirroring his troubled soul whenever he ran across nature's sorrows.

"Poor Arnie," said Marty. "Maybe it's easier for Belinda. At least she can cry when she's hurtin'. The boys, 'specially Arnie, always tried not to cry."

"Funny where they got thet idea," returned Clark. "I never told 'em thet boys aren't to cry."

"Nor me. Guess they pick up some of those things at school. Kids can be heartless with one another."

The milk and cream continued to stream from the separator spouts.
"Funny!" mused Marty. "They are so much alike—an' yet different."
"Like how?"

"Well, Luke is carin' and compassionate, all right, but he . . . he
don't hide from pain none. He gits in there an' fights it. He sure enough
had the right makin's fer a doctor. Arnie, now—he coulda never been
a doctor. Couldn't stand even to be around pain. He'd pull away, I'm
a thinkin'."

Clark appeared to be considering Marty's comment. "I think yer
right," he finally said somberly. "Arnie woulda had a hard time bein' a
doctor all right. He's much better at jest bein' a pa."

Marty smiled. Arnie was truly a good pa. They had wondered at
first if he might spoil his youngsters, but Arnie seemed to know better
than that. Even though it was hard for him, he did discipline and did
it consistently.

It was a good thing Arnie took care of the disciplining. He had three
very rambunctious young sons who needed the strong and steady influ-
ence of a father. Their mother, tiny Anne, was hard pressed to keep
up with them. Marty smiled as she thought of the trio. Silas was Amy
Jo's age. The two of them had been born only four days apart and,
having celebrated their tenth birthday, were not quite a year younger
than Belinda.

The next son was John. He was now seven and in second grade already. Abe, the youngest, was still home but chafing to be off to school
like his big brothers. Anne had all she could do to keep the young boy
busy. He insisted that he learn to read so he wouldn't be left out when
his older brothers had their noses buried in books. Anne had felt that
teaching was the duty of the schoolmarm, but with Abe continually
pestering her, she finally gave in and taught the small boy his letters.
Now the older boys were bringing home storybooks so young Abe
could read, as well.

Marty's thoughts were interrupted by the sound of running feet.
David, Clare's third child, burst into the back entry, his eyes shining,
his cheeks flushed from running.

"Hide me. Hide me, Gramma!" he cried excitedly.

"Whoa," said Clark, who had just finished the separating. "Thought the rule was no hidin' in the house."

David stopped short and dropped his eyes to the floor. He knew the rule. He stood quietly for a moment and then looked up, an irrepressible sparkle in his teasing eyes. "Then hide me outside—will ya, Grandpa?"

Clark laughed. "Now, where would I hide ya?" he asked the small boy.

"I dunno. But you have lots of good ideas. 'Member?"

It had been a while since the children had talked Clark into joining them in their game.

"Please," coaxed Davey.

Clark looked at Marty and laughed again. She knew he had been hoping to head for his favorite chair, prop up his leg, and bury his face in a favorite book. Instead, he took Davey by the hand.

"Who's 'it'?" he asked.

"Dan. An' he really looks hard," warned Davey in a theatrical whisper.

"Has anyone tried the rhubarb patch?" Clark asked him, matching his tone and volume.

Davey shook his head, his eyes shining with glee as he acknowledged the potential of the large rhubarb leaves.

"Then how 'bout we try it?" asked Clark as the two left the house.

Marty finished up her evening duties and set out the cream and milk to cool.

She gave one last wipe to the table and had scarcely turned around when she heard the dog barking. They had not been expecting company. It was getting on toward dark. *Who's coming at this hour?* she wondered as she peered out the window.

Through the evening gloom, she immediately recognized the horse at the hitching rail. Luke's black doctor's bag hung from the horn of the saddle. The noise in the yard quickly changed from cries of "One, two, three," or "Home free!" to shouts of "Uncle Luke!" Marty went to the door to add her welcome.

Belinda had already claimed Luke's attention, pouring out her sad story about the sparrow and its untimely death. Luke hunched down in front of her to listen attentively.

"An' if you woulda been here, it might not have died," Belinda finished, just a hint of reproach in her voice.

Luke did not say, as he could have, that he had more important things to be doing. He did not even excuse himself with the fact that he had no way of knowing about the bird. Instead, he laid a gentle hand on Belinda's shoulder. "I'm sorry," he said. "I'm sorry I didn't come sooner."

From the expression on her big brother's face, Belinda would know he meant it. Though still a child, she also knew Luke should not have to feel guilty that he wasn't there when he was needed.

Looking as though she might begin to cry once more, she swallowed her tears and reached out for Luke's hand.

"It's okay," she comforted. "Ya didn't know. It was hurt pretty bad an' maybe . . ." She let the sentence remain unfinished and brushed at her wet eyes.

"What brings ya out this way?" asked Clark as Marty joined them at the front gate.

"Baby Graham just arrived," announced Luke with a grin.

"Oh!" exclaimed Marty, her eyes shining. "Lou's? What is it?"

"Another girl."

"My land! That makes 'im five girls now." Marty laughed. "Ma was a hopin' fer a boy this time. Her with all those granddaughters and us with all the grandsons! Seems it should even out like."

"Well, when I left, Ma Graham was busy fussing over that girl like it was the only thing she ever wanted," said Luke. "If she was disappointed, I sure didn't see it."

"'Course!" responded Marty. "'Course she would. Jest like I fuss over each new grandson. I am sure glad I've got Amy Jo close by, though."

Just then Kate's voice drifted over the farmyard. "Amy Jo, bring the boys in now. It's time ya be gittin' ready for bed."

Marty saw the disappointed looks on four small faces, but they moved to obey their mother.

Luke reached out a hand to rumple the hair of young Dack as he passed.

"We'll see you tomorrow. Remember. You are all coming for dinner after church."

The frown turned to a grin, and young Dack skipped ahead to join his older brothers and sister.

"Can ya stop in fer coffee?" asked Marty of their youngest son.

Luke grinned. "Thought you'd never ask," he quipped, flipping the reins of his horse over the hitching rail. "It's been a long day. I thought that baby was never going to make an appearance. Guess she just wanted to keep us all in suspense as long as she could."

Marty led the way back in and placed the coffeepot on the stove. When she had cut some slices of pumpkin bread and placed them on the table, Luke didn't even wait for the coffee but reached out to help himself.

"You ought to teach Abbie how to make this," he said around the mouthful.

Marty smiled, thinking of the wife Luke had brought back with him from the East, where he had trained as a doctor. Abbie was a dear girl with a heart as big as Luke's, but she had not had the advantage of knowing how to make good use of garden produce. She had been raised in a city, where a garden other than flowers was unfamiliar. But she was trying. She had her own vegetable garden now. She loved to watch things grow and was learning how to use all its produce.

"She's welcome to the recipe," responded Marty with a pat on Luke's shoulder as she went for the coffee. A secret smile creased her face as she remembered her own early culinary efforts as Clark's new wife.

Luke pulled a small book from his pocket and began to pencil in an entry. "That's thirty-seven," he said.

"Thirty-seven what?" Belinda piped up from her perch on the woodbox.

"Thirty-seven babies. Thirty-seven that I have delivered since becoming a doctor."

"Thet's quite a number," remarked Marty.

"It's been almost seven years already. Seven years! Just think of it."

"It's hard to believe," said Clark. "Seems ya jest got yerself back."

"Deliverin' babies must be 'bout the nicest part of yer work," Marty commented as she poured the coffee.

"It's exciting, all right—but I like the rest of it, too. I think I'd soon get weary of just waiting on little ones to decide it's the right time."

"Do you like makin' stitches?" asked Belinda. Her question reminded Marty that the young girl should be getting ready for bed.

"Belinda, ya hurry an' wash fer bed now. It's already past yer bed-time," she chided mildly.

Belinda no doubt wished she had kept quiet—maybe her mother wouldn't have noticed her. She looked as if she was about to argue when she caught her father's eye. It told her plainly that she was not to question her mother. Reluctantly she rose to do as she was bidden.

"As soon as you're ready, I'll tuck you in," Luke called after her, and she cheerfully rushed out to do her washing up.

True to his word, after another piece of pumpkin bread, Luke went to tuck Belinda in. He felt a special closeness to his little sister. He remembered he had looked forward for a long time to having a family member younger than himself. Belinda was special to him in another way, as well. Luke could already sense in her a kindred spirit. Belinda loved to nurse things back to health.

He smoothed back her hair with a hand still smelling of medicine. Belinda told him she loved the doctor smells. She turned her face slightly toward the hand and breathed more deeply.

"Do you like makin' stitches?" she repeated the question that had gotten her noticed in the kitchen.

"Sure. Sure I do. I'm sorry that folks need stitches—but I'm glad I know how to sew them up properly."

Belinda's eyes shone. "I would, too," she confided.

Luke brushed back the wispy gold hair that curled around her face.

"I wish I was a boy," sighed Belinda.

"A boy?" There had been a time when Luke had hoped Belinda would be a boy. Now he wondered why. This dear little sister was one of the most special people in his world.

"Why?" he asked. "Why a boy?"

"Then I could be a doctor," answered Belinda. She sighed more deeply and looked into Luke's eyes. "Iffen I was a doctor," she said, "I'd never have to wait for someone else to come. I could help things myself."

"Like the little bird?" asked Luke softly.

Belinda just nodded, her eyes looking troubled again.

"You don't need to be a doctor to learn to help things," Luke assured her. "You could be a nurse."

"Could I?" breathed Belinda, her eyes wide and shining at the thought.

"Of course."

Belinda smiled—then a dark frown replaced the happiness on her face.

"It'd never work," she said mournfully. "Mama would never let me go way back east to learn how to be a nurse."

Luke hoped he could keep the amusement from showing on his face. "Maybe not," he said evenly. "Maybe not—at least not now. Mama didn't want me to go away when I was eleven, either. I had to do some growing up first."

"But . . . but . . ." began Belinda, and Luke interrupted her.

"It's hard to wait to grow up, isn't it?"

Belinda nodded solemnly.

"That's what I used to think. That's why I tagged along with Dr. Watkins. I wanted to learn all I could—as fast as I could."

The disappointment did not leave Belinda's eyes. "But Dr. Watkins is dead now," she said.

A stab of pain went through Luke as he thought of the kind doctor. He had died only two years after Luke took over the practice. The doctor had been out fishing all alone, and Luke often wondered if he could have been saved if only someone had been with him at the time. But all of Luke's *if onlys* could not bring their dear doctor back.

He shifted his eyes to Belinda's face. "Well, *I'm* here," he stated simply.

She stared at him for a while. "Would you teach me?" she ventured.

"Why not? I think you'd make a good nurse. If you work hard and—"

"Oh, I will. I will. I promise!" she exclaimed, sitting up to throw her arms around her brother.

Luke tweaked the soft cheek, then kissed his sister's forehead.

"Then you'd best get some sleep," he said. "Being a nurse is awfully hard work. You'll need your rest."

Belinda held him close for a minute.

"Thank you, Luke," she whispered.

"Sure," he responded and kissed her again before tucking the blankets under her chin.

Luke joined his parents again in the big farm kitchen, and his mother poured one more cup of coffee for him.

Luke stretched his legs wearily.

"So you had you quite a time with Belinda today?" he asked.

"She sure made a fuss all right," responded Marty. "Yer poor pa was 'bout to head fer town without even havin' him some supper."

Luke looked at his father and grinned. "Didn't know you felt so strongly about sparrows," he joked. "Seems to me I remember you destroying a nest or two when I was a kid."

Clark ran a hand through his thick hair, then smiled a bit shamefacedly at his son. "Ya won't go mentionin' that to Belinda, now, will ya?" After Luke laughed, Clark said, "Ya think I spoil 'er?"

Luke sobered and looked at his father. "I didn't say that," he said slowly. Then he added with his own look of embarrassment, "If you'd brought her in, you know who would have been looking up medicine for 'bird shock' and fighting to save that little birdie's life."

They all laughed.

Marty looked at her son and said solemnly, "I worry 'bout her, Luke. She is so tenderhearted I fear lest she won't be able to cope with the world out there, with life and death. She grieves so when anything is in pain."

Luke was silent for many moments.

"She wants to be a nurse," he finally said slowly.

Marty's eyes were wide as she gasped, "Belinda? Why, it would kill 'er! She would never be able to stand seein' folks who were hurt and in pain."

"Did ya talk about it with her—discourage her somehow?" asked Clark.

"Me?" responded Luke and shuffled about uncomfortably. "Well, no . . . not really. Fact is, I . . . I . . . well, I promised to help her."

Both his parents looked at Luke as if he had lost his senses.

"But . . . but, she'll never be able to—"

"It'll break her heart fer sure."

"Maybe not," stated Luke. "I know she can't face the suffering of any little creature now. But maybe—just maybe—learning to do something about the suffering is just what she needs. Don't you see? If she feels she is actually helping those who suffer, then she might make a good nurse. A great nurse! She'll try . . . she'll really try hard. . . ."

Luke let the thought drift away, carefully watching the eyes of his mother and father as he spoke.

Marty shook her head and reached for her coffee cup, toying with the handle. Clark unconsciously began to rub his aching leg.

"I'd like to take her with me on some of my house calls," said Luke matter-of-factly.

Two heads jerked up. Two pairs of eyes fastened on Luke's face to see if he was serious. No one spoke.

"That okay?" questioned Luke.

There was silence as Clark and Marty exchanged unspoken messages. "Well?" Luke pressed.

Clark straightened in his chair. He cleared his throat and looked again at Marty.

"Sure," he began slowly. "Sure . . . when the time comes . . ."

"Pa," Luke cut in. "Pa, I think the time has come."

"But she's jest a child! Only eleven," Marty exclaimed.

Luke paused a moment, then said, "I knew when I was eleven. I knew." His quiet voice had gotten their full attention.

Marty finally said, "It's just so sudden. It jest . . . well . . . we haven't had us time to think on it . . . to pray. How 'bout we talk it over some?"

Luke placed his cup back on the table and rose to his feet.

"Sure," he said, smiling. "Sure. You think about it, talk it over, pray. I think Belinda and I can wait for that."

Clark rose from the table, too.

"I best be running along," said Luke. "Abbie will want to know all about that new Graham baby."

He leaned over to kiss Marty on the cheek, then reached for his coat.

"Don't worry, Ma," he said. "She's still a little girl. She won't be leaving you for a long time yet. And we won't push. If it's not right for Belinda—why, we'll steer her in another direction."

Marty smiled weakly at Luke. She patted his hand as if to say there was no one else she would even consider entrusting their Belinda's future to, and he squeezed back with the unspoken message that he understood.

THREE

Sunday

In spite of her resolve to pray rather than to worry, Marty awoke the next morning still troubled. If only they could be sure they were doing the right thing. Was Belinda really cut out to be a nurse? Could she even know at age eleven? Was she ready to go with Luke on house calls? It was true that Luke had started accompanying Dr. Watkins when he was very young—but Luke had been older than eleven.

Belinda had no such doubts.

"Guess what?" she informed them proudly at the breakfast table. "Luke says I can go with him when he goes out to take care of sick people."

Marty looked at Clark. They had talked long into the night about Luke's suggestion. She wasn't sure if they were ready yet to allow Belinda this experience, but they finally had agreed that if this was what Belinda really wanted, they would not refuse their permission.

"Are ya sure ya wanna go?" asked Clark.

It was a needless question. Belinda's eyes fairly glowed with anticipation.

"Can I?" she pleaded.

"Yer ma and me are talkin' it over," answered Clark.

"Why do you want to do this?" asked Marty softly.

Belinda looked puzzled by the question. She seemed to feel her mother should understand without it being explained.

"Why?" repeated Marty. "Ya know Luke sees some pretty bad things at times. People really sick. Some hurt bad. You're wantin' ta see thet?"

Belinda grimaced and looked rather sober.

"'Member the little bird," Marty continued. "It was limp and suffering. Well, sometimes hurt people look thet bad, too. Do ya really think ya can stand to see people hurt like thet?"

It was a fair question, and Belinda's expression indicated she knew it. Her face went pale, and she was quiet for a while. "I'll hate that," she answered honestly. "I know I'll hate that part of it. But someone has to be there to help 'em git better. That's what Luke does. But sometimes he needs help. He doesn't have a nurse to help him. I could be a nurse. I could hand 'im things an' help 'im sew up people an'—"

"All right," said Marty with a nod of her head. "Iffen ya really want to. I . . . I guess I thought ya might like to be a schoolteacher like Clae or Missie, but iffen yer really sure . . ."

Belinda's face was still white, but she shook her head solemnly. "I'm sure," she said. Then for a moment she looked doubtful. "I *think* I'm sure." She hesitated before she spoke again. "I'll never know unless I try, will I?"

Clark nodded. "Guess not," he said. "But we don't believe us none in rushin' in, either. Yer awful young to be thinkin' on nursin'. Yer ma and me will give it some more thought."

Belinda's nod indicated she understood that for now the matter was to be dropped.

Following the Sunday morning service, they all went to Luke and Abbie's for dinner as planned. The various family members shared in providing the food. There were too many of them to be expecting one woman to do all the work.

Tables were set up under a large maple tree in the backyard, and dishes of summer foods began to pile up on them as the teams brought each family from church.

The cousins had a delightful day. There were enough of them to form several games when they all got together, and they began to sort themselves out according to ages and likes and to gather in various spots in the yard for some good, clean Sunday afternoon fun.

Nandry's children were the oldest, but not all of them were there that day. Tina was already married and living in a small town several miles from her parents. It was difficult for Marty to believe she actually had a married grandchild—even if that grandchild was the eldest of her foster daughter's children.

Andrew was now eighteen and working on a neighboring farm, so he did not join the family for Sunday dinner, either. Mary and Jane were both there, but they considered themselves too grown-up to join in the childish play. Instead, they busied themselves with caring for Luke's two little sons, the youngest members of the family.

A smile played on Marty's lips as her eyes traveled lovingly over the family.

Clark must have caught the look.

"What're you grinnin' at?" he asked playfully.

"Jest thinkin'," said Marty. "Look at the size of this family—an' half of 'em aren't even here. Clae an' Joe are missin', Missie an' Willie are missin', and Ellie an' Lane are missin'. What would we ever do iffen we could *all* be together?"

Clark's eyes followed her around the circle. He, too, smiled at his family.

"We'd manage," he said comfortably. "Somehow we'd manage."

Then he turned back to Marty. "How many we got, anyway?" he asked her.

Marty laughed at his sudden question.

"Ya don't even know yer own offspring," she teased.

"Jest never sat me down to count," responded Clark.

"Well, best ya sit ya down and figure it out," said Marty pertly. "Me, I'm needed in the kitchen," and so saying, she lifted the hem of her skirt and climbed the steps to Abbie's back door.

After dinner, when they were all relaxing on the back porch, Clark brought up the matter of family numbers again.

"Got it figured," he said to Marty as she lifted young Aaron onto her lap.

"Got what figured?" asked Marty.

"Our offspring. Counted up thirty-eight of 'em."

"You what?" asked Arnie, leaning forward in his chair.

"Counted up the offspring."

"Whose offspring?" Luke wanted to know.

"Our offspring. Yer mother's an' mine. Thirty-eight—thet's what I counted."

"Can't be," said Luke, disbelief in his tone.

"Figure it yerself. 'Course I counted the ones we got by adoption, by you young'uns marryin', an' by us joinin' families—the whole bunch. Anyway, we got 'em—I counted 'em."

"Thet's cheatin' a bit, ain't it?" asked Arnie with a good-natured grin.

"How so? They're all ours, ain't they?"

Dack came thundering up the steps, hooting like an Indian on the warpath. His shirttail was out, his coppery hair every which way, and his trouser knees green with grass stains.

"'Ceptin' him, now," laughed Clark, catching Dack around the waist as he ran past. "Don't know iffen I'm gonna claim me thet one."

They all joined in the hearty laughter, and Clark tossed his wild grandson up into the air and swung him in wide arcs while the little boy squealed with delight. As soon as he was placed back on the ground, a small fist reached out to pound on Clark's artificial leg.

"Knock, knock," cried Dack. "Knock on wood."

"Iffen thet boy ever gits 'im the wrong leg, Pa ain't got no one to blame but hisself," said Clare. "Thet little game of his might backfire some."

Clark had to complete the game to Dack's satisfaction.

"Who's thet knockin' on my wood?" he said, pretending to be upset, and Dack squealed again and dodged out of reach of his grandfather.

The young girls were far outnumbered when the Davis family met for Sunday dinners. Since Nandry's two older girls stayed with the women or appointed themselves babysitters for the youngest members, Belinda and Amy Jo were left to find their own amusement. Most of the time they chose to play the games the boys were playing, but on occasion the boys got too rough, and the two girls went off to find fun of their own making.

They were used to being together. They had shared the same farmyard for all of Amy Jo's days. The difference of nearly a year in age had never been a concern. Nor had the fact that they were very different in temperament. Belinda was softhearted and serious, while Amy Jo was carefree and teasing. She loved a dare, both to give and to take, plagued her mother with her carelessness, and playfully tried to outdo her father in practical jokes. Kate longed for the day when her tomboy daughter would be more ladylike, but father Clare seemed to enjoy the young girl's infectious laughter and rowdy spirit.

In spite of the personality differences, the girls got along well. It would be incorrect to say that Amy Jo was the leader and Belinda the follower, though it was Amy Jo who thought up the mischief for the two. Belinda led the way in other things—like shouldering responsibility, consideration for others, and spiritual aptitude. She often repeated spiritual or moral lessons she had learned at church or from her parents. If the little admonitions caught Amy Jo in the right frame of mind, she accepted them readily, but if she was not so inclined right then, she in turn reprimanded Belinda for "being so bossy."

But their little quarrels were always over quickly. For though Amy Jo had a shortness of patience, she also had shortness of memory, and soon she had quite forgotten what the fuss had been about. Indeed, she often seemed to forget there had been a fuss at all.

It was usually Amy Jo who suggested they desert the boys and find their own fun. Not that she didn't like the boyish games—Amy Jo had enough of the tomboy in her to enjoy most anything, but she also liked to be the leader and sometimes the boys were not too anxious to let her do the leading.

And so it was that after a few games of tag, followed by Red Rover, Amy Jo suggested to Belinda that they leave the boys to their own "silly" playing and go make some dandelion chains. Belinda was happy to comply. She had been bursting to tell her good news to somebody, and

Amy Jo was the perfect candidate. Belinda wasn't ready to share it yet with the boys. They might laugh and tease.

"Guess what," said Belinda when the two had settled themselves in the shade of the maple, laps filled with dandelion stems. "Luke's gonna take me with 'im."

"Where's he goin'?" asked Amy Jo, sounding a bit put out, probably because she hadn't been asked to share the adventure.

"No place," said Belinda, slightly miffed at Amy Jo's density.

"Then how's he gonna take ya?" countered Amy Jo with a toss of her reddish brown curls.

"Silly," said Belinda in disgust. "I mean, to make his house calls. He's gonna let me go along."

Amy Jo looked shocked rather than impressed. "Whatever for?" she questioned impatiently.

"So I can learn," declared Belinda. This conversation was not going at all as she had planned.

"Learn to what?"

"To sew up people and fix broken bones an'—"

"Yuck!" interrupted Amy Jo and stuck out her tongue.

Belinda bit her lip. She was tempted to call Amy Jo a child, then get up and move away, dandelion chains and all. Instead, she quietly began to count to ten like her father had taught her.

"Ya really wanna learn that stuff?" asked Amy Jo.

"'Course," answered Belinda, a stubborn set to her jaw.

"I wouldn't," Amy Jo shook her head confidently. "I hate blood an' messy cuts an' things. I wouldn't wanna do that at all."

"Well, someone has to do it," began Belinda, but Amy Jo cut in quickly, "Let Luke. He's the doctor. What's he makin' you do it for? He gits paid to fix people so why should . . ."

But Belinda could bear no more and closed her ears to the rest of Amy Jo's opinions on the matter. She pulled one of her golden braids and sighed deeply. Amy Jo simply did not understand. Belinda wished she had never told her precious secret. She would say no more—at least not until she could find someone who would really appreciate her wonderful opportunity.

FOUR

House Calls

Belinda was so anxious to get started on her new venture that Luke had a hard time keeping her eagerness in check. He wanted to talk once more with Clark and Marty and get their final decision. He finally found a little free time on a Saturday afternoon.

"Belinda's pushing for an answer," he said from his place at the kitchen table. "She isn't in a frame of mind to wait much longer. Have you had a chance to think and pray about this?" he asked.

Clark nodded and reached for a ginger cookie. "She can go."

"But . . . but not just anytime," Marty quickly added as she stood beside Luke pouring fresh lemonade.

"We been thinkin' ya might be able to sorta pick 'n choose the times," Clark explained. "So thet she won't be exposed to too much, too quick like."

"Exactly," agreed Luke. "Exactly my thinking. That's why I said house calls instead of working at the office. I have some idea ahead of time what I'll be finding when I make a house call. Office—well, I never know what might come in."

Marty breathed a sigh of relief.

"Truth is," Luke went on, "I'm on my way out to the Vickers' now. Their oldest son, Sam, cut himself with an axe on Wednesday. I stitched it up fer him at the office, but I said I'd stop by and see how it is doing today. Wasn't too bad a cut, but it will need the dressing changed. Can she come?"

Clark and Marty exchanged glances and the decision was made. Clark nodded their agreement.

"Good!" said Luke. He finished his cookie and reached for another.

"I'll call 'er," said Marty. "I set 'er to straightenin' fruit shelves in the cellar."

Belinda arrived in a flurry of excitement. She was ready to grab her coat and go out immediately with Luke to his buggy.

"My, my!" said Marty with a laugh. "Jest don't get ya in such a state! Ya need to change thet dirty dress and wash those hands afore yer able to go anyplace."

Belinda ran to the sink, quickly swishing water over her hands and face, then upstairs to change.

She was back in a wink, and Marty reached for the brush to straighten her tangled hair.

Belinda wriggled impatiently. "Hurry, Mama," she pleaded. "I don't want Luke to go without me."

Luke laughed. "I'll be here. Do as your mama says. We don't want you going in there all rumpled and scaring my patient, now, do we?" He rose from the table to get the pitcher for another glass of lemonade for Clark and himself.

It wasn't a long ride to the Vickers'. With Belinda on the buggy seat beside him, Luke talked to her about the case, using the proper terms and explaining about sutures, surgery, bacteria, and antiseptics. Belinda listened wide-eyed, her expression indicating how impressed she was with her big brother.

"Oh, Luke, you know so much!" she enthused. "Thanks—thanks so much for havin' this idea an' for bringin' me along."

Luke laughed and told her she probably should wait a bit with her thanks until they'd made their first call.

When they reached the Vickers', young Ezra was sent to take the doctor's horse. With black bag in one hand and Belinda by the other, Luke proceeded to the house. They were met at the door by Mrs. Vickers. She looked a bit surprised to see Belinda.

"This yer baby sister?"

Luke said that it was.

"My child, yer a growin' up. Most old enough to be of some help to yer mama," said Mrs. Vickers.

"Today she's going to be of some help to me," Luke put in with a grin in Belinda's direction. "Wants to learn about medicine."

Mrs. Vickers frowned. "A girl?" The question was full of unspoken dubiousness.

Belinda looked quickly at her brother, then said, "Lots of girls train to be nurses now. An' Luke told me we're going to need lots more of 'em in the future."

"Well, I guess yer mama knows what she's doin'," answered Mrs. Vickers, but her expression indicated that she seriously doubted it. "Never let a girl of mine be a doin' it, though." Then under her breath and with a click of her tongue, she continued, "Nursin'. Never thought I'd hear me the day."

With Luke's arm protectively across Belinda's shoulders, Mrs. Vickers led the way to the bedroom.

The bedroom needed a good airing out, and Belinda felt her stomach lurch a bit at the stale air. Her palms were sticky with sweat and her heart was hammering.

On the bed lay Sam Vickers, his leg propped up on a pillow. Beside him on the bed lay several thongs of cowhide leather. *He must be braiding a rope of some sort,* Belinda thought. He looked bored and frustrated, and Belinda could imagine he wasn't too easy a patient for his mother to care for.

"How are we doing, Sam?" greeted Luke.

Sam's answer was a scowl.

"Bed getting a little uncomfortable?" continued Luke.

"Sure is," grumbled Sam. "Never be so glad to git outta a place as I will be this here bed."

"Well, if your leg is doing okay, maybe we can get you to a chair now and then."

Sam did not look impressed. A chair probably didn't sound all that much better.

Luke opened up his black bag and took out a few items that he placed on the table by the bed.

"It been givin' you much pain?" he asked Sam.

Sam shook his head, but as Belinda looked in his eyes she wondered if he was really telling the truth. She stole a quick glance at Luke and thought that he might be questioning the boy's truthfulness, as well.

Luke proceeded to unwrap the injured leg.

"I see it's been doing a bit of bleeding," he commented.

"Not much," Sam mumbled. "Maybe bumped it in the night or some-thin'." It was obvious he wasn't going to let any bleeding keep him a prisoner in his bed if he could help it.

Belinda watched the sure hands of her brother as they unwound the bandages. There had been bleeding, all right. The closer Luke got to the wound, the redder the bandages were becoming.

Belinda shut her eyes tightly just as Luke went to remove the last strip of bandage, and then she scolded herself and opened them again. *Can't be a nurse with my eyes shut.*

The bandage stuck. Luke lifted his eyes to Mrs. Vickers hovering at the door.

"Could you bring a pan of hot water and a clean cloth, please, ma'am?"

Mrs. Vickers went to do his bidding.

Soaking off the bloody bandages was a slow process. At least it seemed awfully slow to Belinda. She marveled at Luke's patience.

At last the final bit of gauze was lifted from the cut, and Belinda caught her breath as she saw the angry red tear in the flesh. It had been stitched carefully so there was no gaping, but it was still inflamed and fiery looking. Belinda lifted her eyes back to the face of the patient. *It must be very painful. How did Sam . . . ?*

There was pain in Sam's eyes. Without even thinking, Belinda reached out a hand and brushed the shaggy hair back from his forehead. For just a second their eyes met. A message of sympathy passed from Belinda to Sam, and then the spell was broken. Quickly Belinda withdrew her hand and stepped back, and Sam restlessly moved his head on the pillow.

Luke saw it all—saw the genuine care that prompted Belinda's action, saw the brief moment of accepted sympathy on the part of Sam, and saw the hasty retreat by both of them. *Why do we do it?* Luke wondered to himself. *Why do we feel we can't honestly, openly express our concern for another?*

At the same time, Luke was encouraged by the compassion in Belinda's eyes. Yes, she might very well make a good nurse. She could feel, she could empathize with the patients. That was promising in someone of her age. *Perhaps she isn't too young after all.*

Luke continued with his treatment, watching Belinda closely for her reactions. He did not want to push her into a profession where she did not belong. Though he did see hesitation, even shock, at the injury and pain of the patient, he did not see Belinda flinch away. She faced the procedures honestly, squarely, though she certainly did not seem to enjoy them for their own sake.

When the leg had been carefully rebandaged, Luke assisted Sam to a chair in the family living room. Belinda placed the cushions as Luke lowered the young man to the seat. She eased another cushion under the extended leg. And she went back to the bedroom to retrieve the braided thongs so Sam might have something to busy his hands as soon as he felt up to using them.

Luke was impressed. He didn't say anything about it then to her, but he did give her a warm smile and her shoulder a slight squeeze to tell her that she had done a good job as his assistant. Belinda beamed. He would let her accompany him again.

Over the months that followed, Luke carefully chose cases that would be appropriate for Belinda to see and provide some assistance. These times were limited. She could not go where communicable diseases were treated. He did not take her when he feared the case might be too hard for a young girl to stomach. He did not take her when he feared the procedure would be a long one, demanding his undivided time and attention. But he did take her on a number of calls when he felt she could learn some of the principles of home care.

She was always eager to learn. On the way to the case he would explain what they would be treating and how they would go about it. She learned the names of his instruments and their use. It wasn't too long before Belinda was able to pass the instruments to him when he asked for them, if his hands were busy with other things.

Luke was amazed at how quickly she caught on. His voice held admiration and excitement whenever he reported to Clark and Marty. They exchanged glances of both relief and awe. Maybe they had done the right thing. They continued to pray for guidance.

Perhaps the only one to chafe about the arrangement was Amy Jo. She complained loudly and often about "Lindy bein' gone all the time." Not only was Belinda occasionally gone, but when she was home, Amy Jo said she just sat there poring over "some boring old medical book." She wasn't fun like she used to be, and Amy Jo did wish Belinda would just forget the whole thing.

But Belinda wasn't about to forget it. Daily her interest seemed to increase rather than diminish.

Summer came again and with it another break from school. Amy Jo said she was looking forward to the summer because it meant free time—more time for play. She sent a meaningful glance toward Belinda. But Belinda looked forward to the summer because it meant more time to be with Luke—more time to make house calls. Now she would be able to go on more than just Saturdays.

Her excitement mounted just thinking about it. And Luke had promised that in a couple years he would talk to her parents about letting her help in the office in town.

FIVE

A Surprise

"Belinda! Belinda!"

Marty's voice rose above the usual clamor of the farmyard flocks and herds. Belinda and Amy Jo, who were in the loft of the barn enjoying a new batch of kittens, heard the excitement in her voice. Belinda bounced to her feet. Perhaps Luke had come and they were going on another house call.

"I've gotta go," she informed her playmate.

Amy Jo pouted. "Yer always runnin' off," she said. "We never git to play anymore."

For a moment Belinda hesitated. She did feel bad when Amy Jo was upset. She was about to apologize when her mother called again.

"Belinda! Amy Jo!"

At the sound of her name, too, Amy Jo also scrambled up. The two of them hurried down the ladder and to the house, reaching the kitchen door breathless and flushed.

"There you are," said Marty to them as they followed her into the kitchen. Belinda had seen the shine in her eyes, and she knew her mother had news of some sort. So it wasn't just going to be some household chore.

"What is it?" she asked, puffing out each word.

"Clare jest got back from town, and there was a letter from Missie." She put a hand on the shoulder of each girl. "Ya can't guess what she has to say!"

Belinda couldn't remember seeing her mother so excited for a long time.

"Did she have another baby?" she asked.

Marty laughed. "No. No new baby. But it's something you'll . . . you'll find most interestin'. Both of ya." Marty picked up the letter that lay on the kitchen table and nodded toward two chairs. The girls obediently sat down.

"Listen to this," Marty instructed, and the girls prepared themselves to listen. Amy Jo cast a look in Belinda's direction and rolled her expressive eyes. The look said clearly, *All this fuss over a bit of news in a letter,* and Belinda nearly choked on a giggle bubbling up inside her.

"'We'd like to ask a big favor of you,'" read Marty. "'Ya know that Melissa is gittin' to be quite a young lady now. She has finished all of the grades in the local school. She thinks that she would like to be a schoolteacher. We still are very short of teachers here. Melinda—you remember Melinda, her teacher—thinks that Melissa would make a good teacher, and we'd like to give her the chance.'"

Marty hesitated a moment and glanced expectantly at the two girls. They waited for her to turn back to the letter before they dared to look at each other, and when she did continue, they both had to hide girlish snickers behind their hands. *Why all the fuss about a far-off relative, a relative we haven't even met, wanting to become a schoolteacher?* was their unspoken question to each other.

"'So, we have been thinkin',''' Marty read on, "'would you mind if Melissa comes out to stay with you while she gets some more trainin'?'"

Marty again looked up at the two girls.

It took a few moments for it all to sink in, but when it finally did, it was Amy Jo who cheered loudly.

"Oh boy!" she squealed. "Someone to play with while yer off with Luke."

Belinda was a bit hurt by the outburst.

"She'll be livin' at our house," she countered.

"Yeah, but—"

"Girls!" Marty interrupted. "Stop yer fussin'. I thought you'd be thinkin' on Melissa, 'stead of fightin' over who'd git her."

Belinda and Amy Jo had enough good training to feel a bit embarrassed.

They waited quietly for Marty to continue.

"'She will need a couple more grades in your local school, and then she will go on to take her normal school training. By then she should have adjusted enough to being away from her family so it won't be so difficult for her. We thought if she could be with you first, it would be much better for her than sending her directly to the big city.'"

It was beginning to seem more real.

"'She will arrive about a week before classes begin. We will send her out by train.'"

Amy Jo reached over and poked Belinda, mouthing some words that Belinda did not catch.

Marty continued, "'If it's okay with you, we sure would appreciate it. It's goin' to be awfully hard for us to let her go. I understand much better now how you felt, Mama.'"

Marty's voice trailed off, and her eyes began to mist. Belinda knew that tears were coming. But Amy Jo brought a quick halt to any sentiment.

"You an' Grandpa gonna let her come?" she asked in her usual forthright fashion.

Marty looked with loving exasperation at her young granddaughter. Only Amy Jo would have found it necessary to ask such a question. But then she did not usually think before she spoke.

"'Course," said Belinda, giving Amy Jo a gentle poke. "Ya know very well thet Ma and Pa'd never say no."

Amy Jo just shrugged.

The excitement of it all began to sink through to Belinda. *It will be so nice to have another girl in the house—almost like having a sister.* Belinda caught herself. She did have sisters—her foster sisters, Nandry and Clae, but they were much older and had children of their own even older than herself. And she had Missie and Ellie—but the truth was she had never yet seen Missie, and Ellie had left home for the West when she, Belinda, had been only a few months old. She had never had a sister around to share a room—or secrets—or anything else with. *Oh, true, there's Amy Jo,* she thought. Amy Jo was almost like having a sister— even if she really was a niece. *But Melissa will be right in the house with me,* she exulted silently. She knew better than to say something like that aloud in Amy Joe's presence.

Belinda's eyes traveled to the calendar on the wall. The letter had said Melissa would arrive a week or so before school. How many more weeks would that be? Quickly Belinda counted—*three or, at the most, four.* She could hardly wait. *Boy, the weeks are going to pass awfully slowly!* She turned back to her mother, her eyes now reflecting Marty's shine. She jumped from her chair and threw her arms around Marty's waist. *No wonder Mama was so excited!*

"Does Pa know? Does Pa know?" she implored.

"Not yet," said Marty. "He's over to the Grahams' helpin' Lou. He should be home 'most anytime now."

"Oh boy!" exclaimed Belinda and turned to Amy Jo. The two of them joined hands and danced around the kitchen. "Melissa's comin'! Melissa's comin'," they chanted.

Marty watched the two girls, laughing at their foolishness, but truth was, she sort of felt like joining in their dance. *It will be so good to have Melissa,* she rejoiced inwardly. It would be a little bit of Missie back home with them again. Marty's eyes grew teary, and she brushed at them with a corner of her apron.

What will she be like? she wondered. *She's most grown-up now. Well, no, not quite. She's only about nine months older than our Belinda.*

Marty turned back to her youngest. Belinda was acting awfully child-ish at the moment, but there were times when Marty had to realize that Belinda, too, was quickly growing up. She was a mature girl for her age in many ways. Yes, Melissa could well seem quite grown-up. They'd need to remember that in their dealings with the girl. Marty brushed at her tears again and turned to gaze out the kitchen window. It was going to be so wonderful.

Belinda couldn't wait and rushed out to greet Clark with the news. For a moment he looked as if he thought she was "funnin'" him, but when he looked over her head into the flushed and happy face of Marty, he grinned and flipped his work-worn hat into the air.

"When?" he asked. "When's she comin'?"

"In just three or four weeks," Belinda told him with great excitement.

"Jest early enough to git herself settled afore school classes begin," added Marty.

Clark grinned again. "Thet spare bedroom gonna need some fixin' up?" asked Clark.

Marty hadn't thought that far ahead. Belinda protested that she hoped Melissa would be able to share her room. But she soon stopped that line of argument, wondering aloud if perhaps Melissa would rather not do that.

Marty nodded somewhat absently to Belinda. She was busy thinking about Clark's comment. The room should be freshened up, all right. Perhaps she should sew new curtains and make a new spread, as well. It had been a long time since the spare room had seen anything new. *Maybe Belinda would like to help in the planning.* Marty's mind continued to busy itself with many ideas, and she had the room nearly made new by the time she turned to walk the path back to her kitchen. But for the moment, getting supper on the table had to be her main concern.

Belinda had gone on down to the barn with Clark, and Marty could hear her telling him other news from the letter as they went. Marty could not resist climbing the stairs for a quick peek into the room that would be for the girl. The door had not even been opened for several weeks. It smelled a bit musty and unused.

Her eyes traveled over the walls, the floor, the curtains, the bed. Clark was right. The room did need sprucing up. *Let's see,* Marty mused, *this was Missie's room before she was married. Melissa will be staying in her own mama's room!*

Suddenly three or four weeks did not seem like a very long time after all. My, she had so much to do! Marty hurried back down the steps and to the kitchen as if getting supper quickly out of the way would be a great help in preparing for the arrival of her granddaughter. She chuckled to herself. That was silly. There wasn't one thing she'd be able to do tonight to prepare for Melissa's coming.

Marty talked it over thoroughly with Clark, and they agreed on her plans for the room.

"I do wish we knew a bit more about the girl's likes an' dislikes," stated Marty. "It would be jest like me to go an' choose a color she detests."

Clark smiled and patted her hand. "You'll do jest fine, Marty. Remember how well ya did with the chinks in our first log cabin home?"

Marty looked at him quickly to see if he was teasing her. She was deciding whether to be put out with him or not, but then couldn't help but laugh at the memory of her vigorous scrubbing of the log walls and the wet, muddy chinking falling out on the floor in clumps. Clark finally laughed, too.

"Well, it sure weren't funny then," Marty reminded him, wiping her eyes. "I was a feared the whole house was goin' to come down around our ears!" Marty and Clark looked at each other awhile, remembering those long-ago days.

"Well, anyway," Marty said, back to the present, "I'm serious about fixin' up this room for Melissa." She paused to think a moment. "Belinda likes soft blues and greens but doesn't care for loud, bright colors. Amy Jo loves bright reds and yellows and never picks a soft color in anything. Now, how do I know what Melissa might choose?"

Clark didn't say anything, but his face indicated he didn't seem to think it was much of an issue.

"Use soft colors on the walls and curtains and spread," he suggested, "with a bit of brightness in some pillows an' rugs."

Marty looked at him in amazement. Maybe he had more sense about such matters than she had thought.

She nodded her head, in her mind picturing the room fresh with pale flowered wallpaper, fluffy curtains—maybe white eyelet fluttering at the window and a matching spread with lots of soft ruffles on the bed. Scattered on the bed would be bright pillows, maybe in shades of greens, yellows, and even blues, depending on the wallpaper pattern. On the floor could be homemade rugs. Patterned in bright colors and—

Clark interrupted her thoughts. "I'll do whatever you want—wallpaper, paint—whenever yer ready," he was saying. "But you an' Belinda will need to take care of the rest. I never could sew on a patch, much less make somethin' fancy."

Marty smiled a bit distractedly at his comment, her mind still busy with the room plans.

"Clark," Marty said reflectively, "I think I'm goin' to invite Amy Jo to come along with Belinda and me on our shoppin' trip. I sure don't want her feelin' left out, with Melissa livin' right here with Belinda an' all."

Clark nodded in agreement. "We'll want to be careful to make Amy Jo feel a part of things, seein' she and Belinda have been more like sisters than anything else all these years," he commented.

And so their plans were made. Marty checked with Kate before telling Amy Jo about the trip to town. Kate was happy to have Amy involved in the choosing of the new things for the room. She, too, was aware that with three, it was easy for one to feel left out at times. She and Marty discussed the situation and agreed that they would keep their eyes and ears open for possible problems.

Right after the morning chores had been done, Marty announced the shopping plans to two excited girls, and they ran to get ready for the trip into town.

The first duty was to select a pretty wallpaper. Just as Marty would have guessed, Belinda picked a soft cream with a mint green print on it, but Amy Jo insisted that it was "too dull." She wanted lavender with large yellow roses. Marty, finally at her wit's end, decided to leave the wallpaper till later and took the girls to look at what was available in yard goods. Here again there was a difference of opinion. Marty loved the gauzy white for Priscilla curtains, Belinda favored the fluffy green organza, and Amy Jo insisted that a bright yellow with a bold pattern of purple flowers was the prettiest.

"And think how beautiful it will be with that wallpaper pattern, Gramma!" Amy Jo enthused while Marty inwardly cringed. "Ya know, the same colors, but opposite—the flowers yellow on the wallpaper an' . . ." she chattered on while Marty tried to figure out what to do.

She began to wish she had left both girls at home and gone with her own inclinations. She suggested they take a break and go to the hotel dining room for a cup of tea. The girls agreed, really not all that interested in tea, but they knew the hotel served some pastries to which they were partial.

Marty needed that cup of tea. She sipped it slowly, trying to sort out just how she would get around the differences of opinion. At last she decided to broach the subject head-on.

"Seems—" she began, "seems we don't agree much on how Melissa's room should be done. Now, we don't have Melissa here to do her own decidin', and it would be rather foolish to wait an' jest move her on in and then move her out again whilst we do up the room. Still—it would be so much nicer iffen she could make her own choices, but—"

"Why can't she, Mama?" interrupted Belinda. "She could share my room until her room is all finished—then we wouldn't need to move her in an' out."

Marty hadn't even thought of that possibility. "Why, Belinda, thet might jest work! Let me see . . ." and Marty was off in thought, busy with more plans. It did make more sense to let Melissa do her own choosing. But what if her preferences tended toward those of Amy Jo's? Well, it would be only two years and Melissa would be moving on again. Marty supposed that she could stand nearly any color scheme for her granddaughter's sake. She could always shut the door, she decided with an inward chuckle.

"I like yer idea," Marty said to Belinda at length. "Maybe we should jest wait. Melissa could do the choosin', an' she'd feel more at home that way."

Belinda grinned.

"Ya don't mind sharin' yer room fer a piece?" Marty inquired.

"I don't mind," Belinda assured her. She not only didn't mind, but she was looking forward to the opportunity.

Amy Jo scowled as only she could. Marty and Belinda both knew she was displeased about something.

"Ya jest want her in yer own room so thet ya can be friends faster," she pouted.

"Friends?" responded Marty, her head coming up. "Melissa is Belinda's niece—an' yer cousin. Ya don't need to worry none 'bout bein' jest friends. Yer *family*—both of ya."

But Amy Jo still frowned at Belinda.

Marty finished her tea and gathered her belongings.

"Well," she said, "I guess thet's what we'll do. We'll jest leave it until Melissa gits here. I think I'll work on some new rugs, though. I can put in enough colors thet they will go with most anything. Don't want to leave everything until last."

The girls still dawdled over their pastries.

"I'm gonna go git the groceries I be a needin'," Marty informed them. "When ya git done here, ya join me at the store."

They both nodded.

"Now mind yer manners—and don't go gittin' yerselves in any trouble," admonished Marty, and she smoothed out her skirts and started for the door.

Amy Jo frowned at Belinda again.

"Yer happy 'bout it, ain't ya?" she said in an accusing voice.

"'Bout what?"

"'Bout waitin' till Melissa gits here. 'Bout not pickin' the room colors. 'Bout Melissa stayin' in yer room with ya."

Belinda shrugged, trying not to look too happy about the turn of affairs. "Guess so," she said. She didn't think it would be right to deny it, either.

"Well, I'm not. I wanted to help choose, too. I liked the colors I picked. An' I jest bet Melissa woulda liked 'em, too."

"Maybe," said Belinda.

"I wish I could have 'em in *my* room," went on Amy Jo, sounding determined to be negative. "I never picked my colors yet. It's been the same, *the same,* ever since I was borned, I think."

Belinda doubted that, but she didn't say so.

Amy Jo sighed. "I'll never git my own colors. Mama wouldn't even like 'em. Green an' white—thet's all she ever likes."

Belinda saw nothing wrong with those colors, but she thought it best not to say so.

They finished their cakes, and Amy Jo lifted each remaining crumb to her mouth on the tip of one long, tapering finger. Belinda watched her. She had never noticed how long and slender Amy Jo's fingers were before. She compared them to her own. Her fingers were not as long, but there was a certain strength there in her slender hands. She turned them over and over. She couldn't help but picture a scalpel there—a syringe. She forced her mind back to the present.

"We'd better go," she said. "Mama said she wouldn't be long."

Amy Jo pushed back her empty plate and reluctantly trudged from the room after Belinda.

SIX

Planning

During the next three weeks, even the thrill of accompanying Luke on his calls took second place in Belinda's mind. All she could think about was Melissa's coming. What would she be like? Would they like each other? What about Amy Jo? How would things work out with three of them to get along instead of just two?

Belinda wasn't the only one holding her breath and wondering about the future. She knew Amy Jo wondered—and at times even shed a few tears. Amy Joe said she was sure the two girls, sharing a room up in the big house, would forget all about her. When Belinda attempted to remonstrate with her, Amy Jo had interrupted with, "Well, I don't care." She tossed her head and flounced off. But Belinda knew Amy Jo did care, and she was troubled.

Marty and Belinda were working together over pie crusts in the big farm kitchen.

"Excited 'bout Melissa comin'?" Marty asked.

"Oh yes!" admitted Belinda. "I can hardly wait."

"Been thinkin'—it might be a bit hard fer Amy Jo."

Belinda did not argue.

"We need to be extry careful not to let her feel left out," went on Marty, and Belinda nodded, knowing her mother was really meaning "you" when she said "we."

"Have ya thought on any way we might do thet?" asked Marty.

Belinda hesitated. "No," she said slowly. "Not really . . . but I . . . I've been thinkin' on somethin' I'd sure like to do fer Amy Jo."

"What's thet?" asked Marty.

"Ya know Amy Jo's room?" ventured Belinda.

Marty nodded.

"Well, it's pale green an' white. It's been those colors—well, since she was born, I think."

Marty nodded again.

"Amy Jo doesn't like those colors," Belinda dared to say.

"She doesn't?"

"No. She's sick, sick, sick of green an' white. She wants somethin' bright, or somethin'—somethin' darin', I think."

Marty nodded once more.

"Ma, do ya think Clare an' Kate would let Amy Jo have new colors?"

"I dunno," she said slowly. "Does this mean a lot to Amy Jo?"

"I think so," answered Belinda. "She feels kinda sad 'bout Melissa." Belinda wondered if her mother might misunderstand and was quick to add, "Oh, she's excited 'bout it—same as me. But—she's sad, too, 'cause she won't have Melissa livin' at her house an'—"

"I think I understand," said her mother.

Belinda stole a glance at her mother's face to see if she did understand. After studying it, she felt sure that Marty really did understand what she was trying to say.

"I'll have a chat with Kate," said Marty. "Maybe iffen yer pa an' me offer to help with the wallpaper an' the material, they'll let Amy Jo do her own choosin'. She's got a birthday comin'. We could do it fer her birthday."

Belinda wanted to hug her mother, but her hands were all covered with flour. She smiled happily instead.

"Thanks, Mama," she said appreciatively.

But it was really Marty who felt the best about the conversation. She was pleased to know that Belinda cared enough to be thinking about Amy Jo, and was concerned that Belinda might consider only her own excitement about Melissa's arrival.

Marty decided she would tell Clark all about it when they had some time alone to talk. She was sure he would be pleased as well as she was with the maturity of their daughter. She did hope that Clare and Kate would see the offer of a new room for Amy Jo as a show of love rather than any kind of interference.

Marty thought about the colors and prints Amy Jo was likely to pick, and she was secretly glad they would not be decorating a room in her home.

You've made us all different, Lord, she prayed quietly, *and bless this lively and beloved granddaughter of ours. . . .*

Over coffee at Kate's the next morning, Marty discussed the idea of redoing Amy Jo's room as her birthday gift. Kate was thrilled.

"I should have thought to let her do her own choosin' before," said Kate.

"I saw firsthand some of Amy Jo's choices," Marty informed Kate with a chuckle. "Ya better be preparin' yerself is all I can say. I hope ya like yer rooms colorful an' bright."

Kate laughed. "I've seen a few of her choices. They are a bit shockin', aren't they? Well, I guess we will jest learn to live with 'em. I'm realizin' more an' more it's like you an' Pa have often said, they grow up awful fast, an' soon they won't be with us at all." Kate poured more coffee, then went on reflectively, "Besides feedin' an' clothin' and trainin' our children, Clare an' I need to be listenin' to 'em an' learnin' to know 'em as people on their own whilst we've still got the chance."

Marty nodded, thinking of her own scattered family.

"Ya know how Amy Jo has always liked to be drawin' an' colorin'?" Kate continued.

Marty smiled in acknowledgment, remembering Amy Jo drawing and coloring pictures even before she started off to school. They often laughed about her color choices, but Amy Jo had loved the brightness and insisted on using the most colorful watercolors she had.

"I've been talkin' to Clare," went on Kate. "I've been thinkin' on gettin' Amy Jo some things for drawin' an' paintin' fer her birthday. Let her show her love fer color in her own way. What d'ya think?"

Marty quickly agreed. "Maybe we shoulda done thet ages ago," she mused aloud. "Why didn't we think of it?"

"Guess we've been too busy thinkin' shoes an' vittles," Kate responded.

Marty nodded. It did seem to take all a parent's time just thinking of the physical needs of the family. "I think she'd love it," Marty went on after giving Kate's suggestion some thought. "She's always loved bright an' colorful things."

"Maybe Clare could make a little table for her room so she could work with a bit of privacy," Kate went on as though to herself. "Wouldn't she love thet, though?"

"When shall we tell her?" asked Marty, anticipating her granddaughter's surprise and joy.

"Let's leave it fer her birthday surprise. It's only two months away. By then the excitement of Melissa's comin' will sort'ave died down. Then she can do her own pickin' and have her room the way she likes it by Christmastime."

Marty agreed, but here was something else she would have to wait for, along with Melissa's arrival.

When Marty shared the secret plans with Belinda, she was almost as excited as they expected Amy Jo to be. If Marty thought, however, her own waiting was difficult, it paled compared to Belinda's eagerness to tell her beloved niece and friend.

Marty helped to fill the days before Melissa arrived by thinking of things they could do that the girl might enjoy when she joined the family—a picnic before the weather turned cold, a visit to Ma Graham, dropping by the schoolhouse where she'd be attending. . . . Marty's thoughts were kept as busy as her hands with the rugs for the floor.

Belinda was not so fortunate. Every day seemed to drag by slower than the one before. Amy Jo accused Belinda of forgetting all about her now that Melissa was coming. She hinted that Belinda would disregard their friendship from past years and like Melissa better. On more than one occasion, Belinda nearly told her about the coming birthday surprise, but she always managed to hold her tongue.

Belinda was especially glad when Luke dropped by to pick her up on the way to make a house call. It did help to distract her from the tedium of the wait.

Then a telegram arrived. They crowded together to read it at the same time.

"'Melissa to arrive on 25th by stage. Stop.'" Clark carefully read. "'We love you all. Stop. Willie and Missie.'"

August twenty-fifth! That was only two days away. Belinda thought she'd never be able to bear it. She turned to run to tell Amy Jo and then checked herself. Maybe that wouldn't be so wise. Amy Jo might misunderstand her excitement. Instead she decided to do one last thorough cleaning of her room—the room Melissa would be sharing with Belinda until her own was ready.

She crowded her things together in the tiny closet so Melissa might have room to hang her clothes, then emptied half of the drawers in the tall dresser. She pulled out a wooden box her father had made years ago for her doll things and carefully folded her extra clothing into it. Then she carried the box to the empty room that had been shared by Arnie and Luke. She was glad her mother hadn't suggested Melissa use this room until the room that had been Ellie's was ready for her. *Funny,* Belinda thought. *Mother still thinks of the front bedroom as the "boys' room."* She hadn't even thought of putting Melissa in there.

Well, Belinda didn't mind. Her niece! Just think! She would soon be meeting her niece for the first time! And her niece was almost nine months older than she!

Belinda's heart pounded with excitement and her stomach churned with just a bit of concern. What would it really be like? Well, she would soon learn. It wouldn't be long now.

Marty's heart was also racing. She could not count the number of times when she had ached to hold and to know her granddaughter— their Missie's "baby girl." Melissa Joy was no longer the baby in age or birth sequence—she had a younger sister, Julia, whom Marty had never seen, either. But Melissa had been "on the way" when Clark and Marty had spent their difficult winter at the ranch of Willie and Missie. She had been the little one they had hoped to hold before they left again for the East. But Melissa had kept her appointed time for delivery and had not put in her appearance until after the grandparents had gone back home. So Melissa seemed special to Marty somehow. And now . . . now she was a young lady. A girl on the verge of womanhood . . . and Marty had never seen her.

Melissa's coming was an aching reminder to Marty of just how much she missed Missie and Ellie. She longed to see for herself how they were keeping, to hold their children in her arms.

Marty recalled all the fun she and Clark had shared with Melissa's brothers, Nathan and Josiah. *My, how they would have grown by now,* she marveled. They were well into their teens—almost men. Marty reminded herself that they would not be wanting to sit on Grandpa's lap for a story or cuddle close with Grandma for a bedtime lullaby. Those days were over—never to be reclaimed. She thanked God for the time they had been able to have with the growing boys.

And Julia. Julia was now a little girl of ten. Would Marty have the same privilege of one day welcoming Julia into their home? Would Julia also wish to be a schoolteacher? Marty decided it did no harm for her to hope so.

Ellie, too, was a mother now. Their daughter, Brenda, was almost seven, and twin sons, William and Willis, were busy four-year-olds. Tears wet her eyes as Marty yearned to see them, to get to know them as more than just names of their faraway offspring.

But Melissa—Melissa was like an earnest, a promise of things to come, a little part of those Marty loved from out west. Was she like

Missie? Like Willie? Marty had not even seen a tintype of the young girl.

Oh, how she wished her "western family" could all come for a family reunion. But at least Melissa could catch them up on all the news—that is, if Melissa was the kind of person who would talk freely to them. Would she be shy? After all, she didn't know them—not any of them. Marty felt her stomach tighten again, and, as many times over the past few days, she bowed her head. *Lord, please bring Melissa safely here, and help us to get to know each other quick,* she prayed earnestly, *and help her not to be fearful. . . .*

SEVEN

Melissa Joy

The whole household was in a frenzy of excitement and activity. Marty had checked and rechecked the supper preparations. Belinda had dusted, straightened, and fussed over her bedroom that they would share. Amy Jo had made any number of trips to the big house to see if it was time to leave. Even Clark paced around restlessly, caught up in the anticipation. Only the horses, already hitched to the buggy, waited patiently.

At last the slowly moving hands of the clock allowed that they could begin their trip into town without being ridiculously ahead of schedule, so they scrambled excitedly into the buggy and Clark clucked to the team.

"What do you think she'll be like?" asked Amy Jo of Belinda for the umpteenth time.

Belinda sighed deeply. If she only knew. It would be so much easier welcoming this niece if she knew what kind of a person she was.

"Do ya think she's skinny or fat?" Amy Jo pursued her quest for information.

"I don't know," answered Belinda patiently.

"But ya can guess," insisted Amy Jo.

"Okay," responded Belinda just a bit testily. "I guess she's in between."

Amy Jo held her tongue but not for long.

"Does she look like her ma or pa?"

"We've never seen her—none of us."

"But didn't Aunt Missie ever write who she looks like?"

This question caused Belinda to stop and reflect. But after a few minutes she was unable to come up with any answer. She leaned forward and tapped Marty on the shoulder.

"Mama, did Missie ever say who Melissa takes after?"

Marty, too, thought for a few moments before responding.

"No-o," she said slowly now. "Don't recall she did, but I . . . I s'pose she'll look like her ma. No reason fer her not to."

The answer was unsatisfactory to Belinda, but she didn't say so.

"Well," whispered Amy Jo relentlessly, "she might be real fat. She might even be ugly."

Belinda recalled a comment of her mother's from a few days back. Marty had said it was far more important how Melissa *acted* than how she *looked*. Would Melissa be difficult to get along with? Belinda had heard her ma and pa on more than one occasion talk about how the ranch hands doted on the girl. They enjoyed the boys, but she was their favorite, and they were her self-appointed protectors. Yes, Melissa Joy could well be spoiled.

Belinda had a fleeting wish that she could escape the smartly moving buggy and return home to her own room. Maybe she shouldn't have been so quick in offering to share it. Maybe it would have been better if Melissa had stayed in the West instead of coming here to continue her schooling. Maybe . . .

But Amy Jo was asking questions again. "What if she has freckles?"

"Nothin' wrong with freckles."

Amy Jo tossed her head and scowled. "Oh yeah," she sputtered, "*you* can say thet. You ain't got none. Iffen ya had 'em, ya'd know there's somethin' wrong with 'em, all right."

Belinda gave her an impatient look. They had discussed freckles many times in the past. She knew Amy Jo had always hated her own scattering of freckles. Belinda always felt that the discussion led nowhere and accomplished nothing.

"You've hardly got any, either," she said. "Don't know why ya fuss 'bout 'em so."

276

"Well, iffen ya had 'em you'd—"

"Girls!" said Marty sternly.

Belinda and Amy Jo exchanged glances, knowing better than to continue the bickering. Amy Jo gave Belinda an angry look and mouthed a few words Belinda did not understand. Belinda looked away. At least now Amy Jo might be quiet for a while.

But not for long. "How big do you think she is?"

"She's past fourteen."

"Not 'old.' *Big*. How tall?"

Belinda shrugged. Amy Jo's guess was as good as hers. She couldn't understand why the girl persisted. Perhaps it hadn't been so wise to invite Amy Jo to meet the stage with them.

Amy Jo toyed with the ribbon on her long reddish brown braid. In spite of being peeved with her, Belinda found herself marveling at Amy Jo's unique coloring. It wasn't often that auburn hair was paired with large violet-colored eyes.

Without thinking Belinda blurted out, "*You* don't look like yer ma."

Amy Jo's head swung around to stare at Belinda, her lovely eyes wide with questions. Marty, too, turned to listen from the front seat.

Belinda hastened to explain her sudden comment. "I mean—ya don't look *only* like yer ma. Ya got her eyes, and her chin, too, I think, but not her hair color or the shape of her face."

"Ma says my hair is the same color as my gramma Warren's," declared Amy Jo, flipping one braid back over her shoulder.

Belinda nodded.

"An' my face is shaped like Pa's," Amy Jo went on.

"Ya see," pointed out Belinda, "Melissa could have bits—I mean, parts—of things that are like any of the family. She doesn't have to look like her ma or her pa—at least not *jest* like one of 'em."

Amy Jo scowled, not willing to part with her owlishness. But she did stop asking questions that had no answers.

As they continued the journey into town, Marty thought more about the two girls' recent discussion about looks and Amy Jo's last declaration on the subject. *Like yer pa's*, Marty agreed silently, *an' like his pa's*.

Every once in a while she caught a fleeting expression or a turn of Amy Jo's head that reminded Marty of Clare's father—her first husband, Clem. Those reminders were not disturbing or sad—simply a memory of a long-ago time.

The long ride to town finally ended. Now they faced a wait for the stage to arrive. Marty fervently hoped it would not be late.

"Why don't you two go git yerselves some ice cream?" Clark offered, fishing some coins from his pocket, and the girls gladly accepted the money and ran off down the street.

Marty turned to Clark, relief showing in her face. Clark no doubt had read her thoughts. He knew how much quibbling children bothered Marty.

"They're jest all keyed up, thet's all," he said. "They'll calm down once the stage gets here."

"I do hope so," murmured Marty with a sigh. "Oh, I hope this works. I hope it don't turn out to be two girls against one. I couldn't stand the bickerin' iffen it did."

"Now don't ya go borrowin' trouble," said Clark as he flipped the reins of the team over the hitching rail.

Marty stood still, her brow creased in thoughtfulness.

"Maybe we should have at least asked a few questions," she continued. "Clark—we really know nothin' 'bout this granddaughter of ours."

"Know all we need to know," responded Clark comfortably, reaching out to take Marty's arm and steer her across the dusty street. "We know she's our granddaughter, and we know she needs a place to stay whilst she gits her schoolin'. Now thet there is enough, to my way a' thinkin'."

Marty sighed again and lifted her skirts to keep the dust from sifting up onto them with each step. Clark might be right, but she did hope they weren't in for any unhappy surprises.

Marty did some shopping in the local store. She really didn't need further provisions, but it helped to fill the minutes until the stage was due. With time left over, she decided to look at the yard goods. Melissa might be needing some new frocks for school. Missie had written nothing about it, but it wouldn't hurt for Marty to know what was available should she need to do some sewing.

She noticed that the bright bolt of colorful print Amy Jo had picked for the curtains and bedspread was still on the shelf. She wasn't surprised. She couldn't imagine anyone else wanting it. Marty considered buying it on the sly and tucking it away until Amy Jo's birthday surprise, but she decided against it. Amy Jo was so changeable she might pick something entirely different by the time her birthday rolled around.

Where are the girls, anyway? Marty checked the store clock. They were taking an unusual amount of time to get their ice cream. *They haven't gone and gotten themselves in some kind of trouble!* Marty laid aside the bolt of blue gingham she was holding and went to look for them.

She didn't need to look far. They were stationed on the sidewalk in front of the stagecoach office. The two girls had claimed a bench there. They sat sedately swinging their legs and talking excitedly.

Looks like they're friends again. Relieved, Marty turned back to the yard goods. There were some very pretty pieces, and she decided to buy a length for a new dress for Belinda, who was quickly outgrowing her frocks. Marty could not decide between two pieces of material and ended up taking them both. She would need another one soon anyway, she reasoned, and this would save her an extra trip into town.

Purchasing the yard goods and the thread took several minutes, and Marty was glad for the distraction from waiting. She chatted with the store owner as the yard goods were measured. To her chagrin, her voice sounded almost as high-pitched and excited as did Belinda's and Amy Jo's.

At last she went to join the girls. Clark was already there, seated on the sidewalk talking with the local livery man. Marty slowed her steps. She must get her emotions under control. She was acting like a giddy schoolgirl! What kind of a grandmother would Melissa think she had?

Marty decided to take her parcels to the buggy and stow them beneath the seat. Clark offered to do it for her, but she declined. Then Belinda jumped up and said she'd run them over, and Marty knew Belinda would most likely "run," all right.

"I'll go with ya," Amy Jo offered enthusiastically, jumping up.

"No—no, thet's fine," assured Marty. "There's still lots of time. I'll jest take 'em on over. Give me somethin' to do."

By the time she returned, others had gathered to meet the stage, as well.

Some were strangers to Marty, but she also noticed neighbor folk and some from the little town. They exchanged greetings and pleasantries.

"You expectin' someone in on the stage?" asked Mrs. Colson, the new grocer's wife.

Marty didn't suppose she'd be standing there in the heat and dust unless she was waiting for someone, but she smiled warmly and informed Mrs. Colson that their granddaughter from the West was joining them for the school year.

"How nice," said Mrs. Colson with a matching smile. "I got a sister comin' in. She jest lost her husband a couple months back an' don't know what to do with herself."

Marty murmured her sympathy and understanding.

"I do hope me thet she ain't a burden," Mrs. Colson went on quite frankly. "Some people in their grievin' feel thet the whole world should grieve with 'em. I ain't got the time nor the inclination to—"

But the stagecoach rounded the bend, and her words were covered by the cheer that went up from the waiting group. Though Marty did not join the cheer, the whole of her being suddenly seemed to strain forward. She wondered for a moment if she'd be able to stay on her feet, and then the dizziness quickly passed. She stepped forward to take Clark's arm, more for emotional support than for physical aid.

Clark, as always, sensed her emotion and reached down to gently squeeze the hand that rested on his arm.

What if Melissa missed the stage—or changed her mind at the last minute? flashed through Marty's mind. She shook the thought aside as Belinda pressed in against her, excitement making her tremble.

"Mama," she asked, tapping on Marty's arm for attention as she'd done when a youngster. "Mama, how will we know her?"

Marty's face turned blankly to Belinda's upturned one. She had no answer. She had never seen her granddaughter and had not thought to ask for any "sign." She just thought . . . just thought they'd know her *somehow*. What if they didn't? What if they had to ask? *How embarrassing!* thought Marty in panic. But Clark was speaking.

"Well, now, I don't s'pose there's gonna be too many fourteen-year-old girls a travelin' all alone on thet there stage," he said confidently.

The worry left Belinda's eyes. Marty reached down and pulled her close. She wondered just which heart was beating the hardest.

In a flurry of trail dust, the stage skidded to a stop. The driver threw the reins to the waiting liveryman and jumped to the ground. The door was opened, and a well-dressed man stepped down. Marty's eyes quickly noted that he wasn't an acquaintance, and she dismissed him.

A matronly lady was next, and Marty looked over at Mrs. Colson. But it was not she who claimed the woman. A man stepped forward, one Marty did not know, and the two embraced and walked off toward a bay team that stood at the nearest hitching rail.

Marty's heart continued to hammer away in her chest.

A younger man descended. He cast a glance in their direction at the two girls, nodded his head at the nearby men, claimed one piece of luggage, which he shouldered, then walked toward the hotel.

Marty could feel Belinda quivering. The suspense was tying them all in knots.

And then a young lady—no, a child, or was she a young lady?—stepped carefully down from the stage. A mass of curly brown hair hung beneath her hat, and deep brown eyes looked curiously around at the crowd. Marty started to dismiss her. *Missie has fair hair,* she argued with herself. And then the girl smiled. Smiled right at them. And Marty recognized Missie's smile, and she knew with a quickening of her heart that she was looking at Melissa Joy.

Clark must have known it even before her, for he had already stepped forward and was even now reaching to claim the hand luggage the girl carried.

But she didn't offer her luggage—she offered herself. With a glad little cry she threw herself into his arms. It was enough to propel Marty forward. With tears streaming down her cheeks, she hugged the girl to her, all doubts scattering like leaves in the wind as she held her close. In that one brief instant, she felt she already knew her granddaughter. *She is lovely an' sweet—she's our Melissa!* Marty rejoiced.

EIGHT

Getting Acquainted

The ride home was a merry one. They quickly discovered Melissa was not shy. She chattered excitedly about her experiences on the trip. She gave them all an extra hug from Missie and Willie. She told them about Nathan, Josiah, and Julia. She talked about her father's new barn and her mother's huge garden down by the spring. Marty drank it all in, plying her with questions. There was so much she wanted to know, so much she longed to hear.

Belinda and Amy Jo hardly got a word in edgewise. It did not seem to bother Belinda. She sat quietly, listening to all the information about her western family. Amy Jo did not look so complacent. As befitting her nature, she no doubt wished to be a part of the conversation with lots of questions of her own.

She finally nudged Belinda with an elbow. "Bet they don't even know we're here," she grumped, sounding like she was back to her sour mood during the ride into town.

It didn't matter all that much to Belinda. She knew she would have lots of time to talk to Melissa later. After all, they would be sharing the same room.

Amy Jo must have thought of the same thing.

"But why should *you* care?" she challenged. "Ya'll be a livin' with her. In the same room even. Ya can talk as much as ya like."

"She's gonna be here fer a couple a' years," Belinda reminded her quietly.

"Two years," sighed Amy Jo. "Two years of not talkin'."

"Don't be silly," said Belinda. She was truly weary of it all.

"See," pouted Amy Jo. "Ya don't like me already."

"I do like ya," hissed Belinda in her ear.

"Ya do not. I *knew* it would be like this. I knew ya'd like her better."

"Oh, stop it," Belinda chided. "I don't even know 'er yet. Iffen ya keep on bein' so silly, nobody'll like ya."

Amy Jo turned to her corner to pout, and Belinda went back to listening to the conversation. Melissa had been tucked in securely between her grandma and grandpa so they might get acquainted on the way home.

". . . And Mother said to be sure to give it to you the minute I arrived," Melissa was saying, and then added with a laugh, "I hope she meant the minute I arrived at the farm, because it's packed securely in my trunk."

Marty and Clark joined in her light merriment.

It was the first that Belinda had known anyone who said "Mother" rather than "Ma" or "Mama." It sounded so grown-up somehow.

Melissa was going on with her description. "And Julia sent you a doily she made all by herself."

"Tell us about Julia," coaxed Marty. "Is she like you?"

"Oh no," and Melissa laughed again. "She's not at all like me. She does have brown eyes. Guess we all have Father's brown eyes. But she is quite fair—more like Mother—and she is very quiet. Mother says God must have known that our house could only bear one talker—and that's me."

Melissa laughed again, a joyful little laugh that seemed to make the sun shine just a bit brighter.

"Julia is . . . Julia is sweet," said Melissa reflectively. "She's very unselfish, and she helps Mother without her having to ask, and she loves animals, and . . . and . . . I'm really going to miss her," she said quickly, and there was a hint of tears in her voice.

"But Mother says that time will pass very quickly," Melissa continued bravely. "I sure hope so. I'm going to miss all of them. I've never been away from the ranch before—not even for overnight. We used to coax Father to let us go with him to the city, but he never took us—only

Mother. She did all of our shopping. Father isn't too fond of the city, I guess. But, my, I did see some interesting things on the way out . . ." and she was off again with her entertaining descriptions of people, places, and events, as she had covered nearly half a continent by train.

"There was this young gentleman who offered to help me with my things," Melissa was saying, "but Mother and Father gave me strict orders not to talk to strangers, so I just smiled as politely as I could and said I wasn't allowed to accept help. He was nice enough about it."

"An' how are yer brothers?" asked Marty.

"Fine! Nathan is taller than Father, and Joe—he wants to be called Joe now—Joe is just a couple of inches shorter. But he might be the taller of the two when he stops growing. At least, that's what Mother thinks."

"Oh my," Marty exclaimed. "Oh my. I never dreamed of them bein' that big—"

"Father is helping Nathan to buy his own spread. It's not far from ours. He wants to ranch, too. And Joe has some cattle of his own. He loves his cattle, but he says he might just wait and share the ranch with Father. Joe is more of a 'homebody'—at least that's what Mother calls him."

"Nathan have his eye on any young lady?" Clark interrupted to ask.

"We've been teasing him about my teacher's daughter—Elisa is the same age as Joe—but he's not saying anything yet," Melissa responded.

"An' yer pa?"

"He's just fine. He loves having Grandpa LaHaye there with him, but Grandpa is at Uncle Nathan's ranch right now—though he did come over to tell me good-bye. They all came over, Uncle Nathan, Aunt Callie, and the family. And they all sent their greetings."

"Is Cookie still with you?"

"Oh, he'll never leave. He's family!"

"How many of the hands are still around—the ones thet we knew when we were a stayin' out there?"

Melissa stopped to think about it. She said she wasn't sure who had been there when her grandparents had visited the West, so she would just name all the ranch hands.

"Well," she began slowly, "let's see. We have Jake and Browny and Clyde and Tom and Hooper."

"They're all new," put in Marty. "This Tom an' Hooper, we didn't know 'em."

"And there is Shorty and Burt and Charlie."

"Didn't know any of them, either. Is Smith still there?"

"No, Smith left when I was small."

"Does Wong still do the cookin'?"

"Wong? No, Wong died. About five years ago. We have a friend of Wong's from San Francisco now—Yen Soo."

"Oh," said Marty. "I'm sorry to hear thet Wong died—we liked him."

"Mother liked him, too. She had a hard time getting used to Yen at first."

"What happened to Wong?"

"We really don't know. He refused to go to a doctor. He said he had his own medicine, but he just got weaker and weaker. Cookie nursed him for months. But he didn't get better."

A silence hung over them for a few minutes. Clark and Marty looked at each other, no doubt silently pondering whether Wong had ever come to know the Lord.

"Well, thet's our farm, jest up there," Clark told Melissa.

"Oh, it looks lovely—so big. I mean, the house looks so big. Ours is adobe and built low to the ground, but yours looks so tall—and so white. I love it! Mother said that I would."

"You will have yer own room, of course," put in Marty, "but it needs redoin', an' we thought ya might like to choose yer own colors. So we decided thet while we were workin' on it, ya could jest spend some time with Belinda in her room—iffen ya don't mind."

For the first time Melissa turned around to look at Belinda. She gave her a glowing smile.

"That will be fun," she assured them. "Julia and I share a room at home. I was afraid I would be lonely." Then she added, "Do you mind, Belinda? I mean—you've had your own room—"

"I don't mind," Belinda said immediately, shaking her head. She would have said more—more about looking forward to it, counting the days, hoping that Melissa might never move out—but she caught Amy Jo looking at her and she decided not to make further comment.

"We were goin' to have the whole family in fer supper so ya could meet them all," Marty said, "an' then we thought it best to take it a bit slower. You'd never git us all straight at one time," she laughed softly. "So it will be jest the five of us to supper. Amy Jo will join us at table."

Melissa flashed Amy Jo a smile that Amy Jo returned, a little crooked and wobbly. Melissa turned back to her grandmother.

"Mother says that Uncle Clare and Aunt Kate live right near you—right across the yard. That must be so-o-o fun!"

"It is," smiled Marty. "You'll git to meet 'em all in good time."

And then Clark was halting the team and helping each one safely down. All but Amy Jo—she jumped down herself, casting a peeved glance over her shoulder as Clark helped Melissa over the wheel.

"I'll bring in thet luggage later," Clark informed them and began to unhitch the team.

The rest of them proceeded to the house, Melissa exclaiming about everything as she went. Over and over she made comments like, "Oh, Mother told me about this," or "It's just like Mother said!" Marty said that Missie must have done a thorough job of acquainting her daughter with her new surroundings, and Melissa nodded vigorously in agreement.

Belinda was asked to show Melissa their room and invited Amy Jo to join them, but she shook her head. She'd help Marty with the final supper preparations, she said.

Belinda led the way to the room, and Melissa exclaimed many times about how much she loved it. Then Belinda took Melissa to see the room that eventually would be hers, explaining that Melissa was to choose her own wallpaper and curtains and spread.

"Oh, I'll love it. I'll love it!" cried Melissa. "Mother has always done the selecting. I've never even been to the city. When do we get to go shopping?"

Belinda shook her head. She wasn't sure what to say. Would the yard goods in their little town suit Melissa?

"We don't go to the city much," Belinda said slowly. "We shop in town nearby here."

"They have those things here?" asked Melissa incredulously.

Belinda nodded. Of course they had those things.

"Mother always had to go to the city for shopping. They had only very crude, basic things in the local stores."

Belinda did hope Melissa wouldn't consider the store-bought yard goods "crude."

"Your town will be just as much fun as a city," Melissa assured her. "I still get to pick."

The supper hour was a busy time. Melissa still chatted away—although, in her defense, much of it was in answer to the many questions she was asked.

As soon as the meal was over and the family had read the Bible and prayed together—"We do this, too," Melissa told them—she began clearing away the supper dishes.

"Do you like to wash or dry?" she asked Belinda.

Marty was pleased to see the young girl offering to help. She cast a glance at Clark to be sure he had also noticed. Clark had and nodded to her in answer.

"You'll need to tell me about my chores," went on Melissa. "Julia and I had a list. Once in a while we'd change jobs—just so we wouldn't get bored doing the same things over and over. Mother didn't care—just as long as all of the chores were properly done."

Belinda nodded, glad to have someone to share the household duties.

"What do you like to do, Amy Jo?" asked Melissa.

"I don't live here," Amy Jo was quick to inform her.

"Oh, I know—you live in the log house. Right? That must be so much fun! I've never lived in a log house—but my mother lived in a soddy once. Anyway, I just meant for tonight—for now. What would you like to do for now?"

Amy Jo, who hated to wash the dishes and wasn't too fond of wiping them, either, said, "I'll put things away."

Clare came over to help Clark with the luggage. Melissa seemed to have brought enough things for three or four girls. One trunk was especially heavy.

"Whewee!" exclaimed Clare. "What's thet little lady got in here? Gold?"

"Didn't see much gold layin' round when I was out there," Clark responded.

"Oh, Grandpa," Melissa exclaimed, sounding like she was enjoying the teasing.

The luggage was all carried up to Belinda's room. Melissa could now begin to unpack. Belinda showed her the empty drawers and the closet space, and she and Amy Jo both lounged on the bed to watch the unpacking.

Belinda was sure that Melissa's things would never fit in the allotted space. *She must have scores of dresses,* Belinda thought with a twinge of envy.

Melissa's clothes were of fine quality and good workmanship. Belinda was sure her ma would not need to worry about preparing Melissa's wardrobe for the school term. But it was not the clothes that took all the space—Melissa's garments were really no more plentiful than Belinda's own. Books filled the heavy trunk and seemed to be Melissa's prized possessions—treasured volumes obviously captured her time and attention. Belinda and Amy Jo looked on in wide-eyed disbelief.

"Where'd ya git 'em all?" asked the candid Amy.

"As gifts," responded Melissa. "I love books. That's what I always ask for when Mother and Father go to the city. That's what I ask for on birthdays and Christmas—and other times, too."

Belinda let one finger trace the leather cover of a book lying on the top of the stack.

"Do you like books?" Melissa was asking.

Belinda nodded, but Amy Jo spoke for herself.

"I love 'em. I *love* 'em—but I've never see'd so many—not in all my life."

"You can borrow my books if you wish," Melissa was quick to inform them.

"Oh, could we? Could we? I'd love to. What's this one?" asked Amy Jo, hopping off the bed to carefully lift one from the trunk.

"It's a book on nature," replied Melissa.

"It's got lots of pictures!" exclaimed Amy Jo excitedly.

"Illustrations," Melissa corrected softly.

"How'd they git these pictures?" continued Amy Jo, ignoring Melissa's comment.

"An artist drew them."

"Drew 'em? Ya mean—with a pencil?"

"Or paints—or inks."

"Drew 'em," Amy Jo mused in a daze. "They look so real."

Melissa was called downstairs to come meet her aunt Kate and three boy cousins. Amy Jo did not move from her seat on the edge of the bed. Her eyes were fixed to the pages of illustrations. *How could anyone make such true-life drawings!* she marveled. But she'd sure like to try. She'd *love* to try. Something deep within her responded to the artwork in the book. Her eyes grew bright with hope as she studied the work. *Oh, if only I had such a book.* Her eyes went back to the trunk. So many—she'd had no idea this cousin from the West would have such treasures. And to think that she would be willing to share them! It was almost too good to be true.

Amy Jo sat for a long time, slowly paging through the fascinating book.

Clark and Marty knew Melissa must be terribly weary after her long trip. She did not protest when they suggested bed, saying that they could catch up on the rest of the news later.

Clare, Kate, and their family had returned to their log home across the yard, Amy Jo tightly clutching the illustrated nature book that Melissa had been more than willing to lend. Amy Jo promised she would be back in the morning as soon as her chores were done.

Marty sat quietly fingering the gifts from Missie that Melissa had promptly dug from her opened trunk as soon as she was able. The evening had been a satisfying and exciting beginning for all of them.

Melissa followed Belinda up the wide stairway and into the bedroom still strewn with books from her unpacking. As she gathered them up, she was glad she did not need to spend this first night alone in another room. She missed Julia. She missed her mother and papa. She even missed her two teasing big brothers.

Belinda folded back the spread, looking a bit shy.

"Do ya want the back or the front side?" she asked Melissa.

"You pick," encouraged Melissa. "It's your bed."

"I don't care," insisted Belinda.

"Then I'll take the back. That's where I sleep with Julia."

Without further comment the two prepared for bed, said their prayers, and climbed between the fresh sheets. They said a simple good night to each other and did not talk any further.

Melissa's tired thoughts took her back over the miles to those she had left behind—to her home, her room, her family as she had left them. Oh, how she would miss her family! But she took herself firmly in hand and told herself she was going to really like it here on the farm, with her wonderful grandparents whom she loved deeply already. And Belinda and Amy Jo . . .

And then she was asleep.

Belinda's thoughts went forward as she lay in bed beside Melissa. What were the days ahead going to be like? Would they like each other? Would they become good friends as well as kin? How would Amy Jo feel? She had seemed so happy over the books that Belinda was sincerely hoping Amy Jo would now also be pleased Melissa had come.

It was not long until Melissa's even breathing told Belinda she was asleep. Still, Belinda could not stop her thoughts from tumbling over one another. It was all so new and different—so strange. It was much later before she was able to quiet her busy mind and follow Melissa to dreamland.

"She's a real sweetheart, ain't she?" asked Marty after she and Clark had settled themselves in bed.

Clark chuckled. "Sweetheart—an' a real chatterbox," he responded.

"She had a lot to talk 'bout. I'm glad she's not tight-lipped. I woulda hated it iffen she had come from Missie an' not told us anything 'bout what's goin' on there."

"She does a bit of talkin'," Clark agreed, and he chuckled again.

"She's a pretty little thing, too," Marty commented further. "Those flashin' dark eyes an' that glossy brown hair. Her smile is like her ma's, though—but her colorin' sure isn't."

"Uh-huh," agreed Clark.

"An' she has nice things, too. I didn't know iffen I'd hafta git out my sewin' machine to have her ready fer school, or what."

"Missie wouldn'ta sent her to us without the things she be needin'."

"No, I guess not. I shoulda known better."

The pressure of Clark's hand on hers didn't mean "I told you so," but Marty realized Clark was right when he encouraged her not to worry about things.

There was silence for a few minutes.

"She's not 'uppity,' though," continued Marty.

"Ya thought she might be?"

"I wasn't sure. Ya know how Missie always talked 'bout all those ranch hands makin' such a fuss over her an' all."

"Well, I'm right glad she's not spoilt none," Clark was quick to point out.

Silence again.

"Did notice me one thing, though," said Clark thoughtfully.

"What's thet?"

"Did you notice how edjacated she be?"

Marty was silent. She had noticed *something,* come to think on it, but had not put it into words. "She's had her one more year of schoolin' than Belinda," she said at last.

"It's more'n thet. She talks—well, she talks careful like . . . not . . . not like you'd 'spect someone from out west to talk."

"Her ma an' pa was both edjacated."

"Yeah, but she's even more careful than either of 'em. Didn't ya notice?"

"Guess I didn't."

"You will," promised Clark.

"Maybe it's got somethin' to do with her wantin' to be a teacher."

"Missie was a teacher."

Marty thought about it. Melissa did talk more carefully than any of them. Well, it wouldn't hurt for them all to pay a bit more attention to how they spoke. It might be especially good for Belinda and Amy Jo.

"Ya know what thet there trunk was full of?" Marty asked. "The one thet ya groaned over carryin' it up the stairs?"

"What? Felt like bricks."

"Books."

"Books?"

"More'n half full of books," announced Marty. "Saw it myself. An' she was quick to share 'em with the other girls, too. Didn't ya see Amy Jo a huggin' one to herself like she'd never let go of it?"

"So she's a book lover, huh?" mused Clark. "Maybe *thet's* why she talks so proper."

"Could be," agreed Marty. But after thinking about it for a minute, she added another thought. "Do ya s'pose thet some of it might be Melissa's schoolteacher, Henry's wife, Melinda? 'Member how careful she always spoke?"

"I'll jest bet yer right. She probl'y drills her students on proper word talk. Melissa might notice a difference round here," said Clark. He was quiet for a few moments. "We'll hafta tread careful like," he went on. "She's got an awful lot of changes ahead of her."

"She has at thet," agreed Marty. "Won't be hard to be thoughtful of her. She's 'most won my heart already."

Clark reached out a hand to smooth Marty's hair back from her face. "I'm glad she came," he said softly. "Glad we're gettin' a chance to know her a bit. Makes one glad an' sad all at one time, don't it—doesn't it?" he corrected himself.

Marty agreed. As usual, he had read her thoughts perfectly.

NINE

Cousins

The rest of the family were all anxious to meet Melissa, so after the next Sunday's church service, they planned to gather at Clark and Marty's. They had all been introduced to her in the churchyard, but Marty was sure Melissa would never be able to keep all her cousins straight after just one meeting. And it was important to Marty for Melissa to really know her own kin.

Melissa had already mailed a fat letter home to her family, telling all of her experiences on the trip east and how exciting it was to meet her grandparents. She covered a whole page about Belinda and another about Uncle Clare and his family.

Marty had carefully planned the Sunday dinner and the time the family would spend together. The grown-ups were to sit at the table in the big kitchen, but the children would be allowed to take their dinner out on the wide back veranda. Marty debated about where to put Melissa. Would she feel more comfortable with the youngsters or the adults? Marty was getting herself in a stew over it when Clark interrupted her little argument with herself.

"Be good for Melissa to git to know her cousins afore school starts. Why, with the knowin' of all of 'em, she oughta know 'bout half the school." He chuckled at his own little joke.

Marty knew he was exaggerating, but she made no reply. Clark's comment served to make up her mind. She would put Melissa on the veranda with the rest of the youngsters. There were already enough adults at the table. Mary and Jane always wanted to sit at the table with the grown-ups. That made twelve and that was about all the big table could hold. Marty instructed Belinda about the setting of the table.

It wasn't long until the teams began to arrive, filling the farmyard with excited voices as cousins noisily greeted one another.

Melissa, who was busy helping cut apple pies, smiled as she heard the racket.

"Wouldn't Mother love to be here?" she commented.

Marty smiled back, sure that Missie would.

Arnie's family was the first to come into the house. Clark took care of introductions.

"Now, ya've met Arnie an' Anne at church. They have three rascals. They all look alike—only come in different sizes. Silas is the oldest. He's thet big fella carryin' thet lemon pie."

Silas smiled a rather shy smile, and Melissa greeted him warmly.

"Then there's John. Don't call 'im Johnny. *He* might not mind—but his ma won't like it." Clark winked playfully at Anne, and she smiled at the good-natured ribbing.

John gave his cousin a big grin, and Melissa smiled back immediately.

"An' this here little fella—make thet, 'this here big fella'—is Abe."

Abe grinned quickly and looked ready to bolt. They all could tell he would rather be out with the boy cousins his own age. Melissa chuckled as he give her a quick hug and then was gone.

Luke's family came in next, Abbie carrying a large potato salad. This family had been introduced at church, and Melissa now was able to repeat all their names. Thomas and Aaron were both anxious to get out to play, as well. Aaron was the baby of the bunch. Clare's Dack and Thomas were about the same age. Aaron wrapped his chubby arms around Melissa for a big bear hug, but Thomas backed shyly away.

Clare and Kate joined the group. Except for Amy Jo, their children did not come inside, but Melissa had already become acquainted with Dan, Davey, and Dack.

Nandry and Josh were the last to arrive. Mary and Jane, both a bit shy, welcomed Melissa. Somewhat plain and retiring like their mother, they were friendly and warm after they got to know Melissa better. Mary went to work in the kitchen and Jane went in search of Aaron, her special charge. Aaron did not object. He basked in all the special attention showered on the youngest. Free to pick his activity, his first choice was Grandpa's porch swing, and Jane willingly obliged.

They were just ready to sit down to their chicken dinner when Dan brought a wailing Davey in. He had fallen from the steps and cut his forehead. Uncle Luke had him patched up and smiling again in no time.

The mothers fixed plates of food for all who were to eat on the veranda. Even Aaron was allowed to join them, "all by myself," he announced proudly as he knelt on the bottom step in front of his food placed on the next step up. Belinda promised to keep an eye on him. Melissa wouldn't have known what went on around the big folks' table, but her delighted expression indicated she wouldn't have given up her spot on the veranda for the world.

Over the babble of excited voices, Dan and Silas tried to outdo one another in telling jokes. Most of them were corny, but their audience laughed heartily anyway.

Amy Jo spent most of her time scolding her young brothers. Dan was too silly, Davey too careless, and Dack too . . . too *everything,* she announced in exasperation while she went to get a rag for his spilled milk.

John was sitting nearest to Melissa. He eyed her openly and then asked in awe, "Do ya got yer own horse?"

Melissa nodded. "I have three of them, in fact," she told him.

"Three! Wow! All yer own?"

"All my own."

"What're their names?"

"Sandy—he was my first horse. He's getting quite old now. Pepper is black and really pretty, and there's Star. She has a white patch on her forehead that looks like a star. She's Pepper's mother."

"Wow!" said John again.

"Do you have a horse?" asked Melissa.

"No. Not my own. We have a pony—but we all gotta share it."

"Do you like horses?"

John's face answered the question even before he said, "Sure do. I'd give anything to have my own. Anything!"

"I've got a book about horses," offered Melissa. "You can look at it if you want to."

John's face lit up. He'd love to look at a book about horses.

"It tells all about the different kinds and how to train them and everything," Melissa said.

"Wow!" said John again.

"I'll get it for you as soon as dinner is over," promised Melissa.

From that moment on, Melissa could have asked whatever she wished and John would have done his very best to oblige her.

True to her promise, after they had finished their meal she brought the book for John to see. Several other cousins clamored to be close enough to look at the pictures, too.

"I have other books," said Melissa generously. "Would you like to see them?"

Several of the cousins declared that they would, and Melissa turned to Belinda.

"Do you mind if we go up to your room?" she asked, and when Belinda assured her that would be fine, Melissa led the way up the stairs. Soon the bedroom floor was covered with young bodies poring over all the exciting books. John was given the book about horses and the others were allowed to choose ones of interest to them.

"Boy!" said Silas. "How'd ya git ya so many? It's even more'n we have at our school."

"They've all been given to me," explained Melissa as she gently caressed the cover of one of her treasures.

Never had the household been so quiet on a Sunday when all the Davis family members were gathered together at home. Soon this little fellow or that began to coax for a book to be read aloud, and one after the other Melissa read some of the shorter ones. All eyes were on her face, all ears attentive to the reading.

Downstairs the adults interrupted their conversation to wonder where all of the children had gone.

"With this much peace an' quiet, they're all either asleep or in a heap of trouble!" Luke declared from his comfortable position on the davenport.

Kate eventually climbed the stairs to peek into Belinda's room. There she saw arms and legs crisscrossed over the rug-covered wooden floor as children listened in fascination to the voice of Melissa. Kate stood and stared in disbelief before she tiptoed back down the stairs.

"Yer never gonna believe what I jest saw," she informed the others. "The whole passel of 'em, all in Belinda's room, listenin' as quiet as can be whilst Melissa is readin' to 'em."

"You're kidding," stated Luke.

"Cross my heart," Kate insisted. "The whole bunch of 'em—jest spellbound."

"We shoulda brought thet there little gal out here years ago," Clare said loudly. "Jest think of the gray hairs it woulda saved."

The others laughed.

Marty could not resist quietly going up to see for herself. Just as Kate had said—there they all were, sprawled on the bed or on rugs and pillows across the floor of Belinda's room, all eyes fixed on Melissa. No one even stirred as Marty peeked around the door.

Well, I declare, she said to herself. *If that don't beat all.*

She went back down the stairs to assure the rest that Kate had not been fooling.

"Never seen nothin' like it," she stated. "Every last one of 'em. Quiet as you please."

"Guess she'll make her a schoolteacher, all right," said Arnie. "Anyone who can keep my three rascals quiet can handle 'bout anything."

"Sure didn't take her long to get acquainted," put in Luke.

"She already shared one of her books with Amy Jo," Kate told them. "I've never seen the girl so excited. Been copyin' it, she has. Tries to draw every picture. Some of 'em are kinda hard, too, but Amy Jo does a fair job of 'em, iffen I do say so." She paused to gaze reflectively out the window. "She sure has been eager to git to 'em. Never argues 'bout her chores now, 'cause she knows thet she is free to draw jest as soon as they are done."

Marty's eyes filled with tears. "It sure is nice to have Melissa here," she said softly. "Missie's gonna miss 'er. She's the sweetest thing ya ever saw."

Clare nodded in agreement. "She's sweet, thet's fer sure—but let's not put the burden of perfection on 'er."

Marty looked at Clare in surprise.

"Meanin'?"

"Well, she's human after all, Ma. Let's leave her some room to make some mistakes—have some flaws. She's gonna find plenty of 'em in us, her kin. Reckon we ought to allow her a few, as well."

Marty reflected on that for a while. Clare was right. Melissa was bound to have *some* weaknesses. They just hadn't seen them yet. Well, whatever they were, Marty would still love her, she decided. But even as Marty assured herself of that, she couldn't imagine anything that could possibly be wrong with Missie's little girl.

In spite of the rather rocky beginning during their drive home from the station, Marty was very happy at how well the three girls seemed to be adjusting to one another. There were times when two of them were together when the third girl was not included, but it was not a case of two shutting the other out. When the third girl arrived on the scene, she was always warmly welcomed to become part of the little group. There was no gossiping or vying for position or attention that Marty could see, and she thanked the Lord for that.

All three had their own unique personalities. Amy Jo, vibrant, alive, and artistic in nature, was apt to act and react spontaneously and sometimes to regret it later. She was quick to speak her mind, but quick to initiate a restoration of the relationship if she felt she had done or said something out of line.

Belinda had always been warm and compassionate. She felt it deeply if someone hurt her or was hurt. She was slow to become upset and quick to offer her aid. She loved to share and give. At times her loving nature brought her pain, and she suffered deeply with the suffering of another. But Belinda did not find it as easy to put aside words spoken in the heat of the moment. Often, the impetuous and careless barbs of Amy Jo could cause Belinda grief for days. She forgave, but it was difficult for her to get over the memory of her pain, and it affected her appetite, her rest, and her very being.

Melissa was somewhere in between the two. She loved to be with people and to share in their experiences. She was open and caring without taking charge, as Amy Jo was wont to do. Melissa was a communicator, though she chose her words with more care and consideration of the other person's feelings than Amy Jo, and her words never seemed to be used as a weapon. Melissa spent very little of her time alone, whereas Belinda could entertain herself with her own thoughts and company for hours on end. Amy Jo liked people if she was in the right mood.

And so the three girls interacted with one another, learning and growing from their friendship. Marty felt the experience would benefit all three of them.

All three went to town with Marty on the day Melissa was to choose her room colors and fabrics. From her previous experience, Marty wondered at the wisdom of taking three girls to choose for one room, but Amy Jo and Belinda wanted to be a part of it, and Melissa begged for them to be included. Clark smiled encouragingly at Marty as he handed her the reins for the team. She was sure he understood her misgivings.

The girls had worked themselves up to a feverish pitch at the thought of their trip to town. Amy Jo this time was doing most of the high-spirited chattering.

"I already found the most beautiful print," she was informing Melissa. "You'll jest love it—I know ya will."

"Oh, Amy Jo," admonished Belinda. "Remember, Melissa gits to choose for herself. We aren't gonna tell her what she should git."

"I won't tell her," replied Amy Jo rather hotly with a toss of her red-brown braids, "but that doesn't mean I shouldn't even show her the pretty piece we found before."

"Sure you can show me," offered Melissa. "And you can show me your choice, too, Belinda."

"I haven't chosen one," said Belinda. "Ma and I decided thet you should choose."

"And I will," Melissa said excitedly. "I can hardly wait. I wrote Mother and Father all about it."

"I jest bet you'll love the colored print. It is so . . . so . . . *vibrant*!" exclaimed Amy Jo. "Vibrant" was a new word she had found in one of Melissa's art books, and she loved it. The family would hear the word over and over during the next few months.

"Maybe Melissa doesn't like 'vibrant,'" Belinda said softly.

"Oh, Lindy," Amy Jo responded impatiently. "Do you think she's a child? She'll say if she likes it or not."

Marty feared a quarrel was about to commence.

"I think we'll go to the hardware store first an' pick out the wallpaper," she hurried to inform the girls, snapping the reins over the horses' backs. "Then we'll go look at the yard goods."

Her little plan for diverting an argument did not work. Amy Jo began to suggest a "good choice" for Melissa's walls. Belinda frowned, and Marty felt she had to move the conversation onto other ground entirely.

"Jest up ahead there is the school, Melissa," she announced, pointing to a white building set back in some trees. "Would ya like to stop an' peek in the winda? The door will likely be bolted, but we should be able to git us a bit of a look-see."

It worked, at least temporarily. The girls were soon excitedly talking about school. Marty sighed with relief and urged the team on a little faster. They would stop briefly at the schoolhouse, but then there was still a long road into town. Could she manage to keep the conversation even and controlled?

TEN

School

It was a weary Marty who turned the team back over to Clark when they arrived home. His eyes questioned her as he helped her down over the wheel, but he asked nothing aloud.

"Later," she whispered to him, and he nodded.

The three girls were gathering parcels and carrying them into the house.

"When will you do the wallpaperin'?" Amy Jo was asking. "I'll help."

"Grandpa will be doin' it," Marty called out as the three moved through the door. "I think he'll ask Clare if he needs 'im any help."

"Aw," groaned Amy Jo over her shoulder. "It woulda been fun iffen we three coulda did it."

"Done it," corrected Melissa evenly, no scolding in her voice.

"Grandpa will do the wallpaperin' tomorra," Marty went on as she joined them in the kitchen. There was no way she would be talked into allowing three young girls—at least these three—the opportunity of messing around in the wallpaper paste.

"What 'bout the curtains?" continued Amy Jo, her freckled face crinkled in disappointment.

"I'll sew up the curtains an' spread," answered Marty.

"Then we don't git to do nothin'," argued Amy Jo.

"You did the choosin'," Marty reminded her.

And what a job that was! she could have added. Belinda, though she had said very little, liked the soft pastel prints. Amy Jo had argued vociferously for the "vibrant" colors. Melissa had held her ground and picked a blue-and-white gingham. And her walls would have tiny blue flowers in vertical rows on a white background. For accents around the room she chose some bright blue for toss cushions, tie-backs, and bows for trimmings.

It wasn't what Marty would have selected. An all blue-and-white room seemed a little boring to her. But Marty did not try to sway Melissa. They had promised her own choice, and Marty intended to keep her word.

"I'll do the kitchen work while you sew," offered Melissa, and Marty nodded her appreciation.

"I still wish we could do some work on the room," grumbled Amy Jo.

"Ya can," said Marty with a tired sigh. "When yer Grandpa's done his paperin', ya can scrub the floor an' move back the furniture."

At Amy Jo's look of disgust, Marty added, "Maybe Melissa will let ya help arrange the furniture a new way," but Amy Jo was not to be cheered up so easily. Her disagreeable attitude quickly changed to one of defeat when Marty held her ground with an even and determined look of her own. From long experience Amy Jo knew when her grandmother was serious—it would be the girls' job to clean the room and move Melissa in after it had been redone.

"'Course we will," Belinda was saying. "That will be fun. We can put everything jest where Melissa wants it."

Marty watched Amy Jo as she looked around, her expression moving from *there's nothing for it but to cooperate* to *it might be a little fun at that.*

Marty sighed, then smiled and shook her head.

The room was papered, the curtains and spread made, and the little pillows stuffed with soft, old material. The girls began their housecleaning as Marty finished off the last of the sewing.

Melissa set up the ironing board and carefully ironed the new curtains, ruffle by ruffle. Belinda scrubbed the floor, and Amy Jo dusted the furniture but mostly fluttered about giving orders and excitedly exclaiming over everything.

The bed and dresser were moved back into the room with the help of Clare, who had come to see how the job was progressing. He said some nice things about its appearance and left the three girls to do the arranging. They all agreed, much to Marty's relief, that the bed should be under the window, the new curtains framing its head. The dresser fit nicely on the north wall, and the desk Clark was working on would stand in the corner near the door with the bookshelves.

By the end of the week the new room had its new occupant. Belinda told her mother that she really didn't want Melissa to move, but they were just across the hall from each other, and she knew it really was nicer for them each to have their own room. She did like her times alone and would soon have wearied of constant company, she said.

When it was all done, Marty had to admit that Melissa had chosen well. The gingham curtains and the bright splashes of blue went nicely with the light-patterned wallpaper. The shelves of books also added to the cheeriness and hominess of the room, and with the bright scatter rugs on the floor the room looked inviting and warm, as well as light and airy.

Marty sighed wearily as she retired that Saturday night. She was glad they had allowed Melissa the privilege of picking her own colors. She was also glad that the process did not need to be repeated in the near future. It had been tiring having the three girls excitedly rushing about the house, continually asking about her sewing progress. And though they had willingly worked in the kitchen, Marty really preferred being in charge there herself. She found herself redoing some of the tasks the girls had hurried through. So Marty was glad it was over and she could stretch out beneath the warm comfort of the soft quilt and let the kinks of the week's "busyness" gradually work out of her back and arms.

In just another week all the children but young Dack would be off to school for another year, and her days would be more her own, Marty reminded herself. She both welcomed it and was dismayed by it. The years were passing by so quickly. Before they knew it, Belinda, too, would be grown and moving on to a life of her own. *It will be so lonely in the old house when that happens,* Marty mourned. She thought of the last few busy, bustling days. She couldn't manage all that activity as well as she used to. But she wasn't ready to settle into a quiet and uneventful life, either.

When the first day of school arrived, it nearly matched the week Melissa's room had been redone for noise, commotion, and activity. Melissa and Belinda both fussed with their frocks and their hair—Melissa had three different dresses on before settling on a pale yellow with blue flowers. Belinda decided on a pink print. They each tried several hair styles and finally both went back to the comfortable familiar, the sides pulled back in a bow. They dashed back and forth between their rooms, exclaiming over this, agonizing over that, until Marty felt that she would never survive until they were finally out the door.

In her new bright green dress, Amy Jo stopped by for the two girls, and at last they were all on their way. Each girl looked feminine and appealing and strangely at ease, while Marty still felt her head spinning. She sighed as she watched the three join Amy Jo's two younger brothers, and then all five of them walked down the long lane to the road that would take them to the small country schoolhouse. Even from where she stood at her kitchen window, Marty could hear their excited voices drifting back to her. It was always that way on the first day. At the end of the day, too, they would come home eager to inform Marty and Clark and anyone who would listen about all the experiences of "first day." After that, Marty knew from past experience, the family was fortunate to get any information at all.

Marty turned from the window, poured herself a fresh cup of coffee, and sank wearily into a kitchen chair. The back door opened, and Clark's head cautiously peered around it.

"It safe to come back now?" he queried.

Marty smiled. "They all be gone, iffen thet's what ya be meanin'."

"They sure do git excited. I couldn't stand all thet flutterin' about.

Guess I must be gittin' old," and so saying, Clark entered the kitchen and tossed his worn farm cap into the corner. "Any coffee left in the pot?"

Marty looked from Clark to the cap on the floor. She made no comment, but Clark responded to her look. "No use hangin' it on the peg. I'm gonna go right back out again."

Marty made a move to get up from her chair for Clark's coffee, but he stopped her with a gentle touch on the arm, and she relaxed again.

Clark reclaimed his breakfast cup, crossed to the kitchen stove where the coffeepot still steamed, and poured himself another cup of the hot, dark liquid. He took the chair opposite Marty at the table.

"How ya holdin' up?" he asked in a teasing voice, but Marty could also sense his genuine concern.

She smiled. "Fine, I reckon—though it sure do slow a body down some."

"The first day of a new school year is always excitin', I remember, but didn't it seem to you thet they were flyin' higher 'n a kite this time?"

"Maybe so . . . maybe we jest fergit . . . I dunno." Marty took another sip of her coffee. "Maybe Melissa bein' here has somethin' to do with it. The other two are so anxious to show her off to all their school chums. Then, too, I s'pose thet new teacher also has 'em worked up some. They always seem to be a bit on edge until they know jest how a new teacher will be."

"Seemed nice enough to me," responded Clark.

"Good," said Marty. "It's so important for children to have a good teacher."

Marty drained her cup, but she didn't leave her chair. She sat companionably while Clark finished his.

"So now do ya git to rest ya some?" Clark asked.

Marty looked around her at the table covered with dirty dishes and the kitchen still untidy from preparing the breakfast and making school lunches. She didn't bother to reply. Clark could see the answer for himself.

"Least it'll be a bit quieter," he continued.

"Oh, they'll calm down in a day or two," Marty assured him. "They always do. Afore we know it, things will be so routine again thet we'll all feel a mite bored."

Clark nodded his head.

"Iffen I was you, though," went on Marty, "I'd be 'bout as far away as I could be, come end of the school day. They always come back even worse than they went off. Gotta tell every little thing thet happened the first day. Who did what an' went where an' got whatever—from the whole summer long."

She stopped with a twinkle in her eye and said, "On second thought, maybe ya'd like to be here to help do some listenin'."

Clark laughed. "Thanks for the invite," he said, setting his empty cup back on the table. "But, no, I guess I'll head me fer the farthest field."

Marty reluctantly lifted herself from the comfortable kitchen chair and began to stack the dishes.

"An' what 'bout you?" Clark asked her. "How ya plannin' on pro-tectin' yerself from the onslaught?"

"Ya ain't got any rock thet needs pickin' in thet far field, have ya?" asked Marty.

Clark laughed again and went to retrieve his cap from the corner. "Guess we'll make it somehow," he said confidently. "We always do."

Marty knew he was right. She stirred herself to hurry more with the dishes. She had bread to bake and a stack of laundry waiting for her.

"Think I'll look round fer a job thet might take the help of a young'un," Clark continued. "Got me a feelin' it's gonna be a powerful long day fer young Dack."

It was Marty's turn to smile. True, it would be a long day for Dack. It also was a wonderful excuse for Clark to enjoy his grandson.

In spite of her dire warnings to Clark, Marty found her excitement mounting as the clock on the wall shelf announced it was almost time for the children to be returning from school. She crossed to the window and looked out to the road several times before she heard the dog bark his welcome and knew the children would soon come bursting through the door.

Marty set out some glasses and poured cold milk. She wasn't sure just how many of the young troop would stop at the big house. She knew Kate's family would be eager to tell about their day, as well.

Marty heard the excited voice of young Dack as he enthusiastically welcomed home his brothers and the girls.

Amy Jo was first through the door of Marty's kitchen. She led Belinda and Melissa. The boys had gone on home to the log house.

"Gramma," exclaimed Amy Jo, "guess what happened at school today!"

"How 'bout ya jest tell me," responded Marty, lifting fresh sugar cookies from the cooling rack to a plate. "Never was very good at guessin' games."

"We got a new teacher!"

Marty looked up. "We already knew thet," she said. "'Member—we talked 'bout it fer the last several days. Yer grandpa helped to move her in."

The new teacher was a recently widowed lady from a nearby town who had been most happy to get the job. She had moved into the local teacherage just as soon as she was sure the job was hers, and Clark had been one of the men who had driven a wagon over to load her furnishings.

The girls looked at one another and snickered behind their hands. Marty could not understand the joke.

"I know ya told us 'bout the teacher," explained Belinda, "but we didn't know 'bout her family."

"She has a family? I *didn't* know 'bout thet. I thought thet she was alone when yer—"

"She was," Belinda said quickly. "Her family was at their grandparents' or aunt's—or somethin'."

"I'm glad to hear she has family," said Marty as she poured one more glass of milk and set it on the table.

The girls looked at one another again, a general tittering accompanying the glances.

"So what does she have fer family?" asked Marty, innocently enough.

This brought outright giggles from all three girls.

Amy Jo was the first to recover sufficiently to speak. "A boy!" she gasped out.

"A boy?" Marty looked at the giggling girls. Even Melissa was acting like a silly schoolgirl. Marty had expected her to be at least a bit more mature than the two younger girls.

"Well, does this here boy have three ears an' one eye, or what?" asked Marty.

All three girls groaned in unison. Marty wasn't sure how to interpret the answer.

"Oh, no-o," said Amy Jo. "He's . . . he's . . . well, he's *vibrant*."

"Don't be silly, Amy Jo," chided Belinda. "Boys aren't vibrant."

"Well, he's . . . he's . . ." Amy Jo began again, but Melissa cut in. "Divine," she finished with an exaggerated sigh.

All three girls went back to giggling. Marty was beginning to get the picture. Her sigh was even deeper than Melissa's. Was she ready to deal with three young girls in the middle of schoolgirl crushes over the same boy?

"You'll like 'im, Mama," said Belinda, turning in her chair to look at Marty. "He is so mannerly and so tall and so—"

"Divine," repeated Melissa.

More moans and groans, finished with giggles.

"Well, it do seem thet this boy has made hisself quite an impression," ventured Marty. "I sure hope thet his mama is equally qualified. Haven't heard one comment on what ya all think of yer new teacher."

After a pause, "She's nice," offered Belinda, "an' Jackson treats her so . . . so . . ."

"Gentle," put in Melissa.

"Yeah, gentle."

It seemed that "nice" was all Marty was to hear about the new schoolmarm.

Amy Jo reached for another sugar cookie. "An' he even treats his little brothers good."

Marty was sure that to Amy Jo, treating younger brothers "good" must be going the second mile indeed.

"He has brothers?" asked Marty.

"Two. An' he doesn't even fight with 'em and they go to 'im when they need help with their work—"

"How old are they?" asked Marty.

"One in grade one an' one in grade four, an' they really like Jackson, ya can tell by the way they—"

Marty was tiring of all roads leading back to this Jackson. "Is thet all thet happened at school today? Jest this here Jackson making his impression on ya?"

Melissa stepped away from her chair and toward Marty. "Oh, Grandma," she said, "he is really nice. He is tall with broad shoulders and blondish hair and a little mark in his chin, sort of like a dimple. And he is real smart in school. He has only one more year to be taught by his mother because she has taught him everything she can, almost, and then he wants to go on to school somewhere and train in some occupation—maybe banking, or some such thing—that is, if they can afford it. His father died, you know—with consumption—and they don't have much money, so he might have to go to work instead. He's only sixteen, but he's strong, so he could get a job easily enough, but he'd—"

"Whoa!" said Marty, holding up her hand while Melissa stopped midsentence.

There was silence for a moment as Marty looked around the kitchen at the three girls. Marty was the one who broke it. "I'm sure he is a fine boy—but there must be other things thet took *some* of yer time at school today."

The three girls looked blank. Finally it appeared Belinda had come up with something. Her face brightened. "I asked the teacher an' her family fer supper," she informed Marty.

"Supper?" Marty wheeled to face her. *"Supper?"*

"Oh, not tonight," Belinda quickly amended. "Jest sometime."

Marty made no comment. She had been given quite a start.

"Ya always invite the teacher—sometime," Belinda added, "so I thought I should tell her 'bout it."

"I see," said Marty as she turned to put another stick of wood in the stove. "I jest hope thet ya made yer new teacher an' her two younger sons feel as welcome at their new school today as ya must have made this here Jackson fella," she remarked.

Three heads dipped slightly.

"An' I hope ya all three behaved yerselves like the ladies ya been taught to be," continued Marty, turning back to look at each one squarely.

The girls stole looks at one another.

"An' I hope ya all are prepared to spend yer school time learnin' what the teacher's tryin' to learn ya."

Three solemn pairs of eyes studied Marty. She decided she had pressed it far enough.

"An' what did ya think of yer first day at this new school, Melissa?" she asked, changing the subject.

"I like it," answered Melissa politely.

"An' did the other young'uns make ya feel welcome?"

"Oh yes," said Melissa, nodding her head vigorously.

"Good! An' ya liked the students?"

More snickering. Marty knew she shouldn't have asked that last question.

"So . . . ya all like this here Jackson?"

The girls did not answer with words, but their eyes admitted the fact.

"An' he liked us, too," ventured Amy Jo.

"All of ya?"

They all nodded.

"Well," said Marty matter-of-factly, dusting the wood chips from her hands after feeding the fire, "thet sounds safe enough. No boy I know of can manage three girls at once. Long as this here Jackson don't go an' pick out jest one, guess we needn't worry none."

The girls looked at one another, the unspoken questions on their faces: Was Marty talking to them—or to herself? They couldn't be sure, but her words seemed to get through to them. Would Jackson continue to consider all three of them his friends? Would he "pick" one of them? If so, which one would it be? And how would the other two feel? They turned back to their milk glasses with more serious faces.

"Now, ya best hurry up with yer milk an' cookies," instructed Marty. "Ya need to change so thet ya can care fer yer chores. An', Amy Jo, I'm sure yer mama will be wantin' to see you at home."

And so saying, Marty turned back to her kitchen counter and supper preparation. Further talk would need to wait, but she was resigned to a lot more of it in the days and weeks to come.

ELEVEN

Back to Routine

Marty watched the days on the calendar pass—busy ones with fall canning and gardening, but rather routine. For Belinda and Melissa the days were also full. They trudged the distance to school, where the new teacher insisted upon close attention to what they were being taught. They walked home again to the many farm chores that awaited them. Amy Jo always joined with them, as well as Dan and David.

Clark's days were filled with harvest work. He and Clare worked together in the fields, and when they had finished their own tasks, there was usually an ailing neighbor to help. By the time all of the crops had been brought in, the fall winds were chill and hints of winter were in the air.

Marty had been wrong about one thing: the girls did not quickly settle back to their normal emotional levels. They still returned from school in an excited frenzy each day and always the talk was of Jackson. Jackson did this and Jackson said that, until Marty was truly weary of it all.

Marty still had not had the opportunity to meet Jackson or his schoolteacher mother. She had thought they would join the community in Sunday attendance at the little church, but so far the Brown family felt strong ties to the small church in their former town. Every Sunday, according to reports, they hitched their one horse to a light buggy and drove the fifteen miles back to worship with the lifelong friends who had supported them in their bereavement.

So Marty tried not to lose patience as the three silly girls sighed at the end of the school day over young Jackson. If Marty had listened, she would have heard many things about him that she would have admired—both true and imagined. But she did not listen. She was tired of the tales. She was tired of the swooning. She wished Jackson had never arrived to upset her three girls and her world.

She even considered forbidding the girls to talk about Jackson once they were in the kitchen, but she decided not to, in case the regulation would blow the situation way out of proportion. After all, it was a passing fancy. At their age, if the girls were not moping around over Jackson, they undoubtedly would have found someone else to pine over.

Marty still had not invited the teacher and her family for dinner. True, she had been unusually busy with her fall work, but Marty had always been busy and still had found time to invite guests. However, this year's teacher had not yet been given an official invitation. Eventually Clark commented on it.

"Not plannin' to have the teacher in this year?" he asked her one night when they were preparing for bed.

Marty's head immediately came up. Even that simple statement had her on the defensive.

"'Course," she answered a bit too quickly and sharply. "Been busy."

Clark didn't pursue it further, but his eyes told her he knew he had somehow hit a raw nerve.

Marty quickly repented. She had answered a simple question with a sting in her voice. How could Clark know she dreaded the thought of bringing that young man Jackson into her home, where she would need to watch firsthand three silly girls tittering and swooning over him. Yet it seemed foolish to admit to such a ridiculous feeling.

She sighed as she slipped on her nightgown. The girls had been continually pestering her about it. She wouldn't be able to put them off much longer. Every other day, it appeared, they were informing her of which neighbor family had had the Browns over for supper. Marty could not hold out much longer without seeming aloof and uncaring in her neighbors' eyes. Yet perhaps the neighbors did not have daughters who talked and giggled incessantly about one tall, good-looking, mannerly young fellow. Marty sighed again.

"Somethin' troublin' ya?" asked Clark patiently.

"It's jest this here Jackson fella."

"Teacher's son."

"Ya've heard of 'im?"

"How could one live in this here household an' not hear of 'im?" inquired Clark with a grin.

Marty felt some of the weight shifting from her shoulders. She was even able to laugh in return.

"Guess yer right. It's been 'most unbearable, hasn't it? I git so sick of hearin' all the tales of Jackson I could jest scream at times. 'Jackson said this'—an' it might be somethin' as simple as, 'It looks like it might rain,' but, oh my, it's so intelligent or so funny if *Jackson* says it."

Clark laughed in return.

"They're jest young girls growin' up," he reminded her. "The others all muddled their way through thet stage, too."

"Did they, Clark?" Marty asked seriously. "I've been tryin' an' tryin' to remember, but I really don't recall Nandry or Clae or Missie or Ellie actin' like this. Did they?"

It looked like Clark was thinking deeply as he unstrapped his artificial limb and laid it aside.

"Don't recall 'em carryin' on like this, either, come to think on it," he answered and let one hand reach down to gently massage the stub of his leg.

"I know thet they noticed the young fellas," Marty said, "but they didn't fill their days an' their minds with 'em like these girls do. I don't understand it—an' I guess I don't much like it, either."

"I s'pose part of it is havin' the three of 'em so close together in age. They jest sorta egg one another on, so to speak."

Maybe that was it. Maybe they would be sensible, too, if they were each on their own instead of comparing and adding to and outdoing one another's stories. Marty folded back the blankets and fluffed up the pillows.

"Well, as I see it," Clark picked up the conversation again, "we'll jest have to hold steady an' keep on prayin' for some sense to return to our girls, an' fer the strength to endure all the swoonin' an' talkin' till it do." He smiled slightly. "We need ta jest hang in there, knowin' thet 'this, too, shall pass.'"

"Yer right," agreed Marty with another sigh. "An' I gotta git busy an' have thet teacher in."

The two knelt together for prayer before retiring for the night. Marty slipped her smaller hand into Clark's large one as they prayed together for each one of their family members, and for the needs of the community that were known to them, and especially for wisdom and understanding in all of their relationship—including three young girls caught in the time between childhood and womanhood.

Amy Jo's birthday arrived. The four from the big house joined Clare and Kate's family for the birthday supper. For Amy Jo it was a momentous event—for a few months she was the "same age" as Belinda, and to Amy Jo that was very important.

Her young brothers were excited, too. A birthday was a celebration, and they reveled in sharing the birthday meal and cake and begged to help her open the presents. Clark and Marty's gift was a note—a note explaining to Amy Jo that by the permission of her pa and ma, Marty would take her into town and let her do her own choosing for new wallpaper for her room and yard goods for curtains and matching spread. Amy Jo bounced joyfully up and down, her auburn tails bobbing out behind her. Marty was sure there was no other gift they could have given her that would have made her more excited.

Her parents' gift to young Amy Jo brought equal excitement. There, in a neatly wrapped package, were art supplies and a simple book on sketching. Amy Jo was wild with her good fortune. She could hardly wait to begin her efforts. Marty wondered fleetingly if the family would constantly be plagued at awkward moments with requests to pose for a portrait, but she said nothing.

In spite of her granddaughter's joy, Marty really was not looking forward to the trip to town to make the purchases for the bedroom, but she kept her promise at the very first opportunity. Not surprisingly, Amy Jo insisted that Belinda and Melissa also accompany them. Marty knew that she would be weary when the day was over—unless, of course, Amy Jo stayed with the same choice she had made previously. In that case, the mission could be accomplished quite quickly.

It was not to be. Amy Jo decided to go with something completely different. She wanted something "vibrant." Marty wondered just how much more vibrant than the bright purple flowers a piece of yard goods could be, but she held her tongue and suffered through the long decision making. Amy Jo took her time, vacillating between a daring yellow with scattered red flowers and leaves, and a smoky blue with green and lavender splashes. Marty had never known that such colorful prints existed.

Amy Jo finally settled on the smoky blue and tried to match the wallpaper to the yard goods. Marty was sure the room would seem dark—though hardly dreary.

They did find a wallpaper with the same colors—the background was a bit more blue with an all-over pattern of small purple flowers and green leaves.

But Amy Jo insisted that it would look just right.

Clare was persuaded to put up the paper the very next day while Kate sewed the curtains and Marty made the spread. Amy Jo moved into her "new" room, exclaiming over and over how *vibrant* it looked. Marty had to admit that, surprisingly, the room did look quite homey and inviting. She was glad to move on to other things. Winter was upon them and she hadn't yet had the teacher's family in for supper.

TWELVE

Emergency

About the only events that distracted Belinda's attention from Jackson were the house calls she was able to make with Luke. He still stopped by for her when he had a case in the country that he thought would be suitable for her involvement. Now that she was back in school, those times were less frequent, and Belinda undoubtedly would have chafed over the situation had not her life and her mind been so busy with Melissa, school—and Jackson. As it was, she squealed her delight whenever she saw Luke's buggy pull into their lane.

Amy Jo still turned up her nose over Belinda's medical interest, wondering aloud how anyone could possibly enjoy seeing blood and fevers. Melissa, on the other hand, openly admired Belinda, though she had no desire to accompany her. She was considerate, however, about shouldering some of Belinda's responsibilities in the kitchen on those days when she went off with her doctor brother. Melissa always asked for a full report on the patient when Belinda returned home again, but she did turn a bit pale at times when Belinda described some aspects of their care.

A brisk, cold wind blew in with Luke when he turned his team into the yard one Saturday morning. Belinda flew out the door to meet him at the hitching rail.

"Get back in there and get a coat," he scolded her. "Winter is here, and you're out here like it was a summer day. I'll be called out to doctor you next!" He may have been a doctor, but he was also her brother, so Belinda ignored his protest, assuring him she felt warm and would use the blanket if she got cold.

"Where we goin'?" she asked him.

"Out to the Simpsons'. Thought it about time you saw a broken bone. But hurry. We don't want to make the poor boy suffer any longer than we have to. A broken limb can be awfully painful."

Belinda ran back to the house to inform Marty. "We're gonna set a broken bone," she called over her shoulder as she rushed back out the door. "It shouldn't take long."

Luke had already swung the horses around, and the buggy left the yard at a brisk trot. While they traveled Luke told Belinda about bones—the structure of the human body and what the large bones were called. They went over the names until she had them well in her memory. Then he went on to describe different kinds of breaks and the basic treatment for each. Belinda listened with wide eyes.

"What kinda break is this one?" she asked, hardly able to wait until they got there and she could see for herself.

"I wasn't told. I was just informed that the young Simpson boy had broken a limb in a logging accident of some kind."

"Which limb?"

"I don't even know. I'm guessing it's a leg. Usually when a log rolls, it gets the leg," replied Luke and clucked again to hurry the team.

For the first time in several days, Jackson was far from Belinda's thoughts. "Are ya gonna take 'im to town?" she asked.

"Not likely. Once it's set, he should be able to rest in his own bed. I'll stop by often to see how it's coming."

"I don't think I know the Simpsons," said Belinda.

"They're new. Just moved onto the old Coffin place."

"Oh. Will they be comin' to our school?"

"I don't know a thing about the family."

"It would be nice," said Belinda. "Iffen they have school-age young'uns, thet is."

They turned the team down the rutted, overgrown lane and pushed them hastily toward the simple log dwelling. Belinda was scrambling quickly down over the wheel when she heard the most agonized scream she had ever heard in her life. She felt, rather than saw, Luke stiffen. His head jerked up, and his body seemed to become a machine of action. Without even a backward glance, he grabbed his black bag and sprang toward the house. "You tie the team," he called over his shoulder.

Belinda stood shaking. Luke had said that broken bones could be painful, but never had she dreamed they could make one scream so. Another scream pierced the air, and Belinda broke from her frozen stance and began to flip the reins of the horses carefully around the post. Luke might need her help. She should get to him quickly.

But when Belinda reached the door of the log cabin, she was met by a heavyset woman in a worn and dirty apron. She placed herself solidly in the doorway, her legs slightly akimbo. Belinda could see that her eyes were red from crying and her brow covered with sweat.

"The doc says you're to stay out," she said tiredly.

Belinda could not understand the order. Luke had brought her along to learn how to set a bone. He might even need her assistance, and here was this woman trying to bar her entrance.

"But—" began Belinda, peering over the woman's shoulder toward the door at the back of the room.

"It's not a pretty sight in there," the woman continued, and her whole body trembled.

Another cry rent the stale air of the little cabin. For a moment Belinda went all weak and she, too, trembled. She had never heard such a sound in all her life. Scuffling noises came from the small room. Belinda wondered wildly just what was going on. Luke might need her. He might even be in trouble. How was she to know?

With one quick movement she ducked around the woman and ran to the room from which the awful cry had burst. Luke had already laid aside his heavy coat and even removed his jacket. His shirt sleeves were rolled up and he was bending with deep concentration over a form on the bed. A man and a boy also stood over the writhing form, pinning it to the bed sheets. Sweat beaded the brow of the man, and the boy's lip trembled.

"I thought I told you to stay out," said Luke without even turning around.

Belinda took a deep breath to help control her shaking. Her eyes were getting more accustomed to the darkness of the room. Only one small, dingy window let in any light. She looked back at Luke's strong back. The muscles rippled beneath his thin shirt as he fought to administer some kind of drug to the thrashing patient. In spite of a wave of nausea sweeping through her, Belinda swallowed hard and stepped forward.

"I thought ya might need me," she said determinedly.

"Can you?"

"I . . . I think so," she replied, swallowing hard.

"I do need you—badly—but I don't want—"

"What should I do?" asked Belinda quickly.

"Get a lamp. I need more light."

Luke had not turned to look at Belinda, his full attention concentrated on the injured young man.

Belinda swallowed again and hurried from the room. She must not waste time. Luke needed a light. He needed her.

The woman stood in the kitchen, her head leaning against the wall. Great sobs shook her body. Belinda wished to go over to her and offer some kind of comfort, but there wasn't time yet. "We need a lamp," she said firmly, but the woman did not seem able to move.

Belinda cast her eyes about the kitchen. There was a lamp on a shelf near the stove. She lifted it down and shook it to check the fuel supply. It did have oil. Hurriedly she struck a match on the stove surface and lit the lamp, then hastened with it to the bedroom.

The boy on the bed was no longer screaming. He was not thrashing around as much, either. Belinda breathed a little sigh of relief. The drug Luke had given must already be working. She pushed forward with the lamp, holding it out in front of her so it would shed light on Luke's work.

It was then she saw the patient. It was not a broken leg that Luke bent over. Neither would Belinda have called it a broken arm. Mangled and crushed beyond recognition, the appendage was only blood and bits of tangled flesh and bone. Belinda felt her stomach lurch. For a moment she was sure that the rush of blood leaving her head would put her on the floor. She reached awkwardly for the bedpost with one hand, the lamp clutched in the other, and hung on for dear life as she fought for control. The room gradually stopped spinning, but Belinda feared she would lose her breakfast. Wave after wave of nausea swept over her. Luke had no time for a second patient. Belinda fought with all her strength to bring herself under control. Luke would need her help. He would need all the help he could get.

The youth showed no sign of struggling now. Mercifully the drug had claimed him. Luke bent over the bloody mass that had been an arm and carefully examined it. Belinda held the lamp as steadily as she could, trying to avoid the scene before her, but her eyes kept returning to the sight.

Luke straightened and looked directly at the large man who still held his son, even though it was no longer necessary.

"I'm sorry, sir," Luke said as gently as he could, "I'm going to have to take the arm to save the boy."

A convulsive sob shook the man. One large hand reached up to cover his face as he wept uncontrollably. The other hand remained on the shoulder of the boy on the bed. Luke reached out a hand to another younger boy, who also stood with his hands still holding his brother.

"You can go now, son," he said softly.

The boy dashed from the room, and they heard the front door open and slam shut again. Belinda distractedly thought that he should remember a coat. She had discovered it was colder than she had thought on the way here.

"I'll need lots of boiling water and some clean cloths," Luke informed the man. "You needn't worry about him throwing himself around now. He's beyond the pain."

The man wiped at his wet face with a ragged, dirty sleeve and hurried to do Luke's bidding. Belinda moved in closer with the lamp. Luke looked about the small room and dirty bedding, but he muttered to Belinda there was no way he could move the boy into his office in town.

"I'm going to need your help, Belinda. Do you think you can manage?"

Belinda nodded, her insides still churning, but she was determined.

"Put the lamp on that little table and pull it as close to the bed as you can. I'll need your hands to help me with this surgery."

Belinda placed the lamp and returned to do whatever else Luke needed.

The rest of the morning was only a blur in Belinda's memory. She worked alongside Luke as one in a trance. She knew that she responded to each of his orders. She handed him his instruments, reached out supporting hands, acted as she was directed, but she did it all in some kind of stupor. At one point the boy stirred slightly, and Belinda had to administer more chloroform. Her hand trembled as she held the cloth with the chemical to his nose and mouth. Luke watched carefully and told her when to draw it away.

The surgery seemed to take forever. By the time the stub of the limb was bandaged and the instruments cleared away, Belinda was beyond exhaustion. So was her brother, the doctor. He leaned his head wearily against the post of the bed and a tremor went through his body. Belinda had never seen him like this before.

He did not succumb to the moment for long. He again turned back to his patient and checked his eyes and took his pulse.

"Watch him carefully for any change," he told Belinda. "I'm going to get this mess out of here," and, so saying, Luke began to bundle the remains of the crushed limb in bloody rags so that he could dispose of it all.

Belinda allowed herself to sit on the edge of the bed. It was the first time she had taken a really good look at the patient. He was young, no more than seventeen or eighteen, she guessed. And he was deathly pale. She had never seen anyone quite so white. His breathing seemed shallow but steady. She wondered how long it would be before the anesthesia wore off. How would he feel when he wakened? There would be enormous pain, Belinda knew. He would be suffering for many days—weeks, even. But he would not have an arm. Belinda thought about the anguish he would feel. What a terrible thing to happen to a young man. To lose his arm just as his life was opening up to adulthood.

Belinda thought of Clark and his missing leg. It had been hard for her pa, she knew that. Even though it had happened before her birth, her mama had told her about the pain and suffering that went with the experience. But Clark had been a grown man—a man mature enough to accept his situation. And Clark had the Lord to help him. Faith in his heavenly Father had somehow gotten him through. What about the young man before her? Did he know the Lord? For some reason, Belinda feared not. Without taking her eyes from the pale face before her, Belinda began to pray, her voice no more than a whisper.

"Oh, God," she implored, "I don't know this boy. I don't know iffen he knows you, but he's gonna need ya, God. He's gonna need ya to help him accept this awful thing thet has happened in his life. He's gonna need ya to help him git better again." Without thinking Belinda reached out a hand and brushed the hair back from the pale, sweat-dampened forehead. *His hair is a nice color—almost as shiny an' black as a raven's wing* was the thought that flashed through her mind. The face was finely formed and well proportioned, the nose straight and even. Belinda suddenly realized that in spite of the paleness and an unkempt appearance, the boy was very nice looking. Self-consciously her hand drew back. What was she doing gently stroking the face of an unknown boy? A flush warmed her cheeks.

Luke returned, bringing with him the parents. His eyes searched Belinda's face. He seemed pleased with what he saw there.

"You can leave now," he said softly. "I'll stay with him."

The woman was bending over her son, sobs shaking her body, when Belinda slipped quietly from the room. She didn't know where to go. It was really too cold to wait outside. She did long for some fresh air, though, so she grabbed Luke's coat, wrapped it tightly around her, and left the small cabin.

There was a woodpile in a shed nearby. Belinda decided she would carry in some wood and make some coffee—if she could find the grounds and a pot. She was sure the family could do with some activity to momentarily divert them from the tragedy. Even a cup of coffee might bring some kind of relief and refreshing.

Belinda was not in a hurry. She needed to stretch her legs a bit—work the knots out of protesting muscles. She strolled back and forth, studying the farm before her.

Kinda run-down looking, she noted. Belinda had forgotten that it had been without tenants for a number of years. The new folks certainly had their work ahead of them. The buildings were ramshackled, the fence rails down, the garden area showing unsightly weeds, even through the early sprinkling of snow.

Belinda wondered just where the young boy had been working when it had happened. Luke said a logging accident. Was he hurrying to get in a winter supply of wood before the colder weather struck? Belinda lifted her eyes to the wooded area at the far end of the field. Was that where tragedy had struck this young man and his family?

At last Belinda turned back to the small log shack that housed the family wood supply. She went in to pick up an armload for the kitchen stove. Her eyes had not yet become accustomed to the darkness when a slight movement startled her. She jumped, a quick intake of breath escaping her lips. It was the younger boy who crouched in the corner. Belinda quickly regained her composure.

"I'm sorry," she said. "I didn't see ya there."

The boy said nothing. It was just as Belinda had feared—he had run from the house with no coat.

"Ya must be cold," said Belinda. She was glad he was at least out of the cold wind.

The boy still said nothing, only hugged his knees to his chest.

Belinda tried a smile. "Yer brother is gonna be fine now," she told him.

The boy began to sob uncontrollably. Belinda wished to comfort him but she wasn't sure what to do. She just let him cry.

After several minutes he began to mop his tears on patched shirt sleeves. "He's not gonna die?" he asked in disbelief.

"Oh no!" said Belinda. "Dr. Luke is with him. He'll be okay now."

The boy succumbed to a fresh burst of tears. When they had subsided he mopped up again, then turned large, dark eyes to Belinda.

"I was so scared he'd die," he told her shakily. "I didn't think anyone could live with an arm . . . with an arm . . ." He couldn't go on.

There was silence for a few minutes.

The boy broke it. "Will his arm ever get better?" he asked quietly.

Belinda did not know how to answer. Was it her place to inform the boy of his brother's amputation? Shouldn't Luke or his parents be telling him?

"Will it?" the boy insisted.

Belinda decided it would be worse if she tried to evade the truth. She crossed closer to him in case he needed her, crouched down, and looked him squarely in the eye. "Not . . . not really," she said, "but it will heal now."

His eyes grew big. "Wha'd'ya mean?" he asked her.

"The doctor . . . the doctor had to take off the arm . . . then sew it up . . . to save yer brother."

"Ya mean, cut it off?" His eyes were wild with fright and shock.

Belinda nodded slowly.

"But he'll *hate* that. He'd rather die! Don't'cha see? He'd rather die."

The boy leaped to his feet, his eyes challenging Belinda. By the time he finished his speech, his voice was a high-pitched scream. Belinda wondered if he was going to kick at her angrily. She was sure the temptation was in his mind. And then his whole body slumped dejectedly, and he threw his arms about her and cried, the deep sobs shaking the slender body.

There was nothing Belinda could say. She just held the weeping boy and cried along with him.

Much later than their parents had anticipated, Luke and Belinda turned in from the road. Marty had been frequently checking out the kitchen window, her eyes scanning for any sign of them. It was with great relief she saw Luke's team of blacks coming up the lane.

Luke came in with Belinda, though the hour was getting late.

Marty met them at the door, the questions showing in her eyes. It was evident from the extreme weariness of both her offspring that something unexpected had faced them at the farm home.

"It wasn't just a break," Luke informed her quietly.

"Ya like a cup of hot tea and a sandwich?" Marty asked him.

"That would be nice," said Luke, and he shrugged out of his coat, then unwrapped the blanket Belinda had clutched about her.

"Ya be needin' me, Ma?" asked Belinda in a weary voice.

"No. No, guess not," Marty responded, then cast a glance Luke's direction.

"I think I'll go on up to bed, then," said the young girl.

"Don't ya want somethin' to eat?"

"No. Thank ya, Ma. I'm not hungry. Jest awful tired."

Luke's eyes told Marty to let her go.

Marty pulled Belinda close for a moment and then kissed her on the forehead. Belinda looked like she was glad for the comfort of her mother's arms and gave a weary smile.

Marty reminded her that Melissa was staying overnight with Amy Jo, so she'd be able to get to bed and rest right away. Belinda didn't look like she would be up to answering any questions.

Luke pulled out a chair and sat down at the table. Clark joined him but shook his head no at Marty's offer of a cup of tea. Marty busied herself at the stove and cupboard and soon had a roast beef sandwich, made with thick slices of homemade bread and farm butter, to set before her weary son. She poured two cups of tea and sat down to join him.

"I take it this was a tough one," Clark was saying.

Luke nodded his head. "'Bout the worse thing I've seen yet."

"Not a break, ya said."

"Crushed. Crushed beyond recognition."

"Did Belinda—?" began Marty, but Luke stopped her question with his hand.

"I told her to stay out, but she came in anyway. Said I might need her help." He swallowed a sip of the hot tea and sat silent for a minute. "I did. I sure did. I don't know what I'd have done without her."

"She could . . . could face it?"

"At first she nearly passed out . . . I saw that. But she fought against it, and she helped through the entire surgery. Did everything just like I asked her. She was a real brick about it. I was proud of her."

Marty shuddered and pushed back her cup. She did not want the tea after all. In her mind's eye she was seeing again the crushed leg of her husband.

"She's made of good stuff, that kid of yours," Luke was saying, and there was pride in his voice.

"Ya don't think it was too much fer her?" asked Clark.

"I would never have knowingly decided to let Belinda see what she did . . . not at her age. I would have kept her out of there if I could have . . . if I hadn't needed her in order to save that boy's life. There was no one else to help me. Belinda knew the names of each of my instruments as I called for them, and we were fighting against time. I hope . . . I hope and pray . . . that it wasn't too much for a girl her age. I . . . I don't think it was. I think . . . I think she'll be fine. We've got us a nurse, to my way of thinking."

Marty felt both pride and concern at the words of her son. She would watch Belinda very carefully during the next few days—maybe try to get her to talk about her feelings and thoughts on it all.

"An' the patient?" asked Clark. "He's gonna make it?"

"He's a kid of seventeen," said Luke with deep compassion. "He'll make it—physically. He's out of danger now, barring complications. But whether he'll make it emotionally or not, only time will tell. It's going to be tough. I don't need to tell you that."

Clark nodded solemnly.

"I was wondering . . . would you mind making a call in a few days? Give him a bit of time to get used to . . . his . . . his misfortune, then just stop by?"

Clark nodded in agreement.

"And, Pa," said Luke quietly, "wonder if you'd mind leaving your artificial limb at home."

Clark said nothing. Just nodded again in understanding.

"Well," said Luke, getting to his feet. "I'd best be getting on home. Abbie will be concerned." Luke looked evenly at Clark and Marty and then turned toward the stairs. "First, I think I'll just go up and say good night and thanks to my little sister."

THIRTEEN

The New Neighbors

Marty did watch Belinda carefully over the next few days. The girl did not seem withdrawn or troubled, but she was much more solemn than she had been. She did not join in with the other two girls in the sighing and tittering over Jackson. Overnight, it seemed, she had become more mature—above such childish games. Marty did not know if she was thankful or regretful. Belinda was still very young. Marty worried about the experience robbing her of even a brief moment of girlhood.

When Melissa returned home to the big house from her overnight with Amy Jo, she wanted to know all about Belinda's last "adventure." Belinda answered her questions very briefly. A boy's arm had been crushed in a logging accident, she informed Melissa, and Luke had needed to amputate the limb.

Melissa grimaced and looked over at Clark and glanced at his leg.

"Was it awful?" asked Melissa.

"Yes," answered Belinda briefly and went out to get the clothes off the line.

Clark and Marty waited for a few days, and then as Luke had sug-gested, they hitched the team and went to call on their new neighbor. Clark felt a bit awkward returning to his crutch. He had almost forgot-ten how to use it.

The ride to the Coffins' old farmstead was a quiet one. A cold wind whipped about little flurries of snow, and Marty shivered against the cold. What would happen when they got to the new neighbors? What would they say? What *could* they say? There really weren't any words in the world that would comfort them.

"Looks like winter's really settlin' in," Clark mentioned as he hurried the team with a flick of the reins. Marty shivered again. The thought of winter somehow fit with thoughts of the visit ahead.

As they turned the team down the lane to the log house, Clark and Marty both noticed the condition of the farmyard.

"Things sure do go down quickly when a farm is left vacant," Clark commented, and Marty silently agreed.

Clark tied the team. They both had expected someone to come to the door, if not out to the yard, to welcome them, but there was no sign of movement anywhere. Clark led the way up to the door. A wisp of smoke was struggling from the chimney, fighting its way against the wind and snow. Marty pulled her coat more tightly about her and, too, fought her way against the wind.

Clark rapped loudly on the wooden door. They could hear some shuffling inside, but the door did not open. Clark rapped again.

The door opened a crack, and the pale face of a young man peeked out at them. He looked pained and hesitant.

"What d'ya want?" he rasped out.

"We're neighbors—from down the road a piece," Clark responded. "Jest thought we'd pay a call."

The door opened a bit farther. Marty could see the bandages over the stub of an arm. There were traces of blood showing on the whiteness. She shivered but not from the cold. She wasn't quite prepared for this.

"Nobody home but me," the lad said, still not inviting them in.

"Then guess we'll jest visit with you a spell," answered Clark cheerily, and he moved slightly to usher Marty in before him.

The boy moved back from the door, allowing it to open wide enough for their entrance. Marty could tell that it was only manners, not desire, that allowed them into the cabin. Her heart was deeply stirred for the young man.

He turned to them. "Won't ya sit," he said gruffly.

Clark did not take the chair nearby, the one that had been offered. He helped Marty out of her coat and seated her, then walked across the room to a chair near the window. His crutch thumped strangely on the wooden floor. There had been a time when the thumping crutch had sounded familiar. Now, after a number of years with the artificial limb, it sounded strange and eerie.

The boy had noticed. Marty saw him stiffen.

Clark seated himself and laid the crutch aside. He turned to the young man.

"Don't think I've heard yer name," he began. The boy didn't respond, and he went on, "Understand yer pa jest bought the place here."

"We're jest leasing," answered the boy. "Got no money for buying."

"Heard about yer accident. Powerful sorry. Terrible pain, ain't it?"

The dark eyes of the boy shadowed. Marty wondered if he was about to ask Clark what he knew about the pain, but his eyes fell again to the stump of a leg. He didn't say anything, just nodded dumbly.

"The worst should soon be over now," Clark continued. "It should soon be lettin' ya get some sleep at night."

Again the boy nodded. He still said nothing. Marty concluded he did not want to discuss his missing arm.

"Care for some tea?" the boy finally asked into the silence.

"That would be nice," exclaimed Marty, sounding a bit too enthusiastic to her own ears. The young fellow moved forward to lift the teapot from a cupboard shelf and put in the tea leaves. The kettle on the stove was already hot, and he poured the water into the pot. It slopped over some, hot water sizzling as it hit the iron of the stove surface. Clearly he was still adjusting to managing with only one hand.

"Can I give ya some help—" Marty began, rising from her chair, but as she caught the quick glance of Clark, she sat back down and busied herself with easing imaginary wrinkles from her full skirt.

The boy fumbled with cups from the cupboard. He handled them without too much problem, but when he went to slice some dry-looking bread to go with the drink, Marty turned away. She could not bear to see him struggling with the small task.

She could feel the tears stinging her eyes. *Why? Why should one so young face such pain and loss?*

Marty let her eyes move over the small room. She needed something— anything—to fill her thoughts.

The room was dingy and sparsely furnished. The little that was there needed care. The bare wooden floor was in need of scrubbing. Dirty dishes were stacked on the bit of available cupboard space. The stove was covered with charred bits of remaining spills. The walls and windows were empty of anything that would give the place a homey look. Marty shuddered again and turned back to the young boy. It was clear that the family was not very well off. Marty felt pity for them rising within her. Determinedly she shook it off. She felt sure they would not welcome her pity.

"Just pull up your chairs," the boy was saying, and he placed the bread and tea on the table.

"'Fraid we're outta butter," he acknowledged without any real apology in his voice. He was just stating a fact.

Clark helped Marty move her chair to the table and then he pulled his own forward. Marty ached to be allowed the privilege of serving the tea, but she held her tongue. The boy poured. Some of it splashed on the table without comment from anyone.

"Where you folks from?" asked Clark as he sipped the tea.

"We jest came back from the West," said the boy. "Afore that Pa worked in a hardware store. He was sure the West would make us a better living, but we had us some hard luck."

"Sorry to hear thet," responded Clark.

"My pa got sick with some kind of lung fever, and Ma an' me just couldn't keep things going. He's some better now, but by then we'd lost our claim. Pa tried to get jobs in various towns, but there wasn't anything there, either. So we came on back. Got this far on the cash we had. We heard 'bout this here place. Fellow in town said we could live here cheap. Just a few dollars a month, but it needs lots of fixing. Can't rent the land though. Guess one of the boys still farms it."

That would be Josh, the Coffins' son-in-law. Clark and Marty knew that Josh farmed his father's land along with his own.

It was not intended as a hard-luck story, they could tell, just a brief statement of how things were.

"Where're yer folks now?" asked Clark.

"Logging," replied the boy. "This fellow said we could help ourselves to all the logs we wanted. We need firewood, and Pa reckoned anything extra we could take out we could sell for supplies."

Logging! Both his pa and his ma. Logging to try to get fuel supplies so that the family could survive the harshness of the prairie winter. Marty shivered again. Logging had already cost the young boy his arm.

"I got me a whole root cellar of vegetables and fruit," Marty said. "I was wonderin' what to do with all the extry. It'll jest up and spoil a sittin' there. I hate haulin' out rotten vegetables come spring. We can jest bring some of 'em over here fer the use of you folk."

Clark caught the look on the face of the young man. The family did not ask for charity. The boy threw a glance toward Marty, and she stumbled on quickly, "In exchange for some of the logs, thet is. Thet is—iffen ya be carin' to trade?"

The boy relaxed. "I reckon we might," he said evenly. "I'll ask Pa."

Marty wasn't going to worry about what they would do with the extra logs.

"I'm a member of the school board here," Clark was saying. "Ya got any sisters or brothers of school age?"

"One brother. He should be in school, right enough, but I don't know as Pa can spare him. He's out logging, too."

Marty's head came up, concern gripping her heart. *Oh, Clark, we've got to stop him,* she wanted to say. *He might get hurt, too!* But she did not say it. It was really out of their hands.

They drank their tea and ate their bread, Clark dipping his in his cup. Marty wanted to chide him, but the fact was, she wished she dared do the same thing. The bread tasted rather old.

Marty looked out at the weather. The snow had increased. She thought about the man, woman, and child out in the woods chopping trees on such a day, but she made no comment.

"I was wonderin'," Clark was saying. "I have me a surplus of dry firewood—but I could sure find ways to use green logs. I'm wonderin' iffen yer pa would be willin' to make a swap. I'm in no hurry fer the green. Anytime next spring will be jest fine. I can git the firewood over to ya right away—git it outta my way."

Relief showed on the young face. "Reckon Pa would make the trade," responded the boy.

"We'll plan on thet, then," Clark said and rose to go.

They thanked their host for the tea and shrugged into their warm coats. Clark was about to lead Marty to the waiting buggy when the young lad stopped them.

"I didn't catch your name," he said.

"Clark. Clark an' Marty Davis."

"My doc's name is Davis."

"Yeah, he's our son." There was pride in Clark's voice. But the shadow in the eyes of the young boy quickly snatched it away.

"Yer wonderin' iffen he coulda saved yer arm, 'stead of takin' it, aren't ya?" Clark said softly.

The boy turned slightly away. He swallowed hard. The tears that started to form were not allowed to fall. It was several minutes before he could speak.

"Naw," he said. "Naw, not really. Ma an' Pa told me he didn't have any choice." He swallowed again, obviously working to get his emotions under control. "He's . . . he's been back a number of times. He's . . . he's a fine doc. Nothing he could have done different."

Marty watched as Clark put out a hand and let it drop to the muscular shoulder. He said nothing except what the boy might understand from the slight pressure of his hand, and tears filled her eyes.

They turned to leave when the boy spoke again. "Ma said there was a girl . . . she helped the doc. Ma says I owe both of them my life. You wouldn't . . . you wouldn't know who she was, would you? I forgot to ask the doc."

"Belinda," said Clark. "Belinda. She goes with Luke some. Wants to be a nurse someday."

"Belinda," repeated the boy. "I . . . I guess I'm beholden to her. I'd like . . . I'd like to tell her thank you someday."

Clark nodded. "I think thet could be arranged," he said with a smile, and followed Marty out into the bitter wind.

Talking It Out

Marty kept thinking they would get their daughter back again, but Belinda was still thoughtful and quiet.

"Land sakes," said Marty to Clark as they prepared for bed one night, "I'm havin' me one awful time tryin' to keep up to all these suddenlike changes. Our Belinda—she's gone from one stage to the next before I can scarcely turn my head. A gigglin' young girl one day, an' the next, a serious young lady. Do ya think we'll get Belinda's childhood back fer a bit? I wasn't quite prepared to let 'er go jest yet."

Clark drew Marty close. He held her quietly for a few minutes, his hand stroking the long hair that she had unpinned to fall down around her shoulders.

"I've noticed it, too," he said. "Thet there accident seems to have changed our Belinda."

"Do ya think it's eatin' away at her, Clark?"

"She doesn't seem bothered—jest more serious somehow."

"Guess what she went through would sober up anyone," Marty reasoned.

"It's hard to let her grow up so fast . . . I know thet . . . but truth is, I rather like 'er this way. She's kinda . . . kinda sweet, don't ya think?"

Marty smiled. "She always was yer pet. Didn't expect thet to change none jest because she adds a few years." She reached up to playfully pat Clark's cheek. "I'd expect ya to think she's sweet."

"I jest mean . . . well, she seems miles ahead of Amy Jo in her bearin'. She acts an' looks like a grown-up somehow. Even more than Melissa. Ya noticed thet?"

"I've noticed," said Marty.

There was silence for a moment.

"Clark, do ya think we should sorta help her talk it out? I mean, iffen this accident is botherin' her, we don't want it to turn up later in her life with scars we never guessed were there."

Clark thought about it. "Wouldn't hurt none, I guess."

"Speakin' of scars," went on Marty, "did ya see the young man again when ya took over the foodstuff and the firewood?"

"Saw 'im," Clark answered simply, knowing whom she meant.

He drew back and walked to the window. He ran a hand through his hair and stood quietly looking out at the night sky. Marty knew he was troubled. She crossed over to stand beside him and look out across the dark outlines of the farm buildings by moonlight. She laid a hand gently on Clark's arm but waited for him to speak.

"He's hurtin', Marty. Really hurtin'," Clark finally said, his voice low.

"But he seemed so . . . so acceptin' when we saw 'im before."

"I don't think the reality of it all had hit 'im yet. He was still in so much pain with the arm . . . he was still in deep shock over the whole thing. But now . . . now he knows thet it's fer real . . . permanent . . . an' there's nothin' to be done 'bout it. He'll always be a one-armed man. Thet's tough. Thet's really tough."

"Do ya think the parson could help him any?"

"I thought so . . . until I talked to the parson. He'd already been there . . . twice. He didn't even git in the door."

Marty's eyes grew large with concern.

"Did ya . . . did ya say anythin' 'bout how God helped us when—?"

"Tried. Wouldn't hear it. Luke says they won't even let him make doctor calls anymore."

"Oh my!" exclaimed Marty. "Might thet make a problem with the wound?"

"Not physically. Luke says the arm has healed nicely. Shouldn't be infection or anythin'. But emotionally . . . well, Luke worries a fair bit 'bout thet."

"Oh dear!" Marty lamented.

"Is there anythin' we can do, Clark?" she finally asked.

"I've been thinkin' and thinkin' on it. Can't think of one thing— 'cept pray."

"Did he ask 'bout Belinda again? We had promised to arrange fer 'im to see her. He wanted to thank—"

"Thet's another thing. He said to fergit the whole thing. Doesn't want to see her. Says she didn't do 'im such a favor after all."

"Ya mean—?"

"Says he'd be better off dead."

Marty's breath caught in a quick little sob. Clark put his arm around her.

"I was so taken with him," she said. "Strugglin' with thet heavy teapot an' thet dry bread, as mannerly and self-possessed as ya please. I thought he was so plucky an' brave an'—"

"Now, let's not think less of the boy," Clark was quick to say. "He is all those things. It's normal what he's feelin'. Remember, we had God and His help . . . or I might have done exactly what this here boy is doin'. It's a tough thing he's goin' through . . . an' understandable how he's feelin'. I jest hope an' pray he's able to sort it all out and git beyond it . . . thet's all. Talk 'bout scars. This young fella's got scars all right . . . an' the worst an' deepest ain't on thet arm."

Marty thought about the Simpson family. So nearby, yet so shut off from the help of their neighbors. She wished there were some way— *some way* they could reach out and break down the walls.

"They didn't refuse the food—the vegetables an' fruit?"

"No-o. But I think they would have iffen they hadn't been on the brink of starvation. They are proud people. It hurt them powerful to take it. Man insisted thet he'd work it off."

"So what did ya do?"

Clark shrugged. "Told 'im he could. Now I gotta come up with somethin' fer 'im to do."

"Oh, Clark. What will ya give 'im? Ya got everything done that needs doin'."

"I dunno. It's gotta be somethin' in outta the cold. His coat is so thin ya could sneeze clear through it."

"He could build some more fruit shelves in the cellar."

"Ya needin' more?"

"Not really. But it's warm—an' there's room there—an' it wouldn't hurt none."

"It's an idea," said Clark, reaching out to pull the window shade down. Then he turned to climb into bed. Marty turned to follow him. She was surprised to find she was still holding her hairbrush.

"An' the firewood?" asked Marty as she returned the brush to her dresser.

"He's determined to pay fer thet, too. Guess we'll have us more green wood come spring."

"What ya gonna do with it?"

"Dunno. I'll check with Arnie an' Josh. See iffen either of 'em have any need. We should be able to figger out somethin'."

"Funny," murmured Marty as though to herself. "I don't care none fer a grown man with his hand out . . . but pride can sure enough be a hurtful thing, too."

"Makes it a bit hard to be neighborly," agreed Clark. "Still, a man needs his dignity. We've got to allow 'im thet."

Clark blew out the light and they pulled the warm blankets up around their chins. The winter nights were cold, and there was no heat in the upstairs rooms except for what drifted up the stairs from the stoves below.

"Ya don't have sewin' thet ya need done, do ya?" Clark asked. "Clothes? Quilts? Rag rugs? Anythin'?"

Marty turned to him in the darkness. "Nothin' I can't git done over the winter. Why?"

"I was wonderin'—maybe the missus could help earn 'em a bit, sewin' or somethin'."

Marty was silent. There really wasn't that much the household needed. And she liked to do it. The long winter days and even longer evenings were made more bearable by the things that took shape in her hands. She looked forward to the projects and planned for them all fall as she worked hard in her garden patch. And now—?

"Might be," she answered Clark. "I'll see what I can come up with."

Marty finally had an opportunity to talk with Belinda. She had been watching for an opening. She did not wish to force the issue but did want to give the girl a chance to express her feelings concerning her involvement in the amputation. But it was difficult to find time.

The occasion turned up when Melissa was sent on an errand to Kate's. She asked for some extra time there because Amy Jo had sketches she was anxious to show her. Also, now that Amy Jo had gotten some practice, she wanted to try her hand at drawing some of her kin. Melissa was picked for the first sitting.

Luke had stopped by on his way back from delivering a baby. Belinda, as yet, had not been invited to participate in a delivery. She had coaxed—more with her eyes than words—to be able to go with Luke on one of his happier duties as a doctor, but so far Luke had held back.

After Luke had drunk his coffee to warm up some from the cold and eaten some of Marty's sponge cake, he put on his coat again and left for home.

Belinda, busy stirring up a batch of cookies for school lunches, opened the conversation.

"I fergot to ask 'im how the boy who lost his arm is doin'."

Marty looked at her daughter. She wasn't sure just what to say. Belinda seemed to sense her unrest. Her eyes turned to Marty questioningly.

"He's okay, isn't he? He didn't git infection or—?"

"No, no. He healed nice. Thet is, his arm healed."

"What're ya meanin'? He wasn't hurt anyplace else. Luke checked him carefully fer cracked ribs or—"

"No, no," Marty said again. "Nothin' like thet."

"What is it, then?" asked Belinda. "I can tell yer holdin' back somethin'."

"He's havin' a tough time adjustin', thet's all," said Marty slowly.

Belinda looked relieved. "I would, too," she said simply. "Thet's to be expected. Luke talked 'bout it on the way home. He said thet workin' it through is one of the stages of acceptin' an amputation."

Marty nodded her head in agreement.

"So when Luke talks to 'im, does—?"

Marty didn't allow her to finish her question. "The boy won't see Luke any more."

"Ya mean Luke has quit callin' already? Why, he told me thet he'd keep goin' back jest to be sure thet—"

"They won't let Luke call. Told 'im not to come anymore."

"They did? Who did? The pa? Don't he know thet—?"

"No," said Marty. "It was the boy."

There was silence.

"I've got to git over there right away," said Belinda firmly. "I shouldn't have waited so long. He'll think . . . he'll think I don't care. Do ya s'pose Pa would—?"

"He doesn't wanna see you, either," Marty said softly.

Belinda's eyes turned to Marty. Marty could see the protest there.

"But ya said—"

"I know what we said."

"He wanted—"

"I know. But he changed his mind."

"But why?" Belinda cried.

"I can't answer thet. 'Cept . . . 'cept he's hurtin' on the inside now. He can't understand why it shoulda happened. He's sufferin' with it in a new way. He says he wishes he'd died—"

"Can't we do somethin', Ma?" Belinda cried.

"Yer pa's been tryin'. They're proud people. Hard to do things fer. They insist on payin' fer everthin', an' they can't accept the help of neighbors." Marty hesitated. She sighed deeply and turned to the troubled eyes of her youngest. "The worst is," she said slowly, "they can't seem to accept the help of God, either."

"I wondered," said Belinda. Then to Marty's surprise her lip began to tremble, and the next thing Marty knew she had thrown herself into her mother's arms and was weeping against her shoulder.

Marty let her cry. Her own tears fell in sympathy and love. The poor girl did feel this whole thing very deeply.

At last Belinda was able to talk. "Oh, Ma," she said, still clinging to Marty. "It was awful. So much blood an' . . . an' raw, mashed flesh and bits of broken bone . . . everywhere. I never knew . . . I never knew anything could look so . . . so awful!"

Belinda shuddered and Marty tightened her arms.

"An' there he lay. Quiet and still . . . almost like he'd already died."

Belinda stopped and blew her nose.

"But he wasn't quiet at first," she hurried on. "At first he screamed . . . it was awful. We heard the screamin' 'fore we even got to the house, an' Luke . . . he jest grabbed his bag an' ran an' left me to care fer the horses. Then when I got to the house the woman . . . did ya see the woman?"

Marty shook her head no.

"Well, she's big, an' she stood there—legs apart an' arms spread out—barrin' the door so I couldn't go in. 'The doctor told ya to stay out,' she said, and I heard the boy screamin' and throwing 'imself about. An' I knew Luke might need my help, so I ducked an' went past her."

Belinda stopped again, obviously reliving the scene in the crowded bedroom of the log cabin.

"An' there he was—his pa—his pa an' a younger brother holdin' 'im down. Luke was . . . Luke was tryin' to give 'im somethin' to make 'im quiet. An' the blood . . . the blood was everywhere an' the . . . the mash . . . it was jest a *mash*, Ma, thet arm! I remember I thought, *He's dyin'. Luke will never save 'im,* an' then I remembered how Luke always says, if they're still breathin', ya *fight.* An' I looked an' he was still breathin' an' I prayed an' then I took a deep breath and started fightin' down the heaves that wanted to come. It was awful. My head went round and round an' my stomach churned and my legs went soft as jelly. But I didn't go down. For a minute I . . . I wished I could jest pass out, an' then . . ."

Belinda's face had drained to white. Marty feared she might faint now.

". . . then I made up my mind to help. Luke needed me. I could see thet. The father wouldn't be any good. 'Sides, he was too big . . . there wasn't room. An' he didn't know the first thing 'bout Luke's instruments. An' he looked 'most as pale as his son on the bed.'"

Belinda stopped again. Marty did not prompt her.

"Funny," she mused. "Once we started workin', it was all different somehow. The mass of blood and flesh no longer seemed like an arm. It was somethin' to fight against . . . somethin' thet was threatenin' to take a life. We had to stop it, Luke an' me. I forgot all 'bout bein' squeamish. I jest wanted to git thet job done in time to stop thet boy from dyin'. It was . . . it was so important, Ma. Can ya understand thet? There was death an' pain in thet room . . . an' only Luke an' me to fight against it."

Belinda's eyes were big with the enormity of her thoughts. They had fought against death—she and her doctor brother—and they had won. Marty wanted to cheer for the victor, but instead she began to weep softly, the tears gently rolling down her cheek.

Belinda's eyes glistened. "Ya shoulda seen 'im, Ma. Ya shoulda seen Luke. He was wonderful. He knew just what to do. An' he hurried . . . but so careful. An' he got thet blood stopped. An' he did . . . he did beat death. Oh, Ma! Now I understand . . . I understand why Luke wanted to be a doctor. It's not the broken bones or the bad cuts or the bursted appendixes. It's not the awful things he sees. It's the chance to fight those things . . . to bring healin' an' help. Thet's what doctorin' is."

Marty took her daughter by the shoulders and looked deeply into her eyes, shining with tears but also with joy. Marty was no longer worried about Belinda. Marty feared no emotional scars in spite of Belinda's traumatic experience. Marty saw only a peace, an acceptance. Belinda had found a way to reach out to others who were in pain.

"An' ya want to help," Marty said softly. It was a statement, not a question.

"Oh yes," Belinda responded breathlessly.

Marty drew the young girl into her arms. "Then help, ya shall," she said simply.

They stood for a moment and then Belinda pulled back, her eyes shadowed again. "But, Ma, it doesn't seem right to fight to save lives an' then—only to have 'em wish they had died."

"No," agreed Marty gently. "It doesn't seem right."

"Then we hafta do somethin' fer thet boy."

"We'll keep prayin'," said Marty. "God will show us what else to do."

"Ya shoulda seen 'im, Ma. After . . . after it was all over. Luke left to . . . to care fer the . . . the mess . . . an' he left me to watch the boy. He was so pale an' so . . . so . . ." Belinda hesitated. Marty waited. "He's good-lookin', Ma," she admitted softly, honestly.

"I noticed," said Marty with a smile.

Belinda flushed slightly. She turned back to her cookie batter on the counter. For some reason Marty knew that the sharing time had come to a close.

"We've gotta do somethin'," Belinda said again, but she was speaking more to herself now than to her mother.

FIFTEEN

Sunday Dinner for the Teacher

On a cold day the Brown family was due to join the Davises at the Sunday dinner table. Now that winter had arrived, the Browns no longer drove the fifteen miles to their former church but were attending the community church close to the teacherage and schoolhouse.

Marty had already met the "divine" and "vibrant" Jackson at Sunday services. He *was* nice looking, for a young fella, she concluded. And he was gentlemanly and proper, and he did not put on airs—in spite of the fact that all the young girls were continually fluttering around him. His two brothers seemed like nice enough youngsters, too, and Marty was impressed with Mrs. Brown, the widowed schoolteacher.

So it was without hesitation, and a twinge of conscience for not having done so sooner, that Marty extended the dinner invitation to the Brown family. They gratefully accepted, and Marty began thinking ahead for her meal planning.

When Amy Jo heard the news, as would be expected she coaxed, begged, pleaded, and bargained most persuasively to be included. Marty could have made room at the big table for Amy Jo, but she saw no reason to encourage the silliness of the girl, so she said a loving but firm, "No, not this time." Amy Jo was quite put out. For a few days she did not even drop in to visit at the big house. Marty knew her granddaughter—impulsive and easily peeved but essentially goodhearted—eventually would get over her miff and cool off enough for them to have a sensible talk about the matter.

The Davises met the Browns after the service at the back of the church and offered to guide them back to the farm.

"Oh my," said Mrs. Brown. "We have a bit of a problem. Young Jordan only wore his lighter coat. I had told him—but you know children. I should have checked before we left the house. Anyway, we must drop by the teacherage to get his warmer coat before coming out. If you just give us the directions, I'm sure we can find you with no trouble."

Marty agreed. The directions would be straightforward enough and were easily followed. She was about to say so when she felt a tug at her sleeve. Melissa stood there looking demure.

"Someone could ride with them," she said decorously, "and show them the way."

It sounded sensible enough to Marty.

"I'm sure there's no need," Mrs. Brown assured them. "We hate to make trouble—"

"Oh, it wouldn't be any trouble at all. Would it, Grandma?"

"No," responded Marty. "No trouble at all."

Without thinking further about it, Marty turned to Belinda. She was used to giving Belinda instructions, and Belinda was totally familiar with the country roads, so it was the most natural thing for her to send Belinda along with the Browns.

"Jest grab yer coat an' go along with the Browns," Marty said. "They need to drop by the teacherage fer a moment."

To Marty's surprise, Belinda hesitated. It was not like Belinda to resist a direct order.

Marty, puzzled, looked at her. "Yer coat?" she prompted.

Then Marty's eyes followed Belinda's to the downcast face of Melissa, and she knew Belinda's hesitation had something to do with the other girl.

"I jest thought thet . . . thet maybe I should go with you an' Pa,"

Belinda said carefully, "to help git dinner on an' all. Melissa can go with the Browns. Won't you, Melissa?"

Melissa's face brightened. Marty nodded her agreement. She was still mystified over the peculiar behavior of the two girls when she saw Melissa reach out and give Belinda a quick hug, then wrap her coat tightly about her in preparation for the trip with the Browns.

Strange creatures—girls, thought Marty with a shake of her head as she reached for her own coat on the peg.

"So what was thet all 'bout?" she whispered to her daughter after the others were out of hearing.

"Oh nothin'," said Belinda with a shrug. "Melissa likes Jackson, thet's all."

"Oh," said Marty, the truth finally dawning. Then she added, "Thought thet you liked Jackson, too."

"Not the way Melissa does," said Belinda.

"I see," said Marty.

They left the church just as the Brown's sleigh was leaving the yard. Marty could not help but smile to herself. *Melissa must feel just a mite disappointed,* she noted. The young Jackson sat in the front driving the gray. His mother shared the seat with him, and tucked in the back along with the two younger boys was Melissa. Marty was quite sure it hadn't all worked out according to Melissa's desires.

They had been home only long enough to get the food ready to serve when their dog announced the arrival of the guests. Clark went out to lead the team to the barn, and Marty went to the door to welcome the Browns. Belinda stayed where she was, busy in the kitchen.

Melissa showed them in, careful not to precede Mrs. Brown but not too concerned about the two young boys. She was busy casting sidelong glances at Jackson. He seemed to take it all in stride.

Jordan spotted Clare's David across the yard and was momentarily sidetracked. The two had become friends at school and concluded they should get in some playing time before dinner. Mrs. Brown intervened and urged Jordan on to the house.

Mrs. Brown was a delightful guest. She complimented Marty on her home, exclaimed over the delicious aromas from the kitchen, said nice things to Belinda, who was giving special attention to making the table look attractive, and thanked Melissa again for her kind escort. It all seemed sincere and natural, and Marty found herself liking the new woman even more.

Marty, with Belinda's help, soon had the food on the table and began to seat her guests. Without giving too much thought to the arrangements, she put Mrs. Brown between the two younger boys to her right and Jackson down beside Clark so they could share some man-talk. She motioned for Belinda to sit next to him and Melissa beside her. Belinda immediately suggested, "I think thet Melissa should sit in the middle. It's easier fer me to wait on the table iffen I sit on the end."

Melissa quickly took the middle chair before someone changed the arrangement. Jackson held the chair for her to be seated while Melissa flashed him the most winning smile. Marty only nodded dumbly.

They all took their places, and Clark led in the table grace. The meal was a success in every way. The food had turned out to be tasty, and the Brown family were natural conversationalists. Even the children had manners and a sense of decorum rarely seen in ones so young. Young Jordan only whispered twice to his mother to be allowed to go out to find David.

Marty found herself wondering about the deceased Mr. Brown. How had he died? And when had the death taken place? She felt a deep sympathy for the young widow. *It must be hard to raise a family—especially boys—alone.* Marty felt a chill at the very thought. She didn't know what she'd ever have done without Clark when the boys were growing up, not to speak of their daughters.

"Is the teacherage meetin' yer needs?" Clark was asking the woman. As chairman of the school board, it was up to him to find out.

"It's fine," said Mrs. Brown. "A bit crowded for the four of us, but fine. I guess we had a few more things than we really needed, but I just couldn't part with them—just yet."

She did not explain, but Marty felt she understood.

"Ya lived right in town before?" Marty asked.

"Yes. My husband worked in the bank in Chester."

Marty was picturing a big frame or brick house with delicate curtains covering the windows and flowers blooming along a neat boardwalk up to a white front door.

"It must be quite an adjustment fer ya," she said, compassion in her voice.

"Yes," admitted Mrs. Brown. "Yes, it is."

"Had you taught before?" asked Clark.

"I was a schoolteacher when I came to Chester. That's where I met Carl—Mr. Brown. I taught for two years before we married—and a bit when the other teacher was down with pneumonia one winter. But Carl—Mr. Brown—wanted me to be at home. And then Jackson arrived, and I was happy to forget about schoolteaching. I likely would never have taken it up again if . . ."

But Mrs. Brown stopped. "I was so glad when I heard of the opening here," she continued, changing directions. "It was truly an answer to prayer—for all of us. We are so thankful for the opportunity." She turned to Clark, the person who had hired her. "I do hope I will live up to your expectations, Mr. Davis. If ever you question my—"

"We are pleased with your work," Clark was quick to inform her. "Very pleased."

Mrs. Brown did not seem entirely comfortable.

Clark went on, "Now, no more talk of school," he said kindly. "Today you are not the schoolteacher—an' I am not the chairman of the board. We are neighbors—neighbors an' fellow members of the church. Let's fergit school an' jest have us a good neighborly visit."

Mrs. Brown smiled warmly. "I'd like that," she said simply, looking relaxed again.

So the visiting turned to other matters. The three Brown youngsters were included. Clark knew how to make each one feel welcome at his table.

After dinner Belinda and Melissa volunteered to do the dishes. Jordan—anticipation brightening his face—and Payne were allowed to run out to join Dan and David, who were towing their sleds toward the banks of the nearby creek. Marty led Mrs. Brown into the family living room to look at some new quilt patterns. That left Clark and Jackson. Clark suggested checkers and was answered by an enthusiastic grin.

Belinda could tell that Melissa was hurrying her through the dishes. She didn't have to ask why. Though Melissa had stopped giggling and tittering over Jackson, Belinda knew she still had a special interest in the boy. Belinda had noticed her giving him coy little smiles and watching for opportunities to be around him.

"I think Jackson likes me," Melissa whispered confidentially to Belinda as the girls worked at the dishes.

Belinda did not respond.

"Have you noticed the way he looks at me?" asked Melissa.

"How?" asked Belinda. She had noticed no difference in the way Jackson looked at Melissa or anyone else, but she didn't dare say so. Melissa seemed just a tad annoyed by the question. She no doubt had been hoping Belinda would simply say yes.

"Well . . . well . . . like he likes me," she finished lamely.

"Maybe so," said Belinda, refusing to take the bait. "Can't say I'd noticed anything particular."

"And we had such a good ride over here together," she continued, changing her approach. Belinda wanted to smile. She had seen with her own eyes the seating arrangement for the ride over.

Suddenly Belinda felt sorry for Melissa. Melissa really did like Jackson. Belinda liked Jackson, too, but she understood there was some difference in the way the two of them felt about the boy. Well, she wouldn't stand in Melissa's way. She loved Melissa. She had no desire to hurt her. After all, Melissa was a very generous person. She shared her books, she shared her wardrobe, she shared her friendship. It was asking too much to expect her to share her first love, as well. So Belinda held her tongue and smiled at Melissa in hopes that it would give her encouragement.

When the last of the dishes had been returned to the cupboards, Melissa removed her apron, rubbed a bit of sweet cream into her hands, and went to join the others in the living room. Belinda remained in the kitchen, wiping the table and hanging up the dish towels. She couldn't see what was happening, but she could figure it out by what she was hearing through the door.

The checker game must have ended in a draw, with Clark winning one match, Jackson another, and the third a stalemate.

"Yer good, boy," Clark congratulated him warmly as they pushed back the board and rose to their feet.

"Pa an' I used to play a lot," Jackson explained.

"Bet ya miss 'im."

"Yeah," the boy said quietly, sadness in his tone. "Yeah, I sure do."

Melissa's voice interrupted the conversation. "Care to see where the boys are sledding?" she asked Jackson.

"Sure," he replied.

"I'll get your coat," said Melissa.

She hurried through the kitchen to the coat pegs and was soon wearing her own coat and carrying Jackson's over her arm. Then she led the way back through the kitchen to the side door.

Belinda was still there. She had not yet removed her apron but was busy polishing the big black stove with a scrap of newspaper. Jackson stopped beside her.

"We're goin' out to see where the boys are sleddin'. Want to come?"

Belinda looked from Jackson to Melissa.

"I'm not quite done," she said simply. "You go on—"

"We'll wait," said Jackson. "Got lots of time. What you gotta do yet? Let me help." And so saying, Jackson took the paper from Belinda and began to vigorously rub the iron surface. Belinda cast Melissa a helpless look over his bent shoulders.

"Really, I . . . I was goin' to . . ."

Belinda lifted a stove lid and tossed the used paper into the firebox. She reached for a few sticks of wood to replenish the fire. They would want coffee or tea later, but already the cake was sitting in the pantry. There was really nothing else that needed doing. She had no more excuses.

She smiled at Jackson. "Well . . . I guess it's all done," she answered honestly.

"Then get out of that apron and grab your coat," instructed Jackson, and he reached to give the bow a playful tug.

Belinda moved away toward the hook on the wall, apparently to hang up her apron, but it was really to get out of reach of the boy.

Jackson lifted her coat from the coat hook on the back porch and
held it for her. She shrugged it quickly onto her shoulders, avoiding any
further help from him and any eye contact with Melissa, and the three
of them went out into the brightness of the winter sunshine, squinting
against the sun on snow.

From the creek came the shouts of young boys and the barking of
the two farm dogs. The snow crunched underfoot, and even though
frost hung thick in the air, the wind was not blowing and the day felt
almost mild.

Belinda breathed deeply. She loved the crisp feel of winter. As long
as one had a warm meal and a warm coat . . . For some reason, the face
of the young boy who had lost his arm suddenly appeared in her mind.
She knew instinctively that he would not be dressed for the sharpness
of the winter weather. She sighed deeply. He had so many needs, that
boy. She didn't even know his name. But Belinda ached to help him. She
had been praying, just as her ma had suggested, but so far God hadn't
seemed to give her any answers.

Jackson must have heard her sigh, and she could feel him looking at
her. "Something wrong?" he asked, concern warming his voice.

Belinda felt her cheeks coloring. Surely he couldn't read her thoughts!
"No . . . no-o. Nothin'. I like the winter, thet's all. I mean, it's so—"

"Me too," Melissa the chatterbox broke in, obviously having no intentions of being left out. "It's so clean and fresh and bright. So bright!
I think that it's even brighter than the West," she prattled on. "The sun
seems so . . . so . . . intense here . . . or something. Oh, it's intense out
west, too. Intense and bright and it shines most all the time, but here,
there seems to be something different somehow."

Jackson glanced from Melissa back to Belinda.

"Do you like the winter, Jackson?" Melissa pressed.

"Guess so," he said laughing lightly. "Never thought much about it.
Guess I just like summer a bit more."

"Oh, me too," gushed Melissa. "I love the summer and the flowers
and the birds! Out west we have wild flowers that grow all over on the
hills. I used to go out and pick handfuls and handfuls of them in the
spring," she enthused.

"'Fraid I don't pick too many flowers." Jackson laughed again.

Melissa gave him a teasing smile. "Wouldn't be expecting you to be out picking flowers," she said. "It's not the kind of thing that a man does."

Jackson flushed a bit. He probably hadn't missed her term "man." But Belinda found herself wondering why Melissa had said that. Why, Clark, her pa, picked flowers all the time. He was always bringing in a handful of one kind or another. *And Ma always looks at him kind of special,* she noted to herself, *when he gives them to her.* Her brothers brought flowers to Ma, too. She had seen them herself. Whatever was wrong with a man picking flowers if he wanted to?

Belinda was still sorting it out when Jackson unexpectedly asked her, "Warm enough?"

"Fine. Jest fine," she quickly responded.

They reached the creek and stood watching the shrieking, sliding, tumbling boys as they frolicked on their favorite sliding bank. Jackson was grinning. "It looks like fun," he commented.

Belinda smiled in reply. "It is," she said. "I've spent hours out there."

"You have?"

She nodded.

"Never had a sled," said Jackson. "There wasn't anyplace to use one in town."

"Oh, you've missed a lot of fun," Belinda told him. "There's nothin' quite like thet fast 'whish' as you come down the hill. 'Course our hill isn't very big, but . . . it . . . it's fun."

"Shall we try it?" asked Jackson enthusiastically.

Belinda looked down at her skirts. She knew that tumbling in a snowbank was often a part of sledding.

"I'm hardly dressed for it," she laughed, but Jackson persisted.

"We'd be careful. I'd sit in the front. All you'd need to do would be to hang on."

"I'll go," Melissa offered.

Both Jackson and Belinda turned to look at her. Her cheeks were flushed and her eyes bright with challenge.

"I'll go with you. I'm not afraid," she insisted again.

Without comment Jackson turned his attention back to Belinda. His eyes seemed to ask her if she had changed her mind.

"That's a great idea," Belinda was quick to agree. "Take Melissa. This is her first winter here. She's never slid down the hill before, either." Belinda did not add that she thought Melissa was foolish to be even considering it now in her Sunday skirt.

Dan shared his sleigh and Jackson settled in the front, holding fast on to the rope that worked the steering bar. Melissa climbed on behind him and without hesitation wrapped her arms around him to hang on for dear life. Belinda, watching, wondered if she hung on a bit tighter than was really needed, but of course she made no comment. The sled did go "whish." Jackson, laughing and shouting, sounded like he was thrilled with the ride. He asked for another. They went down again, Melissa hanging on just as firmly. Jackson "whooped" as the sled sped down the short hill.

He called up to Belinda, "It's great! How about trying it with me? See, we didn't fall off. It's a snap!"

Belinda just laughed and shook her head.

"One more, just one more. Please?" Melissa begged the boys with pleading enthusiasm.

The next ride was not the "snap" Jackson had described. Midway down the hill the sled seemed to develop a mind of its own. It veered off the well-traveled path and hit a bank of snow. From there, matters only got worse. The sled bounced farther afield and struck a rock. Before Jackson could correct its course, the sleigh plunged into a snowdrift and skidded to a stop on its side, spilling its two passengers in a cloud of snowy dust.

The young boys at the top of the hill howled with glee, no doubt thoroughly enjoying the entertainment. Belinda stared openmouthed, fearful that one of the two might be hurt in the spill, but when they both climbed, a trifle unsteadily, to their feet, she relaxed. Melissa did look a bit the worse for wear. Her skirt, hanging crazily because of a huge tear at the waist, was covered with snow and her coat, also snow-covered, was hanging open as though it was missing all its buttons. Jackson brushed the snow from his coat, grinning sheepishly.

"Whoops!" he called up the hill to Belinda. "Guess it's not without some risks after all."

Belinda laughed, glad that no one had been hurt.

Jackson helped Melissa brush the snow off her coat, and asked her if she was all right. She assured him rather stiffly that she was fine, probably embarrassed at the state of her clothes. He righted the sled and started up the bank.

"Now will you ride with me?" he called laughingly to Belinda as he slowly made his way back up the hill, dragging the wayward sled with him.

"No, sir. I still will not," answered Belinda cheerfully.

Melissa, after rummaging around in the snow to locate her missing buttons, left quickly for the house to change her clothes and get herself back in order.

Jackson handed the sled back to Dan and thanked him warmly for the ride. "I'd like to try it again sometime," he informed the boy and Dan grinned, happy to have made an impression on an older fellow.

Belinda's eyes followed Melissa. "I'd better git in," she said to Jackson. "Mama might need me. She'll want to serve coffee soon."

He moved to fall into step beside her, but she waved him away.

"Why don't ya stay out an' have another ride or two?" she said. "Dan won't mind. We'll call ya as soon as lunch is ready."

"You sure?" asked Jackson, eyeing the hill again.

"I'm sure. You might not git another chance. Spring can come pretty early in these parts."

"Before Christmas?"

"Ya never know."

He grinned. "Think I will," he said. "Thanks."

Belinda nodded and hurried off toward the house. She needed to check on Melissa. She prayed that there had been damage only to Melissa's clothes and not to her pride—or to their friendship.

Belinda found Melissa in her room. She had removed the torn dress, but she had not put on another. Instead she lay on her bed, her face buried in her hands, her shoulders shaking with sobs.

"Melissa," cried Belinda in alarm. "Were you hurt?"

Melissa looked disgustedly up at Belinda, her eyes swollen from crying.

"As though you care," she challenged.

Belinda was taken aback. She crossed to the bed, sat down, and laid a hand on the girl's arm.

"Ya know I care," she insisted. "Are you sure you're all right?"

Melissa drew herself up and climbed off the bed. "Don't get your hopes up," she threw at Belinda, "I don't need a nurse."

Belinda was completely baffled by the whole exchange. She decided to change the subject.

"We're gonna have coffee soon. I'm jest goin' to git it on now."

"Well, I won't be there," spat out Melissa.

"You *are* hurt. Where?"

"I'm not hurt," Melissa insisted impatiently. "I'm just not coming down, that's all."

"But what—what will I tell folks? They'll all wonder—"

"Tell them anything you want to. I don't care," and Melissa tossed her hair back with an angry move and reached for her bathrobe.

Belinda stood to go. She wasn't sure what to do. She didn't know what was wrong. She still wondered if Melissa really had been hurt and was refusing to say so. She wished Luke would miraculously arrive.

"Is there anythin' I can do?" she asked, genuinely sympathetic.

Melissa gave her an angry look. "It would seem that you have already done enough, don't you think?" she spat out.

Belinda frowned. "What do ya mean?" she asked. What in the world had she done to make the girl so angry?

"'What do ya mean?'" Melissa mimicked. "You know exactly what I mean. You've been butting in on me and Jackson all day. You know he likes me—and you know I like him—yet you just keep on butting in—spoiling everything!"

The long speech ended in uncontrollable tears. Belinda stood staring at her overwrought and unreasonable niece. *Where did Melissa get such an idea?* was her frantic thought. She had purposely tried to stay out of the way. And she had bent over backward to—but it was clear Melissa was not going to listen to reason.

354

Belinda heard her mother calling her. She slipped from the room without further comment, but her heart was heavy as she went back down the stairs to help in the kitchen.

Not much had been said while their guests were still there, but as soon as the Browns had left, Marty wanted an explanation concerning Melissa. There was little Belinda could tell her. She hated to "tell on" Melissa, but there was no way she would lie to her mother. So she finally just told the truth as simply as she knew how.

Marty's eyes widened as they sought Clark's above Belinda's head. "Yer sure?" she asked. "Yer sure she thinks ya were cuttin' in?"

Belinda nodded.

"An' she's jealous?"

Again Belinda nodded.

"I find thet hard to believe," stated Marty. "Surely she'll see things different in the mornin'."

But Melissa did not see things differently in the morning. She did her chores and prepared for school, but she was not her usually cheery, chattering self. And she carefully avoided any conversation with Belinda.

"Oh, dear Lord," prayed Marty, watching the girls walk down the lane to the road, a careful distance between them. "We've got us one of them triangles. What do we do now?"

SIXTEEN

Pride

At Christmastime, neighbors tried to share food baskets with the Simpson family, but each visitor was turned away at the door. The community all wanted to help, but they did not know what to try next. The minister also was turned away again when he tried to visit—it seemed that the family wanted no comfort or aid from God, either. Marty's heart ached over their destitute and pride-filled condition, and Clark muttered under his breath. Sheer foolishness and pigheadedness, that's what it was.

The debt for the firewood and groceries still had not been paid. Clark would have gladly considered it a gift, but he knew the family would not. Until they felt they had paid the debt, Clark was well aware he would not be able to help them further.

He decided to drop in on them one more time. At first he planned to take Marty with him. Then he figured it might look too much like a neighborly call, so they talked it over and Clark decided to go alone. He wanted it to seem as businesslike as possible.

All the way over to the Simpsons', Clark tried to think of jobs that needed doing. He really could think of none. Clark reflected on the plans he and Marty had made. It wouldn't be easy for Marty. In fact, it wouldn't be easy for either of them, and he feared they both might feel a bit guilty of dishonesty in the whole affair. It was hard to tell the Simpsons that they needed help when in truth they did not.

Marty had been able to come up with a short list of things she could have Mrs. Simpson sew for her. Then there was a quilt that was promised to Nandry's Mary for her birthday. Marty supposed she could use some help in the quilting, though she enjoyed it and usually did her quilting alone.

Still, those jobs wouldn't take much time.

So they had tried to figure out something else for the woman to do, but each time they came back again to the sewing.

"How much in yard goods do ya have on hand?" Clark had asked Marty.

"Four or five pieces, I reckon," she had replied.

"Well, can't ya find some way to make use of 'em?"

"I had purposes in mind fer all of 'em," Marty had told him, "but I just don't need 'em yet. One was to be a dress fer Belinda, but it's too grown-up a print fer her yet—well, at the rate she's maturin', maybe not that long," she quipped. "And one is fer aprons fer Kate, and one is fer the backin' fer Amy Jo's quilt when she finishes school an' another fer—"

"I'll go to town," Clark had said. "I'll go to town an' buy some material with no purpose at all."

"Then what'll I have 'er do with it?" Marty had protested.

"I dunno. We'll think of somethin'—how 'bout a new dress fer you?" Clark said with a smile and a hug.

"Oh, Clark, I don't need somethin' new," Marty protested.

"Maybe not, but maybe Mrs. Simpson does," was his gentle rejoinder, and she nodded her head in agreement.

And so he had gone to town and had come home with six lengths of yard goods. He had chosen some pretty pieces—or the clerk had, Marty wasn't sure which, she told him with a twinkle in her eye—but she also said she still hadn't figured out what to do with all of them. And who knew if Mrs. Simpson could even sew? She might only spoil the pieces.

Clark just shrugged his shoulders. "Throw 'em in the ragbag, then," he had stated, at which Marty had looked dismayed.

It would have been so much simpler, so much less costly, if the family had just allowed the neighbors to outright help them.

Clark reviewed all of this in his mind as he coaxed the team forward. He was busy trying to properly prepare his words to the Simpsons. What could he say that would be totally truthful and would not offend them?

Clark tied the team and walked toward the door. His artificial limb was making his leg ache again. Or maybe it was just the cold—Clark didn't know for sure. All he knew was that shivers of pain were shooting from the stump clear up to his hip.

He rapped loudly on the door and Mr. Simpson answered. He appeared ready to launch into his usual "we-don't-take-any-charity" speech, so Clark began quickly, "Came to see 'bout clearin' thet debt fer the wood and foodstuff."

The door opened a bit wider and the man stepped back.

The woman was busy at the stove. By the smell that filled the room, Clark decided she was making stew for supper. It smelled good. Clark sniffed appreciatively and gave her a smile and a nod.

Clark looked around for the boys, but only the smaller one was present, listlessly playing cat's-in-the-cradle with a piece of twine in a corner of the room.

The man motioned toward a chair, though he did not ask Clark to be seated, nor did he invite him to remove his coat.

Clark sat down and unbuttoned the coat to hang loosely.

"I'm listening," growled the man, standing with hands on his hips.

"Well, I figured as how ya might be anxious to git the weight of this here debt off a' yer shoulders," Clark began. "I have a few jobs round the place thet I could put ya to doin' as soon as ya can spare the time."

"Time, I got lots of," the man replied without a smile.

Clark nodded.

"How many days?" the man asked.

"Not sure. Two—maybe three."

"That won't pay off our debt," the man stated sullenly.

"It'll pay off the vegetables," responded Clark. "Yer gittin' out green logs next spring in exchange fer the firewood."

Mr. Simpson nodded. Maybe it would cover the vegetables. He seemed to feel that the matter was closed.

"My wife has some sewin' that . . . that . . . she could use some help on," Clark continued. "Wondered iffen yer wife might be interested."

"Thought you said the work I did would pay it off," the man answered irritably.

"So it will," Clark said without ruffling. "The sewin'—thet would be fer a wage."

Clark saw the woman at the stove swing her head upward. He pretended not to notice.

"Yer wife can't sew?" asked the big man with a hint of sarcasm.

"She can sew first rate," Clark was quick to defend Marty. "No harm in a woman gittin' a bit of help with her chores now an' then. We've got ourselves lots of grandkids—"

The man mumbled something under his breath. "So what're you offering to swap?" asked Simpson.

"Thought we might pay in cash," said Clark. "We could swap, but we don't know iffen there's anythin' we got thet ya might be needin'. But good help, now—thet's hard to come by."

The man's eyes narrowed in obvious interest. He turned to the woman.

"You want to do that, Ma?" he asked her.

Clark was pleased he had asked, not ordered. He must have some good qualities in him under all that gruffness.

The woman responded with a nod of agreement.

"What're you paying?" asked Simpson.

"What d'ya think is fair wage?" Clark countered.

"Ten cents an hour," said the man.

Clark took his time before answering.

"Was thinkin' on fifteen," he finally informed the man. "Don't wanna git the reputation of not bein' willin' to pay a fair wage."

"Fifteen," agreed Mr. Simpson, and the two men shook on it.

"I'd best be gittin' on home, then," said Clark, rising to his feet. "It gits dark powerful early these days, an' I got me chores to do."

"We'll be over first thing in the morning," the man told him.

"Then I guess I'd best tell ya where to find us," Clark said with a hint of a smile. It did not bring any kind of friendly response to the face of the man. Clark pulled a stub of pencil and a piece of paper from his pocket and busied himself drawing a simple map. He was bending over the table when he heard the door creak open and close again. Out of the corner of his eye, he saw movement, but he purposely did not look up from drawing.

The older boy had come home. Clark finished his crude map and his bit of explanation before he lifted his head.

The boy still had not moved from the door nor removed his skimpy coat. The one sleeve had been tied into a clumsy knot to keep out the cold. A gun was tucked under his good arm, and in his hand he carried a couple of rabbits and a grouse. Clark nodded a greeting and eyed him evenly.

"Ya must be a good shot," he acknowledged with genuine warmth.

The boy nodded in return, tossed the game into the corner, and hung the gun on the wall pegs.

"Do ya always have thet kind of luck?" Clark asked with a grin.

"Mostly," said the boy simply and slipped the coat off his shoulders.

Clark moved toward the door. He buttoned his coat against the cold and reached to reclaim his hat from where he had dropped it by the chair. He could feel the boy's eyes on him.

Clark looked at him, wondering what was going on in his mind.

He had almost reached the door when the boy spoke.

"Thought you claimed to have only one good leg," he said with a bit of rancor in his voice.

Clark looked down at his legs. They both looked good all right. His trouser legs fell full and nearly to his boot tops. Only if one looked closely would he have seen that the boots did not match.

"No," said Clark with a smile. "Me, I got two good legs. Now, one I borrowed, I need to admit, but I got me two."

He reached down and hiked the pant leg quickly upward, exposing the wooden leg with its straps and braces.

He saw the woman wince before she turned quickly away and the younger son, who had sat quietly in the corner of the room, suddenly leaned forward, his eyes round with wonder.

"It works 'most as good as my old one did," Clark went on. "Oh not quite. But Luke, my doctor son, he insisted thet I git me one. I fought it at first, but now I don't know what I'd do without it. Frees my hands up"—Clark extended his hat in both his hands—"an' makes things a heap easier fer me."

The boy said nothing.

Clark turned back to the man as he slipped his hat back on. "Well, we'll see ya in the mornin', then," he said and nodded his good-bye.

He let himself out the door, closed it firmly behind him, and limped his way to his restless team. He wasn't sure if he had made any head-way or not. His prayers as he drove home were even more fervent as he prayed for each member of the Simpson family.

SEVENTEEN

Hired Help

Clark and Marty were still at the table the next morning, enjoying a second cup of coffee after the hurry of getting the youngsters off to school, when Marty heard the dog bark. She leaned forward and lifted back the curtain. To her surprise two people were walking up their lane.

"Now, who d'ya s'pose is out walkin' at this hour?"

Clark joined her at the window.

"Must be our hired help," he exclaimed. "Never thought 'bout not havin' 'em a team or wagon."

Marty frowned. "Ya mean the Simpsons?"

"Thet's them."

"Oh, dear, Clark," Marty cried as she jumped up from the table, one hand quickly trying to smooth her hair. "I sure don't know how I'm gonna use me hired help! Never had such help in my whole life. Why, I don't even know how to go about givin' orders."

Clark laughed. "Jest pretend it's one of your young'uns," he told her. "Ya never had problems tellin' 'em what to do."

"Well, she'll hardly seem like a young'un. An' she might resent the tellin', too. Who knows jest what we got ourselves into?"

"Do ya have a paper all set out?" asked Clark.

"A paper?"

"Yer gonna have to keep track of the hours. She gits paid by the hour, ya know."

"No," said Marty, shaking her head, "I don't have me a paper."

Clark went to the door. "Come on in," he invited, and held the door wide for the two.

They came slowly in, looking carefully about them. Marty had never been so conscious of her own well-being and cozy, comfortable surroundings as she was at that moment. Why had God blessed her with so much when some had so little?

"Jest hang yer coats there by the door," Clark was saying.

Marty went to get two cups from the cupboard. She wondered if they had even had breakfast, but she didn't dare ask.

"We were jest having another cup of coffee before settin' to work," Clark informed them. "Won't ya sit yerselves down an' join us?"

Marty moved the plates left behind by Melissa and Belinda and wiped the table for the guests—well, hired help. Clark lifted the family Bible from the table back to its shelf in the corner.

"Yer nice an' early," Clark commented. "I like a man to be early. We'll git us a good start."

Marty poured the coffee, and Clark passed the cream and sugar. The two helped themselves, at first tentatively, then more liberally.

"Ya got any more of those cinnamon rolls?" Clark asked Marty. "Thinkin' I might like one with my coffee here."

Clark had just finished a hearty breakfast, but Marty understood and moved quickly to the pantry to bring out half a dozen of the rolls. She placed them in the middle of the table and had hardly let go of the plate when Clark reached for one. Marty was surprised that he helped himself even before offering one to the Simpsons.

"Jest help yerself iffen ya care to," Clark said around a bite of roll.

Then it dawned on Marty why he had done that. Both Clark and Marty knew that the rolls were for the benefit of the Simpsons. But Clark did not want them to catch on to that fact and was afraid they would not avail themselves of the rolls if they were the only ones at the table eating. So when Marty sat back down, she, too, helped herself to a roll, though she didn't know how in the world she would be able to get it down. Both the Simpsons helped themselves to the rolls and ate heartily.

The four really didn't visit over their rolls and coffee. The new neighbors had very little to say. They seemed restless and anxious to get started, and Marty guessed that at fifteen cents an hour they wanted to waste no time.

"Best we git ourselves goin'," Marty finally said. "Do ya mind givin' me a hand with the dishes so we have the table to work on fer the cuttin'?"

Then Marty got out a piece of paper and wrote Thursday across the top. She looked at the time, sure to read it to the minute, for the lady's eyes were on the clock, too.

"It's seven forty-six," said Marty. "We'll start countin' the time right now." Marty cast a glance toward the big stove. "My lands," she said. "We still didn't drain thet coffeepot, an' I do hate bein' wasteful. Could ya drink another cup?"

And without waiting for an answer she rose to get the coffee and refilled the cups.

"It won't be wasted time," she informed the woman. "I'll use the time to explain to ya what we'll be doin'."

They drank their coffee slowly. Now and then Clark or Marty gave some explanation about what the two would be expected to do. They seemed to be satisfied with this procedure.

At length Marty felt she could stall no longer. Clark sensed it and rose from the table and led the way out of the kitchen. The man reached for his coat, but Clark stopped him.

"Won't be needin' thet jest now," he said. "First job is more fruit shelves down in the cellar. It stays shirt-sleeve warm down there."

The man left his coat, cast a glance at his wife, and followed Clark.

Marty scurried about her kitchen, her thoughts running ahead of her. They would need to get the dishes out of the way. The kitchen floor should be swept. She planned to mix up a batch of fresh bread. Could the woman be trusted to do the cutting on her own? Oh, well. If worst came to worst, she could do as Clark had said and throw the piece into the ragbag.

The woman spied the dishpan on the peg beside the stove and went to get it.

"The water's there in the reservoir," said Marty and nodded toward the end of the stove.

The woman could not help but show her pleasure at the convenience. She lifted out dipper after dipper of the hot water until she had all she needed in the dishpan.

Marty let her begin washing up the dishes. *Pretend she's one of the young'uns,* she repeated to herself as she dried them and put them away. She hoped that the pretending would work.

They finished the dishes with hardly a comment. *Well, she sure won't be hard to listen to,* Marty said to herself with a hint of a smile. *Never seen such a quiet one.*

Then Marty realized she hadn't been doing much talking, either. Well, she'd change that.

"Hear you've lived in the West," Marty commented warmly.

The woman nodded her head.

"How long were ya out there?" asked Marty.

"About twelve years," said Mrs. Simpson.

"Did ya like it?"

She looked at Marty. Now the questions were getting personal, her look seemed to say. She shut her lips tightly and shrugged her shoulders. Marty got the message. She must be careful not to pry.

Marty left her to wipe the table and went for the broom. When she had her pile of kitchen wood chips and breakfast crumbs gathered, she swept them into the dustpan and pulled back the lid of the stove to dump them in. The stove needed more wood and Marty reached for a few more sticks.

"You let it burn between meals?" Mrs. Simpson asked in disbelief.

Marty nodded. "Wood's one thing we've plenty of," she said, "an' this kitchen stove is the main source of heat fer the house."

The woman said nothing.

"I be needin' to mix up my batch of bread," Marty went on. "I'll jest git it outta the way before we start our sewin'."

Mrs. Simpson nodded.

There was silence in the kitchen for many minutes as both women attended to their respective chores. Down in the cellar the sound of a hammer began to beat out a rhythmic pattern. The men were at work.

The stove was wiped up, the dishwater was discarded, and the pan hung back on its peg.

"What do you want me to do next, Mrs. Davis?" the woman asked.

"Jest call me Marty," Marty responded. "I'm more used to thet." Then she hurried on. "We'll start on some sewin' jest as soon as I finish this kneadin'. 'Most done now."

"And what do I do while I'm waiting?" asked Mrs. Simpson.

Marty wanted to say, "Just sit ya down," but she didn't dare. She cast her eyes about her kitchen, looking for some job—any job. It was tough having hired help.

"The back porch could be swept," she said at last.

The woman took the broom and dustpan and moved to the back porch. Marty hoped it was not too cold. The back porch, though enclosed, did not get the heat of the rest of the house.

Marty finished her bread mixing just as the woman returned with the broom.

"I'll git the material," Marty announced and went for the yard goods. She decided to bring only two pieces at a time. She didn't want it to look as if she were flaunting their wealth. She had noticed the tattered and mended garment the woman was wearing. It had recently been washed, but there was nothing to disguise the fact that it was almost worn through in the spots where it had not already been mended.

"This is the one thet I want to start on," said Marty, "an' here is the pattern. Now, the machine is right in the family livin' room there. An' the scissors and thread are in thet basket beside it."

Marty didn't know what to do next. She didn't want to appear like she was hanging around to see if the woman knew what she was doing. Yet she really had nothing else to take her immediate attention. She could churn some butter, but there was such a tiny dab of cream to be churned—she had just done the churning the day before. She could do some baking—but she didn't need anything baked at present. She wanted to take up work on the braided rug she had been working at and had intended to fill her day with, but it seemed foolish and awkward for her to be doing hand sewing while her hired help used the machine. She could—

Marty stopped herself.

"I'll be upstairs," she told the woman. "Iffen ya need anything, jest call," and she turned to the steps that led her up to her bedroom.

Marty had already made her bed and tidied her room for the day. She wandered aimlessly around for a few minutes, fluffing pillows and arranging curtains. Then she sat down on the side of her bed. It was cool upstairs.

This is silly, she told herself. *Completely silly. Here I am, a grown woman, 'most a prisoner in my own home.* Her thoughts fluttered back and forth. *How am I ever gonna make it through the next few days? How many days is Clark hirin' 'em, anyway? An' what am I gonna do with my time?*

Marty shivered. It was too cold to stay upstairs for long. She grabbed a warm shawl from the chair beside her dresser and wrapped it tightly about her shoulders.

You could pray, a little voice from somewhere within her said. *Remember how you are always saying that you wish you had more praying time?*

Marty flushed, even though there was no one in the room with her—no one visible, that is.

She knelt beside her bed. She began slowly, willing herself to concentrate on the needs of family and friends. Before long she found herself truly communicating with God—talking to Him from her heart and hearing His responses the same way. It was a time of refreshment and uplift for Marty.

Every one of her family members was remembered in a special way. She remembered her far-off daughters, her sons-in-law, and each of their children. She included Nandry and Josh and each of their children. She prayed for Clare and Kate and for Amy Jo, that her life and her artistic talents would be used for God's glory. She remembered each of the three boys. She asked God to be with Arnie and Anne and their boys.

She prayed for Luke in his doctoring and for Abbie and the children as they were so often alone.

Marty prayed especially for Belinda, that God would direct her in her future plans and make her useful in His kingdom. She asked God for wisdom in their relationship with Melissa, Missie's little girl who was so far away from home, and she asked for special wisdom and help in dealing with the little rift and misunderstanding that was making tensions between Belinda and Melissa. She prayed for the neighbors; she prayed for the church. She prayed for the new schoolteacher, that God would comfort her in her widowhood and help her in her adjustments and in raising her three sons.

And Marty, with tears, prayed for the Simpson family. She prayed that their somewhat awkward attempts to help would turn out for good. "An' help me to think of things fer her to do," she requested. She pleaded for special help for the young boy's adjustment to the loss of his arm.

Marty earnestly prayed on. There was no need to jump up and run to care for this task or that task. And then Marty thought of her batch of bread. *Why, it must be almost covering the cupboard by now,* she thought as she sprang to her feet and flung the shawl aside to hurry down to the kitchen.

She needn't have worried. Mrs. Simpson had seen to the punching down of the dough. She was now sitting at Marty's machine, the treadle humming along smoothly as neat seams took shape beneath her skilled fingers. Marty felt like rubbing her eyes. *The woman must be a professional seamstress!* she marveled.

"My!" said Marty. "Yer awful good at thet!"

The woman never lifted her eyes from the cloth. "Used to work in a dress shop back east before I was married," she said simply.

"My!" said Marty again.

She watched for a few minutes more, then roused herself.

"Well, I guess I'd better start thinkin' on dinner. My, how the time has flown."

Marty saw the woman's eyes also travel to the clock on the mantel, and she could almost hear the calculations that were taking place. *Three and a half hours at fifteen cents an hour makes fifty-two and a half cents.*

Marty decided to make some milk pudding. It would be ready in plenty of time to cool. She would also fry up some pork chops and potatoes. She had carrots to warm, too. Her bread would soon be ready to make into loaves. She moved about her kitchen less self-consciously and even began to hum softly to herself. It had been a long, long time since she'd had so much of her morning to spend in prayer. *Maybe hired help isn't so bad after all,* she concluded.

EIGHTEEN

Adjusting

Gradually Marty adjusted to having another woman sharing the work in her home. Each morning after the dishes and early morning chores were finished, Marty climbed the steps to her room for prayer. Though she did not always use as much time as she had that first morning, she did appreciate the extra minutes she was able to spend on her knees.

Gradually the new garments took shape under the experienced eyes of the hired seamstress. Marty was excited and pleased. Surely there was need for this woman's sewing skills in their little town. Marty had overheard the local women talk about how difficult it was to find someone to sew up yard goods in proper fashion. *Well, there'd be no complaints about this woman's sewing,* Marty felt sure of that.

Marty even brought out the pieces of material she had tucked away for future use and had Mrs. Simpson sew them up, as well. *No point in harboring them,* she decided. Each of the girls could do with a new dress for Sundays.

Mr. Simpson had long since finished his assigned tasks and returned to felling trees in the woods near their home, so his wife walked the distance to the Davis' alone. But still the two women did not really visit, though they occupied the same house for a time each day.

Marty shivered each time she saw her neighbor trudging up their lane in the chill of the early morning, or begin the trek back home at the end of the day. But she really could think of nothing to do about it. *If she just wasn't so proud,* Marty kept saying to herself. *If she just wasn't so proud, we could help her more.*

But the woman *was* proud—just like her husband, and Marty did not dare to suggest anything that might smack of charity.

Marty gathered up all the sewing she could find and let the woman do it for her. Then she went to Kate's and carried back all the mending and stitching that Kate could gather together—quite a bundle because of their three active boys. They then finished off the rugs Marty had prepared for her winter's sewing projects and went on to the quilting. Even in that close proximity, they mostly worked in silence—Marty had quickly run out of one-sided conversation topics. But, surprisingly, the quiet had not felt awkward. When the quilting, too, was done and Marty could think of no other sewing projects, she suggested they have one last cup of tea together while she figured the amount still owed.

It seemed strange to Marty, and she had an idea it was to Mrs. Simpson, knowing this was their last time together. Marty had come to enjoy the silent presence in her home. She poured the tea, sliced the cake, and picked up her piece of paper with its calculations.

"The way I figger it," she said, "I still owe ya a dollar and ten cents."

"That's right," said the woman, surprising Marty. Marty had not been aware that the woman was also keeping a tally on the account. She was glad their figures had agreed.

Marty got out her handbag and counted out the money, which the woman promptly put in a little cloth bag and tucked in the front of her dress.

"Ya know, I've been thinkin'," said Marty, trying to tread very carefully. "Ya really do lovely work, an' I know thet there are a number of women in town who've been lookin' fer a seamstress. Would ya be interested—?"

The woman did not even let Marty finish. "I do not have a machine now," she said abruptly.

Marty did not let that stop her. "Ya could use my machine." At the look on the woman's face, she was quick to add, "I'd rent it to ya at a set rate."

The woman relaxed some, but then said, "It's a long way to town. How would I ever get my orders?"

"We go in every week," said Marty as offhandedly as she could. "Ain't no problem to pick ya up an' drop ya off."

"We live beyond you," the woman reminded Marty.

"Well . . . not much beyond us. Wouldn't be—"

"I could walk on over to catch the ride, I suppose," the woman said.

"Fine," said Marty, trying to keep her voice matter-of-fact. "Thet would be fine.

"We're goin' into town tomorra," continued Marty after a pause. "Why don't I jest take in a sample or two of yer work an' ask around a bit?"

"How much would you be charging for the machine?" asked the woman.

"Ah . . . let's see. Ah, ten cents should do nicely."

"Ten cents an hour. I wouldn't be making much—but it might help some. Do you think that folks will be willing to pay fifteen cents an hour for the sewing?"

Marty didn't remind her that she had just finished paying her fifteen cents per hour and her own machine had been used.

"I didn't mean an hour," Marty said. "I meant ten cents a day. An', yes, I think thet yer work is well worth fifteen cents an hour. Yer good— an' yer fast. Folks should expect to pay thet much fer the work ya do."

The woman said nothing, but her eyes took on a bit of shine.

"I'll do it, then," concluded Marty. "I'll see what I can find out."

"I'd be obliged," mumbled the woman, the closest she had come to admitting that she was accepting something from another.

She rose to go.

Marty smiled warmly. "I guess this needn't be good-bye, then. I mean, ya'll still be comin' over to use the machine an' all."

"If the plan works," said the woman shortly.

"Iffen it works," repeated Marty.

The woman nodded.

"I've enjoyed havin' ya here," Marty said a bit self-consciously. "It's been nice workin' with ya."

Mrs. Simpson nodded again.

"An' we'd be so happy iffen ya'd join us in worship at our church. It's not fancy like, but you an' yer family would be most welcome—"

She was cut short as Mrs. Simpson's eyes sparked and she flung a hand toward her tattered dress. "Like this?" she hissed. "Like this to your church? No, I'm thinking that not much of a welcome mat would be extended to people looking like this."

Before Marty could even respond, the woman grabbed her coat from the coat peg, and without waiting to put it on, she pushed her way out the door and was gone.

Marty stood looking after her in stunned silence. Though her eyes remained dry, her heart cried out in silent prayer. *Oh, God,* she prayed, *forgive us if we have unthinkingly given that impression. Why would she think we wouldn't welcome her the way she is? I so much wanted her to know she was welcome into my house and she'd be welcome into your house, too, but somehow I have failed you again, Lord. I've failed you again.* And the tears came then.

But soon from somewhere within, Marty heard a reply. *Be patient,* the gentle voice said. *Just be patient. I have never failed you, and I am with the Simpsons, too, even when they are not aware of it.*

Marty did check for sewing work when she went into town. The first place she went was to the dry goods store. She showed the clerk behind the counter some of the work that Mrs. Simpson had done for her, explaining that the woman would be happy to do sewing for the ladies of the town. The shopkeeper was impressed and said she was sure she could find customers. Marty knew this would increase sales in yard goods, so this would be a help to both Mrs. Simpson and the shop owner.

The woman promised to put up a notice where interested women could sign their names and indicate what kind of sewing they wished to have done. Marty was to check the list the next time she was in town.

The next Saturday, Marty was thrilled to see the list of names. It looked like her machine would be kept busy for several weeks. She picked up the yard goods and the patterns that the ladies had selected and took them home for Mrs. Simpson. Somehow she would get word to her neighbor that the arrangements had been made and that there was much sewing to be done.

NINETEEN

The Triangle

The situation had not improved greatly between Belinda and Melissa. Marty kept hoping and praying that things would work themselves out. Clark had been so sure the simple solution to the problem was just to ignore it. It was a part of growing up, he said, and if allowed to take its course, it would eventually go away. Well, this time Clark seemed to have misread the state of affairs. The problem had not gone away.

Marty longed to sit the two girls down and talk some sense into them, but she really could not see where Belinda had been at fault in the matter. And Melissa might feel she was being "picked on" if Marty were to talk to her alone.

Marty found it hard to believe that their generous, sweet, sensitive Melissa could have such a stubborn streak. Well, Clare had cautioned them that she would not be perfect.

Because of the strained relations, Melissa was spending more and more time over at Kate's. She did enjoy being with Amy Jo, and she liked the young boys, too. She spent hours reading to them and coloring pictures or making cutouts. Melissa was a born teacher. She was the happiest when she was in charge.

Belinda did not seem to suffer greatly from Melissa's absence. She

carried on her duties cheerfully and went out with Luke at each opportunity. Always, when she returned home, she had a full report for
Clark and Marty. Marty herself was finding that she was learning a
lot about medicine. *It's no wonder both Luke and Belinda find it so
intriguing,* she noted to herself.

Marty wondered if Kate might be feeling Melissa was spending far
too much time at the log house. She decided to walk over for coffee and
have a chat with Kate.

She was met at the door by Dack. "Do ya want to read to me,
Gramma?" he asked hopefully before Marty even had her coat off. He
no doubt was restless with being shut indoors with his siblings off at
school and was glad to see her.

"Dack," scolded Kate, "let yer Gramma catch her breath." She turned
to Marty. "He thinks thet's all people have to do since Melissa spoils
'im so."

Marty laid aside her coat and sat down at the kitchen table. Her
fingers traced the pattern on the oilcloth as Kate busied herself fixing
a cup of tea for each of them.

Kate handed Dack some raisins. "Here ya are," she said to the small
boy. "Why don't ya go have yerself a party with the dolls?"

Dack left, looking excited about getting "official permission" to set
Amy Jo's dolls all in a row and share his raisins with them. Later he
would go down the row, eating the raisins on behalf of each doll baby,
Kate explained with a wry smile.

"Is yer seamstress all done now?" she asked as she sat down with
two cups of tea.

Marty nodded, then smiled. "An' guess what?" she admitted a bit
sheepishly. "After all my fussin' 'bout it, I'm actually missin' her."

Kate laughed with her.

"Yet it sure wasn't her talkin' thet I miss. Never saw such a quiet
woman in all my born days."

"Thet's what ya told me before," responded Kate. "Well, there're
plenty of days I'd sure settle fer a bit of peace and quiet. I'll be right
glad when thet youngest can be off to school with the rest of 'em, I'm
thinkin'."

Then she smiled knowingly. "Least, thet's what I tell myself now," she added. "I know when the time actually comes an' the house gits quiet, I might be changin' my wants some."

Marty nodded agreement. She knew what it was like to see the last one go off to school.

"How's Amy Jo doin' with her art?" Marty asked.

"Ya know, Ma, I think she really has talent. Clare an' me jest can't believe some of the work she does. An' it helps so much fer her to have all those books of Melissa's to learn from, too. Bless Melissa, she's been so good 'bout sharin'! I do hope we aren't hoggin' her too much. I know she's here a lot an' we love to have her, but I sometimes think ya must think we are pretty selfish."

"No," said Marty. "Iffen yer enjoyin' her, I won't be begrudgin' ya." She paused. "I am a bit perplexed, though," she said slowly.

"About what? Melissa?"

"Yeah."

"Somethin' wrong?"

"I dunno," said Marty. "Thet is, I don't know iffen it's worth stewin' 'bout or not. Clark says to jest leave it an' it'll go away, but it's been a fair while now, an' it ain't gone away yet."

"What's thet?" asked Kate, looking sober.

"Well, ya know 'bout this here Jackson thing?"

"Ya mean all the girls moonin' over 'im?"

"Yeah. You'd think he was the one an' only boy on the face of the earth."

"I agree with Pa," said Kate comfortably. "They'll grow out of it in time. All girls seem to go through a silly stage—some worse'n others."

"Oh, it ain't the moonin' I worry 'bout. Least not directly. It's more'n thet. Melissa hasn't said anything?"

"Not to me, she hasn't. Maybe to Amy Jo. They seem to have lots of little secrets they share in her room and giggle or groan over. Me, I pay 'em no mind. I remember goin' through thet myself."

Marty smiled. She might have gone through it, too, but it was a long time ago. "Well, it's more than that," she tried again to explain. "Melissa seems to have a real crush on Jackson. An' she was sure thet he liked her, too. Special like. Well, when we had the Brown family over a while back, Jackson seemed to pay more mind to Belinda than he did to Melissa."

"So-o," said Kate, sounding like she was getting the picture. "How'd Melissa take thet?"

"Not well, I'm afraid. She accused Belinda of cuttin' in, an' she's been miffed with Belinda ever since."

"I see," said Kate as she got up to pour more tea.

From the bedroom they could hear Dack scolding a doll for not waiting her turn.

"Have ya talked to Melissa?" asked Kate, setting the teapot on the back of the stove.

"No. I've been followin' Clark's advice—waitin' fer it to go away."

"An' it hasn't?"

"Well, not yet it hasn't, an' last night when they got home from school, Melissa seemed more angry than ever. Didn't say nothin'. Jest changed her clothes and headed over here. How did she seem to you when she got here?"

"I didn't notice anything different. But she an' Amy Jo went right to her room," said Kate. Then she asked, "Did ya learn what happened?"

"I asked Belinda. She tried to shrug it off. Said Melissa had seen Jackson give 'er a wink, in teasin'."

"How does Belinda feel about Jackson?" asked Kate.

"Well, iffen she cares for him, she sure doesn't let on," responded Marty. "But then, right now, 'bout all Belinda seems to care fer is her house calls with Luke."

"She is excited 'bout thet, isn't she?" said Kate. "Me, I could never stomach the sight of blood. Amy Jo is jest like me thet way. We can't even wrap up a cut finger or pick out a sliver without going all queasy. Clare has to do it."

"I don't care for blood, either," admitted Marty, "but I'm beginnin' to understand what Belinda finds so excitin' 'bout it."

"How is the boy doin' who lost his arm?"

"We haven't seen or heard much 'bout him fer quite a while. His ma worked fer me day after day, but she never said one word 'bout 'im, an' I didn't dare ask. She was touchy 'bout things she considered personal."

"I do hope he doesn't let it bitter 'im none," said Kate.

Marty told Kate that she and Clark had been praying for him along that very line.

"I really don't know what to say 'bout Melissa," said Kate, returning to the former issue.

"I thought she might have said somethin' while she was here," said Marty. "Somethin' thet would give me a hint as to what to say or do."

"No, nothin'. She doesn't spend all that much time talkin' to me. She is either whisperin' with Amy Jo or readin' an' playin' with the boys."

"Well," said Marty, setting her empty teacup back on the table, "I don't wanna be borrowin' trouble. Maybe it'll jest pass over like Clark says."

"I'll keep my eyes and ears open now thet I know," promised Kate.

Marty stopped in Amy Jo's room to see Dack before leaving for home. He had almost finished the raisins. The last doll still claimed a little pile. Dack pointed at her reproachfully. "She won't share," he stated. "It's not nice not to share."

Marty agreed that the dollie should share, and Dack scooped up the few remaining raisins and popped them all into his mouth.

"There!" he exclaimed triumphantly. "Now she'll learn ta share."

Marty laughed and gathered the chubby little boy into her arms for a hug. "I'm glad yer learnin' 'bout sharin', Skeezix," she said, calling him her special name. "How 'bout sharin' dinner with Grandpa and me tomorra?" Marty invited, and Dack gave a whoop and ran off to the kitchen to get his mother's agreement.

Marty felt better as she walked back to her house. If Kate knew nothing about the ruckus, then maybe it wasn't too serious. Surely Amy Jo would talk to her mother about it even if Melissa didn't. Perhaps Marty had blown it all out of proportion in her thinking. Clark was likely right. Eventually the whole thing would just go away.

But it wasn't to be that easy. Before the girls even reached home that afternoon, Marty could tell that something had happened to make matters worse. The two girls were not even walking together. Melissa stormed on ahead, her every stride announcing the fact that she was very angry. She burst into the house and, without acknowledging Marty's greeting, stomped up the stairs and slammed the door to her room. Marty could hear her crying all the way from the kitchen.

"Well!" said Marty, even though there was no one there to respond. "Well!"

Belinda walked in a few moments later, her cheeks streaked as though she also had been crying—and Belinda did not cry easily. Unless it was to mourn over hurt pets or birds. Marty wondered what had happened now.

Belinda did greet her mother, but she, too, passed and would have gone straight up to her room had not Marty stopped her.

"Wait," she said. "Wait a minute. Don't ya think I should know what's goin' on?"

Belinda hesitated. Then the tears began to flow again.

"It's thet dumb Jackson," she wailed.

"Dumb Jackson? Why, I thought ya liked Jackson."

"Well, I don't," insisted Belinda. Then she quickly amended, "Well, I do. I do. He's . . . he's . . . but I don't like him as much as Melissa does. She . . . she . . . an' he . . . he . . . he jest makes trouble."

"Trouble? How?" asked Marty.

"He . . . he . . . keeps doin' things . . . sayin' things . . . an then Melissa gits mad at me."

"What did he do now?"

"Yesterday he wanted . . . wanted to help me with my geometry. I told him, 'No thanks,' 'cause I was nearly done. The day before he asked to sit with me at lunch hour, but I made an excuse, an'—today, Ma—today he asked iffen I'd go with 'im to the church picnic!" she ended in a rush.

"The church picnic? The church picnic is months away yet."

"I know . . . but he said he wanted to ask early so thet no one else would ask me first," Belinda acknowledged with downcast eyes.

"I see," said Marty. "An' Melissa found out about it, huh?"

"Found out?" cried Belinda. "She was standin' right there when he asked me!"

"Oh my!" said Marty. "Oh my!"

It was clear that someone was going to have to talk to Melissa. And she, Marty, seemed to be the one.

She wiped her hands on her apron and reluctantly climbed the stairs, silently asking the Father for wisdom.

She rapped on Melissa's door, but there was no answer, so she waited a moment and then opened the door gently. Melissa was lying on her bed, her head buried in her pillow. Marty crossed to her and lowered herself to the bed, reaching out to smooth back the girl's long curls. Melissa's reply was a fresh burst of tears. Marty let her cry.

When she felt she had waited long enough, she began carefully, slowly, "Ya really do like Jackson a lot, don't ya?"

Melissa nodded and gave a shuddering sigh.

"I remember," said Marty reflectively, "I remember when I was yer age, I liked a boy a lot, too."

No answer.

"I thought he was the smartest, the handsomest, the nicest boy I had ever seen—an' he was, too."

"Was it Grandpa?" asked Melissa in a muffled voice from her pillow.

"Grandpa? Oh my, no. I didn't meet yer grandpa till many years later. Then I finally learned the truth. Yer *grandpa* is the smartest and the handsomest and the nicest man I've ever seen."

Melissa was quiet. Marty let her be.

"What happened to the other one?" she asked at length, just like Marty had hoped she would.

"Clifton? Thet was his name, Clifton. Well, Clifton . . . it seemed like he cared more fer another girl than he did me. It nearly broke my heart. Her name was Cherry, and she had long blond hair and big green eyes. She was older'n me—maybe two years. Fact is, she and Clifton were 'bout the same age. She loved to tease. Was worse than a boy 'bout it. At first I thought she really didn't care fer Clifton at all, jest wanted to flirt with 'im to make me mad. An' it did make me mad, too, ya can bet it did. But . . . I guess maybe she really did care for Clifton after all. Still . . . I never liked her. In fact, it was a long, long time until I could bring myself to forgive 'er."

Marty waited again.

"So-o," said Melissa.

"Well, she married Clifton, Cherry did. I could hardly stand it at first.

Jest thinkin' 'bout it made me angry inside. An' then one day I did some thinkin' on it. Me moanin' around wasn't gonna git me Clifton. An' there I was spoilin' all my growin'-up years a weepin' over 'im. 'Now, is he really worth it?' I asked myself. 'Is he really worth spoilin' my life for?' I decided right then and there thet he wasn't, an' I dried my eyes and went on out an' had me a good time."

"And you forgave her?"

"No-o. Not then. Not for many years, in fact. Ya see, I wasn't a Christian when I was a girl. So I was still foolish enough to carry thet grudge. It wasn't until I was grown-up and met yer grandpa's God and became a believer thet I had sense enough to see I didn't need to forgive Cherry. I needed Cherry to forgive me."

"What did she say?" asked Melissa.

"Say?" queried Marty. "Oh, ya mean when I asked her forgiveness? Well, that's the sad part. I never got to ask Cherry. I was way out here and Cherry had never left our hometown. I wrote a letter. It came back to me. All it said on the envelope was one word—'Deceased' it said, jest like thet, 'Deceased.'"

"You mean—?"

"Cherry died. I found out later that she had died in childbirth. But I've always felt sad I wasn't able to tell her thet I was sorry—to ask her forgiveness. Ya see—I hadn't been very nice 'bout it all. It really wasn't Cherry's fault thet Clifton liked her better'n me."

Melissa began to weep again. Marty reached down and gathered the girl in her arms.

"Oh, Grandma," she sobbed, "I like him so much."

"I know," said Marty, stroking her hair. "I know."

"I don't think Belinda even *likes* him," continued Melissa, sounding exasperated.

"She likes 'im," said Marty. "She jest doesn't like 'im in the same way you do. An' she feels bad thet he keeps doin' an' sayin' things thet hurt ya."

"Did she say that?" asked Melissa, turning swollen eyes to look at Marty.

"She said thet."

"I guess I should talk to her," Melissa whispered, and a fresh batch of tears started.

"Thet would be a good idea," said Marty.

"Do you . . . do you think she'll forgive me?" Melissa sobbed.

"Oh my, yes," Marty assured her. "But I tell ya what. Before ya go off to have yer talk with Belinda, why don't ya an' me jest have us a little talk with God? Ya see, there's someone else involved here thet we haven't even talked 'bout."

Melissa's eyes studied the face of her grandmother.

"Jackson!" went on Marty. "Jackson is in this, too. Now he is a fine young man an' apparently . . . well . . . sometimes we don't do a whole lot a choosin' in ones we love—our heart seems to jest do it fer us—an' it appears thet fer now, Jackson thinks his heart has chosen Belinda. Time will tell thet, of course. Ya all are very young, an' sometimes . . . well, sometimes the heart changes its mind again. But, in the meantime . . . well, we don't want to hurt Jackson, do we?"

Melissa's eyes dropped to her hands, twisting her handkerchief round and round. She shook her head. She did not want to hurt Jackson.

"So we need to pray . . . fer all three of ya. Fer Belinda, fer you . . . an' fer Jackson. Thet each one of ya might be able to let God help ya with yer choosin'. Ya see, He knows! He knows how things should be for our very best. So iffen we leave it to Him, He can work it all out."

Melissa nodded, sniffed, blew her nose on her rumpled hanky, and they knelt down beside her bed together.

The days that followed were much happier for everyone, and Marty thanked the Lord daily. There were still times when Jackson unintentionally hurt Melissa with his continued interest in Belinda, and Belinda cringed inwardly and subtly tried to divert his attention toward Melissa. But even though Melissa still cried alone in her bedroom once in a while, the tension between the two girls was gone. They could even talk about the situation together, and at times they brought their problem to Marty. It always seemed to help when the three of them prayed together about it.

TWENTY

Helping Luke

Belinda arrived home from school in a rush. From her flushed cheeks and heavy breathing, Marty knew she must have run a good deal of the way. When Marty had first caught sight of her slight figure flying up the lane, her heart had started to pound. Surely something was wrong! But the girl's first panted words put her mind at ease.

"Luke stopped by the school," she gasped out. "He's goin' out to change the bandages on the little Willis girl. He said fer me to join 'im there. He might need my help."

"Is thet the one with the bad burn?"

Belinda nodded, still puffing.

"Ya gonna take the sleigh?" asked Marty.

"No, I'll jest ride Copper. Thet'll be faster." And Belinda was off up the stairs on the run. Marty knew that as soon as she changed clothes for riding she would be back down.

Marty grabbed a warm sweater from the clothes hooks by the door and headed for the barn. At least she could saddle the horse and save Belinda that much time.

Copper, in the corral beside the barn, came when Marty shook the pail containing a small amount of oats. The other horses came, too. It was not a problem for Marty to catch Copper. It was a bit of a problem for her to get rid of the other horses.

She led Copper into the barn and was almost done saddling him when Belinda appeared, still breathless. Marty wasn't sure if it was from running or from excitement.

They led Copper from the barn, and Belinda mounted.

"Now, mind ya, don't run 'im too hard," Marty cautioned her. "Luke won't be that anxious fer ya to git there."

Belinda nodded, called a good-bye, and was off down the lane. It was then Marty remembered that Belinda hadn't even taken time for a snack, and the youngsters were always hungry when they got home from school. Well, for Belinda, her daily bread seemed to be her nursing.

Belinda pushed Copper. She was mindful of her mother's admonition, but she did not want to keep Luke waiting. She had not been there when Luke had first tended the child, but he had explained to her in detail about the burn the little girl had received. He was quite concerned. Besides causing the young child a great deal of pain, Luke was afraid it might become infected and cause permanent damage to the arm. So Luke planned on keeping a very close eye on the girl. This meant a frequent change of bandages—and that was a difficult, painful process. Because of the oozing of the open sores, the bandages stuck—sometimes badly, and they had to be carefully and slowly soaked off. It was important to be patient in the process, both to prevent pain and to cause as little damage as possible to the wound beneath.

Belinda wasn't sure what her role would be. She had never been with Luke on a burn case before. Burns made her stomach flip. She had once burned herself when she was a little girl—not bad as burns go. In fact, they hadn't needed a doctor; her ma had treated it herself. But it had been terribly painful, and Belinda had not been able to use two of her fingers for days. At the time, she wondered if they would ever be useable again. Of course they were. In fact, now Belinda had a hard time remembering which fingers it had been.

But this burn—according to Luke—this burn would be different. The little girl had spilled hot grease all down one arm. Some had splashed on her chest, too, but those burns weren't too deep.

Even as Belinda felt herself drawing back from what lay ahead, she pushed Copper as fast as she dared toward the neighboring farmhouse. Luke needed her. The little girl needed her. They must do all they could to save the use of her arm.

Luke's team was already there, tied to the hitching rail out front, when Belinda urged Copper down the lane at a gallop. She hastened to dismount and wrap the reins securely about the rail. If he was not tied carefully, Copper had a bad habit of leaving for home before his rider. Belinda hurried to the house.

The lady of the home greeted her. Belinda did not know the family well. They did not have school-age children as yet and did not attend their church. Belinda had seen them occasionally at community gatherings or on the street in town. She nodded to the woman now and her eyes searched the room for the patient.

Luke sat on a couch on one side of the room. A little girl—perhaps three years old—with a big bandage sat on his knee. He was letting her play with his stethoscope. She put the instrument in her ears, as she had seen the doctor do, and grinned impishly at him.

She doesn't look too bad, thought Belinda. *Why, she can even smile!* Belinda had expected to encounter screams of pain.

"Well, here's my nurse," Luke announced to both the mother and the little girl. "Guess we'd better get to work, huh?"

The woman took Belinda's coat, and Luke sent Belinda to the washbasin in the kitchen to carefully wash her hands. She knew when she had finished, he would also insist on pouring a strong-smelling disinfectant over her hands. She didn't mind the smell, but the kids at school teased her about it—it stayed with her for days. But Luke always insisted on the thorough cleansing, and Belinda did not even think of arguing about it.

"Now, Mandie," Luke said to the little girl, "let's take a look at that arm of yours."

The little girl pulled away. She did not want her arm touched. Instinctively, she knew it would be painful. She could bear the present pain—it still hurt, but it was bearable. But it had been worse. The memory of the pain she had endured made her draw away.

Luke gently lifted her and placed her on the table to take advantage of all the light he could. The child began to cry. Luke tried to soothe her, but the tears and shrieks only increased.

Luke turned to the mother.

"You might want to go for a bit of a walk, ma'am," he said softly to the woman. Already her eyes were filling with tears. She slipped on a warm coat, lifted the baby from the floor, and wrapped him securely in a blanket.

"I'll be at the barn iffen ya need me," she murmured.

The door closed gently, and the woman and baby were gone.

"Now," said Luke above the cries of the child, "I'd hoped you could keep her attention elsewhere, but that's not going to work. You'll have to hold her while I get this bandage off. First, let's get organized."

Luke poured hot water from the kettle on the stove into the basin and added some of his strong-smelling disinfectant. He swished the water round and round, making sure the sides of the basin had been cleansed, then he walked to the door and down the path a few steps to dispose of the water. When he returned, he poured more warm water into the basin and again added disinfectant. With the basin on the table, he laid out sterile pads and all of his instruments. Then he nodded to Belinda, who was holding the child, trying to comfort and assure her.

Belinda placed the little girl back on the table and the screaming began again. They would not even be able to converse during the procedure. Luke nodded to Belinda above the child's head, and she took a firm hold of the little girl.

Belinda never would have dreamed that one so small could be so strong. It was all she could do to hold on to the child.

The first several rows of bandage came off quickly and easily, and then it began to get more difficult. Luke soaked and cut, soaked and cut, and the size of the bandage gradually decreased. And all the time they worked the little girl screamed and fought.

Belinda wished Luke could hurry. She was getting exhausted. She wondered how the little one had the strength to go on fighting against the procedure.

But Luke did not hurry. He took his time, and carefully, oh, so carefully removed each layer.

By the time he was down to the last of the bandages, Belinda was aching and covered with perspiration. The bandages, put on so clean and sterile, were now heavy with blood and liquid from the oozing sores. The smell was a strange mixture of the body fluids and the medication Luke had used on them before. Belinda wondered for a few minutes if she was going to be sick, but she fought firmly against it. This was not the time to be feeling queasy. She held fast to the little girl.

"Doesn't look too good," she heard her brother say over the cries of the child, and Belinda let her eyes drop to the burned arm.

Her stomach lurched, and she shut her eyes and counted, trying to shut out the sight. The wound looked terrible.

"I'm gonna have to clean it up," Luke almost hollered at her in order to make himself heard. "Don't like to use chloroform on one so little, but might have to put her under for a bit."

Belinda watched as Luke poured a small amount of chloroform on a clean cloth. Then with a quick but gentle movement, he covered the child's nose and mouth. Almost immediately Belinda felt the small body relax in her arms. Luke carefully laid the little girl down on the clean sheet covering the kitchen table.

"We're going to have to work quickly," he said. "I didn't want to give her much. Now, you keep a close eye on her. Check her pulse often just as I showed you, and watch her breathing. I'll do this as fast as I can," and so saying Luke took his scissors and began to trim away the burned and lifeless flesh.

Belinda was glad she had something to do other than watch Luke. She checked the small girl's faint pulse, thankful that it remained even. Her breathing, too, did not alter. Belinda lifted the eyelid and studied the pupil's response to light. The child seemed to be doing fine.

"I don't think she'll stay under much longer," Belinda informed Luke, watching her eyelids flutter. "Do you want to give her a bit more?"

"I'm almost done. We'll try to make that do. I don't want to give any more if I can help it."

Luke was just finishing up the removal of the infected flesh when the girl began to stir. For a moment she looked about her uncertainly, and then she began to scream again. Luke moved her to a sitting position, and Belinda held her, talking to her soothingly.

The heavy medication on the bandages was nearly overpowering. Belinda felt her legs turning to rubber. She held the tiny arm as Luke pressed the sterile cloths carefully onto the burned area and began the process of rebandaging. Still the girl screamed. Belinda did not know if the cries now were from pain, fright, or anger—or all of them.

At last the job was done and Luke lifted the wee girl into his arms. Speaking softly in a hushed voice, he began to walk the floor with her, gently rocking her in his arms and murmuring soft words of comfort.

Gradually the child calmed. Luke continued to croon, telling her over and over what a brave, big girl she was and how she was going to be all better soon.

He turned to Belinda, who had collapsed into a nearby chair. "You might want to tell her ma that she can come in now," he suggested.

Belinda reached for her coat. *Fresh air!* she thought in relief. She left the house and headed for the barn.

The woman was lying facedown on the hay. Beside her, bundled warmly against the weather, slept the baby.

"Ma'am," said Belinda, bending over the grieving form, "ma'am."

The woman stirred, turning a tear-streaked face to Belinda.

"We're all done. Ya can come in now."

"Thank God!" the woman muttered, and Belinda looked at her carefully.

How did she mean the words? They had not sounded like a small prayer of thanks, the way they did when her ma or pa spoke them. No, they had sounded quite different somehow. Belinda wished she knew what to say.

"Yes, ma'am," she faltered after a moment. "We do thank God. It's only Him thet can make the treatment work—make thet arm to heal."

The woman looked at Belinda with a very strange expression on her face, then lifted herself from the hay, gathered up her sleeping baby, and hurried to the house.

By the time they reached the kitchen, Luke had completely calmed the child. He had bathed her teary face with a warm cloth and smoothed back the tangled hair.

Except for the swollen eyes, one would not have known she had just been through such an ordeal.

The child reached for her mother, and the woman hurried to lay down the baby so she might take the little one from Luke.

"I'll see you again in a couple of days," Luke was telling her.

"How . . . how many more times do we need to go through this?" the young mother asked him, her eyes filled with agony.

"I really can't say," Luke said honestly. "The burn doesn't look good at this point. It's going to be a fight to keep out infection. We'll have to keep a close watch on it. But I hope . . . I hope the healing process soon begins. Once it starts to heal properly, it might improve quite quickly. With a child, it often does," he assured her, patting the child's head.

Luke smiled at the woman. "We'll do the best we can," he promised her.

She nodded. She was too overwrought to even think of a thank-you, but Luke understood.

He gathered all his belongings, threw the dirty bandages into the kitchen stove so the woman would not need to see the reminder, and reached for his coat.

Outside, Luke laid his hand on Belinda's shoulder. "Thanks," he said. "I never could have done it without you."

She smiled weakly.

"Do you mind coming back a few times to give me a hand?"

"No . . . I don't mind. I'll help."

"It's not very nice, is it?"

"No," admitted Belinda.

"It's always so much harder for me when it's a child," said Luke, shaking his head. "I just hope and pray I never need to treat one of my own. I don't know if I could bear it—or any of our family's children, for that matter. It would be so hard. The poor little things just can't understand the pain—and the treatment."

Luke shook his head. Belinda knew that he felt it deeply.

"You okay?" Luke sincerely asked her, searching her face.

"Fine," said Belinda.

"You looked a bit pale in there."

Belinda smiled again. "I felt pale for a few minutes, too."

Luke gave her a quick hug and turned to untie his team.

"I have to go on to the Williams'. They think they have a case of measles. Let's plan to meet here on Thursday right after school, okay?"

"Yes," said Belinda, "I'll be here."

"Maybe next time it won't be quite so bad," said Luke, "but . . . I can't make any promises."

Belinda nodded and mounted Copper. She was anxious to get home.

TWENTY-ONE

An Accident?

Belinda let Copper choose his own speed going home. It was a good thing the horse knew his way. Belinda was not paying much attention to the animal—her mind was still full of what she had just seen.

Belinda thought the amputation of the Simpson boy's arm had been terrible, the worst thing she had ever seen in her life. But the little girl's burns today would certainly rate a very close second. It was a terrible thing to see, and imagining the child's unbelievable pain, Belinda cringed each time the mental picture flashed into her mind.

Maybe I'm not cut out to be a nurse after all, she wondered as she rode. It was so painful to see the suffering. Maybe she should do like Melissa and become a schoolteacher. An artist, like Amy Jo, was out of the question—she didn't have an artistic bone in her body.

But then Belinda thought about Luke, about his dedication to this service, this ministry to people. She pictured him again as he carried the child back and forth in the kitchen, soothing and comforting her. *Luke needs me,* she thought. There were too few nurses, he had said. Doctors could not handle all cases on their own. They needed assistants. Deep inside, Belinda knew this was her dream, her calling.

Of course she would not enjoy seeing the pain. Of course she would find some cases distasteful and troubling. But someone needed to be there, to fight against pain and suffering as Luke was doing. He would always be there, and with God's help she would be there, too.

As Copper ambled along toward home, Belinda's thoughts turned to Jackson. She *liked* Jackson, but she just couldn't seem to make him understand that she *loved* nursing. At this time she did not want to even think about boys. In the first place, she was way too young, though she did admit to mildly enjoying the girlish flirtation games on occasion. But, on further thought, Belinda could think of no good that would come of flirting. If the boy responded—well, that meant even more trouble, for Belinda knew if she wished to be a nurse, she would need to dedicate the next several years of her life to training for it. What would she do with a special beau then?

Besides, Melissa was the one who seemed to really care for Jackson. Melissa was young, too—too young to be thinking seriously about fellows. But Melissa seemed inclined to think about them anyway, and it certainly didn't help matters that she had about made up her mind Jackson was the fellow for her. Now, it wouldn't have been so bad if Jackson had shared the attraction. But Jackson's attention had obviously been captured by Belinda, and the whole thing was very difficult to deal with. Fortunately, Amy Jo's painting had captured her imagination, so Belinda didn't have that niece to worry about, too. She was glad Jackson would be going off to school someplace come fall. Perhaps that would solve the problem for all of them.

Without warning, a shrill crack suddenly split the air. Before Belinda knew what had happened, Copper had spooked, tossing his head into the air and leaping wildly to one side. Belinda grabbed for the saddle horn and the reins but was unable to control the animal or her own body.

Frantically, she realized she was flying through the air. Time seemed to freeze before she struck the ground. When she did land with a sickening thud, all of the air was knocked out of her body, and she lay there on the ground in a daze. Copper tossed his head again in fright and headed for home at a gallop.

In the bush next to the road, the hunter must have heard the commotion. He had not seen or heard anyone around when he fired at the rabbit and would never have shot if he had. But from the noise on the nearby road, he feared that the gunshot had meant trouble for someone. He quickly ran over to check.

The first thing he saw was the fleeing horse, his head held to the side to avoid stepping on the dragging reins. Then the hunter looked the other direction and saw a motionless form lying on the roadway. He cried out in alarm as he ran to the body.

It was a girl, lying in a crumpled heap like a discarded sack. He knelt beside her, nervously looking for signs of broken bones or other injuries.

What should he do? Where should he go for help? He wished that horse was still available. He stared anxiously down the road, hoping the animal had stopped, but it was just disappearing over the crest of the hill.

The girl moaned softly. He turned back to her, fervently hoping she was not seriously injured. He dared to touch her face—to smooth back her hair. *What should I do?* he lamented.

The girl moaned again and began to stir. He watched her face carefully. *Who is she? Where does she live?* He should go for help. Get her parents. Something. But he couldn't leave her here alone. He cradled her head carefully. *What if her neck is injured?* his frantic thoughts tumbled over themselves.

She moved again and he saw her eyelids flutter. Was she coming around? Would she be okay? *Oh, please, God, please, God,* he pleaded with a God he neither knew nor understood.

Belinda fought against the unreal world she so precipitously had entered. *What happened? Where am I?* She struggled to fill her aching lungs with air. She hurt. Her whole chest hurt.

Gradually she began to breathe again. The pain was subsiding and her thinking began to clear. She forced her eyes to open. Someone was bending over her, gently stroking her face as though coaxing the life back into her body. She strained to make her eyes focus on the world swirling around her.

And then she saw the dark eyes and the black hair. She knew who it was immediately. It was the boy, the boy with one arm. She fought to get control of her breathing, straining to sit up. *What happened anyway?* she tried to ask.

"Easy," he was saying softly. "Easy. Don't try to move yet."

"What . . . ? What . . . ?" tried Belinda again, but her voice would not work properly. She let her head drop against his supporting arm, closed her eyes, and willed the world to stop spinning.

What had happened? Where was she? Why was she here? Slowly, oh, so slowly, things began to fall into sequence. She had been helping Luke. They were done . . . had finished the bandaging of the little girl's burned arm. She was on her way home. She was riding . . .

"Copper," said Belinda, straining to lift her head again. "Where's Copper?"

"Sh-h," the boy hushed her. "Take it easy. Yer gonna be all right. Jest rest a few minutes."

"Copper," repeated Belinda.

"Copper?" asked the boy, wondering what Belinda was muttering about, and then it must have dawned on him. "Is Copper a horse?"

Belinda looked at him, her head still foggy. *Of course Copper is a horse. My horse. And he should be here . . . somewhere.*

"I'm afraid Copper went on home," the boy said.

Belinda's head was clear enough now for her to understand the implications.

"Oh no," she groaned, moving her head to the side.

The boy looked relieved.

"Oh no," said Belinda again. "Ma'll be frantic!"

"What?" questioned the boy.

"Ma . . . she'll be worried sick when thet horse comes in without me. I gotta git home . . . fast as I can."

Belinda struggled to get to her feet, but the boy held her. Belinda was surprised at the strength in his one arm.

"Don't," he said. "Not yet. You might be hurt bad . . . have a broken bone or somethin'. It's not safe to move jest yet."

"I'm fine," Belinda protested. "Really!"

"You don't seem so fine to me," he insisted. He stared into her face, his own flushed with emotion. "Thet is, you might be hurt some. We don't know yet."

Belinda wondered why the boy seemed flustered, but she did not try to figure it out. All she could think about was her mother. She knew Marty would fear the worst when Copper arrived home riderless. She had to get home—and quickly—but first she would just rest a minute and be sure that she was really okay. The boy was right about that.

She closed her eyes and relaxed. The trees had stopped swirling around, her breath was coming much more easily, and her chest no longer hurt. Here and there she felt bruised, but nothing seemed unbearably painful. She was bound to ache some, and would doubtless be quite sore for a few days, but she did not think she had broken any bones. Bit by bit she mentally went over her body. No, she was sure she was all right.

She looked up at the boy again. His eyes were anxiously studying her, his face now pale. She did not try to fight against the arm that held her. Instead she spoke to him, evenly and coherently.

"I think I'm ready to get up now. I'm sure I have no broken bones. I jest had the wind knocked outta me, thet's all."

"Yer sure?" He still did not release her.

"I'm sure," she assured him. "Iffen ya'll jest help me to my feet . . ."

"Take it real easy," he cautioned, "and let me know if anythin' gives you pain."

He stood to his feet then, gently lifting her along with him. Belinda felt things beginning to spin again, but she held tightly to his arm and closed her eyes until the whirling stopped.

"How is it?" he asked solicitously.

"Fine. Be jest fine in a minute. No . . . no bad pain . . . jest a few bruises."

Belinda tried a smile. It was a bit weak, but the boy responded, his dark eyes lighting up.

"Yer a good sport," he said admiringly.

At that Belinda chuckled softly. "A good sport? Well, I didn't exactly choose this way to—"

"I know," said the boy. "It was my fault. I'm sorry." His eyes were shadowed with remorse.

396

"Yer fault?" asked Belinda. "How . . . yer fault?"

"I didn't notice you comin'. I shot at a rabbit, an' the noise frightened yer horse. I didn't even know you were around till I heard the commotion. I . . . I . . . but it was already too late. Yer horse was runnin' off, an' you were a layin'—"

Belinda stopped him. "Did ya git the rabbit?" she asked softly.

He looked at her as though he wondered if she were teasing him. Then she smiled, and the next thing they were laughing together.

"I dunno," he said truthfully. "I think I did."

"You'd best go see," Belinda prompted him. "Don't wanna waste it."

"Yer serious?"

"It was nearby, wasn't it?"

"Right over there, behind those bushes."

"Then go check. I'll brush a bit of the dirt offa me and then I'd best be gittin' home."

He soon was back with the rabbit, grinning as he held it up for her inspection. Belinda could see that it had been a clean shot. *Must be good with a gun,* she thought.

"Good meat, rabbit," he informed her. "I should know. Thet's about all we've been eatin' this winter."

Belinda nodded, still busy trying to remove the dirty snow and road grit from her clothes. He reached out a hand and brushed her hair gently. "You got it in your hair, too," he said softly.

Belinda tried a step. Her legs seemed to be working fairly well, but he quickly reached out and took her arm.

"Why don't I git rid of this first?" he said, indicating the gun and the rabbit that lay at his feet.

Belinda waited until he had moved to a nearby tree and deposited the gun and the game in the branches. "I'll pick it up on my way back home," he informed her. "Now, let's get you on home before yer mama comes lookin' for you."

They walked very slowly at first, his hand carefully assisting her. She was not in any real pain, but she did notice there were many parts of her body that seemed to be crying out for attention. She would be stiff and sore tomorrow, that was for sure. At least they did not have far to go.

"Is it okay?" he asked her repeatedly, and each time she stoutly insisted that she was fine.

They had not gone far when they heard a horse rapidly approaching, and Clark came over the nearest hill, riding Copper at a brisk gallop. As soon as he reached them he slid to a stop and dismounted in one fluid motion.

"Ya all right?" he asked Belinda anxiously.

"I'm fine," she answered, "jest a little bruised, thet's all."

"What happened?"

"Ol' Copper here spooked an' threw me."

"It was my fault," explained the boy. "I shot at a rabbit."

"An' he got it, too," Belinda put in admiringly while the boy colored and looked away, embarrassed.

Clark's eyes went from one to the other of them. The boy still supported Belinda protectively.

"Well, I'm glad yer okay," Clark said quietly. "An' yer mama will be greatly relieved, too. Didn't know what to think when thet horse came in like he did. I tried to tell yer mama that he jest might have slipped rein again and left ya stranded at wherever ya were. But we had ta check to be sure."

"I tied him carefully like ya said," Belinda informed him.

"Well, let's git ya up on this horse," said Clark.

"You ride, Pa," Belinda argued, thinking of Clark's leg.

But he would not hear of it, and soon Belinda was boosted up into the saddle, and they were on their way home again at a brisk walk. Neither thought to question whether or not the boy should continue on with them. He could have gone back for his gun and his rabbit and gone home. But for some reason he did not, and Clark and Belinda both accepted his presence without discussion.

Marty hurried out to meet them when they entered the lane.

"What happened?" she asked, her eyes large with concern.

"She's jest fine," Clark quickly assured her. "Jest took a bit of a spill. Ya know ol' Copper. He spooks awful easy."

Clark lifted Belinda down and went on to the barn with the horse. The boy took her arm again, and with Marty fluttering anxiously on the other side, they went into the house.

When they were safely seated at the kitchen table, and Belinda was sipping a cup of hot tea, Marty turned to the boy.

"So you two finally met?" she commented. "Seems it's accidents thet bring ya together."

The boy looked puzzled.

"Guess Belinda will have plenty of tales to tell in comin' years 'bout her nursin' experiences," Marty went on with a little chuckle. "Thet's where she was tonight, too—when this happened—helpin' Luke. But I guess ya knew all 'bout thet. Tonight's was a burn case."

The boy turned to Belinda, his dark eyes wide . . . questioning. This . . . *this* was the girl he had been told was there when they took his arm?

TWENTY-TWO

Introductions

Belinda, having recognized the boy immediately, had assumed he knew who she was, as well. But of course he would not have known who she was. He had been unconscious the whole time she was with him after his accident.

Belinda noticed shadows darkening the boy's eyes. She saw the questioning look on his face. His lips parted as though he was going to say something, and then they closed tightly and he turned away.

He did not bolt, though she feared for a moment that he might. The knuckles on the hand that gripped the edge of the table were white. His face was even paler than it had been when he had bent over her in the road. She wanted to say something—anything, but didn't know what it would be.

Clark's appearance helped to break the tension. Understandably having no idea of the undercurrent in the room, he hung up his coat and hat on the proper pegs and walked toward the table.

"Sure can tell thet summer is 'most here," he said in a good neighborly fashion. "The days are gittin' to where they're worth somethin' again, an' the air is actually warm. Be mighty glad to see warmer weather, too. I've had 'nough winter fer a while."

There was no comment from the two seated at the table. Marty brought thick sandwiches and milk for each of them. Belinda looked carefully across at the boy. Would he refuse it? She was afraid he might. But no, he mumbled a polite thank-you and began to eat the sandwich.

"How's yer pa doin' on his loggin'?" Clark asked the boy.

His eyes lifted from his plate and met Clark's. "Fine," he replied but said no more than that.

"It's nice havin' yer ma comin' to sew most days," put in Marty. "I enjoy her company."

The boy nodded.

Clark pulled up a chair and joined them at the table. Belinda said nothing. Inside she felt a deep ache. She couldn't explain it—she just knew that she felt something, an emotional pain, much more keenly than she felt her aches and bruises from the fall.

Something was terribly wrong. She had hoped the Simpson boy had adjusted to his arm being gone, had learned how to go on without it, had understood those who had been forced to take it to spare his life. But from the dark shadows in his eyes and the frown on his countenance, she knew it wasn't so.

Does he still hold the surgery against Luke? Belinda wondered. *Perhaps he does*—but her mother was talking. From the looks directed her way, Belinda knew the question must have been directed to her.

"Beggin' pardon," she responded and shook her head slightly.

"Yer not hurt, are ya?" asked Marty, coming forward to touch the girl's forehead.

"No, no, I'm fine—really," Belinda quickly answered.

For just a moment Belinda saw concern in the boy's eyes again, and then it was gone and the darkness returned.

"I'm fine," Belinda insisted again, "I jest wasn't listenin'. Was thinkin'—thet's all."

"I asked about the little girl. How is she?"

"Mandie?"

"Is thet her name?"

"Mandie. Mandie . . ." Suddenly Belinda could not remember the family's last name. Near panic seized her. Was there actually something wrong? Had she hit her head? And then it came to her. "It's Willis," she said with confidence and relief. "Mandie Willis."

Marty looked at her quizzically and Belinda hurried on. "She's . . . she's . . .." She wanted to say that the little girl was just fine, but in honesty said instead, "She's burned real bad. Luke is worried 'bout infection. We have to go back on Thursday."

Marty frowned in concern. "Terrible thing, those burns," she said. "'Specially fer a little child."

Belinda nodded.

"Ya've hardly eaten a thing," Marty scolded. "Ya missed yer supper an' now—"

"I'm jest not hungry," said Belinda and pushed the plate away from her.

"But ya need—" began Marty and was interrupted by Clark.

"Might be better fer her stomach if she don't put nothin' in it fer the present."

Marty removed the plate.

"So what did ya do?" she asked Belinda.

Belinda looked at her, not understanding.

"How did ya help yer brother?"

"Oh! I . . . I held Mandie . . . while Luke took off the old bandage an' . . . then I . . . I watched her after she was put to sleep, to see thet . . . thet . . . she was okay an' . . . an' everythin'."

All the time they had been talking Belinda could feel the eyes of the boy on her face. She couldn't read the expression in his eyes, but she really did not want to know. Did he hate her for her part in his tragic surgery? She wished she could go to her room. That he would go home.

"I think thet's enough medicine talk," Clark said, and Belinda sighed in agreement.

Clark's hand slowly, unconsciously, moved down to rub his injured leg. Though he was not aware of his action, the boy noticed it. *How much does his leg still hurt him?* he wondered. Did it still shoot fire up the limb, making it seem like it was still there and badly damaged? Did the pain never quit? "Phantom pains," they called it. Well, phantom or not, the pains were very real. The boy winced just thinking about it.

"Don't believe I've been told yer name," Clark was saying. "We never were introduced proper like. I'm Clark Davis, this is my wife Marty and my youngest girl, Belinda. But then, ya already know her."

He didn't. He hadn't. Not really.

The boy mumbled his acknowledgment to the introductions. When Belinda was presented, his eyes met hers for a moment, but the distance was still there.

"An' yer name," Clark prompted.

"Drew. Drew Simpson. Andrew really, but everyone calls me Drew."

Belinda repeated the name mentally. *Drew*. It suited him somehow.

"Well, Drew, we're right glad to make yer acquaintance. An' we are thankful to ya fer carin' fer our Belinda."

"It was my fault—"

"Nobody's fault," Clark stopped him. "Thet fool horse always was bad fer spookin'. Don't know how to go about gittin' 'im over bein' gun-shy. He's always been thet way. Well, we'll jest watch 'im a little more closely, thet's all."

Drew had finished his milk and sandwich. Marty offered him some crumb cake, but he politely turned it down.

"I've got to get home before my folks get to worrying about me," he said and reached for his cap. "Didn't realize how late it's getting."

Both Clark and Marty thanked him again. They invited him to return anytime in the future. Drew did not say whether he would accept their invitation. For just a moment his shadowed eyes met Belinda's and then he turned away. She wanted to say something. To thank him for his kindness, but she choked on all of her intended words.

And then he was gone, the door closing firmly behind him. Marty was speaking as she cleared away his dishes, "He seems like an awful nice young boy. I do hope he ain't harborin' any bitterness over his arm."

Belinda excused herself. She wanted the privacy of her own room.

Spring almost too quickly was overtaken by summer, and after school was over, Belinda busied herself with accompanying Luke on more house calls. Mandie's burned arm gave them a real scare. Luke even worried at one point that she, too, might lose it. But he fought—my, how he did fight—and the arm finally began to heal. It would always bear ugly scars, but she still had the use of it.

Belinda did not see Drew again, though she frequently wondered about the boy. Was he still harboring his grief? She did not know. They did see his mother—almost every day, in fact. She still came to sew. Over the days and weeks Marty had seen the woman's eyes go from despair, to acceptance, to hope, to renewed faith in life. True, the family was still in difficult circumstances, but they were on their way to independence. Well, they had always been independent enough, but now it looked like they might one day be able to take what they considered to be their proper place in the community.

The woman now wore a new dress, one she had made for herself. She even walked straighter with more confidence now that she was no longer wearing the many-times-mended garment. There were even moments of brief conversation between her and Marty as they took little breaks for tea and discussed weather, gardens, or neighborhood events.

Marty learned that Mrs. Simpson's two sons had never been to school—not for a single day of their lives. And yet both of the parents put great stock in education and had taught the boys everything they could, bringing home extra books to help them keep up with other youngsters their age. Mr. Simpson himself had been a college graduate, Marty discovered to her great surprise. And Mrs. Simpson had at one time tutored special English classes to immigrant families. Marty understood a bit more about the pride that kept them from "accepting charity."

But though Belinda saw Mrs. Simpson often, she did not ask about Drew. Not that she did not care. It was just that she feared to ask the question because the answer might not be the one she wanted to hear.

Jackson still hung about—"a hard one to avoid," Belinda told her mother ruefully. Even though school was out for the summer, Belinda saw him each Sunday at church, and he always lingered about, looking for some opportunity to serve her or suggesting some outing they might enjoy together. Belinda tried to be kind and firm, but Jackson did not seem too good at taking hints.

Melissa still sighed with longing for Jackson to take notice of her. There were other boys who would have gladly showered Melissa with their attention, but she ignored them completely.

How foolish we are, thought Marty as she watched silently from the sidelines. *Each wantin' exactly what one can't have.*

When fall came, Jackson packed his bags and went off to school in the city. He'd been counting on an intimate chat with Belinda to ask her if she would wait for him, but he could never get an opportunity. Belinda was always busy. He never saw a girl so taken with her work. So Jackson went off to college with a heart slightly heavier than his steamer trunk. A year was a long time to be away, and Belinda was growing up awfully fast. His only hope was that her nursing would keep her so busy she wouldn't notice the other boys who hovered around.

The school year began with Marty dreading the thought that this would be the last one at the local school for both Belinda and Melissa. But as she watched them go off together, she was pleased that they were chattering and enjoying each other's company. *It should be an easier year for all of them,* Marty thought with relief, *having Jackson a good two hundred miles away!* Marty sighed and shook her head. *Poor Jackson!* She did feel sorry for him. He was a fine young man.

Well, the girls were still young. There would be lots of time for beaus. She could just imagine Missie praying that Melissa would meet no fellow of special interest while she was back east going to school. Missie would not be any more anxious to lose her Melissa to the East than Marty had been to lose her Missie to the West.

Marty sighed again and turned from the window. She was afraid the year ahead was going to pass all too quickly.

TWENTY-THREE

Birthday Party

The team moved at a brisk trot, faster than usual, Marty felt, as she cast a quick glance Clark's way. But she did not question him. He urged the horses on, not holding them back as he normally did when they were homeward bound on a beautiful June day. Marty turned in an attempt to enjoy the wild roses that lined the roadside. Their fragrance reached out to her as the light wagon hurried on by. They truly were pretty, but Marty found that her thoughts were on other things.

Strange, mused Marty to herself without making any comment aloud. Still, the whole thing did seem unusual.

Marty was very aware that today was her birthday—and though Clark had given no signals to indicate that he remembered, she was sure he had not forgotten. Clark had never forgotten her birthday in all the years of their marriage. Yet, birthday or not, he had seemed awfully anxious to hustle her away from the house, and his excuse of "Ma Graham needin' some cheerin' up" now seemed a tad flimsy.

Marty had agreed to accompany Clark to the Grahams', expecting to find a lonely and somber Ma, but she had been her usual cheerful self, serving Marty tea and fresh strawberry shortcake and bringing her up-to-date about all the new achievements of her many grandchildren.

Clark had left Marty to visit and went on to town. Marty was very cooperative with the plan, whatever it was, but she found herself watching the clock and chafing a bit as the afternoon slowly moved along. Clark's return seemed to take longer than usual, and Marty was getting anxious to return home. When he finally did arrive, she said good-bye to Ma Graham and climbed into the wagon with an assist from Clark.

Her birthday always meant a family dinner. The offspring took turns year by year hosting the celebration. Marty did not try to keep track of where the birthday dinner had been or where it might be this time. The girls always knew, they informed Clark, and without discussion of where they were to celebrate, Clark always got Marty to the right home at the appointed time.

Most years Marty enjoyed the little game. She purposely tried not to think of whose turn it should be so that she could savor the "surprise," but as Clark clucked again to the team, Marty found her mind reviewing the last few years of birthday dinners.

It had been at Arnie and Anne's last year, and the year before, at Nandry and Josh's. Before that? Marty had to really concentrate. Oh yes. It was at Clare and Kate's. But, no, surely this year it was to be at Kate's or they would be late for dinner. And it sure looked as if they were headed for home.

It was a weekday, so the dinner would be the evening meal. They always had an early dinner together when the celebration occurred on a weekday, and even then it tended to be rushed. Marty cast an anxious eye at the sky. It was getting late. Before too long the cows would need milking. Marty stirred restlessly on the seat. She did hate being rushed. Time with family always seemed so short.

It must be at Clare and Kate's, she concluded. There just wouldn't be time to drive to one of the other homes. *I'm mistaken about three years back. That year must have been at Luke's and—but no,* she interrupted herself, *I can distinctly remember Kate's chicken and dumplings.* For some reason, she decided, Luke and Abbie were unable to have the family this year and so Kate was taking their turn.

Marty's thoughts turned from speculation to worry. *Was Abbie not feeling well? No one had told her—*

"Did ya have a good chat with Ma?" Clark's voice broke into her thoughts.

Marty blinked in surprise and shifted her attention back to her husband. His face was relaxed, his hands firmly holding the reins as he expertly guided the team down the country road.

Why was he asking about Ma in the middle of thoughts of birthday? And then Marty realized that just because her mind was totally absorbed with her birthday dinner, that was no reason Clark's thoughts should be taken with it, as well. Perhaps this time he *had* forgotten. *Perhaps . . .* Marty felt a little stab of disappointment. But *once* in all of the years of their marriage? Surely she could forgive him this once.

"Oh yes . . . yes," Marty stammered. "We had us a good chat. Ma's as perky as can be. Full of plans and tales of grandkids an' . . ." she hesitated. "Where'd ya get the idea that she was feelin' down?" she asked, turning on the seat so that she could look full at Clark's face.

"Feelin' down?" Clark echoed. "I don't recall ever sayin' Ma was down."

"But ya said . . . ya said she needed a bit of a visit . . . some cheerin' up, ya said."

Clark just smiled his teasing smile. "I know yer visits always cheer Ma up. Jest by yer bein' there I know."

But Marty was not in the mood to listen. Something seemed to be wrong here. A little hurt stirred within her. Had her whole family forgotten her birthday?

She strained forward as the team slowed to make the turn up the lane that led to their farm. Her eyes scanned the hitching rails expecting to see signs of Arnie, Luke, and Josh, but no teams stood placidly swatting at annoying flies. No wagons sat empty in the farmyard.

They have, sighed Marty. *Ever' last one of 'em. They've all forgotten.*

Marty felt an unaccustomed heaviness as Clark helped her down from the wagon. Was age catching up with her? She hadn't noticed it before. Oh, true, she was slowing down some. She was aware of it as she hoed her garden or hung out the wash, but she had done nothing all day long and yet she felt weary—nothing, that is, except to "cheer up" Ma Graham.

Marty turned to go up the walk to the front door. She was almost there before she realized that Clark, who usually went right on down to the barn with the horses, was at her side. Ignoring her questioning look, he opened the door for her, and she led the way onto the big back porch.

Her mind was already in the kitchen. The hour was late. What would she prepare for their supper? She hadn't planned on having to get the meal this night. It should have been her special birthday dinner. She wasn't to have—

"Surprise!" "Happy Birthday!" exploded all around her as she opened the door into the kitchen. She heard her own voice catch in a gasp and felt Clark's hand of support on her arm.

"Oh my!" said Marty, taking a step back from the noise and confusion. "Oh my!"

They were all there. Every one of them. The horses and wagons had been carefully hidden from sight. The trip to Ma's had been a ruse—one that Ma herself had helped plan and support. Clark had gone to town and whiled away the hours until the time he was told to have Marty back home.

But this time it was the girls' surprise. Belinda, Melissa, and Amy Jo. They had insisted to the family members that it was "our turn" to have Marty's birthday dinner. They had even gotten an excused absence from their schoolteacher in order to have the afternoon free to prepare the meal. They had cooked every dish from start to finish. Marty could only exclaim over and over as she hugged the three and tried to swallow the tears crowding against the back of her throat.

A small bouquet of fresh spring wild flowers graced the table, which was carefully set with Marty's good china. Everything was in readiness, and Clark quickly urged the family to take their places at the table "before the food gets cold," the girls insisted.

After Clark's prayer, the mothers fixed plates for the younger ones and the older children waited on themselves. With a flurry of noise and commotion they headed for their favorite spot on the back veranda. When things quieted, the adults began their meal, Belinda, Melissa, and Amy Jo hovering nearby to pour the coffee and wait on the table.

The gravy was just a bit lumpy, the biscuits a bit too brown, and the fried chicken a teeny bit dry, but to Marty, the meal was delicious and she kept telling the girls so, over and over.

"Did we surprise you? Did you guess?" Amy Jo kept asking.

"I had no idea," Marty assured her. She didn't add that she'd been a mite worried that her family had forgotten her. "Ya did it all? Yerselves?"

The girls laughed merrily, pleased that their plan had worked so well, and pleased, too, that Marty seemed so surprised at their achievement.

"We all shared in the cooking," Melissa explained. "Even Amy Jo. She did the potatoes and the cole slaw."

"An' Melissa did the chicken an' the biscuits, an' Belinda the vegetables," Amy Jo quickly put in, wanting to give proper credit where credit was due. "And Belinda made the cake, too," she added as an afterthought.

"It's yer favorite. Spice," Belinda told her.

After the meal was over, the children were called in from the porch and the whole family joined together in the singing of "Happy Birthday," the little ones anxious for the fun of handing out the gifts. Marty exclaimed over and over as the lovingly chosen and handmade gifts were presented to her.

The three girls saved their gifts until the other members of the family had all presented theirs.

"I wanted you to have this, Grandma," said Melissa, passing to Marty a carefully wrapped gift in light-blue paper.

Marty unwrapped it to find a beautifully bound edition of *The Pilgrim's Progress*. Marty knew it was selected from Melissa's private library, making it all the more meaningful to her.

Amy Jo came next. Her gift was not as carefully wrapped, but the colorful paper was festive. Marty began to unwrap the present, noticing that her hands trembled from excitement.

She lifted away the paper and found herself looking straight into the eyes of Melissa—from Amy Jo's first attempt at a portrait. There really was a likeness, and though Amy Jo's art would need years of polishing and perfecting, Marty was amazed that the girl had done so well. "Oh my, Amy Jo! You did good—real good on this picture," Marty exclaimed, and other family members began to crowd around to see Amy Jo's art. There were many congratulations and enthusiastic comments, and Amy Jo beamed her pleasure.

When the excitement died down, Belinda pressed forward. She handed Marty a small package. "Remember the lace collar ya saw and liked?" she murmured. "Well, I couldn't afford to buy it, but I found a pattern almost like it, an' I crocheted ya one myself. It's not as nice but—"

Marty slipped the lace collar out of the paper. Belinda had done a beautiful job. Marty traced the delicate floral pattern with a tip of her finger.

"Why, it's even prettier," she said softly, her eyes thanking Belinda even more than her voice did. "Thank ya, Belinda. Thank ya, everyone. I do believe this is the nicest birthday I ever had."

Clare began to laugh. "Ma," he said, "seems to me ya say thet every year."

"An' every year I mean it, too," insisted Marty.

Then all eyes turned to Clark. The family knew well the tradition of Clark presenting the final birthday gift.

"My turn, is it?" said Clark, rising to his feet.

Clark's hands were empty.

"Well, this year," he said slowly, "I have nothin' to give." He hesitated. All eyes were on his face. No one spoke. Clark cleared his throat. None of his children believed for a minute that he had nothing to present to Marty.

"Leastways," he continued, "nothing here at hand. My gift is outside. In the garden. Anyone who wants to see it has to follow me out there."

No one remained behind. Clark led the way, taking Marty by the hand and leading her to the end of the garden. All the other family members trailed along behind, several of them making guesses as to what the gift might be. Marty heard the laughing and the teasing voices all around her, but her mind was busy trying to guess, too, what Clark had gotten for her.

"There it is," Clark said, halting before a small, waist-high tree. It was not magnificent in appearance, but Marty knew it must be "special." She reached out a hand and turned the tag that hung from a small branch, fluttering in the soft evening breezes.

"'Jonathan Apple,'" she read aloud and then, with a little cry she threw her arms around Clark's neck. "Oh, Clark, where did ya find it? Where did ya get it from? I been a wantin' one but no one round here—"

"I sent away fer it," said Clark as he held her. "Sneaked it in here an' planted it yesterday. Was scared half to death thet you'd catch me at it."

Marty looked around at her family. She reached out to try to pull all three of the young girls into her arms at one time. Each one of her gifts was so personal, so special. Her family knew her well. Her family showered her with love. She felt blessed beyond expression. Her eyes brimmed over with tears.

"Go ahead," she challenged them with a smile, "laugh iffen ya want to, but this truly—*truly* has been my best birthday ever!"

TWENTY-FOUR

A Caller

All through the spring and summer Drew struggled with his bitterness. Why had he lost his arm? If there was a God who cared about him, why had it been allowed to happen? Why hadn't the doctor just let him die? He would rather be dead. At least he *thought* he'd rather be dead. Yet, at times, even Drew breathed deeply of the fresh spring air or exulted over the brightness of the summer sky, or tilted his head to catch the song of a bird.

Almost daily he thought of Belinda. And always his thoughts were troubled. He did not know how to sort out his feelings toward the young girl. Why was she so interested in nursing? How could she stand to see her brother cut people up? Didn't she have any kind of feeling? At the same time that he questioned her interest in nursing, he admired her in a strange sort of way. He was quite sure he wouldn't have been able to face some of the situations that Belinda did.

How does she do it? WHY does she do it? The whole thing puzzled him. He couldn't understand her. He couldn't understand this whole strange family. And Drew certainly could not understand his inner conflict.

In some way, Drew took pleasure in his self-pity. And yet there was something else that kept fighting to be free of the bitterness. He seemed to be at war with himself. He wondered why he didn't just give in to his bitter feelings.

But just as he felt ready to give up his anger, his stump of an arm would catch his attention and a new wave of pain would sear, seemingly from fingertip to shoulder. Sobs of pain and anguish would cause Drew to bury his head in his pillow or flee the house in renewed bitterness.

And so Drew struggled with himself. One minute he was content to wrap himself securely in his shell of bitterness and pain, and the next minute almost responding to the urge to try to find some other way to live with what "fate" had handed him.

Another thing puzzled Drew. He felt there was something different about his mother, subtle changes he couldn't put into words. Was it just his imagination or was it really there?

For the past several years, Drew's mother had been shut away in silence and self-pity. She had not wanted to go west, had resisted with all her being. Oh, not in so many words. That was not her way. But they all knew how she felt. It showed in the tightness of her lips, in the stiffness of her stance, in the darkening of her eyes. Though she had never been one to laugh and chat easily, she became a woman living in a shell. It was as if the real person did not even share the dampness of the crowded soddy with the rest of the family. She became cold and withdrawn, even from her children.

There had been one thing that had seemed to bring life and fire to Drew's mother, and that was lesson time. How her dark eyes flashed if the boys were reluctant to study. Her chin thrust forward stubbornly when she declared that she did not intend to rear unlearned children—west or no west. Their father, too, made sure time was found each day for books and learning.

At the beginning of the new school term, Drew had watched his younger brother Sidney being ushered off to school. Now that Sid was dressed in proper garments, their mother had insisted he should be in a real classroom where he belonged. Drew watched her holding her breath that first morning. *How would he fare among the other students?* Drew knew this was her worry. Would the youngster have years of catching up to do? But the first report of Mrs. Brown was filled with incredulous praise. The boy was unbelievably ahead of his age group, she stated, and she commended the Simpsons heartily for their excellent job in supervising the boy's education.

Drew knew his mother had been tempted to send him, too, off to the local school. She undoubtedly would have insisted, had it not been for his age and his missing arm. She did not say so, but Drew knew that her mother-heart, though shriveled and broken by her hard life, ached for him. She knew it would be difficult for him to face the world.

Drew's father did not seem to feel comfortable in Drew's presence. He did not discuss the accident or Drew's handicap. In fact, he seldom talked to Drew at all. But he did make it quite clear that he did not wish to have Drew back in the woods felling trees.

Even Sidney let his eyes skim quickly over the empty sleeve and then directed his gaze elsewhere. Drew began to feel he would go through all of life with people conveniently overlooking him.

So Drew was left to his gun and his wandering. He probably would not have been able to make it through those first difficult months had he not known that the family needed meat, and that he, even though missing a limb, was still able to supply it.

But in recent weeks Drew had been sensing a newness of life and hope in his mother. Oh, true, she still had very little to say, and she still never laughed, but her eyes looked different somehow. She seemed . . . she seemed warmer, less chilled and cut off from the rest of the family. Could it be that something was changing on the inside? *And if so, why?* Drew wondered. Was it simply because she was winning the struggle for survival? Oh, they were still in need—that was for sure—but they were not in debt to any man. They had lost nearly everything they'd owned, so there was really nothing more for anyone else to claim. But they were dressing better now—were eating more than rabbit stew. His mother even had her own garden, and come fall she would not be beholden to the neighbors.

But was that the whole reason for the hope in her eyes? Or did it have something to do with that Davis family? She shared the house with

Mrs. Davis three times and even up to five times a week. Was some of that other woman's optimistic spirit rubbing off on her?

Drew watched his mother closely, hoping with all his heart that the change might continue and that she would begin talking to him, chatting as mother to son, perhaps even allowing him a chance to talk about his missing arm. He studied his mother carefully each day when she returned from the Davis farm.

Drew did not understand the Davis family. But he could sense that they were different in some way. He had never seen a woman who seemed to be as sensitive—as caring—as Mrs. Davis. Drew longed to see that look of love and caring in the eyes of his own mother. *If only . . . if only . . .* his heart kept crying. *If only we could talk. If only Mother felt free to speak what she feels. If only she would ask me how I felt.*

And what about the Davis father? The guy with just one leg? How had it happened and how come he could accept it . . . even *joke* about it? Why did he seem to have such a warm and generous spirit? His little schemes of the year before had not been missed by Drew. He knew Clark had "invented" ways to help the family through their first winter. He had seen the Davis' woodpile. He had seen the farm. Drew knew Clark wasn't the type of man to need outside help to keep things in order. *What makes the fellow tick, anyway?* he asked himself.

The whole thing was beyond Drew. He couldn't figure out any of it. He stayed as far away from the Davises as he could get.

One fall day when the wind was rattling the red and gold leaves and the geese were crying overhead, Drew found himself walking toward the Davis farm. The gun was tucked in the crook of his missing arm. He always carried it that way. It made him feel that his arm—such as it was—was still good for something. But today the gun was forgotten. He would not have thought to shoot even if a rabbit or a grouse had crossed his path. Drew, deep in thought, decided he had to find some answers. With sudden resolve he quickened his step toward the only person who might be able to help.

Drew was relieved to find Clark clearing fallen leaves out of the spring. Drew did not wish to go near the house. He did not want to risk a chance meeting with Belinda.

"Drew!" Clark greeted him warmly. "Out huntin' again I see. No luck?"

Drew laid the gun aside, his cheeks flushing a bit. He hadn't really been looking for game.

"Not yet" was all he answered.

"I'll jest be a minute here," Clark told him, "and then we'll go on up to the house an' see what Marty might have to munch on."

Drew leaned over the gurgling water and swept more leaves out into the current with his right hand.

"Were ya left- or right-handed?" Clark surprised him by asking.

"Right," answered Drew.

"Thet's one thing about losin' a leg," Clark stated matter-of-factly, "don't make much difference." When Clark chuckled, Drew smiled to join him.

"How's yer pa doin' with his loggin'?" Clark asked further.

"Good," said Drew. "He found himself a mule somewhere. He's real pleased with himself."

"Thet'll help him a lot," said Clark. "Don't know how he managed last winter without one."

"Oh, he and Ma just hooked on ropes and hauled them out. I'm after Pa to let me get back to helpin' him," Drew went on.

Clark looked directly at the boy. He commented, "He don't want ya in the woods?"

Drew shook his head. "Won't let me go near—ever since the accident. Thinks it's his fault, I guess. That's just silly. Wasn't anybody's fault—just one of those things."

Clark was silent for a few moments while he scooped out soggy leaves and tossed them aside. "Guess I can understand his feelin's," he said.

Drew nodded. He guessed he could understand his pa's feelings, too, but it did seem foolish when his pa needed all the help he could get.

"Well," said Clark, straightening up, "guess thet'll be good enough fer now. I'll need to clean it once or twice yet 'fore winter freezes it in."

A flock of Canada geese passed overhead, calling out their forlorn cries. Clark and Drew both looked skyward.

"Always did think thet the cry of a goose is one of the saddest sounds I know," Clark observed. "Does it hit ya thet way?"

Drew nodded solemnly. It did. He wasn't sure why.

"I don't know what there is about it," Clark went on, "but it 'most makes me shiver." And his shiver was obvious to Drew.

"Let's go git somethin' to warm us up," he suggested. "Marty'll have somethin' hot fer sure."

Drew sucked in his breath. If he went now he might never find the courage to talk to Mr. Davis again.

"I was kinda wonderin' if I might talk to you some?"

Clark's face softened. He lowered himself to a soft bed of leaves and nodded to the boy to go on.

"I . . . I hate to take your time like this but . . . but . . ."

"I've got me more time than anythin' else," Clark assured him.

"Well, I . . . I . . . noticed . . . truth is, I've been wondering. You see, I figured if anyone should know what someone goes through in losing a limb, then it should be you."

Clark broke a small twig and cast it into the spring water. The current swirled it around a few times and then carried it off downstream.

"I only lost a leg, boy," Clark said softly. "Ya lost an arm. Now I ain't even pretendin' thet there ain't a big difference there."

The boy swallowed hard. Clark was making light of his own loss.

He looked at Clark evenly. "I happen to know myself well enough to know that I wouldn't take kindly to losing a leg, either," Drew said.

Clark nodded.

"How long ago?" Drew asked.

"Long time now," said Clark, leaning back against a tree trunk. "Long, long time. Before Belinda was even born."

"How'd it happen?"

A shadow passed briefly over Clark's face, telling Drew even more than his words did.

"Couple a kids were messin' around in an old mine shaft," Clark began. "It caved in on 'em. I went in to get 'em out. They were 'most buried in it. Afore I got the second one out, it caved in again. The heavy timbers got me."

"How'd you get out?" asked Drew.

"Men—friends from our son's ranch—dug fer me."

"Did you . . . did you give yer permission to the doc? To take yer leg, I mean?"

"Nope!" said Clark. "Didn't know a thing 'bout it. Actually, I didn't lose my leg right away. An' there weren't a doc within miles, far as anyone knew. It was Marty thet tried to clean it up an' disinfect it. It was crushed, too. An awful mess, they tell me. Then gangrene set in. I shoulda died, I guess, but God had other plans. Sent along a doctor— right from among the neighbors—and he took care of the leg while I was wild with fever."

Drew felt himself go weak as Clark told the story simply, without drama. He could picture too well the scenes that Clark briefly described.

They sat silently for many minutes.

"What did you think when you . . . when . . ."

"When I came to my senses and knew what'd happened?" Clark finished for him.

The boy swallowed hard and nodded. He could not speak.

"Well, at first . . . at first I thought my whole world had fallen apart. I wondered how I would ever be a man again . . . how I'd care fer my family . . . what I'd think about myself. Fer a while . . . fer a little while . . . I wished I had died . . . at least thet's what I *thought* I wished. But not fer long. God soon reminded me thet I had a lot to live fer. That my family loved me and would keep right on lovin' me—one leg or two—an' thet God hadn't forgotten me. Thet He was still with me, still in charge of my life. It took a while, but God helped me to accept it. Don't miss it too much anymore at all."

"It still hurts you, though, doesn't it?"

Clark's head came up. "What makes ya say thet?" he asked, looking carefully at Drew.

"I've seen you. I've seen you reach down and rub it. I know . . . I know how bad it can ache. Even though it's gone, it can still—"

"Phantom pain," Clark finished for him.

The boy nodded.

"Yers bother ya much?"

"Sometimes. Sometimes it's not bad."

Clark nodded knowingly.

"How long you had thet . . . thet . . . ?" the boy began.

"Wooden one? 'Bout five years now, I guess. Works real good, too. Don't know how I ever got along without it. Luke, my doctor son, talked me into it."

"They don't have . . . they don't have . . . things for arms, do they?"

"'Course they do. Not jest like this. Sorta has hooks an' things, but Luke could tell ya all 'bout 'em."

Clark stopped while Drew suddenly put his head down on his one good arm, sobbing convulsively. He felt Clark quickly put an arm around him and draw him close.

"Cry," Clark said, his voice sounding a little shaky, "go ahead an' have a good cry. I did. Let me tell ya, I did. Scream, iffen ya want to. Git it all out. Ya got somethin' worth cryin' over. Go ahead, boy."

Drew shook with his sobbing. "I hate it!" he screamed out. "I hate it! I don't have an arm. I don't have a God. I don't have *nothin'*."

Clark still held on to him, then passed him a large checkered handkerchief and let him blow. With an arm still around him, Clark spoke quietly. "Son," he said. "I can't do nothin' 'bout gittin' ya an arm but . . . but I do know where ya can find yerself a God."

Drew looked up, no longer ashamed of his tears.

"Ya don't even need to go a lookin' fer 'im," Clark said, "fer, truth is, He's been lookin' fer you. He loves ya, son. He loves ya. An' He wants to come into yer life, ease yer hurt and give ya a real reason fer livin'."

Drew felt himself shaking his head. "I . . . I . . . I've done lots of wrong things. I don't think thet God would want—"

"That's the beauty of it," Clark continued. "He doesn't need to wait until we're without wrong. He'd wait forever iffen He did. We've all done wrong. The Bible tells us thet—an' there's no way we can change from our sinfulness on our own. And there's a serious penalty for sin— death." He paused and looked into Drew's wet face.

"But the Bible also tells us thet while we were yet wrongdoers, Jesus

420

Christ loved us enough to die fer us," his voice continued, strong and confident. "Now, thet means thet the death penalty fer those wrongs—those sins of ours—Christ paid. So we come to Him and jest thank 'im for what He's done and accept the new life He offers. Thet's all there is to our part. An' then He does His part. He forgives us our wrong-doin' . . . an' He gives us the peace an' fergiveness we been lookin' fer. It's as simple as thet."

Drew couldn't believe what he was hearing. It sounded way too good to be true.

"How . . . how do you do it?" he asked.

"Jest pray . . . jest talk to yer heavenly Father 'bout it. Ya ever prayed, boy?"

"Only once," the boy admitted. "At least I guess I prayed. It was when Belinda got hurt. I was so scared, I—"

"An' God answered yer prayers, didn't He?"

"Did He? I never thought about it. I . . ." Drew paused to think about it a moment. "Will you show me how?" he asked.

Clark's arm tightened around his shoulders. "I'd be most glad to," he assured him.

TWENTY-FIVE

Sorting It Out

There was much joy in the Davis household later that evening when Clark told his good news to the family. Clark led the family group in special prayer for young Drew, and Marty allowed her tears to fall freely while the others' eyes were closed.

Though Belinda's face took on a special shine over the announcement, she said very little. And then when she was finally free to slip away unnoticed, she went to her room and fell down beside her bed.

She wept there. She wasn't sure just why. There were so many emotions swirling around within her. She was thankful that God had answered her prayers. She hoped that Drew would now be at peace with himself. She prayed that his bitterness would be gone. She knew that there would still be many bad days in store for him, but with God's help and the prayers and support of friends, he could make it; she knew he could.

Would he be able to forgive her also? She prayed he would understand that she and Luke had only done what needed to be done. That they sorrowed with him over his loss nearly every day.

It was a long time until Belinda felt relieved enough of her burden to be able to prepare for bed. Even as she crawled between the soft flannel sheets, she wondered if she would see Drew again. Yes, she would, she reminded herself. Her pa had said that Drew had promised to come with them to church on Sunday. For some strange reason Belinda's heart gave a little skip. What would it be like? What would they say to each other? Would he smile? Belinda went to sleep with a strange feeling of anticipation. She hoped the days until Sunday would pass quickly.

The next day, a Thursday, Luke stopped by at school to ask if Belinda would be interested in helping with a birthing. Lou Graham's wife was expecting again, and she had told Luke she would not object to Belinda being present.

Belinda squealed with enthusiasm and rushed home to change her clothes. She would meet Luke at the Grahams'.

"Don't dawdle," he warned her. "You never know how much time you might have—or might not have—when waiting on a baby."

Belinda laughed and promised she would hurry.

Belinda barely made it to the Grahams' in time. The delivery was the most exciting event she had ever witnessed. Over and over again she thought of the story her mother told of how her sister Ellie had been the only one to assist at Belinda's delivery. She wondered if Ellie had been as excited as she was now.

Once it was well on the way, the birthing was all over so quickly. Belinda was given the privilege, under Luke's watchful eyes, of taking care of the new little girl. After bathing her and wrapping her in her warm flannels, Belinda placed her gently on Mary's arm. The woman beamed down at her new offspring.

"Meet Amanda Jane," Mary said. "Amanda, this is Belinda, yer nurse. Didn't she do a fine job, now?"

Ma Graham moved forward to claim her new granddaughter, and then before Belinda could turn around, all the family members were pouring into the room, squealing and shoving and coaxing to hold the new sister.

Belinda was in an especially lighthearted mood as she mounted Copper and set out for home. She could hardly wait to share the experience with her family. *Why, even squeamish Melissa will enjoy this story,* she thought.

Belinda, her thoughts on other things, was brought swiftly back to the present when Copper flicked his ears forward and looked off to the side. Belinda tightened her grip on the reins. Perhaps a small animal was in the bush. But it was Drew who stepped from the undergrowth, his rifle tucked firmly under his arm and whistling softly to himself.

Drew seemed as surprised to see Belinda as she was to see him. They just looked at each other, neither one speaking. There was so much that could have been said, but no words came. It was Drew who finally broke the silence.

"Don't worry," he said, "I won't shoot."

Belinda began to laugh softly. "Good enough," she replied.

Drew laid down the rifle, lest even the sight of it should make Copper bolt, then moved toward Belinda.

"I was hoping to see you before Sunday," he said simply.

Belinda's eyes met his. They were still deep and dark, but there was no shadow in them. She waited for Drew to speak again.

"Have you been helping your brother again?" Drew asked.

Belinda nodded and smiled.

"Where this time?"

"The Grahams'. Lou Grahams'. They jest had 'em a new baby girl. It was my first time fer a delivery."

He smiled easily up at her. "Guess that beats taking off arms, huh?"

Belinda's eyes dropped.

"Are you in a hurry?" he asked quickly. He probably wished he hadn't joked about his accident.

"Not . . . not really."

"Would you mind if we talked a bit?"

Belinda shook her head.

Drew looked up at her and laughed. "Would you mind coming down off your horse before I get a crick in my neck?"

It was Belinda's turn to laugh. She passed him the reins to dismount. Drew could not hold the horse and assist Belinda, as well. But she did fine on her own.

"I'll tie him," he said.

"Tie 'im tight," called Belinda. "He loves to break free an' go on home."

"Seems this horse of yours has lots of bad habits," said Drew, and Belinda laughed again.

Belinda stood still until Drew joined her.

"Would you like to sit?" Drew asked, and he led Belinda to the side of the road to a fallen tree resting against another one and just the right height for sitting. Before Belinda could protest, he removed his coat and spread it on the log for her, and she scooted up onto it.

Belinda wasn't sure what this conversation was going to be about, so she let Drew do the leading.

"I suppose your pa told you about the other day," Drew began.

Belinda nodded. The boy would think she was tongue-tied if she didn't soon come up with something more than gestures.

"I don't know how it works . . . but it does. I really . . . feel different. Somehow, I . . . just . . . I just know there really is a God . . . and that He really does change you when you ask Him to."

"I know," smiled Belinda. "He changed me, too."

"You know . . . I didn't know much about God," Drew went on. "I'd heard people talk about Him. Mostly cussing. But . . . when you got thrown that day and I was scared to death, something deep inside me told me there really is a God who I could pray to. I prayed. I didn't even know how . . . or what to say or anything, but I prayed for you."

Belinda's eyes were about to fill with tears. "I've been prayin' fer you, too," she admitted.

Drew swung around to face her. "You have?" he asked incredulously.

She nodded her head again. "Ever since . . . ever since that day . . . I even prayed for ya when ya were still layin' there. Right after we had . . . had taken yer arm. Luke took out the . . . crushed pieces . . . an' I watched ya an' . . . an' prayed."

"What did you ask?" asked Drew.

"That you'd get better. Thet you'd . . . you'd git over it. Wouldn't be bitter."

Drew became very quiet. He was staring at the clenched fist on his one remaining hand. It slowly relaxed. He finally said, "Bet you thought God hadn't heard your prayer, huh?"

"Sometimes it takes a while," answered Belinda simply. "We need to learn patience when prayin'. Pa is always sayin' thet."

"I like your pa," said Drew.

"Me too," said Belinda with warmth and another smile.

"Well, it might have taken a while longer than it should have. If . . . if I just hadn't been so bullheaded, but I want you to know that God did answer your prayer. All of it."

"I'm so glad," Belinda said, and her eyes misted again.

They sat silently, each wrapped in thought.

"You really like your nursing times, don't you?"

Belinda nodded.

"Why?" asked Drew. "I mean you're so young . . . and . . . and . . ."

"I . . . I've always hated to see things suffer," Belinda said in answer to his question. "Even when I was little. I would find birds or little animals an' . . . I'd try to make 'em well again. Sometimes I would even take 'em to Luke. He'd help me. We'd do all we could to make 'em better again. Luke, he . . . he hates to see sufferin' too. An' he will do anything—anything—to help people."

"Funny," said Drew. "I thought much differently about the two of you for a long while."

"I know," acknowledged Belinda. "I'm sorry." Her voice was no more than a whisper.

"I'm the one who's sorry. I . . . I was stupid, that's all. Full of self-pity and . . . and anger. I should have been thanking you for what you did, and instead I was acting like a . . . a baby."

"Oh no," protested Belinda. "I knew how you felt. I mean—well, Pa, he's been through that, too, an' we knew—"

Drew laid his hand on her arm, his hand warm against her skin. She felt protected somehow, but she didn't understand the feeling. They sat in silence for several minutes, and when Drew spoke again, the subject had changed.

"This your last year of school?" he asked her.

She nodded.

"Then what?" he asked again.

"Luke's gonna let me work in the office in town. He'll train me and I'll help him there an' with his house calls. After thet . . . I don't know."

Drew was silent.

"What 'bout you?" asked Belinda.

"Well, I've wanted to get some training, too," he told her. "It would be tough, I know that . . . but I've wanted to be a lawyer."

Belinda's eyes widened.

"A lawyer?"

"Guess I want to help people, too. Only in a little different way."

"Like?" asked Belinda.

"My pa wouldn't have lost everything he owned if he'd had a lawyer. The other fellow had no legal claim on it, but he had more money and more power than my pa. He ate up one little rancher after another."

Belinda nodded her understanding.

"Why . . . why do ya say you '*wanted* to be'?" she asked him.

He looked down at the dangling sleeve, Belinda's eyes following his.

"It would've been tough enough when I . . . when I had . . . both arms, but now . . . well . . . I'd . . . I'd never be able to . . ."

Belinda let her eyes rest on his arm for only a moment. Then she looked back into his face. "Thet makes no difference," she boldly stated. "Ya don't need two hands to think—an' lawyers mostly think—an' talk. Ya can still do thet."

He looked doubtful.

"'Course ya can," continued Belinda. "Ya got a good head—jest like yer brother. So—you haven't been to school? In the classroom? But ya been taught. Taught real good, too. Yer ma and pa have helped both of you learn what ya need to know. Teacher's always talkin' 'bout how much Sidney knows. An' I'll bet thet ya know even more, and you can keep right on learnin', too. Ya can still study. No reason ya can't still be a lawyer iffen ya want to."

"You . . . you really think I could?" he stammered.

"'Course!"

His hand tightened on her arm, and Belinda could tell he was feeling very moved—whether about her words or something else, she didn't know.

They sat silently, Belinda swinging one free leg back and forth gently.

She was deep in thought, wondering just how she could help Drew realize his dream.

He interrupted her thoughts. "Do you have a beau?"

Belinda blinked.

"Do you?" he pressed further.

She shook her head dumbly.

"I . . . I'd . . ." he began.

But Belinda cut in quickly with, "I don't think I should have one now. I mean—it'll take a long time to learn about nursin'. It wouldn't be fair to . . . to ask a boy to wait."

Drew sucked in his breath. "Yeah," he said at last. "Yeah, it will take me a long time to become a lawyer, too."

Belinda nodded, and a little thrill went through her at his words. *He is believing in himself again,* she exulted silently.

"So I guess we both have to wait, huh?" said Drew.

"I guess," replied Belinda. But her smile held more hope than her words.

Silence again. This time it was Belinda who broke it. She stood up, looking over toward Copper.

"I'm glad we had this talk," she said honestly, smiling shyly. "I was worried some about Sunday. I . . . mean . . ."

"I know what you mean," answered Drew. "I was worried some, too."

"I better git home," continued Belinda. "They'll be lookin' fer me."

"I'll get your horse," said Drew.

Drew led Copper to the road and Belinda followed. He handed her the reins as she went to mount. Belinda guessed he wanted to have his hand free so he could help her.

She paused before putting her foot in the stirrup, and Drew stepped close to her.

"Thanks, Belinda," he whispered, and she turned to look at him.

She hadn't realized he was standing so close. She hadn't realized just how compelling his dark eyes were. They held hers as he stepped even closer. His hand went out to rest on her waist, and he drew her slightly nearer. Then he bent his head and kissed her firmly, yet gently.

It took Belinda's breath away. She had never dreamed it would be like that. So sweet, so tender. Her first kiss.

LOVE TAKES
WING

To Aunt Laurine—
with love and thanks
for who you are
and what you mean to me.
God bless!

Characters in the
LOVE COMES SOFTLY series

Clark and Marty Davis, partners in a marriage in which each had lost a previous spouse.

Nandry and Clae, foster daughters raised by Clark and Marty. Nandry married Josh Coffins, and their children are Tina, Andrew, Mary, and Jane. Clae married Joe Berwick. Their children are Esther Sue, Joey, and Paul.

Missie, Clark's daughter from his first marriage, married Willie La-Haye and moved west to ranch. Their children—Nathan, Josiah, Melissa (who came east to live with Clark and Marty while she finished high school, then went on to train as a schoolteacher), and Julia.

Clare, Marty's son born after her first husband's death, married Kate. They live in the same farmyard as Clark and Marty. Their children—Amy Jo, Dan, David, and Dack.

Arnie, Clark and Marty's first child. He married Anne, and they have three sons—Silas, John, and Abe.

Daughter Ellie, married Lane Howard and moved west to join Missie and Willie. Their children are Brenda, William, and Willis.

Son Luke, trained to be a doctor and returned to the small town to practice medicine. He married Abbie. Their children are Thomas and Aaron—and now new baby daughter, Ruth.

Daughter Belinda, Clark and Marty's youngest child. She was trained as a nurse.

Jackson Brown, the school friend who greatly impressed Melissa, Amy Jo, and Belinda when he first arrived at the country school. Melissa was the one who really carried a torch for him, though Jackson preferred Belinda.

ONE

The End of a Long Day

Belinda pushed wisps of gold-brown hair back from her flushed face and took a deep breath. It was "one of those days"—again! The whole week seemed to have been filled with emergencies. One right after the other.

Why are people so careless? Belinda asked herself a mite crossly.

She tossed her soiled white apron aside and began to clean up the bloodstained operating table.

The last case of the day was a boy who had caught his hand in a piece of farm machinery. Luke had worked hard and long to try to save all his fingers, but neither he nor Belinda were too hopeful about the outcome. She felt tired, overworked, and anxious about the state of young Jamie's fingers.

I should be getting used to such things by now, she admonished herself. After all, hadn't she been assisting Luke in surgery for over a year? But there didn't seem to be any way she could get used to the pain she felt when she looked at the suffering reflected in a patient's eyes—especially when it was in the eyes of a child.

She sighed again deeply and breathed another prayer for young Jamie.

"I'll do that," said a voice from behind her.

She hadn't even heard Luke enter the room. She turned, intending to argue that cleaning up was part of her job, but he continued, "I know you're in a hurry. It's only an hour until the train will be in."

Belinda's thoughts now focused on the event that had been filling her with excitement this whole week. She had been counting the days—the hours. How could it have slipped her mind? It must have been the injured boy who had taken her complete attention while they worked to save his hand. But now with Luke's reminder, Belinda's excitement flooded through her again. *Melissa is coming home!* She now was finished with her teacher's training in the East and would be spending a few weeks at the farm before continuing on to her home and family in the West.

Belinda glanced down at her soiled dress. She sure didn't want to leave Luke with the cleaning, but she did need a bath to freshen up, and she just had to do something with her wayward hair. Missing out on welcoming Melissa on the afternoon train was almost unthinkable. It had been a long time—a long, *long* time since she had seen . . . well, had seen her niece, who was only a bit older than she and had become a dear friend during the two years she had lived with the Davis'. Belinda was glad she didn't have to explain their complicated family very often.

She gave Luke a warm, appreciative smile and turned reluctantly from the untidy surgery.

"Sorry," she apologized.

But he assured her, "No reason for you to be sorry. It isn't your carelessness that has been filling our office with accident cases."

Belinda reached up and pulled the pins from her hair, letting it tumble down about her shoulders. She eased slender fingers through the curls to gently shake out the tangles.

"Have ya ever seen a week like this one?" she asked her brother soberly.

"It's been a bad one, all right," Luke admitted. Then he sighed deeply and said, "I sure hope it's about to come to an end."

Belinda agreed.

"Now you'd best hurry," urged Luke. "You don't want to be late for that train."

Belinda scurried from the room. She did want to be there when the train pulled into the local station. Her whole family would be waiting for Melissa. Would she have changed much? Would the two of them still be able to share secrets and understand—sometimes even without words—how the other was feeling? Was Melissa still pining over Jackson Brown, or had she found another young man? What was teacher's training like? Did she like the city? Belinda had so many questions.

Yes, they had written frequently, but it just wasn't the same. There were some things that were not easy to put down on paper. Belinda did hope there wouldn't be any awkwardness between them. She was filled with anticipation and just a bit of apprehension.

She set the portable tub on the mat in her small upstairs room at Luke and Abbie's house and carried pails of warm water to fill it. As she settled into her bath, her thoughts went back to the first time the family had gathered to wait for the arrival of Melissa. That time she had been coming from her home in the West. None of them had known what to expect as they waited for the stagecoach to arrive. Belinda could still remember the butterflies and the questions. What would she be like? Would they like each other? Would they be able to get along? Maybe it would be like having a sister her own age.

And so it had turned out—Melissa had been like a sister, even though she was in fact a niece. Belinda had grown to love her dearly and had missed her greatly when she went away to normal school. And now the days had ticked by and Melissa was coming home again—this time by train from the East. And the train was coming to their very own town.

This was a new and welcome luxury to the people of their community. They were getting used to hearing the whistle and the *clickity-clack* of the metal wheels on the iron tracks, but Belinda still had not quite gotten over the thrill of it all. Often she dreamed of boarding the passenger car and being taken to some faraway place that she had only seen in picture books. But so far it only remained a dream.

She did not allow herself the pleasure of a long soak in the tub. There just was not time. The train, though sometimes late, was far more dependable in its travel than the stagecoach had been, and Belinda knew if she did not hurry she would miss the excitement of Melissa's arrival.

She rushed around as she dressed and hurriedly pinned up her hair. With each glance toward the dresser clock, her heart beat faster. She was going to be late in spite of her scurrying about. She still had the tub to empty and—

She called an answer to a gentle knock, and Abbie opened the door only wide enough to poke her head into the room.

"My, don't you look nice," she said with a smile, then quickly added, "Luke said to tell you to leave the tub. We'll take care of it when we get back."

Belinda glanced sideways at the tub. She did hate to leave things undone, but Luke was right—there just wasn't time before going to the station. She nodded to Abbie in resignation.

"Everyone ready?" she asked, and Abbie indicated they were as she pulled on a glove.

Belinda grabbed her own gloves and a small handbag. She took one last look in the mirror to be sure that her hat was on straight, smoothed the hipline of her skirt, and hurried downstairs after Abbie.

Thomas and Aaron had already left the house and were waiting at the end of the walk. Aaron, the younger of the two, was giving Thomas a ride on the front gate, even though both boys had been told not to swing on it. As soon as their mother appeared, Thomas dropped quickly to the walk and turned his attention to the ants that were scurrying back and forth across the boards, as though he had been studying them the whole time.

"Thomas," Abbie said sternly, not to be fooled, "what have we told you about swinging on the gate?"

Thomas just lowered his head and did not answer.

"There's a nice swing in the backyard," Abbie continued. "I've told you before that the gate will sag if you swing on it."

Still Thomas did not respond.

Abbie hurried down the walk, and when she reached the small boy, she laid a hand on his shoulder. "No dessert for dinner," she said quietly but firmly.

Belinda saw his eyes quickly lift to his mother's face. Thomas loved desserts.

"Now, let's hurry along," Abbie prompted both boys, dismissing the matter. "We don't want to make Aunt Belinda late for the train."

"But Papa—" began Aaron.

"Papa says for us to go ahead. He'll join us at the station."

Belinda felt another pang—she should have been the one cleaning up the surgery room instead of leaving it for Luke.

Abbie must have sensed her hesitation, for she quickly added, "Papa says it's more important for Aunt Belinda to be there on time. She has missed Melissa more than any of us."

So saying, Abbie herded her charges toward the train station at a brisk pace. Belinda didn't protest further and fell into step.

The Davis family had never gathered to meet the train before, only the stagecoach. Clark and Marty, already waiting on the wooden platform near the tracks, had come into town from the farm by wagon. Beside them stood Amy Jo, her brownish red hair swept rather carelessly into a loose knot on the top of her head. Her green velvet hat looked none too secure to Belinda's eyes, but Amy Jo wore her apparel in the same lighthearted fashion that she did everything else. She smiled and waved exuberantly at Belinda in greeting.

"Isn't this jest too exciting?" she enthused. "Imagine traveling by train—all by yerself. Wouldn't you jest . . . jest *die*?"

Belinda doubted that she would die—but there was something inside that did yearn to have such an experience. She greeted Amy Jo warmly and then turned to her mother and father.

"I was afraid ya'd been held up," said Marty, "an' I knew how special this is fer ya."

"We *were* held up," responded Belinda. "In fact, I should be back scrubbing the surgery—but Luke let me go."

"Isn't he gonna make it?" This time Marty's question was directed to Abbie.

"He hopes to," Abbie answered, "but he did need to do the surgery first. He never knows when he might need it again, and one can't stop and do the cleaning up then."

Marty nodded in understanding, and Clark asked, "Would it help iffen I were to—?"

He didn't have a chance to finish his question. Abbie knew what he was about to ask and answered quickly, "No. No, he wouldn't want that. No use you missing the train, too."

"I *should* have stayed—" began Belinda, but Abbie reached out to give her shoulders a quick squeeze.

"He wouldn't have let you, and you know it," she said firmly, closing the matter.

Amy Jo moved over and crowded in against Belinda. "Isn't this . . . isn't it jest . . . jest . . . ?"

For a moment Belinda's mind flew back several years, and she could imagine Amy Jo finishing her sentence with *vibrant*, a word Amy Jo had chosen to describe almost everything during her early teen years. But this time Amy Jo picked another word, one she had recently discovered. In Belinda's view it, too, was a little overdone.

". . . jest *wondrous*!" she finished excitedly.

Belinda smiled. Amy Jo had not changed. She still gushed and glowed over most of life. Things would never be dull as long as Amy Jo was around. Belinda reached out to clasp the long slender fingers and gave them an affectionate squeeze. Amy Jo pressed closer, her excitement spilling over and making them both almost tremble.

"What d'ya think she's like?" she prodded.

Belinda looked a bit blank. Amy Jo knew Melissa as well as she did, she wanted to say.

"She'll have changed, ya know," Amy Jo pressed on. "Be more grown-up, more sophisticated. More . . . more . . . worldly."

Marty turned to the two girls, a slight frown on her face. Belinda knew her mother would not care for the word *worldly* in regard to her dear Melissa, and Amy Jo must have sensed it immediately, also.

"I . . . I mean . . . more . . . more knowledgeable of the world. More . . . more . . ." She faltered to a stop, grasping Belinda's hand until her fingers hurt.

A distant train whistle drew all eyes to the track. Somewhere out there, around the curve hidden from view by poplar trees, the train was making its way, far too slowly, toward their town, their station, the platform where they all stood. And sitting no doubt sedately and newly educated all alone on one of the upholstered seats was their Melissa. A stir of excitement ran through the little cluster on the wooden planks of the platform.

"It's comin'!" shrieked Aaron, and Thomas answered with a long hooted whistle of his own.

Just as the train rounded the bend, Belinda saw Luke take his place beside Abbie and sighed with relief. And then she forgot everything and everyone except for Melissa.

Would she have changed? How much? Belinda fervently hoped her niece hadn't become too sophisticated . . . too worldly-wise, as Amy Jo was hinting.

And then the huge engine was rattling along beside the platform, and smoke and soot were shooting out through the afternoon air, making people step back sharply and cast anxious glances at their Sunday-best clothing.

The metal wheels squeaked and squealed as the train ground to a halt, and the loud hiss of steam spilled out into the quietness of the springtime air. The train gave one last shudder and settled into quietness.

A conductor soon appeared, methodically setting into place a wooden step and opening doors. There was movement at the windows as passengers started to shift about inside, putting on coats, gathering belongings, and preparing to exit. Others stayed seated. This was not their destination, so they had no reason to stir. They looked with little, if any, interest at the crowd on the little platform and the wine-red station behind them. There was nothing much noteworthy in this small town, much like most every other stop on the tedious western journey.

Belinda noticed one matronly lady glance carelessly out the window and then raise a gloved hand to her mouth to cover a yawn. Belinda found herself looking quickly around her. Were they all really that boring? Was the little town truly that unexciting? Perhaps so. Belinda had never known anything else with which to compare her surroundings. Briefly she visualized herself stepping up onto the iron steps and entering the passenger car, bags in hand, traveling to wherever the train might take her.

The thought was fleeting, for coming toward them, arms filled with small packages, was a more mature and even prettier Melissa.

At her glad little cry, the group surged toward her. Belinda, too, moved forward, then realized that Amy Jo still held tightly to her hand.

Melissa passed from one to another, tears wetting her cheeks as she greeted each family member with hugs and kisses.

"Oh, Belinda!" she exclaimed when it was Belinda's turn. "Look at you! You're so . . . so grown-up. And so pretty! Oh, I just . . ." But Melissa didn't finish her statement. Instead, she threw her arms about Belinda, and the two girls held each other tightly.

When the whole group had expressed their welcome, the family cluster moved from the platform with Melissa's luggage to the wagon, all talking at once.

Belinda thought back once more to the first time Melissa had been met by the family. In so many ways this was the same. And yet so very different. There was no reserve here now—not from anyone. Amy Jo, who had felt left out of the conversation the first time, made sure she was not left out now.

Questions and answers filled the air until it was difficult to sort out who was answering what. Even the two young boys fired rapid questions at their older cousin, most of them in regard to the train. How fast did it go? Had she seen the coal being shoveled into the engine? Had the train—? Melissa laughed and hugged them both with a promise to tell them all about the train trip.

"Are ya all ready to come out to the farm tonight?" Clark was asking Belinda.

"My things are all packed and waiting. We jest need to stop off at Luke's and pick 'em up," Belinda answered, savoring the pleasure of a whole week off to enjoy Melissa's company.

"Ya sure you won't need me?" Belinda asked Luke one more time. He was tucking her things in beside Melissa's luggage when the wagon stopped at Luke's house.

"'Course I'll need you," Luke responded, but at the flicker of concern in her eyes, he quickly added, "But for a few days I'll manage—somehow. And if I really get into difficulty, I'll send for you."

"Promise?" asked Belinda.

"Promise," Luke assured her.

Belinda turned to give each of the boys a quick hug and climbed up into the wagon beside Melissa and Amy Jo.

The trip to the farm was filled with more chatter—and this time it wasn't just Melissa who talked nonstop. Belinda soon began to feel that the conversation was almost as exhausting as the surgery. She hoped she soon would have Melissa to herself for a more quiet conversation. Belinda was sure she wouldn't really know if Melissa had changed until then, when the deeper thoughts and feelings of the two girls could be expressed.

Until that time, Belinda knew she must be patient. The rest of the family wanted to have time with Melissa, too. She belonged to all of them. When they got to the farm, there would be a family dinner to welcome back Missie's "little girl." After dinner there would be a large stack of dirty dishes to be dealt with. There would be no time for a girlish chat on this night.

Belinda allowed a small sigh to escape her. It was hardly audible with the grinding of the wagon wheels and the chattering of Melissa and Amy Jo, but it brought Marty's head around as she studied the face of her youngest.

Marty didn't ask the question, but Belinda could sense it. She smiled at her mother to reassure her.

"I'm a bit tired," she admitted. "It's been a very long day. Started even before sunup with the Norrises rushing their baby in with croup."

Marty nodded in understanding. Clark overheard and turned his head.

"A week's rest will do ya good," he said, then turned back to guide the team. "You've been workin' awful hard. Yer lookin' a mite pale," he threw over his shoulder.

"I'm fine—really," insisted Belinda and suddenly felt uncomfortable as the chattering stopped and all eyes rested on her.

"One good night's sleep and I'll be right as rain," she said firmly, hoping that folks would forget her and get on with the catching-up again.

TWO

Girl Talk

When the last family wagon had left the yard and the last dish had been returned to the cupboard, Belinda was far too weary to suggest a chat. Melissa looked weary, too, in spite of the fact that she still was chatting away about her year out east and her excitement with being back.

Amy Jo reluctantly wrapped her shawl about her shoulders and headed for the log house across the farmyard, promising that she would be back again first thing in the morning.

Belinda tried to stifle a yawn, but it was getting hard for her to keep her eyes open.

"Ya be needin' yer bed," Clark commented, and Belinda could only nod in agreement.

"You must be weary, too, dear," Marty said to Melissa, giving her granddaughter an affectionate pat.

Melissa smiled. "I am," she admitted. "Terribly! But I'm still not sure I'll be able to sleep. It's just so good to be back with you all."

Belinda watched her mother's smile. She knew Marty had been afraid Melissa would be so taken with eastern civilization that she would almost forget her country relatives. But the girl had come back with her teacher's certificate and her genuine love and appreciation of family still intact. Belinda was as relieved as her mother.

"Ya best git on up to bed—both of ya," Marty said, looking from one girl to the other. "Plenty of time to catch up on all the news."

They slowly climbed the steps together and did not even pause to visit at the doors to their rooms, but with a promise of a "good talk" on the morrow, they hugged good-night and went to bed.

Belinda was so weary she could hardly lift her warm flannel gown over her head. Kneeling to say her evening prayers, her brain refused to function and her petition was shorter than normal. With a slight apology to God, she slipped between the soft sheets and was soon sound asleep. She did love being home in her own bed, much as she loved working with Luke and living with his family.

Belinda slept much later than usual the next morning, oblivious to the sounds of the stirring household. She was unaware that Amy Jo had already made her appearance to a "sh-h-h" from her grandmother and that the sun was well on its way into the late spring sky.

Melissa, too, had slept late, though she did awaken before Belinda. After eating one of Marty's hearty breakfasts, she left with Amy Jo to go look at some of her recent sketches and drawings.

It was almost ten o'clock before Belinda even stirred. As she looked at the little clock on her dresser, she could scarcely believe her eyes—she couldn't remember ever sleeping so late. A bit embarrassed, she hurriedly dressed, made her bed, and tidied her room. She couldn't resist a peek through Melissa's open door and could see for herself that Melissa had already left a neat room and gone out to enjoy the new day.

Belinda descended the stairs, and she felt her face flush as she heard Marty busily stirring in the kitchen. What would they think of her idling abed so long?

As Belinda came into the kitchen, Marty's head turned from her task. "My churnin' didn't waken ya, did it?" she asked worriedly.

"Oh my, no," responded Belinda. "Fact is, I guess nothin' wakened me. I jest slept on and on."

"Ya had a lot of catchin' up to do," insisted Marty. "Ya likely shoulda slept longer."

"Mama," said Belinda in disbelief, "look at the time. It's 'most ten. I'll be willin' to bet ya never slept this late in yer whole life."

"Nor do I have my sleep interrupted night after night," Marty said. "At least not since ya got old 'nough to sleep through the night," she commented with a chuckle. "Ya jest sit yerself down at the table now. I'll git ya some breakfast." When Belinda started to protest, Marty shushed her with a raised hand. "I don't get many chances ta feed ya anymore, Belinda. Let me do this."

Belinda nodded her agreement and pulled out a chair. "It *has* been bad recently," she said as she sat down, "but it's not always like this."

"Well, ya need a few nights of good sleepin'," Marty went on. "I'm glad ya got one to start out with."

Belinda smiled. It *was* nice to have her mother fussing over her again.

"Not much breakfast," Belinda quickly said as she noticed Marty getting out the frying pan for eggs and bacon.

"Ya need to eat," Marty insisted, turning to look at her. "Yer gittin' thin."

Belinda looked down at herself. Perhaps she had lost a few pounds— but nothing much.

"It's 'most dinnertime. If I eat a big breakfast now, I won't want any dinner."

Marty's eyes rested on the clock. She finally nodded in agreement. "Well, let me fix ya some bread and butter," she said, moving to slice some bread from the homemade loaf. Belinda noted that she sliced off two thick pieces and spread them both with butter and jam, but she did not complain when Marty put them in front of her on a plate.

"Thanks, Mama," she said as she took a bite. "I think I'd be havin' to let my dresses out if ya was feedin' me all the time." They laughed comfortably together as Marty sat back down at her butter churn and starting the handle humming.

"Where's Melissa?" asked Belinda around another bite.

"Oh my! I promised the girls I'd let 'em know the minute ya stirred!" Marty jumped up from her chair to head for the door.

"Let them be," Belinda waved her hand to stop her mother. She laughed softly. "As late as I've slept, a few more minutes won't hurt anything. Amy Jo was most anxious to get a chance to talk to Melissa anyway. We'll jest give them a few more minutes while I have my breakfast, and then I'll go on over."

Marty settled down again, this time at the table for a few quiet moments alone with Belinda.

"Ya do look a mite better this mornin'," she observed.

"I feel better, too," admitted Belinda.

"Ya looked awful worn out last night. Thet nursin' be too hard on ya, I'm a thinkin'."

"Oh no." Belinda was quick to defend her work. "Usually we get lots of sleep. Well—anyway, enough sleep. But recently we've had so many emergencies—accidents and illnesses. It's been a bad time for Luke, too. He really is far too busy. This town could use another doctor."

"I never thought on thet," remarked Marty, looking surprised.

"Luke says it himself," went on Belinda. "And Abbie—well, she says it often."

"Maybe Jackson will come back here to practice," commented Marty. "His mama would sure like thet."

It wasn't the first time Belinda had thought about that possibility. Jackson had changed his mind about banking and had now completed two years of training toward becoming a doctor. Luke had mentioned Jackson's name several times when he talked about the town needing another medical doctor. Belinda hardly knew her own mind on the issue. She did hope fervently that Jackson had not decided on a career in medicine simply because of her own interest in nursing. But she couldn't help but wonder.

When Jackson first left their area, he had written Belinda often. Belinda enjoyed the newsy letters telling of his new experiences, the long recitals of what he was learning in his classes and from the library textbooks. But soon the letters started to become more personal than Belinda was comfortable with. She thought Jackson seemed to be taking too much for granted. As difficult as it had been for her, she wrote Jackson, telling him she felt they were unwise to keep up the distant relationship. Jackson had written back a very kind and understanding letter. Still, Belinda had some misgivings. Jackson's words had implied quite clearly that this was "for now."

"How much longer does Jackson have?" Marty was asking.

Belinda's attention moved back to her mother.

"Ah . . . ah," she stammered and then got her thoughts back in order. "Luke says he will be ready in two years, I think," she responded.

"Can Luke wait thet long?"

"He might have no choice. It's hard to find doctors willin' to work in small towns."

"Has he talked to Jackson?"

Belinda thought about that one. She wasn't sure, though one night she had heard Abbie urging Luke to get in touch with the young man before someone else spoke to him.

"I don't know," she said, "but I think he may have."

"I hope so. Fer Luke's sake. An' fer the sake of Abbie and the boys. Luke doesn't see nearly enough of 'em."

"Thet's what worries Luke," Belinda said thoughtfully. "He doesn't seem to tire like I do, but he does dislike bein' so busy. He enjoys the boys so much and says they are growing up far too fast. He'd like more time to do father-son things. Take them fishin' and play ball and such."

Belinda rose slowly from the table, reluctant to break off the visit with her mother but anxious to see Melissa—and Amy Jo, too. Though not too far from each other, they seemed to have few chances to really talk anymore.

"I'd better go," she told her mother. "The girls will think I've gone and died in my bed."

Marty smiled and rose to return to her churn.

"I'll be back to help ya with dinner," Belinda promised.

"No need," said Marty. "I've got it all ready to jest put on the stove. You go ahead and enjoy your visit. The days will go fast enough."

Belinda knew that was true. She stacked her dishes on a corner of the cupboard and left the house.

The morning sunshine felt warm and welcome on her hair. She turned her face to it and breathed in deeply of the spring air. Above her, birds twittered and frolicked, looking like they, too, were thankful to be alive. It was nest-building time.

Belinda found Melissa and Amy Jo on the lawn swing sipping lemonade and chatting intently. Both girls called to her and motioned her over to join them.

"Yer lookin' better," said the frank Amy Jo. "Ya looked awful last night."

Belinda smiled.

"Not awful," corrected the more tactful Melissa, "but awfully tired."

"Thet's what I said," Amy Jo hastened to assure her. "Awful!"

The three laughed.

"So are ya caught up on all the news?" Belinda asked Melissa.

"Oh my, no," Melissa countered. "That will take much longer than we've had. I doubt we'll get it all said in the next two weeks."

At the mention of "two weeks," Amy Jo's face fell and she quickly said, "Don't talk about it. I don't want to even think about Melissa leaving again."

"I do," said Melissa evenly. "I haven't seen Mother or Father for almost three years."

Amy Jo immediately turned sympathetic. "Have ya missed them terribly?"

"I've missed them. Sometimes a lot. Other times not so much. But I've missed them. And Nathan and Joe and Julia." Melissa's face became very thoughtful. "I've even missed the ranch hands and my horses," she admitted.

"If I left home, I don't think I could stand it," said Amy Jo, shaking her head. "I'd miss everyone so much."

Melissa nodded. "I'm glad I came," she informed the two girls. "Really glad I came. But I will be glad to get home again, too."

"I'm glad ya came, too," said Belinda softly. "It would have been a shame not to get to know ya."

"It would have been jest awful," wailed Amy Jo. "Jest awful!"

"Even more awful than I looked last night?" teased Belinda, and they chuckled again.

"I think it's good to see more of the world than your own little nook,"

Melissa said. "I love the West, but I'm glad I dared to leave home for a time and get to know a bit more about our country. One can get so . . . so . . . ingrown."

Ingrown, thought Belinda. *Guess that's what's happening to me. I know nothing about the world except these few miles around where I was born and live. Nothing!*

"An' ya never would have met *Jackson*!" squealed Amy Jo, and the girls laughed merrily.

"Jackson," Melissa chuckled. "You know, there was a time when I thought that life just wouldn't be worth living without Jackson."

"Is it?" wailed Amy Jo in mock surprise.

Melissa laughed again. "Well," she said, her large brown eyes rolling heavenward, "if I learned nothing else at normal school, I did learn this. There are lots of young men out there. And some of them—a few of them—are even as exciting as Jackson."

"No-o-o!" groaned Amy Jo.

"On my honor," said Melissa in mock seriousness, raising her right hand.

From there the talk went on to Melissa's year at the school and the school parties and church functions that she'd attended and the escorts she'd had for such occasions.

Amy Jo clasped her hands together, moaning openly at the very idea of being a popular young lady in such a circumstance. Belinda listened quietly, though she did have a few questions of her own she wished to ask Melissa. She wasn't sure if she would enjoy so many beaus or not, but it was interesting to think about it. One thing for sure was that she was no longer concerned about Melissa being heartbroken if Jackson should choose someone else.

THREE

A Neighborhood Party

A party in Melissa's honor was being planned. It was really Amy Jo's idea, but Marty saw it as an opportunity for the youth of the community to get together for a fun fellowship time and heartily endorsed it. Belinda, who usually wasn't too keen on parties, found herself looking forward to the Saturday evening event.

The guest list included past school friends and young people of the local church. The invitations went out, and Amy Jo was very worried about how many would be able to come on such short notice. "What if nobody comes," she was constantly wailing till she nearly drove everyone to distraction.

But on the evening of the party, the teams and saddle horses began to arrive shortly after seven, and the Davis farmyard soon was filled with tethered animals and various kinds of horse-drawn vehicles. It had been some time since so many of the girls' schoolmates had been together, and there were lots of excited greetings and laughter as the group gathered in the large backyard.

The festivities began in the nearby pasture with a game of softball, the fellows playing and the girls wildly cheering them on. Then a few girls joined the game, Amy Jo one of them. She was used to playing most of the games that her younger brothers played and saw no reason to be left out. She coaxed Melissa and Belinda to play, but Belinda declined. She had never cared much for sports of any kind and did not want to embarrass herself by showing her lack of ability.

Melissa hesitantly joined the game. Her sports skills were no greater than Belinda's, but she was going to make the most of her lack of expertise. Joe Parker coached her running. Tom Rankin helped her to cover third base, though his spot was really shortstop, and Sly Foster showed her how to hold and swing the bat. Melissa looked as if she was actually enjoying the game of softball.

The game continued until almost sundown. When it became too dark to see the ball, the group switched to other running games. Belinda excused herself, saying that she would prepare the fire for the corn roast to follow.

She was laying the kindling wood in the open brick pit Clark had built in the backyard for just such occasions when a voice spoke to her from the soft twilight. "May I help?"

It was Rand O'Connel, a young man Belinda hadn't seen since school days. Belinda thanked him and moved aside so that Rand could take over the task.

"Hear you've been nursin'," he commented as he carefully placed the wood.

Belinda nodded her head and then realized that in the near-darkness a question should be answered aloud. "Yes," she said. "Helpin' my brother Luke."

"Do ya like it?" he questioned further.

"Oh yes. Least most of the time. Sometimes it can get a bit hectic."

"Pa says yer good at it," went on Rand, and Belinda puzzled for a moment and then remembered that Mr. O'Connel had been in to have stitches because of an axe cut on his foot.

"How is yer pa's foot doin'?" she asked.

"Fine now. Doesn't even limp."

"That's due to Luke—not me," said Belinda.

"Pa knows thet. But he also said ya took his mind off the pain, knew what to do until Luke got there and how to help Luke when he did the sewin' up."

452

Belinda felt herself flushing at the praise and dropped her eyes.

"Do ya farm with yer pa?" she asked to cover her embarrassment. "I haven't seen ya around since . . . since grade school."

"Jest got back. Been helpin' my uncle down state."

"Oh."

"He has him a dairy farm and needed a hired hand."

"Are ya goin' back?" asked Belinda to keep the conversation from dying.

"Nope. Not to milkin'," he said simply.

"So, what do ya plan to do now?" asked Belinda.

Rand lit a match to the kindling and watched as the small flame began to lick at the fine wood splinters. Around them the darkness was closing in. The shrieks and calls of the players filled the air all about them, making the evening feel friendly and warm.

"Fer now, I plan to jest look around here fer a job," responded Rand, his eyes still on the growing fire.

"What kind of job?" Belinda asked.

"Can't be choosy," he acknowledged. "Take whatever I can git. Heard of anything?"

"No-o. Not that I recall. But it shouldn't be hard to find something. Yer big—an' strong. Should be lots of work—"

And then Belinda realized what she had just said about him and stopped in embarrassment. Rand said nothing. She wondered if he had even heard her foolishness. Much to her relief, he seemed totally taken with tending the fire.

The firelight was casting dancing shadows over his features. She had forgotten what he looked like. She had forgotten most everything about Rand O'Connel. Not that she had ever really noticed him much in the past. He had been just a boy—a fellow student at their small school, neither stupid nor brainy, loud nor shy. He had just been there. By the light of the fire, she took a good look at him now.

His dark hair fell boyishly over his forehead, and he unconsciously brushed it back with a work-toughened hand. The hair at the nape of his neck curled over his shirt collar, and Belinda realized that if the rest of it hadn't been cut short, it would probably curl over his whole head.

His eyes were deep set and fringed with dark lashes. His nose had the slightest hump, suggesting that it might have been injured at some time. There was a small indentation in his cheek that looked almost like a dimple—though, looking at the young man, Belinda dared to think he'd not take kindly to anyone calling it such.

He must have felt her eyes upon him, for he turned to look at her. Belinda shifted her gaze quickly away and pretended to be busy brushing the wood chips from her long skirt.

"I hear Melissa's been away at school an' is a full-fledged teacher now," he said after a brief silence that hung awkwardly between them.

Belinda, glad for something to break the spell, answered in a rush, "Yes, thet's right. She loved normal school—but she's glad to be home, too."

"Is she stayin'? Here, I mean? I thought her home—"

"Oh, it is. I mean, she's jest here for a brief spell. Two weeks in fact—and part of thet's already gone. Then she's going home. To her real home. I've jest gotten used to thinkin' of this as her home. I mean . . . this seems like home for her . . . to me. She was with us for more'n two years and then back for visits an' . . . I really will miss her," she finally finished lamely.

Rand just nodded his head. He seemed to have been able to follow her rambling.

"She excited about teachin'?" he asked.

"Oh yes. She's always wanted to be a teacher. And they need lots of teachers in the West, too."

"I'm glad she likes it."

He seemed so sincere, so genuinely pleased for Melissa that Belinda looked at him intently, wondering, *Is this another of Melissa's secret admirers? Is he wishing her well, even though his real desire is for her to stay in the area?* Belinda concluded that he well could be. She felt a strange sympathy for Rand. He seemed like such a nice young man. Belinda was sorry he might suffer over Melissa's coming departure.

But Rand went on in a matter-of-fact voice. "Glad she's found what she wants to do. Must be nice to decide an' then jest go on out an' do it." He laid a bigger stick of wood on the fire.

Now Belinda was puzzled. Perhaps he *was* smitten with Melissa—but he also sounded almost wistful about her goal of teaching. Was there something Rand wished to do—to become—that seemed beyond him? Belinda hardly knew what to say next. This turn in the conversation was a surprise, a puzzle to her.

Before she could think of what response to make, Rand looked at her and smiled. In the firelight she saw his eyes lighten, his cheek crease into a deep dimple.

Now that is definitely a dimple, she caught herself thinking and shifted her weight from one foot to the other in an effort to hide her embarrassment over the unbidden thought.

"Have me the feelin' thet nursin' or teachin' jest isn't in the same class as milkin' cows," he said, laughing good-naturedly.

Belinda smiled back and took a minute to answer. "Maybe it is," she said slowly. "If one enjoys milkin' cows."

He sobered, then nodded his head. "Might be at thet," he agreed, then repeated, "if one enjoys milkin' cows."

The fire crackled, and the calls and laughter reached out to them from the nearby game. But a silence fell between them as each studied closely the orange-red fingers of the flickering flames.

Belinda gathered from his statement that he had never been fond of farming. She also sensed that there was something else he felt he would enjoy. Whatever it was, he seemed to consider it unobtainable. Was it? Or was that just Rand's assessment of the situation? Belinda knew it really was no business of hers—and yet she was interested and concerned for him. She really did care. Would he feel she was interfering if she pressed further? She finally decided to risk asking, hoping that Rand would not see it as prying into his personal life.

"What *might* ya like to do?" she asked softly.

Rand laughed quietly as though his dream were too farfetched to even mention. Then he turned and studied Belinda carefully to see if she really was interested in hearing. From the look on her face, he must have concluded that she was.

When he answered, he spoke softly, as though his words were for her alone.

"Had me this crazy dream, ever since I was a kid, of makin' things—buildin' with my hands," he said, stretching out his hands before him.

Belinda's gaze fell on the outstretched hands and she saw strength and creativity in the long fingers and broad palms.

"Thet's not one bit crazy," she responded before she could check herself. "No reason in the world why ya can't do thet."

Rand swung to face her. "I ain't got no money to train," he said rather stiffly, "an' I wouldn't know where to go to git trainin' even iffen I did have the money."

"Then learn by doin'," Belinda put in quickly. "Try! Be willin' to try! You might fail—but you'd learn from yer mistakes. Next time you'd know how to go about it better. Watch others and learn from them. There's lots of ways to learn if you really want to. I couldn't go off to school, either, so I'm learnin' from Luke. Maybe a builder would let you work with him. . . ."

Belinda might have gone on and on had not Rand stopped her.

"I never thought on thet," he said, shaking his head in wonderment. "Never once thought on it. Do ya really think someone might—?"

"'Course! Why not?"

The voices of the others were drawing closer. Belinda could hear the chatter of Amy Jo and the ladylike laugh of Melissa as they all came to take part in the roasting. But before they reached the yard and the crackling fire, Rand reached out and gave Belinda's hand a quick squeeze.

"Thanks." He spoke simply, and Belinda gave him a brief smile.

She was surprised at the amount of empathy she felt for him. It must be tough to be a young man with dreams and little hope of seeing them realized. If he did become a builder, then there was Melissa who would be hundreds of miles away—

Before Belinda could stop herself she said, "And I'm . . . I'm sorry," her voice almost a whisper, "thet Melissa is goin' back west. She is very sweet . . . an' terribly pretty, an' I know . . ."

Rand looked puzzled. "Melissa? Why? I think she should go where she feels home is—where she is needed."

"But—" began Belinda.

Rand seemed to catch on then. "Ya think I . . . I like *Melissa*?"

Belinda just nodded.

"Why?" he asked simply.

"Ya asked about her—talked about her. I . . . I thought—"

He shook his head. "She seems nice—sure—an' pretty, too, I guess, though I really hadn't noticed." For a moment he hesitated. The group was entering the yard. Taking a deep breath, he hurried on. "Guess I've only been seein' one girl tonight. For a long time, in fact." And Rand gave Belinda such a meaningful look that she flushed with embarrassment. Mumbling something about seeing to the food, she fled to the security of the farm kitchen.

FOUR

Such a Short Time

As the girls put the clean dishes back in the cupboard, they discussed the party.

"We should do it oftener!" exclaimed Amy Jo. "I haven't had so much fun for jest—years."

Melissa looked rather dreamy. "Me too," she admitted. "It was even more fun than the parties at school back east."

"Really?" demanded Amy Jo. "Ya really had more fun?"

Melissa nodded. "Part of it was having you and Belinda with me," she admitted. "You make everything more fun."

Amy Jo sighed.

"Did I say something wrong?" asked Melissa quickly.

"No . . . it's jest . . . well . . . it's never as much fun when yer not here. Belinda jest works all the time, an' I . . . I jest help Ma and hang around . . . an' . . ."

Melissa stopped to put her arms around Amy Jo's neck, and Belinda felt an odd stab of guilt. *Life must be hard for fun-loving Amy Jo,* she thought to herself. The girl loved people and parties and all the merriment that went with them. Belinda didn't really miss the fun and excitement of parties. Oh, she liked people, too. But she was usually too tired to even think of social events and companionship, with nursing taking so much of her time and energy. Maybe . . . maybe if Jackson did come back to help in the medical practice, some of that would change. Maybe there would be time for other things. . . .

Tears had formed in Amy Jo's eyes. "I . . . I jest wish ya didn't have to go."

Melissa's eyes filled, also. She shook her head slowly. "Oh, I'm so mixed up," she said frankly. "So mixed up. I want to go and I want to stay. I . . . I just wish there weren't so many miles between here and home. If only we could visit more . . . could stop in for a week here or there whenever we took the notion. I miss the folks . . . but I know I'll miss you just as much."

Belinda, too, had joined her tears with the others. All three stood wiping eyes and noses. The joy of a few moments before had simply melted into sorrow at the coming parting.

"I shouldn't *ever* have come here," sniffed Melissa. "I didn't miss you all one bit before I got to know you."

Amy Jo looked up with a start, then began to giggle. At first Belinda could see nothing funny and then the thought of how the three of them must look, all huddled together wiping tears and moaning over the fact that they had gotten to know and love one another, struck her as funny, also. She joined the laughter, and Melissa, thinking of her absurd words, laughed harder than anyone.

"We're silly, aren't we?" ventured Amy Jo. "We all know thet we wouldn't have missed these years fer the world . . . an' yet . . . it's so hard to think thet they're over."

Belinda poured out three glasses of milk and nodded toward the table. She helped herself to a slice of johnnycake and moved to a chair.

"I don't know 'bout you," she said, "but I was so busy servin' the food thet I scarcely ate a thing. I'm hungry."

The other girls followed suit. Melissa chose two gingersnaps, and Amy Jo helped herself to sugar cookies.

"But it was a good party," insisted Amy Jo, no doubt intent upon getting them back in a festive mood.

"I had quite forgotten there are so many charmers around here!" exclaimed Melissa.

"Charmers!" howled Amy Jo. "Don't ya mean farmers?"

Melissa doubled over in laughter. Even Belinda smiled.

"Be serious, Amy Jo," giggled Melissa. "Some of these fellows are so-o good-looking. And strong. And they are so . . . so anxious to help a person."

"Help *you*, ya mean," argued Amy Jo, even though she'd had her share of "help" in the games, as well, Belinda had noticed.

Melissa giggled again, then sobered.

"I'm sure there won't be nearly as many young men back home," she said quietly.

"See! Thet's another reason ya should stay here," insisted Amy Jo.

Melissa seemed not to hear. "In fact," she went on slowly, "I can't really remember much about the boys at all. They all seemed like such kids."

"They *were* kids when you left," Belinda reminded her. "Don't forget that they have been growin' up, too, while you've been gone."

Melissa nodded. "Still . . . I can't really think of a single one I would be interested in."

"Stay here!" Amy Jo begged. "There's no future in being an ole-maid schoolteacher."

Melissa made a face and dunked a cookie daintily in her milk. She took a bite and rolled her brown eyes heavenward. "There *are* a number to choose from here, I will admit!" she exclaimed around the mouthful.

"So stay!" said Amy Jo.

"Amy Jo," scolded Melissa good-naturedly. "I didn't come to find a beau. I came to get my teacher's degree."

"So-o," said Amy Jo, "who's to complain iffen ya get lucky?"

Belinda smiled and Melissa laughed heartily. Amy Jo did have a tendency to speak her mind, but she was a lot of fun.

"Talking about young men," said Melissa, finishing her cookie and turning her eyes toward Belinda, "what about that wondrous young fellow"—she flicked a playful glance at Amy Jo—"giving you all the unneeded help with the fire?"

Melissa opened her eyes wide and stared meaningfully at Belinda, and she felt her face coloring and quickly got up to pour herself another glass of milk.

Amy Jo waved a hand carelessly in dismissal. "Thet was jest Rand," she stated.

"Just Rand? What do you mean '*just* Rand'? Where did you find him anyway?"

"He's a neighbor. At least was." Amy Jo stopped answering the questions meant for Belinda and turned to ask one of her own.

"I haven't seen him around fer ages. Where's he been?"

"He was workin' for an uncle . . . someplace," Belinda said as evenly as her voice would allow.

"Is he back to stay now?"

"Didn't say. He's lookin' for work wherever he can find it."

"Don't tell me you're going to let him get away?" asked Melissa with a teasing smile. "Where'd you meet him anyway?"

"He went to our school."

"I don't remember him. And I'm sure I wouldn't have forgotten—" began Melissa.

But Belinda interrupted. "I had forgotten ya didn't know him much. Guess he left after your first year here. He was a couple of grades ahead of me."

"Oh! What a shame!" said Melissa, her brown eyes exaggerating her disappointment.

"Ya wouldn't have noticed him anyway—ya were too busy moonin' over Jackson," Amy Jo reminded her, and Belinda was thankful that the conversation was headed in another direction.

"Dear old Jackson," said Melissa. "Wonder what he's going to do with himself after he's done his training?"

Amy Jo was quick to answer. "Might even come back here iffen Uncle Luke can talk him into it. I heard Uncle and Pa talkin'. We really need another doctor here, they said."

Melissa turned her eyes back to Belinda, unasked questions in them. Belinda pretended not to notice.

"Here?" Melissa mused thoughtfully. Then she turned to smile at Belinda. "So-o, you might win after all."

"Don't be silly," began Belinda. "I never wanted Jackson."

"That was the strange thing about it," Melissa said slowly. "I did. At one time, I did. But I couldn't even get him to *look* at me."

Belinda felt the color rising in her cheeks.

"Belinda never wants anybody," put in Amy Jo, "but none of 'em seem smart enough to notice thet. They all chase her anyway."

"Don't be silly," Belinda said again.

"It's true," insisted Amy Jo. "Jest look at Jackson—an' Walt Lewis at church, an' Tyler Moore, an' this here Rand. I bet ya we'll see him hangin' around in the future an'—"

Belinda couldn't think of anything else but "Don't be silly" one more time and went to rinse the milk from her glass.

"'Me thinks thou doth protest too much,'" spoke Melissa, moving to slip an arm around Belinda's waist, and Amy Jo laughed at Belinda's discomfort.

Then Amy Jo must have caught a glimpse of the wall clock, and she jumped up from the table. "Wow!" she said. "Look at the time. I've got to git home before Pa comes lookin' fer me. I'll never be able to git up fer church in the mornin'."

Belinda grinned. "I'll just bet ya you will," she countered. "If yer pa has to carry ya."

"Yer right," admitted Amy Jo. "He'll see thet I'm there all right."

She hurried out the door, and Melissa and Belinda put out the light and climbed the stairs by the light of the moon through the window.

Belinda tried to hang on to each precious day with Melissa, but each one just flew by. Melissa swung between excitement and melancholy, but Amy Jo seemed to have just one mood. She was down—really down. She just *knew* she would lose all interest in her world when Melissa stepped onto that westbound train.

Belinda was working in the kitchen when Kate came to share afternoon tea with Marty.

"I'm worried 'bout Amy Jo," Kate admitted. "She jest dotes on Melissa, an' I'm afraid what it will do to her when Melissa goes off home."

Marty had also sensed the loss Amy Jo was facing.

"Clare an' me have talked an' talked about it. It would be so much better fer Amy Jo iffen she had some kind of work, like Belinda, but she ain't at all interested in nursin'. I've talked to her about tryin' to git a job in town, in the store or some such. She has no interest. She's never wanted to teach. Jest likes to draw an' paint—an' I don't see much future in thet fer a girl way out here."

Marty nodded solemnly.

"We've been thinkin' thet she needs to git away from home fer a bit. She's always known jest us—jest life here on the farm. She needs to—what do they say?—'expand her horizons,' get acquainted with somethin' more." Kate twisted her empty cup in obviously nervous hands.

"I came to talk to ya about it. Clare an' me jest don't know whether it's wise or not, an' we'd like yer honest opinion. Clare is talkin' it over with Pa." Kate stopped to take a deep breath. "Ya know thet Amy Jo has always teased 'bout goin' off to art school, an' me an' Clare jest have never felt right 'bout it. Well, we still don't. But maybe . . . jest maybe a girl has to try her own wings a bit."

Marty was about to shake her head. She knew little about the big cities that offered art classes, but she wasn't sure that an immature, strong-willed, impulsive girl like Amy Jo should be away on her own.

"Well, we still don't think thet art school be the place fer her," went on Kate, much to Marty's relief, "but we been wonderin' if maybe a trip west would be good fer her."

"West?" asked Marty, surprise in her voice and face.

Belinda swung around from the cupboard, wondering if she had heard Kate correctly.

"Well, she's got lots of kin there, an' Melissa has already done a fair bit of travelin' on her own and could look out fer her, an' she could jest spend some time drawin' an' paintin' new things, an'—"

"Ya mean, let 'er go on out with Melissa?"

Kate nodded, her face still full of questions.

Marty thought for a few minutes and then her eyes began to shine. "I think thet's a good idea," she said, and a small smile began at the corners of her mouth. "Never did care fer the idea of Melissa travelin' thet far all alone."

Kate let out her breath. "Ya don't think me an' Clare are bein' foolish?"

"No."

"Spoilin' her jest because she's our only girl?"

"Oh no. Like ya say, it should be good fer her to see another part of the world. She needn't stay long." Marty thought for a minute, then went on. "We'll all miss her. She has her own way of makin' things seem more fun."

"I know," sighed Kate. "I can hardly bear the thought of givin' her up—even fer a short time."

Belinda moved forward. The two ladies at the table seemed to have forgotten all about her.

Kate looked up, her eyes misted with tears. "We haven't said anything to Amy Jo yet," she hastened to tell Belinda.

"Of course," Belinda assured her. "I won't mention it."

"Thanks," Kate murmured and rose from the table. "I'd best git back. I left Amy Jo doin' one last sketch of Melissa." She stood for a moment deep in thought. "Iffen Pa thinks thet it's not foolish . . . then I guess we'll let her go," she stated.

Belinda wondered if Kate was secretly praying that Clark would veto the idea.

But Clark did not. He heartily approved of Amy Jo being given the chance to see the West.

"I jest wish ya was free so thet ya could go on out with 'em," he told Belinda.

"Oh, I couldn't—not now," Belinda was quick to inform him. "Luke is just so busy. He needs me right now. It will be different if another doctor comes."

And then for the first time Belinda let herself think about how much she would like to be going with the other two girls. It would be so much fun to travel together—to see another part of the world. It would be awfully lonely with both of them gone. Belinda was glad she would have plenty of work to fill her days. She didn't know how she would ever bear Melissa and Amy Jo both leaving her behind if she weren't so busy.

When Amy Jo was told the good news, she went wild with excitement, just as Belinda had known she would. Melissa was glad for a traveling companion and immediately began to share with Amy Jo all the things they would see and do together. Both girls begged Belinda to try to get some free weeks so she might join them, but Belinda answered firmly that until another doctor arrived, she was needed here.

A wire was sent off to Missie and a reply came back directly, saying they would be thrilled to have the company of Amy Jo for as many months as her parents would be willing to let her stay.

Bags, trunks, and boxes were packed in a flurry of excitement. Belinda missed out on some of the commotion. She had to go back to Luke's to take up her responsibilities in the practice. But she had the afternoon off to see the girls board the train. Never had she seen anyone so eager as Amy Jo.

"Oh, I wish thet ya were comin', too," she enthused. "Then it would be jest . . . jest *wondrous*!"

Belinda nodded. "I wish I were, too," she admitted.

"I'm going to miss you so-o much," sniffed Melissa. "You've been just . . . just like a sister. I wish we weren't so many miles apart."

There were tearful good-byes all around. Even Clark wiped his eyes and blew his nose. The girls had many messages to convey to the loved ones out west and were told over and over how to behave themselves among strangers. At last, all too soon for those who stood on the wooden platform once more, the westbound train was chugging off, its whistle sounding shrilly on the afternoon air. Belinda waved her handkerchief with tears running down her cheeks as two excited passengers leaned from the window to wave back.

As the train rounded the distant bend, Belinda turned from her family and the dusty platform, glad that Luke needed her.

FIVE

Back to Work

After her two nieces departed, Belinda's days—and often nights—were filled, as before, with assisting Luke. But the weekends at the farm no longer seemed as inviting and pleasurable. Being home with Clark and Marty was a nice break from the medical practice. But it certainly was not the same without Amy Jo breezing cheerily in and out of the farmhouse, and no longer could Belinda tell herself that "soon Melissa will be back" to share the big house.

The boys in the nearby log house missed their big sister, too, though Dan and David were reluctant to admit it. Dack had no inhibitions about such sentiments and expressed his feelings openly, often lamenting the fact that his folks had allowed Amy Jo to leave.

"She will be home again in a few months and you will appreciate her even more," his mother assured him more than once.

Kate now visited Marty far more frequently. Often she brought handwork with her. She could hardly bear the "empty nest" and left it with the least excuse. Some days she even went to the fields with Clare, driving the team while he pitched hay or loaded rock.

Marty, too, said she missed the energetic Amy Jo. The days slipped by with no Amy Jo bouncing in and out asking favors, eating cookies, running errands, or bringing bits of news. Marty wondered aloud if she should take to the fields herself, but as it was, she had all she could do to keep up with housework and garden.

As fall arrived the family began to count the days until Amy Jo would be back home. Then one of her fat, newsy letters had an unexpected request. "Please, please," she begged, "could I just stay for a few more months? I just love it out here. The people are so friendly, and there is so much to draw and paint. I've learned so much more about color. You wouldn't believe the colors out here. They are *wondrous*! So different than around home."

Much to Dack's disappointment, Clare and Kate reluctantly agreed that she might have a bit more time and come home in time for Christmas.

Belinda couldn't help but be disappointed, as well. She had been looking forward to having her niece back and hearing all about Amy Jo's adventures.

Belinda took a few days off to help Marty with the fall preserving. Marty, thankful to have her youngest at home even for a short time, chatted as they worked, catching up on their mother-daughter talks.

The snow came early, and Marty said she was doubly glad that she'd had Belinda's help to get in the garden. The menfolk had not been so fortunate with the crops. One field was still unharvested and probably would remain so until spring, with the look of the late fall storms. Clark and Clare discussed the situation and decided to turn the cattle into the field. The herd could forage for what was there. Then at least the whole planting would not be lost.

Minor farm accidents and a nasty flu had kept Luke's surgery full. Now measles had visited the neighborhood, and many children and a few adults were down with the disease. So Belinda had little time to really mope about. Still, she looked forward to Amy Jo's letters and read and reread every incident until she had them almost memorized.

Christmas was approaching, and Belinda began to count the days again. Amy Jo's return would not be long now. Belinda expected news of her arrival date with each new letter that came, but each time she quickly scanned the pages, the homecoming news was missing.

Belinda was sure Clare and Kate would never agree to Amy Jo's missing Christmas.

When another bulky letter arrived with her name on the envelope, Belinda tore it open, quickly looking for a date, but again it was not given.

She was very surprised to read:

Remember when Melissa said there weren't many fellows to choose from out here? Well, she was wrong. One of them is calling on her. She might have forgotten about the young men out here, but believe me, they didn't forget about her! And it didn't seem to take her long to remember Walden when he asked if he could call. Walden came to see her almost as soon as she got home. I guess he was just waiting for her to get back.

So Melissa had a beau! Belinda was not surprised. "Bet Missie was glad ya waited till ya got home," Belinda murmured to her faraway niece, then continued on with Amy Jo's letter.

And just listen to this! Amy Jo went on.

Walden has a younger brother named Ryan. He is just wondrous! I could write pages and pages about him. They are the sons of a neighborhood rancher. Their pa helped Grandpa build the little church. And Ryan is calling on me. Isn't that just wondrous! They usually call on us together. Walden and Ryan both plan on ranching with their pa. Melissa says that the ranch is plenty big enough to support three families. They have a sister, too, but she is crippled. Was thrown from a horse when she was a child and has never had proper use of her legs since. It is really sad, but she is a nice person and doesn't let it get her down. She loves art, too, and I have spent some time helping her to learn to sketch. She really isn't awfully good at it yet, but she does her best.

Belinda smiled. Amy Jo was as candid as ever. Belinda couldn't help but wonder about the poor girl who couldn't walk. Would she have been able to overcome the fall if she'd had proper medical attention?

Well, I've got to go, Amy Jo's letter finished up.

> *Wally and Ryan will be here soon and I must get ready. I will tell you more about him next letter. I would love for you to meet him, but until you do, I'll describe him the best I can in a sketch.*
>
> *Oh yes. Please, please don't say anything to the folks yet! I don't want them getting all upset about this. I'm not sure yet how Ryan really feels about me, and until he makes his intentions known, there is no use causing any fuss. You understand!*
>
> *I guess I should say that I wish you were here. I do miss you— terribly—but I'm afraid I don't wish you were here. If you were, then Ryan likely would have picked you, and I just would have died if that had happened.*
>
> *I love you,*
> *Amy Jo*

Belinda stood with the letter drooping in her hands. *Amy Jo has a beau—little Amy Jo—and she doesn't want the fact known!* Belinda's thoughts whirled. *Is it honest for me to keep it from Clare and Kate?* she wondered. But if she were to tell, what could she say? *Amy Jo likes a young man but she isn't sure yet if he likes her?* That would accomplish very little. No, she'd keep quiet, at least until more facts were known. No good would come of her telling now.

She turned her eyes back to the letter and then remembered the last page—Amy Jo's sketch of her "wondrous" Ryan.

Belinda's eyes looked at an ordinary yet pleasant face. Amy Jo's drawing had even seemed to capture a joyful twinkle in his eyes, and his mouth parted slightly with a hint of a smile. He was boyish looking, but Belinda reminded herself that Amy Jo was not much more than a girl. But youthful or not, they suited each other somehow, this young man and Amy Jo. Belinda could see why they might take to each other.

Carefully she folded the paper and tucked it and the letter into her top dresser drawer. Deep inside she felt a stirring of loneliness as she had never felt before. Was life passing her by?

The news did not need to be kept secret for long. Amy Jo's next letter to her folks told them all about Ryan Taylor. She begged and pleaded for them to please, please, give her one more extension of her visit. She wanted to spend Christmas with Ryan and his family. She would be home early in the new year—at least by Easter, she promised—and she sent her love to each one of them, thanking them for their patience and understanding.

Clare and Kate were dumbfounded. They had not realized that their little girl was so grown-up that she might fall in love on her trip out west. Belinda was quite sure they would have kept her closer to home if they had even considered such a possibility. Now the damage was done. Amy Jo was miles away and felt herself deeply in love with a young man that her parents had never seen.

A long letter from Missie, which soon followed, helped the situation a bit. She wrote to Clare and Kate, giving them a detailed account of Ryan and his family. He certainly seemed to be an upright and worthy young man, but that fact did not move him one mile closer to the Davis farmstead. Still, it did manage to reassure Clare and Kate to some degree. It did nothing for Dack. He fretted and cried and declared that Christmas just wouldn't be Christmas without his big sister.

Belinda felt the same way, but she didn't add to the gloom of the family by stating it.

Three days before Christmas, Luke's Abbie had a baby girl. The precious little one added new meaning to the season for all of them. She had arrived two weeks early, but though she was tiny, she was wiry and healthy. Belinda felt she had never seen anyone so small and so sweet.

So they missed Luke's family at the Christmas dinner table, too, but the rest of the family gathered as usual. Belinda did not linger for long. If Luke should be called out on an emergency, someone would need to be with Abbie and the children. She ate as hurriedly as she dared, shared in the opening of the gifts, and then saddled Copper and headed for town. Marty was sad to see her go, but she told her that she knew Belinda's responsibilities made it necessary.

"Yer first Christmas," Belinda crooned to the tiny Ruth Ann as she held her that evening. "What did ya think about it? Oh, it was a little different this year. No big dinner for ya with all of the cousins and aunts and uncles. Not much fuss and bother in presents because we didn't know ya were coming quite so soon. But the real Christmas—that was the same. This is Jesus' birthday, Ruth Ann. Ya *almost* shared His day. I wonder if He was ever as tiny as ya are." Belinda's finger stroked the soft cheek. "His mama didn't have much of a Christmas, either, thet first year. No presents—until later when the wise men came—no warm room or fancy dinner. But she did have some guests. Strangers—not family. Shepherds. Not too polished, I would think.

"But I'm sure she was happy, because she had her little Son. She knew He was special—but she didn't know then jest *how* special. And she didn't know all about the heartache she would suffer because of what people would do to her Son. She just loved and enjoyed Him that first Christmas." Belinda paused in her soliloquy to lift the baby to her shoulder.

"We don't know what lies ahead for you, either," Belinda continued, "but we know God loves ya—and we all love ya, and I hope and pray that everything waiting for ya in life will be jest good things."

And so saying, Belinda kissed the soft little head and tucked the baby in her crib until her next feeding. Christmas really had been rather special after all.

SIX

Rand

Belinda was getting Ruthie ready for bed when she heard a rap at the door and Luke answer it.

"What now?" moaned Belinda. She had been looking forward to a free evening. But instead here was another emergency call for the doctor. Then Belinda heard a male voice say, "Good evening. Is Miss Davis in?"

Luke replied that Belinda was.

"I'm Rand O'Connel" was the reply. "May I speak to her, please?"

"Come in," invited Luke, and Belinda found her heart skipping and her mind all flustered.

My, I must look a sight, she admonished herself and couldn't resist a quick peek in the mirror at her flyaway curls. She heard Luke invite the guest into the parlor, and then he came through to the kitchen to inform Belinda that she had a caller. "I'll finish with Ruthie. You go ahead," he told her.

"I'm 'most done," replied Belinda, her head still whirling. "I was jest ready to take her on in to her mama."

Luke gently eased the baby from Belinda's arms and walked toward the bedroom, whispering sweet talk to her. Belinda stood in the middle of the kitchen floor watching him go and wondering what on earth she should do next.

Awareness that someone sat in the parlor waiting for her to make an appearance finally spurred her into action, and she rushed upstairs to her own bedroom, stripping away her soiled apron as she went.

There wasn't time for a thorough cleanup. She pulled off her wrinkled dress and slipped into a fresh one, then attacked her hair with a brush. Its unruly curls gave her some trouble, but Belinda managed to get most of it tucked into the pins. Taking one final look at herself in the dresser mirror, she drew a deep breath and went down to meet her caller.

Rand was seated where Luke had left him on the parlor sofa, twisting his hat nervously back and forth in his hands. At the sight of Belinda, he quickly rose to his feet and managed a smile that showed his dimple. Belinda smiled in return, though her nervousness refused to leave her.

"Good evening," she greeted him in proper fashion.

Rand nodded his head slightly and responded in kind.

Belinda didn't know what to say next. Scrambling through her haphazard thoughts, she eventually stammered out, "Please . . . please be seated." She held her hand toward the sofa and then moved to a parlor chair to seat herself.

"I was wondering iffen we might walk instead," Rand answered. "It's a lovely evenin' . . . an' . . . I thought ya might like some fresh air."

"Thet . . . thet would be nice," Belinda said in relief. It would be so much easier to walk and chat than to sit and chat. "I'll just grab a coat."

On her way she informed Luke and Abbie of her plans.

"I won't be long," she promised.

She was turning to go when Abbie stopped her. "Belinda . . . feel free to help yourself from the kitchen to serve your young man refreshments."

It was meant sincerely and Belinda appreciated it, but the phrase "your young man" brought the color to her cheeks. Rand was not "her" young man. She scarcely knew him. They had been youngsters in the same country school—nothing more.

She murmured a thanks to Abbie, determined to straighten out the misunderstanding on the morrow, and went to join Rand.

He was still standing, waiting for her. As soon as she appeared, he moved forward to help her with her coat, then opened the door to allow her to pass out into the twilight.

Rand was right. It was a perfectly beautiful evening—crisp, yet not the bone-chilling cold of winter. The promise of another spring was in the air, and off in the distance Belinda thought she heard a bird singing.

Rand fell into step beside her and they walked a few paces in silence. Breathing in the evening air, Belinda looked skyward where the stars were just beginning to make an appearance, and sighed.

"Long day?" asked Rand solicitously.

Belinda shook her head and laughed slightly. "Not particularly. Just routine things. The evening always affects me this way. I guess it's my favorite time of day—but I haven't been seeing much of it recently. Baby Ruthie always needs her bath then, and the boys need to be tucked in."

"I thought you were a nurse," Rand said good-naturedly, "not a nursemaid."

"Oh, I am," Belinda quickly explained. "It's just thet Abbie hasn't really gotten her strength back since Ruthie arrived. Luke still sends her to her bed early—and I love to help with the little ones. Ruthie is such a dear, and the boys are no problem at bedtime . . . much." She finished her speech with another little laugh. "Sometimes they test me," she admitted.

Rand was watching her as she spoke. He nodded his head and gave her a smile.

"I . . . I haven't seen you around," Belinda said to change the direction of the conversation away from herself, and then bit her tongue. He would think she had been watching for him, expecting him to call. *What a foolish thing to say!* she berated herself silently.

But Rand answered matter-of-factly, "I've been away." He added softly, "I took yer advice."

"My advice?"

"After givin' it some thought, I remembered a man down near my uncle who was a builder. I decided to go see him. He put me right to work—jest like ya said. I've learned a lot over the past months."

By the time Rand had finished, Belinda was beaming with pleasure.

"Really? I'm so glad!" she exclaimed.

He smiled warmly, and from the expression on his face, Belinda sensed that he really couldn't believe he was actually going to have his dream come true.

"I'm so glad," she repeated.

"I owe it all to you, ya know."

"Nonsense!" said Belinda. "Yer the one who had to take the risk and—and do all the work. And yer the one who had the ability in the first place. I really had nothin' to do with it."

"Not true," insisted Rand. "I would never have tried iffen it hadn't been for you. When we talked thet night, suddenly you made me realize it all depended on what I was willin' to do 'bout it. Dreams are fine . . . iffen they don't jest stay dreams. But they git ya nowhere iffen ya don't put some effort 'long with 'em."

They walked on in silence for a while. Belinda was truly pleased that Rand had found the courage to take the first step toward becoming a builder. He did seem like a nice young man.

"So now what?" she asked softly, hoping he wouldn't misunderstand the question and give her interest greater importance than she intended. "What will you and the man down south be building next?"

"I won't be buildin' down there anymore. He kindly taught me all he could . . . then gave me his blessin' an' sent me on my way to build on my own."

"Here?" asked Belinda in surprise.

"Here," he laughed. "And thet's why I came to see ya first. I wanted to properly thank ya."

Belinda flushed slightly. "But there's no—"

He held up his hand. "I know what went on in my head," he laughed, "an' I had already given up the dream until ya urged me to try and suggested a way to start. So I know I owe ya a heap of thanks."

Belinda smiled and nodded her head playfully. "Fine," she said. "I accept yer thanks. I'm mighty glad to have had a part in yer decision. I think you made the right one."

Rand chuckled along with her.

"Now, fer a properlike thanks, I'd like to take ya out to supper," he continued.

"To supper?"

"Over to the hotel dinin' room."

"There's no need fer thet," Belinda hurriedly replied.

Rand stopped walking and placed a restraining hand on Belinda's arm. He looked down at her, his eyes studying her face in the soft dusk. "I'd like to," he said intensely. "Please?"

Belinda was flustered. Yet what harm could it do to go to supper with a young man in the local dining room? Especially if he felt honor bound to express his thanks. She swallowed and nodded her head in agreement.

"Fine," she managed. "Fine. If ya like. It would be very nice to go to supper."

Rand released her arm. "Thank ya," he said fervently. "Tomorra?"

Belinda nodded again, trying hard to think ahead to what day "to-morra" was and what commitments she might have. She could not think of any, but she hoped she wasn't making an arrangement she would need to break. "Tomorra," she agreed.

She could scarcely see Rand's face now in the gathering darkness, but she did see him smile.

"I'd . . . I'd best be gettin' on back," Belinda said, and they began to retrace their steps.

It was a quieter walk back through the darkness. Rand reached out a hand to her elbow on occasion to steady Belinda as they walked over the uneven planks of the boardwalk. She knew the familiar walk like her own bedroom, but she didn't pull away from the offered assistance. Rand was a mannerly young man and would offer the same kindness to any lady he accompanied, she told herself.

"What will ya build first?" she asked in the darkness.

"I start on a house tomorra. The fella who has the hardware store don't wanna live above it anymore. His wife wants her own house . . . an' own yard. So he's havin' me build it for 'em."

"That's wonderful! What is the house like?"

Rand chuckled softly. "I wish I knew. That's the only . . . the only 'fly in the ointment,' so to speak. His wife still hasn't made up her mind, so the next few days are gonna be spent tryin' to get 'er settled on what she wants."

"I wish ya well," laughed Belinda.

They reached the doctor's house, and Rand opened the door for Belinda. She suddenly remembered Abbie's offer.

"Would ya care for some coffee . . . or . . . or lemonade? Abbie said we could use the kitchen."

"Not tonight, thank ya. I still have lots of work to do on buildin' plans iffen I'm gonna be ready to show Mrs. Kirby some ideas tomorra."

Belinda's eyes fell to the parlor clock. "Oh my!" she exclaimed. "It's already late. I'm sorry we took so long."

"Nonsense," Rand declared. "I won't sleep tonight anyway," and he chuckled.

"I s'pose yer pretty excited," agreed Belinda. "Guess I would be, too, if I was about to build my first house."

"The house has little to do with it," Rand informed her, leaving Belinda to puzzle over his statement.

"See ya tomorra night," Rand went on. "What time?"

"I . . . I guess we should make it . . . say six-thirty. If thet's okay with you."

"Six-thirty," agreed Rand. "I'll be here."

Just before he closed the door, he turned back to Belinda. "Thank ya," he said sincerely, "for agreein' to walk on such short notice. It was bold of me to jest drop over . . . but I didn't know how else to see ya."

"It was nice to see you," Belinda heard herself saying and wondered at her frankness. Then with a smile and a tip of his hat, Rand closed the door and was gone.

SEVEN

Supper

Belinda rushed through the surgery cleanup the next day so she might have plenty of time to make herself presentable. She had never been out to supper with a young man before, and her stomach was so knotted up just thinking about it that she wondered if she even would be able to eat.

Over and over she reminded herself that this was simply an opportunity for Rand to say thank-you for what he considered to be her part in nudging him toward his dream. Belinda quite successfully talked herself into its "common courtesy" aspect rather than seeing it as a social occasion, even though she still felt she deserved no such gratitude.

Luke and Abbie didn't look quite as convinced when Belinda explained to them the reason for her not sharing in their usual evening meal. They said nothing, but Belinda noticed the twinkle in Abbie's eyes as she nodded a bit knowingly toward her husband.

Aaron and Thomas, along with their older cousin John, who was there for a visit, didn't seem to catch the lack of special significance in the event, either.

"Why are ya goin' ta eat with a man?" asked Thomas.

"Because . . . because he has asked me," responded Belinda. "He wants to say thank-you by taking me to supper."

"Can't he talk?" inquired Aaron.

"Of course," Belinda answered, her cheeks flushing.

"Then why don't he jest say it?" demanded Aaron.

"Well, he has said it."

"Then why do ya hafta eat over there? Why don't ya eat here with us?"

"Well, he . . . he . . . wants to say it again . . . in another way." Belinda felt flustered. How could one explain such a thing to children?

"I think it's dumb," put in Thomas.

"I think it's dumb," echoed Aaron.

"It's not dumb. It's . . . it's a . . . a social nicety," argued Belinda. "A . . . a kindness. Mr. O'Connel is bein' a gentleman."

The boys thought about that for a moment. Belinda was hoping she had finally succeeded in making them understand and was about to shoo them from her room so she could finish pinning up her hair in peace.

"Can I come, too?" asked Aaron.

Belinda stopped her pinning and spun to look at the young boy. His earnest eyes looked intently into her face.

"Not . . . not this time," she answered, trying not to seem unkind.

"Why not?" he insisted.

"Because . . . because . . . ya haven't been asked," Belinda said evenly.

Thomas reached out a hand to draw his younger brother back. "He don't got nothin' to thank *you* for, Aaron," Thomas reminded him.

Aaron reached a hand into a trouser pocket and pulled out a fistful of childish treasures. "I'll give him my blue marble," he offered.

"Don't ya understand nothin'?" put in the older, wiser John, who had been quietly listening to the whole exchange. "Aunt Belinda is goin' to eat with him 'cause she wants to. It's called courtin'. Pa told me. O'Connel says 'thanks' an' takes her to supper, then she says 'thanks fer the supper' by invitin' him to tea, then he says 'thanks fer tea' by takin' her on a buggy ride. It's called courtin'." John finished his factual recital while Belinda stood with her mouth open. She wanted to protest, but John already was gathering his two younger cousins and herding them toward the door.

"I still wanna go," insisted Aaron.

"People what's courtin' don't take nobody with 'em," explained John patiently.

"Why?" demanded Aaron.

"I dunno. They jest don't. They always jest . . ."

The voices faded down the staircase, and Belinda could hear no more. She turned back to her mirror, not knowing whether to laugh or cry. Her brush was still in her hand, and with trembling fingers she finished her hair. She noticed that her cheeks were flushed, and she prayed she would regain her composure before Rand arrived. It seemed that young John had undone her whole carefully thought-out explanation for the evening.

Rand was there promptly at six-thirty. Belinda heard Thomas answer the door and hurried from her bedroom before the young boys might have a chance to question him or make any inappropriate comments.

Only a few minutes' walk brought them to the town hotel, and as Rand had already spoken to the dining room host, they were quickly seated. Belinda then had the difficult task of deciding what she would like for supper. Her head was not working well. Over and over the words of her nephews chased around her brain.

"Might I suggest the fresh lake trout?" Rand asked, and Belinda quickly nodded. Fish would be a nice change and it would also save her the task of deciding.

After their order was given, they had too much time to just sit and feel uncomfortable, to Belinda's way of thinking. Rand seemed perfectly at ease, and Belinda couldn't help but wonder where he had found his confidence.

She could think of absolutely nothing to say and felt very foolish just sitting there studying the hands that fluttered nervously in her lap.

"Did ya have a busy day?" Rand questioned, and Belinda drew a deep breath, thankful for something to talk about.

She explained briefly some of the events of her day and then asked him about his activities. Rand smiled as he described how he and Mrs. Kirby had gone over and over the house plans.

"Things are far from settled," he informed her. "She still isn't sure jest what she wants."

"Best not to rush her then, I guess," spoke up Belinda. "Buildin' a new house takes a great deal of thinkin'-on fer a woman. She'll want to be sure it has all the things she's been dreamin' of. If they are left out, she will keep thinkin' of them after she's all moved in, and wishin' that they'd been added. Ya wouldn't want yer first customer to be eternally dissatisfied."

"Where'd ya git so smart?" Rand teased with a chuckle. Then he went on, "I've been thinkin' the same thing. In fact, I talked to Mr. Kirby. Said thet it might be wise to give his wife more plannin' time. Wilson wants a storage shed built, and they need a new barn at the livery. Maybe I'd best start there before I take up on thet house."

"What did Mr. Kirby say?" asked Belinda.

"He agreed—rather reluctantly. I think he's jest anxious to git this buildin' over. I'm sure he's heard nothin' but 'new house' fer the last several months."

From then on, conversation was much easier. In fact, Rand was interesting to talk to and soon had Belinda completely at ease. They talked about the small town, the new developments, the hopes for its future now that the railroad came through, and the need for another doctor, and they laughed over some of the memories of their shared school days in the little country school.

In no time, it seemed to Belinda, their plates of food arrived. As they enjoyed the tasty meal, the conversation continued. All too soon supper was over and there was really no reason to linger.

"Thank ya," Belinda said sincerely as Rand led her from the dining room. "That was very nice. And now yer 'thank-you' is more than paid in full."

Belinda's thoughts went back to John's comment. Her simple "thank-you" did seem inadequate. She felt she owed Rand more than that. But even as the invitation to tea lingered on her lips, she refused to utter it. This was not a courtship. This was one friend expressing gratitude to another. She would not consider it to be any more than that.

They walked home slowly, enjoying their chat and the stroll.

"Where are yer two nieces?" Rand asked. "Wasn't one going back west?"

"Yes. Melissa. But it turned out that Amy Jo went, too. She was to be gone only a few months, but her visit has been extended on and on. She still isn't home."

"You must miss 'em."

"Oh, I do."

"Will Amy Jo be back soon?"

"I hope so. It seems such a long time . . . but I fear . . . I fear she might not come back at all."

"She likes the West?"

"More than the West. She's found a young man out there," Belinda said simply.

"Is she thinkin' of marryin'?" Rand asked in surprise.

"She hasn't said . . . but I'm thinkin' she is."

"Isn't she younger than you?"

"A little."

"Do her folks think she's ready to be married?"

Belinda laughed softly, a complete change from her former mood. "Do one's folks ever think a girl's ready to be married?" she joked.

Rand smiled, then surprised her by asking, "Do you . . . *you* think she's ready?"

"I don't know," responded Belinda slowly. "She was always kind of flighty—carefree—but she sounds more serious now. Maybe she is."

They walked in silence for a few more moments.

"Are you?" asked Rand quietly.

"Me? What?" pondered Belinda. She had entirely lost the thread of the conversation.

"Ready fer marriage?" he said simply.

"Oh my, no!" exclaimed Belinda, her cheeks flushing and her composure fleeing. "I . . . I haven't even thought on such a thing. I'm nowhere near ready. I . . . I . . ."

Rand did not press her but, seeing her obvious embarrassment, quickly changed the conversation.

"Luke has him a nice house. It has lots of special features. Thet's the kind of houses I want to build—'stead of just straight box type. Wonder iffen he'd be so kind as to let me peek in his attic someday to study the rafter structure."

Belinda was surprised at the sharp turn in subject but managed to say she was sure Luke wouldn't object. His house had been purchased, along with the practice, from the late Dr. Watkins.

With the talk back on safer ground, Belinda regained her composure and enjoyed the rest of the walk home.

She thanked Rand for the meal and the lovely evening, but she did not extend an invitation to tea.

"May I see ya on the weekend?" Rand asked, but Belinda was quick to turn him down.

"I go to the farm for the weekends," she said. "It's the only time I get to see the folks."

"I understand," he said kindly. "Then perhaps I will see ya in church on Sunday."

Belinda nodded.

After he had left, Belinda chided herself for not being more hospitable. He was a fine young man and she could do with friendship. *But why, why,* she asked herself as she pressed cool hands to warm cheeks, *why do I get the feeling that he is thinking differently about it than I am?* Was there more to his simple question concerning her preparedness for marriage than he had expressed? Surely it was all in her head. She determined to put it from her thinking completely.

Rand was in his usual place in church on Sunday with a row of neighborhood young men and did not greet Belinda more than by doffing his hat and wishing her a pleasant good morning.

She saw him chatting with Clark for some length after the service, though, and was careful to keep herself busy with some of her friends.

On the way home Clark began to share the earlier conversation with Marty, and Belinda could not help but overhear.

"Thet young O'Connel fella is back. He's been learnin' the buildin' trade an' now wants to do his buildin' hereabouts."

"Thet's nice," said Marty agreeably. "Does he think there'll be enough work?"

"He's already lined him up several jobs. Seems ambitious enough."

"Thet's nice," said Marty again.

"He was wonderin' iffen some of our young fellas might be interested in workin' fer 'im," went on Clark.

"Some of ours?" asked Marty, taking a new interest in the conversation.

"Yeah. Clare's or Arnie's. Promised I'd ask."

"They're jest boys," offered Marty.

"Old enough to work. I was doin' a man's job by the time I was their age."

Marty nodded.

"Do ya think any of 'em might be interested?" she asked.

"Don't know," responded Clark. "But I'll mention it like I promised. Clare's Dan might be. Don't think he has him much interest in farmin'.'"

It was true. They had all sensed it.

"What do ya think Clare will say about it all?" asked Marty next.

"S'pose he'll want Dan to be a doin' what brings 'im pleasure," Clark responded and clucked to the team to hurry them up.

Belinda thought the conversation was over. But Clark continued, "Good to see thet young fella back again. Seems like a fine young man. I'd be right glad to see Dan workin' with the likes of 'im." And then as an afterthought, "Now why ya s'pose Amy Jo couldn't have stayed on here an' taken up with 'im 'stead of goin' off west an' meetin' someone we don't even know?"

"Who knows the ways of the heart?" asked Marty, and the conversation finally took a different turn, much to Belinda's relief.

EIGHT

Amy Jo

A wire from Amy Jo simply stated that she would be home for Easter as promised. They should meet the afternoon train on Good Friday. She did not mention her young man, and the family wondered if the little romance had ended. Kate privately told Marty that she prayed it might be so, though she did hope her impetuous daughter had not been hurt by the whole experience.

The wire arrived only two days before the specified Friday, and once again the whole family was in commotion preparing for Amy Jo's return.

Belinda was glad she was busy with patients so she wouldn't be anxiously counting down the hours until Friday's train. To get herself through the long evening wait, she busied herself in Abbie's kitchen doing some special baking. Thomas and Aaron pulled up chairs and leaned on the counter, watching the dough taking shape in the blue mixing bowl.

"Wha'cha makin'?" Aaron began.

"Cookies. Can't ya tell?" Thomas told his brother. "See, she's got sugar an' eggs an' butter all stirred together."

"It might be cake," defended Aaron. "Mama puts all them things in cake."

"This time it is cookies," Belinda explained.

485

"What kind?" asked Aaron.

"Applesauce cookies," answered Belinda.

"Ummm," said Aaron. "My favorite."

"You say thet 'bout any kind," rebuked Thomas.

"That's 'cause I like 'em," said Aaron with a stubborn set to his chin.

"They're not yer favorite, then, iffen ya like 'em all," argued Thomas.

Belinda was in no mood for childish spats. "They are Amy Jo's favorite. Her *true* favorite," she informed the children.

"Are ya bakin' 'em jest fer her?" asked Aaron dolefully.

"Yes—but no. Not all fer her. We'll give her some—but you can have some, too."

Aaron seemed satisfied.

"When's she comin'?"

Belinda lifted her eyes to the clock. "In about . . . about forty-two hours," she responded.

"Forty-two? Thet's a long, long time!"

"Does two days sound better?" asked Belinda.

"Two is better'n forty . . . forty what?"

"Forty-two."

"Yeah, forty-two. Two's better'n that."

"Ya silly," cut in Thomas. "She comes when she comes. Don't make no difference what ya call it." Then he seemed to reconsider his statement for a moment and directed a question to Belinda. "Is forty-two and two days the same long?"

Belinda smiled. "Two *whole* days make forty-eight hours, but it's not quite two whole days now. Instead of forty-eight, it's about forty-two," she explained to the boy.

"It still seems a long time," insisted Aaron.

"We only got the message this mornin'," Belinda reminded them.

"Forty-two is still a long time," Thomas agreed with his brother.

"Bet the cookies'll all be gone by then," Aaron said, eyeing the dough as it was placed on the cookie pans.

"We'll hide some," suggested Belinda.

Aaron grinned. He loved secrets. Then he sobered. "But only a few many," he cautioned.

486

When the first cookies were taken from the oven, Belinda poured two glasses of milk and sat the boys at the table with three cookies apiece. They chattered contentedly as they ate, and Belinda found their company a distraction for the long evening hours.

"Ya gonna hide some fer 'Connel?" Aaron asked.

"Fer what?" she asked, perplexed by his question.

"Not 'what,'" corrected Thomas. "People aren't 'whats,' Papa says." He stopped to dip an edge of his cookie into his milk and then sucked the moisture out.

"'Connel," repeated Aaron.

"Oh, you mean Mr. O'Connel."

"S'what I said," remarked Aaron, then followed his brother's lead in dunking a cookie. Not quite as adept at dunking, a soggy piece of his cookie fell into the glass, and he ran to the cupboard for a spoon.

"Are ya?" he asked as he returned to the table.

"No-o-o. He lives at Mrs. Lacey's boardinghouse. She cooks for him."

"Bet he doesn't git cookies like this."

"Aaron," Thomas spoke impatiently. "Jesus didn't say we gotta share with *ever'body*."

"That's not what I meant," hastened Belinda. "God wants us to share with others. It's jest that sometimes—" Now she was talking herself into a corner. She would never know how to explain to the two boys. She quickly changed her tack.

"How would ya like to take a couple cookies to yer papa? He is busy in his office, but I think he would like some cookies and milk."

The boys loved the idea, and Aaron was given a small plate with the cookies and Thomas a glass of milk and they marched off to take the offering to Luke. Fortunately the more careful Thomas had the glass in hand.

By the time Belinda finished her baking, "hid" a few cookies to present to Amy Jo, and cleaned up the kitchen, it was late and she was ready for bed. She mentally scratched this first day from her calendar and hoped the next day would be filled with lots of activities and jobs that needed to be done. *I'm awful glad,* she told herself as she climbed into bed, *that Amy Jo didn't send that wire any sooner!*

487

The next day turned out to be rather quiet in the doctor's office, so Belinda asked Abbie if there were any errands she could run. Abbie did need a few things from the store, so Belinda donned a light shawl, her spring hat, and set off with a basket over her arm.

The purchases did not take long, and she whiled away a few more minutes looking in shop windows. The afternoon still stretched on before her, and she did not look forward to trying to find something to fill it.

She finally strolled toward home, studying neighborhood gardens and the spring flowers beginning to make their appearance. She was so preoccupied she went right on by Luke's house without even realizing it.

"Out for an afternoon walk?" The nearness of the voice startled her and she jumped. "I'm sorry. I didn't mean to catch ya off guard," the person apologized as she turned to see who it was. "You were jest so deep in thought."

Belinda looked up to see Rand smiling down at her. "I . . . I guess I was," she admitted, looking about her to get her bearings. "I . . . I was off doin' some errands fer Abbie, and comin' home I was . . . was admirin' the spring flowers an' I 'most forgot what I was about, I guess." She laughed at herself and turned to start back in the right direction.

"May I walk along with ya?" he asked. "I'm headin' fer the hardware store."

"Certainly," answered Belinda and shifted her basket only to have it gently taken from her hands.

"I heard around town that ya have some good news."

"Oh yes! I can hardly stand the wait for Amy Jo's return. I guess thet was why my thoughts were so far off a moment ago."

He nodded and fell into step beside her.

"What happened to the young man—her beau?" he asked after they had walked a short distance together.

Belinda lifted her eyes to look at him. "We don't know," she said honestly. "Amy Jo said nothin' about him in the wire. Perhaps . . . perhaps it wasn't so serious after all."

"That's unfortunate," said Rand. "I hate to hear of love gone sour."

Belinda wasn't sure if the comment was teasing or serious. She could think of no response, so she kept her silence.

"What's Melissa doin' these days? Teachin'?"

"Yes," Belinda answered, wondering again if it could be that Rand was interested in Melissa. "She got herself a school the very first term after she got back home. It's close enough that she can stay at home and ride horseback to classes each day."

"That's nice," responded Rand. And then he added, "I don't suppose she'll do thet fer too many years."

Belinda looked at him questioningly.

"Must be lots of ranchers out there who can see how pretty she is," he explained. "One of 'em is bound to catch her eye one of these days."

"She . . . she already has a beau," Belinda offered, carefully watching Rand's face.

He brightened. "Has she, now?" he said. "Thet's nice." Then he quickly added, "Is Melissa older or younger than you?"

"Older," said Belinda. "A bit."

"An' she's yer niece," he noted with a grin. Belinda smiled and nodded.

They had reached Luke's gate, and this time Belinda had no intention of missing it again. She reached for her basket and said she must be getting in to see if she could be of any help to Abbie.

Rand slowly gave up the basket and tipped his hat, saying he hoped to see her again soon. Then he was gone, and Belinda went around to the back door and into the kitchen.

I never even thought to ask him how his building is goin', she chided herself. *He'll think me most uncarin'.*

The next morning Belinda and Luke were so busy she began to fear they would still be in the office sewing up cuts and administering medication when Amy Jo's train whistled its way into town. *Why couldn't some of the cases have been spread out over the past two days?* was her unreasonable question, which she had more sense than to express aloud.

But Luke must have read her agitation anyway.

"Don't worry," he soothed. "When it's time for that train, you'll be on the station platform. Anything that's going on here I can handle."

Belinda still fretted. She had already missed the morning Good Friday service at church. *If only patients could be regulated,* her thoughts continued to whirl around, *instead of coming by bunches at the wrong times!*

She turned her attention back to the task at hand and hoped that by the time the train was due, the office would be cleared out.

At last the final patient was on the way out the door, and Belinda took a deep breath and looked around her. There was cleaning up to be done, but the clock on the wall said there were still forty-five minutes until train time. If she hurried, she would make it just fine.

"I would like to say I'll do the cleaning," said Luke, "but I promised the Willises I'd drop by. Mrs. Willis hasn't been able to shake that nasty cough she developed when she was carrying her last child."

"It's fine," responded Belinda. "I have plenty of time."

"Do you mind giving Abbie a bit of help with the youngsters?" asked Luke. "I know she wants to meet the train, but it's kind of hard for her to carry the baby and watch two rambunctious boys."

Belinda smiled. "I'll be glad to help," she assured him. "Those boys and I have a few cookies to deliver."

Belinda hurried to clean the room and sterilize the instruments. Amy Jo would soon be back home where she belonged. Belinda hoped her niece would never be tempted to leave home again. It was far too lonely without her.

Belinda finished her duties and rushed up to her room to get ready. She took the remaining applesauce cookies from their hiding place and carefully placed them in a small decorated tin. *Aaron will want to carry them,* she noted to herself. Leaving them on the kitchen table, she went to see what assistance she could give Abbie.

Abbie was just putting the blanket around the baby. The two boys were already on the front step. Belinda gave the cookie tin into Aaron's care and offered to carry the baby.

It was only a brief walk to the station, but by the time they arrived, Belinda's arms were tired. She couldn't believe how much little Ruthie had grown in such a short time. She wished they had one of those baby prams she had seen pictured in the Sears Roebuck catalog.

When they joined their excited family on the platform, Clark took Ruthie, and Belinda was glad to give her arms a rest. Cousins shouted at one another and raced about. Scoldings followed and then threats, and finally the younger members were firmly seated on the bench beside the station and, much to their chagrin, told to remain there until the train arrived.

Finally the far-off whistle was heard and then the distant thunder of the metal wheels told them that the train would soon be there.

Kate stood with pale face and hands clasped tightly together. "Oh, I can hardly wait to see her," she said to the little cluster of family. "I never dreamed when we let her go thet she'd be gone so long. When she kept stayin' an' stayin', I felt so frightened . . . so frightened she wouldn't be comin' back. I'm so glad . . . so glad thet she is. I jest hope she isn't hurt over thet there boy. But there are lots of fine young men around here fer her. She's still so young . . . so young."

Belinda had never heard Kate go on so. She attributed it to nerves.

"I jest hope she won't miss the West too much. Maybe she'll have it all outta her system by now. Same with thet young man. My, I hope she doesn't moon over losin' him. I scarce could bear a mopin' girl." Kate turned to Belinda. "You'll have to watch out fer her. You always was good at talkin' her outta her dark moods. You could introduce her to some of the young people in town here—like thet O'Connel boy. Pa says he's real fine. Dan's gonna go work fer 'im as soon as school classes are out."

That was news to Belinda, though she wasn't surprised. She was surprised, however, at her feeling of reluctance to be a matchmaker between Amy Jo and Rand. She felt hesitant. Were they right for each other?

Then the train was pulling up beside them, and they all moved back a step so Kate might be the first one to greet her girl.

Will she have changed? wondered Belinda. Maybe she'd had her heart broken by the young Ryan. Belinda hoped not. Amy Jo had seemed so taken with him. Yet Amy Jo was impetuous. Perhaps she had now forgotten all about him.

And then Amy Jo was stepping down from the passenger car. Radiant, her brownish red hair was swept atop her head becomingly and her light green traveling dress fit her to perfection. Her complexion was flawless with no longer a trace of the hated freckles. She walked with poise and decorum. Amy Jo had left a girl and had come back to them a young woman. Belinda held her breath.

Kate swept Amy Jo into her arms and held her closely, weeping with joy. It seemed a long time until Belinda had her turn.

"You look wonderful," she said with a slight laugh. "Jest . . . jest so . . . so . . . vibrant!"

Amy Jo laughed merrily.

"That's what love does for one," she whispered in Belinda's ear.

Belinda pulled back to look into the violet eyes.

"Ya mean ya still . . . ? But yer home now . . . many miles from . . ."

But Amy Jo silenced her with a little shake of her head. She turned glowing eyes to the family group.

"Everyone!" she called excitedly. "Everyone! I want ya to meet Ryan. We've come home to be married."

Belinda hardly heard the gasps around her she was so busy trying to get her own startled thoughts under control. She raised her eyes toward the enthusiastic Amy Jo and for the first time noticed a young man who stood behind her. At Amy Jo's words he took a step forward and reached out a possessive hand to take Amy Jo's arm. He smiled and tipped his hat to Kate, then to Marty, and Belinda saw Kate's face grow even paler.

"Oh my!" Belinda said under her breath. "Oh my!" Then she looked again into the deep blue eyes and tanned face of the young rancher. Amy Jo had sketched a good likeness. Belinda felt she would have known the young man anywhere. This was indeed Amy Jo's Ryan.

After the initial shock, the family was quickly captivated by Amy Jo's young man. Even Kate, who could hardly face the idea of losing her Amy Jo to the West, had to admit that Ryan would make a wonderful son-in-law.

"Iffen she had jest given us a bit of warnin'," Marty kept saying, shaking her head, "we all wouldn'ta stood there with our mouths a hangin' open."

But warning was not Amy Jo's way. That would have spoiled her "surprise." The young man Ryan did apologize several times to Clare and Kate. "I wanted to ask for her hand proper like," he informed them, "but Amy Jo wanted to make the announcement herself."

It seemed he was willing to let Amy Jo have her own way in all matters concerning their wedding.

"I want to be married on June first," Amy Jo insisted. "Thet is the day Melissa and Wally have chosen, and Ryan and I decided thet as we couldn't have a double wedding, the family being scattered so, we'd do the next best thing and be married on the same day—her out west and me here."

Kate was sure she could never be ready for a wedding by the first of June, but Marty and Anne and even Nandry all pitched in, and things for Amy Jo's trousseau began to take shape.

"Why don't we git Mrs. Simpson to sew the gown?" asked Marty. "She does a wonderful job, and she is so quick with her stitchin'."

Mrs. Simpson was still very much in demand as a seamstress and had even been able to purchase her own machine, so Marty saw very little of her. But arrangements were made, and Amy Jo's cream-colored wedding gown was coming together under the skilled hands.

At first it didn't seem real to Belinda. But as item after item—two new everyday dresses, a travel outfit, snowy white underthings, as well as two quilts, dish towels, and other household linens—was spread out on the bed in the spare bedroom at the farm, she had to admit it was indeed true. *Our Amy Jo is getting married!* Amy Jo, their little girl. Amy Jo, their bit of sunshine. And many miles away, somewhere out west, Melissa, too, was excitedly preparing for her big day. Belinda tried to put her feelings into words, and she finally concluded she felt as if she were being left behind.

The frantic preparations kept Belinda more than occupied until June the first arrived. The day was beautiful, and she slipped a cool mint green dress over her head as she got ready to join her lovely niece at the front of the church, where she would solemnly declare her love and commitment to Ryan.

"Oh my!" Belinda couldn't help but exclaim when she caught her first glimpse of the bride standing in the middle of her family's living room. Kate was fluttering around her, making sure the dress was hanging properly on the slim figure.

"That soft, creamy material an' the lace trim are jest *perfect* with your hair," Belinda commented, giving Amy Jo a careful hug. "It's truly *wondrous!*" And they laughed together.

Later, Belinda could not keep the tears from forming in her eyes as she listened to the two young people make their promises. Amy Jo was no longer theirs. She belonged to Ryan now, perhaps at the same moment that Melissa, too, was repeating her marriage vows.

It was a lonely and rather subdued Belinda who went up to bed that night after the festivities of the day were all over and the wedded couple had left for their honeymoon trip, home to their West.

Belinda wondered who would shed the most tears that night, she or Kate. She knew they all would miss Amy Jo, their "vibrant" one, something awful.

NINE

An Accident

Belinda for sure had missed Amy Jo while she was out west, but it had always been with the hope she would be coming home soon. Now Amy Jo was making a home of her own many miles away.

Melissa, too! she mourned. *And all at the same time!*

"I know ya miss the girls," Marty commented to Belinda. "Maybe Luke could get along without ya for a few weeks an' ya could go on out ta see 'em."

"Mama," Belinda reminded her, "a few months ago I woulda jumped at the chance. I was so lonely for them both, and I'da given anything to be able to see them. But not now. Now they're both new brides. They wouldn't want me hangin' around. Besides, I would feel out of place. It's not the same as it used to be. We wouldn't have the same—the same closeness as before."

Marty nodded her agreement at Belinda's assessment. It wasn't the same anymore.

Belinda looked about at her world. Why did things have to keep changing? Spring, without slowing down even for a minute, was turning to summer and then would come fall. In the fall little Thomas would be off to school. The next thing they knew it would be Aaron's turn—and then wee Ruthie's. Already she was sitting up alone, reaching for things, and pulling herself up in her crib. She had scarcely even been a baby at all.

Things had seemed so simple, so secure when Belinda had been a child going to school and sharing girlish games with Amy Jo, her constant companion. But life went on and no amount of "digging in one's heels" seemed to slow it down.

Belinda thought she had never been so lonely in her life. She would have had a most difficult time of it had she not been so busy. Luke was right—they certainly needed another doctor in the town.

The thought of another doctor immediately reminded Belinda of Jackson. What was Jackson like now? He had been a nice young fellow when they had been schoolmates. Was it possible that after all this time she might feel drawn to him? Belinda allowed herself a few minutes of imagining and then sharply rebuked herself—by now Jackson likely had another girl. *Perhaps he's even married,* she told herself with a shake of her head.

But Belinda didn't really think that Jackson had married. She saw his mama every Sunday at church, and Mrs. Brown spoke often of her son and his medical career—she had never mentioned anything about his marrying or even having a young lady, to Belinda's knowledge. Belinda decided to push the thoughts of Jackson aside and think instead about Rand.

Rand dropped by occasionally, and in Belinda's loneliness she welcomed his company. The little town seemed so confining and the beloved farm home so very lonely. Rand was awfully busy, working from sunup to sunset every day of the week except Sunday, and there was very little time for him to make calls. He had been to the Davises for Sunday dinner on a few occasions, but Belinda hesitated to offer an invitation too often lest he get the wrong idea.

When summer had turned to fall, Rand stopped by one evening and suggested a walk. Belinda was only too glad for the diversion. He apologized for his busyness and asked Belinda how her days had been filled.

"'Ills an' spills,'" Belinda responded. "That's what Luke calls it. Sickness and accidents. That's about all I see or do."

Rand looked thoughtful. "Is nursin' losin' some of its charm?" he inquired.

Belinda flushed. "No. No, not really. Fact is, I don't know how I'd ever bear livin' without it. I'm jest . . . jest restless, I guess."

"Still missin' Amy Jo?"

Belinda nodded. She didn't trust her voice.

"Maybe you've outgrown nursin'," said Rand. "Maybe it's time fer ya to take on a new challenge."

"Like what?" asked Belinda innocently.

"I can think of one," admitted Rand. When Belinda did not question him, he went on slowly, "But I promised myself thet I wouldn't speak of it yet. Not till I have this Kirby house finished and the cash in the bank."

Rand's statement puzzled Belinda, but her attention was captured by the Kirby house. "Mrs. Kirby finally got worked out jest what she wants?"

"I've been buildin' on it fer the past two weeks."

Belinda smiled as she imagined the excitement of watching something take shape under one's hands. "Oh, I'd love to see it sometime. Could I?"

Rand laughed at her enthusiasm. "I'd love to show ya," he promised, "but not yet. There's not much to see now. But jest as soon as I have somethin' to show, I'll give ya the grand tour—how's thet?"

Belinda smiled her thanks in anticipation. *Jest think of havin' your own house,* her thoughts raced. *Melissa and Amy Jo both have their own. . . .*

"Dan likes working with ya," she said, to slow down her imaginings.

"He's good," said Rand. "Fer a fella so young, he catches on real fast. An' he isn't afraid of work, either."

They had reached Luke's front gate. Belinda stood silently gazing at the night sky. She was about to say that she should go in, but she lingered, enjoying the lovely evening and the company.

Rand surprised her by reaching for her hand. "I'm sorry I've been so busy," he said softly. "Once I git a house or two built an' git some cash on hand, I can slow down some."

"I understand," said Belinda, touched that he would care about her loneliness. He was really very kind.

"Could we go for a drive on Sunday?" asked Rand, and Belinda assured him she would enjoy that.

"Should I come out to the farm to get ya in the afternoon, an' bring ya back to town?"

Belinda thought quickly and said that would work fine.

"See ya then," Rand whispered, lifting her fingers to his lips before releasing her hand. Then he was gone, his long strides taking him quickly toward the boardinghouse.

Belinda stood watching him go, her heart fluttering and bewilderment on her face. She looked down at her slender fingers as though expecting his kiss to show there, and her breath caught in a little gasp. What might that Sunday drive hold for her, she wondered. She opened the gate quietly and thoughtfully made her way up the walk.

But it turned out that drive was not to be.

After the morning service that Sunday, the family gathered at Clark and Marty's for dinner. Nandry's Mary and Jane had both married and now had homes of their own, and on this Sunday Mary was with her Jim's family, and Jane was down with a bad cold. So Belinda was the only girl there. The boys played their games in the yard as usual and the men talked on the back veranda until the call for dinner.

Belinda was about to give the signal when there was a commotion in the yard. Someone was running and there were frantic calls and yells of "Come quick! Come quick!"

"What is it?" Belinda heard Clark call, and young John screamed back in fright, "The bull's got Abe. Quick! He'll kill 'im. Quick!"

Clare was on his feet in a flash. The bull was a new one to the farm and no one knew his temperament. All the youngsters had been warned to stay away from his pen until he was declared safe. Now Clare was running toward the barnyard with Arnie and Luke right behind him.

Belinda heard the farm dogs barking and the cattle bawling. The whole place seemed to be in an uproar.

"Grab a pitchfork!" Clare shouted over his shoulder, and Luke veered toward the barn to comply.

Clare flung himself over the bullpen fence. Belinda could see nothing more after he entered the corral, but she could hear shouts and dogs barking and angry bellows from the bull.

"Oh, dear God, no," Belinda heard someone say beside her and realized that her mother had joined her on the veranda, her eyes fixed on the fence beyond.

"Mama, go back in," warned Belinda.

But Marty held her ground, and soon Kate and Anne had joined her. "What is it?" Kate choked out.

Belinda could not answer. Her eyes on the bullpen, she prayed that Clare would be there in time. Arnie, too, had climbed the fence to face the enraged bull, and Luke was running toward them, pitchfork in hand.

It was Arnie who came back over the wooden fence, the limp form of his young son in his arms, while Clare and the dogs distracted the bull. Only when Luke challenged the bull with the pitchfork did he break away from Clare and run bellowing toward the far end of the pasture.

Dinner was forgotten as Abe was placed on the living room sofa and a white-faced doctor uncle bent over him, checking his vital signs and feeling for broken bones.

Belinda could see that Clare, too, needed a doctor, but he waved her aside and lifted the rifle from the back porch.

"I won't have a critter on the place that endangers children," he muttered through stiff lips, and a few moments later they heard the crack of the gun.

Arnie sat silent, head in his hands and his shoulders shaking. He could not bear even to look at Abe.

"He's dead," he kept murmuring. "I know he's dead."

There was too much happening for Belinda to sort it all out. Youngsters were wailing, women were crying, grown men were trembling with the tragedy.

Then Belinda's training and experience as a nurse suddenly took over. Luke needed her. This was an emergency. She was supposed to know how to act in an emergency.

True, it had never been a loved one before. That made it so different. She remembered many years before when she had heard Luke say that it was always so much harder when it was a child, and that he hoped and prayed he would never need to tend one of his own family.

And now Abe lay deathly white and blood-spattered, and Luke would need to fight with all he knew to try to save him. Belinda braced her shoulders, wiped away her tears, and steeled herself to join him.

Luke's hand was still on the boy's pulse. Belinda could not voice the question she knew she should ask, but Luke sensed her presence and, without looking up, spoke to her in a low voice. "We need to get him to town. He needs attention immediately. I have nothing here. He shouldn't be moved, but we have no choice. He's in bad shape, Belinda."

"Have ya . . . have ya . . . found where he's hurt?"

"He has some broken ribs. I hope his lungs are okay, but I'm worried. His left arm is badly broken. His neck and back seem all right, thank God."

Belinda looked down at the ashen face of her nephew. It all seemed so unreal—like a nightmare.

"Clare needs some tendin', too," she said, "but he wouldn't stop fer me to check him. I don't know where he's hurt, but I saw blood, and his shirt is all torn and dirty and—" Suddenly the tears were streaming again, and Belinda wanted to throw herself into her mother's arms and let the sobs shake her body. She fought hard to control herself and finally managed to stifle the flow.

"I'll tell Pa we need the team," she said to Luke and turned back to the family members who crowded in about them, hankies to white faces and tears flowing.

"We need to get him to town," Belinda said as calmly as she could. "Luke has nothin' here."

"Then he's . . . he's still . . ." sobbed Anne, unable to finish her question, and Belinda reached out a hand to ease her into a chair.

"He's hurt . . . bad," Belinda said honestly, "but we'll do all we can."

It was a long trip into town. Clare drove the team, brushing off any questions about his own condition. Anne had been so distraught that Arnie had left her in Marty's care. Belinda prayed silently all the way as she sat beside the boy on the floor of the wagon, his father on the other side, holding his hand. She knew Luke was praying, too, and that those at the farm would be doing the same. Abe roused on the way and cried out because of the intense pain, then slipped into unconsciousness again. Belinda's heart nearly broke to hear Arnie's sobs.

At last Clare pulled the team up before the doctor's residence, and Luke and Arnie gently carried the youngster in to the surgery table. Luke carefully went over the young boy once more. Though the ribs were broken, Luke thanked God that there was very little blood showing on the young boy's lips. Perhaps the internal injuries were not too great. A careful check of his pulse and breathing told Luke he had not gone into shock.

Luke administered drugs and, with Belinda assisting him, set the mangled arm the best he could. He let Arnie and Clare in to see the boy before sending them back to the farm with the latest news of his condition. Then began the long vigil.

Abe was in and out of consciousness. When he awoke he murmured pleas for his mother, and Anne was soon there to whisper soothing words through trembling lips. Luke did not want Abe stirring because of the broken ribs and so kept the boy sedated much of the time. Family members came and went quietly, suffering with Abe as their hearts ached for his parents.

But eventually the boy began to improve, and by the time a week had passed, Luke was gently propping him up with pillows to discourage pneumonia. By the end of two weeks the family was confident that Abe would get better. He still had a long way to go, but daily they prayed their thanks to God that his life was spared.

Clare had a multitude of bumps and bruises, but miraculously no broken bones. He said the farm dogs took the brunt of the bull's charges, finally distracting the animal from him.

When Abe was well enough to be moved on home, Luke and Belinda were able to again get a full night's sleep. But it wasn't over yet. Luke's doctor eyes told him that. He would need to have a chat with Arnie— and how he dreaded it.

TEN

Concern

Luke watched young Abe closely, making regular house calls to Arnie's. He said he was pleased with the boy's general progress. Still, Belinda had a strange feeling that Luke was looking for something and was not completely satisfied with how things were going. She didn't quite dare ask him about it, afraid of what he would say.

Arnie hardly let Abe out of his sight. He was constantly reminding the lad to be careful, to watch his step, to slow down when running. Belinda even wondered if all Arnie's worrying and fussing over him might turn his son into a sissy.

"What was Abe doin' in thet bullpen anyway?" she asked Dack one weekend when she was home. "Didn't he hear Clare say that everyone was to stay away from thet bull?"

"Our ball went in there, an' Abe thought he could jest climb in and out real quick an' no one would ever know," Dack explained, looking very serious.

Belinda shook her head. "When adults make rules, they have reasons," she said. "Abe is sufferin' because of his disobedience—and the rest of the family has suffered, too, because of him. Besides thet, yer pa lost an expensive bull."

"I know," said Dack, his head lowered. Then his face came up. "But it wasn't my fault, Aunt Belinda. Honest."

Belinda reached out to ruffle the mop of red hair. "I'm not blamin' you, Dack," she said. "And I shouldn't scold ya. I jest don't want ya to forget the lesson."

Rand had met the farm wagon that Sunday on its frantic rush to town, and Belinda had quickly explained the circumstances. He of course understood their ride would have to be postponed, and a few weeks later made the same arrangements for the coming Sunday. She bundled up warmly against the brisk fall wind and settled herself on the high buggy seat beside him. He explained that he was borrowing the buggy until he had enough put aside to buy one of his own.

"Where would ya like to go?" he asked her.

"I can't think of anyplace in particular," Belinda responded. There was really nothing that scenic in the area. Belinda had seen the neighborhood farms dozens of times. She was not aware of anything new unless some farmer had put up a new hog barn or machine shed. True, the fall leaves could be beautiful, but most of the color of the fall already lay strewn over the pastures and fields.

"We could drive into town and see the Kirby house," he suggested.

"Is it ready?" she asked in surprise.

"No, not finished yet. But at least there is enough of it fer ya to get some idea of what it will be."

"Oh, let's!" cried Belinda.

"Yer sure ya'll be warm enough?" he wondered.

She assured him that she would and the team was turned toward town.

"How's Abe?" asked Rand, and Belinda told him the boy seemed to be recovering nicely. Their talk continued with little bits of news from town and community. Belinda noticed again that Rand was an easy person to talk to.

When they reached the building site, Rand tied the horses securely and gave Belinda a helping hand down over the buggy wheel.

"It's a bit awkward to get into the house yet," he admitted. "I was goin' to wait until the steps were in place before bringin' ya on over."

Belinda laughed. "I'll manage fine," she said, eyeing the makeshift stepping blocks.

The house was bigger than Belinda had imagined. She wandered through the main-floor rooms, trying to picture in her mind's eye what they would look like when they were completed and furnished, with a family living in them. *It must be fun to have a house,* she mused. For a moment she almost envied Mrs. Kirby.

"This must be the parlor," she commented as she walked. "And the dining room and kitchen through there, with a pantry over there. But what's this?"

"Mrs. Kirby wants a mornin' room," answered Rand.

"A mornin' room? I've never heard of such."

"All the finer homes have them—accordin' to Mrs. Kirby. The ladies of the house sit in them and do needle work while the maids clean the rest of the house."

Belinda looked at Rand in surprise. "Is Mrs. Kirby going to have herself maids?"

Rand laughed. "Not thet I know of—but she will have her mornin' room."

Belinda smiled. "Maybe it'll give her a sense of well-being," she offered, feeling she should defend Mrs. Kirby for her little quirk.

"Maybe so," responded Rand.

"And what's this?" asked Belinda, indicating another room off the main entry.

"Well," smiled Rand, "tit for tat. Iffen Mrs. Kirby was to git her mornin' room, then Mr. Kirby insisted on a library."

"My," said Belinda. "It will be a grand house, won't it?"

Belinda's eyes traveled upward. There was no stairway to lead to the second floor, only a ladder leaning against the opening. Belinda did not think she should attempt it in her Sunday skirts.

"How many bedrooms?" she asked.

"Four—and a nursery."

"I didn't know the Kirbys had any family thet young," Belinda noted.

"They haven't. Their youngest is eight or nine. But I guess it didn't sound right to Mrs. Kirby to have a fine house without a proper nursery. Maybe she'll use it for a sewin' room or somethin'."

"My! It must be nice to have so many rooms thet ya can have one jest fer sewin' in," marveled Belinda.

She continued her wanderings from room to room, running her hand over the smoothness of polished wood or studying the delicate colors of stained-glass inserts over the windows.

"It's goin' to be one grand house," she said with awe in her voice. "Mrs. Kirby is a lucky woman."

She wasn't conscious of the high praise she was giving to the builder, but she did notice Rand seemed to be pleased with her comments.

"I'd like to see it again—when ya get nearer to bein' finished," said Belinda. "Do ya think the Kirbys would mind?"

Rand smiled. "Guess it's mine fer the time bein'," he said. "I'll be glad to show it to ya as many times as ya wanna see it." He took Belinda's hand to help her down the improvised steps. Belinda thought about it later and realized her hand in his felt natural, not awkward.

Belinda was in the office when Arnie brought Abe in for another checkup. His uncle Luke looked him over thoroughly and declared the ribs as good as new. He then sent Abe in to have cookies and milk with Thomas and Aaron. There was nothing unusual about that, so Belinda was unprepared when Luke pulled a chair up beside Arnie and haltingly began, "Arnie—there's something we need to talk about."

Arnie's eyes swung to Luke's face, and Belinda could read fearful questions there.

"He's not healin'?" Arnie asked quickly. "But you said—"

"He's healing. He's doing fine," Luke interrupted.

"Then what's the problem?" Arnie demanded.

"The ribs are great, the lungs just fine. All the bumps and bruises are completely healed . . . but I'm worried about the arm."

"Hasn't it healed?"

"It's healed . . . sure. But it was a bad break . . . and I didn't have

the equipment to set it properly. It needed care that I couldn't give
and—"

"What are ya tryin' to say?" Arnie interrupted. "Yer talkin' riddles.
Ya set it, didn't ya?"

"I set it . . . like I told you. I did the best I could under the circumstances, but—"

"What circumstances?"

"That arm needed the care that only a large hospital could give to
make—"

"Then why didn't ya say thet before?" Arnie's voice was harsh with
emotion. "Why'd ya let us think everything was goin' to be jest fine?"

"Arnie," said Luke patiently, "Abe was badly hurt. I was concerned
about saving his *life*! I knew at the time that the arm needed special
care—better care than I could give it in my simple office, but I did the
best I could here because Abe was not in any condition to be moved
to a hospital at the time. The trip might have killed him. Can you understand that?"

Arnie nodded slowly. "Well, it's done now," he said, working hard
on swallowing. "Guess we made out okay. Abe is alive an' seems fine,
an' iffen the arm has healed all right—"

"But it hasn't," replied Luke carefully. "That's what I'm trying to
tell you. Abe still needs special care for that arm."

"But ya said it's healed."

"It is," Luke answered slowly, "as far as the break itself."

"Then what needs doin'?"

"It's healing crooked, Arnie. Crooked."

Arnie just sat staring into space, trying to understand the words.

"What's thet mean?" he asked finally.

"It means if it doesn't get treated properly, the arm will get worse.
Abe won't have full use of it. In time it might not function well at all."

Belinda looked first at Arnie and then at Luke. So that was what had
been bothering her doctor brother.

"What . . . what can be done?" asked Arnie, his voice tight. "It's
already set."

"That's not a big problem. They rebreak it. The only thing is, the sooner it is done, the more successful it will be."

Arnie swung about to face Luke, his eyes dark with anger. "Are ya suggestin' thet I take my son to some city hospital and put 'im through his pain all over again—on *purpose*?"

For a moment Luke was shocked to silence.

"Well, forget it," rasped out Arnie. "The boy has suffered quite enough. Iffen you'da set it properlike in the first place—"

But Arnie stopped short. The expression on his face said he knew he wasn't being fair. Luke had done his best. He had saved the life of his son. Arnie looked as though he wished he could take back his words.

"Arnie," said Luke gently, "I don't blame you for feeling that way. Honest, I don't. And I wouldn't even suggest such a thing if there was any other way. But I've been watching that arm. It's getting worse. It needs to be fixed and the sooner the better. I know a good doctor. He does amazing things in corrective bone surgery. He would take Abe's case, I'm sure he would, and there's a good chance—a *good* chance that the arm would heal properly—be almost as good as new. This doctor—"

"I said no." Arnie's voice was low but the tone unmistakable. "I won't put him through all thet."

Luke took a deep breath. "If you don't," he said firmly, "you'll have a crippled boy."

The tears ran down Arnie's cheeks. He brushed them roughly aside. "He's been through enough pain already," he insisted. "What kind of pa would I be to put him through more?"

"A loving pa," Luke said, laying a hand on Arnie's arm, his voice little more than a whisper.

Arnie spun around to face him. "You doctors!" he cried, choking on his words. "All ya wanna do is play God. Ya don't think nothin' 'bout the pain ya cause. Ya jest gotta fix, fix, fix. Well, I won't have them experimentin' on my son jest to git glory in the doin', ya hear? The matter is closed. I never wanna hear of it again. An' one more thing, I don't want ya sayin' a word of this to Anne. She's suffered enough havin' to watch her boy fight to live. It would jest make things worse. Ya hear?" And Arnie slammed out the door, calling for Abe as he went.

Belinda took a deep breath and looked over at Luke. He stood leaning against the wall with his head down, his face in his hands, and he was weeping.

ELEVEN

Sorrows

Belinda could sense the heaviness in Luke as he went about his daily medical rounds. She longed to share his burden in some way. She knew Luke had done his best, but she also knew he felt his best hadn't been good enough, that he had failed a child—and, even worse, a family member.

One wintry day when the foul weather seemed to be keeping away all but the emergency cases, Belinda decided to broach the subject of young Abe to her doctor brother. She knew there was no way for her to ease the pain Luke was feeling, but she felt that even talking about it might help some.

"Have ya talked to Pa and Ma about Abe?" she asked softly.

Luke raised his eyes from the column of figures he was adding. He shook his head, his face thoughtful.

"Do ya think ya should?"

"I don't know," Luke hesitated. "Some days I think I've just got to talk to them and on other days . . . I don't know. It might just make things worse."

"Worse how?"

"Arnie already avoids me."

Belinda nodded in agreement. She had noticed it also the last time the family had gathered for Sunday dinner. Quiet and morose, Arnie hadn't entered in with the usual man talk and good-natured banter. In fact, Arnie seemed to have retreated from the warmth of the entire family. Marty had noticed it, too, and worried that he might be coming down with something and should be taking a tonic.

"Abe seemed chipper enough," Belinda finally commented after the silence.

Luke was still deep in thought. He turned his eyes back to Belinda as she spoke.

"He's chipper," he responded, "but he's not using that arm well. If you watch him, he handles almost everything with his other hand."

Belinda hadn't noticed, but then she hadn't been as attentive as Luke. Thinking back, she realized now that Luke no doubt was right.

"What happened, Luke?" she asked softly.

"One of the bones that was broken was in the elbow and it was pushed out of proper position. I figure that the bull must have caught the arm between his head and the hard-packed earth and twisted as he ground it. You've seen certain critters do that. They aren't content to just butt things. They grind at them with those rock-hard heads of theirs."

Yes, Belinda had seen them do that.

"Well, this bone was dislocated, so to speak, as well as broken, and I couldn't get it to line up properly. I hoped—and prayed—that it might adjust itself as it healed, but deep inside I knew it would really take a miracle for the bone to align on its own." Luke sighed deeply, his eyes troubled. "Well, this time we didn't get our miracle," he stated simply.

"And ya think they can do thet in the city—set it right?"

"I'm sure they could. They have a team of doctors and all the latest equipment. I'm sure they could do a good job for the boy. I got to watch a doctor do a very similar procedure when I was in training. I couldn't believe what he accomplished."

"Is it . . . is it terribly painful?" went on Belinda.

"There's pain . . . of course. After all, it is a break. And also surgery. But they have good sedatives. Good medication for pain. And the main thing is that the patient is whole again. It's worth the additional suffering for a while if Abe gets his arm back."

Belinda understood Luke's reasoning. If it were his son, he would do all he could to give him a whole and usable body. But this wasn't Luke's son. And Arnie had never been able to stand to see suffering of any kind. He shrank back from it, hating it for its very sake. Arnie would find it hard to make a decision that would cause suffering to anyone, especially his child, even if the purpose was to bring healing.

"What happens if nothin' is done?" Belinda continued.

Luke shook his head. "It'll get worse and worse. He may lose use of the arm entirely as time goes on. It might not grow with the rest of the body. Might even begin to shrivel some. At best, the elbow will be stiff and unbending. To say it simply—the boy will have a crippled arm."

Belinda cringed. She remembered, years ago, seeing such a boy. She had gone to another town with her ma and pa, and they were riding down the street in an open carriage when they were halted in the street for some reason. Belinda had looked about her while the horses fidgeted and impatiently tossed their heads.

At first she had enjoyed looking in the windows of the nearby shops and watching the people in their colorful garments as they hurried back and forth on the sidewalk. And then her eyes had landed on a young boy on the street corner selling papers. In his one hand he held high the latest edition as he called out the headline to the passersby and urged them to buy their copy. But it was the other hand that drew Belinda's attention. The whole arm was twisted off to the side in a strange way, the hand small and the fingers bent.

She had been shocked at the sight and unable to understand why the boy's arm looked like that. Even at her young age her heart was tender with sympathy. She had tugged on her pa's coat sleeve and pointed a finger at the young boy, asking what was wrong with him.

Concern in his eyes, her pa had gently pulled her arm down and turned to look at her intently.

"He's crippled, Belinda," he had said softly. "I don't know how or why, but his arm's been damaged somehow. Like my leg was damaged," and he tapped on his wooden one. Belinda stared up at her pa with wide eyes. She was so accustomed to his handicap that she didn't even think about it.

At just that moment three young boys came around the corner. Belinda saw them stop before the newspaper boy. *Maybe they're goin' to help him,* she thought. But they began to dance around, calling out such things as, "Claw hand, claw hand," and "Crooked arm!" Then they had snatched his papers and begun throwing them about on the street. Clark saw it all, too, and before Belinda could understand what was happening, her pa had jumped from the carriage. Seeing him coming, the boys turned and ran from the scene.

It had taken Clark many minutes to help the young lad gather his papers back in the stack, and then Belinda had seen him slip the young boy a bill, pick up a paper, and join the family, his jaw set and his eyes filled with anger.

By then Belinda was in tears, and Clark reached out to draw her close while Marty fished in her handbag for a fresh handkerchief, clucking all the time over the injustice of it all.

"Why . . . why did they do thet . . . be so mean?" Belinda had quavered out.

Shaking his head, Clark said, "I don't know, little one. I don't know," he soothed. "Our world is full of unkindness. It wasn't meant to be . . . but it is. Thet's why it's so important that we, as God's children, never add to the grief of any of His creatures. He put us here to love an' help an' heal, an' we need to be extry careful thet we're a doin' thet. Not hurtin' or harmin' our fellowmen."

But Belinda still was unable to understand why the boys would taunt and tease the boy, and she could not erase the scene from her young mind. There followed a time when she had bad dreams about it and would waken in the night crying, and Marty would come to her bed and comfort her.

And now . . . now their own Abe was destined to be crippled. Belinda felt she understood Luke's concern. Surely . . . surely there was something to be done about it . . . some way to make Arnie see reason.

"Well, I think we have no choice," she said firmly. "Ma and Pa have to know. They are the only ones who can talk some sense into Arnie."

Belinda placed the sterilized instruments in a sheath of clean gauze and returned them to the cabinet.

"But Arnie would be angry . . . I know he would," Luke said thoughtfully.

Belinda nodded. "Fer a time. But surely in the end he would see thet we've done the right thing. Surely . . . surely when young Abe is . . . is whole again, he will be thankful thet we persisted." Belinda lowered herself to a chair near Luke and allowed herself a few moments of deep thought. "It's a terrible thing to be handicapped if it doesn't really need to be," she finished sadly.

Luke lifted his pencil back to the paper before him. He shook his head and sighed again deeply. "Maybe you're right," he said wearily. "Maybe I shouldn't give up so easily. If only there was some way to do it without hurting Arnie further."

Strange! mused Belinda. *It's Abe's accident, Abe's pain, but it's Arnie who's sufferin' the most.*

"It's too cold for you to be riding horseback," Luke said on Friday afternoon after the last patient had been sent on his way. "I'll get the team and drive you home."

Belinda did not protest. The buggy wasn't a lot warmer, but if she were to take Copper, by the time she reached the farm her feet and hands would be numb and her cheeks tingling. Besides, this would give Luke an opportunity to speak to Clark and Marty, and Belinda was convinced that such a talk was a must.

The two rode most of the way in silence. They were both weary and had already discussed the main things on their minds—and besides, they felt comfortable with silence. Now and then, they would discuss something briefly and then fall silent again.

Marty was at the door to meet them.

"My, my!" she exclaimed. "I was worryin' some 'bout ya comin' on

horseback, but Pa said ya'd jest stay on at Luke's fer the weekend."
Belinda had often stayed in town for one reason or another.

Marty hurried about the big farm kitchen, putting on the coffeepot
and slicing fresh bread for sandwiches.

Clark came in from the barn to join them at the table. He gently
massaged his injured leg to take the sting of the cold from it without
attracting too much attention. Luke, as usual, noticed but made no
comment.

Belinda knew without Luke's saying so that he would talk to his
ma and pa about Arnie and little Abe. She didn't particularly wish to
be involved in the conversation, knowing it would be difficult for all
involved. Excusing herself "to change into a housedress," she left the
kitchen and climbed the stairs to her room.

She spent some time changing from her office clothing, puttering
around tidying her dresser, and straightening a few drawers, and at last
she went back down to the kitchen. All during this time she had been
praying for her family.

Luke and her parents were still seated at the table when Belinda
entered the room. The coffee cups were empty and pushed to the side.
Belinda read concern and distress in the three faces. Marty's eyes were
red from weeping, and she held a damp handkerchief in her hands,
abstractedly twisting it back and forth. Clark's hand rested gently on
the worn family Bible, and Belinda knew they had been drawing counsel
from its pages.

Belinda poured herself a glass of milk and joined them at the table.

"We've got some money laid aside," Clark was saying softly, "an'
we'd be glad ta help. I s'pose such an operation would cost a great deal."

Clark reached out and took Marty's hand, and Belinda saw them
exchange silent messages—Clark seeking her agreement and her giving
it without hesitation.

"It would cost, to be sure—the trip, the hotel, the surgery," Luke
answered them. "It would cost. But Arnie didn't mention money. That's
not what's holding him back. If he was convinced it was the right thing
to do, he wouldn't stop to consider the money. He'd take Abe tomorrow.
Even if he had to sell his farm to do it," said Luke.

Clark nodded. They all knew Arnie would do that.

"We jest have to convince 'im thet there's more'n one kind of pain," Marty said thoughtfully. "Abe might suffer far more from a useless arm than from the operation."

Belinda wondered if her mother was remembering the young lad on the street corner.

Luke suddenly looked at the kitchen clock and stood to go. "I've got to get home before it gets dark," he said. "Promised the boys we'd play some Snakes 'n Ladders tonight."

"We'll talk to Arnie," Clark promised. "First chance we git, we'll talk to 'im."

Luke nodded, looking satisfied with that. Surely Arnie would listen to his parents, whom he loved and respected. He shrugged into his coat and hurried out to his team.

Clark and Marty did talk to Arnie. Anne was there, as well, and she was shocked to hear about the condition of her son's arm. Arnie had said nothing to her.

But though Clark and Marty urged Arnie to take Luke's advice, Arnie held firmly to his position. His young son, just a child, had suffered enough. His own father should not put him through any more. Besides, who knew for sure if the operation would even be successful. Luke himself had admitted that there wasn't one-hundred-percent certainty. What if Abe went through the pain and ended up with no improvement?

Clark and Marty returned home with heavy hearts.

The next Sunday only Anne and the boys were in church, and she offered no explanation. Afterward she simply said that they would not be joining the rest of the family for Sunday dinner.

The pain in Marty's heart grew worse. Besides the anguish over her grandson's arm, her family was no longer a close-knit, openly loving unit. She wiped tears and tried to swallow the lump in her throat as she dished up the fried chicken. Where would it all end?

TWELVE

A New Kind of Suffering

The situation did not get better. Arnie was not back in church during the next Sundays. Anne came with the boys a few times, and then she, too, began to miss more often than she attended.

"Surely they will all be there fer Christmas Sunday," Marty said hopefully to Clark, but she was wrong. Again they were missing, and word came through Clare's children from school that Arnie's family wouldn't be coming home for Christmas celebrations. They would be sharing Christmas dinner with Anne's folks.

The pastor called on them but was given no real explanation for the change. It seemed that things just kept "croppin' up" on Sundays. Then Arnie resigned from the church board.

Hoping that *something* would help, Clark and Marty called at the farm. They were welcomed openly by the children, civilly by Anne, and reluctantly by Arnie. After a short and strained conversation over teacups, they left for home, their hearts even heavier than before. There seemed nothing more to do but wait and pray.

Marty's heart ached as she felt the burden of it. "I never woulda dreamed," she confessed to Belinda, ". . . I never woulda dreamed it could happen to us. Ya hear of such things in families—rifts thet break a family apart, but I never woulda dreamed it could be *our* family."

"Do . . . do the rest know?" asked Belinda soberly. "Missie and Ellie and Clae?"

"I finally wrote 'em," Marty confided. "I waited an' waited, hopin' an' prayin' thet things would . . . would heal. Thet Arnie would change . . . but I finally decided thet they should know." Marty stopped to blow her nose. "They were the hardest letters I ever had ta write in my entire life," she continued, "even worse'n when I had to write on home 'bout yer pa."

Belinda nodded.

"Clare went to see Arnie, too—did ya know?"

Belinda hadn't, but she wasn't surprised.

"It was way back 'fore Christmas. He didn't git nowhere, either."

Marty stopped to think back over the exchange between the two boys.

"What did Arnie say?" asked Belinda quietly.

"Said lots of things. Mean things. Things thet Arnie—our old Arnie— never woulda said."

Marty brushed at more tears.

"He said it was no one else's business. Said he and Anne loved Abe the way he is—crippled in others' eyes or no. Said Luke had no business bein' a doctor iffen he . . . he couldn't even proper-set an arm." Marty's voice broke in a sob, and the tears ran uncontrolled down her cheeks.

"An' then he said thet the whole thing was really Clare's fault. He never shoulda had him an unsafe bull in the first place."

Belinda blinked back her own tears. It was hard to believe that her own brother—tender, sensitive Arnie—could say such cruel things. He had always been so loving . . . so caring. *Arnie must be deeply hurt to have changed so much . . . so completely,* she told herself inwardly.

"I've never felt so heavyhearted in all my life," admitted Marty. "To see those I love so much hurtin' and not speakin' is jest more'n I can bear."

"How's Pa doin'?" asked Belinda.

"Never saw yer pa suffer so. Even his leg didn't lay 'im as low as this has. His leg was jest . . . jest flesh an' bone . . . but this . . . this is . . . is flesh an' *blood,*" Marty sobbed again.

"How's Abe?" asked Belinda after a pause.

"The boys see 'im at school. Say he's fine. Jest fine . . . though he don't use thet arm much a'tall. They say it's beginnin' to twist off to the side some. Dack had 'im a fight over it last week. One of the other boys called Abe some name. Dack wouldn't even say what it was . . . but the teacher sent him home with a note to his pa an' ma, after givin' both fighters the strap."

Marty halted her account long enough to wipe her nose again.

"Clare went on over to the school an' had 'im a long talk with Mrs. Brown. Guess she was real nice 'bout it, but Dack has been warned no more fightin'."

Marty shook her head slowly. "Maybe we're in danger of takin' the family fer granted," she said. "When ya have it all together, lovin' an' supportin' one another, ya don't realize how blessed ya are. Iffen ya got yer family, then ya have most of what ya really need."

Belinda wiped her eyes and rose from her chair. "I hear Pa out on the porch. I'll bring 'im a cup of coffee to chase away the winter chill."

Marty nodded, but she knew it would take more than hot coffee for the chill on his soul.

Marty finally decided to take matters into her own hands. On the first day the cold let up some, she asked Clark for the team, bundled up warmly, and set out for Arnie's. The boys were at school and Anne was alone in the kitchen when Marty arrived. Anne seemed genuinely pleased to see her mother-in-law and expressed sincerely how she had been missing their visits.

"Me too," Marty said frankly. "An' thet's exactly why I'm here. It's jest not right fer a disagreement to keep the family apart. The boys need their cousins . . . an' their aunts and uncles . . . an' their grandma an' grandpa, too. An' we need them . . . an' you an' Arnie. Ain't right or natural fer a family to be apart like this."

Anne nodded, but she made no comment.

"I came to talk to my son," went on Marty. "Is he here?"

"He's at the barn," Anne said softly.

"Did he see me comin'?" asked Marty outright.

"I think maybe . . . he . . . he might. Yes, he did." Anne hung her head.

"Then I guess I'll jest have to go out to his barn," said Marty briskly, and she moved to put her coat back on.

"No. No, don't do that," Anne quickly responded. "I'll go. I'll go get Arnie . . . tell 'im you want to see 'im."

"Ya think . . . ?" Marty began and Anne nodded. Surely Arnie would have to agree to see his own mother.

Arnie did come. His face looked drawn, his expression distant, but he nodded agreeably while seeming to steel himself against whatever Marty had come to say.

He sat down at the table with her and accepted the cup of tea from Anne. Marty made small talk about the weather and the children and asked a few questions about his stock. Arnie appeared to relax some.

Marty reached out a hand and laid it on Arnie's. She had to be careful, very careful in what she said. She knew Arnie so well.

"Arnie," she said, and in spite of her resolve, the tears began to form in her eyes. "Arnie, you have always been the tenderest member of the family . . . have felt things the deepest . . . an' said the least. I . . . I know how the hurtin' of young Abe has brought ya deep pain. We have all suffered—we love the boy—but you have suffered the most."

Marty paused. Arnie's eyes were fastened on his cup, but he had not withdrawn his hand. Marty took courage and went on. "We miss ya, Arnie—you an' the kids—an' Anne. We need ya—as a family we need ya. It's jest not the same when yer not there. The family isn't . . . isn't whole anymore. We all feel it. It hurts. Real bad. It's not as God intended it to be."

Arnie stirred and Marty was afraid she was pressing too far . . . too fast. She withdrew her hand and sat silently for a moment. Then she said carefully, "We've pushed ya . . . an' we're sorry. We haven't been . . . been thoughtful of yer feelin's like we shoulda been. We know thet ya can't stand to see anyone ya love suffer."

Then Marty changed direction, her voice taking on a new lilt. "Well, we won't push anymore. We'll promise ya thet. Abe is a dear, good boy. We got no shame concernin' 'im jest the way he is. An' maybe thet arm will git better 'stead of worse. God has done such miracles before. But whether He chooses to heal our Abe or not won't make any difference to how we feel 'bout 'im. He's ours . . . an' we love 'im an' miss 'im."

Marty waited for some response on Arnie's part, but he said nothing. Anne was standing by her kitchen cupboard crying softly, silently.

"Would ya come back, Arnie?" Marty pleaded. "Would ya come back to yer family? To yer church? We love ya, Arnie. We need ya. Please. Please come home."

Marty's tears were flowing unashamedly as she made her plea, and suddenly Arnie's face convulsed, and he laid his head down on his arms and let the sobs shake his body. Marty leaned over to hold her broken son. She soothed and comforted and stroked his hair much as she had done when he had been a child. Then she kissed his cheek and slipped into her coat. She had done all she could.

Arnie did come back. He came to church the next Sunday, though he sat stiffly in the pew. The children were thrilled to be back, and Marty noticed a more peaceful look in Anne's eyes.

Arnie also joined the family at Clare's house for dinner. Marty had warned all of them that not one word should be said about the young Abe and his need for corrective surgery. Everyone was very cautious about the words they spoke—so much so that the conversation often lagged. At times the tension in the air was so heavy that one felt choked by it.

The family was back together—at least bodily. But it wasn't the same, not the same at all. They all tried so hard—too hard—to make things seem as they had always been. The chatter, the teasing, the concerns over one another's affairs—all meant to bring back the feeling of family—all failed miserably in doing so. There was a strain about it all that seemed to draw more attention to the fact that there was friction, not harmony, in the family circle. The unity had been broken. The bond had been weakened. They were not as they had been.

Marty talked to Clark about it on the short walk home. She longed for the old relationship to be restored, but she was at a loss as to how it could be done. She didn't have any answers, and there seemed to be so many troubling questions. Marty wept again as she walked.

Belinda, too, suffered under the strain of the family rift. It weighed heavily upon her as she went about her daily nursing duties. There were times when she wished she could get out from under it all, even for a brief season. She often thought of asking for some time off so she might go out west for a visit, but she always dismissed the idea. Luke needed her. It sounded like in just a few months they might get their new doctor, and then she would be free to take some time for herself. She would hang on until then.

Rand still called when he was free. He had taken Belinda to see the Kirby house on a number of occasions. Belinda thought it was beautiful and was amazed that Rand could build such a lovely home. Rand smiled at her praise, his eyes saying more than he dared to say in words.

Once the Kirbys were established in their new home, there was no longer that small diversion. Rand was busy working on another house for the town grocer but not nearly as grand as the Kirbys'.

Belinda got through the days as best she could, finding pleasure in the company of her young nephews and little Ruthie. *Children,* she often thought, *they seem to somehow put the world to rights again. If only we could be more like children.*

Belinda ticked off the long winter days one by one, looking forward to spring. But one morning the unexpected broke into the routine of their days. A message was sent from the local station that someone traveling the train had taken suddenly, seriously ill and the doctor should come at once. Luke left hurriedly, telling Belinda to prepare for the patient in his absence.

Belinda at once set about making up a bed on a cot in the surgery. She had no idea what the problem was or if the patient was male or female, young or old, but she did the best she could to be ready.

An older woman was rushed from the train to the surgery, lying quietly in the back of Tom Hammel's wagon. Belinda had never seen anyone quite like her before. Her clothing was very stylish, though the elaborate hat had been laid aside to accommodate the makeshift pillow. Her face was ashen in spite of powder and rouge. A fur wrap lay loosely about her shoulders. She looked to be tall and thin and very regal looking even in her present state, and Belinda felt herself quiver with excitement, in spite of her deep concern for the patient.

THIRTEEN

The Patient

For the next several days, Belinda's time was taken up with the careful nursing of the woman. Twice Luke feared they were losing her, but each time she managed to hang on to life. Her condition was diagnosed as a stroke, and Luke was concerned that there would be some lasting paralysis to her right side. Belinda hoped not, and daily as she nursed the sick woman she prayed that she might totally recover.

Three days later a gentleman arrived at their door. Abbie had answered the knock. Luke was out in the country making a house call, and Belinda was sitting with her patient. She could hear the conversation from the next room.

"Good day, madam," the man said properly, and Belinda could visualize him doffing his hat.

Then he continued. "I understand that Mrs. Virginia Stafford-Smyth is being cared for at this address."

"That's . . . that's right," responded Abbie. "She was brought in to us from the passing train." The name of the woman appeared on her luggage and was one of the few things they had managed to learn about her—that and her Boston address.

"I came to see her," said the man simply.

Abbie hesitated. "She's . . . she's very ill. My husband—the doctor—has not allowed visitors."

Belinda could not help but smile. No one in the small town even knew the woman, much less was interested in visiting her—however, Abbie was following Luke's usual orders in such circumstances.

The silence that followed alerted Belinda to the fact that Abbie might need some help. She checked her patient and rose from the side of the small cot in the already overcrowded little surgery.

"May I help you, sir?" she asked politely when she reached the door. "I'm Mrs. Stafford-Smyth's nurse."

"Oh yes," said the tall man, standing erect with his bowler hat firmly in gloved hands. He looked relieved to see someone with a position of authority.

"I'm Windsah. Mrs. Stafford-Smyth's butlah," he explained in precise eastern tones. "We received a telegram that she had been taken ill. I've come to take charge."

A *butler!* thought Belinda. *Whoever would have thought we'd ever see a real one way out here?* Excitement coursed through her, but she kept her professional demeanor and answered firmly, "Dr. Davis is in charge of Mrs. Stafford-Smyth at the present. I'm afraid ya will need his permission to see the patient. She's been very ill."

"Oh, deah!" said the man a bit impatiently. Belinda had never heard an accent like his before.

"I came all this way on that abominable train," he explained. "And now you say I can't see Madam."

"I'm sorry," said Belinda. "I'm sure the doctor will allow ya to as soon as he returns, but until then I'll have ta ask ya to be patient."

"Very well," agreed the man and lifted his bowler hat toward his bald pate. Then he hesitated and lowered it again. "I suppose there is accommodation for one in this town?"

"A hotel," responded Belinda. "Over three blocks and down Main Street."

"That little building called the Red Palace or some such thing?"

Belinda allowed the flicker of a smile. "The Rose Palace. Yes, that's the one."

"I noticed it on the way ovah," said the man. "It didn't appear to be much of a spot. Palace indeed!" He clicked his tongue in derision. "I suppose it shall have to do." Then he turned to go, placing his hat on his head as he did so.

Belinda stood looking after him, wondering about it all. After seeing the usual farmers and local townspeople as their patients, it seemed so very strange to be nursing a woman who had her own butler. And it seemed more strange that a butler should be coming to "take charge" of her. Where were her family members? Didn't they have time to look after their own?

But Belinda had little time to ponder it all. She turned back to the bedside of her patient.

"Mrs. Stafford-Smyth," she said softly. "Mrs. Stafford-Smyth, do ya hear me? Windsor was just here to see you. He has come all the way from Boston—yer home."

But as in the past there was no flickering of eyelash or indication that Mrs. Stafford-Smyth had heard.

"Keep talking to her," Luke had said. "Maybe one of these times we will break through." So as Belinda nursed her charge, she talked. But to this point there had been no response whatever.

When Luke arrived home he was told about the strange visitor and, after checking the patient, went to see if he could locate the man. Belinda was sure he would have no problem spotting him in the small inn.

He indeed had no problem and was soon home again, Butler Windsor in step beside him.

Luke brought the man directly in to see the patient, and Belinda stepped aside to allow him access. He bent over her solicitously, and Belinda saw his face drain of color.

"She is in a bad way, isn't she?" he said in a hoarse whisper.

He straightened up, shaking his head. "I had hoped the telegram was exaggerated."

He then looked around the room, his eyes taking in the cabinets for medications and instruments, the spotless table that served as Luke's surgical table, the two high stools, the small desk and one oak chair and the corner basket where waste materials were gathered. He looked back again at the cot with its snowy white sheets and woolen blanket.

"Oh, deah me," he murmured. "Madam shouldn't be in a place like this."

Surprised at his own frankness, he hastened to explain. "Whenever Madam has been ill, she's always been in a hospital—in her own private room."

"There is no hospital in our little town, I'm afraid," explained Luke. "This is the best we have to offer."

"How beastly inconvenient!" the man exclaimed, and Belinda turned to hide her smile.

"She should nevah have gone on this trip to begin with," he persisted, "but she would have her own way. Madam can be so stubborn at times." He shook his head in exasperation as though he were speaking of a wayward child.

"Well, nothing to be done about it now but to make the best of it, I warrant."

He turned back to Mrs. Stafford-Smyth, his face showing his concern. "How long did you say she has been like this?" he asked.

"She was brought to us on Tuesday," Luke informed the man. "She had taken ill on the train and they stopped to deliver her to me."

"And she was like this from the beginning?" he asked further.

Luke nodded his head. "There has been very little change," he offered.

"Beastly!" said the man again.

As Belinda slipped from the room, she heard Luke begin to explain Mrs. Stafford-Smyth's condition to the butler and heard his tongue-clicking in return. He was a funny fellow, but he certainly did seem genuinely concerned about the elderly woman.

Belinda busied herself in the kitchen and soon carried a tray of tea things to the parlor. Putting them down on the small table next to the sofa, she returned to the room where the elderly woman lay.

"Excuse me," she said softly, "but I thought ya might like a cup of tea." She looked knowingly at Luke and nodded her head slightly toward the door. The man looked as though she had just offered him a ticket back to civilization.

"Oh my, yes," he agreed. "It is long past propah teatime." He followed Luke from the room.

Belinda poured two cups of the strong, hot tea. Their guest accepted one appreciatively, breathing deeply of the aroma from the cup. She then passed him a plate of Abbie's gingerbread, and he accepted a slice with a slight nod of his head. Belinda, glad to have been able to help restore some order to his world, excused herself and went back to her nursing duties.

Windsor—Belinda did not know if it was his first name, his last name, or all the name that he had—spent the next several days at the local hotel until he was assured that Mrs. Stafford-Smyth, his "charge," was going to recover. He often came to the little room where her cot had been placed and visited with Belinda while she cared for the elderly lady.

Belinda found him most enjoyable in spite of his stuffiness. To her amazement he even had a sense of humor—of sorts. He turned out to be deeply committed to Mrs. Stafford-Smyth, and Belinda could not help but admire that in him.

Still, Belinda did wonder if his frequent visits had something to do with the fact that she always served him tea. The hotel's, he complained, was only lukewarm and weak as rainwater.

Belinda smiled and made sure that the pot was boiling, the teapot heated, and the tea given a long time to brew.

Belinda did not discover much about her patient from the tight-lipped butler, who made clear he considered it poor breeding indeed to discuss one's employer. However, he did give out bits and pieces of information in their chats together over teacups.

He had worked for Mrs. Stafford-Smyth for forty-two years, beginning in her employ as a young man and serving no other. Mr. Stafford-Smyth had been a busy city lawyer, but a heart attack had taken him to an early grave.

"Has the family always lived in Boston?" Belinda asked.

"Oh, indeed, yes," answered the butler quickly, as though to even consider any other locale would be a travesty to all that was held sacred.

"Does Mrs. Stafford-Smyth have a family?"

The man sat silent for some time as though weighing whether the question should be considered too personal to answer, but at length said quite simply, "She had two children. She lost one in infancy and one as an adult. She has two grandsons—but they are *abroad*."

Belinda understood from his terse answer that she was to pry no further.

It was on their third day of vigil together that Mrs. Stafford-Smyth roused slightly. At first she seemed totally confused. She pushed at Belinda and looked about her in bewilderment and some fear. Belinda was glad the butler was there to move to her side. The woman quieted when she saw him and settled back again on her pillow.

"Madam must rest," he said gently but firmly. "You have been very ill," and he took her hand and held it until she relaxed again.

Belinda offered the woman some liquid, and she accepted a few sips willingly. One of Luke's greatest concerns was that they had been able to get her to swallow very little.

She did not stay awake for long, but from then on she roused every few hours, and each time she seemed a bit more alert.

Eventually she was able to make her requests known and after several days was even able to form words, though her speech was labored and slurred.

It was at that point that she was moved to a room at the local hotel, and after conferring with Luke and then with Mrs. Stafford-Smyth at length, Windsor decided that he needed to return to Boston to look after the affairs of her house.

"Don't worry . . . nurse will care for me," the lady managed to say, and Belinda understood that she was expected to stay in her employ. But even Belinda could not nurse twenty-four hours a day, seven days a week. So Mrs. Mills continued on the night shift and Flora Hadley on the occasional day.

Mrs. Stafford-Smyth improved slowly but steadily with each new spring day. Luke was pleased and thankful that she was getting her speech back so quickly—but then Mrs. Stafford-Smyth was not at all like her silent butler and she practiced continually. She loved to chat, and she engaged Belinda in conversation most of her wakeful hours.

"What did he tell you about me?" she asked one day, and Belinda knew that she was speaking of Windsor.

"Very little," Belinda replied as she fluffed a pillow. "He seemed to feel thet butlers should be seen and not heard."

Mrs. Stafford-Smyth began to chuckle. "Exactly!" she said. "Exactly! That describes my Windsah perfectly."

Belinda smiled at the word "my." *Just how does Mrs. Stafford-Smyth mean the word?* she wondered.

"Well, *I'm* not hesitant to talk," the woman said. "What would you like to know?"

Belinda smiled. "Whatever you would like to tell," she responded.

"I'm a widow," she began.

"Windsor did tell me that," said Belinda.

"What else?"

"Thet yer husband had been a noted lawyer. Thet he died quite young with a heart attack. Thet ya lost both of yer children."

"My," said Mrs. Stafford-Smyth. "How did you evah coax all of that from him?"

"He *was* a mite reluctant," smiled Belinda. "But he did like my tea." They laughed comfortably together.

"Mr. Stafford-Smyth was only thirty-nine when he had his heart attack," the woman went on thoughtfully. "So young and with so much promise." She thought for a few minutes and then hurried on. "We lost our Cynthia when she was only two. It was whooping cough that took her. My husband was still with me then, so I had someone to share my sorrow, but when I lost our son, Martin . . . I had to bear it all alone."

"I'm . . . I'm so sorry," said Belinda.

"Martin was only thirty-two when he died. He had been to Europe several times with me. He liked it much bettah than Boston, I'm afraid. Then he fell in love with a French girl and they were married. He brought her home to Boston, but she nevah really did care for it, so they were back and forth—back and forth. Finally they bought a new home in Boston and tried to settle down. They had two sons, but they still both loved to travel, so the boys were raised more by nannies than by their parents. I guess there's no harm in that—if one has good nannies. Just because one is a parent doesn't mean that one knows about children."

Belinda found herself wanting to argue the issue, but she kept silent.

"Anyway," Mrs. Stafford-Smyth went on, "on one of their trips abroad there was an accident. They were both killed. They were buried in France. Of course I went over for the funeral. I was devastated. Martin was all I had left. Except for the boys. I brought them to my house and we raised them—my staff and I—with the help of their nannies, of course. They are both grown men now—and I don't see them much. Right now they are in France visiting their family on their mothah's side. Some days I feah I have lost them, too."

She paused, and Belinda was afraid the woman might start to weep, but instead she shifted herself on the pillows and lifted her chin.

"So I travel," she said. "Just as much as I can. 'Gadding,' Windsah calls it, and he doesn't approve of it much. Usually I take my nurse with me, but this trip—well, we already had our plans made, our tickets purchased when she took sick. Gall bladder. She had to have surgery. Well, one can hardly travel after surgery, can one? Windsah and I had quite a fuss ovah it. He said I should cancel my plans and stay at home. I said I was old enough to care for myself." She smiled. "So I went."

There was a pause. "Evah been to San Francisco?"

Belinda shook her head.

"Well, I have. All the way from Boston to San Francisco. Just to see what it was like." She smiled again, then sobered. "My, what a long, long dusty trip. And the trains! Some of them are so dirty and appalling and nevah on time." She shook her head again at the thought of it. "But don't evah tell Windsah I said so," she hastened to add. "He already thinks he's been proven right."

Belinda smiled. She did enjoy getting to know Mrs. Stafford-Smyth but didn't like the thought of this fascinating lady leaving them when she was recovered and would be able to travel home. However, she was a long ways from total recovery yet.

"I think ya should rest a bit now," Belinda cautioned, and without fuss the woman allowed herself to be tucked in and the drapes pulled to shut the sunlight from the room.

FOURTEEN

A Busy Summer

"You've been so busy I've scarcely seen ya," Rand commented, sounding rather disappointed, and Belinda had to admit he was right.

"You've been pretty busy yerself," she reminded him.

"I'm hopin' things will slow down some fer me now," he said gently. "Now thet I have the house fer the grocer done, seems I should catch my breath and look to other things as well as buildin'."

Belinda wasn't sure what "other things" Rand was referring to. Perhaps he meant that he didn't want to build every waking minute, she decided.

"How's yer special patient?" he asked her.

"Oh, she's doing much better. Luke feels thet she should get completely well. Well, almost completely—she may always have a bit of trouble with her left side. But it's jest a matter of time now."

"Time?" said Rand with a trace of complaint in his voice. Then he softened and added slowly. "Seems to me such a long time already."

"I suppose it seems thet way to Mrs. Stafford-Smyth, too," Belinda responded.

"Yeah," agreed Rand with a sigh. "I reckon it does."

They walked in silence. Belinda was enjoying the warm summer evening. She didn't get out nearly as often as she'd like, and Marty had commented on her paleness the last time she went out to the farm.

"So ya think ya'll be needed fer some time?" Rand was asking.

"Oh, she's not nearly well enough to travel yet. Especially alone."

"Couldn't thet there butler fella come an' get her?" Rand suggested.

"Thet would be awkward. She still needs help with dressing and all."

"What about her old nurse? The one ya said had her gall bladder out?"

"We haven't heard from her for some time," explained Belinda, since one of her tasks was to assist Mrs. Stafford-Smyth with her mail.

Belinda wondered why Rand had so many questions about her patient, but before she could inquire, he had switched the topic entirely.

"Hear there's a church picnic on Saturday. Sure would like to take ya iffen yer free to go."

Belinda thought for only a moment. "I'd love to go!" she responded enthusiastically. "It's a long time since I've done anything like thet. I'll see if I can work out the schedule with Flo."

For the first time this evening, Rand gave her a full smile. She noticed again his deep dimple. She had been missing Rand's company, she realized, surprised at the discovery.

"You've already finished yer second house?" Belinda commented to keep the conversation going.

"Jest this week," said Rand.

"I didn't even get to see it," Belinda lamented.

"Ya haven't been seeing much of its builder lately, either," Rand said with a wry grin. "I was about to hit my thumb with my hammer or fall off a ladder or some such thing jest so thet I might git to see the town nurse."

Belinda blushed but brushed his teasing aside. "I haven't even been seein' my own ma and pa for jest ages," she confessed.

"Well, we'll take care of thet on Saturday," promised Rand.

And Belinda smiled. She really looked forward to the day off.

Belinda was able to arrange for Saturday off, and she left with Mrs. Stafford-Smyth's orders to "have fun as young girls were meant to do," and prepared for Rand's coming with extra care.

Such a long time since I've been on an outing, she exulted as she bathed and groomed her hair.

Lighthearted, she chose her favorite dress, a full-skirted soft blue gingham with lots of bows and flouncy frills. *It kind of matches my feelings,* she decided as she held it up to herself in front of her bedroom mirror.

She was ready with time to spare, so she spent the extra moments playing with Ruthie. She had missed having time with her little niece.

They were busy with a game of peekaboo when a male voice interrupted them. "Now, if that doesn't make some picture," he said.

Belinda swung quickly around. She had not heard anyone knock on the front door.

But it was in the entrance to Luke's office that the male figure stood. Belinda's eyes traveled upward over sharply pressed suit pants, white shirt with rolled-up sleeves, and broad young shoulders. Then she looked at his face and a little gasp escaped her lips. "Jackson! I didn't know ya were here yet." Luke had told her that Jackson was planning to join the practice, but she didn't realize it would be this soon. She could not remember his being so tall—so good-looking. She flushed in embarrassment and turned her eyes back to Ruthie.

"My niece," she said, disentangling Ruthie's small fist from her bodice frills as Jackson moved into the room.

"I've already met the little charmer," said Jackson evenly. "It's her aunt who has eluded me."

"I . . . I hadn't even heard ya were . . . were back," Belinda repeated defensively.

He crossed to sit down on the sofa beside her. "Actually," he said, "I just arrived on Thursday, and I spent a few days with my mother. Then Luke said I should pop in and take inventory of his office supplies to see if I have any ideas on what we might add."

"Luke will be so glad to have ya here," said Belinda. "He's been worked near off his feet."

"I heard that it's his nurse who puts in long hours."

Jackson seemed to be studying Belinda's face, and she found herself flushing again.

"Not . . . not really," she stammered. "I'm taking the whole day off today."

"You are?" said Jackson. "Splendid! The inventory can wait until another day. Mother said there's a picnic out at the church. I'd love to go and see how many of our old friends are still around."

"That's a great idea," put in Belinda. "Folks would all love to see ya."

"Then let's go," he prompted and stood, offering a hand to help Belinda to her feet.

"Well . . . I . . . I . . . I can't," she stammered, not accepting the hand.

"You can't go? But I thought you said—"

"I . . . I did. I mean . . . I . . . I am going but I . . . I already—"

A knock on the door saved her from explaining further. Belinda lifted small Ruthie into her arms and went to answer it. She felt quite sure that she knew who was there, but she wasn't sure he had come at the best of times.

When Belinda opened the door, Rand stepped inside without comment. But he whistled softly as he stood studying her in the blue gingham dress. Belinda couldn't help but note when she dressed that it emphasized her wide blue eyes, fair skin, and cheeks just touched with pink.

"My feelings exactly," said another voice, and Rand lifted his eyes from Belinda to the tall, well-dressed young stranger.

Belinda's cheeks turned even pinker as she looked from one to the other. "Rand," she said, "this . . . this is Dr. Jackson Brown. Jackson, please meet Rand O'Connel."

For a moment Rand stood in silence, seeming to measure the man before him. Then he stepped forward, offered his hand, and said, "Welcome to town, Doctor. You might not know it, but seems I've been waitin' on ya fer a long, long time."

Jackson obviously did not understand the implication of the words, but he took the offered hand and shook it firmly.

"If you'll excuse me," said Belinda, "I'll give Ruthie back to her mama and grab my shawl."

It was then Jackson must have realized what was happening. His eyes clouded for a moment and then he straightened his shoulders. He must have been deeply disappointed, but neither was he a man to give up easily.

"And if you'll excuse me," he said to Rand, "I have some inventory to care for. Nice meeting you, Mr. O'Connel," and he turned back to the office.

"And nice to meet you, Doctor," put in Rand just before Jackson closed the door.

The picnic outing did not go as well as Belinda had hoped. It was obvious to her that the relationships in her family had not healed. She had prayed that over the months things would return to normal. She could see at a glance that they had not. For the first time in her life, she thought that her mother looked old. There was a weariness about Marty that surprised Belinda. Her mama shouldn't have changed that much in only a few months' time.

Then Belinda saw young Abe, and she could see further deterioration in his arm. Abe hardly used his left hand at all, and Belinda knew that Luke's worst fears were being realized.

As she gazed around at the laughing, chattering picnickers, she realized that most of the girls her age were already married or being courted. That left very few of her old friends with whom to sit and chat. And just seeing her old classmates made her miss Amy Jo and Melissa even more.

The quiet ride home probably was not what Rand had planned it would be. But he must have sensed that Belinda was troubled about something.

"Ya seem bothered," he finally broke the silence.

Belinda responded with a sigh.

"I'm sorry to be such sour company," she responded. "It's nothing, really. Least not any one thing. Just a lot of little things all pressin' in together."

"Care to talk about 'em?" asked Rand. "All these 'little things'?"

Belinda smiled in appreciation. "Thanks," she said, "but I think not. Not right now, anyway. I haven't sorted through 'em myself yet."

Rand nodded in understanding and drove on without further comment.

They were almost home when he startled her with a question. "This here new doctor—Dr. Brown? Ya knew 'im before?"

"We . . . we went to school together," she answered. "His ma was my teacher. She still teaches at our school. Been there for several years now."

Rand's eyes narrowed. "An' he'll be workin' with ya now?"

"He's to be Luke's associate," she answered simply.

"How do you feel about thet?" asked Rand.

Belinda frowned slightly. She really wasn't sure, but she answered as truthfully as she could. "Luke has been countin' on it fer some time. He will have more time with his family now. Thet's what he's wanted fer such a long time."

"An' you?" asked Rand.

"I . . . I guess maybe I'll have more time, too," Belinda stammered.

Rand smiled, his expression saying *That's what I have wanted . . . for a long time, too.*

He drove for a moment in silence.

"This here doctor . . . he's not married?"

"No-o," answered Belinda.

"Got 'im a girl?"

"I . . . I wouldn't know. We haven't been in touch fer . . . fer some time."

Belinda took a quick glance at Rand, and his face seemed rather stiff. She felt very uncomfortable, and she was relieved to see the doctor's residence just ahead.

FIFTEEN

Confusion

"And how are ya feelin' this mornin'?" Belinda asked Mrs. Stafford-Smyth upon entering her room.

"Oh, it's good to see you!" exclaimed the elderly lady with feeling. "I've missed you all weekend."

"Problems?" questioned Belinda with a frown. She did hope nothing had gone wrong while she had been away.

The woman shook her head and waved a pale hand feebly in the air. "No, nothing . . . nothing specific," she admitted. "Flo does her best and so does that deah Mrs. What's-her-name, but it just isn't the same as when you are heah. They never seem to know . . ."

She went on and Belinda let her talk, much relieved to know that there really was nothing seriously wrong with the woman.

Belinda busied herself checking her patient's temperature and pulse as Mrs. Stafford-Smyth poured out her woes. Without comment about the complaints, Belinda fluffed up the pillows, politely asking, "Would ya like to sit up in a chair fer a few minutes?"

"Oh my, yes," responded the woman. "I am so sick, sick, sick of this bed." Then she hurried on. "You see, that's exactly what I mean. Those . . . those other two. They nevah think of things like that. They just do the 'necessaries.' It's as though they don't want to bothah . . . just want to get the day ovah with."

"I'm sure they don't feel thet way," Belinda assured the elderly lady. "It's jest thet they haven't had much experience in bedside nursing care. Mrs. Mills has nursed neighbors fer years, but most of her time has been helpin' mothers an' newborn babies. Flo is just being trained in nursin'. Luke wants to have a second nurse available so thet one doctor an' one of the nurses might get some time off now and then. He is even talkin' of trainin' a third girl to help jest so she'll have some knowledge if he ever needs to call on someone. Mrs. Mills is gettin' older an' won't want to nurse much longer."

"Well, I think it's a splendid idea to train others. Believe me, I do," insisted Mrs. Stafford-Smyth. "But you must admit that some folks are fah more adept at sensing needs than othah people are. You are one of those few, Belinda. You seem to feel for the patient—to understand the hardness of the bed and the misery of lying day aftah day on one's back."

She hurried on. "I know you need time off. No one can work day and night. But I do hate the days or nights when you are not heah. Things just always go so much—"

"And how is our patient this morning?" a man's voice asked along with a rap on the door for their attention.

Belinda recognized Jackson's voice before she turned around to invite the tall young man to enter. Mrs. Stafford-Smyth's face showed her surprise, and her eyes were filled with questions.

"Mrs. Stafford-Smyth," said Belinda without really looking directly at Jackson, "this is Dr. Brown, Dr. Luke's new associate. Dr. Brown, Mrs. Stafford-Smyth of Boston."

Jackson crossed to the bedside and took one of the lady's weak hands in his, smiling at her warmly. And though the patient was not aware of it, Belinda watched his trained eyes already picking up much information about her physical condition.

"And how are you feeling this morning?" he asked her sincerely.

She didn't answer his question. Instead, Belinda could tell she was studying him, her eyes—as sharp in their own way as his—assessing everything about him.

She must have been impressed by the nicely dressed, professional young man, because she finally answered him, respect in her tone. "You caught me by surprise," she responded slowly. "I was expecting my favorite Doctah Luke to be in to see me. Now I see a good-looking young man who appeahs to me to know what he is doing. How can such a small town have the honah of two such notable doctahs while the city of Boston suffahs with old has-beens and young, smug up-starts?"

Jackson laughed heartily, patting her hand as he did so.

"Doctah Brown, you say?" Mrs. Stafford-Smyth said, turning toward Belinda. "Where did you evah find him, my deah?"

Belinda could feel her cheeks flushing. She could also feel Jackson's eyes upon her. She did wish that Mrs. Stafford-Smyth were not quite so forthright.

"Dr. Brown grew up in our community," she explained, hoping her voice was even and controlled. "His mother is the schoolteacher in our country school. Dr. Luke has been in touch with him all through his trainin', hopin' to entice him back to our little town."

The elderly lady's eyes again rested on Jackson. "I still say it is unfai-ah," she protested good-naturedly.

Jackson became serious and all-doctor then, examining the patient, asking questions, and jotting items of note on the small pad he carried.

Mrs. Stafford-Smyth cooperated. Belinda had the impression that she rather liked doctors fussing over her.

"We have some new medication I would like to try," Jackson told the woman. "It has been used with good success in the hospital where I took my training. I will explain to Nurse Davis the dosage and how it is to be administered."

Mrs. Stafford-Smyth nodded in agreement.

"Now I do believe," went on Jackson, "that when I arrived, I heard some talk about sitting up for a short time. I think that's a splendid idea. Could I help you to settle Mrs. Stafford-Smyth before I go, Nurse Davis?"

Belinda nodded and went to prepare the lady's chair by the window. Then, with Jackson's help, Mrs. Stafford-Smyth was carefully positioned on the chair, the draperies pulled back, and the window slightly raised so she might enjoy the freshness of the summer day.

Belinda thanked Jackson and was about to turn back to her patient when Jackson surprised her with a request.

"May I see you for a moment please, Nurse?" he asked.

Belinda felt a twinge of concern. Had he noticed something about her patient she had failed to see? And then she remembered the new medication—he had said that he would explain to her the proper use and dosage.

"I'll be right back," she assured Mrs. Stafford-Smyth, "and I will be jest outside yer door. If you should need me, I'll—"

"Nonsense," said the lady. "I'm fine. I haven't breathed such wonderful ai-ah for weeks."

Belinda smiled and followed Jackson to the hallway.

"She's really doing remarkably well," he commented after the door had closed gently behind them. "I am convinced that she has had first-rate care."

"Luke has—" began Belinda, but Jackson interrupted her.

"I know that Luke has handled her treatment well—but I was talking specifically about nursing care."

Belinda could only flush at his compliment. "Thank you," she stammered, her eyes dropping.

Jackson stood for a moment looking down at her.

"I was hoping you'd have dinner with me this evening."

Belinda looked up quickly. The invitation had caught her completely by surprise.

"I . . . I thought you were goin' to explain the medication . . . to tell—"

"I didn't bring it with me," hastened Jackson. "I have a supply at the office. I'll bring it this evening and explain it all to you then."

His eyes seemed to be pleading, and she wasn't sure just why. Was it necessary to meet over dinner to discuss the medication? Would a doctor ask his nurse to discuss cases over a meal? But she had worked only for Luke, and they were occupants of the same house. They could discuss cases anytime. Maybe it wasn't unusual. How was she to know? She found her head nodding in agreement. Instinctively she knew that working with Jackson was going to be different than working with her brother Luke.

"Very well," she responded, licking her lips to moisten them.

"When are you off?" he asked next.

"Mrs. Mills comes at seven."

"Fine. I'll see you then."

"But . . . but . . ." argued Belinda. "I . . . I should freshen up some before . . . before dinner."

"Of course," he smiled. "I was thoughtless. How much time do you need?"

"It's going to make supper—er, dinner—very late," Belinda reasoned. "Ya'll be starved by then."

"Tell you what," he bargained. "Why don't we both catch a little something to eat around four, and then we'll be able to wait until eight with no problem."

Belinda felt she had been invited into some kind of conspiracy—actually, it was rather exciting. She nodded, a smile playing about her lips.

"I'll leave orders downstairs to send something up to the room for you and Mrs. Stafford-Smyth," he went on, and when Belinda was about to protest he waved it aside.

"I'll see you later," he promised with a smile that both dismayed and warmed Belinda. He touched her arm gently and was gone.

Belinda stood slowly shaking her head, watching his brisk strides take him down the corridor. Just before he rounded the corner, he turned slightly and gave her a little wave of his hand. She blushed, not expecting to get caught watching him walk away.

She pushed the door open gently and returned to her patient, glad to have something with which to occupy her time and attention.

"How are ya?" she asked solicitously. "Are ya tirin'?"

"Oh my, no," said the woman forcefully, "and don't you dai-ah try to put me back in that stuffy old bed yet."

Belinda smiled and went to freshen the bed while her patient was out of it.

"My," went on Mrs. Stafford-Smyth, "such a nice young man! You're a lucky girl."

Belinda lifted her eyes from the bed she was remaking, about to ask the lady what she had meant by her statement. But Mrs. Stafford-Smyth went on. "He likes you, you know. Anyone can see that. Have you known him long?"

Belinda wanted to deny the lady's assumption, but she wasn't sure she could truthfully do so, so she skipped it and went to the woman's question.

"We went to school together for a couple of years. He was a year ahead of me, an' he left to go take his trainin'."

"And did you develop your interest in nursing before or aftah you met him?" questioned Mrs. Stafford-Smyth frankly.

Belinda felt her face coloring but she answered, perhaps a little too quickly, "Before. I guess I've always been interested in nursin'. When Luke discovered my eagerness to learn it, he promised to help me. I was only a little girl then."

The lady smiled, then nodded. "See! It's like I said. Good nurses are born, not made."

They were silent for a few moments. Belinda continued straightening up the room, and Mrs. Stafford-Smyth sat looking out upon the sun-drenched world beyond her bedroom.

"I must say, though," she mused, "it certainly has complicated things for me!"

"Complicated things? Meanin'?" Belinda asked, not following the woman's train of thought.

"I had been hoping I might soon be ready to make the train trip home."

"The new medication won't complicate thet, I'm sure," Belinda quickly assured her. "In fact, it might well hasten thet time fer ya."

Mrs. Stafford-Smyth's eyes began to shine with excitement, the first that Belinda had seen there. Then the woman sobered again.

"That wasn't just what I meant," she continued. "I had . . . had been planning for some time to ask if you would accompany me."

Belinda's breath caught in her throat in a little gasp. She had never even thought about such a thing. The enormity of it caught her totally by surprise.

"You mean . . . travel with ya by train . . . all the . . . the way to Boston?" she asked.

"If you would."

"Oh my," said Belinda. "I never thought I'd see the likes of Boston."

"Would you consider it?" asked Mrs. Stafford-Smyth.

"I . . . I don't know. I'm not sure thet Luke could manage—"

"He would have Flo—and the new nurse he's training. You said so yourself."

"Yes, but . . . but Luke hasn't even started trainin' the second girl yet, an' . . . an' Flo . . . well, she's not ready yet to take over—"

"It wouldn't be for a week or so yet—and besides, there are two doctahs now. They can relieve each other."

That was true.

"Maybe they could . . . could manage for a short time," began Belinda. "How many days would the trip take?"

Mrs. Stafford-Smyth did not answer at once. She hesitated, looking steadily into Belinda's face. Then she spoke slowly. "That's the complication. I had wanted you to stay on with me in Boston . . . indefinitely . . . as my private nurse . . . and now . . . now this young, good-looking doctah appeahs . . . and it is very plain to me that . . . that he has othah plans for you."

Belinda began to flush deeply. "Oh . . . I . . . I believe you are . . . are mistakin' friendship fer . . . fer something more," she argued. "Jackson—Dr. Brown and I were classmates, not . . . not . . ." She faltered to a stop, feeling she had already said too much.

Mrs. Stafford-Smyth did not appear to be convinced.

"Did you write?" she quizzed.

"Fer . . . fer a short while," answered Belinda honestly.

"Did he return a married man?"

"No-o-o."

"Has he ever spoken of anothah young woman?"

"No," Belinda quickly explained, "but we have not been writing lately. There might very well be a young woman . . ."

But Mrs. Stafford-Smyth just smiled a knowing smile. "I rest my case," she said.

Belinda's head began to whirl. What was Mrs. Stafford-Smyth telling her? Surely, after all these years Jackson could not still think . . . ? Why had he invited her to dinner to discuss a case that could have been taken care of at the office or here in the sickroom? *What is going on? Oh my!* she thought. *Oh my!* But Mrs. Stafford-Smyth was speaking again.

"If I should be wrong—or if you should be interested," she began, "my offah stands. I would welcome you as my traveling companion and as my nurse in my home in Boston for as long as it would convenience both of us. The salary will be negotiated at such time as you decide. I will not pressure—but it would please me very much if you should decide to accept my proposal."

Belinda could only shake her head. It all seemed like a dream.

"Oh my," she said hesitantly. "I . . . I think I would enjoy the trip . . . but to stay on . . . well . . . thet's quite different. I've never been away from my family . . . and . . . well, I guess I sorta feel I'm needed here. Luke needs me an' . . . an' Mama needs me. Now that things are . . . are . . . now that Dr. Brown is here an' you are feelin' much better . . . I . . . I plan to go home more. I . . . I jest don't know . . ." Her voice trailed off.

"We'll let it rest . . . for now," said Mrs. Stafford-Smyth.

Belinda was glad to dismiss the amazing idea from her mind and turn to other things.

At four o'clock sharp there was a rap on the door and a young girl from the hotel kitchen staff stepped aside when Belinda opened it.

"I was ta bring this to yer room at four," she offered.

"Oh my. Oh, oh yes," responded Belinda. She had quite forgotten Jackson's suggestion. She took the tray from the girl, thanked her sincerely, and turned back to the room.

Mrs. Stafford-Smyth, who was tucked back in her bed propped up with pillows, looked quizzically at her.

"Dr. . . . Dr. Brown ordered it," explained Belinda. "He thought thet a bit of refreshment might be . . . might be a good idea."

"What a thoughtful young man," commented the elderly lady. She eyed the tray filled with hot tea, pastries, and fresh fruit. "It does look good, doesn't it? Could you help me sit up just a bit more?"

Belinda looked in surprise at her patient. Mrs. Stafford-Smyth, who had needed to be coaxed and cajoled into eating even a small portion of her meals, was prepared to attack with enthusiasm the tray of afternoon tea things.

Perhaps we should have thought to try this long ago, Belinda told herself. *She might have taken to "tea" more quickly than to "dinner."*

Belinda poured two cups of the steaming tea, added sugar and cream to Mrs. Stafford-Smyth's at her bidding, and then the two ladies settled down to enjoy the dainties from the tea tray. It was almost like having a party, and Belinda enjoyed the bright chatter of Mrs. Stafford-Smyth as she recalled some of the teatimes she had shared with others in her home in Boston.

I must remember to tell Jackson—Dr. Brown—over supper—dinner— how good this has been for Mrs. Stafford-Smyth, Belinda told herself.

Perhaps it would not be long, after all, until the elderly lady would be able to return to her dearly loved Boston.

SIXTEEN

Dinner

Belinda had ample time to bathe, do her hair, and dress carefully. She had gotten quite a few questions from her two small nephews and a few good-natured remarks from her brother Luke when her plans for the evening were known. She tried to brush it all aside and convince them that this was nothing more than a doctor-nurse consultation in regard to a patient. But by now she had difficulty convincing even herself of that.

She told herself that she would not dress "special," but even as she made the determination she found herself lifting a soft, full-skirted pink taffeta from her closet. She knew it was by far the most becoming dress she owned. She slipped it over her head and studied herself in the mirror, deciding just how she should style her hair to go with the gown.

She had just finished adding a touch of scent to her wrists and temples when she heard the knock at the front door and Luke admitted Jackson to the family parlor. Belinda felt her pulse quicken—merely because this would be a special evening out, she said to herself, and for Belinda those were few indeed. With heart pounding and cheeks warm, she waited for Luke's summons before leaving her room to meet her caller.

Jackson did not compliment her with words, but his eyes shone with appreciation as he looked at Belinda. She took a deep breath in attempt to calm herself as he held the door for her, but his light touch under her arm as they walked down the front steps sent a thrill through her that was both pleasurable and unnerving.

Belinda walked by his side as calmly as she could manage, anxious to take her seat in the hotel dining room before the whole small town was abuzz with the fact that she was out strolling with the new doctor.

The dinner was an enjoyable experience for both of them. Jackson talked easily, sharing with Belinda stories of his experiences in medical training and his excitement over new medicines and treatments that were constantly being discovered.

"The field of medicine is moving forward so quickly that it is difficult for us doctors to keep up," he said, genuine awe in his voice.

Belinda could not help but feel some of his enthusiasm. For a moment her old wish came to mind. *I wish I'd been a boy. Then I could have been a doctor.* But she did not dwell on it for long.

When there was a bit of a lull in the conversation, Belinda dared present a question. She didn't know how Jackson would respond to being asked about a patient—by a mere nurse. She was so used to working with Luke, and they discussed all cases openly.

"What . . . what do you think about Mrs. Stafford-Smyth and her progress?" she ventured rather timidly.

"From reading all of Luke's reports and examining her today, I would say that she has made a remarkable recovery," he answered without hesitation.

Belinda relaxed. It was good to hear another doctor fresh from the latest in medical training agree with Luke about her patient. She had really become quite attached to the elderly lady, in spite of the obvious difference in their social backgrounds.

"I think that getting her up for a brief time was an excellent idea," Jackson continued. "Did she tire quickly?"

"She surprised me. But I didn't leave her up quite as long as she would have liked. I was afraid she might overdo."

"Good for you," encouraged Jackson. "She should gain her strength back quickly now as long as she doesn't do something foolish and have a setback."

"She is beginning to talk about traveling home to Boston," Belinda said slowly.

"Home? That might be rushing things a bit. Unless, of course, she has someone who will come and travel with her. Even then I would give it another week or two at the least."

A week or two. That really wasn't very long.

"Someone mentioned a traveling companion," went on Jackson.

"Yes," said Belinda, "but we just heard from the woman. She hasn't recovered well after her surgery. She isn't able to come."

"Well, Mrs. Stafford-Smyth definitely won't be able to travel by herself for some time yet," said Jackson soberly. Then he brightened. "But perhaps something else could be arranged. I would like to see you freed up from your heavy responsibility as soon as possible."

Belinda looked up quickly. "I've rather enjoyed nursin' her," she said.

"I'm sure you have. And you have done a commendable job. But there comes a time when one must move on to other things . . . don't you think?" and Jackson smiled at Belinda in the soft light of the lamp.

She nodded. *Perhaps it is time to move on to other things,* she agreed, but she did not voice her thoughts to Jackson. Something told her that she and Jackson might not quite be thinking along the same lines. She wondered just what he might say if she were to tell him about Mrs. Stafford-Smyth's complimentary proposal. But she decided that this might not be the time. After all, the two doctors did need a nurse to assist in the office, and Flo was not yet knowledgeable enough to take over all the duties. Belinda decided she would not concern Jackson with the possibility that she might ask for a few months' leave. At least not just yet.

"Now, about that medication," Belinda began, but Jackson stopped her with a chuckle.

"In my hurry to pick up a very attractive young lady, I'm afraid I've forgotten to bring it," he said. Then he added quickly, "I'll be sure to bring it with me when I come to check Mrs. Stafford-Smyth in the morning."

"So . . . so you will be coming again tomorrow?" asked Belinda shyly.

"Luke and I went through all the patient files, and Mrs. Stafford-

Smyth is one of the patients that we agreed I will take," answered Jackson simply.

Belinda nodded. "And the . . . the directions for giving the medication?" she prompted.

"Very straightforward—nothing other than one tablet morning, noon, and night—with water."

Belinda blinked. *Hadn't Jackson indicated complicated instructions when he'd mentioned the new medication earlier? Or had she imagined it?*

Jackson was talking about his desire to help bring culture, in some small measure, to their town.

"It would be so enriching and relaxing," he said, "to attend a play or a concert now and then," and though Belinda had never had the pleasure of either, she quite agreed.

"It would also help young suitors, such as myself," Jackson went on with a knowing smile. "What is there now to offer a young woman except a walk in the fresh air or a ride in the country?"

Is Jackson thinking of courting someone? He couldn't mean me! Belinda's thoughts rushed frantically through her mind. To cover her confusion, she tried to make a little joke with, "Well, there *are* the school programs each spring." She was very relieved when they laughed together and Jackson, as far as she was concerned, completely changed the conversation.

"Mr. O'Connel seems like a fine young man."

"Yes," agreed Belinda innocently. "He is."

"Is he from the area or did he move in?"

"He grew up here. Went to our school, in fact. But I guess thet was before you came. He was ahead of me. He left to go off to work fer his uncle down state."

"Was he just paying a visit in the area when—?"

"Oh no. He's back to stay."

"What does he do?"

Belinda thought it was nice of Jackson to be so interested in Rand.

"He's a builder," she replied. Thinking of the fine house Rand had built for the Kirbys made her eyes brighten. "He built the most magnificent house," she continued enthusiastically. "He had a fella come and help him with the most ornate parts—the gables and fancy trimmin's an' all—but he built most of it himself."

"Is it the building or the builder that makes your eyes shine?" Jackson asked softly.

Belinda flushed. "Maybe . . . maybe it's just the lamplight reflectin' in my eyes," she countered. Then she responded truthfully, "Rand is a good friend."

"Just a friend?"

"Of . . . of course," Belinda answered.

"Nothing more? Because, if you have an understanding . . ." Jackson spoke softly and left the sentence dangling.

"We have no understandin'," Belinda offered quietly, though she did wonder why it was necessary for her to explain this to Jackson. She noticed his look of relief. He nodded and smiled at her.

"Then," he said with mock formality, "since there is nothing else for one to do in this small town, may I escort you for a walk in the soft-gathering twilight?"

Belinda smiled at his playfulness and fell into the mood of the moment. "Thank you, kind sir," she answered and accepted his proffered arm for a leisurely stroll back to Luke's house.

Dusk gathered about them, making the dust and grit of the little town less noticeable. The scent of the garden flowers drifted out on the hint of a breeze, caressing the senses with feelings of warmth and goodwill. Belinda breathed in deeply. It was good just to be alive on such an evening. She was glad Jackson was back, that she had been out for dinner, and that the lovely evening was perfect for a walk.

They were nearing Luke's house, carefully picking their way along the wooden sidewalk, when they turned a corner and almost ran into a figure in the semidarkness.

"Excuse me," a voice said, and Belinda recognized Rand at once.

"Rand!" she exclaimed without thinking, and his head abruptly came up.

"Belinda," he returned with equal surprise.

"I didn't expect to—" she began.

But Rand interrupted her brusquely. "Obviously not."

What does he mean by that? she found herself wondering.

But Jackson was saying, "Miss Davis kindly consented to be my dinner guest."

"So I was told," Rand retorted.

"Have you been visitin' Luke?" Belinda asked, feeling her question quite a safe one, but to her amazement Rand answered that query curtly also.

"No. I was not calling on Luke." Then he added more quietly. "I went to see his sister."

"Oh! I'm . . . I'm sorry I wasn't home. I . . . I didn't know ya were plannin' to call. I . . . I . . ."

Rand seemed to soften then. He turned to Belinda with apology in his voice. "I'm sorry," he stammered. "I shouldn't have jest taken it fer granted. I jest never thought . . . had never . . . never concerned myself with . . . with makin' plans ahead before."

It was true. Rand had been accustomed to dropping over casually whenever his busy schedule would allow. If Belinda should happen to be busy with a patient, he would visit briefly with Luke and then go on back to the boardinghouse.

"But I see," went on Rand, "that from now on, I'll need to make my plans known."

He spoke to Belinda, but his eyes never left the face of Jackson. Belinda felt very uncomfortable and uncertain. *What is happening here?* she wondered.

Then Rand tipped his hat and bid them a good night, and Belinda felt Jackson's hold on her arm tighten as he guided her carefully over the uneven boards of the sidewalk.

SEVENTEEN

Looking for Answers

"I've missed you around here, Belinda," Luke said as he entered the office the next morning. Belinda was gathering her things before departing for her day of nursing at Mrs. Stafford-Smyth's hotel room.

Belinda smiled at her older brother. "I've been missin' you, too," she said honestly. "Fact is, I feel thet I haven't seen much of any family fer some time. I'm lookin' forward to Ma's birthday supper."

Belinda noticed the slight frown that creased Luke's forehead.

"Can't you make it to the birthday dinner?" she asked quickly.

He tried to smile at her. "I'll be there," he said simply.

Belinda's eyes were still full of questions, and Luke reached out and laid a hand gently on her carefully pinned hair. When she had been a little girl, he used to muss her curls, she remembered, but he did not muss them now—he must have decided she would have too much work pinning it back up.

"Sorry to be so . . . so obvious," he said. "It's just that family dinners aren't what they used to be."

"Ya . . . ya mean Arnie?"

Luke just nodded.

"Have ya . . . have ya seen Abe recently?" Belinda asked.

"It's just getting worse all the time."

"And Arnie still—?"

"I haven't talked to Arnie about it since I promised Ma I'd—" Luke stopped abruptly. He was silent for a few minutes and then continued. "It's not just Arnie. It's the whole family. Have you seen Ma and Pa lately? They both look like . . . well, like old, worn-out people. They look like they don't sleep nights or . . . or even eat properly."

"I don't think they do," said Belinda, her voice full of grief. "Last time I was home I heard them talkin' in their room in the middle of the night, an' . . . an' when it came to mealtime, Ma mostly just pushed things back and forth on her plate."

"I worry about them. I took out some tonic to them, but I've no idea if they are taking it or not." Luke shook his head. "I worry, but worrying doesn't help. I pray . . . but I feel like my prayers are getting nowhere."

Belinda looked at her brother. His young shoulders seemed to sag beneath the heaviness of the load. For an instant she thought of trying to talk some sense into Arnie herself, but she quickly dismissed it. She wouldn't know what else to say and, besides, Ma had promised Arnie that no one would bring up the matter again.

"Wish I could get out to a few of the special meetings."

Luke's statement surprised Belinda. "Special meetin's?"

"You hadn't heard? They have a revivalist coming to the church. It seems like it's just what I need. I feel—"

But Belinda interrupted, her eyes shining. "Thet's it! Thet's it!" she cried. "We need to get Arnie out to those meetin's. Can't ya see? If Arnie would get things in his life straightened out an' let God lead him—then God could talk to him about young Abe, an' the family wouldn't need to. Oh, Luke, this whole thing—this whole tension and the heartache of Ma and Pa—it could all be straightened out if only . . . if only Arnie would let the Lord show him what to do."

Luke nodded thoughtfully.

"Oh, Luke! Let's pray and pray some more until Arnie goes," she pleaded.

Luke put his arm around her shoulder and gave her a squeeze. Belinda's excitement was infectious—or maybe it was her faith.

"Yes, let's pray," Luke agreed.

"So how was your dinnah with that new young doctah?" Mrs. Stafford-Smyth asked Belinda forthrightly.

Belinda felt the color rise in her cheeks but kept her back turned and her hands busy with morning duties. "Very nice," she answered evenly.

"Did you know that the young gentleman—the builder—stopped by heah a few moments after you had left last night? Said he had come to walk you home."

"Rand?"

"Yes—that Rand. He seemed terribly disappointed when we said you'd already left. Said he'd stop by your place a little latah in the evening."

Belinda wondered why Rand had been telling her his personal plans, but then she couldn't help but smile. With the direct questioning of Mrs. Stafford-Smyth, he very likely had little choice in the matter.

"He seems like a nice young man, also," went on Mrs. Stafford-Smyth.

"Also?" echoed Belinda.

"Well, the young doctah. Both of them seem like fine young men. I don't know how I would evah make the choice if I were you."

Belinda frowned.

"But girls have changed since the days when I was being courted," the frank woman went on. "Why, I knew a girl back in Boston—she had three beaus all at once. She went with one to the opera, one to church doings, and the other out boating each Saturday afternoon. Managed all three of them—just as slick as you please. She said she enjoyed all of the activities, but the church-go-ah would nevah be seen at the opera—and the opera-go-ah didn't care for open air and sunshine, and the boat-ah refused to darken the door of a church. 'Course it was a bit difficult for her to arrange her days so that the one didn't meet the othah, but—"

But Belinda turned to her with flushed cheeks. "I'm afraid you have this all wrong," she said firmly. "The two young men in question are friends—both of 'em. I went to school with 'em as a . . . a child . . . and have no reason not to keep up their friendship. They are both fine young men, with high principles an' moral conduct, and I don't need to sneak around an' . . . an' . . . assign different days of the week or . . . or appropriate activities fer . . . fer . . ."

Mrs. Stafford-Smyth did not seem at all taken aback by Belinda's defensiveness and out-thrust chin. The lady smiled demurely. She seemed to enjoy seeing Belinda a bit worked up over something.

Mrs. Stafford-Smyth simply said, "You needn't defend your actions to me, my deah. I understand perfectly that you look at things a bit differently than your young men do."

The phrase "your young men" bothered Belinda, and she was about to tell Mrs. Stafford-Smyth so when there was a gentle rap on the door. It opened and Jackson stepped into the room. In his hand he held the bottle of medication he had promised to bring. He greeted them both cheerfully and handed the bottle to Belinda with a friendly wink. She felt her cheeks grow even hotter and turned to the window to let in a little of the morning sunshine and fresh air. Jackson moved on to the bedside of the patient. Soon the two were engaged in jovial banter, and Belinda, with attention diverted from her, was able to regain her composure.

"While you are here I'll slip down for Mrs. Stafford-Smyth's breakfast tray, if I may?" Belinda said to Jackson. When he nodded his agreement, she smoothed her white apron over her full skirts and left for the kitchen. She was glad to get out of the room. But even away from the sharp eyes of Mrs. Stafford-Smyth and the smiles of Jackson, she felt ill at ease. What if . . . what if Mrs. Stafford-Smyth was right? What if both young men really did see themselves as suitors? Belinda enjoyed their company—their friendship, but she had no intentions of letting it go beyond that. Not with either of them. Surely they didn't think . . . ? But Belinda shook her head in frustration and confusion. She did wish that men weren't so . . . so presumptuous.

That night Rand arrived at Luke's with a box of nicely wrapped candy and an invitation for supper the next Saturday night. Belinda smiled her thanks, but she really wished she could refuse the gift. She liked candy, but she did not want it from Rand. She wanted only his friendship—the outings and the long, quiet talks and his listening ear. Why . . . why did he need to go and make things difficult?

The next morning when Belinda arrived at Mrs. Stafford-Smyth's room, she saw a pretty bouquet of flowers on the bedside table. She smiled at the elderly woman.

"Flowers," Belinda commented. "Isn't that lovely—someone has brought ya a nice bouquet."

"Not so," said the elderly woman with a mischievous smile. "Read the note."

With a puzzled frown Belinda moved to the bouquet and picked up the piece of paper beside it. *To the busiest little nurse in town,* it read. *How about dinner on Saturday night? J.B.*

Belinda's face burned with anger and embarrassment. Why would Jackson go and do such a thing so . . . so publicly? Why involve Mrs. Stafford-Smyth, who already was suspicious of his intent? Belinda's chin lifted as she moved to pull back the heavy drapes and open the window. *Things are getting out of hand,* she thought, and she didn't like it one little bit.

Belinda turned down both Saturday-night dinner invitations. It was easy to come up with an excuse. She was going home to her ma and pa. Never had she felt a need to escape more than she did on that occasion. Never had she been so relieved to lay aside her traveling hat and pull up a chair in the quietness and peace of her mother's kitchen.

"You look tired, dear," Marty observed as she served the tea.

"I am. A bit," admitted Belinda. She sighed deeply and reached up to loosen the combs in her hair, letting the heavy, long tresses fall down about her shoulders. "It's been a long, long time since Mrs. Stafford-Smyth was brought to us," she observed.

"But I thought she was doin' much better."

"Oh, she is. She doesn't even need constant care now. We had a cot moved into the room, an' Mrs. Mills is able to sleep there at nights. And we are able to go for her meal trays, an' she can sit up for longer periods. She really is doin' jest fine . . . but I . . . I guess the strain of it all might be catchin' up with me."

"How much longer?" asked Marty.

"She's talkin' daily 'bout going home now. I don't think we'll be able to keep her much longer."

"Will she be able to travel alone?"

Belinda looked carefully at her mother. "She's . . . she's asked me to accompany her," she answered slowly, watching for Marty's reaction.

Marty took her time in responding. "An' ya think ya'd like to." It was more of a statement than a question. Belinda's mother knew her daughter well.

"I . . . I thought it would be a nice change. See a bit of the country. I've never been east before, and I . . ."

Belinda wished she could bring herself to say openly that she needed to get away . . . needed time to be able to think. The two young men in her life were crowding her, making her feel she was being pushed into a corner. She wanted to get away to where she had room to breathe. But Belinda said none of those things.

"I think it would be good fer ya," said Marty, tiredly pushing a stray strand of hair back from her face. "Days I wish I could jest do the same," she admitted.

Belinda turned a concerned face to her mother, then reached out a comforting hand and touched her cheek. "Luke an' I are both pra-yin' . . ." she told Marty, "prayin' thet those special meetin's might turn things right around. God can, you know. Arnie can still—"

"It's more than jest our young Abe. Luke was right 'bout 'im, of course. The arm has gone bad. But it's . . . it's beyond thet now. Some-times I look at Arnie an' I see such pain in his eyes I can scarcely stand it. I think he is hurtin' far more than thet boy."

"He still comes to church?" Belinda asked. Since being so busy and having so few weekends at home, she had been attending the church in town rather than the one out near the farm.

"Oh yes, he's there. Doesn't take part in anythin', though. Jest sits. I sometimes wonder iffen he's even listenin'." Marty sighed deeply.

"Is he still angry with Luke?" asked Belinda.

Marty shrugged her shoulders. "He doesn't say . . . but I'm guessin' he's still angry with Luke an' Clare . . . an' . . . maybe even with God. I don't know."

"We need to keep prayin'," insisted Belinda. "If we all jest pray . . ."

Marty nodded and managed a smile. "Prayin'? Thet seems to be all yer pa an' I do. Sometimes even in the middle of the night we spend us time a prayin'. This has been hard on yer pa. I worry 'bout him sometimes."

Marty stopped and Belinda reached out again to take her hand. She worried about both of them. She had never seen anything as difficult for Clark and Marty as the rift in the family circle.

The meetings began with the special speaker in the small country church. Arnie went to the first meeting and then declared himself too busy to go back on successive nights. Anne could go if she wished, he said, but he had other things he needed to do.

But Luke went. Every night he could possibly get away—even on those nights when his doctoring duties made him late for service—he rushed to finish his work, dressed quickly, and went to join the others. He had been feeling a "dryness"—a need for spiritual refreshing. The strained relationship with Arnie had cut him deeply. He knew instinctively that only God could meet his inner need and, ultimately, mend the broken family relationships.

EIGHTEEN

Changes

As much as Belinda would have liked to do so, she could not avoid either Rand or Jackson. As soon as she was back in town, Jackson was either at the bedside of Mrs. Stafford-Smyth or in the small office where Belinda picked up her nursing needs and left her daily chart.

He always smiled and teased a bit, and asked for dinner dates or evening walks. Belinda put him off the best she could, but she knew that one day soon there would be some kind of showdown if she didn't escape.

Rand, too, was a problem. Nearing completion on another house, he had hinted once or twice that as soon as it was finished, he would like to begin work on a house of his own. At first Belinda had been surprised, but then it seemed reasonable enough that a builder would make himself a place to live rather than continue to pay rent at the local boardinghouse. She had smiled and commended him.

Then one day Rand followed up on his intentions. "Could I drop by some sketches, so thet ya can do some lookin'?"

"Well . . . I . . . I," she began, but Rand only smiled and said he'd bring over the sketches the next evening.

Belinda went to work the next morning feeling desperate. Had Rand really meant what she feared he might? Had she been giving him the wrong impression? She hadn't intended to. She needed . . . she desperately needed some time away from all this.

She pushed her troubled thoughts aside as she entered her patient's room. She did not wish to bother Mrs. Stafford-Smyth with her problems. "Ya look very chipper this mornin'," she informed her charge, and Mrs. Stafford-Smyth responded that she was feeling much improved, too.

After Jackson came and had completed his regular morning check, Belinda turned to her patient. "I'm going to slip down to the dining room for a cup of coffee with Dr. Brown," she said very matter-of-factly, though Mrs. Stafford-Smyth smiled knowingly and Jackson gave her a broad grin as he held the door for her.

"What a pleasant surprise," he noted when they were alone in the hall.

Belinda only smiled. "I'd like a full and honest report on our patient," she informed him.

"Oh my," he laughed. "I had hoped that you found my company irresistible."

Belinda did not say any more about Mrs. Stafford-Smyth until they were seated at a corner table with steaming cups of coffee and fresh morning muffins before them. "Mrs. Stafford-Smyth talks daily about returning to Boston," she began. "What I want to know is this: is she well enough to travel?"

Jackson's eyes lit up. "I'm sure that traveling would not in any way be a hazard," he answered truthfully, then hastened to add, "providing of course, she has able assistance."

"And would you call me 'able assistance'?" asked Belinda with a teasing tone.

Jackson set his coffee cup back down and stared at Belinda. "What are you saying?" he asked.

"Mrs. Stafford-Smyth has been after me for some time to travel home with her," responded Belinda. "I have been puttin' her off . . . but recently I've been thinkin' it might be a nice change."

Jackson looked shocked, but he seemed to quickly regain control and even managed a smile. "Perhaps it would," he answered. "You have been quite . . . quite confined, haven't you? A little break for you might be nice and then when you return . . ." Jackson did not finish his sentence.

"How long do you think you would be gone?" he said instead. "A couple of weeks?"

"Thet's . . . thet's not quite what Mrs. Stafford-Smyth has in mind," answered Belinda evenly. "She wishes me to stay on as her private nurse."

Belinda saw the shadow pass over Jackson's face and linger in the depths of his eyes. "But surely you're not even considering . . . ?" he began.

"Yes," Belinda nodded. "Yes, I am."

"But . . . but . . ." began Jackson, "you can't be serious."

Belinda did not waver. "Why?" she asked simply. "I talked to Luke about it last night. He says thet Flo is quite able to handle the office duties now. He said you had been particularly intent on trainin' her—"

"I *was* intent on training her," Jackson said abruptly. "I've been most anxious to relieve you of your constant nursing . . . but not so that you could go to Boston. Only so you would be free to consider . . . consider other things."

The silence hung heavy between them. Belinda, uncomfortable, toyed with her teaspoon, unable to look up at Jackson.

"How long?" he asked at length.

"I don't know," she answered honestly. "It depends on how things go. Mrs. Stafford-Smyth has even mentioned my bein' a travelin' companion fer her trips abroad—"

Jackson groaned. "After all these years," he said softly. "After all these years of waiting, and you are asking me to go on waiting while—"

Belinda's head came up. "No!" she said quickly. "No!"

She looked directly into Jackson's face. "I have *never* asked ya to wait, Jackson. Never. Waiting was . . . was yer idea. I'm . . . I'm dreadfully sorry if ya've had the wrong . . . the wrong impression about . . . about us. Yer a dear friend, Jackson, an' . . . I . . . care deeply fer ya, but I don't . . . haven't ever meant to make ya think thet . . ."

She stumbled to a stop. Jackson sat before her with an ashen face, saying nothing. He reached a shaking hand up to rub his brow. At length he was able to lift his eyes again to Belinda's.

She was also sitting silently, the tears unwillingly forming in the corners of her eyes. She hadn't wanted to hurt Jackson. Hadn't planned to do so. She felt heartless, even though she knew the fault was not really hers.

"I . . . I'm sorry," she whispered softly.

Jackson reached across the table and took her hand gently in his. "My dear little Belinda," he said in not much more than a whisper. "You've always tried to tell me . . . haven't you? But I refused to listen. Refused to believe that it wouldn't work out . . . in time." He paused a moment to sort out his thoughts and then went on softly, "Go ahead. Go to Boston. And if you ever get tired of it . . . or if you ever change your mind, I'll . . . I'll be here . . . waiting."

"No, Jackson, please," broke in Belinda. "Please . . . please don't wait anymore. I . . . I couldn't bear it. I . . . I feel thet so much of yer life has already been spent in waitin'."

Jackson's laugh was strained, but the sound of it relieved the tension in the air. "You make me sound like an old, old man," he chided.

Belinda shook her head in confusion and flushed. "Of course I don't mean thet," she hastened to say, gently withdrawing her hand. "It's jest . . . jest . . ."

Jackson nodded, looking as if he truly understood what she was saying. Even that nearly broke Belinda's heart. Oh, she fervently wished—hoped—he would stop waiting for her and find someone else.

It was no easier breaking the news to Rand. He had come over that evening with the sketches he had promised. After pouring two glasses of lemonade, Belinda reluctantly followed him, with his sketches, to the picnic table under the large elm trees. Rand spread the drawings out before them.

"I want ya to go over 'em carefully," he said, excitement in his voice. "Anythin' thet ya like, jest mark and then we'll do up another sketch combinin' it all together."

Belinda drew in her breath. "I'm . . . I'm really excited about yer house, Rand," she said slowly, "but I don't know how much help I'll be able to give."

At Rand's questioning gaze she hurried on, "You see, Mrs. Stafford-

Smyth is able to travel now, and she has asked me to accompany her back to Boston."

"To Boston?" echoed Rand. "Thet's a fair piece, as I understand it. How long's it take anyway?"

"Fer the trip? I . . . I'm not sure but . . ."

Rand began to fold the sketches, then changed his mind and spread them out again. "Iffen we have it figured out before ya leave," he said, "I could start gettin' things under way whilst ya was gone. Then when ya git back—"

"But Mrs. Stafford-Smyth wants me to stay on," Belinda admitted hesitantly.

"Stay on? What ya meanin'? Stay on fer how long?"

"In . . . indefinitely," Belinda said, her voice low.

"But ya didn't agree to anythin' like thet, did ya?" asked Rand in disbelief.

"Well, I . . . I said that I would consider it and . . . and recently I have thought thet . . . thet I would like to," Belinda finished in a rush, her chin coming up.

"But . . . but what 'bout us?" Rand asked hoarsely.

"Us?"

"Us! Our plans?"

"Rand," Belinda said as softly as she could, "you and I have not talked about any 'plans.'"

Rand flushed and rustled his sketches. "Well . . . well, maybe not . . . yet," he stammered. "The timin' wasn't right. I had to git me some means first. But ya knew . . . ya knew how I felt about ya. Thet as soon as I was able I'd be askin' . . ."

Belinda shook her head slowly, her eyes clouded. "No, Rand. I'm afraid I didn't know. Maybe I should've, but I've thought of you as a dear friend—"

"A friend?" hissed Rand. Then he drew himself up, a set look on his face. "It's the doctor, ain't it?" he insisted. "I knew . . . I knew the minute I saw thet guy he was trouble." Rand's eyes sparked angrily.

Belinda reached out to lay a hand on Rand's sleeve. "No," she said abruptly. "No." She shook her head, tears filling her eyes. "Jackson has

562

nothing to do with how I feel about you. I . . . I . . . care deeply about you, Rand. If there was . . . anyone . . . anyone I would . . . would like to share a home with . . . it would be you." Her lips trembled as she spoke. "But I'm not ready. I . . . I'm jest not ready."

"Yer two nieces have been married fer a couple'a years already," Rand reminded her, then added almost bitterly, "Seems thet by the time a woman reaches yer age, she should be most ready to settle down . . . to know 'er own mind."

Belinda turned away. His words seemed unfair . . . even if they were true. Most young women were married before they were her age. She thought of her nieces. By all reports Amy Jo and Melissa were both very happy. Belinda was happy for them. But she wasn't Amy Jo . . . and she wasn't Melissa. She still didn't feel ready for marriage. Or maybe she just hadn't met the right young man. She didn't know. She was so confused. Maybe there would never be a young man in her life. Well, that was better than trying to live her life with the wrong one. She turned back to Rand.

"I'm very sorry . . . really. I wouldn't have misled you for the world. I . . . I . . . you are special to me . . . as . . . a . . . friend. It's jest . . . jest thet I don't care in . . . in thet way."

Rand took Belinda's hand. But Belinda resisted his effort to draw her toward him.

"Okay," he finally conceded. "Go 'long to Boston. Guess I can busy myself on another house. No rush on this one. But when ya git back . . . we'll . . . we'll talk about it."

"Rand," argued Belinda. "I . . . I might stay for a long time . . . several years. I might not ever come back."

"We'll see," said Rand darkly as he rolled up the sketches. "We'll jest have to wait an' see."

"How soon can you be ready to go?" Belinda asked Mrs. Stafford-Smyth the next morning.

"Am I being evicted?" the woman asked good-naturedly.

Belinda smiled. "No! I thought ya were anxious to be on yer way home, and I asked Dr. Brown yesterday over thet cup of coffee if ya were ready to travel. He assured me there was no reason for ya to stay on here one moment longer than ya want to."

By the time Belinda had finished her speech, Mrs. Stafford-Smyth was beaming. "And you'll go with me?" she asked.

"I'll go with ya," promised Belinda, feeling much relief in just saying the words.

"And stay?" asked the elderly woman.

"And stay!" responded Belinda. "At least fer a time."

"Good!" said Mrs. Stafford-Smyth. She seemed like she was truly looking forward to having Belinda with her. The two of them got on well. And Belinda was surer than ever that she needed a change—as did two young men whose expectations she did not share.

Luke went to the farm for a visit with Clark and Marty. Marty knew the moment she looked at his face that something important had happened, but it wasn't until they were seated around the comfortable kitchen table sharing their coffee and doughnuts that she dared to comment.

"Ya look like a heavy weight's been lifted off yer shoulders," she observed.

Luke smiled. "Not my shoulders—my heart," he said.

Marty's face brightened. She knew Luke had attended every meeting he could, staying behind to share in the prayer times whenever possible.

"Those meetings were just what I needed to get things back into proper focus again," he admitted.

Marty nodded. She had found the special services a time of spiritual encouragement and refreshing, as well. In fact, she and Clark had talked and prayed together one night until near morning, and finally had been able to leave the matter of the family tension in the hands of a masterful God.

"I'm on my way over to see Arnie," Luke went on, and Marty looked at Clark, hardly able to contain her pleasure. God was already answering their prayer.

"To tell 'im ya forgive him?" she asked quickly, eagerly.

Luke looked surprised. "Forgive? I have nothing to forgive him for. No . . . I . . . I am going to beg my brother to forgive me," said Luke soberly, and the tears began to fill his eyes.

"But . . . but I don't understand," said Marty. "Arnie was angry with you . . ."

"And for good reason," Luke explained. "I had no business to be butting into Arnie's life, assuming I knew what was best for his son, demanding he see things my way." By the time Luke had finished his speech, tears were coursing down his cheeks. "I didn't mean to be arrogant . . . and . . . and self-righteous, but I was. I just hope and pray that Arnie can find it in his heart to forgive me."

Marty looked at Clark. His eyes were also filled with tears. He reached out and took the slender, strong hand of his doctor son and squeezed it gently. She could tell he was unable to express his thoughts because of his deep emotions.

Marty wiped at her eyes and blew her nose. When she could speak again she took Luke's other hand. "We'll be prayin'," she said. "Yer pa an' me'll be prayin' the whole time it takes ya to talk to yer brother."

But Clark had found his voice. "I think we should start now," he stated simply, and after they had bowed their heads together, Clark led the little group in prayer.

Luke and Arnie each talked about the incident later from his own perspective. Both said that the meeting of brother with brother was the most emotional thing they had ever been through. After Luke's initial confession and plea for Arnie to forgive him for his arrogance and interference, Luke suggested they pray together. At first Arnie was guarded and defensive, but as Luke began to pray, Arnie, too, was touched with his need to restore his relationships—first of all with his God, and then with his family. Soon he, too, was crying out to God in repentance and contrition.

They wept and prayed together, arms around each other's shoulders. By the time they had sobbed it all out to God and to each other, they both felt spent but, at the same time, refreshed. Nothing was said about young Abe. Luke knew it was not his decision, and Arnie knew he would need to deal with the matter soon and honestly.

Arnie did not put off the matter of Abe's arm for very long. In his head he realized that already too much time had passed since the accident, and he recognized and admitted to himself that the arm was continually worsening. After talking it over with Anne, he called Abe to the kitchen where he and Anne sat at the family table.

Arnie swallowed hard. It was not easy for him to speak honestly with his son about a matter that was so painful and had caused so much heartache.

"Yer uncle Luke has been to see us," he began. When he hesitated, Abe looked from his father to his mother with some fear in his eyes. With effort, Arnie hurried on. "He . . . he's . . . he's concerned 'bout yer arm."

Abe let his glance fall to the offending limb, but his gaze did not linger. Arnie noticed that the boy drew the arm closer to his side.

"Fact is . . . fact is . . ." Arnie found it hard to keep the tears from his eyes and voice. "We've known fer some time thet the arm wasn't healin' right. Luke tried to tell me . . . but I wouldn't listen." Arnie paused to clear his throat and then said, "Luke told me at the time thet ya needed surgery to . . . to right the arm . . . but I . . . I . . ."

But Abe stopped him, his eyes wide with amazement. "They can do thet?"

Arnie looked at the boy, not sure what he was asking.

"Can they, Pa?" Abe repeated. He let his eyes return to the crooked arm, locked into its constant position. "Can they right the arm?"

Arnie nodded slowly, blinking back the tears. "Luke says they can," he said honestly. Then seeing the light suddenly come to the eyes of his son, he hastened on, "Oh, maybe not . . . not perfectly . . . but at least . . . at least they can help it a good deal . . . straighten it some and strengthen it some an' . . . an' give it some movement."

But Abe obviously was not hearing his pa's words of caution. He was hearing words of hope. His eyes were bright with joy as he turned back to Arnie.

"When?" was all he asked.

Anne finally spoke, brushing away tears that lay on her cheeks and reaching to put an arm around her son. "Abe," she said slowly, softly, "I . . . I don't think ya understand. It's not gonna be thet easy to fix. Ya don't jest walk in the doctor's office an' have him . . . do . . . do yer arm. It means a trip to the city . . . examinations, decisions . . . then iffen the city doctors think it will work out okay . . . then they . . . they need to operate . . . to break the arm again . . . an' then try to set it . . . mend it better."

"But . . . but . . ." Abe faltered, his eyes mirroring new despair. "But ya said, Pa, thet it would help some . . . thet Uncle Luke said . . ."

Arnie nodded solemnly.

"Then . . . then . . . ?" But Abe stopped. His eyes misted for the first time. Arnie felt that his son now understood about the pain involved with the surgery.

But when Abe spoke, the pain was not mentioned. "It costs a lot, huh?"

The simple words cut Arnie to the quick. "No," he said quickly, shaking his head and starting to his feet. "No, son, thet's not the reason. We . . . we . . ." But Arnie could not go on, and again Anne took over, reaching for Arnie's hand as she spoke to Abe.

"It was yer pain we feared—not the cost. We . . . we didn't want ya to suffer no more . . . yer pa an' me. We . . . we hoped the arm would git steadily better on its own, but . . . but . . . we think now thet it won't, not by itself." She stopped and, still clasping Arnie's hand, reached out her other hand to Abe.

"So . . . so," she went on hesitantly, "I guess it's really yer decision. Now . . . now thet ya know about . . . about the . . . the surgery . . . the healing again . . . what do you think we should do?"

Abe did not hurry with his answer. He looked steadily from one parent to the other. Then he looked down at his disabled limb. He swallowed hard and licked dry lips.

"Iffen ya don't mind . . . iffen it won't be . . . be . . . too much cost, then I'd like to try it . . . the surgery. Even iffen it jest makes it a little bit better, it would be . . . be good."

The words brought a flood of tears to Arnie. He reached out and drew Abe to him, burying his face against the leanness of the young body. Abe seemed confused by his father's response, but even in his youth he knew Arnie needed him. Needed his love and his support.

"It's okay, Pa," he mumbled, his arms wrapped firmly around Arnie's neck. "It's okay. It won't hurt thet much."

"Don't ya see? Don't ya see?" sobbed Arnie. "We shoulda had it done first off. Luke tried to tell me . . . but I wouldn't listen. It woulda worked better . . ."

Abe pulled back far enough to look into his father's eyes. "Is thet what's been troublin' ya?" he asked candidly.

Arnie only nodded. Abe moved to place his arm securely around his father's neck again. "Oh, Pa," he said with tears in his eyes. "We've been so scared . . . so scared . . . all of us kids. We feared ya had some awful sickness an' might die . . . an' here . . . here it was jest my silly ol' arm. It's okay, Pa." The young boy patted his father's shoulder. "An' ya know what? Iffen ya'd asked me way back then 'bout breakin' my arm all over agin, I'da prob'ly been scared ta death an' . . . an' run off in the woods hopin' it'd heal by itself. Now we all know thet ain't gonna happen," he finished matter-of-factly. "I know ya love me. The pain . . . it . . . it won't be too bad," he reassured them.

Father and son held each other close, and Anne breathed a prayer to God as she wiped her tears. There was much ahead for all of them—for there would be surgery to be faced just as soon as Luke could make the arrangements.

Arnie went to see Luke the next morning, but on the way he stopped to ask forgiveness of Clare and to beg Clark and Marty to forgive him for all the suffering he had caused them in his bitterness. He pleaded to be restored to his old relationship within the family circle, and with tears of joy and prayers of thanksgiving he was drawn back into their loving arms.

NINETEEN

Boston

"Are ya comfortable?" Belinda asked Mrs. Stafford-Smyth. They were settled on the eastbound train for Boston after an emotional and teary good-bye at the station. Most of Belinda's family had been there to see her off. She was glad that neither Rand nor Jackson had appeared, although she had received messages from each of them the night before her departure.

May your trip to Boston be smooth, uneventful—and hasty, said Jackson's light little note tucked into a basket of forget-me-nots. Belinda had not been able to hide her smile.

Rand's message had been more direct. *Sorry for any misunderstanding,* it read. *Whenever you are ready to come back, I'll be here. Rand.* This note came with a small packet of house plans, and etched in a corner in Rand's script was the terse comment, *Study at leisure.*

Poor Rand, mused Belinda. It seemed he was refusing to give up.

But now all of that was behind her. She leaned back against the velvet seat of the Pullman and tried to gather her thoughts into some kind of order.

I'm actually on my way—to Boston! Imagine! She had made the decision, arranged for her absence from her work, checked with her family, planned the departure, and sent word to her new employer's home in Boston. *I guess I'm really grown-up now!* she joked inwardly. She was on her own, bound for a city hundreds of miles from home—and with indefinite plans as to the length of her stay.

Marty had shed some tears, of course. Belinda had expected it. She was Marty's baby—the last of the children to go. Belinda knew it would be hard for her ma and pa, but she was so thankful the clash between Arnie and the other family members had been healed before she left. Again she said a quick prayer of thanks to God. That morning at the station her mother had looked years younger and much more relaxed, even though she was bidding her youngest a tearful good-bye.

Belinda took a few moments to worry about the office. Would Flo really be able to take over all the tasks that had been Belinda's for so long? Would she be skilled enough to assist with the simple surgeries that were done in the little surgical room? Of course, now that Jackson was there, he would be able to assist Luke—or Luke assist Jackson, whichever way it went. Belinda, happy for that fact, was able to dismiss the office from her mind.

Next, Belinda considered her nieces and nephews. They grew so quickly. If she stayed away for any extended period of time, they would grow up without her. She pictured rambunctious Dack. It seemed like such a short time ago that he was a boisterous, sometimes in-the-way little preschooler, and now he was playing boyish games and doing lessons. Even Luke's three little ones were growing up so rapidly. Belinda found it hard to believe that Ruthie was already toddling about and saying words that might not be understood but seemed to mean something to the pint-sized chatterer.

What will they be like when I get back home? she wondered. *They change so quickly.*

Then Belinda remembered Melissa and Amy Jo. Word had just arrived that Melissa was the mother of a baby boy, Clark Thomas, and that Amy Jo would have her turn at motherhood some time in November. It seemed unreal to Belinda. She thought again of Rand's angry words. He was right, Belinda admitted. *Most girls—women—do know their own minds by the time they're my age.*

For a minute Belinda's face grew warm with the memory, and then she straightened her shoulders, lifted her chin, and assured herself, *And I do know my own mind, too. I knew then and I know now that I'm not ready to marry either Rand O'Connel or Jackson Brown. It would be wrong, wrong, wrong for me to do so.*

Feeling better with that matter settled, Belinda turned her eyes back to her patient. "Would ya like another pillow?" she asked solicitously.

"Stop fussing so," scolded Mrs. Stafford-Smyth good-naturedly. "If I want something, I will let it be known. This is your first trip. Enjoy it. Look theah—out the window. See that sleepy little town? The whole country is filled with one aftah the othah. I wondah how folks can tell them apart." She smiled. "Wondah just how many people get off at the wrong stop," she mused on, "thinking that they have arrived home."

Belinda smiled. But she was sure that no homecoming included such a problem. She realized Mrs. Stafford-Smyth saw even Belinda's little town as one of tiny duplicate beads of a necklace stretching all across the great continent. Yet, if she, Belinda, were heading home, she knew no other town would look the same to her as her own town would.

She decided to check with her patient one more time. "Ya promise ya'll ask if ya wish something?"

"I promise," laughed the woman.

Belinda shifted some hand luggage so she could move closer to the window.

"In that case," she said lightly, "I will be glad to accept yer invitation and enjoy the scenery. I've never traveled quite this far from home before," and Belinda settled down to follow the changing landscape as the train rocked and rattled its way east over the uneven tracks.

The landscape soon began to change. The trees were bigger and forests denser. The farms looked different to Belinda than the farms at home. The small towns gave way to larger ones. They even passed through some cities. Belinda, face pressed to the window, found them especially intriguing and couldn't see enough of the people who lined the platforms or walked the streets. *This is a new world from the one*

I've known all my life, she told herself. She could sense it, even though the glass windowpane held her back from it.

They were obliged to make two train changes. Belinda worried that the procedure of getting resettled might be hard for her patient, but Mrs. Stafford-Smyth seemed to handle the situation well. They had plenty of help from the solicitous porters, who probably sensed a good tip from the hand of the older woman.

On the third day Belinda noticed Mrs. Stafford-Smyth begin to lean forward in some agitation. At first Belinda wondered if her employer was experiencing some kind of pain or discomfort. Then she noticed the shining eyes, the flushed cheeks. "We should be in Boston by teatime," the woman exulted, and Belinda understood her excitement.

Belinda tried to imagine what the home of Mrs. Stafford-Smyth was like. Whenever she had asked, the woman had refused to indulge her curiosity. "You shall see for yourself in due time," she answered comfortably, and so Belinda was forced to wait. Now that they were almost there, she found her own excitement mounting.

Just as Mrs. Stafford-Smyth had told her, shortly after two, Belinda began to see buildings crowding in closely on both sides of the tracks. The shrill whistle of the train announced that they were coming to another city center, and then the conductor was walking the aisles, crying his message of "Bos-ton. Bos-ton. Next stop, Bos-ton," and Mrs. Stafford-Smyth began to twitter and flutter and primp for their arrival.

Belinda felt a-twitter, too. She peered from the train window for as long as she dared, trying hard to gather all the information she could by staring out into the busy city streets.

"This is the shoddy part of town," Mrs. Stafford-Smyth said with a wave of her hand. "We'll see the real Boston latah."

Belinda looked around. It did look rather shoddy, but she would not have said so to her elderly charge. She knew how much Mrs. Stafford-Smyth loved her city.

The train was decidedly slowing, and Belinda began to gather bags and packages together. She picked up the hat she had laid aside and carefully settled it back into position on her curls, pinning it securely into place with her hatpins. Then she moved to assist Mrs. Stafford-

Smyth, who was smoothing her grayish hair into place, and Belinda helped her arrange her hat and veil securely.

"What do we do once we arrive?" Belinda asked as she worked.

"Windsah will be theah with the carriage," replied the lady.

"Will you wish to lie down?" asked Belinda, wanting to know how to prepare things for her patient.

"My word, no!" sniffed the woman. "I will ride through my own town sitting up." Then her tone softened. "I'm not sure that I will evah want to lie down again," she added. "Seems I have been lying down for ye-ahs and ye-ahs."

Belinda smiled. "It has really been just months and months," she corrected softly.

Windsor was there just as Mrs. Stafford-Smyth had said. He came aboard and assisted his lady from the train, helping Belinda settle her in the elaborately ornate carriage. Belinda was so busy staring she could hardly keep her wits about her to do what was necessary. At length they were ready, Mrs. Stafford-Smyth ensconced among many pillows, and Belinda sedately seated opposite her beside the butler, Windsor. The driver was given the signal, the whip cracked, and the impatient horses were off with a flurry into the traffic of the downtown streets.

Belinda longed to lean out the window to see all they were passing, but she knew it would not be ladylike. Instead, she sat silently as the good man Windsor inquired about their journey.

"And was the trip tedious, madam?" he was asking.

Mrs. Stafford-Smyth sighed. "Yes," she said simply, "quite tedious. But it would have been much worse had it not been for Belinda. She made me quite comfortable."

The butler did not turn to look at Belinda, but she could tell he was greatly relieved to know she had made things as easy as possible for his madam.

"And how are things at home, Windsah?" asked Mrs. Stafford-Smyth.

"We have done ou-ah best in Madam's absence," he said simply as she nodded.

Belinda turned her head slightly to gaze out the small window of the carriage. Would she ever have opportunity to see all the fascinating things they were whisking by in this wonderful city? Mrs. Stafford-Smyth and Windsor seemed not the least interested.

"Cook needs instructions," Windsor was telling her. "She wishes to know what diet regimen Madam might be on."

"Madam is on no diet," declared Mrs. Stafford-Smyth. "I am so sick of flat-tasting hotel food. I can scarcely wait for the flavahs of my own kitchen. You tell Cook to prepare the usual—and lots of it, because I plan to eat my fill ovah the next few days."

The butler's face barely hid his amusement. "Very well, madam," he said. "And where does Madam wish to be served? In your own chambers?"

"I shall take tea in the drawing room the moment we arrive," said Mrs. Stafford-Smyth. "Then I wish to see my rose garden. I have missed it terribly. Then—"

"But Madam should rest after such a long and rigorous trip," Windsor chided her with just the proper amount of respect and liberty born out of long years of service.

To Belinda's surprise Mrs. Stafford-Smyth did not argue. "Perhaps," she consented, "for an hou-ah or two."

"And does Madam wish Miss Davis to occupy the Omberg suite?"

"No, she shall have the suite next to mine."

"The Rosewood?"

"The Rosewood."

How foreign these terms seemed to Belinda! This talk of "suites" instead of rooms, of names instead of locations. The Omberg suite! The Rosewood suite! It all sounded very mysterious—and so elegant.

But when Belinda got her first view of the mansion Mrs. Stafford-Smyth called home, she gulped and understood why they had to name rooms. She was sure they never would have kept things straight otherwise. Never had she seen so many rooms under one roof—not even at the Rose Palace Hotel.

The house was of brick and stone, and its extensions and gables and additions seemed to go on and on. *I'm glad to be near Mrs. Stafford-Smyth,* she decided with no small amount of relief. She might never find her way otherwise.

The house was nestled on the wide expanse of carefully manicured green lawn, with flowerbeds filled with hollyhock, daisies, and begonias. The driveway of red stone circled to the wide front step, and an arched brick canopy reached out to keep all who arrived protected from the weather.

Mrs. Stafford-Smyth was excited to be home, but she showed none of the awe Belinda felt as her eyes scanned the imposing sight.

"Welcome to Marshall Manor," said Mrs. Stafford-Smyth softly, smiling at Belinda.

"Oh my!" was all Belinda could manage. She felt she had just stepped into a fairy tale. She was glad Windsor, at least, had his wits about him. He stepped down from the carriage to help Mrs. Stafford-Smyth.

Two maids stood at the top of the stairs, ready to be of assistance at the least nod from the butler. Windsor spoke to the one nearest to him. "Madam wants her tea in the drawing room," he said, and the girl bustled off without so much as a nod.

Then Windsor spoke to the second girl. "Show Miss Davis the Rose-wood suite," he said, "so that she might freshen herself for tea. Then escort her back to the drawing room."

The girl nodded to Belinda and led the way through the doorway and up the long circular staircase. Belinda was still gazing about her, enamored by the polished wood, the glistening chandeliers, and the sparkling crystal. Never in all her wildest dreams could she have imagined that such a place existed. *No wonder Mrs. Stafford-Smyth was so anxious to get home!* The place was absolutely breathtaking.

TWENTY

Getting Acquainted

The Rosewood suite was like a dream, too. Belinda, expecting to find a pretty little room in a soft rose color, found instead a suite of rooms done in rich wood paneling, blue velvets, and white lace. Never had she seen anything so exquisite, not even in the picture books Melissa had shared with her during their school days.

A large four-poster bed with a blue spread and lace overlay graced one wall of the large bedroom. The window drapes were also of blue velvet with white lace. On the other side of the room was a marble fireplace with a comfortable grouping of soft chairs surrounding a low, highly polished wooden table. An ornamental lamp was placed on white lace in the middle. At the window was a window seat covered with blue velvet, almost hidden from view by several pillows of blue print fabrics and lace work. The chest of drawers and the tall wardrobe matched the polished wood of the bed. The walls that were not paneled were covered with beautifully patterned wallpaper, with blue as the predominant color.

Belinda just stood there trying to absorb it all.

Wouldn't Mama love to see this, she breathed to herself, well aware of Marty's love for beautiful things.

"The bath is through there," indicated the young maid, pointing to a door off to the right. Her voice brought Belinda back to the present—she was supposed to be getting ready for tea. She flushed and hurried forward.

"I'll wait for you in the hallway, miss," said the maid.

Belinda did not dare linger any longer, though she certainly wanted to. She looked quickly about her, promising herself a leisurely, thorough inspection later, and quickly went through to the small room off her bedroom.

The bath, too, was in blues, but here bright spots of pink and some ivory had been added in place of the whites in the bedroom. It was most becoming, and Belinda wished she could skip tea and just wander the suite at her own leisure.

She poured water from the pitcher to the basin and looked about her for a washcloth. The only ones in view looked so new and so ornate she wondered if they were put there for use or for decoration. She had to use something, so at length she gingerly picked one up, dipped it carefully in the warm water, and wiped her face. Alarmed at the travel grime that showed up on the cloth, Belinda carefully washed it out the best she could and then hung it back on its rack. Hurriedly she smoothed her hair and went to present herself to the maid.

She was led through a long hallway, past many doors, down long winding stairs, and then through another hallway, and finally into a room where a bright fire burned on the hearth. Here, too, homey, elegant furnishings seemed to abound. In the midst of her pillows sat Mrs. Stafford-Smyth, Windsor before her and an older lady standing back slightly, listening carefully to the Madam recounting tales of her illness in the little town out west. For a moment Belinda hesitated. It was only now that she fully appreciated the difference in what Mrs. Stafford-Smyth was accustomed to and what they had been able to offer her.

"Come in, my deah, come in," the lady said cheerily, motioning with her hand to Belinda.

Belinda felt suddenly shy. She could not refrain from looking dolefully down at her crumpled and slightly old-fashioned traveling gown. Surely it—or she—was out of place in this elegant home.

"Would you pou-ah, my deah," invited Mrs. Stafford-Smyth, not seeming the least bit nonplussed by Belinda's appearance. Then she turned to the butler and the elderly woman in the room. "Belinda has spoiled me dreadfully, I'm afraid. She nursed me the total time I was ill. Oh, she had replacements at times, of course, but it was really Belinda who cared for me. I don't know what I should evah do without her. She knows exactly how I like my tea, the right amount of fluffing in the pillows, even how to make me smile when I get out of sorts."

Mrs. Stafford-Smyth gave Belinda an appreciative smile and waited for her "exactly right" tea.

"Ella showed you yo-ah suite?" she asked as she accepted the cup.

Belinda could not keep the shine from her eyes. "It's lovely," she enthused.

"Good! Then you won't be quite so tempted to be running back to one of those young men you left behind."

Belinda could feel the color rising in her cheeks. She poured another cup of tea and handed the cup to the lady who still stood by the serving tray. The woman was obviously flustered, and she nervously indicated that the cup was not for her. Belinda was bewildered.

"Mrs. Pottah does not take tea in the drawing room," said Mrs. Stafford-Smyth simply. "She has her tea in the kitchen."

Now it was Belinda's turn to be flustered. She felt her gaze travel to Windsor. Mrs. Stafford-Smyth seemed to read her question.

"Windsah does not take tea with us, eithah—unless on the rare occasion I can talk him into it."

"I see," murmured Belinda.

The woman called Mrs. Potter moved forward to serve Mrs. Stafford-Smyth some of the dainty sandwiches. She then hesitated, seeming not to know what to do next.

"Serve Miss Davis," instructed Mrs. Stafford-Smyth. "She will be taking tea with me daily."

The woman said nothing, just moved forward with the tray of sandwiches. Belinda was alert enough to realize that what was going on in the room was not the usual—but she had no idea what the usual might be.

After Mrs. Potter had served sandwiches and Belinda had replenished the teacups, pastries were served. Belinda thought she should decline, but they looked so good and she was so hungry after three days of train fare that she could not resist. *I'll work it off later,* she promised herself, and then wondered just how she was to work it off. While Mrs. Stafford-Smyth rested, there would be nothing for her to do, unless of course she could be of assistance in the kitchen.

When Mrs. Stafford-Smyth declared she couldn't eat another bite, Windsor took her arm. "You wanted to see your roses, madam?" he asked with proper respect.

"Oh yes, Windsah, please," she returned and was led sedately toward another door.

Belinda stood, carefully set her teacup back on the tray, and began to help Mrs. Potter gather the tea things. She was stopped by a dark look of disapproval. Not knowing her offense, she drew back, her eyes offering apology.

"I'm . . . I'm sorry," she stammered. "I meant to be most careful."

"Nurse does not need to concern herself with the picking up," the woman said curtly. "We all know our stations round heah."

Belinda frowned. It was all so strange. A room with people, and you had to pick and choose who could be served. Work to do and only those designated for the certain job dared to do it. She had never heard tell of such a way to live.

"And what am I to do?" she dared ask.

"Madam gives your ordahs."

"But . . . but she hasn't given any," Belinda reminded the woman.

"Then I guess you wait until she does," the woman threw over her shoulder as she hoisted her tray and left through the side door.

Belinda, alone in the room, didn't know whether she should exit through the door that had swallowed up Windsor and Mrs. Stafford-Smyth, try to find her way back to her own suite, or just wait right here where she was. It was all so puzzling.

She wandered slowly about the room, admiring each piece of furniture, each ornately framed picture. Her eyes traveled over everything, drinking in the beauty of her surroundings.

Oh, she thought, *I never dreamed anything could be so lovely. I could just look and look and look.* And except for wishing that she had her family near to share her adventure with, Belinda was full of excitement and satisfaction. *It won't be one bit hard to stay on here,* she told herself. *It's like living one's make-believe.* Then she turned to retrace her steps around the room one more time to make sure she didn't miss a single elegant item.

In the days that followed, Belinda became more acquainted with her surroundings. The suite she occupied also had an adjoining parlor room. Here again the basic color was blue, with a pattern of rose and touches of mint green enhancing the design. Belinda could not get her fill of the softness, the coolness, the harmony of the colors. The polished grain of the furniture and elegance of another marble fireplace added to the charm.

Off Belinda's sitting room was a door that led to Mrs. Stafford-Smyth's suite. A button on the lady's bedside table had been skillfully arranged to ring a buzzer in Belinda's room. Belinda soon discovered that there were many such buttons throughout the house. One in the parlor to ring for the maid. One in the drawing room to ring for the butler. One in the sunroom to ring for the cook. It seemed to Belinda that wherever Mrs. Stafford-Smyth took repose, a button was near her elbow.

But Belinda liked the button idea. It meant that she could attend the elderly lady without being with her every waking hour. She asked innocently for other duties about the house to make herself useful and was met with open-mouthed disbelief.

Do they think I'm capable of nothing but nursing? Belinda shrugged her shoulders and went to her own room to mind her own business. It wasn't as though Mrs. Stafford-Smyth kept ringing her buzzer. Belinda had plenty of free time she could have used to lighten someone else's load.

Her dilemma was partly solved by Mrs. Stafford-Smyth when she sent Belinda to the library to get her a book or two. Belinda was told to go to the drawing room and ring the bell for Windsor. He would show her to the library and indicate which new books Mrs. Stafford-Smyth had not yet had the opportunity to read.

Belinda did as she was told, and Windsor led her directly to a room with high-paneled ceilings and shelves upon shelves of books. Belinda couldn't help but gasp at the find. Windsor selected a few volumes from a stack of books that appeared to have been set aside, and Belinda carried them, still in awe, to Mrs. Stafford-Smyth.

"I declare," she said as she entered the room, "I have never seen so many books in all my life. Are they all yers?"

The lady smiled. "Of course. But if you like, we will pretend that it is a lending library. You may help yourself to whatever you like, anytime you wish."

"Oh, may I?" Belinda could scarcely believe her good fortune.

"One hint. Don't evah put a book back where you found it. Leave the book on the big oak desk in the middle of the room. Windsah is absolutely convinced that he is the only person in this house—in the world, I'll wage-ah—who knows the proper place on the shelves for each book."

This seemed a bit foolish to Belinda, especially when she planned to read many of the books. But she did not argue. She would do as she was bidden. As soon as she was excused, she went directly to the library to browse among the books.

It was difficult for her to choose from among so many, but at length she selected three volumes and took them to her room. The rest of the day passed quickly as she became engrossed in a Charles Dickens novel. An American history and a lovely little book of poems were also inviting. She no longer fretted that her hands were not busy—she would keep at least her mind occupied.

Wouldn't it be wonderful, she thought, *to read every book in there before I go home again?* But she knew it would take years and years to devour all the contents of those ample shelves.

Belinda could sense a certain tension in the household. She wasn't sure what it was, but she had the feeling it might have something to do with her. She couldn't think of what she might have done to cause friction, but it was there, nonetheless.

One afternoon when Belinda and Mrs. Stafford-Smyth were enjoying tea in the east parlor, Mrs. Potter entered the room.

"Has Madam decided when she would like her dinnah party?" she asked.

Mrs. Stafford-Smyth did some thinking. "Bring me a calendah, Pottah," said Mrs. Stafford-Smyth, and the woman went to do her bidding.

While she was out, the lady turned to Belinda. "I plan to have some of my old friends in," she confided. "Not a large pahty, but my closest acquaintances. I haven't seen them for so long and it will be nice to catch up on the news of Boston."

She sat silently for a moment, then went on as though talking to herself. "Let's see . . . we arrived home on Monday. We are now to Saturday. We could nevah be ready for dinnah guests by tomorrow. What night would you suggest, my deah?"

Belinda had no idea what to suggest. "How . . . how much time does the staff need?" she began. She had finally learned to refer to all of the household employees as staff.

"Windsah will take care of the invitations. The kitchen staff can be ready for the group I wish to have in two or three days."

"Then perhaps Wednesday evening," suggested Belinda just as Mrs. Potter returned to the room carrying the needed calendar. Belinda felt the woman's cold eyes upon her. She wasn't sure what she had said or done that had caused her to be miffed. Wasn't Wednesday giving the staff enough time?

"Or Thursday . . . or Friday," she added dumbly, watching for some sign of regained favor.

It did not come. But the woman did turn from Belinda and confer with Mrs. Stafford-Smyth. "What day were you thinking of, madam?"

"Wednesday," said Mrs. Stafford-Smyth without hesitation.

"Very good, madam," said Mrs. Potter. "Is there anything in particulah that you would like the kitchen to prepare?"

"I will leave that with you and Windsah," said Mrs. Stafford-Smyth. "You know my agitation at fussing over menus."

"Yes, madam," responded the woman.

"Ring for Windsah, would you please, my deah," Mrs. Stafford-

Smyth said to Belinda, and Belinda pressed the buzzer. Soon Windsor stood before them.

"Windsah, we are planning a small dinnah party for Wednesday night."

"Very good, madam," he said properly. "And how many will Madam be seating?"

"I would like you to invite Mrs. Prescott, and the Judge Allenbys, and . . . let's see. No, not the Forsyths this time. We'll save them for latah. Mr. Walsh. Celia loves to chattah with Mr. Walsh. And . . . one more couple, I should think. The Whitleys. That will do it. Yes, that should be just right, I think. That will mean eight at table. That should do."

"But Madam only named six guests. With herself at table, that leaves one short."

Mrs. Stafford-Smyth, with some impatience, listed off, "The Allenbys, Whitleys, Celia Prescott, Mr. Walsh, myself, and Belinda. That's eight," she corrected.

Belinda had seen a flash of surprise in the butler's eyes when her name was said, though he did not flinch. But the expression on Mrs. Potter's face indicated open resentment.

Belinda had thought nothing of being included in the dinner list, for she had been taking all her meals with Mrs. Stafford-Smyth, but when she recognized the looks on the faces before her, she began to wonder about the arrangements. Was this why she felt hostility in the house?

She dared broach the subject with Mrs. Stafford-Smyth when they were once again alone in the room.

"Did yer old nurse—I've forgotten her name—did she dine with you?"

"Of course not," said the lady frankly. "She ate in the kitchen or in her own rooms. Mostly she had her meals taken up, I think."

Belinda waited for a moment. "Do you suppose it . . . it would be wiser if I had my meals in my own room?" she asked softly.

Mrs. Stafford-Smyth looked surprised. "Don't you like sharing your meals with me?" she asked.

"Of course I do . . . it's jest thet . . . well, I feel that yer staff might think it's not quite appropriate, thet's all."

"Nonsense!" spoke the lady curtly. "This is my home and I can make my own rules." Belinda could see that the lady felt the matter was closed.

"But I *am* another employee," Belinda said candidly.

Mrs. Stafford-Smyth looked up from her needlework. "You are more like the daughter I nevah had," she replied softly, and Belinda was touched. How could she argue against that?

Mrs. Stafford-Smyth had been paying Belinda generously throughout the months of her nursing care out west, and Belinda had tucked away most of the money rather than spending it. But with the Lord's Day and the dinner party coming upon them, she decided that the time might be right to relinquish some of her hoarded funds. She entered the hall that led to Mrs. Stafford-Smyth's rooms, walking quietly, lest the woman was resting. As she knocked gently and was bidden to enter, Belinda slipped into the room.

"I do hope I'm not disturbin' ya," she spoke hurriedly, "but I was wonderin' about doing some shoppin'. Are there dress shops nearby that I could visit? I know my dresses are dreadfully outdated and out-of-place here, and with tomorrow bein' church an' all, I . . . I thought thet perhaps—"

"Oh my," said the lady, "I was hoping we could get by until I could go with you myself—but you are right. You would feel more comfortable with something new tomorrow. I should have thought of church. The fact that I am not quite up to going out yet myself should not preclude you from going. Of course you shall have a new dress—and hat—and a shawl, too, I'm thinking. And then of course a pair of dressy high-topped shoes and perhaps a parasol . . ."

Belinda was about to slow the lady down. She hadn't intended to spend *that* much money.

"Windsah will have the carriage brought round and will direct you to LeSoud's," she instructed briskly. "It is the shop I had planned to take you to myself. Oh my, I do wish I could go with you—but then we'll have othah outings. Bring me my writing pad, would you, deah? I'll just drop a little note to Madam Tilley."

And so saying, Mrs. Stafford-Smyth propped herself up on her pillows. Belinda meekly handed her the writing pad and the pen and ink, and Mrs. Stafford-Smyth began to write a letter for the lady called Madam Tilley. Belinda began to feel more and more anxious as the pen scratched on. It seemed the good lady was willing to spend all of Belinda's hard-earned money. Well, she would just put her foot down once she got to the store, she decided. Mrs. Stafford-Smyth would not be there to give orders then.

Belinda was sent to dress for her outing, and Windsor was given his orders and put his call through for the carriage. Before Belinda could catch her breath, she was traveling down the tree-lined streets on her way to the dress shop, with Windsor in attendance.

This time, without inhibitions, she stared openly from one side of the carriage at every mansionlike home, every expanse of green carpet, every hedge of roses, every fashionable carriage. *This truly is a magic kingdom—no wonder Mrs. Stafford-Smyth loves Boston!* she couldn't help but conclude.

TWENTY-ONE

A New Life

LeSoud's was not like any shop Belinda had ever seen or imagined. Magnificent draperies and glass chandeliers made it seem like a lovely parlor, not a retail establishment. Ornate ivory brocade chairs were grouped around low tables holding silver dishes of sweets.

Windsor stepped forward and presented Madam Tilley with the lengthy instructions from Mrs. Stafford-Smyth and introduced Miss Belinda to the older woman. From there Madam took charge, indicating which chair Windsor should retire to and that Belinda was to follow her.

They passed through to another room, this one smaller but decorated with the same type of furnishings. Belinda looked around her in some bafflement. She could see no gowns for sale.

Madam seated her and then called to a young woman dressed in a stylish black gown, stark in its simplicity but attractive with its flowing lines. The two conferred softly for a few moments, and then the girl, referred to as Yvonne, left and was soon back with three gowns draped carefully over her arm.

From then on things moved quickly. Belinda was ordered to stand, then sit as they twisted and fitted her until her head was swimming. She had no idea what was being decided on her behalf. The two women were not speaking English. Madam would "tut" and "hmm" and Yvonne would "oh-h" and "ah-h" as Belinda lifted her arms to accept one gown after the other over her head.

Then there were shoes to try on along with gloves and shawls and coats until Belinda felt dizzy with it all. In spite of the sense of commotion and things being out of her control, she did spot a gown that she liked. A soft green voile that seemed to suit her slender build, she noted as she looked into the full-length mirror, and it was attractive without being too fussy. She could tell it was something her mother would have approved of her wearing for church.

But that gown, too, was whisked away. Belinda knew not from whence they came or to whence they were returned. She tried to ask, but her voice was lost in the chatter of Madam and Yvonne.

When Belinda finally had her own gown on and had set her hat back on her head and drawn her gloves on her hands, she looked about her in bewilderment. She had come to buy a gown, and from the note Mrs. Stafford-Smyth had sent, she had feared she might have to argue her way out of numerous other purchases. But now it seemed she was not going to buy even the one dress she had sought. She looked to Madam, hoping for some explanation.

"But the gown . . . the green voile . . . I . . . I liked—"

"You were pleased with it—no?" the woman said happily, her eyes taking on a shine.

"Yes. Yes," said Belinda. "I . . . was pleased with it."

"It will be delivered this evening," responded the woman.

Belinda was relieved. She must have somehow conveyed to the two women that she wished to purchase the green voile dress. It was to be delivered.

Belinda now wished she had been able to purchase a light shawl and perhaps some more stylish shoes than the somewhat sturdy pair she had brought from home. *Well, I'll just have to get them later on,* she decided. This shopping trip had garnered the dress she needed. She was thankful for that.

Madam and Yvonne still scurried about the room gathering gowns and shoes and handbags.

Belinda hesitated.

"Was there something more, Miss Belinda?" Madam finally stopped long enough to ask.

Belinda flushed, reaching into her handbag. "The account," she faltered. "I need to pay you for the purchase."

Madam looked surprised. "The account is already cared for," she said quickly, her left eyebrow shooting up. "It is all to go on Madam Stafford-Smyth's charge."

"Oh, but there must be some misunderstandin'," began Belinda. "The . . . the gown is personal . . . for me."

Madam reached down to pick up the sheet of lengthy instructions Windsor had given her. "It is all right here," she explained, her shoulders and eyebrows raised expressively. "Madam has ordered specifically that the purchase go on her account, and we at LeSoud's do not go contrary to Madam." She finished with a firm shake of her head that invited no argument.

Belinda started to speak again but changed her mind. She didn't understand the workings of this new world, but perhaps Mrs. Stafford-Smyth felt it would be less complicated to charge the items to her account and for Belinda to simply reimburse her. Still slightly confused, she followed Madam Tilley from the back room to rejoin Windsor.

As they traversed the route back to the Stafford-Smyth mansion, Belinda thought again about her purchase. She was pleased about the green voile. It would be becoming and appropriate for Sunday and maybe afternoon tea, a tradition to which she had been introduced in the Stafford-Smyth household. She eventually wanted to buy a second dress—one a bit more "frilly" for such occasions as the coming dinner party. But she had been unable to get that message across to the Madam. Belinda sighed. She guessed the voile would have to do for the dinner, as well.

"How did you make out at LeSoud's?" asked Mrs. Stafford-Smyth at tea that afternoon.

"Oh my," answered Belinda, looking up from her teacup. "I've never seen so many lovely things. It was most difficult to make up my mind. I did find a dress, though. It is to be delivered this evening." Belinda put down her cup to look directly at her employer. "But I owe you for it. They . . . they wouldn't let me pay at the store. I . . . I don't even know how much it cost. I couldn't find a price tag on a single thing."

"No," said Mrs. Stafford-Smyth simply, "they do not publicly price their items at LeSoud's."

Belinda thought that strange, but she did not say so. There were many things done in unfamiliar ways in the city, she had concluded.

"And about the cost," went on Mrs. Stafford-Smyth simply, "the wardrobe comes with the position. There will be no need for reimbursement."

"But—" argued Belinda.

"No 'buts,'" the lady interrupted, raising a hand to hush Belinda. "You must realize you have a unique station in my home. You are not just my nurse in the same fashion that Pottah is my housekeeper. No, you are also my companion—and as such I expect you to accompany me into society, to sit at my table, and welcome my guests. Because of that, your wardrobe needs to be more . . . more extensive than you would have need of in the past. I would not ask you to pay such costs yourself. That would be unfai-ah. Do you understand, my deah?"

Belinda thought she did, but it still didn't seem quite right.

"Could I have another cup of tea, deah?" the good lady asked, closing the subject and passing Belinda her cup.

The voile dress arrived that evening. And along with it came boxes and boxes. Belinda held her breath and let it out slowly when a brief check proved they held a multitude of gowns and accessories. *This can't be!* she thought frantically. She must talk with Mrs. Stafford-Smyth quickly, before the delivery boy had a chance to return to the store. Most of what lay stacked about her room had to be returned with him.

Belinda was about to run to the suite next door when she nearly bumped into Mrs. Stafford-Smyth coming toward her rooms.

"They did arrive," she said with some excitement. "I thought I heard some commotion."

"Oh yes . . . yes. But, my . . . there's been a mistake . . . an awful mistake. I do have the green voile, but . . . but it looks like they must have sent most everything they had me try on."

Belinda, concerned that Mrs. Stafford-Smyth might think she'd had the audacity to take advantage of the charge account, had her hands clasped in front of her, and her heart was pounding so loudly she was sure the woman could hear it, too.

"I love looking at new things . . . don't you, deah?" Mrs. Stafford-Smyth smiled in a most relaxed fashion. "Do you mind terribly if we open all the boxes together?"

"But you don't understand," insisted Belinda. "They . . . they have sent things I didn't order."

"*I* ordered them," Mrs. Stafford-Smyth explained matter-of-factly.

"But . . . but . . ." began Belinda.

"My deah, I thought I already clarified the situation for you," the lady said now a bit impatiently. "I wish to take you about with me—as soon as I am able to be about, that is—and I want you to look the part. You are more—much more—than my nurse. You are my companion." Her tone said that this should fully put the matter to rest.

For the first time, Belinda really understood, not just about the wardrobe but about the woman's expectations for her. She had never stopped to look at herself through Mrs. Stafford-Smyth's eyes. Certainly her own worn and serviceable gowns were not in keeping with the elegance of the other woman's clothing. Belinda let her eyes fall to the dress she was wearing. Her best. And yet it was so inferior to the gown of the grand lady who stood before her. And this lady who had everything money could buy was looking for a friend.

"Now, let's see what you have here," said the older woman, her voice again filled with eagerness.

Belinda turned back to the boxes. It was going to take a while for her to come to grips with this new way of living and thinking. In the meantime, she would try to match Mrs. Stafford-Smyth's enthusiasm.

There were many pretty things in the boxes. Belinda could not help but appreciate their beauty. She ran a caressing hand over the silks, the satins, the voiles. They were beautiful. *But won't I always feel I'm in a borrowed dress?* she wondered.

There were hats and shawls, a long coat of fine blue wool, parasols, gloves, handbags, and delicate undergarments and sleepwear. Belinda had never in her life seen so much finery. She would have thrilled at it all had it been really *hers*.

Over and over she tried to articulate her thanks to Mrs. Stafford-Smyth, and the woman, obviously not noticing Belinda's discomfort, glowed with the excitement of all the new clothing.

"You will be the prettiest young lady in Boston," she informed Belinda, while Belinda wondered what that had to do with being a companion to the woman.

When the last box had been opened and the last item was carefully put away in the wardrobe or bureau, Mrs. Stafford-Smyth turned to Belinda with a merry twinkle in her eyes.

"You will wear the blue silk on Wednesday evening," she said. "And do up your hai-ah a bit loosah—Ella will help you. She's very good with hai-ah."

Belinda just nodded. Now she was being told how to dress—she who had often made decisions on her own that could mean life or death for a patient.

She looked at the older lady and nodded dumbly.

The next morning Windsor escorted Belinda to church. She had looked forward all week to this chance to meet with God's people on Sunday. Certainly she met with God every day of the week—but Sunday always seemed to her to be a special time. There was something so uplifting about the service, with singing hymns together and hearing God's Word read and preached. Belinda thought of her family as they would gather back home, and for a few moments she felt homesickness wash over her.

But the Boston church was nothing like the little country church Belinda had been used to. Huge and made of stone, its spires seemed to reach almost to the clouds. Belinda gazed in awe, wishing she could just stand and take it all in. But Windsor was gently nudging her forward.

Inside, the building seemed even more massive. The people moving to take their places in the polished wooden pews looked small and insignificant in comparison.

There was not just *a* minister, but several men on the raised platform, all gowned in deep colors that rippled and flowed as they moved about. Belinda smiled to herself. And the congregation gathering in the pews were outfitted in the latest styles, the ladies in all the brilliant colors of the rainbow. *And I feared my green voile might be too colorful,* she commented wryly to herself.

As the worshipers entered the building, strains of a giant organ rose and fell, wafting up in lovely ecstasy and then bringing the listeners back down to gentle peace again. Belinda turned her face to find the source and saw the front of the church was filled with brass pipes of various sizes and lengths. She had never seen a pipe organ before, but recognized that she was seeing and hearing one now.

Her eyes traveled the rest of the way around the interior, appreciating each glass window. The morning sun caught the brilliant colors, making the artwork of the Good Shepherd reaching for a lamb, the dying Savior on the cross, the gentle Teacher cradling a child, all look warm and alive to Belinda.

Her heart throbbed within her. The beauty and majesty of the place! Oh, how easy it must be to worship God in such a setting! How easy it must be for the city dwellers who met each Sunday in such magnificent buildings to feel close to the Lord!

Belinda could feel her heart swell and lift in sheer praise and gratitude to God for all His goodness. How she wished she could share this wonderful experience with her pa, her ma—with Luke. She looked about her at the congregation. The pews were far from filled, and among the ones gathered there, Belinda could see no shining eyes. Stiff-looking, well-dressed individuals with blank faces and fixed stares sat in cultured rows. Belinda was shocked that they didn't seem one bit excited about being in such a glorious place of worship. She felt a chill pass through her and made a conscious effort to reclaim her excitement of a few moments before. She turned her eyes eagerly to the platform. The robed men were so far away she could scarcely see the expressions on their faces. She listened to voices that seemed to reach her only as an echo, and concentrated hard on what was being read from the large open Bible.

The words were good. They were familiar. It was God's Word and it lifted her spirit. But the beautiful large stone church still seemed cold and distant—the people masked and aloof. There were no welcoming smiles or gentle nods. Belinda wondered what was wrong with her and glanced anxiously down at her voile dress. But it really was not that much different from the gowns of the other women there.

No, thought Belinda, *I don't think it's the dress. It must be me. They must know—without me even saying anything—that I come from the western plains.* And Belinda felt alone and isolated among the Sunday churchgoers.

TWENTY-TWO

The Unexpected

In spite of the wonderful library, Belinda had more free time than she could reasonably fill. Mrs. Stafford-Smyth, now that she was back in her own home with Windsor, the housekeeper Mrs. Potter, Cook, and the two housemaids, seemed quite able to manage for herself. Belinda inwardly chafed, feeling guilty about doing so little to earn her keep and that she really was not needed. About the only duty she performed daily was to pour Mrs. Stafford-Smyth's tea, and she was sure just about anyone should be able to do that small chore.

So Belinda tried to find ways to occupy her days. She did read for a good portion of each day, but she had discovered that even reading has its limits. Belinda felt she must have some exercise, so she spoke with Mrs. Stafford-Smyth about it.

"Of course, my deah," said the woman. "An energetic young woman like you needs to get out. I should have thought of it myself. Just because I'm content to sit and stagnate does not mean that you are. Would you like to ride? I understand there is a good club with horses—"

But Belinda shook her head. She couldn't imagine going off to ride horseback in some society club. She thought of Copper back home with a bit of a pang, then almost smiled to think of him sedately marching round and round a horse ring.

"Tennis? We do have good courts at the back—but of course one can hardly play tennis on one's own."

"Jest—just walk, I think," responded Belinda. She had noticed some differences in the speech patterns out here in the East, and she was trying to adapt her own pronunciations accordingly.

"Oh my," said Mrs. Stafford-Smyth. "You may walk about all you like. The streets belong to everyone and are quite safe, really."

So on Wednesday morning Belinda took to the rather quiet streets. It seemed that those who moved about did so by carriage. She had intended to walk briskly for a half hour or so, but there was so much to see she kept finding herself loitering as she gazed at the sights about her.

She returned to the house invigorated and ready for the luncheon that Cook had prepared. She freshened up and joined Mrs. Stafford-Smyth in the drawing room.

"Did you enjoy your walk?" the lady began and then quickly added, "Yes, I can see that you did. Your cheeks are quite flushed, your eyes glowing."

"It was lovely!" exclaimed Belinda. "A shame that you're unable to join me."

Mrs. Stafford-Smyth chuckled. "There was a day when I might have fretted at being left behind—but no more," she said companionably.

The two chatted about many things over their luncheon plates, and Mrs. Stafford-Smyth was again reminded of why she had cajoled and pressed for Belinda to return to Boston with her. The girl was so vitally alive that just being with her was uplifting to one's spirit. Mrs. Stafford-Smyth truly loved her home, she loved Boston, and she would miss it all terribly if anything should happen to change things for her. She was comfortable at home—with maids fussing about and Cook and Housekeeper and dear old Windsor hovering to answer her every whim. But it was lonely in the big house. A staff of servants was not the same as having friends. And, surprisingly, Mrs. Stafford-Smyth thought of Belinda as a friend.

She knew that Potter, with her rigid rules of what was right and proper, did not approve of the special status that was given the girl. Employees had no right to be served tea with the gentry, according to Mrs. Potter. There had been a time, even only a short time ago, that Mrs. Stafford-Smyth would have heartily agreed. But that was before she had met Belinda—before Belinda had tenderly and efficiently nursed her back to health.

Mrs. Stafford-Smyth had learned a new set of rules in the crude little prairie town. The rule of survival. There seemed to be no social status there, no class distinctions, and Mrs. Stafford-Smyth had discovered in Belinda an open, friendly, clear-thinking girl who would share her thoughts, her feelings, and her humor. To the older lady's surprise she had enjoyed such exchanges. And now, back in Boston, she was not willing to give up what she had learned to appreciate.

She knew the whole arrangement was a mystery to Belinda. She also knew that her household staff must titter and talk and exclaim over Madam's strange desire to treat the girl, an employee, as an equal—but in her own house, she was mistress. *Let them talk and fuss,* she told herself. They'd eventually get used to the idea.

She turned her attention back to the attractive face before her.

"The blue silk will look lovely on you!" she exclaimed, and Belinda looked surprised at her passion and abrupt change of thought. They had been discussing a novel.

Belinda frowned. "You know," she said slowly, "things happened in such a flurry at thet—that dress shop," she corrected herself, "that my head was swimming. I don't even remember trying the blue silk on."

Mrs. Stafford-Smyth just smiled. She knew Belinda might not have tried the dress. Madam Tilley was skilled at her profession. She would have known Belinda's size perfectly by the time she had fitted a few dresses. The blue silk was in answer to one of Mrs. Stafford-Smyth's specific instructions in the letter. But the dress was too expensive, too elegant, to be slipped over clients' heads in the dressing room. Even in a place as refined as LeSoud's.

"What time is dinner?" Belinda asked now.

"Seven-thirty," answered Mrs. Stafford-Smyth, "but the guests shall be arriving around seven. I should like you to be with me in the formal parlor by seven o'clock."

Belinda nodded.

"And I think we shall take our tea in my suite this afternoon. We both will need to rest and prepare ourselves for tonight."

Again Belinda agreed, though she hardly felt in need of rest.

"I thought I might take a book and spend some time in the garden now," Belinda offered. "It's such a glorious day—and the flowers are so pretty."

"Thomas certainly does a nice job," Mrs. Stafford-Smyth acknowledged. "He's a good gardenah. Been with us for thirty-five yeahs. I don't know what I shall do when he wishes to reti-ah."

Belinda took her book and went to the gardens as planned, but she did little reading. The day was too beautiful, the flowers too enticing, the bees too busy for her to be able to concentrate on anything but the loveliness. She sat dreaming away her afternoon, enjoying the sights and scents around her.

"I don't believe I've had the pleasure of being introduced," someone said near Belinda's elbow, and she started in surprise and looked up.

A young man, his eyes deep set and dark mustache well trimmed, stood looking at her. Belinda noted his stylish clothing, and she could tell every item was carefully chosen—yet he managed to give an air of informality that she assumed was the appearance he wished to present.

And then Belinda recognized him as one of the grandsons whose portraits graced the rooms of Mrs. Stafford-Smyth. The two women had talked about the boys on occasion. Belinda smiled in greeting.

"I hadn't heard ya—you were expected," she said easily.

"S-h-h," said the young man, placing a finger to his lips. "I didn't send word on ahead. I wanted to surprise Grandmother."

Belinda laughed softly. "And so you will. She . . . she will be caught completely by surprise."

Then Belinda sobered. "I'm not sure but what she shouldn't have *some* warning," she continued. "She has recently been very ill, you know, and too much of a shock wouldn't be good—"

"She's used to us popping in and out," the young man said with a shrug. "I shouldn't think this will bother her much."

Belinda noticed a strange accent in his speech. She couldn't place it but assumed it had been picked up in his travels abroad. It rather intrigued her. There was something mysterious and pleasing about the man.

He tossed his jacket carelessly on the velvet green of the lawn and sat down on it, close to Belinda's chair.

"You still haven't told me your name," he prompted.

"Belinda. Belinda Davis," she replied.

"*Miss* Belinda Davis?" he asked.

"Yes. Miss," returned Belinda and felt her cheeks flushing slightly under the intense scrutiny of the man.

They sat for a moment, and then Belinda spoke carefully. "You haven't said whether you're Peter or Frank."

He laughed. "Dear Grandmother! She insists upon calling us the American version of our real names. I'm Pierre. 'Peter,' if you wish. I don't mind."

"I'll call you Pierre if you prefer it," she answered simply.

He smiled. "Pierre, then. I do prefer it." Then he said, "I was told by that watchdog Windsor that 'Madam is resting and not to be disturbed.'" He mimicked Windsor's voice as he spoke, and Belinda could not hide her smile. "How is Grandmother?"

"She's doing very well now."

Pierre seemed relieved at the news.

"So what are her plans? Is she going abroad for the winter as usual—or have you heard?"

Belinda shook her head. "I know nothing of plans that go beyond this evening's dinner party," she said.

"A dinner party? Oh, dear! How I dread Grandmother's dinner parties. Such stuffy occasions they are, with all those octogenarians. Have you heard her guest list?"

Belinda found herself enjoying the exchange. She had some of the same feelings this young man was expressing, only she had hardly dared to think let alone say them.

"I've heard the list—but I don't recall all of them. Let's see . . . a Prescott woman."

"Of course. Aunt Celia. She is always invited."

"Aunt Celia?" said Belinda in surprise. "I hadn't realized—"

"Oh, she's not really an aunt. We were just brought up to refer to her as such. She's a good friend of Grandmother's from many years back."

"I see," said Belinda.

"Go on," he prompted.

"A gentleman to chat with Aunt Celia," smiled Belinda. "Mr.—Mr. Walls . . . ?"

"Walsh," Pierre laughed. "Those two have been openly and shame-lessly flirting with each other for thirty years. Don't know why they haven't done something about it."

Belinda's blue eyes opened wide at his frankness.

"And . . . ?" he urged.

"Two other couples . . . one is a judge . . . the other I don't remember."

"No young people?"

"I . . . I don't know any of the guests. I have no way of knowing if they are young or old," Belinda reminded him.

"Let me assure you," he said as he stood from the ground and brushed gently at the sharply creased trousers, "none of them are under one hundred and five."

Belinda could not hide the twinkle from her eyes.

"I'm tempted to sneak away before Grandmother discovers me," he continued. And then he looked directly at Belinda. "You'll be there?" he asked.

She nodded in answer.

"Then the evening will not be a total loss," he said smugly. And with a slight smile, he gave her a nod and departed.

Belinda watched him go. How would Mrs. Stafford-Smyth feel about having her grandson home? What kind of a person was he? Surely he had been teasing about his perception of his grandmother's "stuffy" lifestyle. No one could help but love the house in Boston. *The days ahead might turn out to be rather interesting,* she told herself as she closed the book she hadn't had a chance to read and stood to her feet. It was almost teatime and Mrs. Stafford-Smyth would expect her there.

Belinda was pouring tea when she heard a gasp and looked up quickly to see Mrs. Stafford-Smyth lift a lacy handkerchief to her lips. Following her gaze, Belinda turned to the door behind her and saw the young man standing there, a smile on his face.

"Hello, Grandmother," he said. "I hear you have been ill."

Belinda turned back to her patient, worried that the sudden appearance of Pierre might be too much for the woman. But after the initial surprise, she seemed to regain her composure.

"Petah!" she cried, holding out her arms. "Petah!"

He went to her and knelt before her. She reached out a hand to stroke his cheek, and he patted her arm affectionately. Belinda thought it all very touching.

"It's so good to see you, deah. My, you've . . . you've become quite a man," the grandmother offered with pride.

Pierre just nodded.

"And where is Frank?"

"Still in France," answered Pierre. "He has a girl, you know. He is rather smitten, I'm afraid. He sent his love."

"Sit down. Sit down. Tell us all about yourself," Mrs. Stafford-Smyth urged the boy, and then she turned to Belinda. "This is Belinda," she hastened to explain.

The young man smiled and nodded. "I met Miss Davis in the garden," he offered.

"Good! Good!" Then the woman turned moist eyes back to her grandson. "I'm glad you've come. It's awfully good to see you . . . and Belinda needs some youngah company. You can accompany her to dinnah tonight. We're having guests. Just a few old friends . . . but Belinda could use someone her own age. I don't go out yet. She really has seen very little of Boston, and I wanted her to get to know the town. Of course we have been back only for a little ovah a week, but it would be so nice for her if—"

The young man chuckled and placed a restraining hand on his grandmother's arm. "I promise, Grandmother. I'll stay long enough to show Miss Davis the whole town. And I will be at dinner. And I will not run off and desert you without fair warning. Now—may I have some tea? I missed my lunch, and I'm starving."

Mrs. Stafford-Smyth reached out and pressed her buzzer. From the quickness with which he reached the room, Belinda wondered if Windsor had been standing outside in the hall.

"Bring anothah cup and more tea, Windsah, and have Cook make some sandwiches for Petah," she ordered in an excited tone, then turned back to her grandson to ply him with questions and offer her own bits of news. Belinda had never seen her so animated.

This is good for her, she thought to herself. *I'm glad he's home. She must have missed him very much.*

After what Belinda considered an appropriate time, she excused herself to her own suite. *The two need time to get to know each other again,* she reasoned.

Belinda found herself feeling both excited and anxious as she lifted the blue silk carefully from her wardrobe and laid it gently on her bed. She had never worn such a gown before. She caressed the soft material and then held a fold to her cheek. Ella would be coming any minute to fix her hair. She must hurry. She wanted to be ready on time. Mrs. Stafford-Smyth was counting on her help in greeting guests as they arrived.

And then Belinda remembered Pierre. *Maybe things have changed now . . .* she pondered. Perhaps Mrs. Stafford-Smyth would want her grandson at her side to perform the role of host. Well, she could always slip out to the garden if she was in the way. She still would be ready, as she had been asked.

Belinda lifted the silk and let it slide down over her head and settle over her shoulders. She shrugged and shifted, puzzling as she attempted to adjust it. Something was wrong. The dress didn't fit as it should. She hoisted it slightly, thinking it might be caught. It wasn't. She could not understand it. She looked about. Perhaps there was a piece missing. Surely there was an accompanying neckpiece or an attached shawl. But there was nothing else on the satin-covered hanger. Belinda was still puzzling when Ella entered the room.

"What a beautiful dress, miss!" she enthused.

Belinda managed a smile, but she was still perplexed.

"But it . . . it doesn't fit right. Look. The front of it. It's scooped way down."

"That's the way it's cut, miss," explained Ella. "It's supposed to be like that."

Belinda was astounded. She wanted to argue . . . to protest.

"All the girls are wearing them like that, miss," said Ella, no doubt responding to Belinda's obvious bewilderment.

"Well, I won't! I can't!" stated Belinda firmly. "It's most . . . most improper! Why, I'm . . . I'm indecent."

Ella smiled and shook her head. "Why, it fits you real nice, miss. Madam will be pleased."

Madam? Yes, the dress had been Madam's doing. She had ordered it. Belinda had *not* tried it on before. She would surely have remembered such a . . . a . . . low-cut gown. She felt most uncomfortable in it. Why had Mrs. Stafford-Smyth ever purchased such a dress? Surely she had been unaware of its skimpiness.

Certain now that Mrs. Stafford-Smyth had not known of the actual design of the dress, Belinda knew she must talk with her employer—quickly. She hurried down the short hallway that led to the older woman's suite. She did not intend to appear at the dinner table wearing such a revealing garment, and she was sure that Mrs. Stafford-Smyth would not desire her to do so.

She stopped at the adjoining door only long enough to rap lightly and then went on in. Mrs. Stafford-Smyth had Sarah rushing about the room in last-minute preparations.

Without saying a word, Belinda stopped in front of the older woman and slowly turned completely around so that she could see the dress, both the back and the front.

She had expected to hear a gasp of shock. Instead, a murmur of approval stunned Belinda's ears. "Lovely! Just lovely. It was meant for you. Madam Tilley knew exactly what I wanted."

Belinda whirled around to see shining eyes and a broad smile.

"But . . . but . . ." Belinda began and then realized her protests would not be heeded nor understood by the older woman. *She will think I'm just a simple prairie girl who doesn't know about such matters,* Belinda thought, her cheeks burning.

"Now hurry, deah," Mrs. Stafford-Smyth continued. "Petah will be waiting for us. He's going to help us with the guests." Her face was radiant.

Without another word Belinda returned to her own room and allowed Ella to pin her hair becomingly. She found a lace hanky that she tucked into the neckline, then removed it when it seemed to draw even more attention. She hoped the evening might pass quickly.

TWENTY-THREE

Pierre

Belinda stole down the stairs quietly, hoping not to be noticed. *What else can I do?* she debated with herself. *My employer ordered the dress for me, paid for it, and told me to wear it tonight!* It flashed into her mind that maybe she could have borrowed a shawl, *but it's too late now,* she told herself grimly. Perhaps in the excitement of the expected dinner guests, she could slip in unobtrusively, and Mrs. Stafford-Smyth and her grandson would hardly realize she was there.

It was not to be. The minute the swish of her skirts at the door of the formal parlor announced her arrival, Mrs. Stafford-Smyth turned toward her. Her smile spoke even more than her words. She held out her hands to Belinda and urged her forward.

"Ah yes," she said, slowly looking over the picture that Belinda made in her blue gown. "It becomes you. The colah is just right for your eyes. And your hai-ah—perfect! Ella does such a good job in styling."

Pierre made no comment, for which Belinda was thankful, but she could feel his eyes studying her carefully. Belinda felt dreadfully uncomfortable. *With all the material in this full skirt, you'd have thought they could've spared a bit to cover the bodice,* she continued to fret, but of course she did not voice her complaints as she moved away from their gazes in pretense of pouring punch.

"May I bring you a drink?" she asked Mrs. Stafford-Smyth.

"That would be nice, my deah," the elderly lady responded and seated herself in a green brocaded chair opposite the entrance to the hall, facing the doorway and the guests when they arrived.

The Allenbys were the first to appear. He was a very dignified older gentleman, befitting his honored position. She was a wizened little woman, her face pinched and her eyes sunken and sharp. Belinda could feel herself withdrawing from the open stare of the woman. She learned quickly that Mrs. Allenby's tongue was just as sharp as her eyes.

"And who is *she*?" Belinda heard her say to Mrs. Stafford-Smyth after their greetings were over. Belinda moved out of earshot so she wouldn't have to hear her employer trying to explain their relationship.

Mr. Walsh arrived a few moments later, chuckling over some joke, and spent the entire evening laughing over one thing or another. Belinda did not pretend to understand his strange humor, but she did find him fairly pleasant company.

The Whitleys were admitted by Windsor at seven-thirty, the hour of dinner. He let it be known that he never had been one for pre-dinner chitchat. After all, wasn't the purpose of dining together so one could visit over the meal? His wife said nothing, just looked a bit embarrassed by his blustering.

The minutes ticked slowly by with no moves toward the dining room, so the guests were aware that someone else was expected. Once or twice Mr. Whitley took his gold watch from his pocket and studied it openly.

Since the guests' arrival, Windsor had taken over the duties of serving punch. Belinda knew without being told that she was now to allow things to proceed in "proper" fashion, and she withdrew to one of the matched green chairs.

Pierre eased his way over to where Belinda was fidgeting. "Isn't this fun?" he whispered, with a slight nod toward the older guests clustered about talking of weather and health problems.

Belinda only smiled.

"We could walk in the garden," he added.

"But she will be here any minute," Belinda said.

Pierre laughed. "Aunt Celia? She's never on time for anything. When Aunt Celia is expected at seven-thirty, the only thing you don't know is whether she will arrive at eight or ten."

Belinda looked at him in surprise.

"Mark my word," he challenged, but just then the doorbell rang.

"Ah," he said, pulling out his pocket watch, "she's early—it's only ten minutes of eight."

Mrs. Celia Prescott came in with a flurry of excited comments and overdone apologies. She and Mrs. Stafford-Smyth hugged each other warmly, and then greetings passed all about the room. Mr. Walsh chuckled over each remark and Mrs. Celia Prescott tittered prettily in his direction. Pierre looked at Belinda with an I-told-you-so expression, and she had a hard time keeping from giggling herself.

"You know my Petah," said Mrs. Stafford-Smyth, and Pierre bowed to acknowledge the older woman.

"And this is Miss Belinda Davis," Mrs. Stafford-Smyth went on, and all eyes turned to Belinda.

"No wonder you've been off in hiding, young man," teased Aunt Celia with a twinkle. "In what part of Europe did you find her?"

Before either Pierre or Belinda could respond, Mrs. Stafford-Smyth interrupted with, "Belinda is American."

"Then perhaps we shall see more of your grandson in the future," observed Mr. Walsh with another chuckle.

Again Belinda could feel Mrs. Allenby's sharp eyes on her. She wished with all her heart that she could crawl more deeply into her blue silk dress. To Belinda's relief, the woman said nothing.

Aunt Celia reached over to pat Pierre's cheek. "I admire your taste, deah," she gushed. "I always knew you were discerning."

Belinda opened her mouth to say something, but when she saw Pierre shake his head, she closed it. They all had misunderstood the situation entirely. Was no one going to explain?

Belinda sighed and shrugged and allowed Pierre to lead her in to dinner.

As the meal progressed Belinda was glad for Pierre's presence at her side. She usually had no problem chatting with older people, but the conversation around the table was all foreign to her. They spoke of people she did not know, places she had never seen, and events that were somewhere in their past.

Pierre let the dinner guests chatter on around them. He deftly directed the conversation to things he hoped would be of interest to Belinda. He found her charming and very attractive. He wished to ask her all sorts of questions, but he held himself in check. Where had his grandmother found such a lovely girl, and why was Belinda willing to spend time in a house with only an older woman?

The thought did occur to him that his grandmother was a very wealthy woman and that Belinda might have interest in her money. But Pierre, even with a somewhat suspicious turn of mind, dismissed that thought. She just didn't seem the type, unless she had everyone fooled.

After dinner the men rose in preparation for retiring to the library for a brandy and cigar, and the ladies were invited to the drawing room for another cup of coffee.

When Belinda cast a look of appeal toward Pierre, he immediately rose to the occasion.

"Perhaps you wouldn't mind if Belinda and I took a walk in the garden?" Pierre asked his grandmother.

He noticed that Belinda drew a thankful breath.

"Run along," encouraged his grandmother, beaming as though the idea had been hers. She seemed to be smiling secretly to herself as she led the ladies into the drawing room.

Belinda excused herself and went for a wrap, though the night was still young and comfortably warm. She knew she would feel more comfortable with a bit more covering. Returning to the waiting Pierre, she breathed deeply as she stepped out onto the terrace.

"Thank you," she whispered to Pierre, and he nodded in understanding.

"You mean you didn't look forward to the gossip of the old ladies any more than I did to the stale smell of cigars?" he asked lightly, and Belinda chuckled.

"Yes," she said, "I was thinking about all those wonderful books in the library in all that smoke."

"Oh, those old books will be fine," he said carelessly. "It isn't the first time the room has been filled with cigar smoke."

"Actually," he went on after a few minutes of silence, "I wasn't trying to be a hero. I just wanted to have a very pretty girl all to myself."

Belinda could feel his eyes on her, no doubt measuring her reaction to the compliment. She carefully kept her expression neutral and simply smiled quietly.

"I've chatted on about myself enough," Pierre said. "Now I think it's your turn."

She turned to him and smiled slightly. "I have nothing nearly as exciting to tell," she answered evenly. "I was born, grew up, and lived right in one little town on the plains. And that's about all there is."

He laughed. "I think I am being effectively put off," he said good-naturedly.

"Not really," she assured him.

"You've not traveled?"

"Not a bit till I came to Boston."

"No interests?"

"Oh, I've lots of interests. Simply no means." She spoke frankly, unembarrassed.

"Where did you meet my grandmother?" he questioned.

"She was on a trip—out to San Francisco."

"You were on the same train?"

"Oh no," Belinda hastened to add. "She took ill. Had to stop at our town until she recovered."

"I see," he said. But she could tell he really didn't.

"Grandmother spoke to me again about showing you Boston," he went on. "Would you be interested?"

Belinda couldn't help but feel an expectant thrill go through her. "I'd like that," she said honestly.

"I'd like that, too," he echoed. "Where do you want to start?"

"I . . . I know nothing about the city. Best you do the choosing. You'd know what we should see."

He smiled. "Fine," he said. "You'll have your first lesson at nine tomorrow."

Belinda returned his smile. She was looking forward to seeing more of this beautiful city, to learn of its history and its intrigue.

"I'll be ready at nine," she answered, then added with a little laugh, "Not Aunt Celia's nine—but clock-time nine."

Pierre chuckled with her.

"Are you . . . are you planning to be with Grandmother for . . . for some time?"

Belinda sobered. "I love it here," she admitted. "I've been here only a week and already I love it. Just like yer—your grandmother said I would. But how long I stay"—she gave her shoulders a gentle shrug—"that depends," she added.

"Depends? On what?"

"Your grandmother. Me. How we get on together."

"I see," he said slowly.

"Are you staying long?" she asked, turning the tables.

He paused a moment, then said with a little chuckle, "It depends."

Her words had brought him up sharply, and silence fell between them again as they walked around the lovely garden. *It depends! On how Grandmother and I get on together!* Pierre rolled the words around in his mind awhile. In actual fact that was why he had come home. He was quite sure that his grandmother's will was still unsettled. She had wanted first to "try" her grandsons. Now that Franz was about to settle in France with his new love, Pierre felt it an opportune time for him to "get in good" with his grandmother. Why should this beautiful home, this notable estate, be left to someone quite outside the family? Yet his grandmother was independent—verging on the eccentric. She was likely to do just that if neither of her grandsons showed any interest in the place—or in her. Or in pursuing a course of which she approved.

So Pierre had decided to leave his European playground temporarily and come home to "court" his grandmother. Oh, he had never admitted the truth—not even to himself. But as Belinda asked her question, the reality of the situation hit the young man. He was here to get what he could from his grandmother's will. *Perhaps we are not so different after all,* he concluded with a careful look at the attractive girl by his side. The only fact in his favor was that he was kin.

He glanced at her once more, wondering what she was thinking and whether she indeed was after the same thing he was—his grandmother's money.

Pierre did not sleep well that night. To himself he admitted that he found Belinda attractive. She seemed so honest, so sincere . . . so . . . unsophisticated. Yet she had somehow managed to fool his shrewd grandmother. *She must be far more skilled at deceit than I credit her with.*

He struggled with what to do. He saw his grandmother's deep devotion to Belinda. If he were to question her concerning Belinda's integrity, would she become upset? Would it be better to forget the possibility that Belinda might be after the elderly lady's money and take no chance of alienating his grandmother? Did he really care so much about the estate that he would risk a rift with the elderly woman? After all, he knew that as things now stood, he and his brother would inherit at least some of her money. Perhaps he should be content with that.

And then Pierre thought about Belinda. *What if . . . what if she inherits the bulk of the estate?* Was there another way for him to solve his dilemma? After all, she was pretty and pleasing to be with. She had not seemed immune to his charms. Perhaps they could share the estate in another fashion. But Pierre felt uncomfortable with that. If Belinda was so sly as to ingratiate herself with his grandmother only for personal gain, was she to be trusted as a marriage partner? As any kind of partner? And hadn't he sensed an undercurrent in the room when the staff had been present? Did they know something about Belinda that was not yet exposed?

Pierre tossed and turned and tried to sort the whole thing through, but an answer escaped him.

Finally he decided that he must have an open talk with his grandmother. He knew it was risky, but he had to chance it. With the resolution made, he settled down to a few hours of sleep.

He had made his appointment to meet Belinda at nine, so at eight o'clock, Pierre knocked on his grandmother's door. She was already seated at her small corner desk, her breakfast tray left almost untouched on a low table by her bed.

She smiled when she saw him and leaned to accept his kiss on her cheek.

"Good morning," she welcomed him. "Belinda tells me that you are becoming a tour guide this morning."

He attempted a smile. He had little time, so he decided not to spend it in small talk. "That's who I came to talk about, Grandmother," he admitted.

She smiled at him. "You seem to be off to a good start," she beamed. "Isn't she delightful?"

He did not answer her question. "Where did you meet her, Grandmother?"

"I thought you knew. I took a train trip west, and on the way home I fell quite ill. A stroke, they said. I would have died had it not been for the care I received."

"Died?" he echoed, thinking that his grandmother was perhaps being a bit melodramatic.

"Belinda and her brothah, who is a doctah—and a very good one, by the way—stayed with me day and night for the first few weeks. Then Belinda continued to give me nursing care for several more months."

Pierre thought he could understand why his grandmother felt indebted to the girl, but he was still puzzled.

"So, in gratitude, you invited her here as your guest," he prompted, hoping to get more information.

"Belinda? Oh my, no. She traveled back with me to nurse me on the train if need be. I was still very weak. Still am." She stopped and chuckled softly. "She still insists that I get propah rest and—why, she's already been in heah this morning fussing and—"

"Nurse?" said Pierre. He still did not grasp the situation.

"Nurse!" his grandmother repeated, and seeing the frown on his face, she continued. "Not all nurses are old grannies with head scarves, you know."

"You mean Belinda Davis is a *nurse*?"

"Yes, of course. Didn't you know? That's what I've been telling you."

"She's . . . she's in your *employ*?" He was aghast at the very thought.

Mrs. Stafford-Smyth laid down her pen and looked at her grandson. "What is it that's bothering you?" she asked him. "Are you as stuffy and narrow-minded as Pottah or Windsah? Are you, too, going to insist that because Belinda is an employee, she can't be my deah, deah friend? If I want—"

But Pierre stopped her. "But the place as a *guest* at dinner? The . . . the expensive gown? Surely a working girl—?"

"I've just told you," the woman insisted. "Belinda is *more* than a nurse. She is good company."

"And you purchased her gown?"

Mrs. Stafford-Smyth shuffled angrily at her papers. "Yes," she answered sharply. "I purchased the gown. I didn't want her feeling uncomfortable in the presence of those who call. She's a sensitive little thing. She already feels upset about the coolness of the staff. They feel that she should be treated as one of them."

"But that's exactly what she is. Staff! An employee! Your nurse!"

"She is," admitted the woman.

"But . . . but . . . you led me to believe that she was your . . . your guest."

"I did no such thing," denied the woman. "You jumped to your own conclusions."

"But you . . . you asked me to . . . to escort her about town."

The dark eyes of Mrs. Stafford-Smyth sharpened and focused on the face of her grandson. "I did," she said evenly. "And you should bless me for it! Belinda is an intelligent, independent, sensitive, and attractive young lady. Something that you haven't seen in one little lady for all your lifetime, I'll wagah. If you are so put off by the fact that she has no mansions, no family jewels, then you are not the man I had hoped you to be."

Pierre took a step backward. He knew better than to challenge his grandmother when she was in such a mood.

"Yet you seriously wish me—?"

"Yes," she said sharply. "Yes, I wish you to treat her like the lady she is. Belinda deserves to see Boston—to have a good time. And you should be thankful that you have the opportunity to be the one to escort her."

Her dark eyes snapped with the intensity of her feeling, and Pierre closed his lips tightly against the words he wished to speak. Two pairs of eyes measured each other, and then Pierre took a deep breath and shrugged his shoulders.

"All right," he said resignedly. "All right, Grandmother. I'll play your little game. But if word gets out that your grandson is busy escorting a member of the household staff, you could well be the laughingstock of your friends."

"Then perhaps they have no business being called my friends," she retorted, and Pierre knew that he was dismissed—and defeated.

TWENTY-FOUR

Extended Horizons

True to his agreement with his grandmother, Pierre showed Belinda around the city of Boston. He took her to all the parks, museums, and historical sites. They attended plays and musicals. He even accompanied her to church on Sundays. He could tell that Belinda was enjoying it immensely. She seemed to appreciate his company. But he was holding himself aloof in his ongoing concern about the social level of his young companion.

He knew his grandmother was elated. She made clear she was hoping the relationship would quickly develop into something deeper than friendship. She urged Pierre on to new sights and experiences with Belinda, slipping him extra funds to show her the lavish side of Boston's fine restaurants, theaters, and social gatherings.

Gradually Pierre became more and more troubled about the situation he found himself in. He did find enjoyment in the times with Belinda. He no longer worried that she was after his grandmother's money. In fact, he considered Belinda so naïve that she scarcely knew what money was. She viewed it as something to be slipped to newsboys on the street corners or placed in the offering receptacle on Sunday. No, Belinda was not at Marshall Manor for selfish reasons, he concluded.

But Pierre still puzzled over it all. Did Belinda, could Belinda, ever really fit into the life of high society? She was so open, so unsophisticated, and he knew she understood little of the social classes that existed in Boston. No, he concluded, Belinda was really from a different world than the one he knew. He decided to enjoy their outings, their friendship, and leave their relationship at that, even though he was aware that much of Boston's society, along with Mrs. Stafford-Smythe, already accepted her grandson and the attractive young guest as an established pair.

Mrs. Stafford-Smyth was resting when there came a gentle tapping on her door.

"Yes," she called softly. "Come in."

Windsor entered and stood at rigid attention. "Mrs. Celia Prescott is heah to see you, madam." Then he added in a confidential tone meant only for the ears of his lady, "I must say, she seems to have herself in quite a tizzy."

The good lady smiled. Her friend Celia was often in quite a tizzy over one thing or another.

"Would you take her to the drawing room, Windsah, and have Pottah fix tea? I'll be right down."

"Yes, madam," answered Windsor with a click of his heels. Mrs. Stafford-Smyth smiled. Poor Windsor. He did insist on being socially correct in spite of their long-term friendship.

When Mrs. Stafford-Smyth entered the drawing room a few moments later, she found Celia Prescott pacing back and forth in front of the marble fireplace. A lace handkerchief was being brutally attacked in two agitated hands.

"Celia! So good to see you. Please, won't you sit down?" she greeted her friend.

"Virgie, you'll never guess what they are saying," began Mrs. Prescott excitedly. "It's slanderous, that's what it is. Just slanderous! And you must put a stop to it at once."

"Why whatevah are they saying?" asked Mrs. Stafford-Smyth in bewilderment, wondering if there was some news of her far-off grand-son that had not yet reached her ears.

"Miss Belinda—that fine young lady you have staying heah—?"

"Yes," said Mrs. Stafford-Smyth hesitantly. Surely Peter had not gone and done some foolish thing and unwittingly besmirched Belinda's name—unthinkable!

"They are saying—"

"*Who* are saying?" cut in Mrs. Stafford-Smyth. If she needed to deal with gossipmongers, she wanted to know exactly whom she was deal-ing with.

Celia Prescott became all waving hands and fluttering handkerchiefs. "I don't know who said it," she replied offensively. "I heard it from Alvira Allenby and she heard it from—oh, I don't know."

"And what are 'they' saying? Go on."

"They are saying that the young woman, Miss Davis, is . . . is *hired help*," finished Celia in a horrified whisper.

"And so she is," responded Virginia Stafford-Smyth calmly.

"Well, you must put a stop to it. Your grandson's name and your—she *what*?" shrieked Celia Prescott, obviously only now hearing the words that had been stated.

"Belinda is my nurse. And a most excellent one, too. Is there a prob-lem with that, Celia?"

"Well, I . . . well, your . . . your grandson is . . . is escorting her about town, and folks assumed that he had your blessing and . . ."

"And so he has. I know of no young woman I would rathah see my grandson spend his time with," said Mrs. Stafford-Smyth with spirit.

Mrs. Celia Prescott for once did not know how to respond.

"Ah," said Mrs. Stafford-Smyth. "Here's our tea. Would you pou-ah for us please, Pottah?"

Mrs. Celia Prescott lowered herself to the chair across from Mrs. Virginia Stafford-Smyth and, looking very distraught, fanned herself with her lace hankie.

Potter served and then retreated. Virginia Stafford-Smyth picked up the conversation. "Belinda was the one who nursed me back to health when I was so close to dying," she said simply. "I love the girl as I would my own daughtah. In fact, I've often considered adopting her." She paused and seemed to be off in thought. "I would, too, if I thought for a minute that she would allow it." Then she turned again to her guest. "I've seen a few of the young women that my two grandsons have shown interest in," she confided. "Monied families—looking for more money. Showpieces without an intelligent thought in their empty heads. Society girls! Oh yes! Their family history can be traced back nearly to Adam. But shallow, selfish—" she hesitated, looking away from her guest as she sought for the proper word—"nothing," she finally sputtered. "Just ornamental bits of fluffy nothing.

"Well, Celia," she continued, turning to look at her directly, "as far as I'm concerned, I would as soon see my grandson marry an intelligent char as an empty-headed socialite."

Mrs. Celia Prescott gasped in horror.

"There, now! I've said my piece—now we will have no more of it," said Mrs. Stafford-Smyth, and she cheerfully changed the topic to what play was on at the local theater.

As summer turned to fall, Belinda enjoyed the briskness in the wind and the turning of the maple trees. Never had she seen such glorious fall colors. *The golds and browns back home are no match for these,* she concluded. Pierre often took a team and the small carriage, and they went for drives down tree-lined residential streets and sometimes even out into the nearby countryside. Belinda had passing moments of guilt. She had come to Boston to be nurse and companion to Mrs. Stafford-Smyth. She was the first to be thankful that the lady no longer needed strict nursing care; still it did seem to Belinda that as long as she was salaried, she should be doing something further to earn her wage.

But it was Mrs. Stafford-Smyth herself who kept urging the outings. She took great pleasure in Belinda being shown their beautiful city and surrounding area, she said. Each night she would demand to hear Belinda's full report of what they had seen and where they had gone that day.

Belinda did not realize till later the secret hopes that the lady was harboring. She did know Mrs. Stafford-Smyth had been lonely for years and that she dreaded the thought of Pierre becoming restless and leaving her to go abroad once more. Mrs. Stafford-Smyth continued to urge the two young people to find excitement in the town and friendship with each other, and Belinda thought Pierre's grandmother was simply trying to keep him engaged and too busy to think of leaving again.

The autumn winds became chilly and trips in the open carriage were not as frequent. When the snowstorms moved in, one following the other, Belinda checked her calendar. They had moved into winter. She could scarcely believe she already had been gone from her home for several months.

Whenever she received a letter from her mother, homesickness struck her, a bit stronger each time. She missed her family so much. If only there were some way to combine the two worlds. She tried to compensate by throwing herself into each activity that Mrs. Stafford-Smyth suggested. Every day of the week, it seemed, she and Pierre found something more exciting to occupy their time. Eventually there was not even time to fit in Sunday church services. The day was spent instead with plays or concerts. Belinda had never had such full, fun days in all her life.

One day Belinda unexpectedly was called in to see the older woman. She was shocked to find her taken to her bed, her face ashen, her lips tightly drawn. Belinda berated herself. What had happened? Had the elderly lady had a setback? Why hadn't she, her nurse, seen it coming?

"What is it? Are you ill?" she asked anxiously, placing a hand on the woman's brow.

"I'm fine. Really. I just . . . I just am a foolish old woman, that's all."

"Whatever do you mean?" asked the puzzled Belinda.

"I was . . . was hoping I'd found a way to hold him this time," Mrs. Stafford-Smyth said wearily.

"Hold him? Hold who?"

"Pierre. My Petah."

Alarmed, Belinda said, "What do you mean?" already fearing what the answer might be.

"He's leaving. He just came to tell me. He says he can't bear Boston wintahs. He's . . . he's going back to France."

Belinda had no voice to respond to the woman. She simply stood beside her, her hand gently stroking the cheeks, the brow, the silver hair.

"I thought . . . I thought he seemed happiah this time. That now, with anothah young person in the house, he . . . he might stay."

Belinda still said nothing.

"You . . . you didn't have a lovah's quarrel, now did you, deah?" asked the woman.

Belinda found her voice then. "Oh my, no! Why . . . why we've been nothing more than friends . . . just friends."

The woman looked sorrowful. "I . . . I was hoping . . ." she began, but she did not finish her statement.

With the chill that gripped Belinda's heart, she wondered if she subconsciously had been hoping to hold on to Pierre herself, but she did not confess as much to her employer.

"When . . . when is he leaving?" she asked quietly.

"He has already booked passage. He sails on Friday."

Friday! That was two days hence. That didn't give one much time for good-byes. But perhaps that was the way Pierre wanted it.

Mrs. Stafford-Smyth sighed wearily. "You don't understand, deah," she said. "I realize now that I have no way to hold him heah. No way. If I want to see him and Frank, then I must go to them. They will nevah, nevah come home to me."

Belinda nodded. She thought she did understand.

Belinda tried hard not to let her emotions show as she bade Pierre good-bye.

"I can never thank you for all the . . . the sharing of Boston," she told him. "Ya—you made the city live for me."

Pierre took her hand and held it firmly. "I'm the one to say thanks," he said a bit grandly, then more sincerely, "I have had a good time."

"It's going to be rather . . . well, dreary without you," she admitted. "I don't know how your grandmother and I shall ever bear it."

"Take care of her, Belinda," he said, earnestness now in his tone. "I know that it is unfair of me to even ask it of you when I . . . when

I should be staying here, doing it myself. But I can't. Not just now. I know . . . I know you can't understand that, but I beg you not to think too unkindly of me."

"I could never think unkindly of you," Belinda said sincerely. "And as far as your grandmother is concerned, I'll . . . I'll try," Belinda promised. "I know she will miss you terribly. That she misses Franz. She would love to see Franz and his new . . . new . . ." Belinda floundered.

"New love," prompted Pierre. "Though I am the first to admit that Franz may well have changed loves once or twice since I left him. He has changed often in the past, you know. Although this time, he insists it is different."

Belinda smiled.

"Safe journey," Belinda said simply.

"In France we say, 'Bon voyage,'" he reminded her.

"Bon voyage," repeated Belinda.

He gave her a quick, rather brotherly hug, and then he was gone. Belinda stood and watched the carriage until it was out of sight, a tightness in her throat. She had liked Pierre. She had even thought he might care for her, just a little . . . but now he had turned and casually walked out of her life.

Little did Belinda know that Pierre was running away. He was beginning to care too much for Belinda, but unlike his grandmother, Pierre was thoroughly convinced their two vastly different worlds would not mix. Pierre did not wish to give up his world as he knew it, nor did he feel comfortable about asking Belinda to give up hers. The only answer, in Pierre's thinking, was to put the ocean between them.

TWENTY-FIVE

A Taste of Travel

While one winter storm after another swept through the area, Belinda shivered and watched the wind pile banks of driven snow where banks of flowering begonias had so recently been.

No wonder Pierre escaped, she thought to herself grimly. She would gladly have left for parts unknown herself. Then she shook her head at how sheltered she had become, how dependent on the finer things of life—even good weather. Why, this kind of snow couldn't come close to matching a true northerner out on the prairie....

Dear Ma, she sat down to write, *I do miss you all just awfully. And sometimes I can't quite figure out what I'm doing way out here so far from home. But Mrs. Stafford-Smyth needs someone to be with her and be a friend—even more now that her grandson has returned to France....* She knew her mother no doubt would read between the lines and yearn over her youngest, and that her parents would be praying for her.

Not all Belinda's days were chilly and bleak. On the nicer ones, she bundled up against the cold and went for walks or had the carriage brought around so she might do some shopping for Christmas gifts. She was looking forward to sending packages home for her family.

As Christmas drew closer, Belinda felt a renewed stirring of home-sickness. The letters from her mother continued to arrive regularly, and occasionally Belinda received notes from other members of the family, as well.

Luke wrote with news of the medical practice. Belinda was pleased to learn that they had decided to have Rand build them an office—separate and complete, giving Abbie back the privacy of their home. Luke then planned to convert the old office in the house into a large room for the two growing boys.

The up-to-date reports on Abe's arm informed Belinda that he had been away for surgery—two surgeries, in fact—and though the arm was still not completely restored, it was vastly improved over what it had been. *Abe beams when he shows it off to the family members,* Belinda read, and the tears that blurred the words on the page came from a heart of thankfulness.

Arnie was back in church—and not just sitting stolidly on a pew. He was involved again, and his faith had conquered the last trace of bitterness.

But not all the news was good news. There had been deaths among neighboring families, and Luke had lost a baby in delivery—the first in his experience—and had very nearly lost the young mother, too. He felt the tragedy keenly, and Belinda, understanding her brother, ached for him.

The partnership with Dr. Jackson Brown had been a good one. Luke from the beginning had been deeply involved with the practice of medicine, and he was now able to spend more time with Abbie and their growing family.

Ruthie's chattering had turned into understandable language. Thomas had been teaching her to say "Aunt Belinda," and Ruthie seemed to think their little game was fun. Luke wrote that the sound came out more like "Aw Binna." Belinda both laughed and wept over the little story. It was awfully nice to know she had not been forgotten at home.

Actually, both Rand and Jackson had written to Belinda, too. But when she responded with short, friendly but matter-of-fact notes, the answering correspondence from each of them had soon tapered off. Luke had reported in his letter that *Rand stopped by last Saturday to invite Thomas and Aaron on a little fishing trip—and were they ever excited!* Belinda smiled to herself as she imagined their enthusiastic chatter.

When Belinda had all her shopping done, her parcels wrapped, and her gifts on their way, there seemed to be nothing left to do except to wait out the days until Christmas finally arrived.

Belinda had never spent Christmas away from home before. She wondered just how Mrs. Stafford-Smyth celebrated the day. Surely one could not expect much in festivities with only two people.

Other than Pierre, Belinda still had not made any friends of her own age. True, there were a few young people whom she had met in his company, but now that he was gone, she had really lost contact with them. She supposed if things had been different and she had been included as staff in the big house as Potter seemed to feel was proper, she might have become friendly with Ella and Sarah. As it was, the girls spoke to her politely but did their talking and tittering outside of her hearing when they met each other in the halls or kitchen. Though she had tried to engage them in conversation, Belinda was not considered to be one of them.

The guests who joined Mrs. Stafford-Smyth for afternoon tea or an elaborate dinner were all older folk, and though Belinda was always expected to join them, she really did not feel part of those gatherings, either.

She took up handwork along with her walking and reading, and managed to tick the slow-moving days from her calendar, one by one.

Every day she spent some time with Mrs. Stafford-Smyth. She knew the older lady was as much in need of companionship as she herself. Usually they sipped tea, chatted, and did some kind of needlework before an open fire.

In a way it was cozy—at least to an onlooker it would have seemed so. But Belinda knew that deep down inside she felt a restlessness—a loneliness—and she wasn't sure just what to do about it.

On one such day, while Mrs. Stafford-Smyth was working skillfully on a silk sampler and Belinda embroidered a pair of cotton pillowcases, they chatted easily about many things.

"It's hard to believe that next week is Christmas," Belinda observed. Mrs. Stafford-Smyth did not even lift her eyes from her needlework. Belinda thought at first that she had not even heard the comment. She was about to speak further when Mrs. Stafford-Smyth answered, still without lifting her head.

"There was a time when Christmas brought a flurry of excitement in this house," she remarked. Then she added slowly, almost tiredly, "But no more."

Belinda felt her heart sink. It sounded as though the lady was dismissing Christmas as of no consequence.

"How do you celebrate Christmas?" Belinda dared to ask.

"Celebrate it? 'Spend it,' you mean. Much as we are spending today, I expect."

Belinda's eyes lifted from the pillowcases to study her older companion. She saw a droop to the shoulders and resignation in her face.

"But . . . but it's Christ's birthday!" Belinda could not help exclaiming.

Mrs. Stafford-Smyth faced her then and her eyes brightened for a moment. "Oh, we go to the church service—to be sure. But there are no more stuffed stockings and tinseled tree."

Belinda had a sudden resolve. She needed Christmas. Mrs. Stafford-Smyth needed Christmas. She laid aside her needlework and quickly stood to her feet.

"Let's!" she said excitedly.

The older woman's head lifted quickly and she stared as though Belinda had lost her senses.

"Let's!" said Belinda again.

"What are you—?" began Mrs. Stafford-Smyth, but Belinda interrupted, her eyes shining and her hands clasped.

"Let's have Christmas again! You and me. Let's have the tree and the tinsel and the stockings."

"But—but—"

"No 'buts.' We need Christmas. I've never *not* had Christmas. Why, I would mope and cry all day without it. I just know I would. We can have Windsor get us a tree, and I'll decorate, and Cook can make plum pudding or butter tarts or whatever you like, and we'll share gifts with the staff and—"

The older woman began to chuckle softly. Belinda's fire seemed to have ignited something in her soul, as well. She gently laid down her silk piece and rubbed her hands together.

"If it means so much to you—"

"Oh, it does. It does!" cried Belinda.

"Then go ahead. Do whatever you like."

"No! No, not me. Us! Us! You need Christmas just as much as I do. We'll plan it together."

Mrs. Stafford-Smyth chuckled again. "My, you do go on, don't you? Well, if it pleases you—then of course we'll have Christmas. Ring for Windsah and Pottah. We'd best tell them of our plans as soon as possible. Staff will think I've gone completely mad—but—" She smiled. "Better a little mad than a lot lonely," she finished.

The next few days were spent in frenzied but joyful activity. After a trip out in the country, Windsor produced a magnificent tree. Potter rummaged in the attic and storage rooms until she discovered boxes of old garlands and tinseled decorations. Belinda shook the dust from them and trimmed the tree and hung streamers and garlands. From the kitchen came the scents of spices and baking as Cook prepared festive dishes. Mrs. Stafford-Smyth ordered the carriage and began returning from shopping outings with mysterious parcels and packages. A whole new air of excitement pervaded the house that had for so long been silent and empty. They were going to celebrate Christmas.

"I think we need some guests," said Belinda thoughtfully as their plans moved forward.

"Guests? But all my friends spend Christmas with family—or abroad," responded Mrs. Stafford-Smyth.

"Then we need new friends," said Belinda, biting her lip in concentration.

Mrs. Stafford-Smyth just looked at her in bewilderment.

"I know," said Belinda. "I'll stop by the church and see if one of the ministers knows of any new folks in town who are away from their families. How many should we ask for?"

Mrs. Stafford-Smyth began to chuckle. "I don't know. As many as you like, I guess. The formal dining table seats twelve."

"Then we'll need ten more," concluded Belinda matter-of-factly.

When Christmas Day dawned cold and windy, Belinda thought about their plans as she prepared for the morning worship service. *Will there be any guests on such a day?* She had talked with one of the ministers, and he had agreed to seek out guests to fill their table. But with the weather so cold, Belinda began to have doubts. She was also concerned about Mrs. Stafford-Smyth going to the church—should she be chancing an outing this morning? Perhaps she would prefer to stay at home by the fire.

But when Belinda descended the stairs, she found the lady already clothed in her warm woolens and furs and ready for the carriage trip to the large stone church.

Belinda thought that the music of Christmas was especially beautiful as the well-trained church choir sang the story of Christmas. The deep recesses of the building seemed to echo back the praises. Her eyes filled with tears as she thought of her little church back home and the handful of faithful worshipers who would be gathered there singing Christmas carols and hearing the story of Jesus' birth.

The ride back home was a silent one, with both Mrs. Stafford-Smyth and Belinda busy with their own thoughts.

Tea was served in the drawing room and all of the staff was in attendance. The gifts that had been tucked under the festooned tree were distributed amid cries of appreciation and gleeful laughter. It was a good time, and Belinda felt a closeness to the staff she had never sensed before.

As the five-o'clock dinner hour approached, Belinda paced the room, looking first at the clock and then at the frosted windows beyond which the snow still blew in fitful gusts. *We'll be all alone unless the weather improves,* she warned herself. But at ten of five the knocker sounded, and Windsor admitted a young couple who had been married only a few months. New to Boston, this was their first Christmas away from their families. Shortly after, a family of three arrived. The little boy, Robert, stared in wide-eyed fascination at the decorated tree. His parents had not yet been able to afford such "luxuries." Then a young teacher with her father, and another woman, newly widowed, brought the guest list to ten, just as Belinda had required. None of them were previously known to the household or to one another. Coming from various stations in life by manner and clothing, they very quickly sensed their common bond. It was Christmas and they were lonely. They needed one another.

After the meal and an evening of fellowship with a small gift distributed to each one, farewells were said, and Belinda looked out on the wintry evening with deep satisfaction. *It was a great success!* she exulted inwardly. *And the wind has died down.* It would not be as bone chilling for those who drove or trudged home through the snow.

After Windsor had seen the last guest to the door, Mrs. Stafford-Smyth and Belinda settled before the crackling fire in the marble fireplace for a last cup of hot cider and a few more minutes together to review the day.

"Thank you," said Mrs. Stafford-Smyth softly, and Belinda turned to look at her.

"Thank you for giving me anothah Christmas," the older woman said, and Belinda saw the glitter of tears in her eyes.

"Oh, but I didn't give Christmas," Belinda corrected gently. "He did. We just accepted His gift."

Belinda felt a bit let down after Christmas was "packed away" in the storage boxes and put back in the attic. The old house seemed to settle back into its normal quiet with only the sighing wind or the rustling fir trees to stir one's thoughts. Belinda was tired of reading—tired of needlework and more than tired of winter. Mrs. Stafford-Smyth must have felt the same way.

"I've been thinking," she mused one day as they sat by the fire, "I think that it's time to take a trip again."

Belinda's eyes lifted quickly from her knitting.

"I'm feeling perfectly well enough to travel now," the woman continued.

"There's no need for us to sit heah listening to the wind day after day. We could be out seeing new things and meeting new people."

Belinda's heart quickened in her chest. *Oh yes!* she wanted to cry. *Let's. Let's!*

Instead, she held her peace—and her breath—and let the woman go on. "I think the south . . . maybe Italy or Spain. It's always nice there this time of year."

Italy or Spain? Belinda could not believe she was hearing correctly. She had only dreamed of such places.

"Then we will swing up into France. Visit the boys. I wonder if Frank has married that young woman. We could spend spring there—in France. I like France in spring. We might even slip over to Germany or Austria for a few days. You've never seen Austria, have you? No, I thought not. You'd like it there, I think. The mountains are quite magnificent."

Belinda wanted to jump to her feet and cry, *When? When?* but she sat silently, stilling her wildly thumping heart and listening to Mrs. Stafford-Smyth muse on with her travel plans.

"Yes," she finally said, turning to Belinda. "Let's do that. Ring for Windsah, deah."

Never had Belinda seen Mrs. Stafford-Smyth more eager—more alive. The very thought of going abroad and seeing her grandsons had put color in her cheeks and a new spring to her step. Windsor, with years of experience in such matters, took care of every detail in booking passage and reserving hotel rooms.

LeSoud's provided numerous new items for both travelers, and this time Belinda did not even attempt a protest. She knew so little about travel. How would she know what a young lady needed to be properly outfitted when going abroad? Having no desire to embarrass her employer, she decided to allow herself to be clothed according to Madam's wishes.

The day of sailing finally arrived, and amid steamer trunks and hatboxes and carry-ons, Mrs. Stafford-Smyth and Belinda were transported to the dock where the SS *Victor* lay in the harbor. Belinda, excitement coursing through her veins, kept telling herself, *I'm going abroad!* She was actually going to see some of the places she had only read of, dreamed of. *Imagine!* She, Belinda Davis, small-town girl from the prairie, was going abroad! Why, maybe . . . maybe she'd even be like Pierre and Franz and never want to come back.

TWENTY-SIX

A Discovery

Belinda and Mrs. Stafford-Smyth shared a stateroom, but Belinda could hardly bear to spend any time in it when it was so much more entertaining to be on deck, walking about the ship or enjoying the fine meals in the dining room.

Belinda did not push herself into making new acquaintances. She realized she was considered "staff" and held herself in check, lest others should think she was being forward and presumptuous. But she did enjoy watching and listening to the varied and distinguished company among the passengers.

They had been at sea four days when a strong wind came up, driving many of the travelers to their cabins. Belinda clung to the railings, fascinated by her first storm at sea. She worried that the storm might make Mrs. Stafford-Smyth seasick, then reminded herself that she had come as a nurse and might be able to "earn her keep," after all. But it was Belinda who eventually came reeling into their stateroom needing nursing, and Mrs. Stafford-Smyth who provided the care.

"Some people have a difficult time with the rolling and pitching," the kind woman said in good humor. "It has nevah bothered me," and so saying, she tucked Belinda into her bed and arranged for medication from the ship's physician.

Belinda was awfully glad when the rolling finally subsided and she was able to eat again. Soon she was back on deck, enjoying the fresh sting of the salty air and walking the well-scrubbed planks to get her strength back.

A small town on the coast of Spain was their first stop. Belinda was so anxious to see this new country that she had to consciously slow her step to accommodate Mrs. Stafford-Smyth. The sights, sounds, and smells of the small Spanish port were every bit as exciting as she had imagined. They settled into a small villa with whitewashed walls and a red-tile roof. Greenery crowded in close about it, giving it a protected air. Belinda loved it. The best part of all was that they were still within walking distance of the sea, and Belinda took long strolls daily, breathing deeply of the tangy air and watching the roll of the waves.

They managed frequent shopping trips through the quaint streets. Belinda loved to walk slowly through the aisles or stalls, fingering soft fabrics or admiring fine metal work. She made few purchases, but she thought many times, *Wouldn't Ma like that?* or *That color would suit Abbie,* and on and on with each family member.

And then the two moved on by train to Barcelona, Madrid, Rome, Venice—from city to ancient city—where new sights, new people, and new experiences awaited them. Belinda could not immediately recall whether it was Friday or Saturday. There was so much to do and see that she rushed about from morning to evening trying to crowd it all in. Often Mrs. Stafford-Smyth stayed at the hotel, but she usually knew someone in the city who was willing to show Belinda the tourist sights. And Belinda was quite willing to let her traveling companion rest.

"I think I would like to be in France by mid-May," announced Mrs. Stafford-Smyth one evening, and Belinda nodded, knowing that the woman's heart was already in that country with her two grandsons. France in May would be fine. She intended to thoroughly enjoy each stop along the way, though.

But as the days added up to weeks, Belinda began to feel a different kind of restlessness. Each new city was no longer as captivating. There came days when she didn't bother going out for long strolls to study architecture or visit museums. She sat quietly and listened to the distant church bells, or lay on her bed staring silently at the plastered ceiling.

She tried to sort through her thoughts to understand what was happening to her, but she could find no reason for her lethargy.

Mrs. Stafford-Smyth must have noticed it, too. "Are you feeling ill, deah?" she asked anxiously one day at luncheon.

"No. No, I'm fine," answered Belinda, pushing aside the food still remaining on her plate.

But Mrs. Stafford-Smyth did not seem convinced.

"Maybe we've taken things too fast," she offered. "Tried to see too many cities in too short a time."

Belinda thought about that. Certainly they had covered a lot of ground. But she wasn't sure there were any cities she would have left out.

"I . . . I don't think so," she responded. "I liked each one . . . really I did."

"A little lonesome maybe?" prompted Mrs. Stafford-Smyth. Belinda thought about it. Certainly she missed her family. Over and over she thought of them—wishing she could share her experiences with them. In fact, her journal entries were to help her to do that very thing the moment she got home. She wrote them lengthy letters, as well, posting them from various countries. But as much as she missed them all, Belinda didn't feel that was the reason for her low spirits.

"I'm fine, really," she protested, then added with a forced little laugh, "Maybe I'm like you. Just anxious to see France."

"Well, let's be on with it, then," said Mrs. Stafford-Smyth. "There's no reason we have to wait until May. Let's go directly."

And so they did, arriving in Paris the last day of April. Belinda felt her excitement mount again. Maybe this was just what she needed.

Settled in the hotel room, Mrs. Stafford-Smyth stood at the window, holding back the drapery with one hand and looking out over the city that stretched before her.

"It seems so strange," she murmured. "It is the same . . . and yet so different. It's like having someone you deeply love return after being gone for years and years. You know them . . . and yet you don't."

Belinda stirred uncomfortably. Mrs. Stafford-Smyth's words had a strange effect on her. *That's the way I feel about myself,* she thought restlessly. *Like I don't know myself anymore. Have I lost myself somewhere along this journey?* Then Belinda pushed the thought aside and went to join her employer at the window with the twinkling lights of Paris stretching to the horizon.

From somewhere below them, music floated out on the evening air. Belinda could hear laughter and chattering voices in a language she could not understand. Then a dog barked, and angry shouts answered, and the dog yipped in pain or anger and faded away into the distance.

From somewhere far away bells began to toll. *A church,* thought Belinda. *A church somewhere nearby. Can we go to church come Sunday morning?* And Belinda found herself wondering how many Sundays it had been since she had been in church.

They often traveled on Sunday—or were tired, just having arrived from somewhere, or didn't know where the nearest church was. There was also the language problem. "Why go just to sit?" asked Mrs. Stafford-Smyth. "We can't understand one word of what they are saying," and though Belinda knew it was true, she still missed church. Perhaps now that they were here in Paris, Pierre would take them to a church. Belinda smiled in anticipation.

"I wonder if Frank is married." Mrs. Stafford-Smyth interrupted her thoughts. Then she went on as though to herself rather than to Belinda. "He was always the ladies' man. He had a new friend every time I heard from him. But Petah said that this time it seemed to be different. Well, perhaps my boy is growing up aftah all. Maybe by now he is settled down to married life."

But a surprise awaited them. When they, as arranged, met the two grandsons the next afternoon, it was Pierre who introduced his new wife.

"I sent word to you in Boston," he explained to his grandmother. "Windsor informed me that you had left to travel abroad, but I had no idea where to find you."

Belinda extended her sincere congratulations. Quickly putting their previous friendship in proper perspective, she could be happy for Pierre.

The young woman was pretty, quiet, and very devoted to her new husband. Belinda did not proceed with her plan to ask Pierre for an escort to church in case Anne-Marie could misunderstand the request.

Franz, not at all like his brother, was dashing, bold, reckless in his behavior and dress, and dreamy in his approach to life. He was not married, but he was planning soon to be, he said, and his eyes seemed to see only his young Yvette.

Belinda felt that Mrs. Stafford-Smyth expressed the thoughts of both of them when she said, "Well, it seems that if we are to enjoy the sights of Paris, we must do so on our own. I believe that my two grandsons are living in their own private worlds."

Belinda made every effort to enjoy Paris. It was nice to visit museums and historical sites and shops with Mrs. Stafford-Smyth, who knew the city well, but soon Paris, too, was just another city. The streets were filled with people, not friends, and the noise was simply chatter, not words, and the bells that rang in the distance belonged only to stone buildings, not houses of God.

"Back home, spring will have come," Belinda said listlessly, as they sat in an open-air café one day.

"Ah yes," said Mrs. Stafford-Smyth, lifting her head from her delicate French pastry.

Belinda couldn't stop the sigh that escaped her.

Mrs. Stafford-Smyth went on. "I do hope that Thomas continues to work the gardens. I don't know what I shall evah do when he leaves me."

"It was so beautiful last year," Belinda thought out loud.

Mrs. Stafford-Smyth sat in silence fidgeting with her lorgnette.

"Should we return, Belinda?" she asked suddenly. "Perhaps we have 'gadded about'—as Windsah puts it—for quite long enough."

"I'd like that," said Belinda softly.

And so they made the arrangements, packed their trunks and boxes, and were delivered to a departing ship.

All the days at sea Belinda paced restlessly. Now she did not find even the other passengers of particular interest and barely noticed them.

But someone noticed her, an older man in clergy attire who pulled up a deck chair and seated himself after asking her leave.

"Ah," he said softly when she had nodded for him to join her, "do ye kin the sound of the waves like the soft flutter of angel wings?"

Belinda's head turned toward him and she smiled at his poetic musing. He took her acknowledgment as permission to continue.

"Are ye goin' home or away?" he asked her.

Belinda sat up a bit straighter in her chair. "Home," she said simply and wondered why the words didn't stir her more.

"It's away 'tis for me," the man continued with a heavy Irish brogue. "Me friends 'ave been sayin' for years, 'Come to America, Mattie,' an' I've been stallin' an' stallin', but then I said, 'Mattie, ye'll niver know lest ye go.'"

Belinda smiled.

"But first I went on to see me sister in Paris," he continued as though Belinda would be interested in all the details of his story. "'Ye niver know if ye might niver be back,' I told myself."

Belinda nodded and tried to smile.

"'Tis scary, goin' to a new country," the man continued soberly. "An' at me age, too. I worried some, ye can be sure. But then I said, 'Mattie, why all the fussin'? Ye needn't leave God on here behind ye now. Ye ken take 'im with ye.'"

Something in what the kindly man said stirred a response within Belinda. Was that what she had done? Left God back in her homeland? Was that why her trip abroad had become so dismal, so unsatisfying? She knew she had missed attending church, but had she misplaced God, too? After all, God was not limited to buildings. His true dwelling was in hearts. Had Belinda shut the door of her heart when she stepped on the deck of the sailing vessel? If God had no place in her thoughts or plans from that time on, no wonder she had been miserable.

No! No, that wasn't when it happened, Belinda realized as she thought further. She had left God out of her life even before leaving Boston. Perhaps the downward slide had begun before she left her own small town, maybe starting with her restlessness. Had the restlessness been a result of her constant care of Mrs. Stafford-Smyth? She had allowed her nursing duties to keep her from daily quiet times of prayer and Bible reading. *And I was getting all nervous and upset about Rand and Jackson,* she remembered.

Things had only worsened in the flurry of activity in Boston with Pierre. They had been so busy running here and there that Belinda had put aside her Sunday church attendance, as well. Gradually, thoughtlessly, she had drifted into a life that didn't include God.

Belinda looked across at the gentleman beside her. She did not wish to be rude, but she needed some time alone. No . . . no, she needed time with her God. She had been floundering—starving—and not even realizing why.

"Excuse me, please," she said to the man. "I've enjoyed meeting you, but I . . . I . . . need to return to my stateroom."

Belinda was thankful that Mrs. Stafford-Smyth was not there. She needed privacy. With almost frantic gestures she began to rummage through the baggage stored beneath her bunk. Where was her Bible? She who had read her Bible daily had not held it in her hands for weeks.

At last she drew it forth from the bottom of a suitcase. With tears streaming down her face, she clasped the book to her bosom.

"Oh, God," she prayed, "God, I'm so sorry. Forgive me. Forgive me for forsaking you. I . . . I've been so lonely, and in my foolishness I did not even know why." Belinda fell on her knees and cried out to a forgiving Father.

It was a while before the inner storm was spent and peace again entered Belinda's heart. She rose to sit on her berth and opened her Bible. She sat reading favorite portions from her precious book, thankfully noticing how each passage met her need, and wondering how she could have ever become so careless as to neglect it.

She had been raised with Bible reading. Her earliest memories were of sitting on her father's lap as he read to the family from the Bible each morning. She had always been impressed with the importance of Bible reading and time spent in prayer. She knew! She knew! She had learned it well. She had become a believer herself when she was but a girl and had allowed God to lead and direct her life throughout her growing years. How was it possible for her to let the pleasures of the world and the deceitfulness of living a life of leisure and wealth lead her so far off course? How could Satan so subtly and slowly have drawn her away from her source of spiritual life? It had developed so gradually that Belinda had been unaware of its happening.

It's not that the Lord doesn't want me to enjoy beautiful things and interesting places, Belinda decided. *But He wants me to do those things with Him, not without Him.* Thankful that through the kind words of an elderly man God had jarred her back to the truth, she read on, refreshing her parched soul.

At last, feeling renewed and alive again, she laid her Bible gently on the bedside table. She smiled softly to herself, hardly able to wait to share her new discovery with Mrs. Stafford-Smyth. She had not been the Christian witness to the woman she should have been. She prayed God would help her change all that. And feeling assured that she served a merciful and understanding God, Belinda was confident she would be given ample opportunity to share her faith properly in the future.

The future! Suddenly the thought seemed awfully good to Belinda. She had so much to look forward to—so many decisions of life still to be made. She no longer felt crowded—pushed against a wall. Why, even the thought of Jackson and Rand brought no accompanying anxiety. Belinda felt she was ready to offer honest friendship to both of them. *Friendship—but no more—at least at present,* she told herself and felt no guilt concerning her decision. She smiled again, thankful for the feeling of peace.

She felt no pressure to know what her future held. Perhaps . . . just perhaps God did have a home and family somewhere ahead for her. Belinda would like that, but she was willing to take one step at a time.

A wave of loneliness for the ones at home swept over her. She would love to see them—to see them all. To be held in her father's secure arms again—to share private thoughts with her mother over a cup of tea—to watch Luke's steady hand as he held syringe or needle—to chat, to hold, to laugh and cry with her family.

And then Belinda's thoughts turned to Mrs. Stafford-Smyth—the wealthy woman who was in reality so poor—and Belinda's heart ached for the woman. For the first time in her young life, Belinda began to sense what it would be like to be alone—really alone. The thought sobered and chilled her. She must do more with her—be more thoughtful and loving. More sharing and giving. The lonely woman needed her, not as nursemaid, but as friend. Belinda knew that at least for now, she would not—could not—desert her.

"God," she whispered, "I'll need your leading. Your direction. I want to do the right thing . . . and I trust you to let me know just what that might be. Oh . . . not all at once . . . but step by step. Help me to be patient with what you have for me now . . . an' ready to move on when you give me a nudge. Don't let me rush the future . . . but help me to walk into it with faith and confidence in you." Belinda breathed deeply, at peace with herself. "And thank you, God . . . for a future . . . for the knowledge that you have it all in your control."

Belinda smoothed her dress and raised a hand to tidy her hair, then moved forward to take the first step in her new walk with God.

I must find him and tell him, she said to herself with a smile. *He's a rather strange little man—but his words changed my life. I must tell him—and then welcome him to America. "Mattie" he said his name was, but it's hardly proper for me to be calling him that. I must ask his name.* Belinda opened the cabin door and stepped out into the bright sunshine and tangy sea air.

Barcelona—Rome—Paris—steamship—Boston? What does it really matter? For as the kind man has pointed out, "'Ye needn't leave God behind ye now,'" and wherever one goes—wherever God is, the heart can be at peace, at home.

LOVE FINDS
A HOME

To Ingolf Arnesen,
my Christian brother,
prayer partner, and cheering section—
friend of the Davises, Joneses, and Delaneys.
Thank you for your friendship, support, and prayers.
God bless!

Some of the Characters in the LOVE COMES SOFTLY series

Clark and Marty Davis, partners in a marriage in which each had lost a previous spouse.

Missie, Clark's daughter from his first marriage, married Willie La-Haye and moved west to ranch.

Clare, Marty's son born after her first husband's death, married Kate. They live in the same farmyard as Clark and Marty. Their children—Amy Jo, Dan, David, and Dack.

Arnie, Clark and Marty's first child. He married Anne and they have three sons—Silas, John, and Abe.

Daughter Ellie, married Lane Howard and moved west to join Missie and Willie. Their children are Brenda, William, and Willis.

Son Luke, trained to be a doctor and returned to the small town to practice medicine. He married Abbie. Their children are Thomas, Aaron, and Ruth.

Jackson Brown, the school friend who greatly impressed Melissa, Amy Jo, and Belinda when he first arrived at the country school. He later became a doctor.

Belinda, Clark and Marty's youngest daughter, who trained as a nurse and went to Boston.

ONE

Stirrings

Belinda slitted her eyes open against the rays of the morning sun, then quickly closed them and pulled the blanket up around her face for protection. It was early, too early to rise—but she wouldn't be able to sleep any longer with the sun shining in her eyes.

Even in her sleepy state, she knew something was atypical. Previous mornings she had not awakened with the sun shining directly into her face. *The drapes—why are the drapes not pulled?* she wondered groggily. And then things began to filter back into her foggy consciousness.

It was the moon that had kept her from pulling the drapes across her upstairs bedroom window the night before. *It's so full and golden and shining,* she had commented to herself when she went to shut it out. She had impulsively decided to watch it as she lay in her bed. She would get up later, she thought, when the moon had passed from view and properly close the heavy curtains for the night.

But sleep had claimed her before the moon moved out of sight, and now the sun was streaming in the tall, elegant window, refusing to allow her further sleep.

Belinda pushed back her covers and slowly crawled from bed. If she was to get any more sleep, she had to shut out the early morning sunshine.

Still tired, she yawned as she reached for the pull, but she couldn't resist looking out over the lovely garden at the bright summer day.

Already the elderly gardener, Thomas, was bending over the flower beds, coaxing begonias to lift their bright summer faces to the sun. *What beautiful flower beds he's laid out,* Belinda thought. *Why, Aunt Virgie said just yesterday she doesn't know what in the world she will do should Thomas decide to retire.*

Belinda smiled affectionately as she watched the old man. She did not share her employer's fears. She could see his love for the flowers in his every careful move. One might as well ask Thomas to stop breathing as to stop nursing his beloved flower beds.

Sudden determination made Belinda drop the drapery pull. With such a beautiful day beckoning her, she could no longer stay in bed. She would dress and slip out to join Thomas. Maybe he would even let her pull a few weeds.

Belinda hummed as she pulled a simple gown over her head and tied a bow at her waist. Aunt Virgie would not waken for some time yet, and Belinda would be free to enjoy the early morning hours.

She carried walking shoes in her hand so she would not make any noise and a hat to protect her face from the sun. She left her door slightly ajar so as not to disturb her employer in the next room with the sound of it closing. She slipped silently from the room and descended the steps.

Belinda left the house by the veranda door, pausing on the steps to breathe deeply. The heavy scent and beauty of summer blossoms filled her senses. *It truly is beautiful here at the Stafford-Smyth home,* Belinda decided for the umpteenth time. Her longings to be back in her small-town prairie setting were not because she did not appreciate her present surroundings. Her people, her family, were the reason her yearning thoughts so often turned toward home. And thinking of them, as lately she seemed to do almost constantly, her heart ached for a chance to be a part of their lives again.

But Belinda refused to dwell on her loneliness. As she had often done in the past, she firmly pushed it aside and thought instead of the things she had to be thankful for.

Mrs. Stafford-Smyth had been ill for almost two weeks with a serious bout of influenza, but now, thankfully, she seemed to be gaining strength each day. Belinda was greatly relieved. It wasn't the constant nursing or the loss of sleep at nights that bothered her. It was the worry—the possibility that her friend might not be able to shake the disease.

Belinda loved the elderly woman almost as though she were truly kin. They even enjoyed their own little game of "belonging" to each other. Mrs. Stafford-Smyth had asked Belinda if she minded calling her Aunt Virgie, and Belinda had been pleased to comply. In turn, "Aunt Virgie" always referred to Belinda as "Belinda, deah," with her intriguing eastern accent. The arrangement satisfied them both.

The lady seemed to have long ago concluded that neither grand-son—Pierre and his Anne-Marie, nor Franz and his Yvette—would ever consent to share her Boston home with her. Indeed, Pierre and Anne-Marie had sent word from France that they were soon to be joined by a third family member. Aunt Virgie and Belinda, sharing joy over the great-grandchild to come, had even sat and knitted gifts to send to the new baby. But both had concluded without saying anything to the other that it was most unlikely Mrs. Stafford-Smyth would ever personally see or hold the child.

Belinda stopped to admire a climbing rose. The bright pink bloom filled the morning air with a sweet sunshine all its own. Mrs. Stafford-Smyth said that Thomas had developed the lovely flower in his own greenhouse. Belinda breathed deeply of its scent, then moved on into the garden.

McIntyre, Thomas's canine companion of many years, slipped along-side to sniff at Belinda's hand.

"Good morning, Mac," Belinda greeted him, running a hand over his graying head. "I see you're up early, too." The old dog's eyesight was failing and his hearing was not as sharp as it had been, but he never missed an opportunity to be at his master's side.

Thomas heard the words and straightened slowly, blinking as though not sure he was seeing right. He put one hand to his creaking back, then grinned slowly, showing a few gaps where teeth were missing. "Miss Belinda," he said, "how come ye not be abed?"

"It's too nice a morning to sleep," Belinda answered good-naturedly.

But Thomas responded with a twinkle in his eyes, "'Tis jest the same as any other mornin', h'tis."

Belinda smiled. "I suppose so," she admitted slowly. "I really wouldn't know, I must confess. But once I saw the day, I couldn't resist getting out into it. It will be hot and stifling later on, I'm thinking." And Belinda cast a glance at the bright sky with the sun already streaming down rays of warmth.

"Aye," spoke Thomas. "'Twill be a hot one today, I'm afraid."

"I noticed your rosebush is covered with flowers," Belinda went on. "It smells most wonderful."

Thomas grinned widely at her comment. "Aye" was all he said.

He bent back to his work again, and Belinda ventured closer and knelt down beside him.

"Could I . . . would you mind if . . . if I pulled a few weeds?" she asked timidly.

"Weedin' ye be wishin' for?" His eyes widened, no doubt picturing milk-white hands in such an endeavor. "Ye pulled weeds afore?"

"Oh yes," quickly responded Belinda. "Back home I always helped with the garden."

"Ye had ye some flowers?"

"Oh, not like here," Belinda was quick to explain. "Nothing nearly as grand as this. But Mama's always had her flowers. Roses and violets and early spring tulips. She loves flowers, Mama does. But she spends most of her time in the big garden—vegetables, grown for family use. Mama has fed her family almost all year round from the fruits of her garden." Belinda's voice had grown nostalgic just thinking about it. She could see Marty's form bent over the hoe or lifting hot canning jars from the steaming kettle.

"Aye," said old Thomas, nodding his head in understanding. "My mither, she did, too." Belinda thought his eyes looked a little misty.

"Be at it, then," Thomas gave her permission. "Mind ye pick careful. An' don't prick a finger on a thorn." Then Thomas handed her his own little hand trowel, and Belinda leaned forward and let her fingers feel the warmth of the sun-heated soil.

They worked in silence side by side for some time before Thomas spoke again. "'Tis a new rose I have now. In the greenhouse. It has its first blossom just about to open. Ye wish to see it?"

Belinda straightened her back, smiling her pleasure at the invitation. "Oh, could I?" she asked eagerly.

"Aye," the old man said with a slight nod. He lifted himself slowly to his feet, moving his hunched shoulders carefully up and down to ease the ache. Then he cast his eyes around the yard to find old Mac. The gardener never took a step without checking on his dog. With Mac's senses no longer what they had been, he had told Belinda he feared the dog might not notice his departure.

"McIntyre," he spoke loudly now, "we be movin' on."

Belinda loved to hear him speak the dog's name. He rolled the "r" off his tongue so effectively.

The dog lifted his head, then slowly pulled himself to his feet. He moved to Thomas's side, and as one, the figures moved toward the greenhouse.

Belinda fell into step beside them. She stopped only once—by the side of the climbing rose.

"It's so pretty," she murmured, touching a leaf gently.

"Aye," acknowledged old Thomas with a twinkle, reaching out a hand to stroke a velvety petal. "'Tis Pink Rosanna I call 'er."

"You gave it a name?" asked Belinda in surprise.

"Aye. I always name me new ladies."

Belinda smiled at his description of his new rose hybrids.

At the greenhouse, Belinda waited while old Thomas carefully opened the creaking door. McIntyre found his own gunnysack bed by the entrance and flopped down. Even Old McIntyre was not allowed any farther into Thomas's sanctuary.

Belinda followed slowly, moved to exclaim over and over as her eyes swept the massive foliage and glorious blooms, but she held her tongue.

At last they were standing before a small rosebush. With obvious skill and affection, it had been grafted onto another shoot. Belinda could see the slight enlargement where the grafting had taken place. But her eye passed swiftly from the stem to the delicate bud that was just beginning to unfurl. On the same stem, another bud had formed, and a third one was slowly breaking from curled greenery.

"Oh," murmured Belinda, no longer able to restrain herself. "It's . . . it's so beautiful. I've never seen such a pretty rose—such a combination of lovely colors."

Thomas could not repress his smile or the shine in his eyes. "Aye," he nodded, and his gnarled old hand reached forward to caress the flower.

Then, before Belinda could catch her breath, he lifted his sharp pruning scissors, snipped the flower from the stem, and extended it to her.

Belinda reached out her hand and then just as quickly withdrew it. "But . . . but . . ." she stammered.

"Go on wit' ye, now," the old gardener said, easing the bloom into her hand. "'Tis only fitting ye be the one to have the first bloom." He lowered his eyes to his worn-out gardener's shoes. When he lifted them again, Belinda thought she could see a flush on his weathered cheeks. "I named her Belinda," he confessed. "Princess Belinda."

For a long moment Belinda could say nothing. Her hand slowly curled around the flower and she raised it to her face. Breathing deeply of the fragrance, she brushed her lips against the soft petals. She felt her eyes filling with unbidden tears. "It's beautiful," she whispered. "Thank you, Thomas."

"Aye," the old man nodded. "'Tis my thanks to ye fer bein' so kind to m'lady."

Belinda understood his simple explanation. She nodded in return, then smiled and carefully found her way outside.

As she walked back toward the veranda, Belinda studied the flower in her hands. The soft cream of each petal slowly blended into a deeper yellow, which in turn changed into an apricot. Belinda was sure she had never seen such a pretty rose. *To think Thomas named it after me!* she marveled. She felt at once exalted and deeply humbled.

Belinda lifted her face to the sun, now higher in the eastern sky. The summer day was well on its way. Aunt Virgie would soon be awakening. Belinda knew she must hurry to bathe and change from her soiled gardening gown. No longer tired, there was a spring to her step and a light in her eyes. She was ready to face this new day. She smiled to herself.

Her eyes turned back to the exquisite rose.

What a difference one bright flower can make in a person's life, she mused. But then she corrected herself. *No,* she told herself, *it isn't the flower—pretty as it is. It is a person who has brought joy to my heart. Thomas. A dear old man—just a gardener in some folks' thinking—but a beautiful person. One I have learned to love.*

The thought did not surprise Belinda. There were many older people in this household whom she had learned to love. Aunt Virgie, old Thomas, the straightlaced Windsor, Cook—even the stern-faced Potter. Belinda smiled to herself. She loved them all, actually. They were part of her life. Her Boston family.

Oh, she knew others her own age might pity her, being "stuck in a houseful of the elderly," but Belinda didn't feel shut in, restless, and forgotten. Not since she had given God the proper recognition in her life. She felt loved and protected—and needed. *If only . . . if only I didn't feel so lonesome for those back home, I could be quite satisfied and fulfilled living and working for Mrs. Stafford-Smyth at Marshall Manor,* she thought.

TWO

Aunt Virgie

"Good morning, Aunt Virgie," Belinda said softly, proceeding into the room when she had determined that Mrs. Stafford-Smyth was awake.

The frail woman managed a smile. "Mawnin', Belinda, deah," she answered.

"Did you sleep?" asked Belinda as she went to open the drapes, knowing that it was some time since the older woman had enjoyed a good night's rest.

"I did. Scarce can believe it myself, but I did. Oh, and it felt—it felt delicious, too," she said with emphasis. "But you know what else? I feel that now I remembah *how* to sleep, I could just sleep on and on."

"Then perhaps you should. You haven't slept decently for days—or rather nights," Belinda corrected herself with a sly smile.

Mrs. Stafford-Smyth chuckled weakly at Belinda's little joke. "You need sleep every bit as much as I," she informed Belinda. "You've been up night aftah night. I declayah, I don't know how you do it."

Belinda leaned over the bed and laid a hand on the silvery head. "I'm fine," she smiled. "In fact, I feel just great this morning. I've even been out weeding with Thomas."

Mrs. Stafford-Smyth showed her surprise. "You have—at this hou-ah?"

Belinda nodded. "And you should just see the new rosebush!" she exclaimed, "It's covered with the most exquisite roses. And they smell absolutely wonderful."

Belinda thought of her other bit of news. She hardly knew how to tell it so it wouldn't sound boastful, yet she had to share her delight with the older woman.

"And something else, too," she said, and she couldn't help smiling. "Thomas took me to his greenhouse."

The building was always referred to as "Thomas's greenhouse," and no one else would have dreamed of trespassing. The truth was, the greenhouse, like every other building on the grounds, belonged to Mrs. Stafford-Smyth.

"He did?" said Mrs. Stafford-Smyth, sounding duly impressed.

"He did—and more than that. He showed me a brand-new rose he has developed. He hasn't even set it outside in the gardens yet. It had its first flower—though others are coming quickly."

"I declayah!" said Mrs. Stafford-Smyth, seeming to enjoy the telling of the tale as much as the story itself. "It must be something very special to put that shine in you-ah eyes," she noted.

"You will never guess what he has named the new rose," Belinda said, feeling shy.

"Aftah some lovely lady, I suppose," mused Mrs. Stafford-Smyth. "They always do, it seems."

Belinda could feel her cheeks grow warm.

"Well, I hardly expect he named it Old Prune Face, aftah me," joked the elderly lady.

"Oh, Aunt Virgie," protested Belinda, "no one would ever say that about you."

Mrs. Stafford-Smyth just smiled. "Well, they should," she said matter-of-factly. "I declayah, I looked in my hand mirrah befoah I went to bed last night, and I've lost some more weight. I do look like a prune, foah sure."

She has lost weight, Belinda acknowledged silently as she looked at the pinched face against the pillow.

"Well, now that you are able to eat again," Belinda assured the lady, stroking her hair back from the dear face once more, "Cook'll have you fattened up in no time." She smiled as she fluffed up a pillow and made the woman more comfortable.

"But you were telling me about that new rose," encouraged Mrs. Stafford-Smyth. "What did Thomas name it?"

"Let me show you the rose," said Belinda quickly.

"You mean he picked one—already? He nevah does that."

"Well, he picked this one—the very first blossom," beamed Belinda. "Let me run get it. I have it in a bud vase in my room."

"I declayah!" exclaimed the woman again.

Belinda soon returned with her cherished flower.

"Oh my," Mrs. Stafford-Smyth said, her voice properly respectful, "it is a lovely one, isn't it? I hope he chose an equally pretty name."

Belinda felt her face flushing once more. "Well, he . . ." she began. "He . . . honored me by naming the rose Belinda." Her cheeks flamed, and she wished she had never brought up the subject. Mrs. Stafford-Smyth would think her dreadfully self-centered.

But the older lady beamed. "How very apt." She smiled her appreciation. "Thomas is an astute old gentleman. He named a beautiful rose aftah a beautiful young lady."

Belinda blushed further as she accepted the compliment.

"*Just* Belinda?" asked the woman further. "Often Thomas has added a descriptive word—something else to go with the lady's name."

"Princess Belinda," admitted Belinda, dropping her face to hide her embarrassment.

"Princess Belinda—that is nice. That's quite an honah, you know, to have one feel so about you," said the elderly lady.

Belinda was able to face her then.

"It really isn't me he is honoring," she explained. "The name shows his feelings about you. You see, he named the flower after me because—" Belinda struggled to find the appropriate words—"because he wished . . . he wished to express his appreciation to me for . . . for caring for you. You are the one who is special to him."

Mrs. Stafford-Smyth stared wide-eyed at Belinda. "Me? Why, whatevah do you mean? What did he say?" she probed.

"He said something like 'for carin' for m'lady,' " Belinda said evenly.

"How sweet," murmured Mrs. Stafford-Smyth, reaching up to brush at tears forming in her eyes. She was silent for several minutes as Belinda busied herself about the room. Finally she spoke again, softly. "You know, one gets to thinking sometimes that one is really of no worth at all. Life could just go right on without you, and no one would scarcely notice." She sighed, then went on. "Heah I lie day aftah day, no good to anyone. And then . . . then a deah old friend, a gardenah, shows you he cares. Makes one wish to get bettah again."

"Oh, Aunt Virgie," Belinda cried, moving swiftly to the side of the elderly woman and touching her cheek gently. "The whole household has been tiptoeing about, hardly daring to breathe. We've all been worried half sick that you might . . . might not get better. We all need you . . . love you. Do you really have any doubt about that?"

The lady stirred almost restlessly and smiled back at Belinda.

"I'm a foolish old woman," she answered softly. "I have so much to live foah, so many deah friends. I don't deserve them, but I'm so thankful foah them." She sighed again and stirred in her bed, shoving a pillow away with a pale hand.

"Belinda, deah," she said with determination, "bring me my robe and slippahs."

At Belinda's little attempt at a mild protest, Mrs. Stafford-Smyth hurried on, saying, "One nevah gains strength by lying abed. I've got a lot of convalescing to do if I want to enjoy this summah before it's gone. I'd best get at it. The blue robe, please."

Belinda did not argue further. Once Mrs. Stafford-Smyth had made up her mind, it was useless to argue.

Belinda went for the blue robe, glad that the woman had requested the warmest robe in her closet. As she lifted the garment from the hook, Belinda felt an enormous weight of worry fall from her. It had been some time since she had seen a sparkle in her employer's eyes. Truly she was on the road to recovery. Belinda could hardly wait to rush out to the kitchen to share the news with the rest of the household. They all had been very concerned.

"The first thing you need is a good breakfast," Belinda stated as she helped the older woman into the robe and slippers. About to ring for Windsor and a breakfast tray, she responded to a light tapping on the door. Belinda opened it on its silent hinges. She could see the distress in Windsor's eyes. "Is m'lady awake?" he asked in a raspy whisper.

"Yes. Yes," Belinda assured him. "Come in. She's much better this morning. In fact, I was about to ring to have a breakfast tray prepared."

Windsor could not hide his relief, as practiced as the good butler could be at concealing his emotions.

"Come in, Windsah," called Mrs. Stafford-Smyth.

He stepped cautiously into the room, his hands fidgeting nervously. "Thomas wished to know if you'd like a bouquet, madam," he announced with proper dignity.

"Oh yes," agreed Mrs. Stafford-Smyth, a smile lifting the weariness from her face.

Windsor turned on his heels with a sharp click. "I shall be right back, m'lady," he assured her and left the room with a great deal more briskness than he had arrived.

While Windsor was gone, Belinda hurried about, helping Mrs. Stafford-Smyth with her grooming and settling her in the comfortable chair by the open window.

Sarah came with two trays of nourishing food. For the first time in weeks, Mrs. Stafford-Smyth looked with some interest at the meal. Belinda smiled with relief and set a tray in front of the woman, accepting the other tray of food for herself.

They had just said grace together when there was another tap on the door. Windsor was back again with a bowl of fragrant, freshly cut pink roses. Belinda recognized them immediately.

"That's the new climbing rosebush on the back walk," she commented. "The one I told you about earlier. That's Thomas's new Pink Rosanna."

"Pink Rosanna," mused Mrs. Stafford-Smyth. "What a lovely name." She buried her face in the bowl of flowers. "And what beautiful flowers," she added.

Mrs. Stafford-Smyth stroked a soft petal, then breathed again the sweet smell of the flowers.

"Tell Thomas thank you for the flowers," she said, her voice husky. "I . . . I am deeply, deeply appreciative."

Windsor nodded and departed as Mrs. Stafford-Smyth lifted her head and smiled.

Belinda took the rose bowl gently and set it on the small table close beside the woman.

"We'd best eat our breakfast before it gets cold," she said softly, and Mrs. Stafford-Smyth nodded in agreement and lifted her spoon with some eagerness.

From then on, Belinda noted that Mrs. Stafford-Smyth grew a bit stronger each day. It wasn't long before she was able to be up and about for short periods of time, and then she could walk the upstairs halls. At last she was able to make her way down to the rooms below. She enjoyed the summer sunshine as she sat with her needlework in the north parlor. She spent hours out on the veranda absorbing the smell and beauty of the garden. She presided once again over meals in the dining room. Belinda felt they had all been given a new lease on life. The whole household took on a new atmosphere—of thanksgiving and relief.

Belinda was thankful she could once again leave the house occasionally. She had especially missed the Sunday services at church. She was very glad to immerse herself in the stirring hymns, the Sunday Scriptures, and, yes, even the pastor's message. She could hardly wait for the time when Mrs. Stafford-Smyth would be able to rejoin her in the worship. *But I mustn't rush her,* Belinda reminded herself. *She has been very ill. It wouldn't do for her to have a relapse.*

Belinda was determined she would be patient. But, oh, it was so good to feel the burden of worry slip away from her, from the house and its staff. The summer days seemed brighter, the flowers fairer, the food tastier—everything seemed better to Belinda now that Mrs. Stafford-Smyth was well on her way to full health.

THREE

Plans

As the summer progressed, Mrs. Stafford-Smyth again took over the running of Marshall Manor, giving her daily instructions to Windsor, Potter, and Cook. Belinda was able to catch up on her sleep, her mending, her letter writing, and her shopping. She gave a relieved sigh every time she thought of those trying weeks of early summer. She hadn't realized just how deeply she had worried, how frightened she had been, how wearing were the days and nights when Mrs. Stafford-Smyth had needed her constant care.

Each morning Belinda met Mrs. Stafford-Smyth in the well-lit north parlor, where they breakfasted together and planned their day. Then Belinda read a Scripture portion and led them in a daily prayer. Belinda kept hoping for the day when Mrs. Stafford-Smyth would want to pray aloud, too.

Mrs. Stafford-Smyth did attend church services regularly and gave the staff Sunday morning off so they might do likewise. And though lately she seemed more interested in matters of faith, she never expressed to Belinda her true thoughts on the subject.

Belinda longed to have someone she could discuss spiritual things with, but she was sure the senior pastor of the congregation was much too busy to be bothered by a young woman who just wanted to talk. The associate pastor was a single man, not much older than Belinda herself. Though Belinda knew she might appreciate discussing issues of faith with a seminary graduate, she also knew better than to suggest such a thing. Everyone, including the young minister himself, would surely think Belinda had no other intentions than to snare an eligible young man. Belinda had no desire to provide the opportunity for such gossip.

So Belinda continued on each day, enjoying the time spent in Bible reading and prayer but longing for spiritual fellowship. *If only . . . if only Aunt Virgie could understand and share my feelings about faith,* she kept thinking.

But another thought concerned her. *If Aunt Virgie were to die now, would she be ready for heaven?* The idea troubled Belinda. She loved the woman dearly, and the thought of her not being prepared for eternity made Belinda spend even more time in prayer for her friend.

Toward the end of summer Mrs. Stafford-Smyth decided to host another dinner party. Belinda by now was used to socializing with her employer's wealthy and influential friends. She didn't dread the prospect of another such dinner as Pierre had done during his last visit to the household. *In fact,* Belinda concluded, *it is much better to have elderly company than no company at all.* She and Aunt Virgie needed some kind of diversion.

"What should we serve for dinnah, deah?" asked Mrs. Stafford-Smyth as they sat together in the downstairs parlor.

Belinda looked up from her needlepoint. She really cared little what was served for dinner, but she thought that would be an inappropriate response.

Instead she said mildly, "Perhaps Cook would have some suggestions."

Mrs. Stafford-Smyth considered that possibility. "Yes," she agreed at length. "I'm sure she would—but since this is my first dinnah party in such a long time, I'd rathah like to plan it myself."

Belinda smiled. "If you'd like to, then by all means you must."

"I was thinking of roast beef and Yorkshire pudding," the woman went on. "With asparagus tips and spiced carrots."

"That sounds good," agreed Belinda.

"We'll have a vegetable salad, with Cook's special dressing."

"And her poppy-seed rolls," suggested Belinda.

Mrs. Stafford-Smyth smiled, looking pleased that she had coaxed Belinda into sharing the planning.

"What about dessert?" asked the older woman.

"Oh my," said Belinda with a sigh. "I shouldn't even *think* about dessert. I'm sure I've put on some pounds the last few weeks."

"And well you needed to," Mrs. Stafford-Smyth stated firmly. "You spoke of fattening me up. I declayah, you must have lost about as much weight during my sickness as I did."

Belinda was sure it hadn't been all that much. She wanted to protest but let the matter drop.

"Cheesecake would be nice," Mrs. Stafford-Smyth mused aloud.

"Or fresh strawberry shortcake," responded Belinda.

"Does Thomas still have strawberries?"

"He says he has a second crop," answered Belinda. "He is really proud of them."

"Fresh strawberry shortcake it will be, then. I nevah tire of strawberries, and we might as well enjoy them as long as they last," reasoned Mrs. Stafford-Smyth. "Ring for Cook, deah," she said to Belinda's nod. "I'd like to get this settled now."

Cook arrived with a fresh apron neatly covering her plump form. Seeming to be a bit anxious, as she often was when being summoned to the sitting room, her face soon relaxed as her employer began to talk of dinner plans.

"And Miss Belinda would like some of your tasty poppy-seed rolls," Mrs. Stafford-Smyth went on, bringing a smile to Cook's face. "And for dessert, I understand Thomas has another crop of strawberries. We'll have your strawberry shortcake. With cream. Everyone loves that."

Cook openly beamed in spite of herself. She loved compliments on her cuisine—especially when the recognition came from her revered employer.

"We will serve dinnah promptly at seven," went on Mrs. Stafford-Smyth.

Belinda smiled at the "promptly." She knew that Mrs. Celia Prescott would be invited and, as Pierre had remarked so long ago, "Aunt Celia's never on time."

But on the night of the first dinner party in ages at Marshall Manor, Celia Prescott was *almost* on time. She breathlessly fluttered in and greeted her hostess. "Virgie, deah, I am *so* glad you are up and about again! I was worried to *death* about you. You had that dreadful old flu for such a long, long time, I feahed you'd *nevah* recovah!"

"I'm fine now," Mrs. Stafford-Smyth assured her calmly. "I've had good care." And she cast an appreciative glance toward Belinda.

"I have long since admired your foresight in having your own personal nurse," commented Mrs. Prescott with a hint of envy. "I don't know how you'd evah manage without her."

"Nor I," agreed Mrs. Stafford-Smyth with feeling.

Belinda flushed uneasily, which seemed to please Mrs. Allenby, one of the other guests. Belinda still could not warm to the woman. She seemed to take great pleasure in the discomfort of others. Thankfully, all the guests were now present, and they were able to move to the dining room, where Windsor and Sarah were waiting to serve.

Chatting and laughing together, the evening passed sociably enough. Mrs. Celia Prescott humorously shared her adventures of the summer, to Mr. Walsh's great merriment. Mrs. Allenby gave an occasional imperious sniff as her contribution to the evening, while Mrs. Whitley smiled benignly on all. Her husband made up for her silence by firmly expressing himself on every subject. All in all, it was a lively evening, and Belinda concluded that it was good for Mrs. Stafford-Smyth to have someone besides her to talk to.

But when the evening ended, Belinda felt a strange emptiness. That nagging loneliness gnawed again within her.

You just feel some sort of letdown after all the planning and antici-pation are done, she reproached herself. *Aunt Virgie likely feels it, too.*

Belinda quickly slipped out of her crimson party gown and into a cream-colored robe. She would help Mrs. Stafford-Smyth prepare for bed.

If she feels as I do, she murmured to herself, *she'll need some company for a bit.*

But Mrs. Stafford-Smyth was not feeling at all let down. She was still excited about the party as she welcomed Belinda into her room. "Didn't everything go just fine?" she enthused, and Belinda nodded quietly in response. Aunt Virgie had slipped from her violet gown and into a soft pink robe. Sitting at the vanity, her gray hair loosened from its pins, she was brushing her hair as she talked to Belinda's reflection in the mirror. Her cheeks were flushed and her voice filled with excitement. Belinda took the brush from her and gently stroked the wispy tresses.

"Celia had a wonderful idea," Aunt Virgie began at once. "Just as she was leaving she drew me aside and suggested I spend some time with her and her sister in New Yawk."

Belinda stopped her brushing in surprise at the sudden turn of events.

"What do you think of that?" asked the older woman, turning to face Belinda, who could already see what Mrs. Stafford-Smyth thought of it.

"Why, it . . . it sounds wonderful," Belinda answered.

"Yes," mused the older woman. "Yes, I think I'd like that. I haven't been to New Yawk for yeahs. Haven't been anywheah for such a long time. I think I'd like that just fine."

"It would be good for you," responded Belinda, feeling a strange turning in the pit of her stomach. *What am I to do in the meantime?* she wondered silently. *Stay in this big house all by myself?*

"I could do some shopping, take in a few plays, heah the orchestra again. Yes, I think I'll accept the invitation."

"And when will you go?" Belinda inquired.

"Next week. There isn't much time to prepa-ah, but any shopping that needs doing can be done in New Yawk. It would be exciting to look for a new gown someplace besides LeSoud's."

"How long will—?"

"Six weeks," Mrs. Stafford-Smyth explained. "Six weeks. That should be just right. Long enough that one won't need to rush to get everything done, but not so long as to weah out one's welcome."

Belinda nodded. "You know Aunt Celia's sister well?" asked Belinda.

"Oh my, yes. We were deah, deah friends until she moved to New Yawk. The three of us were always togethah. She's different than Celia— more subdued, more dignified. A real lady in every sense of the word. Lost her husband five yeahs ago. Nevah has recovahed, Celia says. She loves to have company. Celia goes at least once a yeah, but this yeah she has asked for me, too."

"That's nice," smiled Belinda. "The trip will be good for you." She kissed the older woman on the cheek and went to her own room.

But Belinda did not fall asleep very quickly. Her thoughts kept going round and round. What would she *do* all day while her employer was in New York? At times she had felt lonely and at loose ends even with Aunt Virgie at home. She wasn't worried now about the older woman's health. Mrs. Stafford-Smyth seemed to be perfectly well again. But Belinda did feel a sense of panic and loss at the thought of being on her own.

Suddenly Belinda sat straight up in bed, a smile spreading over her face in the darkness. *Of course,* she said to herself. *Of course. Why didn't I think of it immediately? I've been aching to go home. This is the perfect opportunity! I won't need to worry about Aunt Virgie while I'm gone.*

Belinda should have lain down and gone directly to sleep then, but she didn't. On and on raced her mind, thinking of home, trying to envision how each person might have changed, thinking of the fun of surprising her friends, cherishing the thought of spending time with her beloved family. It was almost morning before her mind would let her slip off into much-needed sleep.

I'm going home. Home. It's been such a long, long time.

During the next few days the whole house was in a tizzy. Mrs. Stafford-Smyth had announced her intentions to her household staff, and everyone was busy with preparations for her departure.

Belinda was perhaps the busiest of all. There was the choosing of Mrs. Stafford-Smyth's wardrobe and the packing, the last-minute shopping for small items, the dusting of hat feathers, and the changing of ribbons. Through it all Belinda flitted back and forth with a smile on her face. Soon she, too, would be off on her own journey. "Oh, Ma, I can hardly wait!" she whispered joyfully to herself as she worked.

Windsor entered the sitting room with some garments over his arm. "Madam's cleaning has arrived," he informed Belinda in answer to her unasked question. "I shall take it to her at once."

"I'm going up. I'll take it if you wish," Belinda offered.

Windsor had become accustomed to Belinda lending a hand now and then. But she knew he still had rigid ideas of proper positions and activities for the staff. Belinda was the nurse-companion of his lady. She should not be running errands. But after a pause, he must have decided this was all right and passed the garments to Belinda without argument.

"Thank you, miss," he said stiffly, and Belinda was certain he had concluded it wasn't worth the argument with her. She started off with the clothing, a bit of a smile on her lips.

"Your garments from the cleaners have been returned," she said as she entered the room.

"Oh, good!" exclaimed the woman. "I was beginning to feah that they wouldn't come back in time since they were to have been here yesterday."

"Well, they're here now. Should I hang them in the closet or pack them?" Belinda asked.

"I've left room in that trunk for them," responded Mrs. Stafford-Smyth, pointing, and Belinda felt her eyebrows rise as she moved toward the chest.

My, she thought to herself, *whatever will she do with all these clothes? And her planning to do more shopping, as well! I expect to be gone the same length of time, and I'm using one suitcase and a hatbox.* Belinda smiled again.

"Do you have you-ah packing done?" Mrs. Stafford-Smyth asked.

Belinda was surprised at the question but shook her head. "It won't take me long," she assured her.

Mrs. Stafford-Smyth looked a bit alarmed. "Don't short you-ahself on time," she said anxiously. "The train leaves at ten."

"My train doesn't leave until four," Belinda responded. She had already made the arrangements and purchased her ticket, but at her answer Mrs. Stafford-Smyth stopped midstride, her head quickly coming around to stare at Belinda.

"Whatevah do you mean?" she asked sharply.

Belinda began to flush. It was true she hadn't asked her employer's permission. She had meant to talk to her about it, but they had just been so busy there had never seemed to be time. Surely the woman hadn't expected her to stay and care for the house. There was Windsor and Potter and the maids. Mrs. Stafford-Smyth had never before left anyone else to oversee the staff when she had traveled. Belinda had just assumed she would not be needed. But she had been wrong to assume. She should have asked permission before getting her ticket. After all, she was in the employ—

"What do you mean?" Mrs. Stafford-Smyth asked again.

"Oh, Aunt Virgie," began Belinda apologetically. "I'm sorry. I just wasn't thinking. I guess I've been in such a dither. I should have asked you. I didn't realize you expected me to stay on here and—"

"Stay on *heah?* Well, of course not. I expect you to accompany me—to New Yawk."

"Accompany you?" echoed Belinda dumbly.

Mrs. Stafford-Smyth looked shaken. "Of course."

"But . . . but you didn't say . . . say anything about me going with you," Belinda reminded the older woman.

"I didn't?" Mrs. Stafford-Smyth looked bewildered. "Maybe I didn't. I guess . . . I guess I didn't think that it . . . that anything else would be considered. I just expected you to know. Careless of me. Dreadfully careless."

Belinda felt her heart pounding.

"Well, no mattah," went on the woman. "There is still time for you to get ready. I'll call Ella to help you pack," and Mrs. Stafford-Smyth moved toward the bell.

"But . . ." stammered Belinda. "But I've . . . I've made other plans."

Mrs. Stafford-Smyth stopped with her hand on the buzzer. "You . . . you . . . What plans?" she asked simply.

"I've . . . I've purchased a ticket . . . a train ticket for home," Belinda managed.

Mrs. Stafford-Smyth lowered herself into a nearby chair. "I see," she said slowly.

Belinda rushed to her and knelt beside her. "I really didn't know you expected me to go with you. I thought . . . I thought it was just you and Aunt Celia. I didn't know there was room for more guests than that. So I decided it was a good time for me to . . . to go home for a visit. I'm sorry. I didn't think you'd mind."

Mrs. Stafford-Smyth was pale. Her hand trembled as she reached out to smooth back Belinda's wayward curls.

"You'll . . . you won't *stay* home, will you?" she asked shakily.

"Oh no," promised Belinda quickly. "I just plan to be gone for as long as you'll be away."

Mrs. Stafford-Smyth took a deep breath. "My goodness, child," she said with a nervous laugh. "You nigh scared the breath out of me."

"You didn't think . . . ?" began Belinda, but she realized that it was exactly what Mrs. Stafford-Smyth had thought. Seeing the color gradually return to the older woman's face, Belinda realized just how much it meant to her to have Belinda's company here in the big, lonely house.

And with that realization Belinda knew she could never, never just walk out and leave the woman all alone. The thought sent a chill through her body. She loved Mrs. Stafford-Smyth dearly. The older woman was like the grandmother she had never had the chance to know. But to stay with her indefinitely at the expense of never being with the family she loved was a terrible commitment. Belinda didn't know if she could bear it, if she could really be that unselfish.

"You poor child," Mrs. Stafford-Smyth was crooning softly, her hands again smoothing back Belinda's hair. "How thoughtless I've been. Heah I've sat day after day, not even realizing how lonesome you must be foah those you love. And how lonesome they must be for you! Of course you should go home. I should have thought of it myself. It's a perfect opportunity for you. I'm glad you had sense enough to think of it, even if I didn't."

Her hand stopped, resting on Belinda's head. A shadow passed over her face as she looked into Belinda's blue eyes. "And I will not hold you to that promise," she said gently, though her eyes begged Belinda to return. "You know I love you. You know I want you heah, but I will not ask you for such a promise."

"I'll be back, Aunt Virgie," Belinda said in a whisper, and she leaned forward to kiss the older woman on the cheek.

FOUR

Homeward Bound

The whole Marshall Manor household was in a turmoil of activity the next morning. Breakfast in the north parlor was a hurried affair, nervous maids fluttering nearby while Mrs. Stafford-Smyth went down a long, long list of last-minute instructions with Potter and Windsor. Windsor nodded glumly from time to time. It was clear he thought Madam again was giving in to her penchant for foolish gadding about. He did not sanction such travel, and *Remember what happened last time,* his frown seemed to say.

Belinda was up and down the stairs a dozen times, running for this, tucking in that, securing this, dusting off that. At long last the carriage with Mrs. Celia Prescott pulled up at the front of the house and Mrs. Stafford-Smyth, bag, and baggage were loaded in for the station.

"My land, girl," exclaimed Mrs. Prescott to Belinda, "where are your hat and gloves?"

"Belinda is not accompanying us," replied Mrs. Stafford-Smyth.

"She's not? Well, whatever will you do—?"

"I will manage just fine," Mrs. Stafford-Smyth put in archly. "I haven't totally forgotten how to cayah for myself."

"But I thought . . . I just assumed that—"

"Belinda is going to take a trip home to see her family while I am gone," continued Mrs. Stafford-Smyth.

"You'd . . . you'd let her? She might not be back," argued Mrs. Prescott, and Belinda couldn't help but smile at the genuine warning in the woman's voice. There had been a time when Mrs. Prescott had assumed Belinda to be unnecessary and ill-equipped to care for the well-being of her dear friend, Virginia Stafford-Smyth.

Mrs. Stafford-Smyth drew Belinda to her and kissed her on the forehead. "That is her decision," she said softly. "She knows how much I would miss her."

Unable to say anything, Belinda felt the tears forming in her eyes.

"Good-bye, my deah," said the older woman. "I shall miss you. Tell your mama for me what a blessed woman she is to have such a daughtah."

Belinda swallowed.

"Now, you have a good time, you heah? Do all those things you've been missing." She kissed Belinda again. "Bye now."

Belinda managed a good-bye and waved as the carriage pulled out into the street and passed out of sight.

She turned and slowly made her way into the big house. She hadn't even started her own packing yet. Still, she would not need to take much with her. There were many things hanging in her closet at the farm. She was sure they were more appropriate for farm life anyway, and she would make do with them.

She was met at the door by Windsor. "Would you like me to summon Ella for you, miss?" he asked Belinda.

Belinda was a bit surprised at his concern.

"I think I can manage fine, thank you," she responded.

"But I know you've been much too busy to take care of your own packing," he continued. "As you have seen, Madam always needs so much done before one of her trips—"

"I don't intend to take very much with me," Belinda assured him. She couldn't help but smile at his carefully worded reference to Madam's choice of travel "necessities." "I left some clothing at home in my closet," she explained. "I can use it while I'm there."

Windsor looked surprised, and then Belinda remembered that it had been almost three years since she had been home. A respectable young lady would certainly not return to fashions of three years past. Belinda smiled again.

"Fashions do not change that much—or that quickly—in my hometown," she assured the butler. "I think that along with the few things I take, I'll manage just fine."

"As you wish, miss," he replied courteously, but she could see he was not really convinced.

To Belinda's surprise it did take her nearly till departure time to complete her preparations. *Wouldn't Ma love to see this pink dress? But then I won't have room for the blue one that matches my eyes,* she debated. Eventually she made all the necessary decisions. The stylish blue hat was carefully tucked in the hatbox along with some extra pairs of white gloves. She took one last look around her room, tidied her dresser and her bathroom, and rang for Windsor.

As the butler left her room with her bag and hatbox, Belinda pinned her traveling hat in place and picked up a light wrap. The day was still pleasantly warm, so she would not put it on just yet. She followed Windsor down the steps, smiled a good-bye to the staff, who had gathered to see her off, and climbed aboard the carriage.

As the team moved down the long, circular lane, Belinda turned for one more look at the big house. *Marshall Manor.* It seemed impossible that she had learned to think of the beautiful place as home.

Then Belinda eagerly turned forward. *No, not home,* she corrected herself. Home was where she was going now. Home was Pa and Ma and Clare and Kate. Home was Arnie and Anne. Home was Luke and Abbie. Home was nieces and nephews who had most likely forgotten who she was and what she had once meant to them. *That* was home. Belinda held her breath in excitement and anticipation. She could hardly wait to get home . . . but at the same time she felt a nagging uncertainty.

Will it be the same? Can it possibly be the same? How much has changed? What if . . . what if . . . ? But Belinda finally made herself stop. She would take things one day at a time. For now she would concentrate on her westward journey and seeing again the faces of those she loved.

Belinda was sure the train trip west to her home was taking many times longer than it had taken to travel east to Boston. *At least it sure seems longer,* she told herself. Each stop, each large city and small town they passed meant that much greater excitement and impatience in Belinda. Sitting on the edge of her seat, she strained to see ahead as far as possible and willed the train to move faster.

She was too agitated to pay much attention to her fellow passengers. Usually she liked to watch people around her. She twisted her hands nervously until her gloves were soiled and wrinkled. *I'm glad I brought extra pairs,* she thought distractedly.

Meals were provided with the ticket, but she really did not feel hungry. To help pass some time, though, she did go to the dining car for each mealtime. She even managed a nod and smile when she met an elderly person or a young mother with her children, but certainly not with her usual interest and enthusiasm. Back in her seat, Belinda concentrated on the distant horizon, aching, longing for the train to roll into the familiar station and announce her arrival with a hiss of steam.

The closer she got to home, the more agitated she became. She fidgeted, fretted, and fumbled with her purse straps. Only her good manners kept her from pacing the aisle. *Will this trip ever end?* she asked through gritted teeth.

She had decided to keep her visit a surprise and notified only Luke. She would have enjoyed surprising him, also, but it seemed right that someone know of her plans.

"Don't tell the others," she had warned. "I want it to be a secret." Belinda had no reason to think he would give it away. But as she sat fidgeting on the velvet-covered seat of the passenger car, she wondered if she had done the right thing. *Will the shock be too much for Mama?* she wondered. *What if Luke is busy with a house call or surgery and not able to meet the train? How will I get out to the farm?*

Belinda's thoughts whirled, fretful with imaginary worries. Had she been childish and silly in her desire for surprise? *Well, it's too late now,* she finally concluded. She could only wait to see how it would all turn out.

And then they passed a familiar farm—they were only a few miles out of town. Belinda's throat was dry and her hands moist. *I'll soon be there. I'll soon be home,* she exulted. She tried to calm her racing heart with deep breaths, but it wouldn't be stilled. She leaned back against the seat and closed her eyes, trying to pray. Even her prayer was jumbled.

Oh, God, she managed to get her thoughts together in order to begin, *I'm so excited. So . . . so dizzy with the thought of being home. I've been so lonesome. More lonesome than I even knew. Help me. Help Mama. And Pa. Help me not to shock them too much. And please may they be well. All those I love. I'll . . . I'll just about die if they've noticeably failed in health since I've been gone. I don't think I could stand it, Lord. Just . . . just be with us . . . all of us . . . and help us to have good days together. And . . . be with me . . . and with Mama when the time comes for me to go back to Boston. It'll be hard, Lord. Really hard . . . for both of us.*

The train blew the whistle—long and loud—and Belinda finished in a rush, *And thanks so much, Lord, for giving me this chance to come home.* Back where her heart had always been. As the wheels churned to a stop, she took a deep breath, gathered her suitcase and hatbox, and moved down the aisle toward the exit. Only one other passenger was walking toward the door. *Not many folks get off at this small whistle-stop,* Belinda reminded herself.

And then she was in the open air and down the steps. A kindly porter offered assistance. Stepping onto the wooden platform, she paused to look around and heard her name spoken. There he was—her doctor brother Luke, his arms outstretched toward her as the wind whipped the tails of his coat.

With a glad little cry, Belinda ran toward the open arms. "Oh, Luke, Luke!" was all she could manage.

They walked from the station together, Luke carrying Belinda's heavy suitcase and she the hatbox. "I didn't dare bring the team," Luke was telling her. "I knew Abbie would ask questions if I harnessed the team to go to the office."

"Oh, the office!" cried Belinda. "I can hardly wait to see your new office."

"But not today," Luke pointed out firmly. "I don't plan to do one thing today except escort you to the family. I could hardly *live* with not telling them, Belinda! Abbie and the kids will be so excited. And then we'll need to get you on home to Ma and Pa. They won't believe their eyes. Just to sorta prepare the way, I told Ma that Abbie and I would be coming out to the farm for supper tonight."

Belinda laughed, thinking how smart Luke had been and how much fun it was going to be.

"I told Jackson that I was taking the rest of the day off. Thankfully he didn't ask why," Luke explained.

At the mention of Jackson, Belinda felt a strange sensation in the pit of her stomach. *Does Jackson still think that I should . . . that I might care for him?* she wondered. She hoped not.

But Luke was talking.

"By the way, you wouldn't want your old job back, would you?"

At Belinda's questioning look, he hurried on. "No one has said anything yet, but I've the feeling that I might not have my nurse for long."

"Is anything wrong with Flo?" Belinda questioned.

"Oh my, no," laughed Luke. "Unless you consider being in love as something wrong."

"She's in love? That's nice," Belinda smiled, relieved. "So who's the lucky young man? Anyone I know?"

"Quite well, in fact," responded Luke, looking steadily into Belinda's face. "Jackson."

"Jackson?" Belinda stopped. The news was quite a shock. And then to Belinda's surprise she realized it was not only a shock—but a relief. She no longer needed to worry about Jackson. He had found happiness with someone else. She fell in step again with her big brother. "That's nice," she smiled. "Jackson and Flo. I think they'll make a very nice couple."

"Yes," he grinned at her, looking relieved. "They do make a great couple. We're all happy for them."

FIVE

Family

"I don't believe it. I *can't* believe it!" cried Abbie over and over as she held Belinda close, laughing and crying at the same time. "You're here. Really here! We had started to think you'd never come back."

Belinda understood immediately that Abbie assumed she was home to stay. She decided there would be plenty of time for explanations about that later. Instead, she returned the warm hug, the tears brimming in her own eyes.

"The youngsters!" cried Abbie. "They'll be so excited to see you. They're in the backyard. Luke, will you—?"

But Luke had already thought of the children and gone to fetch them. In they rushed to see the surprise "visitor" their father had summoned them to see.

Nine-year-old Thomas was still running when he burst through the kitchen door, but he slid to a stop, looking at Belinda in unbelief, and then let out a shriek. "Aunt Belinda!" he cried, but his feet did not leave the spot.

Aaron, seven, pushed forward next to see for himself. He took one look at Belinda, then without missing a step he threw himself headlong at her, his small arms wrapping around her legs, his face buried in her skirts. To everyone's amazement he began to sob.

Belinda, perplexed, reached down to hug the boy. "Aaron, Aaron," she whispered. "Aaron, whatever is wrong?" She pushed him back gently, then lifted him into her arms.

He buried his face against her shoulder. "I . . . I thought you weren't never coming back," he cried. "I . . . I . . . every day we prayed for you . . . but you never came home." Belinda just held him and rocked him back and forth, with tears coursing down her own cheeks.

"Shhh. Shhh," she comforted the child. "I'm back. See, I'm back."

Thomas came forward then and wrapped his arms around Belinda's waist. She couldn't believe how tall he had grown.

"Thomas," she said, a hand on his mop of brown hair, "look at you. Just look at you. You've grown two feet."

Thomas grinned, a twinkle in his eyes. "I've always had two feet," he countered, and the kitchen filled with laughter at his little joke.

Belinda sat down on a kitchen chair, Aaron still on her lap. The emotional storm had passed, and he was busily mopping up his face with a checkered handkerchief supplied by his mother. Thomas stood close beside Belinda, carefully studying her face.

"Where's Ruthie?" Belinda asked.

"Pa had to go get her. She went to Muffie's house," Thomas explained.

"Who's Muffie?" asked Belinda innocently. Abbie was clucking her tongue impatiently.

"She's not to go there without permission," she said, irritation in her tone. "She knows that."

"Muffie is a dog," supplied Aaron. "He lives down the street."

Belinda looked at Abbie. *Has Ruthie really gone to visit a dog?* her eyes asked.

"The Larsons—two houses down. They're an older couple—who love children. I think Ruthie would live there if she could. They spoil her something awful." Abbie shook her head. "They have a little dog. Ruthie uses that as her excuse to—"

Just then the back door opened and Luke entered, the errant Ruthie by the hand. Her parents exchanged glances. Discipline would need to be meted out—but not at the moment, they seemed to agree. They would deal with the infraction later.

Ruthie, suddenly shy, was too young to remember her aunt Belinda, though Thomas and Aaron had certainly kept her posted about the fact that she had such an aunt. She clasped her father's hand more tightly and twisted herself behind him.

Thomas urged her to come over. "This is Aunt Belinda," he prompted, tapping Belinda on the shoulder. Aaron's arm tightened possessively around Belinda's neck.

Ruthie finally was coaxed to release her hold on her father and took hesitant steps toward Belinda. Her head was slightly down, her tongue tucked into a corner of her mouth. Shyly she moved forward, and Belinda wondered how she would manage to hold another child. She reached a hand toward Ruthie. The child took it and lowered her eyes, moving her little shoulders back and forth in embarrassment as she stood before them. Aaron pulled her in close.

"It's our aunt Belinda," he explained. "'Member? We told you 'bout her. She's nice. She's home now."

Ruthie managed a shy smile. She even allowed a small hug.

"Ruthie doesn't remember me like you do," Belinda informed Aaron. "She was still so tiny when I left. Just a baby really."

Thomas broke in excitedly, "Does Grandma know you're here?"

Belinda shook her head.

Thomas swung back to his father. "Can we take her out, Pa? Can we? Just think how s'prised Grandma's gonna be."

Aaron scrambled off Belinda's lap so quickly she feared he was falling and grabbed for the boy. But he landed on his feet—*like a cat*, Belinda thought with a smile—and joined with Thomas in pleading for a trip to the farm. Even young Ruthie began to clap her hands and to beg.

"Hush. Hush, all of you," Luke laughed, holding up his hands. "Of course we'll take Aunt Belinda to the farm. But first she needs to catch her breath. Now I suggest we let her freshen up a bit while your mama puts on the tea. We'll have tea together, and then we'll all go to the farm. I told Grandma we'd be out to join her for supper."

Three children cheered loudly, and Belinda was tempted to place her hands over her ears. Instead, she chuckled to herself, *It certainly was never this noisy at Marshall Manor!*

"Thomas, could you hand me that hatbox, please?" Belinda asked.

"You already have a hat on," Aaron reminded her, looking at her curiously.

Belinda laughed. "Yes, I know," she admitted.

"You're going to put it in the box?" asked Thomas.

"Well, that would be a good idea, too, but right now I'm looking for something. . . ." Belinda searched the interior for a moment and came up with a bag of peppermints. "These are for all of you to share," she said, passing the bag of candy to Abbie. "Your mama will pass them out as she wishes."

Three sets of eyes brightened and three pairs of hands reached toward Abbie. She allowed one candy per child and tucked the rest safely away in the cupboard. As Belinda left the room to go wash, she heard Luke begin his discussion with Ruthie.

"Now, young lady, what has your mama told you about running off to see Muffie without asking her for permission?" he began.

Belinda heard a little sob from the girl.

Oh, dear, she thought as she went into the bathroom and removed her hat to tidy her hair and wash her hands and face. *I'm glad it's not me who has to discipline. It must be so much easier to just blink at some things.*

But she knew Luke would not do that, easy as it would have been. "Discipline needs to be consistent," she had often heard Luke say, "or it is not discipline—only punishment." And she was well aware of the fact her brother did not believe in punishment for its own sake.

Belinda's excitement matched the children's during the ride to the farm. Thomas, Aaron, and Ruthie all talked constantly, vying for her attention and pointing out every farm and landmark along the way. Belinda could have named them all herself, but she allowed them the fun of being her "tour guides."

The nearer they came to the farm, the harder Belinda's heart pounded.

Have I done this right? Should I have warned the folks of my coming? she debated within herself again. *What if the shock . . . ?* She took a deep breath and tried to concentrate on the children's chatter, grasping the buggy seat until her knuckles turned white. Luke was already pressing the team as fast as safety would allow.

And then they were turning down the long lane. Belinda had always thought of the white farmhouse as large. She was surprised at how small it looked to her now—certainly small compared to Marshall Manor. Small and quite simple.

But it is home, she rejoiced. Belinda edged forward on the seat and could scarcely wait for the buggy to stop.

"Now, don't you holler out anything to Grandma," Luke warned the children. "Aunt Belinda wants to surprise her." They nodded in wide-eyed understanding, and Ruthie clapped a hand over her own mouth "just in case."

The farm dog welcomed them, even seeming to remember Belinda. He stopped at her side long enough to lick her hand and wag his tail, and she patted his head fondly. "You remember me, don't you?" she murmured with satisfaction. Then the dog scampered away, far more interested in the children who ran on ahead to the house.

Marty appeared at the door, drying her hands on her apron. "You're earlier than I expected," she called. "How did you get away from the office so soon?" She leaned down to hug Aaron and Ruthie. "How's school, Thomas?" she inquired.

Belinda, screened behind Luke and Abbie, could hardly contain herself. She wished to rush headlong into her mother's arms. She suppressed the urge and swallowed away a sob from her throat.

"Ready," whispered Luke, and Belinda nodded, tears in her eyes and a smile on her lips. The three adults moved toward the farmhouse. Marty was still busy chatting with the three youngsters. Belinda could hardly believe they hadn't even suggested they had a surprise for Grandma, though they were casting furtive glances toward the approaching adults.

Belinda had almost reached her mother when wee Ruthie could keep quiet no longer. "Look!" she exclaimed, pointing a pudgy finger at Belinda.

Marty looked up. Luke reacted quickly, stepping aside at just that minute.

Belinda heard Marty's gasp. With a cry of "my baby" she threw herself toward her youngest. Belinda met her halfway and, weeping, they wrapped their arms around each other. Marty was whispering words of love and endearment over and over, but now she was saying "Belinda," not "baby." Belinda did not remember her mother calling her "baby" before. *Is that really how she thinks of me?* she wondered for a moment.

"Oh, Mama," Belinda finally managed, "I'm so glad to see you!"

Marty pulled a handkerchief from her apron pocket and wiped her eyes and nose. She held Belinda at arms' length and studied her face carefully. "You've changed," she said at last, nodding. "But I don't see nothin' but maturity in your face. You've grown up, Belinda," and she hugged her close again.

For Belinda's part, her mother looked very much the same as she remembered her. *Thank you, Lord,* she whispered. *Thank you for taking good care of Mama.*

The rest of the family demanded equal time, and the two women were forced to draw apart while the children all tried to talk at once.

"Were you surprised, Grandma? Were you surprised?"

"Well—my lands! I guess I was."

"It was a good trick, wasn't it, Grandma? We really fooled you, didn't we?"

"You certainly did. You certainly did. My, my," and Marty cast a loving glance toward Belinda, "it was a good surprise." And she led the way into the big farm kitchen.

"Grandpa will be surprised, too, won't he? Won't he?"

"He will. He sure will."

And so the talk went on, bubbling and humming around her until Belinda felt her head was fairly spinning.

"I'm gonna run and tell Uncle Clare and Aunt Kate," shouted Thomas and headed for the door, then slid to a stop and looked toward Belinda. "Can I?"

"Go ahead," laughed Belinda. "They might as well hear it from you, and I am anxious to see them all."

The house was in even more confusion when Kate and the boys arrived. Only two of the nephews were home. Dan was off with his father on a farm errand. Belinda was startled to note that David was taller than she was, and Dack was very quickly catching up. They gave her boyish hugs and Kate held her fiercely. Belinda wondered if Kate was actually thinking of her own Amy Jo as she hugged so tightly.

"What do you hear from Amy Jo?" Belinda asked when she could draw a breath.

"She's fine, she says. Expectin' her second child any day now." Kate wiped her eyes, drew a deep breath, and managed a smile. "Her first little one will soon be three. Hard to believe, isn't it?"

Belinda nodded, imagining lively Amy Jo as a mother.

"Well, that's the way life is," shrugged Kate. "Ya raise 'em to leave. That's what life is about. Dan, now, he's got a girl. A nice girl, too, so I 'spect it won't be long till he'll be off on his own, as well."

"Is Dan . . . is Dan still working with . . . with Rand?" Belinda couldn't believe the difficulty she was having with the simple question.

"Oh no," explained Kate quickly. "Rand left. He went back to the town—wherever it was—where he lived before. Dan does odd little building jobs for the neighbors, but mostly he farms with his pa."

Belinda was relieved. Her trip home would not be marred by another argument with Rand, though she could have enjoyed a visit with him.

"Rand married a girl from down there," Kate went on. "She didn't want to leave her family, so they settled in the area."

Jackson . . . and now Rand, Belinda mused, her eyes no doubt reflecting her surprise.

But no one noticed, and Dack interrupted the conversation with a question. "Are you going to be a nurse again?" he asked Belinda.

"I'm a nurse now," Belinda answered. All eyes turned to Belinda as she spoke. "In fact, I did a good deal of nursing the early part of the summer. I wrote Mama—Grandma—about it. Aunt Virgie—Mrs. Stafford-Smyth—was very sick. I was afraid we might even lose her."

"You call her Aunt Virgie?" asked Marty.

"Yes, she asked me to," Belinda stated simply, and Marty nodded.

"Is she better now?" asked Marty.

"Much better, though it took her quite a while to get over it. But she's fine now. Just fine. In fact, she's feeling so well she's off to New York for six weeks."

Marty looked at Belinda, her eyes shadowed with questions. She did not speak out loud, but Belinda could feel the silent conversation pass between them. *And while she's in New York, you have come home?* Marty's eyes asked. The question was so real Belinda nodded solemnly in answer.

And you will go back to Boston? Marty's questioning eyes probed, and Belinda answered that with a slight nod, also.

Marty turned her head then, and Belinda expected it was to hide her tears of disappointment.

Thomas now drew their attention. "When's Grandpa coming home, Grandma?"

Marty's eyes moved to the clock on the kitchen shelf. "Soon," she replied evenly. "He should be here soon."

And then the farm dog barked an excited welcome, and they all knew Clark was on his way.

SIX

Seeing Pa

Belinda was so emotionally drained she knew she could not bear another "game." Before anyone could urge her to duck in the pantry or slip into the living room, she rose from her chair and rushed out the door.

The big team hadn't even pulled to a stop in front of the barn before she could see her father's attention fastened on someone flying toward him, arms outstretched.

"Pa," she called in a half sob. "Pa."

Clark looked in wonder, no doubt unable to comprehend what his eyes—and ears—were telling him. And then he flung the reins from his hands, flipped himself over the wheel, and met his girl—his Belinda—with open arms.

"It's you. It's really you," he murmured huskily into her hair as he lifted her from the ground and gently swung her back and forth. Belinda briefly wondered if her ribs might be crushed in the bear hug.

"Oh, Pa," she laughed as she kissed his cheek. "Pa . . . it's so good to see you."

He set her back on her feet and looked deeply into her eyes. "How are ya?" he asked sincerely.

"Fine . . . just fine," Belinda assured him.

He hugged her to himself again, tears unheeded on his cheeks, and she leaned back and wiped them away with a gentle hand.

Then she reached out to set his hat, dislodged in his quick descent from the wagon, back on straight. "Oh, Pa" was all she could say.

"Ya look great. Jest great," he told her.

Belinda laughed. "Not really," she said ruefully. "I can feel my hair slipping over my ears, my dress is wrinkled, my face feels flushed, I've got train soot to scrub away. Why, I must look a sight."

Clark laughed heartily. "Ya look good to me," he insisted. "When did ya git here?"

"I came in on the train this afternoon. Luke brought me out."

"Luke knew?" asked Clark, and Belinda nodded.

"The rascal! Never said a word—unless he told yer ma."

"No—he didn't tell anyone. I asked him not to. But . . . but I later wished . . . wished I hadn't been so secretive. It wasn't fair . . . not really."

"Well, yer here now—thet's what matters," Clark responded and gave her another hug and a kiss on the forehead.

David arrived then. "I'll take care of the team, Grandpa," he offered.

"Thanks, boy," Clark responded, and he motioned toward the house. Belinda allowed herself to be led, her pa's arm still around her waist.

"How's your patient? Mrs. . . . let's see . . . Mrs. Stafford-Smyth. She doin' okay?"

"She's fine . . . now," responded Belinda. "She got over her bout with influenza just fine. She's off to New York for six weeks. Staying with a friend."

And when Clark's arm tightened about her waist, Belinda realized her father would know that "six weeks" meant she was going back.

"How have you been keeping?" Belinda asked solicitously.

"Fine," responded Clark. "Don't I look fine?" he teased.

"You look just great," Belinda responded, laughing. "I don't think you've aged a bit. Oh, a few more gray hairs," she said with a chuckle, "but other than that . . ."

"Thet gray hair," said Clark, removing his hat and running fingers through his still-heavy head of hair, "thet comes from havin' young'uns scattered all over the country from east to west."

Belinda laughed.

"What'd yer ma say when she seen ya?" Clark asked next. "Bet she was fit to be tied."

Belinda smiled, then sobered. "I sure hope it wasn't too foolish of me to come sneaking in," she replied. "But she seems to have handled it very well."

"Good," said Clark as he held the door for her.

They were met by a barrage of shouts, all the children again talking at once. Luke had held them in check so Belinda could have a few moments alone with her father, but now they all wanted to get in on the excitement.

"Surprise, Grandpa! Surprise! Weren't you surprised? Wasn't it a good trick? We already knew. We already knew! Weren't you surprised?"

Clark tried to answer but was drowned out. He held up his hand—his family signal for some order. When the clamoring had turned to a soft hum, he answered their eager questions.

"It was a grand surprise," he informed them. "I never had me the faintest idea thet Belinda was comin' home. It sure was a great surprise. Why, ya couldn't have brought me a better one—an' thet's a fact."

They were about to return to their excited babbling, but Clark again held up a hand. "Now, I need me a cup o' coffee . . . to sorta get over my shock like, iffen Grandma has one handy."

Marty smiled, nodded, and moved to the stove.

"She might even have some cookies and milk fer hungry little people," Clark went on, "seein' as how it's too early fer supper yet. I s'pose she'd let ya have 'em on the back veranda."

Kate went to help get the cookies and milk ready for the children, and Marty hurried to cut some date loaf. "I wish I had some of yer favorite lemon cake on hand, Belinda," she said over her shoulder. "Iffen I'd only knowed . . ."

But Belinda had moved up beside her and was saying there'd be plenty of time to enjoy her mother's lemon cake. Belinda turned to the cupboard. The cups were still in the same place. It was nice to come home and find so many things—and people—unchanged. Belinda poured the steaming coffee into the cups and then went to the pantry for the cream and sugar. They, too, were in their usual spot. Belinda smiled. She could just slip right in at home again and carry on as though she'd never been away. A nice thought.

The commotion subsided considerably with the children out of the kitchen. It seemed like such a long, long time since Belinda had sat at the familiar table, with familiar folks, talking over simple and familiar topics.

She was brought up-to-date on each family member, told news of neighbors, updated on the affairs of the church, and reminded of things from the past. Belinda wished they could just chatter on and on, but Marty broke the spell.

"My lands!" she gasped, staring at the clock. "Look at the time. Why, we'll never be havin' our supper iffen I don't get me busy."

Kate jumped up and moved toward the kitchen door. "Clare'll soon be home, too," she reprimanded herself.

"Why don't ya jest join us here?" Marty invited. "I have a roast in the oven—thet's the one thing I did git done on time. We'll make it stretch."

"I've got a couple pies," Kate responded. "I can bring 'em over."

Marty nodded. "I baked jest one today," she answered. "Yer two sure would help."

"I'll fix a salad, too," said Kate on her way out.

Marty nodded again, then called to Kate, "Do you s'pose you could send David over to Arnie's? They should be told. Tell Anne to bring what she has an' come to supper iffen she wishes—or else come over as soon as they can after supper for coffee."

Belinda smiled, soon to be reunited with her family. At least all who lived nearby. Missy and Willie, Ellie and Lane and all their offspring were still far away in the West. Nandry and Clae and their children weren't close enough to join them, either. But the ones Belinda had grown up with, the family near home—she would soon see them all. *It's so good to be home again!* she breathed.

Late that night when the last team left for home, Kate reluctantly lifted her shawl from the coatrack. "I guess we'd better get on home, too," she sighed. "The boys still have school in the mornin'."

"Aw. Do we hafta?" protested Dack.

"I'll be here when you come home again tomorrow," Belinda reminded him.

"This is David's last year," Kate informed Belinda. "He's our scholar. Likes school much better'n the others ever have. Never have to coax David to get him up in the mornin's," she finished proudly.

"What's he planning to do?" asked Belinda.

"Hasn't decided, but he'd like to go on fer further schoolin'."

"Good for him," Belinda nodded, pleased about David and happy for Kate.

The last good-byes were said, and Belinda settled back at the table with Clark and Marty, still lingering over coffee cups.

"I s'pose yer awful tired?" commented Marty, touching Belinda's cheek softly.

"I am. It's the excitement, I guess. And I couldn't sleep well on the train at all. It rumbles and groans all night long. But, really, it was the thought of coming home that kept me from relaxing."

Marty took Belinda's hand, squeezing it slightly as her eyes filled with tears. "Iffen I had knowed ya were comin'," she admitted, "I wouldn't have been doin' any sleepin', either."

Clark chuckled. "An' thet's the truth," he agreed with a sage nod.

Belinda decided that maybe her plan of coming home unannounced had turned out to be right, after all.

"Arnie looks good," Belinda commented. "Looks even better than he did when I left."

Marty nodded. "Finally got his problems worked out an' his bitterness taken care of," she acknowledged. "Bitterness can age one like nothin' else can."

"It's a fact," nodded Clark. "'Most made an old man of 'im fer a time."

"His Abe's arm looks good," continued Belinda. "Not nearly as twisted as it was. Why, folks wouldn't even notice it much anymore. One can almost forget he ever had that encounter with the bull."

"Three surgeries it took." Marty shook her head, the difficult memory on her face. "Three surgeries to straighten it out again. But worth it—every one of 'em. Arnie can see thet now . . . but my . . . it was a struggle fer 'im to let the boy go under the surgeon's knife."

"I'm so glad he finally consented," Belinda commented.

"Ya wantin' more coffee?" Marty asked suddenly.

"No. No thanks. I've had plenty." Belinda laughed lightly. "I guess Aunt Virgie and I have taken more to drinking tea. I'm not so used to much coffee anymore."

"Well, I sure can fix a pot of tea," Marty replied, jumping up from her chair.

"Mama," Belinda said quickly, reaching out a restraining hand to her mother, "I don't need tea, either. Why, I've been eating and drinking ever since I set foot in the door. I won't be able to even move in six weeks if . . ." Belinda stopped.

The shadow darkened Marty's eyes again. "Six weeks, is it?" she asked slowly.

Belinda nodded, toying with her cup.

"I thought as much," said Marty. She pushed her cup back listlessly.

"It's . . . it's that I can't . . . can't feel comfortable just leaving Aunt Virgie," Belinda began, sensing that some kind of explanation was needed. "She . . . she is so alone. She really has no one . . . no family who cares about her. Her grandsons are in France, busy with their own lives, and she gets so lonely. I can see it in her face. I . . . I . . ." Belinda faltered to a stop.

"'Course," said Clark, reaching for Belinda's hand.

"Is there . . . is there . . . anyone special in the city?" Marty asked.

Belinda smiled but shook her head.

"Ya know," Marty remarked slowly, "it really would be easier iffen there was. I mean . . . fer me. Ya wouldn't seem so . . . so alone yerself then."

Belinda was surprised at her mother's comment but understood. "I'm not an old maid yet, Mama," she reassured Marty with a smile.

"We-ll," responded Marty, "yer not gittin' any younger, either. All the other girls was . . ." but Marty dropped the sentence. Belinda well knew her sisters had married when they were much younger than she was now.

"No one ever said thet everybody has to marry," Marty quickly amended. "Thet's somethin' each person has to decide fer herself."

Belinda nodded.

"It's not so much I want ya married. It's jest I don't want ya all alone an' lonely . . . ya understand?"

Belinda nodded again.

Marty reached over and patted the hand Clark was still holding. "Are ya lonely?"

Marty's question surprised Belinda. For a moment she could not answer. A lump in her throat threatened to choke her. She blinked back tears and nodded slowly.

"Sometimes," she admitted, dropping her head. "Sometimes I get dreadfully lonesome. I'd come home—so fast—if I could see my way clear to do it."

Belinda lifted her face to look from her mother to her father. Their eyes were wet, as well.

Marty patted the hand again.

"Well, ya know what ya gotta do . . . an' ya know thet ya can come home again . . . anytime . . . anytime ya be wantin' to."

Belinda fumbled for her handkerchief. "I know," she nodded. "And that keeps me going during the really lonely times. Thanks. Thanks . . . both of you."

For a moment their eyes held, and then Marty pushed back from the table. "An' now you'd best be off ta bed afore ya fall off yer chair," she urged. "Yer pa and me have kept ya up long enough. We needn't say everything tonight. We have six weeks to catch us up."

"You have anything thet needs carryin' up?" asked Clark, rising from the table.

"Luke took my suitcase up," answered Belinda.

"Ya go on, then," Marty continued. "Yer room should be ready fer ya. I dusted and freshened it up just last week. I'll jest gather these few cups in the dishpan. We'll be right up ourselves—yer pa and me."

Belinda kissed them both and climbed the familiar steps to her room. The door stood ajar, the suitcase at the foot of the bed.

She entered the room and stood looking about her. It was a simple room. The bed was still covered with the same spread Belinda remembered so well. At the window the matching curtains breathed in and out with the slight movement of the night air. Braided rugs scattered here and there brightened the plainness of the wooden floors. Belinda couldn't help but remember that at one time she had considered this bedroom the most beautiful in the world.

It was still very special, in a homey sort of way. She smiled as she crossed to the bed and turned down the blanket, fluffing up the pillow. She would sleep like a baby back in her own bed. Belinda yawned and began unpacking before retiring.

But after three years the bed seemed reluctant to mold to her unfamiliar form, and tired as she was, the clock downstairs had chimed twice before Belinda was finally able to forget the events of the day and settle down to sleep.

SEVEN

Adjustments

Belinda awakened to the crowing of the farm roosters, the bellowing of the cows, and the clatter from the farmyard. She didn't mind. She didn't want to waste precious time in bed anyway. She threw back the blankets and eased herself up, thinking to hurriedly care for her toilet before choosing what she would wear for the day.

But as she poised, one foot reaching for a slipper, she remembered with a start that there was no bathroom in the farmhouse. She would have to dress first. She would need to wash in the kitchen—and she would have to carry and heat water when she wanted a bath.

She hurried to her closet to choose from the dresses that had remained behind when she left for the East. She intended to pick something homey—something simple for her day about the farm. A simple calico or gingham would take the place of her city silks or satins. Belinda immediately spotted a blue print, one of her favorite dresses. Excitedly she pulled it toward her, then stared in bewilderment.

Is it really this . . . this simple, this childish? Why, it looks like a dress belonging to a little girl, she thought, astonished. *Surely . . . surely I was more grown-up than that when I left the farm. After all, it's only been three years,* she argued with herself. *Was I really wearing such . . . such tasteless things before going to Boston?*

Soberly Belinda rehung the dress in the closet and pulled out another one. But she was even more shocked as she studied it. One after the other, she assessed each dress left in her closet. *There really isn't a fit one in the lot* was her judgment.

What do Kate and Abbie wear? Belinda found herself asking. *Do they really look as . . . as old-fashioned as this? Have I just not noticed it before?*

Belinda pictured Kate at their family dinner last night. Yes, Kate did dress very simply, in country frocks much like Marty wore. Belinda had never given it a thought before—but they were dreary and out-of-fashion, though not any different from what the other women in the community wore.

Now, Abbie usually wears brighter things—dresses with a bit more taste and style, Belinda reflected. But even Abbie, though thought of as one of the best-dressed young women in their town, was not what the ladies of Boston would have considered fashionable by any standard.

Belinda had never been conscious of fashion before living in Boston, and even during her time there, she had been unaware that she had developed an eye for style.

The thought upset her. *Am I getting proud and . . . and stuffy?* she asked herself impatiently, and she pulled the blue frock from her closet and tossed it on her bed.

It's a perfectly good dress, she scolded herself. *It's certainly more suitable for farm wear than anything I brought with me.* She slipped her frilly nightdress over her head and put on the simple frock before she could change her mind.

The dress still fit . . . after a fashion. Belinda noticed with chagrin that it didn't quite fit like it had before. Though she had not gained weight over the past few years, the dress was a bit snug in places. Belinda fretted and pulled, but there was no give. At last she tied up the sash, adjusted the collar, and proceeded down the stairs.

Marty was in the kitchen at the big black stove. The room already felt hot to Belinda, and it was just early morning. *Whatever will it be like by nightfall?* she found herself wondering. The early fall weather could still be very warm during the day.

"My, you look nice," Marty beamed at Belinda. She knew Marty enjoyed seeing her back in her old flowered blue calico. Belinda didn't trust herself to comment. She feared her voice might give away her true feelings about the wardrobe upstairs.

"I'll be right back," she informed her mother and set out down the path at the back of the house. It had been a long time since she had used an outside facility, and she found it strangely disagreeable.

When she returned, Marty was dishing up a platter of scrambled eggs and farm sausage. "Pa said to call him in as soon as you were up," Marty informed Belinda. "Would you like to call 'im? He's at the spring."

Belinda nodded, looking forward to a quick morning walk to the spring. It had always been one of her favorite spots—just as it had been her mother's. She nodded again and turned to leave.

"Tell 'im everything is ready," Marty called after her, and Belinda took it as a signal that she was to hurry.

It really wasn't far to the spring, but she ran anyway. She would have enjoyed a leisurely walk so she could smell the fall flowers and enjoy the colors of the leaves. She would walk the path again later—many times, perhaps—and enjoy the smells and the colors to her heart's content.

Just as Marty had said, Clark was there, raking fallen leaves from the crystal water.

"Pa," Belinda called, out of breath, "Mama says breakfast is ready."
Clark looked up from his task.

"My, don't ya look bright and pretty," he responded. Belinda just smiled. Both Clark and Marty seemed to prefer having their little girl back.

"Sleep well?" asked Clark as he set aside the rake.

Belinda wished he hadn't asked. "Well . . ." She hesitated. "It took a long time for me to drop off," she admitted, then quickly added when she saw worry in Clark's eyes, "Guess I was just too excited."

Clark nodded. "A lot happened in one short day," he agreed.

They walked to the house, Belinda almost running to keep up with the long strides of her pa. "My," she joked, "how fast did you walk when you had two good legs?"

Clark chuckled. "Not much faster, I 'spect. I figured as how I wouldn't let the loss of a limb slow me down any more'n I could help."

"Well, it sure hasn't," panted Belinda.

Clark slowed down a bit. "I was jest thinkin' as I was cleanin' the spring," he said slowly, "of thet boy Drew."

Belinda's eyes flickered toward her father. She felt the color strangely rise in her cheeks.

"Ya ever hear from 'im?" asked Clark.

Belinda shook her head.

"He was over a while back," Clark went on. "Called on yer ma an' me."

Belinda looked at her father, and she could feel her eyes widen with her questions. "He's home?" she asked softly.

"Was. Ain't no more. He was jest visitin' his ma fer a spell. His pa passed on, ya know."

"No," said Belinda. "No . . . I didn't know that. What happened?"

"Not sure. Some said heart. It was sudden like."

"I'm sorry," Belinda responded, her voice not more than a whisper.

"Yeah, it was a shame. A real shame. An' as far as we know, him not ever makin' any move toward the church's teaching, either. The missus, now, she comes regular like. Been comin' the last two years. Took a stand about her faith in front of the whole congregation. Really somethin', her bein' such a quiet, sensitive soul."

"What about the . . . the younger boy?" asked Belinda. "The one who was going to school?"

"Sidney?"

"Yes . . . I'd forgotten his name."

"He's still with his ma. Works in town at the feed mill. Rides home every night. Folks say he had his heart set on going fer more education— but he hasn't gone, least not yet."

They were nearing the house. Belinda hadn't asked the questions she really wanted to ask. *What about Drew? Is he still following the Lord? Did he ever become a lawyer as he'd dreamed? Will he ever come* back . . . home? Has he . . . has he married? But Belinda asked none of them. Instead she said, "I'll bet Drew's ma was glad to have him home."

"Yeah," he agreed. "Yeah, she sure was, all right. Sid said thet it was real hard fer her to let 'im go again."

Clark held the door for Belinda and she passed into the big farm kitchen. On the table a steaming plate of pancakes sent waves of warmth upward. The scrambled eggs and sausage, along with the coffee already poured and waiting beside their plates, added to the delicious breakfast smells.

Hurriedly father and daughter washed for breakfast, using the corner washstand and the big blue basin. Belinda had not shared a towel for ages and it was a rather unfamiliar experience for her now.

Turning again to the heavily laden table, she looked at the syrups, the jams, the jellies. Then her gaze went back to the pancakes and the egg platter. *How in the world will I manage such a breakfast? Does Mama really expect me to eat like a farmhand?* Belinda had become used to scones or tea biscuits or, at the most, a muffin with fruit . . . and now . . . ? She crossed to her plate.

"Ya want some porridge to start with?" asked Marty, adding quickly, "It's yer favorite."

To start with? echoed Belinda silently. *Oh my!*

"A . . . a very small helping, please," smiled Belinda. "I . . . I haven't done anything to work up an appetite yet."

Clark smiled. "Well, we'll right that quick enough," he joked. "I got some hay thet needs forkin' this mornin'."

Belinda just smiled and bowed her head for the table grace.

After breakfast they had their family devotions together as they'd always done for as long as Belinda could remember. It was wonderful to hear her father read Scripture again. His voice trembled with emotion as he read the stories that to some had become commonplace. Belinda loved to hear him read. He had always made the Bible come alive for her.

It was Marty's turn for the morning prayer, and Belinda's thoughts traveled across the country with her as she presented each one of her children and grandchildren to her Lord, asking for His guidance and protection for another day. It was a lengthy prayer. Clark and Marty never hurried their morning devotions.

Afterward Clark pushed back from the table and reached for his hat. Marty waved Belinda aside as she rose to clear the table.

"Now, I want you to jest take the day and git reacquainted with yer home," Marty told her.

"But I'm not that rushed for time," Belinda objected. "I'm to be here for six weeks. I can certainly help with the dishes and—"

"No, no," argued Marty. "I've nothin' else to do this mornin'. You jest run along."

Belinda at last agreed. "I guess I'll go back to the spring, then, and finish the raking," she told Marty. "Pa wasn't quite done when I called him for breakfast."

Marty smiled. "I think thet rakin' the leaves from the spring is one of yer pa's favorite tasks," she said softly. "In the fall he does it every few days. It's a good thing thet the wind always favors 'im by puttin' more leaves back in. I think yer pa enjoys the gurgle an' the talkin' of the stream. But I don't think he'll mind sharin' the pleasure with you."

Belinda smiled in answer.

"'Course, it's my favorite spot, too," Marty admitted. "Always did feel I could do my best thinkin' there. An' prayin'," she added without apology.

Belinda understood. The running water had the same effect on her. She had to admit to herself that she was going to the spring now not so much to rake leaves as to think—to recall.

Thoughtfully she walked down the path again, and when she reached the stream she took up the rake leaning against the tree where Clark had left it. She dipped it dreamily into the clear, clean water, wondering as usual how the stream stayed so sparkling, and pulled a few wayward leaves toward the bank.

So Drew has been home, her thoughts began. *It seems such a long, long time since I've seen him—such a long time since I've even heard anything about him. Why, Drew left when I was only seventeen. I'd almost forgotten that Andrew Simpson existed. Almost!* She stopped raking and stared off into the distance.

Yet . . . yet he kissed me . . . once . . . so long ago. We were just chil-dren then. I was only sixteen. It was my first kiss. Such a . . . such a tender, childlike kiss. Like one good friend kissing another. And I thought about it . . . day and night . . . for what seemed like forever.

But it's strange . . . after that kiss, instead of drawing us together, it seemed to drive us apart. Like we both felt embarrassed and didn't know how our feelings should be handled. We only mumbled greetings when we met and avoided looking at each other.

Belinda flushed even now as she thought about it, and then she smiled openly. *We were such . . . such kids,* she admitted. *Both liking each other, yet afraid to let it show.*

She bent to trail her fingers in the icy water. It helped some to state the truth, even to herself. She had never, ever shared with anyone just how much she had really cared for Drew.

Well, I guess he really didn't feel the same about me was her next thought as she straightened up again, *or he surely would have tried to stay in touch—some way.*

With a sigh Belinda scooped out another batch of leaves and depos-ited them on the shore.

But what if . . . what if we were both visiting home at the same time? What if . . . what if we suddenly met on the street in town? Would there be any kind of feeling for each other after all these years? Belinda couldn't help but wonder.

And then she reminded herself that perhaps Drew was married. She hadn't asked her father. It certainly seemed that Drew was settled . . . wherever he was now living. He had just come home to visit his ma, her pa had said. That didn't sound as though he had plans to ever come back to the area.

Belinda stirred restlessly. *Maybe thinking back isn't such a good idea after all.* She finished, leaned the rake back up against the tree, and moved on to explore other favorite places of the farm.

EIGHT

Memories

It didn't take Belinda long to visit all her old farm haunts. The first place she went was to her pa's barn. She hoisted her skirts and nimbly climbed to the barn loft to check for a new batch of kittens. She would be terribly disappointed if there were none. But after a short search, she discovered their hideaway in a distant corner.

As far as Belinda could tell, there were three in the litter, but they were as wild and unapproachable as young foxes. She never did get anywhere near them, though she tried to coax them to her for a good half hour.

"Now, if I'd been here," she informed the tabby cat, "I'd have had those kittens of yours licking my fingers and playing in my lap long before their eyes were ever open."

Looking totally unimpressed, the cat said nothing. She also was too wary to let Belinda near her. The mother herself had likely grown up without being handled, Belinda supposed. She finally gave up and climbed down the ladder.

She then spent some time looking for hidden hens' nests. She and Amy Jo had always enjoyed this little game, arguing over which one was the better at outguessing the farmyard flock.

Belinda found two nests with a total of eleven eggs. She shook them cautiously to test them, concluding that neither hen had been inclined to "set." Belinda bundled the eggs in her skirt and took them to the house to Marty.

Belinda next chose a favorite book and went to the garden swing. She had intended to read, but with the gentle swaying of the swing, memories of her childhood companions, Amy Jo and Melissa, came to her so strongly she couldn't concentrate.

Why do things have to change? she asked herself unreasonably. *Why couldn't we have just stayed in our innocence, our childish bliss?* But even as she asked, she knew the answer. At the time, they had felt they were growing up way too slowly. Each of them, in her own way, had ached and longed to become an adult. And now her beloved nieces Melissa and Amy Jo were both hundreds of miles away, with homes of their own. And she, Belinda, was here for only a short time—as a visitor. Her duties—her life—lay many miles away, too.

The sad, nostalgic thoughts drove Belinda from the swing. She laid aside the book and wandered to the garden.

Belinda noticed that Marty's apple trees were bearing well. She could see where Marty had already picked some from this stem and that. Perhaps the apples had been baked in the pies Belinda had enjoyed the evening before.

She passed on to the flowers. The goldenrod glowed brightly in the fall sunshine and the asters lifted proud heads, their colors varied and vibrant. *Vibrant,* thought Belinda. *Vibrant. Amy Jo used that word for just about everything. She'd found it in one of Melissa's books, and she loved the sound of it.* Belinda smiled to herself. It seemed like such a long, long time ago.

That's what I should have done with my six weeks, she suddenly told herself. *I should have gone to see Amy Jo and Melissa.*

But even as she thought of it, she knew better. *Mama and Pa would never have forgiven me,* she decided, *if I'd gone out west instead of coming here.* Then she admitted, *Really, I wouldn't have liked it, either.*

She moved on, admiring Marty's flowers. *They are pretty,* she mused, *though nothing like Thomas's tailored flower beds.*

What's the matter with me? Belinda thought crossly. *When I'm in*

Boston, I'm longing for the farm. And when I'm on the farm, I'm secretly longing for Boston. Don't I fit in anywhere anymore?

The thought was an alarming one—and Belinda had no answer.

She decided to go back to the kitchen. Perhaps her mother would find something for her to do.

"I've finished my roaming," Belinda informed Marty. "I'm ready to be of some use now."

Marty smiled indulgently at her youngest. "Have things changed?"

Belinda hesitated. How could she express her feelings? To Marty everything must seem exactly the same.

"Things?" queried Belinda almost sadly as she washed her soiled hands at the big basin. "No, not things. Just . . . just us. People. We change. We've all changed, haven't we, Mama?"

Perhaps Marty did understand. It looked like her eyes were misting briefly with tears. She nodded solemnly at her daughter, and Belinda could see that she, too, was remembering.

"Yeah," she agreed in little more than a whisper. "Yeah, we change. Life is full of change. Seems only yesterday thet I . . . thet I first entered thet little log house over there . . . the one where we first lived . . . where Clare an' Kate used to live. Ain't no one lives there anymore. First yer pa built us this fine house, an' then Clare built the house yonder fer Kate. Now the little house jest sits there . . . empty and cold. An' . . . an' some days . . ." Marty hesitated and took a deep breath. "Some days," she finally went on, "I think I know jest what thet little house is feelin'."

Belinda was ready to cry. She hadn't thought much about how her mother felt. Hadn't experienced the pain of watching a houseful of children leave one by one. She thought she understood better now.

"But life is like thet," Marty acknowledged, squaring her shoulders. "One mustn't stay pinin' fer the past. Thet don't change a thing. One must be thankful fer what the present offers—what the future can promise."

Marty lifted a corner of her apron to dab at her eyes. When she looked back at Belinda she was smiling.

"My," she said, "I wouldn't want a one of 'em any different than they turned out to be. Independent! Responsible! Grown-up! I look at folks round me, an' I think how blessed I've been. All good children, with keen minds and sturdy bodies. Thet's a powerful lot to be thankin' God fer."

Belinda knew that Marty meant the words with all her heart. She nodded in understanding.

"Let's have us some tea," Marty hastened on. "I'll git it ready whilst ya call Kate. She gits lonesome, Kate does. She still misses her Amy Jo." Marty shrugged resignedly. "But she always will," she admitted. "Thet kind of lonesomeness never goes away."

Belinda left the kitchen. She did not hurry on her way to fetch Kate. She was looking at things—at life—far differently than she had ever done before.

She had never considered loneliness as something universal. She had never supposed it to be anything other than temporary and something to be resisted. In her innocence, she assumed it should be, and could be, easily disposed of. Fixed up. Remedied. And now her mother was calmly, though with open painfulness, admitting that lonesomeness was an unavoidable part of life.

When one loved, one was vulnerable. There was no guarantee that things would remain constant. Older folks died. Youngsters grew up. Children chose lives of their own. Nothing stayed the same for long.

It was a troubling thought to Belinda. Wasn't there some way—any way—a person could hang on to what was good? Couldn't one have some control of tomorrow?

But she already knew the answer to that. Would Missie and Ellie be living out west if Marty could have held on to them without at least partially destroying them? Would Amy Jo be miles away from home if Kate could have kept her and given her freedom to grow at the same time? One could not control life, it seemed. Particularly the lives of those you loved. To love was to give freedom. To give freedom often meant pain and loss.

Then why even have a family? Belinda asked herself. *Why let yourself love? Maybe without intending to I've chosen a wiser way. If I never love, never marry, never have children, I won't have to face what Mama—or Kate—is facing now. Is that the answer? Perhaps! Perhaps it is!*

For a moment Belinda felt satisfied. She had solved one of life's riddles for herself.

And then another thought came. *But I already love—it's too late. I was born loving, I guess . . . or I was taught to love awfully early. I love deeply. Pa . . . Ma . . . each of the family. Aunt Virgie. Even Windsor and Potter and the household staff, in a special way. I'm not safe. Not even now. There is no way that anyone can be safe from the pain of love. Not ever. Not as long as you love anyone . . . anyone at all.*

And Belinda knew better than to assume that life would be better with no one—not one soul—to love.

I guess it's like Mama says, she admitted at last. *One just has to let go of the past, enjoy the present, and look forward to whatever the future holds.*

She lifted her face heavenward. "But, oh my, God," she said in a whisper. "Sometimes that's hard. Awfully hard."

A few days later Belinda decided to make a visit to the little log house. She asked Marty about it. After all, it had belonged to Clare and Kate long after it had been Marty's home. They might still feel some ownership and not be comfortable with others snooping about. Belinda didn't want to intrude.

"Go ahead," responded Marty.

"You don't think Kate would mind?"

"Mind? Why no. I think she's as happy to be in a new home as I was."

"But I don't want . . ." began Belinda.

"She's moved everything out," Marty assured her. "The house is totally bare now. S'pose it would be wise to tear it down . . . but there it still stands."

"Why . . . why . . . ?" began Belinda, but she didn't finish the question. She couldn't imagine the farmyard without the old house.

But Marty must have misunderstood, and instead of answering why the house would never be torn down, she tried to explain instead why it was still standing.

She shrugged. "I dunno," she admitted. "Maybe yer pa an' me are jest sentimental. I dunno. We keep sayin' things like, 'Dan might want it,' and stuff like thet. We even talk about makin' it into somethin' else—a granary or a chicken coop—but we won't. I think we both know thet." Marty chuckled, amused by the little game she and Clark continued to play between them.

"Well, I need a key. Is it locked?" Belinda asked.

"Oh my, no. Don't s'pose it's ever been locked. Don't know if we even could . . . 'less one put on a padlock of some sort."

Belinda walked down the short trail that led to what used to be Amy Jo's house, feet dragging. She wasn't sure if it was really wise to go there. But she felt she had to—really must do it—if she was to put the past to rest.

The door opened slowly, creaking its complaint on rusty hinges. Belinda pushed harder and managed tó squeeze herself through the small opening that she forced from the tight-sticking door.

The back entry had the same brown walls, the same square in the middle of the floor that opened up to the dumbwaiter into the cellar. More than once she and Amy Jo had been scolded for playing with the ropes.

Belinda stood and looked around. The room seemed very small—and bare. There were no coats on coat hooks. No boots in the corner. No pail of slop for the pigs. No life here at all.

Belinda shivered slightly and moved farther into the kitchen.

Belinda could not believe her eyes. The kitchen looked as if it belonged in a dollhouse. She had always thought it—well, at least adequate if not big, but now it looked so small and simple. Much too simple for a woman to really live with each day. The colors were still the same. There was an outdated calendar on the wall, a picture of a little boy holding a brown, curly-haired puppy on the front. Belinda guessed that Kate had not had the heart to discard the picture when the year ended. The last sheet with its month had been discarded.

Belinda crossed into the room that had been used by the family. Memories flooded her mind as she looked about the small area. Here she and Amy Jo had flopped on the floor, lying on their tummies, to draw. Here they had stretched out before the open fire to eat popcorn and giggle over boys. They had rocked in the big rocker that had sat right over there. They had bundled up baby dolls and propped them against the mantel.

She didn't bother with the bedroom Clare and Kate had shared, and she didn't check the room the boys had used. Instead, she passed directly to the room that had been Amy Jo's. It had always been a pale green and white—until Amy Jo herself had decided to change that. Amy Jo had wanted a room that was "vibrant." She had been allowed to have her way, and "vibrant" her room had become.

Belinda would have been terribly disappointed if the room had been changed—but except for being unfurnished, it was the same. For a minute Belinda stood stock-still, the memories flooding over her and giving her goose bumps. Then she shut her eyes and pictured again the room as she had last seen it. The bed—right there. Against that wall, the dresser with Amy Jo's socks and undies. Amy Jo's nightie always hanging from the peg in the corner. The little desk where she sat to do her drawing. The dolls, the books, the paints and pencils. Belinda could see it all as vividly as if it were actually before her.

And then she opened her eyes slowly. The empty room stared back at her, the marks on the floor where the bed castors had rolled. The smoky blue paper with its small violet flowers and green leaves was marked here and there by a tack or a smudge. There was a rubbed spot where the desk had stood. Amy Jo had spent so many hours at that desk that she must have soiled the paper. Perhaps Kate had even needed to wipe it with a damp cloth on more than one occasion.

Belinda looked again at the room. In her mind she could hear the childish voice of her then-constant companion. "Oh, Lindy!" Amy Jo would exclaim in exasperation, and Belinda smiled. They were so different, but so close.

With a shiver Belinda turned from the room. Memories were not always pleasant, she decided. Memories could bring pain, too.

She retraced her steps without looking back and slipped through the door into the afternoon sunshine. The shiver passed up her spine again. She felt she had suffered a chill. She tugged the complaining heavy wooden door tightly closed behind her.

On the path to the white house, Belinda's thoughts were delivering a sharp message: *Nothing is the same. The place, the family—nothing! I am not the same. I love my family . . . but I don't fit here anymore.*

You don't fit. You don't fit, her shoes seemed to squeak with each step that Belinda took along the path back to the big house. She had a hard time to keep from running.

NINE

Return to Boston

Belinda knew the time of her visit home went far too quickly for her mother, but the days dragged somewhat for Belinda. Each morning as she climbed from her bed to face the inconvenience of no bathroom, she was reminded that she was no longer the young girl who had occupied the room where she now slept. No longer did she fit in with the farmhouse, the outdated clothes in the closet, the hens and horses. Boston had changed all of that. *At least,* Belinda told herself, *it must have been Boston.*

There was only one place where she felt she still fit. The little country church—for though the people dressed plainly, the warmth and the preaching tugged at her heart. She had longed for such messages, had ached to be part of such worshipful services. She had sometimes sensed deeply within herself that something important seemed to be missing in the big stone church in Boston.

Yes, in the little country church Belinda felt at home—all in one piece. Whole and complete. But one could not take refuge in the church all week long.

For Belinda, the family devotional time was an extension of the Sunday worship service. She felt mentally and spiritually restored and nourished during the time spent with her mother and father as they read from the Word, discussed thoroughly each Scripture passage, and spent unhurried time together in prayer.

This is what I've missed the most, Belinda recognized. *The spiritual feeding. The sharing. It's hard to grow if a person is not nourished.*

Belinda decided to make each day at home a source of spiritual refreshment. Often the morning hours slipped by while the three sat and talked and prayed.

"I knew I was missing—what does one call it—'fellowship'? These talking and sharing times," said Belinda one morning as she sat with her mother and father after their devotional time, "but I hadn't realized just how much."

"Don't ya have anyone to talk to?" asked Marty.

"Well, not about . . . about spiritual things. Not really talk."

"What 'bout yer church?" asked Clark. "Does yer preacher give the Gospel?"

"Well . . . yes . . . sort of," faltered Belinda.

Clark and Marty both looked questioningly at their daughter.

"He . . . he preaches that Christ is the Son of God," went on Belinda. "And he preaches that Christ came to bring salvation to man. He even talks about our sin and that we need to turn away from it . . . to repent of our sinful deeds. He uses all the words. Repentance. Redemption. Salvation."

Clark nodded, looking pleased at Belinda's report.

"But he never really tells people how to find that forgiveness or claim that salvation for themselves," Belinda went on. "Sometimes I get so frustrated, wishing that he'd go that one step further . . . that he'd tell folks to ask God for His forgiveness . . . to ask Christ to come into their lives and take over. Trying to be good—all on one's own—isn't the answer."

Clark nodded solemnly. "Does he encourage folks to read the Scriptures for themselves?" he asked.

"No . . . no, I don't think I've ever heard him suggest it."

Clark was shaking his head, his eyes full of concern. "Thet's a shame," he said soberly. "If folks was readin' the Word, they might discover on their own how to find salvation."

"That's why I worry about Aunt Virgie," went on Belinda. "I'm afraid she just doesn't understand that she has to make a decision herself—a commitment."

"We'll pray along with ya," put in Marty. "We've already been a prayin', but now thet we know how things are, we'll do it even harder."

Belinda nodded, appreciating the concern of her parents. She was glad they would join with her in her prayer concern.

Many things began to crowd into her visit at home. Belinda spent some time with Luke and Abbie, with Arnie and Anne, with Clare and Kate, and she enjoyed catching up on the happenings of each family. She and Marty hitched the team and drove to Nandry's, Belinda's foster sister. Nandry and Josh were alone now, too. All their children had homes of their own, and Nandry boasted proudly about their seven grandchildren.

Belinda was also brought up-to-date on Clae and Joe. They had never come home to the little town they had left so many years before—though they had always intended to. And now Belinda felt that she knew the reason. Clae and her pastor husband, Joe, would fit in here no better than she herself did.

Belinda heard all the news of Willie and Missie, Lane and Ellie, and their families in the West. She was especially anxious for every scrap of information she could gather about Amy Jo and Melissa. Without consciously realizing it, she found herself expecting that the two girls would still be there at the farm, now that she was home.

Belinda ached to just flop across her bed, as was their fashion of old, and talk and talk with her two nieces.

Belinda took a few short rides through the familiar countryside on Copper. He proved to be just as self-willed as ever. Belinda never dared dismount to try to tie him up while she investigated a bush or patch of flowers. She knew how skillful Copper was at leaving for home without her. She did enjoy her outings, regardless, and always returned home with flushed cheeks and shining eyes.

One fall day when the wind was rattling the tree limbs and sending showers of autumn leaves scurrying to the ground, Luke turned his team into the farm lane.

"You busy?" he asked Belinda.

"Why, no," she answered, and Marty swung around to question her son with probing eyes.

"I'm not kidnapping her, Ma," teased Luke. "Just wondered if she'd like to make a call with me."

Marty nodded encouragingly as Belinda reached for a warm shawl.

"Is it cold?" she asked. By the expression on her mother's face, Belinda guessed Marty was hoping this little outing with Luke might somehow bring her back to them.

"It's a bit chilly," Luke responded. "I think you'd be wise to take your coat."

Belinda went for her coat and soon joined Luke in the buggy.

"Do you still make a lot of house calls?" she asked him.

"Not like I used to before Jackson came, but yes, I still make my share of them."

"Where are we going today?" asked Belinda.

"Little Becky Winslow has a bad throat. Her mama wants it checked. Didn't want her in my office in case it was contagious," Luke explained.

"I hope it's nothing serious," Belinda commented.

"Doesn't sound like it is, but one always needs to be careful," Luke replied.

They rode in silence for a time, then Luke spoke again. "Well, it's official. Dr. Jackson Brown and Nurse Flo have announced their coming marriage."

"How nice for both of them!" Belinda exclaimed with a smile. She had seen Jackson on one occasion since she had been home. To her relief it had not proved awkward. They had chatted sociably, easily, as two old friends. Belinda was truly happy for Jackson.

"How soon?" Belinda asked.

"Next spring. May. So I won't be losing my nurse immediately. Still, we are training another woman to help in the office. We don't want to be left with no one in an emergency. We had decided long ago that we should have at least two nurses who know the procedures at all times."

Belinda nodded.

"Remember that place?" Luke pointed with a finger. Belinda recognized the Coffin farm. The one that Josh had rented to the Simpsons.

"Pa said that Mr. Simpson passed away," Belinda said, her mind suddenly churning with many other thoughts.

"He did. It was sudden—and unexpected. By the time Jackson got there, it was too late."

"That's too bad," Belinda commented soberly.

"Mrs. Simpson and Sid still live there," Luke went on.

"That's what Pa said. Looks like they've fixed things up quite a bit," Belinda noted.

"They have. Mr. Simpson worked awfully hard to get it back to what it once was. Say what you like about the family—they can't be accused of being lazy. Hard workers, every one of them."

Belinda kept her thoughts to herself for a few minutes as the team traveled on down the road, leaving the Simpson home behind.

"You mentioned Jackson," she said at last. "Jackson was called when Mr. Simpson died. Does that mean they still haven't forgiven you?"

"Oh no. I've been there several times. I just was out on another call when it happened, that's all. Why, Drew himself was in to see me a while back. He was here to visit his ma."

Belinda nodded. "Pa told me," she admitted.

There was silence again. Belinda finally broke it. She wasn't sure what to ask—*how* to ask—but she did want some answers to all her questions.

"Was Drew . . . has he . . . has he changed much?"

Luke shook his head and clucked to the team. "Well, yes . . . and no," he answered. "He's grown-up . . . filled out . . . gotten to be a good-looking man."

Nothing different about that, thought Belinda to herself. He was always good-looking.

"He's . . . he's very mature," Luke continued. "He'll make a good lawyer. A real good lawyer. Just wish we had him here."

"He doesn't plan to . . . to come back?"

"I don't expect so. Guess he really didn't say one way or the other . . . but he did say that he's happy where he is. He's working in a good firm. Getting lots of good experience . . . making good money, too, I'd expect. Not much to come back here for."

Belinda nodded.

"He asked about you," Luke surprised Belinda by saying.

Belinda's eyes widened. "He did?"

"Said he never did thank you—properly—for your part in his surgery."

Belinda felt a swirl of emotions that came with the memory. It had been one of the most difficult experiences of her life.

"What did you tell him?" asked Belinda.

"Just said that an elderly lady had been brought from the train to us and that you'd gone off to the city to become her private nurse. He seemed happy for you."

A few more minutes of silence slipped by.

"Luke," asked Belinda slowly, "do you think the city is where I really belong?"

He was quiet for a while, then said, "That's a question only you can answer." He turned his head to look into her face, and Belinda nodded.

"It's just . . . just . . . I don't know anymore," she admitted. "I . . . I don't seem to fit here."

"What is 'fitting'?" Luke asked. "How does one feel when one 'fits'?"

"Well, I . . . I guess like I used to feel," Belinda stammered. "I never used to even think about fitting before."

Luke nodded. "When I'd been away . . . to get my training," he said slowly, "and came home again . . . well, I wasn't quite sure if this was the place for me or not. I sure didn't fit in the same way I had before, but I decided that there was little use looking back. That really wasn't where I wanted to be anyway—a young squirt tagging along after Doc. So it seemed like the only thing to do was to make myself a new place, a new 'fit.' One of my very own. And I set to work doing that. I feel quite comfortable in my little spot now . . . and Abbie and the kids, they seem happy, too."

"I guess that's what I'm going to have to do," agreed Belinda, and she thought of Boston. She didn't really look forward to settling permanently in the big city, but to her thinking there was really nothing else that she could do—at least for now. Aunt Virgie needed her—and she certainly didn't seem to have a place here in the country anymore.

She sighed deeply. Life could be so complicated.

"Hey," Luke said, reaching across to squeeze her folded hands. "I have faith in you. You'll know the right thing to do when the time comes."

"But . . ." began Belinda, "I . . . I can't just put it off forever . . . and . . . and drift. I have to make up my mind sooner or later."

"And you will," said Luke. "I'm counting on it."

They had reached their destination. Luke hopped down and turned to help Belinda, then tied the team and lifted his black bag from the buggy.

"Let's take a look at Becky's throat," he said to Belinda, and they entered the house together.

It turned out to be simple tonsillitis, and Luke left some medicine and soon they were on their way again.

"It's always a relief when it isn't something serious," Luke said, and Belinda nodded in agreement. *If only life could always be so simple and straightforward,* she thought.

Marty asked Belinda if there were any neighbors she wished to visit. Belinda pondered for a few minutes. All her school chums were married women, and a number of them had moved from the area. She shook her head slowly. "Only Ma Graham, I guess. I don't really know who else is still around."

And so Belinda and Marty hitched the team again and started to the Grahams'.

"It's been a while since I've been over to Ma Graham's myself," Marty confessed. "I keep tellin' myself thet I must git goin', but then somethin' more comes up thet needs doin', and I put it off again."

Marty had been "doin' " all the time Belinda had been home. The garden produce had to be brought in and put in the root cellar, and the apples had to be picked and stored and the kraut had to be made—and on and on it went. Her hands were always busy, yet she had not allowed Belinda much opportunity to help.

"Now, you don't want to go back to Boston with yer hands all stained an' rough," she would scold mildly. "You jest sit there an' talk whilst I work."

Belinda had not cared for the arrangement, and she had usually found some tasks, such as churning butter or mixing up a cake, while the two of them shared the kitchen.

But now it was visiting day. Marty seemed to look forward to the break.

"Ma's been a mite poorly," she informed Belinda.

Belinda quickly turned, concerned, to ask what the problem was.

"Luke says it's jest old age, plain an' simple. She's had a busy life—a hard life, Ma has, an' I guess thet one can't help it when it shows. She blames it all on her gallbladder," Marty went on.

"Has she thought of having surgery?" asked Belinda.

"Well, to do thet, she'd hafta go to the hospital over to the city, an' Ma don't want to do thet. Says she'd rather jest put up with it."

"That might not be a good idea," Belinda continued.

"Well, wise or not, thet's the way us old folks think sometimes," said Marty, and Belinda smiled at her mother putting herself in the same age group as Ma Graham.

They were welcomed with love and enthusiasm by the older woman. "Belinda, let me look at ya!" she cried. "My, don't ya look nice. So grown-up and pretty. My, how the years have flown. Seems jest yesterday ya was here delivering me another granddaughter."

Belinda remembered. It had been the first delivery Luke had allowed her to help with.

And it was on my way home that Drew stopped me, she silently remembered and felt her cheeks flush slightly.

Like Ma said, it had been a long time ago.

"An' you, Marty," Ma teased. "Seems it's been almost thet long since I've seen even you."

Marty laughed and the two women embraced.

Tea was soon ready and the three sat down for a good chat. Time passed quickly as Belinda caught up on each member of the Graham family. Ma even had some great-grandchildren. She beamed as she spoke of them.

All too soon it was time to go. Marty left with the promise that she wouldn't wait so long to be back again, and Ma promised to have one of her boys drive her over to the Davis farm one day soon.

"Thet was a good idea, to visit Ma," Marty said to Belinda on the way home. "I'm so glad ya thought of it. Ma always did hold you as somethin' special."

"I've missed her at church," Belinda said. "It seemed strange not to see her there."

"Well, it's her bad leg thet keeps her from church," Marty informed her daughter. "Ya notice how she can't take a step without thet cane—an' she can't climb steps at all anymore."

Belinda had noticed, and it bothered her. It was just one more thing that was changing—and she was helpless to do anything about it.

Eventually the day came for Belinda to return to Boston. It was cold and windy, and Belinda shivered as she pulled on her coat. She realized now she should have brought something warmer. The weather had been so much milder when she had left Boston that she hadn't thought of what it might be six weeks later.

Her simple country frocks had all been hung back in the closet. Belinda noticed Marty's eyes lingering on them there.

Belinda commented carelessly, "Who knows when I might be back again?" But she couldn't help wondering if Marty thought, just as she did, that she might never wear those dresses again.

"Ya better wrap this heavy shawl around yer shoulders," Marty said, handing her one, and Belinda did not protest.

The trip into town was a quiet one. They seemed to have said everything there was to say. Now the thought of the separation ahead made talking difficult.

"Yer sure you'll be warm enough?" Marty asked anxiously as Belinda returned the shawl.

"It's plenty warm on the train," Belinda assured her.

"Ya won't need to git off?"

"Not until I get to Boston."

"Do they know when to expect ya?"

"I left the schedule with Windsor," responded Belinda. "He'll be there with the carriage to meet me. He is most dependable, Windsor is."

Marty nodded.

The family gathered, as it always did, at the station to see her off. Even the youngsters had been allowed to leave school early so they could be on hand for Belinda's departure. Also, as always there was a great deal of shuffling about and making small talk while they waited for the minutes to tick by.

At last they heard the shrill of the whistle in the distance. The train would soon be pulling into the station. Belinda began her round of good-byes, leaving her ma and pa for last.

She hated good-byes. The tears, the hugs, the promises. She wished there was an easier way to take one's leave. But it was the doubts that made this good-bye most difficult. Belinda had so many doubts—so many questions. She wondered for the hundredth time if she was doing the right thing. When would she be home again? What would bring her back? Some tragedy? She prayed not. But who could tell? Her mother and father were getting older. Belinda had seen firsthand the aging of Ma Graham. In a few years' time her ma and pa could age like that, she knew.

Belinda shivered at the thought.

"You need a heavier coat," Marty said again.

"I have one in Boston, Mama, and I won't need one until I get there. Really. The train will be nice and warm."

Marty held Belinda close as though to protect her from the chill of the wind and the pain of the world.

"Write," she whispered. "I 'most live fer yer letters."

"I will," promised Belinda.

"An' don't worry . . . 'bout home. We're fine," continued Marty.

Belinda wondered just how much her mother knew about the feelings that churned through her insides.

Clark held her then. She felt his arms tighten about her, and for a fleeting moment she was tempted to change her plans. But she knew she had to return to Boston. She kissed her mother one last time and then, amid shouts of "good-bye," she climbed the train steps and selected a seat just as the big engine began to move the cars down the tracks.

Belinda leaned from the window and waved one last time.

The train was taking her back to Boston. *Back to where I belong,* thought Belinda.

But her mind hurried on.

If that is so, she asked herself, *why do I feel so empty inside? Why are my cheeks wet with tears? Why do I feel as if I've just been torn away from everything that is solid?*

Belinda didn't have the answers.

TEN

Back to Normal?

Belinda had arranged her return so she would be back at Marshall Manor the day before Mrs. Stafford-Smyth was due home. This would give her a chance to be settled in and able to give full attention to the older woman upon her arrival.

Dependable Windsor met Belinda at the station, just as she had known he would. Belinda thought he seemed almost glad to see her, though she was sure he wouldn't have thought it proper to admit as much. Belinda smiled to herself as she settled in among the robes he had brought. The cold wind was blowing in Boston, also, and in true Windsor tradition, he no doubt had noticed the light coat Belinda had worn as she left.

The house looked the same—big, beautiful, and inviting. Belinda tried not to compare it with the little farm home she had just left, but it was difficult not to do so. She was looking forward to having indoor plumbing once again. It would be so nice to soak leisurely in a tub filled with warm water from a faucet. Belinda felt as if she had scarcely had a proper bath since she had left Boston. Taking a bath in a galvanized tub just wasn't the same.

Even the usually distant Potter seemed pleased to see her and bustled about asking how she could be of service and what would Miss like for her dinner. Belinda could scarcely believe her eyes and ears.

Windsor insisted on carrying her suitcase and hatbox up the stairs, and Belinda followed close behind, eager to see if her room was really as pretty as she remembered it.

She sighed deeply as she looked about her. Everything was just as she had pictured it. She motioned to Windsor to set her suitcase by the bureau and excused him with a simple "Thank you."

She was looking forward to a nice, sudsy soak. Even as she thought about it, she could hear water running and crossed the room to find Ella already in the bathroom.

"I thought you might like a nice bath, miss," Ella explained, and Belinda gratefully assured her that she would.

"You just hop right in, miss," Ella said on her way out of the bathroom, "and I'll unpack for you. What do you wish me to lay out for dinner, miss?"

Have I truly lived like this? Belinda asked herself. And then, *Yes. I'd quite forgotten. Before I left I'd gotten used to being treated like a . . . a pampered lady of leisure.*

"Something simple," she smiled at the maid, "seeing as I will be dining alone. I really am very tired and feel the need for my bed far more than the need for food."

"Of course, miss," answered Ella.

"You pick something," Belinda called over her shoulder as she headed for the tubful of warm water.

It was delightful to lower herself into the warmth and the suds and let the water soak away the fatigue from her back and shoulders. Belinda would have lingered longer had not Ella called to her.

"I've finished the unpacking, miss, and laid out your gown. Cook said she will serve in half an hour. Do you wish me to do your hair?"

Belinda considered the offer. It would feel good to have Ella do her hair again. It seemed so long since she'd had it done properly. But she was weary—and she had little time. She called back, "No thank you. I'll need to hurry. I'll just pin it up myself for tonight."

"Very well, miss," said Ella, and Belinda heard the door close.

She climbed from the tub and dried on the large, fluffy towel, noticing how soft and white it was.

Perhaps it has been good for me to be away, she told herself. *I'll take more notice of things that I've been taking for granted.*

Belinda hurried, remembering that Potter did not suffer tardiness with pleasure.

She was almost breathless as she entered the dining room. It seemed so strange to sit down to a table all by herself. Especially when she had just come from a family where several plates usually crowded the table.

But for all the material differences, homesickness tugged at Belinda's heart as she seated herself and bowed her head to say grace while Windsor stood by waiting to serve her.

The dinner looked delicious, and Belinda might have enjoyed it more had she been less tired—and less lonely. Out of habit she forked the food to her mouth but hardly tasted a thing. After she had done some justice to what had been prepared, she excused herself and announced that she was retiring for the night.

With no early-rising roosters or bellowing cows to awaken her, Belinda slept late the next morning. When she finally did open her eyes and study her clock, she was shocked to see that it was quarter of ten. She threw back her covers and rang for Ella.

Ella responded immediately, and Belinda stopped brushing her hair long enough to say, "Run my bath, would you, please, Ella? I've overslept. Mrs. Stafford-Smyth is due in at twelve-thirty."

Ella nodded. "Windsor has been fretting," she acknowledged.

"Why didn't someone awaken me?"

"We all knew you were tired, miss. Potter said to let you be."

"Potter?" Belinda's eyebrows went up and then she smiled. There had been a time when Potter would have taken delight in seeing her summoned from her bed.

"Cook said to let her know when you were ready for breakfast," declared Ella, coming in the door.

"No breakfast today—I don't have time," Belinda told her. "Tell Cook I'm really not that hungry."

Ella looked troubled. "She'll insist on some fresh juice at least, miss," Ella dared forecast.

"Some juice, then. Up here. And perhaps a scone. That's all."

Ella left and Belinda hurried to get ready.

At the time previously set by Windsor, Belinda was in the front hall, her hat on straight, her warm coat buttoned properly. She was ready to meet the train.

Belinda felt a surge of excitement as the wheels of the carriage bumped along the cobblestone road. It seemed a very long time since she had seen Mrs. Stafford-Smyth. She was looking forward to sharing the news from her hometown. *Well, at least some of the news,* Belinda thought. She knew she wouldn't share with the older woman all of the thoughts and feelings she'd had while away.

In fact, the more Belinda thought about it, the more she wondered just what she would be able to share. Her trip home had been so . . . so personal . . . even troubling. Maybe she wouldn't dare discuss much of it at all.

But she would ask Mrs. Stafford-Smyth to tell her all about her holiday in New York. There certainly would be plenty for them to talk about. She'd hear all about the plays, the concerts, the dress shops. They would talk about all the things Mrs. Stafford-Smyth had experienced—but they would not discuss the conflicting emotions Belinda had battled, she decided.

The train arrived on time, and Belinda held her coat securely about her and scanned the crowd for Mrs. Stafford-Smyth. Windsor spotted her first. "There's M'lady!" he exclaimed, and even the proper Windsor could not keep an excited tremor from his voice.

Belinda saw her then and ran to meet her.

"Oh, my deah, my deah!" cried the older woman, "how I have missed you."

There were tears in Mrs. Stafford-Smyth's eyes as she held the girl. If Belinda had doubted the reason why she was back in Boston, she understood and accepted it thoroughly now. *She needs me.* She really had no one else. A houseful of servants was not family, even though Mrs. Stafford-Smyth cared for each of them.

Windsor ushered the two of them into the carriage, declaring that he would return later for the luggage.

"And how was *your* trip, deah?" asked the older woman.

"Fine," replied Belinda. "I was able to see everyone—well, everyone who still lives at home."

"That's nice," smiled the lady. But in spite of the smile, Belinda noted with some concern the tiredness in Mrs. Stafford-Smyth's face.

"Have you not been feeling well?" Belinda asked.

Mrs. Stafford-Smyth waved the question aside. "I've been fine," she maintained, "just fine."

Belinda did not press her further. "And how was your trip?" she said instead. "I am so anxious to hear all about it. It must have been terribly exciting."

The older woman looked at her evenly. "Well, I must say, not really," she replied at last.

Belinda was surprised. *Maybe Mrs. Stafford-Smyth's trip has not gone well.* "You aren't telling me something," Belinda said softly. "What is it? Were you sick while you were away?"

Mrs. Stafford-Smyth shook her head, and then tears began to gather and then to run down her face, splashing unheeded into her fur collar. "It's just . . . just . . ." she sniffed and searched for a handkerchief in her pocketbook, "that I couldn't think of anything else but you, deah. I kept thinking you wouldn't come back once you got home again. I lived every day in feah and didn't feel like doing anything. Celia neahly tossed me out she was so annoyed with me, but I . . . I just couldn't help it."

Belinda reached out to take her employer's hand, passing along her handkerchief. "That's all right," she comforted. "I'm here. I came back just as I said I would."

"I'm so glad. So glad," breathed the older woman. "Now things can get back to normal again."

Normal? thought Belinda. She had just moved back and forth between two very different worlds. *What,* she wondered, *is normal?*

But things did fall back into a daily routine. The two women picked up where they had left off, sharing their meals, their handwork, their reading, their lives. Little by little they spoke about some of the experiences of their time apart, too. It seemed that the one had been as miserable as the other—but for quite different reasons.

The windy fall days turned to winter chill, and snow began to pile up on Thomas's flower beds. This time there was no discussion of a trip abroad to avoid the winter. They knew without saying it that they both had consented to suffer it through. Belinda realized she was already looking forward to spring even as she saw the winds tuck the flowers away under their snowy blankets for the winter.

Belinda kept her promise to her mother. Each week she wrote a lengthy letter home and looked forward to the reply that was sure to come. She shared the letters with Mrs. Stafford-Smyth, who seemed to enjoy them almost as much as Belinda did.

When Christmas came, they celebrated with strangers again. In its own way, it was a joyous time. Mrs. Stafford-Smyth had enjoyed planning the holiday event and having the festive table surrounded by dinner guests. Their guests, too, appreciated the time spent in the lovely big house with the kind woman and her staff.

But for Belinda the most special moments occurred each day as the two of them spent time together studying the Bible. Since her trip to New York, Mrs. Stafford-Smyth seemed much more aware and sensitive to spiritual things. Belinda wondered if something particular had happened there.

But her employer never said anything about such an event. Belinda held her tongue but continued to wonder—and to pray.

ELEVEN

An Exciting Event

Belinda knew her folks at home were praying with her for Mrs. Stafford-Smyth. Each morning as the two studied a Bible lesson together, Belinda watched closely for glimmers of understanding on the part of the older woman.

Mrs. Stafford-Smyth did listen attentively. She also attended church services regularly. But Belinda could not help feeling that the woman did not really capture the true significance of the Christian faith. Mrs. Stafford-Smyth seemed to feel that if one tried to be good—was more good than sinful—then hopefully God's scales would tip in the person's favor.

Belinda selected Scriptures dealing with the sacrificial death of the Savior, the need for a personal faith, the glorious hope of heaven because of what Christ Jesus did on the sinner's behalf. But though the woman looked sincere, each Bible lesson seemed to fall on unhearing ears. Belinda thought often of Christ's parable of the seed and the sower. She wondered if Mrs. Stafford-Smyth would ever choose to be "good ground" for the truth or if the evil one would always snatch the seed away before it had a chance to root—to grow.

Belinda prayed more earnestly and searched more diligently for appropriate Scriptures.

One Sunday morning as Easter approached, Belinda left the morning worship feeling rather dry and empty. The sermon, though it had referred to the Cross and what it meant for sinful mankind, seemed without energy—truth, certainly, but without life or passion. It left much to be desired, in Belinda's thinking.

If he only had gone on—told the rest of the story—explained the meaning of it all, Belinda grieved. *But no. He stopped right there— short, leaving his congregation to sort through the whole thing for themselves. No wonder they cannot seem to understand the meaning of the Cross, of redemption.*

Belinda felt like crying as she climbed into the carriage with her employer for the ride home.

"Wasn't that a wonderful sermon, deah?" asked Mrs. Stafford-Smyth as soon as she had properly arranged her skirts.

Belinda quickly turned to look at her. There was something unusual in the woman's tone. To Belinda's surprise the lady's face was shining in a way that Belinda had never seen before. Belinda could not speak. She just nodded dumbly.

"I've heard it ovah and ovah," the older lady went on with reverent enthusiasm, "but you know . . . I've nevah really understood the meaning of it befoah. This mawnin' as I listened, it all came to me just like that. Imagine! The Son of God himself dyin' in the place of *me.* Isn't it *glorious?* Most wonderful! Why, I bowed my head right there where I sat and just thanked Him ovah and ovah. I nearly had one of those—what do they call it?—revival meetings all by myself."

Belinda stared in wonder. Mrs. Stafford-Smyth had gotten what her pastor at home would call "a good dose of old-fashioned religion"— and in a somewhat unlikely place, too. In a rather formal, staid city church.

"Oh, Aunt Virgie!" Belinda cried, throwing her arms around the older woman. She wanted to say, *That's what I've tried so hard to show you. That's what I've been praying for, working for,* but that seemed irrelevant now. The wonderful thing was that Mrs. Stafford-Smyth knew the truth for herself. *I can hardly wait to write home with the good news!* she exulted. She knew her folks would be nearly as excited as she was.

"You know," the woman went on, her face still shining, "all those readings that we've been doing togethah? Do you remembah where you found them? I'd like us to read them all again—now that I think I understand what they'ah really saying. Could we?"

"Why, of course." Belinda was thrilled to agree.

"I can hardly wait to tell Windsah . . . and Pottah. I'll bet they don't understand it, eithah. Cook might . . . there's a feeling I have about Cook. But the girls . . . doubt if eithah of them do. Do you think they do?"

Belinda hadn't gone that far in her thinking. She was a bit chagrined as she thought of the other household members. She had been concentrating all of her time and prayers on Mrs. Stafford-Smyth.

"You know, we should have the whole staff gathah for the Bible-reading times," Mrs. Stafford-Smyth continued. "My, I'd just hate it terribly if any one of them right in my own house missed knowing the truth."

Belinda could not believe her ears, but Mrs. Stafford-Smyth was still not finished.

"That's what we'll do. Right aftah breakfast each mawnin'. We'll all meet togethah in the north parlah. You can choose the reading and then we'll talk about it."

Belinda had a momentary qualm at the thought of leading the whole household in the morning Bible lesson. *What if someone asks a difficult question?* she thought. *I'm certainly no theologian. It wouldn't be at all difficult for one of them to stump me—badly.*

But she nodded her head in agreement. Maybe even Mrs. Stafford-Smyth would be able to help explain some of the scriptural truths.

It was later that evening that Belinda was able to ask the question that had been gnawing at her all day. Seated in the cozy little parlor having tea and biscuits before retiring, Mrs. Stafford-Smyth was still enthralled with her earlier experience. Belinda listened joyfully as she talked, and then when the lady paused, Belinda posed her question.

"What was it that made you see it—understand the truth of salvation—all of a sudden?"

Mrs. Stafford-Smyth stopped, teacup raised almost to her lips, and thought about the question. Then she answered assuredly, simply, "Why, I suppose it was the Holy Spirit. Just like the Scripture tells us, 'He will teach you all things.' I couldn't 'see' it on my own. My spiritual eyesight was 'darkened.' I don't think I wanted to know the truth. I shut it out without realizing it, just like the Scripture says. I wanted to manage on my own. I had to reach the place where I was willing to hear the truth."

Belinda could only stare.

"You read those verses the othah mawnin'," the older lady told her. "Remembah? Of course at the time they didn't mean much at all to me—but I understand them now."

"Of course," said Belinda.

That night as Belinda knelt beside her bed she had something new to pray about—to rejoice over. But she had a confession, too.

"Dear Father," she prayed, "forgive me for feeling that I had to 'convert' Aunt Virgie when it was your business all the time. I know that we Christians are to share our faith—help me to be faithful in doing that. But, Lord, never let me believe it is my doing when someone reaches out to you. It is only through the work of your Holy Spirit that any lost person can be drawn to you, the Father. Aunt Virgie accepted the sacrifice of Christ only because your Spirit helped her to understand it. Thank you, Lord, for showing her. Thank you that she was able to understand and accept it. And now help the two of us as we try to share this Good News with the staff. And remind me—always—that my task is just to share. Yours is to do the converting."

The whole household soon felt the effects of the conversion of their "Lady." Mrs. Stafford-Smyth was open about what had happened. She did not force the issue with others, but she let it be known that she hoped very much for her staff to be in attendance at the Bible readings.

She had Belinda read, gave opportunity for discussion, but pressured no one to accept or refute the truths.

"God will do that through His Spirit," she kept reminding Belinda. "He is the only One who knows the innah parts of the soul." But Mrs. Stafford-Smyth did not lightly regard her Christian duty. She and

Belinda spent much time in prayer every day for each person attending the morning study.

Then Mrs. Stafford-Smyth extended her mission to share the Good News.

"We need to have anothah dinnah party," she informed Belinda. "I don't know if any of my old friends really understand the truth. I believe they think much like I did—that one gives God proper respect and tries to do good toward his fellowman, and, in return, the Lord blinks while the person squeezes through the gates."

Belinda smiled.

Mrs. Stafford-Smyth thought for a while. At length she continued. "You know," she said, "I think it's moah than that. I don't think I understood what sin was. I thought sin was killing folks, or stealing from your neighbah, or cheating the poah. And so it is—but it's so much more. I didn't understand that the sin that broke the heart of God and kept one from entering heaven was the sin of rejection—of not acknowledging and accepting Christ's death on Calvary in my place. That is why God would not have been able to let Virginia Stafford-Smyth enter the gates. I hadn't recognized my sin of unacceptance—unbelief, if you will—and accepted what He did for me on Calvary."

Belinda solemnly nodded again.

"Oh, but it's so wonderful when it is all taken care of," continued the older woman, tears forming in her eyes. And then she hastened on. "Well, we need that dinnah party, that's foah sure."

Potter, Windsor, and Cook were all summoned once more, and Mrs. Stafford-Smyth discussed her plans. All the old crowd were to be invited, she said, and in some way—some way—the Spirit would reveal to her a way to share her newfound faith. She didn't want to depart this world without telling her dear old friends the truth of the Gospel, she informed the staff members.

The night of the dinner party arrived.

"What do you plan to do?" Belinda asked Mrs. Stafford-Smyth as they waited for their guests to arrive.

"I don't know," she replied honestly. She said she still had not received her directions from the Lord as to how to go about sharing.

All the guests had been seated at the dining room table, and Windsor was standing ready to serve at a nod from his mistress. Belinda watched her, realizing she was stalling for a bit of time while she waited for an idea from the Lord.

Finally the guests were all watching their hostess expectantly, and Mrs. Stafford-Smyth began slowly. "Belinda and I have established a new—" she hesitated—"habit," she said, picking up the thread again. "A good habit. We read togethah before we dine. Belinda, deah, would you bring the Scriptures and read that same portion that we read to-gethah this mawnin'?"

Feeling a bit nervous, Belinda went to get the Bible. She settled herself in her chair at the table and began to read. At first her voice was low and trembling, but gradually it steadied. Fidgeting stopped. Dinner guests lifted their heads to catch the words.

Belinda read, "For when we were yet without strength, in due time Christ died for the ungodly. For scarcely for a righteous man will one die: yet peradventure for a good man some would even dare to die. But God commendeth his love toward us, in that, while we were yet sinners, Christ died for us."

"Ah yes," breathed Mrs. Stafford-Smyth as Belinda carefully closed the Book and handed it to Windsor. "Let us pray." The prayer was a thanks-giving for the food that they were to enjoy, but Mrs. Stafford-Smyth also included a thanks for the truth presented in the Scripture reading.

During a few awkward coughs and throat clearings, Windsor stepped forward to serve the meal.

Before the talk around the table had opportunity to stray to other topics, Mrs. Stafford-Smyth turned to Mr. Allenby. "How do you under-stand that Scripture?" she asked simply.

For a moment the dignified man clearly was mentally scrambling around for some explanation, while his shrewd little wife cast furtive glances about the table.

Mr. Walsh spoke up. "Why, it told of the death of the Son of God for sinners," he stated in a straightforward manner.

"For sinnahs," mused Mrs. Stafford-Smyth. "Who are the sinnahs?" And so began a discussion that gathered momentum as it moved forward. Belinda could not help but smile at times. Never had this elderly crowd become so involved in animated conversation.

There were differences of opinion, of course. Mr. Allenby believed that though all of mankind might "err" on occasion, eventually everyone would be ushered in to enjoy the bliss of an eternal heaven. Mr. Whitley disagreed. Heaven was a state of mind, he argued. Mr. Walsh went so far as to declare that heaven was reserved for a "special" group, but he wasn't sure just who or what determined the special ones.

Mrs. Allenby sat silently, her eyes darting back and forth between the speakers, while Mrs. Whitley fidgeted with her napkin and turned from pale white to blushing red and back again.

Belinda could tell Celia Prescott was getting ready to involve herself in the discussion—she was not going to allow the men of the crowd to have all the say. She broke into the conversation with enthusiasm, making her point and then camouflaging it with a bit of humor. Belinda decided that Celia Prescott did not want to be taken too seriously where religion was concerned.

But Belinda watched as gently, and with skillful courtesy, Mrs. Stafford-Smyth steered the conversation in the direction she wished it to go.

"It seems from what you have said"—Mrs. Stafford-Smyth nodded toward Mr. Allenby—"that it isn't possible for anyone to live perfectly. That all of us, in one way or anothah, at one time or anothah . . . well . . . sins," she concluded, pinning him with his own words.

He sputtered a bit, but he finally conceded the point.

Mrs. Stafford-Smyth then turned to Mr. Walsh. "And you think that heaven was made a special place—for those who rightfully belong there."

He chuckled, nodding sociably. Mr. Walsh, with his unique sense of humor, did not seem able to take even eternity seriously.

"Well, I have reason to agree," continued the lady. "If heaven were for everyone, as you believe, John," she said, turning to Mr. Whitley, "then it seems to me it wouldn't be one bit bettah than what we already have heah on earth. Soon we would have the killing, the war, the poverty—all the things we have at hand. That's not the kind of heaven I would look forward to entering."

Heads nodded solemnly.

"So the only thing left," Mrs. Stafford-Smyth went on, "is the business of how one gets to go there."

Mrs. Whitley fidgeted morosely, her face looking pale again. Mrs. Allenby darted a look at her hostess, then seemed to measure her distance to the door. Belinda wondered if she was going to rush out.

The men still seemed perfectly unaware of the direction and intent of the conversation. To them it was a jolly good discussion, with some life—some spirit. They hadn't enjoyed anything quite as much for a long time, their expressions indicated.

"We make our own heaven," argued Mr. Whitley. "If we are miserly and mean and can't get along with our fellowman, we live and die that way."

"But that's not exactly right," argued Mr. Allenby. "There has to be something *beyond* life—we all know that in here." He placed his hand over his chest.

"What gives us the right to determine who gets to heaven—and how? We are no different than our neighbor," said Mr. Walsh with some spirit, looking like he had scored a good point, even though he did not feel too strongly about the matter.

"Exactly!" said Mrs. Stafford-Smyth emphatically, making Mr. Walsh beam even more. "Exactly. We do not have the right to do that."

There were nods around the table, everyone seeming to agree. And then Mrs. Stafford-Smyth folded her napkin carefully, looked evenly at her guests, and continued. "Only God has that right. And He tells us exactly how it's to be. We are all sinnahs—every one of us—just like you said, Wilbur. We won't be allowed entrance into heaven," she said with a nod toward Mr. Walsh. "Not in our sinful condition. That is what the crucifixion was all about—Christ, the sinless Son of God, dying in ou-ah place. The only hope we have of heaven is in recognizing and accepting what He has done for us.

"How did that Scripture say it, Belinda? 'While we were yet sinnahs, Christ died for us.' It's just as you said, Mr. Walsh. Heaven is for a selected group. Those who believe and accept what Christ has done."

She turned then to Mr. Whitley. "And you were right, too—almost. We do determine our own destiny. We don't make our own heaven or hell, but we do make our own choices that determine which place we will go to. God does not condemn anyone. He has provided heaven for the just—through faith. And hell is for the unjust—the unbelievers. By choosing Christ's salvation or by choosing to go ou-ah own way, we determine which one shall be ou-ah abode."

Those around the table drew a collective breath. The conversation had suddenly gotten rather personal. But Mrs. Stafford-Smyth was not finished.

"It took me a long time to see that," she admitted. "Fact is, the truth just came home to me a few Sundays ago. I finally saw it—understood it. So I did just as Scripture says. I repented of my sin and I accepted what Christ did for me so long ago. I thanked Him for it and asked Him to help me live the rest of my life as He wants it lived. I was slow . . . I know. I had heard the message all those yeahs and still didn't properly understand it. I do hope that you all have been much more spiritually wise than I have been. I really don't understand how I could have been so blind . . . for so long."

Then Mrs. Stafford-Smyth flashed her dinner guests a winning smile. "Still," she said kindly, "it is a truth to be thinking on. Not one of us heah is getting any youngah. It is wise to be sure we're ready for the hereaftah." Then after a pause, allowing time for quiet reflection, with a complete change of tone she said, "Windsah, would you serve the coffee, please?"

TWELVE

The Bend in the Road

A few days later Mrs. Celia Prescott came to call at Marshall Manor. She chatted on for a while about the past trip to New York, the new spring fashions, the play at the local theater, but all the time that she babbled on and enthused over this and that, Belinda had the feeling the woman had something else on her mind.

"If you'll excuse me," Belinda said when they had finished their tea, "it's such a lovely day, I think I'll take a little walk in the garden." The two ladies nodded and Belinda left. She couldn't have explained why, but she had the impression Mrs. Prescott might want to talk privately with Mrs. Stafford-Smyth.

Belinda stayed out in the garden talking with old Thomas, enjoying the clear air and bold sunshine, until she heard Mrs. Prescott's carriage leave the yard.

When she went in, Mrs. Stafford-Smyth still sat in the chair where Belinda had left her, her open Bible in her lap. At the sound of Belinda's step she lifted her head. "We need to pray," she said simply. "Celia is . . . is struggling."

"What—?" Belinda began, but Mrs. Stafford-Smyth interrupted her.

"She is just like I was—blinded to the truth. She wants so badly to be 'good enough' to get to heaven on her own. To admit that she is a sinnah—well, that puts her on a common level with all mankind—and Celia has nevah thought of herself as common." But she said this without indictment in her voice.

"How foolish and proud we are," mourned the elderly lady, tears forming in her eyes. "The creature trying to outwit the Creator. Pretending to be something we know we are not. Why do we do that, Belinda?"

Belinda had no answer.

"Well, we will just keep praying," declared Mrs. Stafford-Smyth. "Who knows what the Spirit might do in the hearts of the ones who listened to His Word the othah night?"

One result of that dinner-party discussion was completely unexpected—even to Mrs. Stafford-Smyth and Belinda, who had been praying. It was loyal, dignified Windsor who responded to the truth of the Scriptures as they had been discussed that evening. The butler had stood patiently and unobtrusively by, serving the dinner guests as they animatedly discussed the meaning of the Scripture passage.

But the truths that had been presented so simply had touched the heart of the old man, and in the privacy of his own chambers, he had turned in faith to the Savior.

Mrs. Stafford-Smyth was overjoyed. Though Windsor did not want to be fussed over regarding his well-thought-out decision, it did cause no small stir in the household as it came to be known.

Windsor summoned Belinda, his face ashen white and his voice choked with emotion. "Come quickly, miss," he trembled. "Something is the matter with M'lady."

Belinda sped from the room. She had been sitting alone waiting for Mrs. Stafford-Smyth to join her for breakfast.

"Call the doctor," she flung over her shoulder as she ran.

A shocked Sarah stood at the bedroom door wringing her hands and sobbing. She had discovered her mistress when she had gone in to help her dress. Belinda rushed past her to reach the older woman. *She could be seriously ill* was Belinda's frantic thought. *She might need immediate attention.*

But as she bent over the woman, it was quickly obvious to Belinda that a doctor would avail nothing. Mrs. Stafford-Smyth was gone. She had passed away sometime during the night—without a struggle, probably without pain.

Belinda stood clasping her hands tightly together, too stunned to cry. *Oh, God,* she prayed silently, *what do we all do now? How will we manage to go on without her?*

She reached down to draw the hands over the older woman's bosom and lift the sheet carefully to cover the face.

"Oh, Aunt Virgie," she said aloud, her voice catching, "I loved you so."

The tears came then, deep, sobbing tears. Belinda lowered herself to the floor, leaned her head against the bed, and let sorrow overtake her.

The doctor and Windsor found her there, her body trembling, her eyes swollen from crying.

"Come, miss," Windsor said kindly and lifted her to her feet. He led her from the room while the doctor performed whatever duty was required. She allowed herself to be guided downstairs by Windsor's steadying hand.

"Sit here," Windsor said, lowering Belinda to a chair. "I'll fetch some tea." Belinda wanted to protest, but she didn't have the strength. *What does it matter?* she thought distractedly. *I'll sip from the cup if Windsor wants.*

The hush over the house was broken only by a sob now and then as one staff member or another worked to contain his or her grief.

Belinda remembered very little about the rest of the day—the rest of the week. She moved as one in a dream—unfeeling, unnoticing, except for the huge, painful emptiness within her. Over and over she asked herself, "What will we all do now?" But there didn't seem to be any immediate answer.

She phoned LeSoud's and ordered appropriate mourning garments delivered. Windsor and maybe Celia Prescott took care of the funeral arrangements and sent notices to those who should know. Many bouquets were delivered to the door. Belinda watched as they covered the mantel and then the tables in the parlor. The flowers meant nothing to her. *Aunt Virgie is gone* echoed numbly through her mind, over and over.

Somehow everyone made it through the awful day of the funeral. Belinda watched as the coffin was lowered into the ground. Around the grave stood the friends and the staff of Mrs. Stafford-Smyth. Franz and Pierre had sent telegrams and flowers, not having enough travel time to make it to the funeral.

It all was so . . . so *final* to Belinda. She found it difficult to fathom—to believe that their dear friend was gone. But no one could change the fact.

Back at the house, Belinda laid aside her veiled black hat. She stripped the black gloves from her shaking fingers and turned to Windsor. "Please don't bother with dinner for me," she said through lips stiff with grief. "I'm really not hungry."

He nodded and quietly left.

Silently Belinda climbed the stairs to her room.

Sometime later there was a tap on Belinda's door. She stirred restlessly in her chair by the window. *Who could want me?* she wondered. *And why? Surely no one had the poor judgment to come calling on such a day.*

Belinda called an invitation to enter, dabbing at her tearstained cheeks as she did so. Windsor stood there, rigid as always but with a softness to his face.

"I brought some tea, miss," he explained and moved into the room to set the tray on the low table.

Belinda stirred and murmured a thank-you of sorts.

Windsor straightened—and then broke his code of many years, speaking personally to one he served.

"She had a great feeling for you, miss. You were to her as her own flesh and blood. She told me that often. And . . . and I know you loved her, too, miss. We all did."

He hesitated.

"But . . . but she wouldn't want you grieving like this, miss. So hopelessly. She . . . she went as she would have chosen to go. Silently—quickly. Without pain or fuss. In her own bed. You must allow her the honor of dignity, miss. Even in her dying."

Another pause. Windsor had Belinda's complete attention now.

"And one more thing, miss," he went on softly. "She was ready to meet her Lord. If it had happened before—even only weeks ago—she may not have been ready. We have you to thank for that, miss . . . and I thank you with all my heart."

Windsor bowed and was gone before Belinda could comment.

Somehow they all managed to muddle through one day after another. The house seemed to be managed without Belinda giving it much thought. She had little knowledge of what made such a big house run smoothly, so she was more than willing to let the staff continue on in their own way.

What do I do now? became her constant question. She supposed the staff was asking questions. They all would continue in their present positions for some period of time until the estate was settled. But after that, they would no longer have employment, either.

When she was able to reason clearly again, she sat down on a bench beside a bed of Thomas's roses to try to think through her situation.

Aunt Virgie is gone, she began. *There is no longer any reason for me to stay here.*

She plucked a rose petal from the grass and held it to her lips. Then a new idea came to her, and she wondered why she hadn't thought of it immediately.

I'll go home, of course, she determined. *Back to where I belong.* The plan pleased her.

But then came the unwelcome thought, *I don't really fit there anymore. When I was home for my visit, I felt like . . . like I didn't belong. I have gotten used to a different kind of life—fine living, a big house, nice things.*

But even as the truth of it all came boldly to Belinda, she flinched. "I don't want to be like that," she declared out loud. "I haven't any business expecting to be pampered and spoiled the rest of my life."

Her thoughts continued. *That's not of God. I came here to help an elderly lady who needed my nursing skills. I did that to the best of my ability. Now that she's gone, I'm no longer needed here. Surely . . . surely God won't allow me to just curl up in an easy chair and forget about the rest of the world.*

Belinda was sure God had something else—some other task for her to do.

I'm going back home, she said to herself determinedly. *The staff can continue running the house without me. I'm going home.*

Belinda had not yet worked out what she might do at home. That was the next question she tackled.

I'll do as Luke said, she decided. *I'll find a new spot for myself. I may not fit where I once was, but I need to find my roots again. I'll find a new place of service. It might take me a while to sort it all out—but with God's help, I'll do it.*

With her resolve firmly in place, Belinda rose to move from the garden back inside the manor. A wonderful peace had settled over her. At least now she knew what she would do next. She would go home—back to family and friends—and find some way to serve God in her own town.

Belinda said nothing of her plans to the staff. She had much to do. There would be all the sorting and packing, and she had to make train reservations and write to Luke. *Perhaps . . . just perhaps,* she thought, *he will be able to use a rather out-of-practice nurse.* She felt it would take her a while to get back into formal nursing again—to be able to put in a full day's work. *But I can do it. I'm strong and healthy. There is no reason I can't soon be a help to the medical clinic.*

She certainly wouldn't need all the fancy silks and satins to go back with her to her hometown. Folks would think she was putting on airs if she were to be dressed in so fancy a manner. Belinda wanted no such distance between her and the other townspeople. *I'll have to find out what can be done with these dresses,* she thought.

But the first task was the letter. Belinda sat down at the small writing desk and pulled her stationery forward. She had just dipped her pen for the first stroke when there was a knock on the door. Ella entered when Belinda called, "Come in."

"Windsor asked me to fetch you, miss," Ella apologized. "It seems the magistrate wishes to see you in the library. Windsor is preparing tea."

Belinda frowned as she left the room and made her way to the library. She assumed that this man had something to do with the affairs of the late Mrs. Stafford-Smyth. *But what have I to do with that? Do they have some questions concerning the death? I was, after all, the nurse—though I was not present exactly at the time.* Still, Belinda realized, if there were questions, it was logical to ask the attending medical person.

Nervously she smoothed her gown and made her way down the stairs. She found Mrs. Stafford-Smyth's attorney seated at the big oak desk in the library. He looked quite at home there. Belinda had seen him on more than one occasion.

He rose as Belinda entered the room and motioned her to a chair before him. Then he turned to acknowledge a second gentleman who sat in a chair by the fireplace. "Mr. Brown is our witness," he explained, which made no sense at all to Belinda.

Belinda settled herself in silence and waited for Mr. Dalgardy to begin.

He cleared his throat and tapped his finger on the oak. Then he looked at Belinda over the rims of his glasses and cleared his throat again.

"We have the matter of the will," he said without emotion. "It is time for us to take some action."

Belinda nodded, again wondering what it had to do with her. And then the man began to read in a droning, monotonous voice, legal jargon and long, strange words that meant absolutely nothing to Belinda.

Why is he reading this to me? Belinda wondered. *I don't understand a thing he is saying—and it really has nothing to do with me.*

There was a pause in the reading while Windsor brought in the tea service. Belinda poured and the reading went on.

Eventually a few items began to make sense to Belinda. There was a generous amount stated for both Franz and Pierre. The attorney assured Belinda that he would care for the matter, while she watched him with wide-eyed puzzlement. There were certain items left to each member of the household staff and a provision made for their future. That made sense. Belinda had been sure Mrs. Stafford-Smyth would not leave her staff in need.

And then the man read on. "And to Miss Belinda Davis, my loyal nurse and dear friend, I leave the remainder of my estate in its entirety. . . ." The voice went on but Belinda heard no more. She held her breath and leaned forward in her chair, her hands turning cold.

"Why, whatever does she mean?" she managed to ask.

The attorney stopped reading to look at the girl.

"She never discussed it with you?" he asked simply.

"No," said Belinda, shaking her head emphatically. "No, she never said a word."

"She means—just as it says—that to you she leaves everything that hasn't been previously disposed of."

"But . . . but . . . what is that? I don't understand. . . ."

"I'm afraid it is much more than we can go into just now," answered the magistrate. "The house, the investments, the bank account. We will specify all of it in detail for you in due time."

"The house?" gasped Belinda. "This *house*?"

The man nodded. He seemed to be rather enjoying the effect he was having on the young woman.

"This house." He looked as though he was having a difficult time keeping the composure befitting his position.

"Oh my!" said Belinda, her hands to her lips as she leaned back helplessly in her chair. "Oh my. There must be . . . there must be some mistake. Why, whatever in the world would I do with . . . with this house?"

She closed her eyes and pressed her hand to her forehead, hoping that the room would soon stop spinning.

THIRTEEN

Decisions

"I . . . I think I need a few minutes alone," Belinda managed, and it looked like the elder solicitor smiled in spite of himself.

"Of course," he answered in a fatherly tone. "Of course. I hadn't realized all this would be such a shock to you. We'll come back tomorrow . . . say, two o'clock?"

Belinda managed a nod in agreement.

"Windsor will show you out," she said numbly and fumbled for the doorknob.

Belinda fled to the coolness of the gardens, her head spinning, her brain dazed. She sank onto a white wrought-iron bench beneath a lilac bush and stared unseeingly ahead, trying to clear her muddled brain so she could sort through what she had just been told.

This bush was covered with blossoms this spring, she murmured to herself. Such a strange thought under the circumstances. Belinda reached a hand to the greenery, fingering a leaf. *There's nothing here now . . . nothing. You wouldn't even know it had ever bloomed. Thomas has clipped all the seedpods.*

"How time changes," she whispered. "Seasons come and go . . . life begins and stops. A person has such a short time to make any impression on the world."

It could have been a morbid thought, but to Belinda it began her thinking process toward a plan. It helped her to put things into proper perspective. It helped to clear her foggy brain.

"And now I have this . . . this to contend with," she said, speaking aloud in the quiet garden. "I was going home. Had my mind all made up, and now . . . now I'm trapped . . . there's no other way to say it." Belinda paused to stare mournfully at the lilac bush.

"She . . . she didn't intend for it to be a burden," she continued. "Aunt Virgie didn't mean to force me into a difficult circumstance. She thought she was doing me a favor . . . giving me an honor. But it isn't so. I don't want her house . . . or her money. I never wanted it. I stayed because she was here and needed me. And now . . . now I am still not free to go."

Belinda lowered her head into her hands and began to weep. "Oh, dear," she cried. "Oh, dear Lord. What do I do now? What do I do now?"

With heavy steps and a heavier heart, Belinda found her way to her room. She sat numbly by the window with her Bible. A favorite psalm helped to quiet her heart, and then she prayed. When she arose she washed her face, made sure her hair was in place, and went to the north parlor, where she rang the bell and waited for Windsor. She felt a bit shaky inside, but her lips were firm in determination.

"Windsor, summon the staff, please," she ordered.

It was only a matter of minutes before they all stood before her. Belinda hardly knew where to begin.

"I suppose you know that an attorney paid us a visit today," she began. There was no reaction, and Belinda knew that the household had been well aware of the fact.

"Well, he brought some startling news," Belinda went on. "He read a portion of . . . of Madam's will."

Silence.

"In it she made provision for each of you. I'm sure that the matter will be presented to each of you at the proper time and circumstance. The will also said that . . . that she left the house and . . . and other things . . . to me."

No one in the room seemed surprised. There were a few murmurs of acceptance, even approval.

"Well, I have no idea—none whatsoever—of how to run a house such as this. But together we'll manage somehow. I just felt that . . . that each of you deserved to know how things stand. You all will have your positions . . . as in the past. There will be no dismissals or rearranging of duties . . . unless any of you prefer to find something else."

Belinda looked nervously around the circle. Heads nodded, and she saw relief on some faces.

"Well . . . that's all I have to say . . . for the moment," she concluded. "You may . . . may . . ." Belinda floundered. How did one excuse the staff?

"Thank you," she finally said. "That is all."

The staff understood they could now leave and moved toward the door. All but Windsor. He stood at stiff attention until the others had left and then approached Belinda. With a slight bow he addressed her. "Would you care for tea now . . . m'lady?"

Belinda had never been so addressed before. She understood immediately what Windsor intended. She was now the mistress of the manor. He and the staff would treat her accordingly. Her word was now rule.

The idea made her flustered. It was hard for her to find her tongue. "Why . . . why . . . yes, please. That would be fine," she managed to answer.

Belinda accepted the tea from the hand of the butler a few moments later. She didn't feel like sipping tea. She felt even less like tasting the tea biscuits that accompanied it, but she went through the motions.

Am I to sit each day, pretending to be something I'm not? she thought, sorrow and frustration churning through her. *I will go stark mad. No company. No duties. Nothing of worth accomplished. How will I ever bear such a life?*

Belinda shook her head sadly, set aside her teacup, and slowly went back to her room.

The two attorneys returned the next day as promised. After time with Belinda, during which more details of the will were explained, the entire staff was called so that the portion of the will outlining their future provisions could be read to them. Belinda noticed some tears and heard such comments as, "She was so thoughtful," "Such a dear thing," and "My, how we will miss her."

Belinda had gone into a new kind of shock. On her young and inexperienced shoulders fell the task of running a large estate. An estate she had not asked for—one she did not wish to have. Yet she knew she could not walk out on the new responsibility after having been entrusted with it in good faith. To do so would be an offense to the memory of the deceased and to the staff Mrs. Stafford-Smyth implicitly assigned to her care. *But what am I to do?* Belinda asked herself over and over. *Grow old in this big house . . . all by myself?*

A few mornings later Sarah came to her hesitantly. "M'lady," she said somewhat warily, "I was sent by Pottah to clean M'lady's—Madam's—rooms—and I picked up her Bible and this fell out. It's addressed to you. I . . . I thought you should see it . . . m'lady."

Belinda reached for the envelope. It did bear her name.

She stood staring down at the handwriting of Mrs. Stafford-Smyth, fearful to open it, yet knowing she must. She reached for a letter opener from her desk and carefully slit the envelope, lifting from it a sheet of paper. Belinda's hands were trembling as she held the carefully penned note.

My dear Belinda:

I have no idea when you might be reading this, for at the moment of writing I feel just fine. However, I am reminded that at my age, one must always be prepared.

I have talked with my barrister again today, and I believe that we have all things in order. I realize that parts of my will might be a shock to you.

Had things been different, I would have left more of the responsibilities to my grandsons, but never mind that.

I am leaving most of what has been accumulated in my name to you, dear. This is not to be an "albatross" but a means for ministering. I know that you will, with your good sense, find a way to use it wisely. I leave all of the decisions to you. I trust you completely.

And, my dear, feel no grief or sorrow for me. I have gone to a much better place—thanks to your constant prompting that caused me to recognize the truth.

I have loved you as a daughter. I thank you for your love for me. You have filled the lonely days of an old woman with meaning—and a reason for living. I could never, never repay you.

All my love,
Virginia Stafford-Smyth

Belinda's eyes were so tear filled she could hardly decipher the last few paragraphs. She could hear the writer's beloved voice in the words on the page. As she grasped the letter, a terrible loneliness for Aunt Virgie besieged her.

She turned back to the penned lines again and reread the letter.

"This is not to be an 'albatross' but a means for ministering," she read aloud. "What did she mean?" Belinda wondered. "What was she trying to tell me?"

And then it came to her in a flash of insight. Mrs. Stafford-Smyth was not demanding that she stay in the house—had not even expected her to do so. She had left the house and funds to Belinda so she would put it to some good use. *Of course! It would be selfish—and foolish—to let this huge home and all the rooms sit idle and empty when so many people need a roof over their heads. There is some way—there has to be some way—that it can be used to help people.*

Belinda couldn't help but smile as a new excitement burned in her heart.

"I need to have a good talk with an attorney," she said to herself. "I'm going to need lots of ideas and help to get this going properly."

Belinda felt she should share her ideas with the household staff. After all, their future was involved in her plans, as well. She called them together again after the evening meal.

743

"Sarah found a letter this morning while cleaning Madam's rooms," she began. "It was addressed to me, but I think you all deserve to hear it," and Belinda proceeded to read the message. She skipped a paragraph or two, since those sections were personal and were not pertinent to the mandate she—and they—had been given.

The staff listened attentively while Belinda read, but it didn't look like any of them felt there were any new revelations. Belinda was forced to explain—as she had known she would—her understanding of the line about the "albatross" and the "means for ministering."

"Mrs. Stafford-Smyth had no intention of my keeping this beautiful big house to waste on my own comfort," Belinda informed them. "She wanted me to use it to help others."

Questioning eyes turned toward her. She hurried on. "Now, I have no clear idea how to do that at present. I'm going to need the help of a law firm to discover just what can be done and what would be advised. I just wanted you all to know that I plan to find some way to share the manor with others."

Expressions of both interest and consternation filled the faces arrayed in front of Belinda.

"I want you to know, too," she continued, undaunted, "that I won't make any final decision until we have discussed it together. It is your home, too. I want you all to be in agreement with what is done here."

The ones who were anxious looked a bit relieved by the time Belinda dismissed them. She could imagine that there was a good deal of discussion once they reached the back rooms.

Belinda was weary . . . very weary. There had been so much happening in her life in the last few weeks. And now she had to begin a serious search of Boston for the proper attorney. She dreaded the ordeal, but she would start first thing in the morning.

Belinda had Windsor take her directly to the law firm that had represented Mrs. Stafford-Smyth. Windsor had phoned ahead for an appointment, and Mr. Dalgardy, who had visited the manor with the will, greeted her in his office.

"And how may I serve you?" he asked graciously.

"It's concerning the will of Mrs. Virginia Stafford-Smyth," Belinda began.

"Yes. I assumed it was," the learned man nodded.

"Well, I—that is, you see the will—it doesn't say that I must keep the house. It just says that I have been *left* the house."

"I don't understand," said the man with a frown.

"Well," Belinda went on, "I also have a letter, you see . . ."

"Could I see the letter?"

"Well, I . . . I didn't bring it with me. It was a personal letter," stammered Belinda.

"Was it from the deceased?" asked the gentleman, "or some other party?"

"Oh, the deceased—for sure. I recognized her handwriting at once."

"I will need to see the letter, I'm afraid, if I am to verify that," the man replied distantly.

"Well, it doesn't change the will any. I mean . . . it just . . . it just explains some things . . . to me," Belinda hastily explained.

The man just continued to frown.

"Well, what I mean is . . . I don't think Mrs. Stafford-Smyth expected me to just . . . just live at the manor . . . all alone and . . . and selfishly. I think she meant for me to use it in some way . . . to help others."

Mr. Dalgardy looked doubtful, but he nodded for Belinda to go on.

"Well, I . . . I need to know what one could do with such a house. How one could put it to good use without . . . without destroying what . . . what it is now. And the staff . . . they still need to be able to carry on there as before, you see."

"You want it turned into a public museum?" asked the man.

"Oh no. No, not at all. I don't think Aunt Virgie—Mrs. Stafford-Smyth—had that in mind at all."

"Then, what did she have in mind?"

"Well, I don't know for sure. But it would mean helping people . . . I *am* sure of that. But I don't know what possibilities there are. That's why I need direction . . . advice. I need to know what the city would allow . . . what options one would have."

"I see," said the gentleman, shaking his head slowly.

Belinda was confused. His lips seemed to be saying one thing and his head quite another.

He rose from his chair and cleared his throat. "If you wish the house used to support charity," he began stiffly, "you can always sell it and donate the proceeds."

"But that wouldn't include the staff, you see," Belinda argued.

"They could be given an adequate pension," he maintained.

"Oh, but the house is their *home* . . . has been for ever so many years. I don't think—"

"I'm sorry," the attorney interrupted, standing, "that's the only way I could help you."

Belinda realized she was being dismissed.

She rose shakily to her feet. "I . . . I see," she murmured as she straightened her skirt and lifted her parasol. She was almost out the door before the man called after her, "If you decide you'd like to sell, I might be able to find a buyer."

Belinda lifted her chin and sailed out the door. *Over my dead body,* she fumed inwardly. *I'll never sell Marshall Manor right out from under the entire staff. There must be something else. . . .*

FOURTEEN

The Task

Keen disappointment colored Belinda's voice as she relayed to Windsor the news of her visit with the attorney. She didn't know where to turn next. But Windsor did not seem to be daunted.

"Did you ask Mr. Dalgardy if there was another law firm he might recommend?" he asked Belinda.

She shook her head. "I didn't even think of it," she admitted. "I guess I was just too . . . too upset when he talked of selling Marshall Manor. Why, I shouldn't be surprised but that he had his eye on it himself," she said somewhat indignantly.

Windsor made no reply, just nodded in agreement.

"Well, I suppose we must just go from law office to law office," the butler said matter-of-factly. "I know of no shortcuts."

Belinda sighed.

The day was getting hot. She was glad she had brought her parasol.

"Will we need appointments?" she asked uneasily. "If we have to make an appointment with each law firm, we could be at this for months."

"Usually," Windsor replied, "but they might give some information. At least we could get the name of whom to call from the secretary."

Belinda nodded. "How shall I do it?" she asked.

"Well, m'lady, if you like, I will take those two offices across the street. You try the one at hand. I will ask for information on your behalf, and you could ask if this one is interested in governing your affairs."

Belinda nodded. It sounded simple enough. She gathered up her skirts for the long climb up the stairs to her assigned firm. She could see their sign: Browne, Browne and Thorsby, Barristers and Solicitors.

By the time she reached the office door, she was breathless and perspiring. She paused long enough to wipe her brow, regain her composure, and then tapped on the door.

"Come in," a male voice invited.

Belinda trembled slightly as she approached the large, littered desk. She tried to remember how Windsor had suggested she express her case, but she couldn't.

"I'm Belinda—Miss Davis," she said. "I am looking for a barrister— an attorney who will help me . . . with the . . . the administration of an estate."

"Do you have an appointment?" the man asked curtly, peering sternly over his glasses.

"No . . . I . . ."

"We do not accept off-the-street business," the man informed her firmly.

"But I . . . I . . ." began Belinda but stopped at his frank stare. *Off the street!* she murmured to herself. It sounded so coarse—so vulgar. For one moment she returned the man's bold look and, her face hot, spun on her heel and left the office.

Down, down the long stairway she descended, her flush heightening with each step.

What a crude way of responding, she muttered to herself. *I do hope Windsor is treated with more respect.*

But Windsor had fared no better. It was a discouraging report he brought to Belinda.

"I think we'd best go home, m'lady," he advised. "We will need to spend some time sorting this through if we are to gain admittance."

Belinda agreed. She was hot and tired. And she was in no mood to be patronized and put down any further today.

She did not even notice the beauty of the fall day as the carriage wound its way through the city streets and back to the grand home sitting in the well-to-do section of town.

They spent a great deal of time making calls, following up one possibility after another, making trips to the inner city and rapping on doors and ringing doorbells. But to Belinda's thinking, they were no nearer to solving their dilemma than when they began. She was beginning to feel they might as well give up when the minister of the church made an afternoon call.

"I understand that Marshall Manor has been left in your capable hands," he commented with a charming smile.

And maybe you are wishing to make sure that you and your church stand in favorable light, Belinda thought but did not say. She quickly chided herself for even thinking such thoughts. After all, he was a man of the cloth, and it was due to his sermon that Mrs. Stafford-Smyth had made peace with her God before her death. He was, Belinda admitted, preaching from the Holy Scripture, even if his application was ineffectual, to her way of thinking.

She nodded silently, waiting for the man to go on.

"We at the church just want you to know that, as Mrs. Stafford-Smyth before you, we value you as a member of our congregation. And if there is ever any way we can be of service—"

"As a matter of fact," Belinda interrupted on sudden impulse, "there might be a way. I am in need of an attorney. As you can imagine, this . . . this house and estate . . . well, they involve a great many decisions. And . . . well, I'm not really used to making such judgments on my own. I feel the need for a good attorney to help me in such matters. Would you know of anyone who might be interested in helping me?"

"I . . . I think I might be able to help you," he said with only slight hesitation. "I'll do some inquiring and see what I can discover."

Belinda thanked him sincerely, and the parson went on his way.

And so it was that three days later there was another caller at Marshall Manor.

Windsor opened the door and waited while the man gazed around himself admiring the wonderful face of the building, the lovely lawns, and the flower beds. Windsor cleared his throat, and the man produced a card. "The Reverend Arthur Goodbody informed me that the lady of the house is seeking legal advice," he told Windsor, and Windsor nodded, stepped aside, and ushered the man in.

"I shall call M'lady," he said. "You may wait in the library."

The attorney smiled, followed the butler, and accepted a seat as indicated.

Belinda could hardly believe the good news Windsor brought to her as he handed her the attorney's card.

"The parson has sent him, m'lady," he explained.

"Oh, bless his soul!" exclaimed Belinda. "I had most given up," and she hastened to the library to meet the gentleman.

When Belinda entered the room, she could feel her face was flushed from her rapid descent of the stairway. The attorney was sitting in the chair and staring at the thousands of books displayed on the shelves, looking appropriately impressed. He rose to his feet as manners dictated, but then a frown replaced the expression of admiration.

"I'm Belinda—Miss Davis," Belinda said with a smile. "And you are"—she referred to the card in her hand—"Keats, Cross and Newman," she read out loud and then smiled again. "Which one?" she asked frankly.

"The . . . the Keats one," the man answered haltingly. "Anthony Keats."

"I'm so pleased you have consented to offer your services," Belinda began and then realized they were still standing. "Please be seated," she said, then walked behind the big oak desk and sat down in the chair.

The man looked bewildered, but he sat down.

"I guess I should explain—briefly," Belinda went on. "I want to put this property to good use. But I don't know how to go about it properly. And I don't know my options—my limits. I need legal aid—advice—to help with some major decisions."

"I see," returned the gentleman, but he didn't sound as if he saw at all.

"It's a large house—very big. I haven't even counted the bedrooms," Belinda continued, feeling embarrassed. "Of course some of them are needed by the staff. The staff is to stay on," she hurriedly explained. "This . . . this is their home, too."

The man nodded.

"Of course, I won't be here. I plan to go home just as soon . . . just as soon as I can get this all settled."

"Could I speak with the homeowner?" the man asked cautiously.

Belinda felt her cheeks grow warm again. "I am the owner," she maintained. "That's why I have called you here."

"Ma'am," the attorney said, stopping Belinda cold, "this is a legal matter. I will need some legal papers."

"Like . . . ?"

"A deed."

"Oh, you mean to the house? Yes, I have it now. It was just delivered last week. It is right here," and Belinda crossed to a safe in the wall. When she had opened it with a click, Belinda removed some documents and handed them to the lawyer. He studied each carefully, his eyes darting from the papers to Belinda and back again.

"How did you obtain the house?" he finally asked her.

"Aunt Virgie—Mrs. Stafford-Smyth—left it to me in her will."

"Your . . . your aunt?"

"Well, not my aunt—not legally. I just called her Aunt Virgie. I worked for her. I was her nurse . . . and her friend," Belinda explained.

The frown on the lawyer's face deepened. "And now you wish to dispose of the house?" he asked.

"Yes," said Belinda.

"Because you can't afford to maintain it?" questioned the man.

It was Belinda's turn to frown.

"Do you need the money?" the lawyer asked outright.

"Oh no," Belinda hastened to inform him. "She left a good deal of money along with the house."

The attorney took a deep breath. "You . . . you just wish to be rid of it? To sell?"

"Oh, I don't want to sell," Belinda told him. "My, no. I would never sell Marshall Manor. I just want to . . . to put it to good use. Aunt Virgie said I could—in her letter."

The attorney looked perplexed. Belinda smiled. "Perhaps we should start over," she offered. "We both seem confused."

The man laughed then. "Perhaps we should."

"Here," said Belinda, handing him a package. "Here is the will— and the letter. Read it while I ring for some tea. I feel in need of some. Perhaps you would join me."

Belinda gave Mr. Keats plenty of time to study the legal document and the note. When he laid it aside and removed his spectacles, Belinda began again. "Do you understand now?"

"Understand? No. But things are certainly in order. You have the will, the deed. You are free to do whatever you wish with the property."

That much was good news to Belinda.

Windsor brought the tea tray, and Belinda poured and served the beverage to the gentleman.

"Now, what I need to know is, what ways are there for me to put this house to good use?" she asked after they each had taken a sip of tea.

"You mean—like a public museum, with an entrance fee?"

Belinda shook her head impatiently. *Why does everyone think that I want to use it for income?* she muttered inwardly. *I have no intention of desecrating Aunt Virgie's home for money.* To the gentleman before her she said, "I want to use the home for good. As a means of ministry—just like Aunt Virgie said in the letter."

"In . . . in what manner, ma'am—er, miss?"

"I don't know," responded Belinda. "That's why I need your advice."

"I see," said the gentleman, sounding a bit impatient himself.

There was a moment of silence.

"It would help me tremendously, miss, if I had some . . . some idea as to what you have in mind," Mr. Keats stated at last.

"Well . . . well, I don't know exactly," responded Belinda. "But . . . it seems to me that with so many homeless on the streets and all of these lovely rooms here that . . . well, that there should be some way to get the two together."

The man looked shocked. "You mean . . . like . . . like an overnight hostel?" he queried.

"No, no. Something more permanent than that. So much coming and going would likely ruin the house . . . and run the staff to death. We can't do anything like that."

The man seemed relieved.

"But there must be some way to put this lovely place to good use," determined Belinda. The man rose to his feet and returned the package of legal documents to her. "I'll look into it," he promised.

"Oh, thank you," replied Belinda sincerely. "I was about to give up in despair . . . and I do so much want to get this finalized and return home."

Mr. Keats cast a glance all around him. "The house is beautiful. Frankly, I can't imagine your ever wanting to leave it. But I'll call as soon as I have some ideas," he assured her, and then Windsor was there to show the man out.

FIFTEEN

Dinner

"How nice," murmured Belinda as her eyes quickly scanned the formal invitation in her hand. "It's from Mrs. Prescott," she said, lifting her head to speak to Windsor. "She has asked me to dinner next Thursday."

Windsor gave a slight nod. "You will wish the carriage, m'lady?"

Belinda thought for a moment. "Oh, dear," she said. "I don't even know where Mrs. Prescott lives."

"Mrs. Prescott was never much for entertaining, miss. She came here often, but she was always much too busy—" Windsor caught himself and began to gather up the tea things. "I know the way, m'lady," he said instead. "I have driven Madam a number of times in the past."

The mention of Mrs. Stafford-Smyth brought a momentary pain to Belinda's heart. An evening spent with Celia Prescott might be very difficult. It was bound to bring back many memories of their times together in the past. Belinda wondered if she was quite ready for such an occasion. She stirred restlessly, then rose from her chair and walked to the unlit fireplace. She stood rubbing her hands together in agitation, her eyes staring into the ashes, though actually seeing little. Windsor turned to look at her.

"Maybe I . . . maybe I should just decline the . . . the invitation," she said hesitantly.

"Madam would not wish that, miss," Windsor replied softly, evenly.

Belinda looked up quickly, surprised at the unusual voicing of opinion from someone who had carefully withheld such comments in the past.

"No-o," she conceded. "No . . . I don't suppose she would. But it's . . . it's going to be so sad. . . ."

Windsor nodded.

"Do you miss her terribly much?" Belinda suddenly burst out.

For a moment there was only silence; then Windsor nodded his head. "Most terribly!" he answered, then turned and was gone with the tea things.

Belinda stood looking down into the empty fireplace. *Ashes,* she thought. *Only ashes where once there was a warm and living flame. It's rather symbolic. Oh, I miss her.*

She brushed tears from her eyes and left the fireplace to cross to the window. In the gardens Thomas was working over a flower bed, McIntyre curled up on the lawn beside him, head on paws. The elderly man and his dog seemed such a natural part of the landscape.

Belinda smiled softly. It was a beautiful day and Windsor was right, she admitted. Mrs. Stafford-Smyth would not want her to sit at home. She, Belinda, had to get on with life.

She went to the corner desk and settled down to write her acceptance of the dinner invitation. Then she tucked the note into an envelope, left it on the hall table for Windsor to deliver, and went out to the gardens to see Thomas.

Belinda prepared carefully for the dinner engagement. She felt a great deal of excitement after all and no small measure of curiosity. Why was the woman inviting her to dinner? It was true that while Mrs. Stafford-Smyth was living, she regarded Celia Prescott as one of her dearest friends. It was also true that during the time Belinda had lived at Marshall Manor, they had not been invited to the Prescott home. Belinda had heard the ladies refer to times in the past when they had shared dinner or tea at the Prescotts', but it had seemed that Mrs. Prescott was no longer disposed to formal entertaining. "It just takes so much out of one," Belinda had once heard Mrs. Prescott tell Mrs. Stafford-Smyth.

So why now? Belinda asked herself again. *And why me?* Perhaps Mrs. Prescott realized how deeply Belinda was missing their dear mutual friend. Or perhaps Mrs. Prescott herself was keenly feeling the loss. *At any rate, an evening out will be good,* Belinda decided. She attended church services on Sunday and went on an occasional shopping trip, but that was the extent of her outings. Even a beautiful house could become a bit wearisome when she had only the staff to share it with.

Belinda looked at her reflection in the mirror. The dark blue silk was becoming. As Belinda smoothed the rich material over her hips, she remembered a comment Mrs. Stafford-Smyth had once made. "I don't want anyone ever going into mourning black for me," she had said. "When people think of me, I want them to think colah. Brightness, not morbid black. You weah colah—blues, greens, crimsons—you heah me, deah?"

Belinda had laughed at the time. Mrs. Stafford-Smyth had not looked like a lady about to bid farewell to life. But then she had gone—so suddenly. As Belinda studied her mirrored reflection and the blue silk, she thought again of her former employer's lighthearted words.

"I know you would approve, Aunt Virgie," Belinda whispered softly. "But will others understand?"

Belinda sighed. Celia Prescott might not understand.

Belinda rang for Ella. *Tonight I will have my hair styled,* she decided.

Windsor was waiting when Belinda came down. The evening was warm and the air heavy with the scent of flowers when she climbed aboard the carriage. She was tempted to tell Windsor to just drive—anywhere. It was good to be out. It was good to soak in the loveliness of the neighborhood gardens. It was good to just escape for a few moments and forget the heaviness of her heart. She realized she was actually looking forward to conversation around the dinner table—even if the other guests would be three or four times her age. One of the things she dreaded most about each day was eating dinner all alone.

Soon the carriage was pulling up before a wide entrance. Belinda stared at the ornate columns, the blue-gray shutters, the windows long and lean, the lines graceful. It was a pretty house—though not nearly as magnificent as Marshall Manor.

Windsor assisted Belinda from the carriage. "I shall pass the time with Mallone," he informed her. "Have Chiles ring when you are ready."

Belinda gave Windsor a brief nod and was soon being admitted by Chiles himself. Mrs. Prescott appeared in the hallway, enthusiastic and light as always.

"My deah girl," she exclaimed, "how have you been? I've been thinking of you—constantly."

Belinda murmured her thanks and allowed herself to be drawn into the parlor.

"You look just lovely, my deah," Mrs. Prescott went on. "Just lovely. And so right. I know how Virgie felt about black. She called it a 'disgusting colah.'" Mrs. Prescott laughed heartily at the recollection.

"But come, my deah," she said. "I want you to meet someone."

Mrs. Prescott drew her toward the chairs before the fireplace, and a young man rose to his feet. Belinda had not noticed him when she entered the room. And he certainly had not made his presence known. He looked embarrassed about greeting her now. He extended a hand, quickly pulled it back and tucked it awkwardly behind his back, then slowly began to extend it again.

"Belinda, my nephew, Morton Jamison," Mrs. Prescott beamed. "Morton, this is the delightful young lady I was telling you about."

Morton flushed and fully extended his hand. Belinda took it momentarily and gave a customary shake. "How do you do?" she greeted him with a smile. He muttered in return and self-consciously wiped his hand down the length of his dinner jacket.

"Morton is studying at Yale," went on Mrs. Prescott, and Morton flushed a deeper red.

"I see," commented Belinda. "How nice." She attempted an encouraging smile. The young man was really uncomfortably shy. Belinda felt sorry for him and wished to put him at ease.

"Please, please be seated," she smiled and moved to take a chair herself. With a look of great relief the young man sat down.

"What are you studying?" Belinda inquired.

"I . . . I haven't really decided," the young man stammered. "Maybe . . . maybe business . . . maybe law. I . . ."

"Morton has his daddy's business to run—someday," cut in Mrs. Prescott. "Right now he's preparing himself with a broad background."

Belinda nodded. "I'm sure that's wise," she agreed and gave the man another smile.

Belinda found her eyes scanning the room. It would appear that she was early. Other guests had not as yet arrived. Belinda had already decided that she didn't plan to develop the habit of lateness, as Celia Prescott seemingly had done. She turned back to her hostess, who was speaking again.

"I thought it would be nice for you young folks to get to know one anothah, being the same age—and you alone in that big house and all," she was saying. "You must get awfully lonely."

"That's very kind," Belinda said softly. "I do get lonely at times."

"Well, you just count on us—me and Morton, anytime, deah," fluttered Mrs. Prescott, and Morton shuffled uneasily in his chair.

Chiles entered the room, cleared his throat, and announced in a rather high voice, "Dinnah is served, madam."

Mrs. Prescott nodded and quickly stood up. "Well, well, now. Let's go right in."

Young Morton seemed totally confused. He acted as if he didn't know if he was to escort his aunt Celia or the young lady dinner guest. Mrs. Prescott took charge. "I'll lead the way, Morton, and you bring Miss Belinda," she directed. Morton moved to hesitantly offer Belinda his arm, his face red with embarrassment.

Belinda ached for the young man. He was so obviously ill at ease that she could only sympathize with him. She gave him a smile and fell into step beside him.

His build was slight, making him seem shorter than he actually was, Belinda noticed. His chin was sharp, his nose a bit too long, his mouth too large, his eyes squinty and hidden behind rimmed glasses, his hair stiff and awkward looking. These features taken alone would not have been a problem, but combined as they were on the young man, they did not make an attractive whole.

Perhaps he is so unsure of himself because he is so plain, reasoned Belinda, determined that she would do her best to set the young man at ease.

"I thought it would be nice to have just a cozy little chitchat," Mrs. Prescott explained as she took her place at the table and motioned Belinda to her right, the young man to her left. Belinda had figured out by now that she was the only guest, a mystifying fact she did not have time to mull over at the moment.

Sitting directly across from the young man proved to be more unsettling than if she had sat next to him, Belinda decided. His nervousness was even more apparent when he was forced to meet her eyes. As a result, Belinda, too, became self-conscious and found it difficult to converse.

Fortunately for the dinner party, Celia Prescott never seemed to run out of things to say. She chatted endlessly throughout the meal, and Belinda needed only to give an occasional nod or murmur some acknowledgment. But as the evening progressed, it became more and more apparent that the woman had "set up" the dinner as an opportunity for the two young people to "become acquainted." Belinda began to feel more and more uncomfortable.

"A young woman like you, attractive and poised, ought to be married," said the frank Mrs. Prescott. "And it does seem such a pity that you should bear the whole burden of caring for such a big house and estate all on you-ah own. I told Morton heah that one who has had some training in business affaihs should be handling all of that fuss. My word! I nevah would have wanted to care foah the business end of things like my Wilbur was expected to do. So many things to considah. Now—well, I just live heah. The trust takes care of all the details. I . . ." and she rambled on and on.

Belinda was beginning to get the picture. "Oh, I really don't mind the business details at all," she finally had a chance to say. "I do have a reliable attorney. It makes it much easier. And I also have an excellent staff. They can care for the house and grounds quite well on their own."

Mrs. Prescott looked a trifle disconcerted. "But still," she hurried on, "a young woman like you needs a . . . a husband . . . family. Surely you don't want to live all you-ah life alone. Why—"

Belinda smiled. "Perhaps living alone is preferred to living with . . . with an unsuitable mate," she said evenly. Morton shuffled uncomfortably. It was clear he felt he was being discussed. *Oh dear*, thought Belinda, annoyed with herself. *I hadn't meant . . . I only meant . . .*

Belinda felt sorry for the young man and tried to change the direction of the conversation. "Do you plan to travel this winter, Mrs. Prescott?" she asked.

It seemed to take the older woman a few moments to change the direction of her thoughts. At last she was able to respond. "No . . . no, I think not . . . though I really haven't given it much thought at all. I . . . I, well, it's early yet. I often don't make my plans until much latah."

"Have you seen the new play at the theater?" asked Belinda, determined not to let the conversation return to its former topic.

"Yes . . . yes, I have. Twice, in fact," admitted the woman.

"Then it must be a good one," Belinda enthused, glad for something new to discuss.

"Well, not particularly," said Mrs. Prescott. "I often go two or three times—just for the outing. In fact, the play itself was rather mundane, but the company is always good. I enjoy the time out in the evening. It's always nice to be with othah people."

Belinda nodded and was about to make further comment when Mrs. Prescott went on. "And that's why I worry about you, deah. You nevah get out. Morton would be glad to escort you to the play, wouldn't you, Morton?" Without waiting for his agreement she went on, "And there are any numbah of interesting museums and concerts and such that Morton would be happy to—"

"Oh, I have seen most of the museums," Belinda informed them easily. "When Pierre was home, Aunt Virgie arranged for us to go."

Mrs. Prescott's face clouded with the recollection. Belinda remembered that the woman had confronted her friend Virgie about letting her young grandson escort "common help" about Boston. Now she seemed to be trying to set up her nephew with that same young lady.

Mrs. Prescott flushed slightly. "I'm sure there are new displays since that time, my deah," she said with an indulgent smile. "And one can nevah get too much music."

Belinda had to agree with that. She loved the concerts and did miss them.

"Well, for the moment, I am dreadfully busy," she replied with another smile. "I don't have time for concerts or museums or any such thing. I am totally taken with trying to make all the arrangements for Marshall Manor—"

"That's just what I've been saying, deah," the older woman said with a hint of impatience. "Theah is absolutely no need for you to bothah you-ah pretty head with such things. A capable husband could care for all that. Why—"

But this time it was Morton who cut in. "Aunt Celia, I believe that Miss Davis is quite capable of making up her mind if—and when—she wishes to marry," he said with more spunk than Belinda would have given him credit for. "And I won't be available as escort because I am going back to Yale the first of the week."

"You said . . . you said you hadn't made up your mind," Mrs. Prescott shot back at him.

"Well, I have now," the gentleman replied with determination. "And now I believe we are ready for our dessert. Would you like me to ring for Chiles?"

With a disgusted look, Mrs. Prescott reached for the bell, and Belinda gave the young man a hint of a smile and a nod. Her respect for him had just risen tremendously, but a healthy measure of respect was all she felt.

SIXTEEN

Arrangements

Belinda finally received a message from the attorney she had contacted, Anthony Keats. It said simply that he had investigated the possibilities for the use of Marshall Manor and had some proposals to discuss. He would be happy to drop by the house if she'd like to set a time. Belinda gave Windsor a few appointment times and had him call the law office to arrange one. She found herself getting more and more nervous as the appointed time drew near.

Windsor opened the door to the man and ushered him into the library, where Belinda soon joined him. He looked pleased with himself, and Belinda felt her pulse quicken as she asked him to be seated and then took the chair directly across.

"I have done a good deal of looking into the matter," he began.

Belinda listened with anticipation.

"The first possibility that came to mind was an orphanage," he began. Belinda wondered why she hadn't thought of it, but even as she considered it, she realized the large staff an orphanage would require.

"Of course, an orphanage doesn't seem to fit too well with such a decorous house," the man went on. "One would need to completely strip the rooms and furnish them far more simply and sell or dispose of all the . . . the ornate bric-a-brac. You couldn't have children and all of the beautiful things trying to coexist here."

Belinda followed his logic. It was unreasonable to expect children to live in such a setting. It was also very difficult to consider selling off all the things that Mrs. Stafford-Smyth had collected and viewed as a part of her home. Belinda shook her head. It didn't seem like a good idea after all.

"Now, another good possibility," the man went on, "would be a conservatory of sorts."

"A conservatory?"

"Music—the arts," the man said. "She did enjoy the arts, didn't she?"

"Oh yes. Of course," responded Belinda. "But how—?"

"You could set this up for exceptional students. You have the music room for lessons, the library and three or four other rooms to convert to practice rooms. The bedrooms as boarding facilities. It would work very nicely for music."

Belinda sat very still. It was all such a new thought to her.

"Or any of the arts," he continued convincingly. "If you wished to set it up for painting, you could convert the front parlor to a—"

But Belinda stopped him with a shake of her head. She really didn't want to "convert" the house to anything. She was much more interested in using it the way it was.

"Well, you could set it up as a library. This part of town could use a good library. The front parlor would then be a reading room. The dining room and north parlor additional shelf space—" But Belinda was shaking her head again.

"You have already ruled out a museum," said the man, ill-concealed frustration in his voice.

Belinda nodded. To think of the house as an attraction for the curious just didn't seem right to her.

"I really would like it . . . *lived* in. In its present state," said Belinda.

The man sighed deeply. "Miss Davis, to do that, you may have to sell it," he reminded her. "Who would want—or *need*—a house this size? This . . . this elaborate?"

"It's not a good place for children," Belinda admitted. "They couldn't run and play freely. Staffing it would be a problem. I don't suppose it would work at all for children." She was talking more to herself than to the gentleman who sat before her.

But the man answered anyway. "Exactly! And the children are the only ones who would need such a place. Other folks have homes of their own."

Belinda agreed sadly. It seemed that her plan wasn't going to be workable after all.

"You're right," she agreed with a sigh. "It's just the young—and the old—who often need a place to stay."

And then Belinda sat up straight in her chair. "That's it," she cried in excitement. "That's it!"

"I beg your pardon," said the man.

"The *elderly*. We can make it into a home for needy older folks. It will be perfect! They can enjoy all the pretty things. We won't need as many staff members as an orphanage would. They can live in dignity—with the company of others. They can walk in the gardens, sit in the sunshine. They will have the library, the music room. It's perfect."

The man across from her was staring at her face. Belinda felt really enthusiastic over this new idea. At last he nodded slowly. "It might work," he decided. "If handled cautiously, carefully."

"Oh yes," enthused Belinda.

"How many would you consider?" he asked.

"Six? Eight? No more than a dozen," answered Belinda.

"And how would you find the . . . the occupants?" he continued.

"I don't know, but churches—the city—someone must know of older folks in need of a home."

"They would need to be able to climb stairs," the man reminded Belinda.

"Maybe some sort of lift could be built," she suggested.

"It would mar the structure," he cautioned.

"We wouldn't need to put it in the front hall," Belinda countered. "There's plenty of room to put some arrangement off the north parlor or the library. We'll have someone take a look."

The lawyer nodded his head somewhat dubiously.

"What about help?" he asked. "Will your present household staff agree to such a plan?"

Belinda sobered. "I told them that I plan to do something with the house," she said slowly. "I will need to talk with them about this idea. I wouldn't want to do something against their wishes. This is their home, too."

The man nodded. "Do you want me to discuss it with them?" he asked.

"No. No, I will talk with them about the plan. I'd prefer it that way."

"Then I guess we have nothing more to consider until I hear further from you," the attorney said, tucking his sheaf of proposal papers back in his leather case and standing to his feet.

"I will be in touch," Belinda assured him. "And thank you. Thank you so much."

He didn't seem quite as excited as Belinda was.

Windsor was waiting beyond the library doors to show the gentleman out. As soon as the entrance door had closed, Belinda turned to the butler.

"We need a staff meeting—in the north parlor," she announced excitedly. "See if everyone can be gathered in fifteen minutes—and have Potter prepare tea—for all of us. Thomas, too, if he'll join us. No. No—not the parlor," Belinda changed her mind. The parlor was much too formal. "We'll meet on the back veranda." She would meet with her staff in a place where they felt more at ease.

Then Belinda hurried up the stairs to change into a simple gown. She wanted the discussion to be among equals. They had an important matter before them. One that would affect all their futures.

The staff had assembled on the veranda by the time Belinda returned. Some looked a bit uncomfortable and anxious as she made her appearance, but Belinda quickly attempted to make them feel at ease.

"Potter, would you pour, please?" she asked and settled herself on the top step, where she could look up rather than down on her staff.

"Ella, would you pass the cakes, please? And then we can get on with our discussion as soon as everyone finds a comfortable spot."

Thomas accepted his tea and joined Belinda on the step. McIntyre flopped down on the grass at his feet.

Windsor pushed a chair forward for Potter and another for Cook, then rather reluctantly took one himself. Ella and Sarah stood leaning against the veranda rail.

"I told you all that I hoped to keep Marshall Manor the same—but be able to put it to another use," began Belinda. "Well, the attorney whom I asked to look into the matter was here this morning." Belinda could tell she would not have needed to mention that bit of information. The whole household was well aware of the fact.

"Well, he had a number of suggestions. He proposed that we use it as a . . . a music or arts conservatory, or a library . . . or such. But for all those things the house would have to be altered—remodeled. Well, I don't favor changing it."

There were approving nods from some of the employees.

"We talked about an orphanage—" Belinda noticed nervous glances. "But that, too, would involve a great deal of alteration."

Belinda thought she heard sighs of relief.

"To me, the most logical thing would be a beautiful, natural home for the elderly," went on Belinda. "We could house a limited number of those who need homes. The house basically can be left as it is. All the pretty things can be enjoyed. The occupants can stroll the garden paths, bask in the sun on the benches, or sit in the parlors and do handwork. Those who play can enjoy the piano. Or they can read in the library. And, the best part, there really wouldn't be that much we would need to change."

Belinda watched the faces in the circle around her. Their expressions had gone from concern, to doubt, to acceptance in a few short minutes.

Windsor spoke first. "Would the present staff be expected to proceed as formerly, m'lady?"

"All who wish to," responded Belinda. "Of course, we will need more staff. There will be more people to feed—and care for."

A few more faces relaxed.

"T'won't nobody dig in my flower beds," mumbled Thomas.

Belinda laughed. "We'll keep all hands out of your flowers, Thomas, I promise you," she informed him. A few others chuckled along with her.

"But we would need more help in the kitchen and the laundry. And for the cleaning. I guess we should all sit down and take a good look at what will need doing and decide whose duty it will be. Then we will need to find additional staff. But . . . first I need to know your reaction to the plan."

Belinda let her eyes travel from face to face, but no one volunteered an opinion.

"Windsor, what do you think of the idea?" Belinda finally asked.

Windsor didn't hesitate. "Things will nevah be like they were in the past," he said evenly, "and there is no way to change that. I'm sure that after all consideration, the plan you have chosen is the best possible one, m'lady."

"And you'll stay on in your present capacity?"

Windsor nodded. "Yes, m'lady," he agreed.

"Good!" Belinda exclaimed, her relief evident. "Potter?"

"I couldn't leave the old house aftah so many years," the woman acknowledged, close to tears. "I'll stay."

"Thank you," said Belinda. "Cook?"

The woman just nodded, looking as though her feelings were too close to the surface to trust herself to speak.

"Sarah?"

"I've been meanin' to talk to you, miss," replied Sarah, blushing deeply. "I . . . I'm planning to be married . . . soon. I won't be staying on in any case." She lowered her face and moved one foot nervously across the veranda boards.

"Why, Sarah," exclaimed Belinda, rising quickly to her feet, "how wonderful! I am so happy for you." And she went to give the girl a hug. The whole group seemed to pick up the excitement, and a murmur ran through the staff.

It was a few moments until Belinda continued. "And you, Ella? You aren't getting married, too, are you?" she teased.

Ella blushed. "Not as I've been informed, miss," she answered good-naturedly. "I'll be glad to stay."

"And, Thomas—you and McIntyre will remain caring for the grounds?" Belinda said with a straight face but a twinkle in her eye.

The old gardener grinned, but McIntyre only stirred slightly and rearranged his head on his paws.

Belinda looked back at her staff. "I am so thankful . . . so relieved," she informed them sincerely. "You have all been invaluable to Mrs. Stafford-Smyth . . . and to me. I don't know how the house would ever manage without you." She paused, then said, "Now we will need to do some careful planning. Potter, I will want to talk to you at length about the staff requirements. And, Cook, I will need your help with who else will be necessary in the kitchen. We have so much to do, but at least now we know how we should proceed. Thank you. Thank you all so much."

After giving Sarah one more hug, Belinda nodded to the little group that they were free to go about their business.

The next weeks were busy ones at Marshall Manor. There were many decisions to be made, so many needs to be taken care of.

A contractor came to assess the possibility of a lift. He laid out a workable plan for the back hall at the end of the big library. The arrangement would work well both upstairs and down and not disturb the appearance of the house. He began the installation immediately. Belinda decided she would be very glad when the construction was over and the mess cleaned up. She could tell that Potter would be even more relieved. The housekeeper was nearly frantic during the building of the lift, trying to keep the dust out of "her" house.

After several discussions, it was decided that the house could accommodate ten residents without destroying its charm and character. Belinda hoped it wouldn't be too difficult to find the ten.

Legal papers had to be drawn up to cover all possible eventualities. Belinda had never seen so many forms and documents. She had dreams of smothering in stacks of papers, struggling to get a breath of air. The whole procedure turned out to be an exhausting as well as an exhilarating one. Belinda prayed for the day when it all would be settled and she would be free to return to her own home.

SEVENTEEN

The Unexpected

Belinda dressed carefully in her gray suit and pinned her hat securely on top of upswept hair. She inspected herself in her mirror, hoping she looked mature and responsible. She did not look forward to another trip to the law office. Her days seemed to be filled with legal documents and decisions. She was getting most weary of it all.

Will it never end? she wondered for the hundredth time. She really wished Mrs. Stafford-Smyth had left the responsibility of her estate to the rightful heirs, her grandsons. Then Belinda told herself, *Aunt Virgie was always so kind to me. Surely I can do this small kindness in return.* Belinda turned from her mirror and went down to see if Windsor had brought the carriage.

Belinda reminded herself as she looked about at the lovely autumn colors that this would be her last fall season in Boston. If things proceeded as she hoped, she would be out west, back in her prairie town, before another winter set in.

Belinda sighed deeply. She was so looking forward to getting home. She knew there would be many adjustments. She had left home Belinda Davis, young girl. She was going home as Belinda Davis, mature woman. She had done some foreign traveling, she had enjoyed cultural experiences in music and theater, her manners had been refined to eastern standards—and she had grown up. It would be very different for her in her hometown. She would need to find herself a new spot in the community and in the church life. *But I will do it,* she told herself firmly. She would do it because she didn't want to lose all the worthwhile things her small-town roots had given her. Family. Deep friendships. Faith. Love. Acceptance. A regard for fellowmen not based on position or possessions. Belinda longed to return to the simple absolutes that had framed her growing-up years.

When they reached the law office, Windsor helped her down and promised that he would return on the hour. Belinda shook the wrinkles from her skirts, lifted a hand to be sure her hat was properly in place, and began the climb to the law office on the second floor.

"Good afternoon, Miss Davis," a male receptionist addressed her. She had been in touch with this office so often she was now known by name. She nodded and offered a greeting in return.

"Mr. Keats will be with you shortly," he said. Belinda moved to a chair in the waiting area and sat down.

Are we really getting any nearer to finishing all these arrangements? she asked herself as she pulled off her gloves. *Each time I think the end should be in sight, some new decisions and more papers are needed. Oh, I hope this will all be over soon.*

"Miss Davis," Mr. Keats summoned her into his office. He was beaming, and Belinda hoped it meant much had been accomplished.

"Well, I believe we have all these documents sorted out and ready for your signature," he began and Belinda felt a burden start to lift from her shoulders.

"You say you have the necessary staff in place?" Mr. Keats questioned.

"Well, not totally," Belinda answered. "We have the kitchen help, extra day staff for the laundry and cleaning, but I still need an assistant for Potter."

"Potter? Oh yes. She's your housekeeper."

Belinda nodded. "She's done it all herself in the past—but now with so many decisions and the shopping and all the detail work, she will need someone else to supervise the staff. I have interviewed a number of women, but so far none of them have seemed suitable."

"Well, staff can certainly be a problem," he nodded and spread some sheets before Belinda. "Now, we need your signature on these papers," he continued briskly. "This is to set up the trust fund from which all expenses for the operation of the manor will be paid."

Belinda nodded and took the pen he offered.

"Now, when you draw funds from this account—" the attorney began.

"Oh, but I won't be the one drawing the funds," Belinda interrupted.

Mr. Keats stopped, a shocked look on his face. "What do you mean?" he asked. "We have set up the funds to be self-perpetuating, so that funds will be available for the continued support of the house."

"Oh yes," replied Belinda. "That is exactly as I wished, but I won't be the one paying the monthly accounts. I won't be here, you see."

"Not here?"

"I will be leaving for home just as quickly as we can get things settled. I thought I had told you."

The man looked chagrined. "Well, I . . . I recall some talk. But I thought . . . I guess I thought you had changed your mind. Nothing has been said about your leaving for some time—"

"Oh no," Belinda assured him. "I have not changed my mind. I wish to leave as soon as possible."

"I see," said the man, but there was a deep frown across his brow.

"Is that . . . is that a problem?" asked Belinda.

"Not a problem. We'll have to set things up differently, that's all."

"How . . . ? What will need to change?" Belinda felt her heart sink in frustration.

"Well, a trust. A board. I'll need to do some looking into it."

"Oh, dear!" cried Belinda. "I'd so hoped we could finish it all today."

The attorney shook his head. "The way we have it set up now won't do if you are to appoint someone else to administer the estate," he stated simply. "This was arranged for you to have complete charge of the affairs and to administer them accordingly."

He pulled the papers back and stacked them carefully together out of reach of Belinda's pen.

"Will . . . will it take long?" Belinda asked, her tone agitated.

"That depends. We will need to look into how to set up the administration to best care for the institution and the affairs of the estate. I will need to do some looking into possible alternatives. It would have been much simpler, of course, if you had chosen to run things yourself. But . . . I'm sure something can be worked out."

Belinda was discouraged as she left the attorney's inner office. There were to be more dealings, more decisions, more frustration.

"Good day, Mr. Willoughby," Belinda said, glancing toward the receptionist as she moved toward the stairs. But she saw he was not alone. A tall man, his back to Belinda, was leaning over the desk, discussing some papers.

"Oh, excuse me," Belinda apologized. "I didn't realize—"

But she stopped short. There was something familiar about the man. And then he straightened and Belinda saw one sleeve of his suit coat pinned up.

Can it possibly be? Belinda's heart gave a sudden lurch. Somehow she knew who it was even before the gentleman turned to look at her.

"Drew?"

The man wheeled sharply, his eyes searching the face of the young woman before him. "Belinda! Belinda Davis! Why . . . why . . . ?"

"What are you doing here?" Belinda asked in amazement.

He had taken a step toward her, his hand going out to take hers.

"It *is* you!" he said, shaking his head in wonder. "It truly *is* you! I thought I must be dreaming."

"What are you doing here?" Belinda asked again.

"I . . . I work for this firm," he responded. "And you?"

"You . . . you work *here?* Why . . . why haven't I seen you before? I've been in and out of this office almost daily it seems for . . . for just *forever.*"

"You have?" Drew said in surprise. "You mean . . . you've been *here?* In Boston?"

"I have been for three years," Belinda informed him.

"I can't believe it! Here we are . . . in the same city, so . . . so close to each other and never knowing it. Why didn't someone tell me?"

"I . . . I had no idea where you were," Belinda explained. "My folks said you were somewhere in the East—training, but they never did say where. I don't know that they even knew."

Drew had still not released her hand. "I can't believe this," he said, shaking his head. "We . . . we have so much catching up to do."

Belinda felt suddenly shy. She withdrew her hand discreetly and fingered her gloves. "Yes," she agreed, the color warming her face, "we do, don't we? Why, I know nothing about . . . about what you are doing now or your . . . your . . . situation," stammered Belinda.

"Are you in a hurry?" asked Drew, and Belinda shook her head.

"Then how about a cup of tea together so we can catch up a bit? I have a few minutes."

"Oh, could we?" Belinda quickly answered. "That would be so nice. I need a friend . . . someone I can talk to," she said. She was embarrassed to feel tears stinging her eyes.

"Is something wrong?" Drew asked quickly and reached out his arm toward her.

Belinda took one step back and shook her head. "No . . . no, not really. I've just had too many decisions to make in too short a time. I'm . . . I'm fine."

Drew nodded, then turned to look at the man at the desk. "Mr. Willoughby, I'm going to be out for half an hour or so. Miss Davis is a friend from home."

Mr. Willoughby, who obviously had missed none of the exchange, nodded silently and turned his eyes back to the paper before him. Drew Simpson took the arm of Miss Davis and led her toward the door.

"I still can't believe this," Drew was saying. "Imagine, you in Boston."

Drew escorted Belinda to a small tea shop and settled her at a table. "Now," he said, "we don't have nearly enough time, so we will have to talk fast."

Belinda smiled. She no longer felt desperate—or lonely—or shy. She was so glad to see someone from home. She was so glad to see Drew.

"I heard that you visited home a while ago," she commented.

"You were home?"

"Just shortly after you were. I was sorry to hear about your father."

Drew nodded and Belinda saw the grief on his face. "It was a real shock," he said. "To all of us."

"How is your mother?"

"She's . . . she's fine. She still has Sid, but I'm afraid she never has really adjusted to country living. Still wants Sid to get more education. I've been trying to think of some way . . . but so far . . ." Drew shrugged, then changed the subject. "But tell me, what are you doing in Boston?"

They were momentarily interrupted while the waitress set their tea before them. As soon as the girl moved on, Belinda smiled. "Well, it's rather a long story," she said, "but I will save you all the details. My nursing brought me here."

"You nurse in a Boston hospital?"

"No. No, I nursed privately. For an elderly woman but . . . she is gone now. I'm trying to get the estate settled. That's why I was at the office today."

"I see," said Drew. "So you went right to the top?" he smiled teasingly.

"To the top?"

"Mr. Keats. He's the senior partner."

"I didn't know that," Belinda admitted. "All I know is that settling an estate is an everlasting chore. It seems I've been in and out of the office so often that I should have part ownership."

Drew laughed. "That's how most folks feel by the time they have sorted through legal papers," he admitted.

"But you . . . what are you doing?" began Belinda. "You said you work there. Doing what?"

Drew smiled again. "Exactly what I was told to do, Belinda Davis. If you remember—practicing law."

"You mean you . . . you practice law . . . with them?"

Drew nodded.

"I'm so glad you were able to get your schooling—that you have done your training," she hurried on.

"Finally! Though there were times when I thought I'd never make it, I now am a member of the firm Keats, Cross and Newman. Though my name doesn't appear on the shingle yet."

"That's wonderful!"

Drew sobered. "It is," he admitted. "And I've never forgotten who made me believe in my dream."

Belinda flushed and toyed with her teacup. "I—we've been out of touch for so long, I guess I don't know much about . . . about how you've been."

"Nor I you," he admitted. "I've been calling you 'Miss Davis,' but I know it's highly unlikely you haven't married."

Belinda shook her head. "I haven't married," she said simply.

Drew smiled.

There was silence for a bit.

Belinda broke it. "And you?"

Drew shook his head.

It was Belinda's turn to smile.

"How are your folks?" Drew said, lessening the emotional tension at the table.

"Fine. They said you had called. They were pleased. And Luke was . . . was glad that there is . . . that you have no . . . no hard feelings."

"I like your brother Luke," Drew said slowly. "I hadn't realized what a special man he is until I talked to him this last time I was home."

Belinda felt her eyes mist over. "I think he's special, too," she admitted.

They chatted on for some minutes, talking of the hometown they both knew. Belinda didn't want the little visit to end. And then Drew pulled a watch from his vest pocket to check the time. "I hate to say this, but I must get back," he told her, and Belinda couldn't keep the disappointment from her face.

"We won't lose touch again, will we?" he went on. "I mean . . . now that we know we are both in Boston . . ."

"Oh yes. Let's keep in touch," Belinda said. She was embarrassed that it sounded a bit too eager.

"You have a telephone?"

Belinda nodded and Drew pulled a small pad and pencil from his pocket. Belinda dictated her number.

"I'll be in touch," he promised.

Belinda waited while Drew paid for their refreshments and walked with him back toward the office.

"How will you get home?" he asked her.

"Windsor will soon be here to pick me up," she informed him.

Drew didn't ask who Windsor was, and Belinda didn't think to explain.

They had almost reached the law office when Belinda had a sudden inspiration. "Would you . . . could you . . . I mean, would it be possible for you to take . . . to take my—what do you call it—legal . . . legal case?"

Drew smiled at her fumbling but shook his head. "Mr. Keats, senior partner, is working for you," he reminded her. "I'm just one of the juniors of the firm."

"But you're my friend!" Belinda responded.

"Mr. Keats would say that's all the more reason for me to refrain from acting on your behalf."

"But . . . but couldn't you just give advice . . . counsel?"

"I wish I could," said Drew sincerely, reaching to take Belinda's hand. "I do. Really. But it's one of the rules of the firm. No interference of any kind with another attorney's client."

Belinda shrugged. She had so hoped to be able to talk things over with a friend. However, she did understand Drew's sensitive position.

"Very well," she smiled. "I promise not to plague you about my . . . my legal tangles."

Drew smiled. "Who wants to talk 'legal'?" he asked lightly. "We have too much other catching up to do."

Belinda forgot her worries momentarily and nodded in agreement. "You'd best run—before you get yourself released from your position," she countered.

Drew pressed her hand. "I'll call," he promised, and then Belinda was standing on the sidewalk alone, looking down the street for the carriage and Windsor.

EIGHTEEN

Friendship

All the way home Belinda marveled at her new discovery. *Drew is in Boston!* she told herself over and over. Drew had not married. Drew was . . . was all that she remembered him to be, and more. Belinda feared and blushed by turn. *Is it possible,* she finally allowed herself to wonder, *that after all this time Drew might still feel something for me? Is it possible that I still feel something for him?*

The quickening of Belinda's pulse at the very idea made her realize that the latter was more than possible. It was very conceivable. She scolded herself for her silly schoolgirl attitude and tried to calm her feelings.

But each time she determined to corral her churning thoughts, they somehow escaped and returned to Drew. What might have happened if she had discovered three years ago that they shared the same city? She didn't even dare think about it.

Well, I know now, thought Belinda. *So what does the future hold?* Again Belinda felt her cheeks warm and pushed the thought aside. She dared not dwell on it. She would take things one step at a time. God knew whether it was a good idea or not for Drew and her to be more than "friends from back home."

Belinda tried to turn her attention back to the muddle with the estate, but even the ponderous proceedings now failed to dim her spirits.

I must invite Drew over for dinner. It'll be so nice to have someone to talk to. To really talk to, she concluded, her eyes bright.

I can hardly wait to write home. Won't Ma and Pa be surprised? Belinda's plans continued. They had no idea Drew was here in Boston. "He is with a good firm," they had said. "Doing well." *But no one knew he was practically my neighbor.* Belinda smiled at the thought.

I wonder where he goes to church? she mused. *I must ask him to go with me one day. Maybe we can even—*

Then Belinda again tried to contain her whirling thoughts. *I'll be so busy getting all the estate's affairs in order that I will have little time for other things,* she reminded herself.

Well, Drew is busy, too, she explained to herself. *But he must have some weekends. At least Sundays. We can go to church together and have dinner and talk,* she reasoned.

But first . . . first she would have to await his call.

Belinda hoped with all her heart that she wouldn't need to wait too long.

Drew called that evening. Belinda had told herself all afternoon that she could not even hope for a call so soon, but still she found herself straining to hear the ring of the telephone.

When the telephone did ring, it gave her such a start that she nearly jumped from her chair. She did drop her needlework and was glad no one was there to see her scrambling to pick it up again.

After all, she scolded herself, *the call could be someone else . . .* all the while hoping that it wouldn't be.

Belinda tried to look calm and sedate when Windsor announced that she was wanted on the hall telephone. She laid aside her embroidery and walked slowly and with dignity to answer it.

"Hello," she said in what she hoped was an even voice. "Miss Davis here."

"Belinda," his voice quickly came back over the wire. "I was still afraid that I'd dreamed the whole thing."

Belinda laughed softly.

"How are you?" he asked, and she had the impression that it was much more than a pleasantry.

Lonely, she wished she could say. It would be a truthful answer. But instead she said what she felt was expected. "Fine."

"You were a bit down for a while this afternoon, I felt. Have you got it all sorted out now?"

Belinda could have said truthfully that she had sorted out nothing but that it no longer seemed so important. Instead, she answered, "I'm sure it will all work out. I guess I get too impatient."

"It's hard . . . waiting," responded Drew. "I'm not good at it, either."

There was a moment's silence and then Drew went on with a chuckle. "Which is why I called. I know this is . . . is presumptuous, but I was wondering if you might be free sometime this weekend."

Belinda could not truthfully say that she had to check her engagement calendar. In fact, she did not even have an engagement calendar, so she didn't play any little game. Instead, she said honestly, openly, "I have no plans—other than church on Sunday."

"Good! Then would you like to take in a concert with me on Saturday night?"

"I'd . . . I'd like that very much," she replied simply, her heart racing.

"I wish I could ask you for dinner, too, but I have to work. We've a case coming up, and I've been asked to spend Saturday at the office getting ready for it. I'm afraid I will be able to make it only to the concert . . . this time."

"The concert sounds wonderful," Belinda told him.

"I should have waited until I could make it a proper evening . . . but . . . well, I didn't wish to waste any more time. I still can't believe we've lived in the same city for three years without knowing it."

"If you need to work, why don't I meet you at the Opera Hall?" suggested Belinda.

"Oh, but I hate to—" began Drew.

"I wouldn't mind, really. It would be no trouble at all for me to arrange to meet you there."

Drew was still hesitant.

"Really," insisted Belinda.

"You're a great sport," commented Drew. "But it hardly seems like the proper way to treat a young lady."

Belinda laughed. "Well, this young lady doesn't mind a bit. Honestly. I would rather you took a few minutes for a proper meal than to have to quickly dash home and over here to collect me."

"Thanks, Belinda," Drew finally agreed. "I will meet you there, then. Say, eight o'clock. By the east balcony stairs. You know where I'm referring to?"

"Yes. The one near the water fountains."

"Right!"

"Fine. Eight o'clock by the stairs."

Belinda was about to say good-bye when Drew stopped her. "But wait," he said. "If you have one conveyance there, and I another, how will I take you home?"

"Well," she laughed, "I guess I will come home the same way I went. That will save you a trip across town."

"You don't mind?"

"No, I don't mind. It will be nice to enjoy a concert. It's been ages since I have gone. Not since Aunt Virgie—Mrs. Stafford-Smyth—passed away."

"I'll see you there," Drew said and bade her good-bye.

Belinda lingered thoughtfully in the hallway after hanging up the phone. She couldn't believe that after all these years, she was actually going out for an evening with Drew. She, too, thought it seemed like a dream. A wonderful dream.

Maybe . . . just maybe this is the reason I could never feel anything for Jackson or Rand. Maybe, in the back of my mind, I have always felt like my heart . . . that I sort of . . . belonged to Drew.

She blushed at the thought and hurried in to snatch up her needlework. But she could not concentrate. Eventually she rang for Potter.

"I believe I'll make an early night of it, Potter," she explained. "Don't bother with tea later."

Potter nodded, then asked with concern, "You aren't comin' down with somethin' are you, miss?"

"Oh no. No. Nothing like that. It's been a long day. The attorney still has us tied up in legal wrangling. I guess I feel a bit edgy."

Potter still looked worried.

"It'll all sort itself out, I'm sure," Belinda smiled.

"I was thinking of *you*, miss—not the house. You look rather flushed," Potter responded, and Belinda was surprised. The older woman sounded so genuinely concerned.

"I'm fine. Really," she insisted, knowing why her cheeks were rosy. The housekeeper nodded and turned to leave.

"And, Potter," Belinda called, "on Saturday night I would like dinner a bit earlier. I'll be going out. Could you inform Cook, please?"

Potter nodded, her eyes brightening with unasked questions. "Very well, miss. What time?"

"Around six, I should think."

Potter nodded again.

"Good night, then," said Belinda, giving the matronly woman a smile.

"Sleep well, miss," replied Potter, and Belinda smiled again as the woman left the room. She planned to do just that.

But she didn't. Her mind was far too busy with many things, not the least of which were mental pictures and imaginary conversations with an old friend by the name of Drew Simpson. She finally rose, wrapped herself in a blanket, and sat by the window in her darkened room looking out over the moonlit garden. Then she began, "Dear Lord, you know what I am feeling right now. . . ."

Belinda was in a tizzy on Saturday. She was so restless she couldn't settle down to any of her appointed tasks. She felt annoyed with herself. "After all, it's just a concert with an old friend," she told herself. But try as she might, her heart would not accept the logic of her mind. She finally fled to the gardens and Thomas for some kind of diversion.

Thomas was busy cleaning the flower beds of debris and fallen leaves. The fall flowers were the only ones blooming now. Thomas always liked to have everything nice and tidy long before the winter storms visited the manor property.

"Your mums are beautiful, Thomas," Belinda said, bringing a smile to the old man's face.

"It will soon be time to work with the bulbs," stated Thomas. "Seems every yeah speeds by just a little fastah."

Belinda nodded, though she herself had felt that this year was particularly slow.

"Just bloom and it's time to cut them back," Thomas was saying gloomily. "The season flies by so fast you scarcely get to enjoy them." Belinda thought she knew how the old man felt.

She lingered for a few minutes, patted the head of the docile McIntyre, and then wandered off down the path. There were still plenty of pretty things to see. She would miss the gardens. Probably even more than she would miss the house with all its pretty things.

Belinda managed to tick a few more minutes from her day as she dallied, but soon she could endure no more wanderings and hastened back to the house to study the clock again.

At last she allowed herself to retire to her room to choose her dress for the evening. She pulled gown after gown from the closet and studied them and then hung them back. Drew might judge some of her silks and satins too elaborate for a country girl. On the other hand, she didn't want to look plain and dowdy, either. She looked at another gown, studied that one, and debated it all over again. It did serve to fill in a few more minutes of the long day.

At last Belinda selected a green gown with classic lines. *It has style without being fussy,* she reasoned. *With some simple jewelry and my hair fixed, I'll fit in nicely with the concert crowd and be well dressed without being "showy."* Belinda nodded in satisfaction as she laid the dress on her bed and prepared for a bath.

She had not called Ella to help with grooming preparations for some time, but she allowed herself the luxury of ringing Ella now—partly because she needed someone to talk to. She feared she might fly apart if she didn't have some way to release a little of her pent-up excitement.

Ella responded immediately to the ring. "Yes, miss?"

"Would you draw me a bath, please, Ella?" Belinda requested. "The jasmine scent, I believe. And then I would like you to fix my hair. I am attending the concert tonight with an old friend."

Belinda saw the flutter of curiosity and excitement in Ella's eyes, but the girl avoided asking the questions she obviously would have liked to ask. "Yes, miss," she said again and went to comply.

"It's been a long time since you've been to a concert, miss," Ella dared to say as she came out of the bathroom.

"Yes," agreed Belinda. "A very long time."

She pinned her hair up so that it wouldn't get wet. "I'm quite looking forward to it."

Ella nodded, a smile on her lips.

Then Ella became almost unforgivably bold. "Is your friend visiting in town?" she asked.

"No."

"She lives here?"

"He," corrected Belinda. "He."

"Oh," responded Ella, looking pleased with the information she had ferreted from her young mistress. "I thought maybe it was someone from your hometown."

Belinda could not hide the excitement in her voice. "Oh, he is. But he's in Boston now. He has been here for years, and I didn't even know until the other day. He is an attorney—with the same firm that has been doing my legal work. Can you imagine? Neither of us knew that the other was in the city. We just happened to meet last Thursday."

By now Ella was smiling broadly. "Why, that's smashing, miss," she enthused. "No wonder you're excited—going to the concert—and with an old friend. How nice!"

Belinda agreed.

"Your bath is ready now, miss," Ella told her. "I'll be back in twenty minutes to do your hair."

By the expression on Ella's face as she went out the door, Belinda could imagine Ella and Sarah whispering together shortly and speculating about it all. And, to tell the truth, the thought didn't even bother her.

NINETEEN

The Concert

Drew was already waiting by the stairs when Belinda found her way through the crowded lobby. He eagerly moved to greet her and offered her his arm as he led her toward their seats. "You make that dress look lovely," he whispered for her ears only.

Belinda smiled at the compliment.

"How was your day?" she asked him.

"Long. But profitable," he answered. "I did manage to get a lot done—though the time seemed to do a lot of dragging."

Belinda certainly agreed, though she did not say so.

"Do you come here often?" Belinda asked as they were seated.

"Oh no. Not nearly as often as I'd like. At first I was much too busy studying. And besides, I had to work when I wasn't in class in order to pay my way through school. I didn't have the money or the time to spend in such places as this."

Belinda admired his honesty.

"How long have you been with Keats, Cross and Newman?" she asked.

"About a year." He chuckled. "So now I've finally earned enough

784

to afford an occasional luxury. I decided about six months ago that I should soak up a bit of culture. So I went . . . once."

Belinda's face showed her bewilderment. "Didn't you enjoy it?" she asked.

"The music, yes. But I simply didn't enjoy going alone."

Belinda nodded. "I feel the same way," she admitted. "I have not even gone once since Aunt Virgie died."

"Well, now we have each other's company," Drew said with a smile. "Shall we come every week?"

Belinda smiled back. She wasn't sure if Drew really was expecting an answer or was just teasing her.

The orchestra began to warm up and it became difficult to talk. Drew leaned closer and whispered, "This is the one part of the concert I would gladly forego. Makes one wonder how such a dreadful noise could ever all come together to make any kind of music."

Belinda chuckled at his little joke, feeling close and contented. It was so nice to be with a friend.

The evening was a total delight to Belinda. Every piece that was played was a "favorite." At least that was how the music affected her. Drew seemed to feel the same way. They nodded to each other, whispered little comments now and then, and thoroughly enjoyed their time spent together.

At the break they left their seats and went for a cold drink. They stood in a shadowed recess of the main hall and sipped lemonade punch and made delightful small talk, getting to know each other all over again. Then they joined the crowd drifting back to their seats for the second half of the performance.

"We must do this again," Drew whispered as the last applause was fading away, and Belinda nodded in dreamy contentment.

"I wish I could escort you home," he continued, frowning in a perplexed way, and Belinda earnestly wished he could, too. It was all she could do to keep from suggesting that she send Windsor on home alone and have Drew drive her. But common sense prevailed. After all, it was late, and Drew must be very weary.

"Would you be interested in coming to church with me tomorrow?" she asked instead and Drew's eyes lit up.

"I'd love to," he agreed.

"Fine. The service is at ten o'clock. The church is on First and Maple. I'll meet you there and then you can come to dinner."

"I would like that, very much," he returned with enthusiasm.

They moved through the crowded foyer and made their way toward the street.

"Windsor said he'd wait near that streetlight," Belinda informed Drew, and he steered her in that direction.

Windsor was waiting as he promised, and there seemed to be no reason to linger. So Belinda bid Drew good-night and thanked him again for the concert.

"Until tomorrow at ten," he said softly, and her heart gave a joyful skip. And then Windsor was clucking to the horses and they were on their way, moving briskly through the city streets.

Belinda had quite a time getting to sleep that night. She went over and over each portion of the wonderful evening. She reviewed each part of the conversation, each selection of the orchestra, each moment of their time together—and then she reminded herself that she must get some sleep if she was going to be at her best the next morning. Even so she had a most difficult time stilling her spinning brain and her beating heart.

The next morning Belinda hummed as she dressed in her most becoming suit and pinned her feather-draped hat on shiny curls. It was a beautiful fall morning, and she looked forward to her drive to church. She had considered walking, but if the wind should arise, it could blow her hair and the feathers on her hat and she would get to church breathless and concerned. So she advised Windsor to bring the carriage as usual.

Drew was waiting on the church steps when she arrived, and she greeted him warmly and led the way into the large sanctuary.

"This is enormous," Drew whispered. "Are you sure you won't get us lost?"

Belinda smiled.

"I've never been in such a big church," he commented.

"Where do you attend?" she asked him.

"A little mission—right downtown. You'll have to come with me sometime."

"I'd like that," Belinda replied. They were ushered into a pew and prepared themselves for the morning worship.

Belinda was pleased to hear Drew beside her, singing the familiar hymns. He had a pleasant voice and was not afraid to sing out heartily. Most of the congregation tended to be rather timid about singing.

The minister's sermon was good—correct in content and flawless in delivery as usual.

The two were greeted at the door as they left the sanctuary, and a few of the parishioners nodded Belinda's way. After all, she had been a faithful part of this church for three years.

"How did you arrive?" Belinda asked Drew.

"I hired a carriage," he answered simply.

"You didn't ask the driver to wait, did you?"

"No. I paid him and sent him on his way."

"Good," she responded. "Windsor has been sent along home, too."

"You're going to walk?" teased Drew. "In your Sunday finery?"

"It's only a short distance," Belinda told him. "It will help me appreciate my dinner."

Drew fell into step beside her. "This is a very nice part of town," he commented as he looked about them. "Your former employer must have been a lady of means."

Belinda nodded. She had told Drew very little about Mrs. Stafford-Smyth. "Did I tell you how I met her?" asked Belinda. "No, I thought not. Well, she was traveling. She loved to travel. Went all the way to San Francisco—'just to see it,' she said. She traveled out by train and on her way home she was taken ill—at our town. They brought her to Luke. She was really very sick. Had suffered a stroke. We didn't know for days if she would make it. But she did. Gradually. When she was well enough to travel on home, she asked me to accompany her. I did because I was . . . well, bored, I guess, and had never seen anything but our little town."

"So you came to Boston," said Drew. "Now I remember, Luke told me briefly of your out-of-town patient. I hadn't realized that you had been with her all this time. You stayed on with her, then?"

"I did. I intended to accompany her here and then return again. But she wanted me to stay on and I agreed. I always thought I would stay just a bit longer because she needed me. She was so lonely."

"Didn't she have family?"

"Two grandsons. But they both live in Paris. Their mother was French. Aunt Virgie kept hoping and praying that they would decide to return to America . . . but it didn't work that way. They both married French girls and settled down over there."

"So now she is gone . . . and you are still here?"

Belinda nodded.

"And you have the affairs of the estate to handle . . . rather than the grandsons?"

Belinda could tell that Drew thought the matter rather strange. It would seem so to anyone.

"She left the boys each a sizable amount of money," Belinda said.

"And . . ." Drew prompted.

"She was a very generous lady. She left her staff each part of the estate, as well."

Drew nodded. "And you have to wait for all the estate to be put in order?"

"Right," she responded with a sigh. "I was so in hopes that it would be taken care of by now . . . but it all takes so much time. We still need to—" Belinda caught herself. "But I promised I wouldn't discuss that, didn't I? Firm rules. This is Mr. Keats's affair."

Drew smiled.

They walked along in silence and then Belinda led the way down the long driveway toward the magnificently appointed home.

Drew's eyes widened. "You're not telling me that this is home, are you?" he asked.

"This is Marshall Manor," announced Belinda. "And I know just how you feel. I felt that way myself the first time I saw it."

"I believe it," Drew murmured, drawing in a breath. "I've never seen a house like this one in my entire life. No wonder it is taking an age to settle the estate."

"I suppose that has something to do with it," she admitted and led the way through the front door to the wide entrance hall. Windsor was waiting to take the gentleman's hat and relieve Belinda of her parasol.

"Come," Belinda said to Drew. "I'll show you where you can freshen up. Dinner will be served in a few minutes."

Drew was studying the paintings in the entrance when Belinda came back down the stairs from her room. "I've never seen such grandeur," he admitted. "I can't imagine what it must be like to live here."

Belinda wrinkled her nose. "I must admit to being a bit spoiled," she confessed. "I found it most difficult to go back to farmyard plumbing on my last trip home."

Drew laughed. "I should think so," he agreed.

Windsor announced dinner, and Belinda led the way to the dining room. The table was a large one to be set with just two places, and Drew mentioned the fact after he had seated Belinda.

"It looks good today," she said soberly. "Usually it has only one."

"You eat in here . . . alone?" Drew asked as the first course was served.

Belinda nodded.

"Couldn't you just . . . isn't there a less formal, smaller table somewhere?"

"Off the kitchen," smiled Belinda.

"Well, couldn't you . . . well, use it?"

Belinda laughed softly. "That does not seem appropriate to the staff," she informed him. "They would be uncomfortable if I did such a thing."

"But . . . but I thought you *were* staff," Drew countered.

Belinda laughed heartily. "I was. It was most strange. . . . Aunt Virgie insisted that I eat with her. She was just lonely, I think, and I was the only staff member who hadn't been brought up 'by the rules,' so to speak. So when she expected me to be at the table, I didn't have the sense to object. At first the other household staff were scandalized by it."

"But now she is gone and you are still at the table," observed Drew.

"That's the strange part. Now they would be equally scandalized if I were to suggest eating near the kitchen with them."

"So you always eat here . . . alone?"

"Oh no. Not always here. Sometimes I ask for my meal in the north parlor on a tray. Or in my room. But *never* in the dining hall off the kitchen."

After asking God's blessing on the food, they began to eat.

"Well, I must say, it's the most delicious food I've tasted for quite some time," Drew admitted.

"Oh, Cook is most proud of her culinary skills," stated Belinda.

Drew was still shaking his head. Then he looked directly at Belinda. "I have to admit," he said simply, "you do look perfectly at home here."

Belinda smiled. "I suppose I've had some practice," she responded. "I felt very much out of my element at first. Especially when Aunt Virgie would entertain. She always had guests her own age, and the conversation was from another world than the one I'd known."

Drew smiled. "I can see the problem," he admitted.

"Shall we have coffee and dessert on the veranda?" Belinda asked later. "Thomas does a wonderful job on the gardens. The fall flowers are still very pretty, but I'm afraid we might not be able to enjoy them for long. Thomas says the seasons come and go so quickly that the flowers scarcely have a chance to bloom."

Drew nodded and Belinda rang for Windsor.

She informed the butler of their plans and fell into step beside Drew.

Drew was just as overwhelmed by the gardens as he had been by the house.

"Thomas is always out here working in them," Belinda informed him. "Every day but Sunday. Even in the rain. In the winter he putters in his greenhouse getting plants ready for the next year's planting."

"Well, he is certainly skilled," Drew commented. "This is the prettiest setting I've ever seen."

"I love the gardens—almost as much as old Thomas does," Belinda said.

"I just can't imagine anyone living like this," Drew observed.

"You get used to it," Belinda replied with a slight shrug.

"'Used to it,' " laughed Drew. "Listen to you. Used to it. As if it were a comfortable old shoe or something."

Belinda joined him in laughter. Windsor brought the dessert and coffee. "I'll pour, Windsor," Belinda offered. "That will be all, thank you."

Belinda could feel Drew's eyes watching her carefully, but he made no comment.

Looking about him at the magnificent home, he pondered aloud, "Seems a shame to have it all pass on to someone else. Someone who might not love it in the way your former employer did."

"That's why I don't want it sold," Belinda agreed. "I just couldn't let Aunt Virgie's house be taken over by strangers."

Drew looked surprised. "It won't be sold? But I thought you said you were busy settling the estate."

"Oh yes. I am."

"Doesn't it have to be sold to give each of the heirs the portion mentioned in the will? You said—"

"Oh, the specifics mentioned in the will were quite apart from the house," Belinda informed Drew. "In fact, all that has been taken care of. That wasn't the difficult part."

Drew looked more puzzled.

"The problem has been setting things up for the house . . . and grounds. I don't want things to deteriorate. It takes a good deal of planning to maintain such a place."

"You have to do all of that?" he asked, astonished.

"Oh yes," responded Belinda simply. "Aunt Virgie left it all to me."

TWENTY

Disappointment

Belinda had no idea the effect her words would have on Drew. The impact of the simple statement took the wind from him as forcibly as the long-ago fall from Copper had taken it from Belinda. Belinda's wealth put an impossible barrier between her and a struggling young attorney, he was thinking with great sadness.

Belinda was still speaking. "It's been a great frustration," she said. "We have gone round and round trying to get things set up properly."

Drew nodded dumbly.

"But finally things seem to be drawing to a close. At least that's what Mr. Keats says. I have another appointment with him next Wednesday."

Drew nodded again. He still had not found his voice.

"Mrs. Stafford-Smyth must have thought a great deal of you," he managed at last.

For a moment Belinda did not comment, and when she did, she had tears in her eyes. "We were more like family than employer and employee," she admitted. "She was so good to me. I miss her very much."

Drew would have liked to move forward to comfort Belinda, but he held himself back.

Unaware of Drew's hesitation, Belinda continued to recount her experiences. "She always missed her grandsons so much," she explained, "but she knew they would never move here to America . . . not even for this beautiful home. So she did what she could to keep it like this." Belinda looked about her and waved her hand. "She gave it to me. She knew I would do all I could to keep it just as it is . . . as much as possible."

Drew nodded, his pain still unnoticed by Belinda.

"It seems like . . . like a lot of house for one small woman," Drew said with a sigh, looking around into the large dining room.

"Exactly," agreed Belinda. "That's why I've decided to share it."

"Share it?"

"With the elderly. We are planning to invite ten older people . . . people who do not have homes or families . . . to live here."

Drew's expression showed his surprise.

"So you see," laughed Belinda merrily, "the dining room table will no longer need to be set for one."

Drew managed a smile. "Doesn't it . . . doesn't it bother you . . . having all those people . . . strangers . . . moving into your beautiful home?" he asked.

"Oh no," Belinda shook her head firmly. "It really seems the only way to do it."

"You mean . . . you . . . you need the income for the upkeep?" he finally asked, feeling awkward about the question.

"Oh no. Nothing like that. There's plenty of money for that. The new boarders won't be charged anything. They will be guests . . . for as long as they wish to live here."

Drew shook his head. "I've never heard of an arrangement like that," he said to Belinda.

"I guess others haven't, either. That's what makes it so difficult to set it up. Even Mr. Keats is hard put knowing how to go about it."

"I see," said Drew. The day seemed to have lost its joy. Drew set aside his cup and stood to his feet.

"Well, I guess I shouldn't outstay my welcome," he murmured.

"Your welcome? Oh, you could never do that," responded Belinda. "Come, let me show you the rest of the house."

Drew politely followed Belinda on the guided tour. The more he saw, the more dejected he became.

"You'll come again?" she asked anxiously when he took his leave.

Drew didn't answer her question directly. "Don't forget you promised to come to the mission with me," he reminded Belinda.

"Oh, I'd love to," she responded with enthusiasm, and Drew's countenance lifted for a moment. But then Belinda added, "I might find some elderly people there who need this home."

Drew, disappointed, nodded solemnly and turned to go.

"But how are you getting home?" Belinda asked him.

"Oh, I'll find a carriage," he said, shrugging his shoulders.

"Nonsense," insisted Belinda, "Windsor will drive you."

Drew began to argue, but it looked as if Belinda had quite made up her mind.

"I'll even ride along . . . if you don't mind," she said with a smile, and Drew agreed helplessly.

Belinda could sense it, but she had no idea why Drew seemed to be withdrawn. She was unaware of the discouraging thoughts racing through the mind of her companion since he had discovered her true situation—that she was a very wealthy woman. Instead, she thought about the wonder of their finding each other in Boston. She was reveling in the fact that they were able to enjoy each other's company. She relived the moments spent together and looked forward to many such happy times in the future.

And then Belinda remembered her plans for going home, and her heart sank within her. It was obvious to her that Drew planned to stay on in Boston. He had a promising future with an established law firm. He would be foolish to give up all that for . . . for a hometown girl.

Belinda suddenly shivered. There seemed to be more than a hint of fall in the air. A strange silence fell between the two sharing the carriage.

"I have discovered several ways that we can go," Mr. Keats began on Belinda's next visit. "But in each case it will involve setting up a trust and administrators."

Belinda nodded.

"The main issue is what kind of trust you wish to set up."

"What choices do I have?" asked Belinda.

"Well, we could set it up under the city administration. They do have a concern committee to care for the homeless. Your proposal might fit into their program."

Belinda considered that.

"Or," Mr. Keats went on, "we could set it up under a church. They have contacts with the needy and could administer it as they see fit."

Belinda spent another period of time thinking of that possibility.

"Or," continued the attorney, "we could set it up independently. A board quite apart from either of those. Self-governed and self-controlled."

Belinda thought some more. "I favor that idea," she finally said.

The man nodded. "One needs to be very careful about choosing the administrators," he cautioned.

"How about an attorney, a banker, a member from the city council, and a church official?" suggested Belinda a bit timidly.

The man nodded. "Good choices," he said, looking surprised. "I would recommend a few more."

"Would you serve on my board?" Belinda dared to ask.

Mr. Keats was obviously flattered. "Well, I . . . I would be honored," he replied.

Belinda felt they had finally made a significant step. The rest of the appointment time was spent in discussing possible board members, and when Belinda left, Mr. Keats had her instructions to make the contacts.

Belinda was hoping she might run into Drew. She wanted to share her good news. And then she remembered that her good news was also bad news . . . at least to her way of thinking. Once the manor affairs were settled, she would have no reason to linger in Boston. She would be saying good-bye to Drew again . . . and this time there was little likelihood that their paths would cross.

I could stay right here and run the manor, Belinda thought. *No one would ask me to leave.*

But in her heart Belinda knew that was out of the question. She needed, desperately needed, to touch base with her roots again—to discover the real Belinda Davis. She had been living in another world—in many ways a fantasy world—for too long. She didn't belong there, and she wasn't even truly happy in that lifestyle. She hadn't been raised to be a parlor pansy in some magnificent Boston home. She was a simple person at heart. She had learned from her parents to think of others—to seek direction from God as to how she could serve.

I definitely have to go home. And Drew will be staying on in Boston. There's no use encouraging anything more than friendship. At least I will say my farewell with some kind of dignity, she determined.

In spite of the resolves made on both sides, Drew continued to call Belinda for engagements, and she continued to say yes to each invitation. They attended Drew's small mission church, as previously planned. Belinda was enthralled. It reminded her so much of the small community church back home. The people were openly friendly, the singing so enthusiastic, and the Gospel presented in such a simple but easy-to-understand fashion. Belinda felt right at home. She told Drew her impressions, and he nodded and smiled, looking pleased that she had enjoyed the church.

She didn't find any elderly in need, though she did ask Drew to keep his eyes and ears open.

They attended another concert, enjoyed a Saturday picnic at the park, visited some local museums, and took long walks. And during the time they spent together they were each silently telling themselves that they were enjoying a simple friendship—nothing more—because the circumstances would not allow for anything else. But within each heart, the feelings were growing more and more intense.

Things can't drag on like this, Belinda told herself as the first snowfall of the year swirled about the manor. *I must get things settled here once and for all and be off for home.*

She spent the morning on the telephone, and by the time she was through, five residents had been secured for the manor. The big house would soon be filled with activity.

I still need help for Mrs. Potter, Belinda reminded herself. *Mrs. Simpson!* she thought suddenly in a flash of inspiration. *Drew would be happy to have his mother here,* Belinda reasoned. *She could help in the house and Sid could go to school.* It seemed like a fine plan to Belinda, and she couldn't wait to discuss it with Drew.

When he phoned that evening, Belinda was quick to put her idea to him. At first he seemed a bit hesitant, but the more Belinda talked, the more he seemed to agree.

"Do you think she would consider it?" Belinda asked.

"I'm sure she would," Drew admitted. "She has wanted to return to the city for a long time."

"But would she mind . . . mind working with Mrs. Potter?"

"Mother was never afraid of hard work," Drew answered. He thought for a moment and then said, "We might even be able to find something for Sid."

"I thought he should be in school," Belinda told Drew. "He could help part-time here at the manor with some of the extra chores and take classes at one of the local universities."

"You have thought of everything, haven't you?" Drew chuckled.

"You think it will work, then?" asked Belinda.

"I think Mother would be delighted," Drew said honestly.

So Belinda sent off a letter with two train tickets and an advance of cash enclosed and held her breath until she received the reply. Mrs. Simpson and Sid would be arriving on the twenty-fifth of November. With a great feeling of excitement she called Drew.

It was a cold, wintry day when Belinda prepared to meet the incoming train. She had first thought she would send Windsor on his own but then realized the Simpsons might be more comfortable being met by someone they knew. Drew had offered to meet the train, but Belinda insisted she had more time for that than he did. "Come in the morning to see them," she invited.

Belinda was glad she had decided to meet the Simpsons herself. Both mother and son seemed somewhat uncomfortable and nervous. Windsor saw to the baggage, and Belinda led the two travelers to the waiting carriage.

"It's cold tonight," she told them. "Be sure to wrap the blankets around you." She passed them two of the heavy blankets Windsor had placed in the carriage and proceeded to bundle herself carefully in her own blanket. The two passengers followed her lead.

She chatted about their hometown and drew bits of information from Sid. He had grown up since Belinda had last seen him, and she was impressed. He had turned out to be a fine-looking young man. Mrs. Simpson was her usual quiet self, although she did answer Belinda's questions.

When they arrived at the manor, both of the tired travelers seemed to come to life in fascination with their new abode. Even Mrs. Simpson made some comments about its beauty.

Belinda knew that the rules had now changed. Potter was the administrator of the manor and as such would need to make all the decisions concerning the staff. And the Simpsons were *staff*, even though Belinda would like to have treated them as her guests. So Belinda wisely turned the two weary newcomers over to Potter, knowing they would be served refreshments and shown to their rooms.

Tiredly, Belinda climbed the stairs to her own rooms. She was anxious for a hot bath and a good rest. Drew would be coming in the morning to greet his mother and brother. Belinda could foresee another heart-wrenching day—the emotional trap to keep her here in Boston at odds with her desire to return to her roots.

TWENTY-ONE

Final Preparations

Belinda had hoped to have all the arrangements concerning the manor finished by Christmastime, but as time went by she began to realize that it would be impossible. She eventually gave up on the idea and started to make plans for Christmas in Boston.

Perhaps it is better this way, she thought. *Potter may need my help during her first Christmas as administrator.* But Belinda secretly wondered if another reason for staying on was to delay saying farewell to Drew.

Mrs. Simpson settled quickly and efficiently into her role as housekeeper. She had several staff under her, including cleaning and laundry services. There would be plenty to do once the manor had all its residents in place.

On December 6 the first two occupants moved in. Mrs. Simpson had their rooms all ready for them in accordance with Potter's instructions, and the two ladies were settled into their rooms and then given a grand tour of the house.

One of the new guests had been a piano teacher in the past, and she was delighted to find a music room and an instrument. The other was very impressed with the library. Belinda found the two women delightful and wished she could ask each one for the complete story of her life.

They deserve their privacy, she reminded herself. *They will tell what they wish when they wish.*

And so it happened. Little by little bits of information came to life as the ladies sat in the north parlor at teatime or before the open fire with their handwork or a book.

Mrs. Bailey was a widow. At one time she, with her husband and three children, lived in a modest home on Boston's south side. Her husband was a drayman until a back injury ended his working days. Mrs. Bailey took on the support of the family by taking in laundry, selling baked goods, and sewing. Then even worse tragedy struck. The youngest child fell into the Charles River and the older one tried to save him. Both children drowned. A number of years later, tuberculosis took the life of their remaining daughter. Then the woman's crippled husband passed away, as well.

Belinda found it hard to believe that one person could endure so much personal tragedy. Yet the woman was still able to smile and to thank God for seeing her through all the difficulties. "And now the Lord has given me time to read and a whole library full of books," she rejoiced, waving a favorite title.

The second woman, Miss Mitton, had never married and had taught piano for many years to support herself. But when the number of students dwindled, she had to move from her neat little apartment to a shoddy tenement in the poorest section of town. The move made her bitter and cynical. Why should one in her position and education be forced to live in such abject poverty? Struggling against her situation, her burden grew even greater.

With a feeling of justice finally being given her, Miss Mitton took up her residence at the manor. She held her chin high to let it be known that she really belonged in this class. Though the woman had never lived in such surroundings in her entire life, she was accepted without judgment. Belinda smiled and humored her. She felt sorry for the little woman who tried so hard to be something she was not.

"I should not be forced to accept charity," Miss Mitton insisted one day as she struggled to hold her teacup daintily in shaky hands. "Fate has handed me some evil turns . . . but I really was born and bred in gentility."

"You were very blessed," Belinda said softly. "Like many of us here, I was not. My home was ordinary, though most adequate. We had love and understanding and proper food and clothing. I guess I learned early that velvets and porcelains are not what constitute a 'good' life.

"But please, let us make one thing clear from the beginning. No one at Marshall Manor is accepting charity. This is *home* for you and each resident. We have invited you to live with us because we want you here. A house is lonely if it does not have family. We are now a family."

Miss Mitton's chin lifted a bit higher, but Mrs. Bailey brushed tears from her eyes.

Belinda made another trip to see Mr. Keats, hoping that things were finally in order. He met her at the door with a broad smile. She took that as a good omen.

"Things have progressed satisfactorily?" she asked.

"Yes, quite," he answered, still beaming at his achievement. "Your board is all in order. They've had their first meeting and have established their directives. The banker and I will handle the paying of accounts— with board approval, of course. The minister and two of the other board members will see to finding the residents as needed. By Christmas the manor should be filled, and you should be free to carry on with your other plans—whatever they might be."

Belinda nodded. The long process was finally drawing to a close.

"I've been thinking," she said. "It would be nice to have a spiritual counselor—a chaplain—for the home."

The attorney looked over his glasses. "A chaplain?" he said.

"Yes," Belinda said, feeling somewhat on the defensive. "To lead the daily devotional times and Sunday services should the residents be unable to go out."

"Have the residents requested a chaplain?"

"No-o."

"Perhaps they are not quite so . . . so religious as you seem to be," stated the attorney frankly.

"But they haven't requested *anything*," defended Belinda. "They haven't moved into the manor demanding this or that. But we do need to care for their needs—physical and spiritual."

"I see," said the lawyer, but Belinda wondered if he really did. Perhaps the attorney was not the one she should be speaking to concerning a chaplain for the manor, she decided. *Very well,* she silently conceded. *I'll talk to God about the chaplain.* To Mr. Keats she said, "We do need a physician. We are dealing with the elderly, and it is common for one ailment or another to need immediate care."

The man nodded. "Do you mean a resident physician?" he asked her.

"Oh no, no. But one should be on call. And should drop by regularly."

"I think we can arrange that with no problem. I will look into it right away."

Belinda smiled her thanks.

"But perhaps it would be wise to have a nurse actually in residence," the attorney went on. "She could care for small problems and call the doctor as needed."

Belinda thought it did sound reasonable.

"I understand that you are—were a nurse," the man said hesitantly. "But, of course, with your position changed so dramatically, I'm sure you wouldn't be interested in such a position. However, it should help you in securing a qualified person."

Belinda knew the man considered her to be a wealthy woman, thanks to Mrs. Stafford-Smyth's inheritance. He still hadn't seemed to realize that she was placing it in the hands of others and would not be drawing from it.

"It's . . . it's not that," Belinda stammered. "It's just that I plan to go home."

"Oh yes," the man said with a nod of his head, but she knew he was still puzzled.

"But I'll think about the situation as you have suggested," Belinda agreed.

All the way home Belinda wrestled with her thoughts. *Is a nurse really needed? Am I needed? Is this God's way of showing me that I should . . . that I can stay on in Boston? Might there be good reason to think that . . . that Drew and I could make a life together after all?*

Belinda felt her cheeks flushing. She did care deeply for Drew, she admitted to herself frankly. But she also realized he had really given her no reason to foster such hopes and dreams. He had been kind and caring and had seemed to enjoy her company, but he had never said or done anything to make Belinda think he might love her.

Belinda shoved aside her dreams and tried to still her pounding heart. It would be wrong, a great mistake, for her to change her plans based only on hopes that Drew would someday ask her to marry him, she knew. That would be a very awkward situation in which to place herself. And also an awkward situation in which to place Drew. *No,* she decided, *I will not build false dreams that might never come to be.*

I must look for a nurse, she decided resolutely, and with determination she set out to find the proper person.

On December 10 three more residents moved into the manor. Mr. Rudgers was a tall, thin man with an untidy mustache and a twinkle in his eyes. Belinda took to him immediately. She could well imagine that his humor was going to keep things lively. His eyes fastened on Miss Mitton almost immediately, and Belinda wasn't sure if he had picked her as a likely target for his good-natured jokes or because there was something in the woman that attracted him. Belinda was sure only time would reveal his real reason.

Mr. Lewis, wizened and bent from illness or the heavy burden of life itself, had no twinkle in his eyes, only sorrow. But he asked for little, accepted all with appreciation, and contented himself with a chair in the corner. Belinda hoped that life in the manor would soon erase some of the pain from his eyes.

Mrs. Gibbons was wiry and talkative. She fluttered about here and there, asking questions. And it turned out that the answers were never confidential information. Mrs. Gibbons was very hard of hearing. "Aye?" she would question, a hand cupped to her ear. "I didn't catch thet." But it was a sure thing that everyone else in the room had "caught" it. Belinda felt that with Mrs. Gibbons to prompt and prod, everyone would be acquainted in no time at all.

Three more guests moved in the week before Christmas. The total was now five women and three men. And on December 21, a marvelous thing happened. A retired minister and his wife came to the manor. Their home had been destroyed by fire and they had no means to rebuild. Belinda sorrowed for their loss, but she felt the couple was God's answer to her prayers.

The gentle old man smiled as Belinda asked him about becoming the spiritual director for the residents.

"God be praised, Nettie," he said, addressing his silver-haired help-mate of many years. "He has given us a home *and* a place of service—not a shelf on which to sit."

Tears traced a path down the woman's softly wrinkled cheeks. "God be praised," she echoed.

Belinda rejoiced right along with them. It was almost Christmas, and with the assigning of the elderly couple to Mrs. Stafford-Smyth's former rooms, the manor residents were all in place.

"Potter, you are in complete charge here," Belinda informed the administrator. "I don't wish to interfere—but if there is any way I can help you with your plans for our first Christmas all together, I would be delighted."

Potter smiled. "I'd appreciate that, miss," she acknowledged. "It has been troubling me some."

So the two of them sat down and plotted out the plans for the Christmas celebration. The menu was left in the capable hands of Cook and her staff.

With the help of Sid, Windsor set up a tree in the parlor and decorated the hall with garlands and boughs. Belinda did the shopping, choosing a simple gift for each manor resident. In future years they could exchange names at Christmas and buy small gifts from their allotted monthly funds.

The long dining room table sparkled with the good china and stemware, and the silver candlesticks held decorated candles. Belinda looked at the table, remembering Christmases past, and concluded that the day would be a special one indeed.

The fact that Drew was coming made the day even more special.

This at first had posed a problem for Belinda. All the staff would be having their dinner in the room off the kitchen. That would mean that Mrs. Simpson and Sid would be eating there. *I can hardly ask Drew to eat in the dining room while his mother sits with the staff in a back room,* Belinda sighed.

But a sudden thought made her brighten quickly. She was no longer the mistress of the manor. There was no reason why she couldn't appoint herself a spot at the staff table, as well. Feeling much better, she went about decorating the staff table. She used good linen from the linen closet, set the table up with china plates, found another set of candlesticks, and arranged small pine boughs and cones. It looked very festive, and Belinda was pleased with the results.

When Christmas Eve arrived, all was in readiness. The manor was filled with residents—only Belinda's personal rooms had not been assigned. Belinda still hoped she could turn over her rooms to a resident nurse, but in spite of her inquiries, she had not yet been able to find one.

Maybe it's foolish to even hope for such a thing, she told herself. *I might happen upon a retired minister, but I'm sure I'll not find a retired nurse. We may need to content ourselves with doctors who are willing to make house calls.*

The manor board was established, the funds available for the continued support of the home, and physicians had been found who were willing to serve the residents of the manor. Belinda smiled softly to herself. She thought of the long, long months of planning and preparation. Deep within, she felt that Mrs. Stafford-Smyth would approve of what she had done.

If only . . . she thought. *If only I had a resident nurse, then everything would be properly in place by Christmas.*

Belinda took one more glance around. Things did look nice. So homey. And it felt homey, too.

From the music room came the sound of Miss Mitton playing some Christmas carols. Occasionally the teasing voice of Mr. Rudgers reached Belinda. *He's at it again, pestering Miss Mitton with his jokes and comments,* she thought wryly. But over the few days they had shared the big house, things had changed. Miss Mitton now giggled in response.

From the north parlor came animated chatter, with an occasional loud "Aye?" from Mrs. Gibbons. Through the open library door Belinda saw Mrs. Bailey with two other residents discussing their respective books. The manor was alive.

I wish Aunt Virgie could see this, Belinda thought to herself. *I think she would enjoy all the . . . the commotion.*

Belinda was about to turn to the stairs when the doorbell rang. She looked about for Windsor, but since he was not nearby, Belinda went to the door herself. Foolishly, she hoped it might be Drew coming to wish her a Merry Christmas Eve. Her heart beat a bit faster as she opened the door.

A tall woman stood there, her coat wrapped tightly about her sturdy body, her hat being held in position against the winter wind.

"Oh, do come in, please," Belinda quickly invited, wondering what errand the woman had.

She moved inside, shook the snow from her clothing, and turned to Belinda.

"I am not expected," she apologized, "but if it's possible I would like to see Miss Davis."

"I'm Miss Davis," Belinda responded. "Please come in."

Belinda cast a look about her. There was really no private place to take a caller. The library and the music room were occupied, and the north parlor was more than occupied. She hesitated and then motioned toward the formal parlor. She believed that it was available . . . at the moment.

The woman just stood and looked at her. "But I was . . . I was told that Miss Davis is the mistress here."

Belinda looked down at the dusty apron that covered her simple frock. She didn't look much like the mistress of such a fine manor.

"I'm sorry . . . I've been preparing for Christmas," she explained with a smile. "The boxes I was digging into were dusty."

She removed the apron and tossed it on the hall table.

"Now . . . Miss . . . Miss . . . ?"

"Tupper," supplied the woman. "Mrs. Tupper."

"Mrs. Tupper," Belinda went on, "how may I help you? Do you have a family member staying with us?"

"Oh no," the woman quickly replied. "I've no connections here." Belinda waited.

"But I was told that you need a nurse," the woman said.

"Yes, we do," Belinda replied quickly.

"I . . . I am a nurse, miss," the woman explained. "I . . . I have all of my letters of reference right here," and she began to fumble in her handbag. "I . . . I must apologize for coming in unannounced . . . and on Christmas Eve. But, you see, it was really my only opportunity. If I don't get the job I . . . I need to take the train back home tomorrow."

"Home?" queried Belinda.

"Well . . . it's not really home . . . anymore. But we used to live in Trellis, my husband and I. He's . . . he's gone now. We had him here in the hospital in Boston, but even with the best care we could give him he . . ." She stopped herself a moment, then quickly changed the direction. "So when I heard you needed a nurse, well, I thought I'd inquire. It's foolish, I know," she admitted, tears in her eyes, "but I hate to go home . . . alone. I'd like to stay on . . . here in the city . . . to be near his . . . his resting place . . . at least for a while."

"I understand," said Belinda, her heart going out to the woman. She moved toward the hallway door.

"Please," she invited, "take off your coat and join the others in the parlor before the fire. They are just preparing for tea. It being Christmas Eve, Cook has prepared something special." Belinda smiled warmly and led the way toward the cozy chatter from the north parlor.

Belinda introduced Mrs. Tupper to the residents in the room and saw that she was part of the group before leaving with the references in hand. She settled herself in her room with a cup of tea and carefully read the pages. The woman was well qualified for what was needed at the manor. Belinda smiled to herself. The last detail was in place. She would welcome the widow to the household and inform her that she had the job. *We have our nurse. And just in time, too!* Tomorrow would be Christmas.

Belinda decided to put the woman in the small bedroom at the end of the hall until she herself could vacate the larger rooms. As soon as Christmas was over, she must lose no time in getting her things sorted and packed.

A new thought sobered Belinda. *There's really no need for me to stay on in Boston now. No need at all.*

TWENTY-TWO

Christmas

Even before Belinda opened her eyes on Christmas morning, she could hear stirring in the house. *What is it?* she asked herself. *Why is everyone up so early? Is something wrong?*

Belinda wrapped a warm robe around her and went to investigate.

But the stirring was only the new family members rushing excitedly about. Belinda blinked in astonishment.

"It's Christmas!" shouted Mrs. Gibbons with glee.

"They are like children," Belinda murmured to herself and then smiled indulgently. It was nice to have them so excited about Christmas. She could well imagine that for some of them this would perhaps be the first Christmas Day that had brought pleasure for many years.

Well, there's little use going back to bed now, Belinda decided, so she pulled back her drapes and looked out upon the new morning, clear and crisp.

The sun had not yet risen, but the wind had quieted during the night, and a blanket of newly fallen snow covered everything. Trees lifted frosty branches like long silver fingers pointing toward the sky.

It will be a pretty morning when the sun comes up, Belinda sighed and caught a glimpse of a silver moon just disappearing on the western horizon.

Christmas Day. I'd hoped to be home for Christmas Day. Belinda's thoughts turned, as always, to her own family and Christmases past.

We'll need both big sleighs this morning to get everyone to church. Belinda's practical side took over. *That'll be so much better than Windsor needing to make two trips.*

Potter, of course, did not insist that everyone attend the morning service, but she had given them the opportunity. To Belinda's delight, all ten residents had decided to participate. Windsor would drive the sleigh he had been driving for many years, and Sid would drive the newly purchased one. Even with the two large sleighs in service, there would be no extra room.

At least we shouldn't be cold, Belinda smiled to herself. *Packed in together as we will be.*

Belinda's presence was not required at the breakfast table. Ella brought a tray to her and she lingered over it, enjoying the fruit and scones that Cook had prepared. It was Belinda's favorite breakfast, and Cook knew that. Belinda poured another cup of coffee for herself and watched the sun slowly climb into the sky, making the frosted trees glow a satiny pink.

It's a lovely day even if it's cold, Belinda observed. *I'm going to enjoy the drive to church this morning.*

Belinda was looking forward to this trip for more than one reason. Drew was to join her there. Then he would return with her for an afternoon of family games and fun followed by Christmas dinner. It promised to be a good day.

Everyone seemed in the best of spirits as each helped the other into the sleighs. Even the quiet Mr. Lewis could not keep a smile from flickering across his face now and then. Belinda was pleased to see him responding to the spirit of the morning.

Behind Belinda in the lead sleigh came Sid in the second one. Belinda waved to him and received a cheery wave in response.

Sid was settling in well to life at the manor. He had enrolled in classes at nearby Boston University and spent most of his time poring over his books. The rest of the time he cheerfully pitched in with whatever needed doing about the house and grounds. There seemed to be no end of ways Sid found to give assistance. Both Windsor and Thomas told Belinda they enjoyed the help and company of the young man. And Ella tittered and primped every time Sid appeared. Belinda could not fault Ella. Sid was an attractive young man and one with courtesy and understanding. And Belinda felt sure that with his ambition and discipline, Sid would do what he set out to do. He was much like his older brother. Belinda smiled.

The church service was full of worship and praise, and Belinda felt her whole heart and soul respond. Drew had taken his place between Belinda and Mrs. Simpson and clearly enjoyed the service, as well. Pride glowed in the eyes of the older woman as she sat between her two grown sons. Things had worked out, after all. She looked sincerely thankful as she participated in the Christmas carols.

"How did you all fit?" Drew asked Belinda as they left the church and prepared to climb into the sleighs for the ride home.

"It was quite merry, actually," Belinda laughed. "Much like the sleigh rides we used to enjoy when I was a schoolgirl back home."

Drew smiled and offered his arm to help her in. "Well, I do hope that no one tries to shove straw down my neck," he said wryly.

"Then don't sit too near Mr. Rudgers," Belinda warned. "He might try—that is, if he had some straw."

"Oh, you have a prankster in the crowd?"

"I have a notion he might try just about anything," Belinda agreed. "Although to this point he's spent most of his energy teasing poor Miss Mitton."

"And how does poor Miss Mitton respond?" asked Drew.

"Well," chuckled Belinda, "at first I don't think she was too sure just what to do. She would frown and squirm and try to stay out of his way. I think she felt that teasing was below her dignity. But then she started to warm up to it. The fact is, I think she is enjoying it tremendously. I would expect that it has been a while since a gentleman paid her that much attention."

"Ah, the weaker sex!" said Drew with an exaggerated sigh. "How subtle they are!"

They all managed to squeeze back into the sleighs and then they were off, the horses blowing and snorting, tossing their heads and wanting to run. Mr. Rudgers waved his arm in the air and shouted, "Turn 'em loose, Windsor!" to which Miss Mitton shrieked like a schoolgirl. Belinda gave Drew a quick glance and caught his wink. The whole atmosphere was like one of children out for a romp, with laughter and teasing and a great deal of good-natured banter. Belinda wondered if the sleigh load behind them was having as much fun.

They returned to the manor with rosy cheeks, stamping their feet and looking forward to hot tea.

"That was a wonderful service," said Mrs. Bailey. "Been a long time since I've been to one as good."

"Wonder where they got that minister," said the straightforward Mrs. Gibbons. "Wonder what happened in his past to take the smile from his face. He was so serious about everything he said. Miss! Miss!" she called, trying to get Belinda's attention. "What happened to that there minister?"

Belinda shook her head. "I have no idea if anything happened to him," she responded.

"Aye?" yelled Mrs. Gibbons. "I didn't catch that."

Belinda was unable to answer again. The commotion in the hall was far too great.

Mr. Rudgers was surreptitiously holding one end of Miss Mitton's scarf, and as she tried to remove it, it refused to be dislodged. Even Mr. Lewis chuckled at the bewildered look on the spinster lady's face.

The clamor finally subsided and the residents were ushered into the north parlor for afternoon tea. Dinner was to be served at five.

Belinda watched as they settled themselves about the room in little clusters, already having formed friendships. It was nice to see them feeling at home.

"Come with me," Belinda said to Drew and led the way to the staff room off the kitchen.

"So you've been relegated to 'staff'?" he teased her.

"And I don't mind one bit," Belinda responded merrily. "You have no idea the number of times I've envied them this coziness. Here they sat chatting and laughing, and I sat all alone in that big dining room wishing I had some good company."

"And to you, good company is . . . ?" prompted Drew.

"A friend," answered Belinda. "Any color, size, rank, or station."

Drew nodded in understanding.

"I'll get us some tea," Belinda said. "Just pull up a chair to the fire-place."

It was a cozy room. The staff spent many hours there. Across one end, just inside the kitchen door, was the big, sprawling table where they ate their meals. At the other end of the room several chairs were grouped around a large stone fireplace. Today a fire burned cheerily. The room, far more than simply a gathering place, was a workroom, as well. Mending was done here. A large mangle iron was pushed up against one wall, and beside it, on the workdays of the week, the clean laundry was folded and sorted on a long, narrow table.

"If walls could talk," Drew said mostly to himself, looking about him, "I'm sure this room has buzzed from time to time as people have worked together here."

"That's an interesting thought," Belinda commented as she went for a tray of tea and biscuits.

"Cook says that's all we get," she laughed when she returned with it. "She's afraid we will spoil our appetites for her feast at dinner."

Drew looked over at the prepared table at the other end of the room. "If it tastes as good as that table looks," he told her, "I would hate to do that."

"Did I tell you the good news?" Belinda said as she poured the tea. "We have a nurse."

"Really? How did you find her?"

"Well, actually, she found us," and Belinda told Drew of the arrival of the woman the night before.

"So everything is about settled, then?"

"That was the last detail to be worked out. I had so hoped to have everything in place by Christmas. And here it is. All set. I can hardly believe it." Belinda shook her head, tears close to the surface.

Drew was silent for several minutes as he sipped his tea. She felt his eyes upon her and turned to meet his gaze.

"You know, you are really something," he said quietly. "Who else but you would take this . . . this beautiful inheritance and . . . and share it with a whole houseful of other people? You amaze me, Belinda. You are the most unselfish person I've ever met."

Belinda's eyes fell before the open admiration in Drew's.

"Please," she said in embarrassment, "don't make a saint of me."

"I mean it," he responded softly. "I admire you . . . tremendously."

"I . . . I'm sure that Aunt Virgie expected me to . . . to *use* the house . . . not just harbor it," Belinda explained haltingly.

"But that was because your aunt Virgie knew Belinda Davis," he insisted.

Belinda shrugged slightly and took another sip of tea.

"That's what I love about your family," Drew went on. "That's the way you all think . . . as though life were . . . were meant to be shared with others. Unselfishness is as . . . as natural as breathing."

Belinda thought about his words. Perhaps . . . perhaps that was true of her father . . . her mother . . . even Luke. She had seen it often, had taken it for granted.

"That was what convinced me there was really something sound about the Christian faith," Drew continued. "I saw it lived and breathed in the form of your father."

Belinda's eyes were now filled with tears, thinking of her family . . . her parents . . . on Christmas Day. She swallowed and blinked away the tears.

"I have been blessed," she said softly. "I know that. I remind myself of it often . . . but"—she smiled through her tears—"it's awfully nice to hear someone else say such kind things about your folks."

There was a movement at the door, and Ella entered.

"Windsor and Sid are on their way from the stable," she said. "Shall I bring in their tea, miss?"

Belinda nodded. "And, Ella, let Mrs. Simpson know so she can join us."

They all gathered about the open fire. The intimacy of the moment was gone for Belinda and Drew, but the chatter and laughter continued. Belinda watched Drew and Sid as they joked back and forth and recognized the joy and pride on the face of their mother. *I'm so glad I invited them here,* she thought to herself. *It has brought Drew so much happiness.*

But even as Belinda thought it, she also realized that she had brought to Boston the only reason likely to draw Drew back to their small hometown. His family.

The rest of the day was wonderful. Belinda wandered through the house listening to the friendly talk and laughter as residents played checkers or chess and enjoyed the music that wafted from the music room. Mr. Lewis surprised everyone when he drew a violin from a worn case and began to play the familiar Christmas carols along with Miss Mitton. He was a bit rusty, his fingers arthritic, and his notes not as clear as they once must have been, but the audience was appreciative and responded with applause at the end of each piece. Belinda could well imagine that the old man and his violin had both found a home.

And then it was time for Cook's Christmas dinner—the guests served in the big dining room and the staff in the staff quarters. Belinda was sure the folks who were gathered around the magnificent table in the formal dining room could not have enjoyed the meal any more than the ones in the simple, cozy staff room.

She wondered if there was just a bit of a strain at first as Windsor, Potter, or Cook would look up to see her calmly sitting among them, but the feeling quickly disappeared as the laughter around the table increased. To Belinda's surprise, she discovered a genuine sense of humor in the dignified Windsor.

After dinner they all gathered together in the main parlor and sang some carols. Miss Mitton was disappointed that she couldn't accompany them on the piano, but there was no way to bring the instrument into the parlor.

Belinda asked Drew to read the Christmas story, and he did so with such feeling that many in the little congregation had misty eyes.

Sid led the gathering in a short prayer, and then eyes and thoughts turned to the gifts beneath the tree. Belinda was glad she had managed to find a last-minute gift suitable for the new resident nurse. Belinda asked Ella to do the distributing, and Ella shyly asked for Sid's assistance.

There were hoots and cries of glee around the circle as each present was opened. *It's turned out to be a truly happy party,* Belinda told herself with deep happiness. Then it was time for the staff to go wash dishes and do the necessary household chores. The manor residents returned to their fires.

Drew turned to Belinda. "This has been the most wonderful Christmas I ever remember," he told her sincerely. "Thank you for letting me be part of it."

Belinda smiled.

"Now I should be getting back. You must be very tired."

"Sid will drive you. He has already asked about it," Belinda informed him.

"I . . . I was hoping for a little chance to talk," Drew admitted, looking disappointed.

Belinda's eyes opened wide. "Of course," she responded, her heart all aflutter. "I'll get my wraps."

"You don't mind?"

Belinda shook her head firmly. If there was one thing she was sure of, it was that she didn't mind having a chance for a talk with Drew.

TWENTY-THREE

Farewell

Belinda's heart was thumping wildly in her chest as Drew helped her into the sleigh. It was a beautiful night for a sleigh ride. The air was crisp and the stars overhead were bright. *Will this be a perfect end to an already perfect day?* she wondered. Sid took his seat up front and lifted the reins. "Okay, big brother," he joked, "is it to be the scenic route?"

Drew laughed and told Sidney to pay attention to his driving. Sid waved a hand good-naturedly and clucked to the team.

The snow crackled beneath the runners as they moved off. Belinda felt like a young girl again, off for an evening of fun and adventure. In fact, she felt about as young and lighthearted as she ever remembered.

Drew tucked the blanket closely about her and asked solicitously if she was warm enough.

Belinda wasn't sure if she would have known if she was freezing, but she nodded that she was fine.

"I really enjoyed today," Drew said again. "It was the kind of Christmas one dreams of."

"It was fun, wasn't it?" Belinda agreed.

"Did you see the faces around the Christmas tree?" Drew asked. "They were like children."

"I suppose this was the first real Christmas for many of them in years," Belinda said solemnly. "Some have come from pretty desperate circumstances. Lonely situations."

"It was hard to remember that today . . . watching them."

Belinda thought again about the day. It had been good . . . *perfect,* she decided.

"I have just one regret," she said wistfully.

"A regret?" Drew placed his arm companionably about her shoulders and pulled her closer.

"The nurse. Mrs. Tupper. I wish I would have offered to take her to . . . to her husband's grave. She is still so lonely. I think if I were in her situation—"

"You didn't know?" asked Drew.

Belinda shifted to look at him in the moonlight.

"Windsor took her to the cemetery," said Drew.

"Windsor?"

Drew nodded.

"How do you know?" asked Belinda.

"Sid told me. He offered to do the driving, but Windsor insisted that the drive would do him good."

"Where was I?" asked Belinda.

"You were busy . . . making all your new family feel at home. It was about three-thirty."

Belinda was speechless for a moment. "Dear old Windsor," she murmured at last. "The more I know of him, the more I love and respect him."

"He is rather special, isn't he?" admitted Drew.

The city streets were quiet, but now and then they passed a house where merrymaking was still in progress. Belinda laughed as they drove by one such house where the music and laughter poured out into the street.

"I guess some people like to make the celebration last just as long as possible," she commented.

Drew's arm tightened about her shoulders. She heard him take a deep breath and her heart beat more quickly. "Belinda," he began, "there's something I need to talk to you about."

Belinda felt she might explode with the intensity of the moment. She didn't trust herself to reply, so she simply nodded.

"You remember when we were kids . . . back home?"

Belinda nodded again.

"You remember how I shot that rabbit and spooked your horse?"

Another nod.

"Well . . . I . . . think I fell in love with you that day."

Belinda could not even nod. She had dreamed so often of hearing Drew say those words.

"And then when I discovered that it was your brother who had removed my arm," Drew went on, "I was shattered. I was so angry about losing it that I couldn't accept you. You were . . . were a part of it."

Belinda felt his grip tighten on her shoulder.

"And then, thanks to your pa, and God, I finally got that all straightened out."

Belinda released her breath and drew in again from the frosted air.

"And then one day I . . . I had the nerve . . . the audacity," and there was a bit of a chuckle in his voice, "to kiss you."

Belinda could feel her face flushing and was glad for the semidarkness.

"I meant that kiss . . . with all my heart . . . but . . . well, I knew I had no business, no business at all, expecting a girl like you to feel anything for me. Still, I couldn't help the way I felt. I wanted to see you . . . to come calling. In fact, I did a number of times, but each time I got only as far as your spring, and then common sense would take over and I'd go home again."

"I never knew that," Belinda said in a whispery voice.

"I knew I had to go away and become an attorney before . . . before I ever had any right to try to win you," Drew went on. Belinda shivered from excitement rather than the cold.

"I wanted so badly to come and tell you good-bye . . . to ask you to have faith in me . . . and to wait, but I knew I couldn't expect that from you."

"Oh, but I . . ." began Belinda with a little gasp but then bit her lip to keep silent.

Drew continued. "Well, I thought I was dreaming that day I met you in the law office. Here I was, an attorney now, and here you were . . . in the same city. It seemed like an answer to all my prayers. I couldn't believe that you had not married. There must have been dozens of young men who would have given an arm to have you." Drew stopped, then laughed at his choice of expressions.

I was waiting for you! Belinda's heart cried, though she made no comment. *I know that now . . . but I didn't know it then.*

"I guess . . . I guess I don't have to tell you that . . . I still love you," Drew said softly. "I suppose I always will. I had hoped, with all my heart, that this time . . . that this time I would have been free to . . . to ask for your love in return. But as I've watched you . . . day after day . . . I've realized . . ." Drew's voice fell and his arm tightened again. "I know now I can't ask that of you. If things had been different . . ." The words hung in the air.

Belinda felt something go cold within her. *No! No!* her heart protested. *Don't say that. Don't!* She wanted to throw her arms around Drew and sob against him. But she held herself upright, rigid, and forced herself to listen to what he had to say.

His voice was low, choked. She could tell that the words were as difficult for him to say as for her to hear. "I love you, Belinda, and as . . . as I can't . . . can't ask, I realized as I watched you today that I . . . I just can't go on as we have been . . . as friends. It hurts too much to see you . . . to keep dreaming. I think it would be better for you . . . for both of us . . . if we don't see each other anymore. You need to . . . to get on with your life . . . and I won't stand in your way."

They were almost to Drew's tenement building. Belinda was sure she would never make it. She bit her lip and choked back the tears. Drew was saying good-bye, she tried to tell herself. *Is it . . . is it because he's heard I'm going home and won't ask me to stay on in Boston? Doesn't he know . . . doesn't he realize that a girl will sometimes gladly change her mind?*

Belinda was on the verge of telling him that he had no right to judge what was best for her, but she checked her impulsiveness. There might be something else . . . something entirely different, something he had not said. She would not put Drew in the impossible position of asking for his explanation. He had said that their lives should go separate ways. She must accept that.

"I think far too highly of you to be anything but open and honest," Drew was saying. "I do hope you understand why . . . why I can't bear the thought of just being friends."

Belinda managed a silent nod. She didn't really want friendship, either.

Sid cried out a loud "Whoa" to the team. Drew pulled Belinda close and tilted her face in the moonlight. "Good-bye, Belinda," he whispered and kissed her once again. Belinda could see the tears in his eyes. Then he was gone, and Sid was calling a good-night to his older brother and moving the team forward again.

Belinda pulled the blankets closely about her, but she could not stop her shivering. She fought to remain calm, though her heart still pounded and her head whirled.

"Beautiful night for a drive," Sid called back. Belinda had no answer. She didn't trust her voice. Sid began to whistle, and Belinda pulled the blanket up around her ears to shut out the sound.

Somehow she made it home. She even managed a good-night to all of those still lingering about the parlor. Then she pronounced it a very long day, excused herself, and headed for her room.

She did not even properly prepare herself for bed but threw herself down on the ornate spread, and for the first time since she had been a small child, Belinda cried herself to sleep.

The die had been cast. There was little Belinda could do about it, she told herself over and over. She arose the next morning, washed her swollen face, and began the job of sorting through her belongings.

She was going home as planned. There was nothing to hold her any longer in Boston.

All morning she sorted and packed. She tossed aside all her fancy satins and silks as they were much too ornate for her hometown. Then she eyed them again and thought of Abbie and Kate. With a bit of remodeling they could make quite suitable gowns out of the dresses. The material was lovely. She changed her mind and packed all but the two fanciest. These she would turn over to Potter. The older woman had a knack with a needle. She could do with them whatever she wished.

There was a rap on Belinda's door, and Ella entered. "No one had seen you about, miss. We feared you might have taken ill or something."

Belinda assured her that she had not. "I've been busy," she informed Ella. "I have so much to do."

The maid looked about the cluttered room and her face fell. "You haven't changed your mind?"

Belinda shook her head.

"I was hoping that you would, miss."

"There's no reason for me to change it," Belinda said, and the words took more effort than Ella would ever know.

"It will just be so . . . so different without you here," Ella went on frankly. "The whole staff had been hopin' you'd stay on."

Belinda looked up from her packing, wondering if Ella had exaggerated. . . . Still, it was nice to hear.

"Things are all arranged now," she reminded Ella. "There is no need for me to stay around," she reiterated.

"Well, 'need' is what, miss?" asked Ella frankly. "Maybe the clothes will be washed and the rooms cleaned, but that doesn't mean that you aren't needed. You make this place seem . . . more like a home . . . to all of us."

Belinda swallowed the lump that threatened to choke her. "That is a very kind thing to say, Ella," she said softly, and when she lifted her head to look at the girl, she saw tears in Ella's eyes.

"I'll miss you, Ella," she said honestly.

Ella blinked away her tears and backed toward the door. "I'll get you a tray, miss," she managed and then was gone.

The day did not get easier for Belinda. The news of her resolve seemed to spread throughout the house and bring a feeling of gloom. It was a compliment of sorts, but Belinda feared the new living arrangement could not tolerate such an atmosphere. She gave up her packing momentarily and went down to try to stir up some merriment.

But Belinda was of no mind to stay on any longer than was absolutely necessary. As the days slipped by, she quietly continued her preparations. She planned to be on her way by the end of the week.

When the day of her planned departure arrived, Belinda drew Windsor aside. "Windsor, I should like to be driven to the station this afternoon," she informed him quietly.

The man's eyes grew big with question. "You still plan to go?" he asked hoarsely.

Belinda nodded. "The train leaves at two," she said matter-of-factly.

"We haven't even had a proper good-bye," the butler said in a tight voice.

"Now, Windsor, what is a proper good-bye? We will say one at the door, when I'm leaving."

"That hardly seems adequate, miss," Windsor dared to contradict her.

"Well, any other kind would just be too painful," Belinda admitted, and Windsor nodded his head.

"It will be painful regardless, m'lady," he told her.

Belinda fled back upstairs to do the last-minute preparations.

When the last item had been tucked away, she drew a warm coat about her and let herself out the back door. She followed the garden paths between what had been Thomas's showy flower beds such a short time ago. Here and there a dry-looking stick acknowledged that something had lived in those beds. The snow covered all else. She was sure she would find the old gardener and his dog in the greenhouse.

"Thomas," she called as she entered the sanctuary. "Thomas, are you here?"

"Over here, miss," Thomas's rusty voice answered, and McIntyre came ambling from that direction to greet her.

"'Tis a mite chilly to be out wanderin'," Thomas observed, and Belinda nodded in agreement.

"It's colder than I realized," she admitted.

"You'll be catchin' yer death of cold," the old gentleman worried, looking at Belinda's feet for the warm footwear she should have been wearing.

"I'm going right back in," she informed him.

She let a moment of silence pass and then spoke again. "I came to say good-bye."

The old man's head moved quickly up from the tender shoot he was grafting onto a rosebush. He said nothing, but his eyes quizzed her.

"I'm returning home . . . as planned," she continued. "Everything is arranged here now."

The old man still said nothing. He laid aside his twig and his tools and looked at Belinda.

"Yer sure?" he asked at length.

Belinda nodded, tears in her eyes. This was not going to be as easy as she had hoped.

"Ye don't plan on being back?"

Belinda shook her head.

"We'll miss ye," he said simply and turned away. It was not fast enough for him to hide the tears in his own eyes. There was silence for a moment. Thomas broke it.

"I have somethin' fer ye," he said and led Belinda to a table at the end of the greenhouse.

Curious, Belinda followed. Thomas reached for a small container, and Belinda could see a plant protruding from the soil. He handed her the pot.

"Mind it doesn't freeze," he cautioned.

Belinda accepted the gift, unaware of what it was she held.

"'Tis a Princess Belinda," he said softly.

"Your rose," whispered Belinda, and more tears came to her eyes. "Thank you, Thomas."

He nodded and reached a hand down to McIntyre's head. "We'll miss ye," he said again.

"And I will miss you . . . so much," responded Belinda.

Thomas nodded. He seemed in a hurry to get the awkward good-bye over.

"Thomas," Belinda said on impulse.

The old man lifted his head and blinked watery eyes.

"Would you mind . . . could I give you one quick hug?"

He moved clumsily to embrace Belinda. He held her much longer than she had anticipated and then they bid a quick farewell. Clutching her precious rose inside her coat, Belinda fled to the big house.

The other good-byes were no easier. She longed to just turn and flee from the house, but she knew she couldn't. She probably would never see these people again. She would miss them all so much. Especially the dear staff. They had been like a family for such a long time. It was difficult to think of life without them.

After Belinda said a hasty farewell to each of the new residents, she turned to the members of the staff. Potter blew her nose loudly on her pocket hankie, Cook let the tears run down her cheeks and then whisked them away with her apron, and Ella openly sobbed. Belinda felt she couldn't endure another minute of the emotional leave-taking. She lingered an extra moment to whisper to Mrs. Simpson, "I'm so glad you agreed to come." Then she gave Sid a hug and hurried out to the sleigh after Windsor.

She continued to blow and sniff all the way to the station. And then she still had to say good-bye to Windsor. "I have no words to tell you how much I've appreciated you," Belinda told the stiff butler, holding out her hand to him. He only nodded as he solemnly shook her hand.

"You've been so kind," Belinda went on.

"I've only done my duty, m'lady," he said with difficulty, "but you served when the duty wasn't even yours."

Belinda was puzzled at his statement.

"I saw the love you gave to Madam," Windsor said frankly. "A love that went far beyond duty . . . and I loved you for it."

Belinda was touched. "You see, m'lady," and Windsor leaned forward slightly in a confidential way, "I've never told this to a living soul before, but . . . I loved her, too. Always!"

Belinda reached up on her tiptoes and placed a quick kiss on the weathered cheek; then she turned and ran toward the waiting train.

How beautiful, she thought as she ran, *how beautiful . . . and how sad. He loved her . . . all these years, and he would have died before he let her know. And just because . . . because he saw them as being from different stations in life.*

Belinda climbed aboard the train with the help of the conductor and settled herself for a good weep.

Men can be so foolish! she cried in desperation.

TWENTY-FOUR

Settling In

The long train ride gave Belinda an opportunity to get herself under control. She needed every minute of it, she told herself. She was an emotional wreck. But as the miles ticked slowly by, she began to put things into better perspective.

Being back in her old hometown would be good, she assured herself . . . back again with her family. There would be many adjustments to be made, she was wise enough to realize, but she was capable of adjustments. She hoped that Luke and Jackson would still need a nurse. Nursing was the only vocation she had. There was no other way that she would be able to support herself—and she certainly did not plan to go crawling home again and be dependent on her ma and pa.

Belinda gently fingered the soft green petals of the rosebush she had carefully sheltered from the cold. Thomas had promised that it would be fine in the little pot until spring came again. Belinda intended to nurture it carefully.

When the train did finally pull into the local station, Belinda climbed down the steps to the familiar platform. There was no one to meet her, for she had informed no one she was to be on that particular train. She made arrangements for her luggage to be held in storage until she could get someone to pick it up.

After setting her rosebush securely in the warmth of the station, she set off for Luke and Abbie's. It was midwinter, but Belinda was hardy. Still, she was thoroughly chilled by the time she rapped on Abbie's back door.

"Belinda!" Abbie squealed and threw herself at her sister-in-law.

Belinda returned the embrace. Ruthie came running to see what the fuss was about.

"Well, look at you!" Belinda exclaimed with a hug for her niece. "My, how you've grown."

Ruthie, well pleased with herself, stretched up on her tiptoes to emphasize the fact of her rapid growth.

"Come in, come in," urged Abbie. "Take off your things. How did you get here? I didn't hear a team." Her words came nonstop.

"Well, I didn't get a ride," she said. "I left my things at the station and walked."

"You walked? In this cold? Oh, Belinda. We'd no idea you'd be coming in or we'd have—"

"I know," Belinda quickly replied. "It was my own doing. I didn't warn you."

"Well, we've been hoping each day for a letter," Abbie rushed on. "The boys have hardly been able to stand it. Every day they come home from school and ask if you've sent your arrival date."

Belinda smiled. She intended to make friends with her young nephews again.

"How are they?" she asked.

"Fine. Fine," Abbie assured her, but Belinda detected a flickering of shadow in her eyes.

"How are the folks?" Belinda asked simply.

"Ma is a bit poorly," Abbie admitted before Belinda could inquire further. "Nothing serious, we hope, but Luke has put her to bed. He's out there now . . . just checking."

Belinda felt her body grow numb. She was unable even to voice her concern.

"The flu, Luke thinks," Abbie rushed on. "But it has really taken the starch outta her. It's been a bit hard for Pa."

"Why didn't someone let me know?" Belinda questioned.

"You didn't get Luke's letter? No, I suppose not. It is likely still on its way. Ma just took sick last Wednesday."

Belinda wanted to get home immediately. She was needed to nurse her mother.

"Is there someone who could drive me out?" she asked Abbie.

"I suppose we could get one of the fellas from the stables—but Luke should be home any minute now. He'll take you."

"I'd really like to get there as quickly as I can," Belinda urged and Abbie nodded.

"Of course," she said. "I understand. I wish the boys were home. We could send one of them over to fetch a team. Well, sit down and have a cup of tea to warm yourself up."

"I think I'll just walk over and hire a team," Belinda said, drawing her gloves back on again.

"Oh, I hate to have you do that," moaned Abbie, wringing her hands. "I know you're anxious, but it's so cold."

"It's really not that bad," Belinda tried to assure her. "Don't worry about me," and she gave Ruthie a hug, kissed Abbie on the cheek, and hurried back toward town and the stables.

She was able to find a young lad to drive her out to the farm. They swung by the station, and her suitcases and trunks were loaded. The rosebush was left behind with the station agent's wife, who promised to care for it until some warmer day. Then they were on their way.

Belinda knew it was her anxiety that was making her impatient, but it was all she could do to keep from shouting at the team to hurry. When at last they did pull into the yard, Luke's team was still tethered out front. Belinda was both relieved and frightened. *What is keeping Luke here so long?* she wondered.

She rushed into the house without rapping on the door, and Clark and Luke both looked up when they heard her. They were seated at the kitchen table drinking coffee.

"Belinda!" Clark jumped up from the table. "Where did you come from?"

Belinda was unable to answer. She was being engulfed in a big bear hug.

"I have a driver to pay and luggage to get upstairs," she said quickly as she was passed to her brother for another big hug. "Where's Ma?"

"Up in her room—and she will be so glad to see you. I think she's sleeping right now," Luke answered.

Clark was drawing on his coat to go take care of the driver and the luggage. Belinda started for the stairs as Luke, too, slipped into his own coat.

Belinda tiptoed up the stairs and quietly opened her mother's door. Marty was sleeping. Her face was pale, but she did not look seriously ill as Belinda had feared she might.

She crossed to the bed and gently laid a hand on Marty's brow; she did not feel feverish. Belinda sighed deeply in relief. Belinda bent to press a kiss on her mother's brow. Feeling much more at peace with the situation, she left the room. She was sure her mother needed to rest. They could talk later.

"You found her?" asked Luke as he came through the kitchen with some of Belinda's suitcases.

"She was sleeping, as you said," Belinda admitted. "I decided she might need the rest more than a chat with me."

"She will be mighty glad fer thet chat, you can bet on thet," Clark assured Belinda, laden with suitcases on his way to Belinda's old room.

Belinda removed her coat and hat and laid them on the sitting room rocker. Then she returned to the kitchen and put some wood on the kitchen fire. It was getting close to suppertime. *I hope I still know how to cook,* she joked to herself.

Clark and Luke came through the kitchen with a trunk between them. "My word, little girl," Clark said teasingly. "Ya sure came home with a passel more'n ya left with."

Belinda nodded. She supposed she had.

She checked the coffeepot and was glad to find some coffee remaining. She was cold from the ride. Perhaps the coffee would help to rid her of the chill. She went to the cupboard for a cup.

Clark and Luke joined Belinda at the table. "Now, catch us up on all yer news," Clark invited.

But Belinda had very little news she felt like sharing. Instead, she asked them for the news of home. She was especially anxious to hear about her mother's illness. Luke explained in detail, and Belinda nodded in understanding as he talked.

"Then she seems to have improved?" she asked when he was done with his report.

"Oh, much," he said with relief. "She was even able to take some broth today—and she kept it down, too."

Belinda felt a surge of thankfulness. "Well, I'll be here to care for her now," she said with emotion. Clark and Luke both expressed gratitude for that blessing.

Marty did continue to improve, but it was three weeks before she was totally herself again. With the assurance that her mother was completely well and could once again take over the care of the house, Belinda began to make her own plans.

"I think it's time for me to move on into town," she informed her folks after their devotions one morning.

Clark and Marty both turned to look at her.

"Luke wrote that Mrs. Jenkins needs nursing care. Mr. Jenkins has been having a terrible time trying to run the post office and care for her, and he hasn't been able to find any regular help."

Marty nodded. "We've heard of the Jenkins' situation," she told Belinda. "Neighbors have helped all they could, but her sickness has gone on fer such a long time."

"When do you want to go?" asked Clark.

"This morning," answered Belinda.

"I'll get the team whenever yer ready."

"Give me about half an hour," Belinda told him and left the table to get out the dishpan.

"Now, you don't need to worry none 'bout these few dishes," Marty assured her, but Belinda insisted that they do the dishes together one more time.

"Luke and Abbie will be glad to have ya back," Marty said as she placed a cup back in the cupboard.

"I've been thinking about that," Belinda said slowly. "I don't think I'm going to go to Luke's."

Marty looked surprised. "I'm sure they'll be expectin' ya," she told Belinda.

"I . . . I suppose they will, although I haven't said that I would be asking them for a room. But, Mama, things are different now. I'm not the young girl I was when I stayed with Luke before. I need to . . . to find my own way. I can't . . . can't make my home with Luke and Abbie forever."

Belinda could see the concern in her mother's eyes as she looked at her.

"Ya sound like yer course is all set," Marty said slowly, "as though yer expectin' to always be as ya are now . . . on yer own."

"I'm fine, Mama. I'm sure the Lord will help me find my place."

"Ya do what ya think best," Marty answered softly. "I'm sure thet Luke an' Abbie'll understand."

And so Belinda found herself one small room in the town boarding-house. It was not fancy, but it was clean, and the other residents were friendly. Besides, she had Luke and Abbie nearby. She could easily slip over to their house if she was feeling lonely.

She settled in as permanent day care for Mrs. Jenkins. The poor lady had arthritis so badly she could do nothing for herself. Belinda was determined to give her the best care possible, to ease her pain as much as she could.

It wasn't the life Belinda had dreamed for herself. But with each passing day she became more and more accustomed to it. It really wasn't so bad, and she did have her evenings to spend as she wished. She had no way to travel to the country church she had known as a girl, so she involved herself in the town church as Sunday school teacher of a girls' class and secretary-treasurer for the ladies' mission group. It kept her more than busy, and the days passed by more quickly than she would have dared to think.

Tenderly she nursed her little potted rose. She was anxious for spring to make an appearance so she could set it out in her mama's flower bed. She hoped it would favor her with a bloom its first year.

Belinda did not pretend even to herself that she did not think of Boston and her friends there. She spoke of them often to her family members. But she never spoke of Drew. Her memories of him were far too painful for her to share with anyone. But each night before she retired, she would include him in her evening prayers.

TWENTY-FIVE

A Happy Ending

"I brought in your mail," Mr. Jenkins said to Belinda as he came from the front room of the building that served as the town post office. It was midday and time for his noon meal.

Belinda thanked him and reached for the two envelopes he handed her.

"How's Lettie today?" he asked as he crossed the room toward the bedroom door.

"A little better, I think," responded Belinda, but he had already passed out of earshot as he went to check for himself.

He was soon back. "She's sleeping," he said thankfully, "and she does look a bit more comfortable than she has."

Belinda nodded and poured the soup in Mr. Jenkins's bowl. He sat down to hurry through his lunch before the jangling of the bell would summon him to care for another customer, and Belinda turned again to her mail.

One of the letters was from Ella. Belinda smiled as she laid it aside. She would save the enjoyment of reading it until she was alone.

The larger envelope bore the inscription of Keats, Cross and Newman, and Belinda quickly tore open the envelope.

"Oh, bother!" she exclaimed as she read the contents.

"Something wrong?" asked Mr. Jenkins.

"No, not wrong. Just a nuisance. I need to sign more papers. I thought I had already signed everything they could possibly come up with . . . but it appears they've found more."

Mr. Jenkins merely nodded. It didn't sound like much to fuss about.

"The only problem is that they must be signed in the presence of an attorney, and that means I will have to travel—"

But Mr. Jenkins quickly cut in, "Got one here now, ya know."

"No, I didn't know," responded Belinda. "Since when?"

"Started up 'bout a week ago. Has his office over in thet little buildin' by the hardware store."

Belinda was relieved. "Well, that will work much better. I was worried about having to ask for some time off."

"You can go on over tonight," Mr. Jenkins went on. "I'll watch Lettie. Or you can run over right now . . . iffen ya like."

"No. Tonight will be fine. Then I can get these papers back in tomorrow's mail."

Mr. Jenkins nodded and returned to his lunch. He was almost finished when the bell began to jingle.

"Drat it!" he exclaimed and took another big bite of his slice of bread. "Almost made 'er thet time," and he hurried from the room to his little post office.

While Mrs. Jenkins slept, Belinda washed the dishes and tidied the three small rooms. By the time the woman awoke, Belinda was ready to devote her full attention to her patient. She made her as comfortable as she could and settled herself in a chair by the bed to read to the woman. Mrs. Jenkins seemed to rest much easier if her mind was busy listening to a story.

Mr. Jenkins remembered his promise and appeared at the door around five o'clock. "I believe thet law office closes at five-thirty," he said to Belinda. "You'd best run on if ya want to git thet cared fer tonight."

Belinda nodded, checked her patient once more, and pulled on her coat and galoshes.

It's staying light longer, she told herself as she hurried toward the hardware store. *That must mean spring is somewhere on the way.* It was a pleasant thought.

She found the small building just as Mr. Jenkins had described it. Above the door was a simple sign, "Law Office," and on the door itself the invitation, "Please walk in." Belinda did so.

The room was simply furnished with a large desk, three straight-backed chairs, some shelves lined with large law tomes, and a large set of file drawers. A man bent over the drawers, probably searching for some elusive file folder.

"Come right in," he called. "Be with you in a moment."

Belinda gasped. *Surely*—? The man's head came up and she gasped again.

"Drew?"

Drew stood upright, his eyes mirroring the surprise that Belinda had felt.

"Belinda!"

"I'm . . . sorry," Belinda stammered. "I didn't know—" and she turned abruptly and ran back out the door.

"Belinda—wait," Drew called after her, but Belinda rushed on.

She was blinded by tears and stumbling along through the rutted snow when Drew caught up with her.

"Belinda, please, wait. What is it? Is something wrong?"

He clasped her shoulder and tried to turn her to face him, but she shook herself free and moved on. He fell into step beside her.

"Please, Belinda. Please," he begged. "We need to talk."

Belinda stopped then and lifted her face to meet his look evenly.

"We have already talked, Drew. Remember?"

He flinched as if he had been struck. "I know," he said in a quiet voice. "I know. But what are you—"

"There doesn't seem to be much else to say," Belinda cut in coldly, and shrugging off Drew's hand, she hurried toward the rooming house.

She spent a miserable evening. She still could not believe it. Here she was back home, thinking she had left Drew in Boston reunited with his mother and brother, and here he was establishing himself, it would appear, right back in their hometown. "I can't go through it again . . . the . . . the love and rejection. I can't," sobbed Belinda aloud. She shook with the intensity of the feelings that kept sweeping through her.

Her eyes red from weeping, Belinda did not bother going down for supper. She knew the others would look at her with curiosity and concern. She had no desire to be asked sympathetic questions.

She tried to read, but the pages blurred. She paced the floor and fidgeted by turn. The evening dragged on; then at eight o'clock there was a knock on the door. Belinda decided not to answer it, but it came again.

"Belinda," came a soft call. Belinda recognized Luke's voice. She knew she must answer or he'd be out looking for her. She let him in.

"Hello," he said in his usual jovial way; then he stepped in, walked straight to her window, and stood with his back to her, looking out at the lights of the small town.

"How is your patient?" he asked after a few silent moments.

"She's . . . doing slightly better, I think," Belinda responded.

"Good," said Luke.

Then he continued. "I dropped by home today. Ma looks much better."

"Oh, that's good!" said Belinda. There was a pause.

"The kids want to know when you're coming over," went on Luke.

Belinda managed a smile. "Tell them I'll be over soon," she replied. "I'm looking forward to some free time on Saturday. Maybe I can make it then."

"Fine," nodded Luke.

"You been busy?" asked Belinda.

But Luke didn't bother to answer her question. He turned to look at her and said instead, "We just had a visitor."

"Oh," responded Belinda, her eyebrows raised. "Who?"

"Drew," Luke said, watching her face carefully.

She caught her breath in a ragged little gasp and quickly turned away from her brother.

"Is he the reason you came home?" asked Luke.

"Of course not," denied Belinda. "Why do you ask that? I had planned for months to come home."

Luke nodded. "He seemed terribly upset," he continued.

"Why?" asked Belinda.

"Well, for one thing, he had the feeling that you needed an attorney for something . . . but you left his office without getting whatever you needed."

"I . . . I was just taken completely by surprise," Belinda confessed. "I'd no idea he was back in town."

"I didn't realize that running into old friends was such a—a traumatic experience," commented Luke.

Belinda flushed. "I guess I did respond . . . rather . . . hastily," she admitted.

"I thought perhaps there was something more," Luke prompted.

"Like . . . ?" began Belinda.

"I've no idea. Would you like to tell me?"

Belinda lowered her face and shook her head.

"But he *isn't* the reason you came home?" Luke asked again.

"No-o," Belinda replied, then added honestly, "but he . . . he might be the reason I didn't stay in Boston."

"I don't understand," said her big brother.

Belinda lifted tear-filled eyes. "I didn't know that . . . that Drew was in Boston until last fall. It was so good to see him. I . . . I thought he felt that way, too. I . . . I even thought that he might care. Well, he maybe did . . . in a way. At least he said he did . . . but he also said that because of . . . the circumstances . . . whatever he saw them to be . . . that we . . . he wouldn't be seeing me again."

Luke nodded.

"So I came on home . . . as I had planned. Though I . . . I knew that I'd stay . . . if . . . if he asked me to. But he didn't, and . . . I didn't expect to ever see him again . . . and then quite unexpectedly he . . . he . . ."

But Belinda could not go on. She turned her back again as the tears began to flow freely.

"Did you know that Drew thought you intended to stay in Boston to administrate the home you had established?" Luke asked.

Belinda shook her head, her back still to her brother.

"Did you know that it was always his intention to return here to set up practice?"

"No," she said after a long pause.

"Did you know that he very nearly laid aside his lifelong dream of helping people in his own hometown so he might be free to stay in Boston and marry you?"

Belinda's shoulders shook. "No."

"Did you know that he felt that to ask you to marry him would be denying you of all the good things you had learned to appreciate?"

"No," sobbed Belinda.

Luke moved across the room to place his hands on Belinda's trembling shoulders. "What in the world did you two talk about all that time, anyway?" he asked in a teasing tone.

"Oh, Luke," sobbed Belinda, and she turned to Luke's arms and lowered her head to his shoulder.

He held her, patting her back as she wept.

"You know what I would suggest?" he said softly when the sobs had subsided. Belinda shook her head.

"I would suggest that you start over. And this time really *talk*."

"Oh, Luke," cried Belinda. "I think it's too late."

"Then what's he doing here waiting right outside the door?" Luke asked with a chuckle.

"He . . . he's here?" Belinda was shocked.

"He's here. And he'll be knocking that door down if I don't soon let him in."

"Oh my!" cried Belinda, her hand going first to her face and then to her hair. "I must look one awful sight."

"I wouldn't expect him to notice," Luke replied gently, then gave her one more squeeze before he released her and opened the door for Drew.

"Belinda?" Drew entered the room hesitantly. "May I come in?"

Belinda silently nodded.

"I . . . I've really messed everything up, haven't I?" he said with such a tremor in his voice that Belinda wanted to reach out to him, but she stood rooted to the spot.

"I thought you felt your work was in Boston . . . with the elderly. . . ."

Belinda nodded again in understanding.

"I knew . . . I've always felt that I was to come back here," he went on.

Belinda managed a shaky little laugh. "Silly, wasn't it? We both thought we knew what the other was thinking when . . ."

But Drew had closed the distance between them. He reached his hand to her face and tipped her chin upward. "Is it too late . . . to start again?" he asked softly.

Belinda couldn't shake her head. He was holding her against him. She knew she'd never squeeze a word past her tight throat. She only looked at him and then she shyly put her hands on his shoulders.

"I love you," whispered Drew. "I always have. Would . . . will you marry me?"

Belinda looked for a long time at the man she loved. She wanted to answer. She even tried to say the word, but still she was unable to speak. Her arms slipped around his neck and he must have taken that as affirmation, for Belinda found herself being tenderly kissed.

Belinda judged it to be the most glorious spring she had ever experienced, she told Drew as they sat rocking on her parents' front porch. Each day seemed brighter, cleaner, more perfect than the last. Marty just smiled at both of them. She had watched love bloom before, she told the couple as she refilled their glasses of iced tea.

Drew found a small house on the edge of town and made arrangements to rent it. Belinda spent hours dreaming of how she would fix this and paint that, and Drew proved to be handy with minor repairs.

"It's going to be just perfect," Belinda enthused. "I can hardly wait to move in."

Drew smiled. The place certainly wasn't perfect, he realized, especially after what Belinda had been used to in Boston. But Drew no longer felt worried about asking her to share his dreams. Love was too evident on her face, and he knew instinctively that they would be happy together.

One day as Belinda was tending her special potted plant, she decided she couldn't wait until they actually occupied the small cottage. Her rose needed planting. When the sun came up in the springtime sky, spilling its warm promises upon the earth, Belinda carefully lifted her potted rose and headed for the small cottage.

Gently she eased the small bush from its confining container and placed it tenderly, securely into the hole she had dug.

"Grow, little rose," she whispered as she poured water into the hole and eased the dirt back in place. "I hope you will be happy here. As happy as I intend to be. You are to make our home beautiful on the outside—and I will try to make it beautiful on the inside."

Belinda rose to her feet, studied her soiled hands, and smiled with inner joy.

"Oh, I hope you bloom," she told the rose. "I hope you'll bloom *this year*." She was silent for a moment and then continued. "But if you don't . . . I'll wait. I feel prepared to wait now. I . . . I finally feel settled . . . ready for life."

The wedding was set for August at the little church in the country. By then Drew's law practice was becoming comfortably established. The small cottage was reasonably refurbished and furnished, and Belinda had busied herself with hanging curtains and scattering braided rugs. Though the little house was simple, Belinda was gloriously happy. It wouldn't be long before she would be Mrs. Drew Simpson.

Mrs. Simpson and Sid came by train for the wedding. Drew gently chided his mother when he and Belinda met the train.

"When I asked you in Boston concerning Belinda, why didn't you tell me she had already gone home?" he asked.

"I had me no idea what had happened between you two," Mrs. Simpson admitted. "I felt that there was something strange going on when two very dear friends suddenly didn't know each other's plans."

"So you told me that Belinda would need to speak for herself?"

Mrs. Simpson shrugged. "What else could I say? I had no intention of intruding on Belinda's privacy."

Drew put his arm around Belinda's waist and pulled her close. "Well, I forgive you, Ma—now that things have worked out," he laughed.

Belinda just smiled. Tomorrow was to be the happiest day of her life.

"Are you ready?" Clark asked his youngest daughter, and Belinda smiled her answer.

"It's a shame," said Clark seriously as he bent to kiss the top of her head.

"What's a shame?" Belinda asked innocently.

"It's a shame I have run out of daughters. Each bride jest gets prettier an' prettier."

"Oh, Pa," Belinda laughed, but her cheeks were glowing.

"Happy?"

"I've never been happier. I think I'm about to burst," admitted Belinda.

"Strange," mused Clark. "After all these years . . . you and Drew."

"It's not strange at all," smiled Belinda dreamily. "I . . . I think that it's just as God always meant it to be. He . . . He just had to wait for me to grow up."

Epilogue

Dear Reader,

We are leaving the Davises at this point in their lives for a time. I realize there is much more we could say about their ongoing family—but it has really grown too large and scattered for us to comfortably keep up with all their comings and goings, living and loving.

Many have suggested a reunion to bring all of the western family back to join Marty and Clark at the home farm. It sounds like fun. But it is almost impossible. For one thing, there are now far more characters than a reader—or the writer—can properly keep straight. Secondly, such an event was unlikely in the days that we are reliving in these stories. The distance was too great and the travel too difficult and expensive for all the family to be able to make the trip.

Thank you for traveling with me. I pray as I write each story that something that is told, or even implied, might strike some responsive chord in a heart—somewhere—and that God will speak to you in a special way. He is able to do that, I know—and that is why sharing the stories with you has been so special for me.

God bless!

P.S. It is now some years since I wrote the farewell note above, and I did return to the Davis family for four novels in the PRAIRIE LEGACY series, picking up with Belinda and Drew's offspring. Look for *The Tender Years, A Searching Heart, A Quiet Strength,* and *Like Gold Refined.*

About the Author

Bestselling author **Janette Oke** is celebrated for her significant contribution to the Christian book industry. Her novels have sold more than thirty million copies, and she is the recipient of the ECPA President's Award, the CBA Life Impact Award, the Gold Medallion, and the Christy Award. In addition, the Hallmark Channel has made numerous films based on her books. Janette and her husband, Edward, live in Alberta, Canada.

Books by Janette Oke

Return to Harmony • *Another Homecoming*
Tomorrow's Dream • *Dana's Valley***

ACTS OF FAITH*

The Centurion's Wife • *The Hidden Flame* • *The Damascus Way*

CANADIAN WEST

When Calls the Heart • *When Comes the Spring*
When Breaks the Dawn • *When Hope Springs New*
Beyond the Gathering Storm • *When Tomorrow Comes*

RETURN TO THE CANADIAN WEST

Where Courage Calls**
Where Trust Lies**
Where Hope Prevails**

LOVE COMES SOFTLY

Love Comes Softly • *Love's Enduring Promise*
Love's Long Journey • *Love's Abiding Joy*
Love's Unending Legacy • *Love's Unfolding Dream*
Love Takes Wing • *Love Finds a Home*
Love Comes Softly 1–4 • *Love Comes Softly 5–8*

A PRAIRIE LEGACY

The Tender Years • *A Searching Heart*
A Quiet Strength • *Like Gold Refined*

*with Davis Bunn
**with Laurel Oke Logan

If you enjoyed this book, you may also like . . .

More Fiction From Bethany House

At Irish Meadows horse farm, two sisters struggle to reconcile their dreams with their father's demanding marriage expectations. Brianna longs to attend college, while Colleen is happy to marry, as long as the man meets *her* standards. Will they find the courage to follow their hearts?

Irish Meadows by Susan Anne Mason
COURAGE TO DREAM #1
susanannemason.com

National Weather Bureau volunteer Sophie van Riijn has used the abandoned mansion Dierenpark as a resource and a refuge for years. But now the Vandermark heir has returned to put an end to the shadowy rumors about the place. When old secrets come to light, will tragedy triumph or can hope and love prevail?

Until the Dawn by Elizabeth Camden
elizabethcamden.com

When a new doctor arrives in town, midwife Martha Cade's world is overturned by the threat to her job, a town scandal, and an unexpected romance.

The Midwife's Tale by Delia Parr
AT HOME IN TRINITY #1

BETHANYHOUSE